WHITE PRODIGAL

❧*❧

Book 4 of the

Kestrel Harper Saga

❧*❧

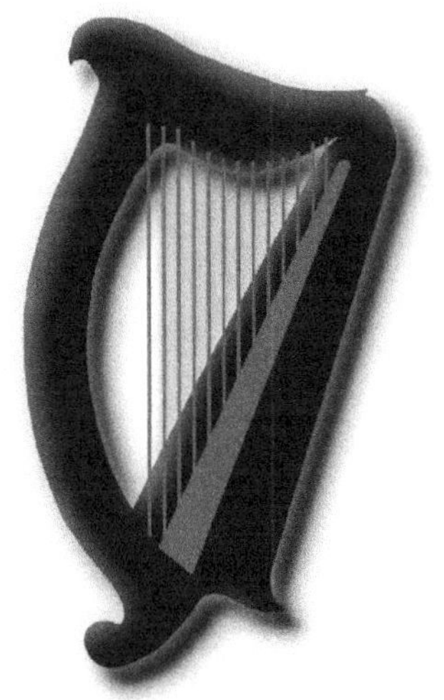

Tamara Brigham

❧*☙

For Angela...
...for your encouragement

❧*☙

Part 1

❧Chapter 1❧

"Kavan!"

Wortham Delamo was too far away to catch the pale man when he snapped backward away from the window sill he had been leaning on, thrown by an unseen force, hand clutching the small of his back, and then spun sideways before collapsing against the wall of their room in the best inn the sea-side city of Pa'aliaka had to offer. There was agony etched on the bard's unaging features, though there was no sign the captain could see of physical injury. The pupils of his emerald eyes were dilated, full of unshed tears, the witness to something far away that Wortham could not view.

Lifting the slender man in his bearlike arms, Wortham carried him to the bed, thinking to settle him there and fetch a physician, but Kavan clung to him with incredible strength, whimpering like a terrified child, and though the Elyri's unusual behavior was disconcerting, it was reassuring to know he was not lost. He was present enough, aware of his surroundings and not sucked into some distant place, to seek the comfort of his dearest friend's company. Such an occasion was so rare that the captain felt obliged to accommodate Kavan's wishes, though at the first hint of physical distress, he would find a way to summon a physician with or without Kavan's permission.

Pregnant, volatile clouds pushed towards the coast from across the eastern sea, blanketing the horizon. Thunder crackled in the distance for the first time that evening, charging the hot night air. There had been no trace of an impending storm all day, and when the four travelers took rooms for the evening, it was with the expectation of a night's rest in decent beds and a calm start for their journey north at the first light of dawn. Watching the clouds roll closer as he cradled Kavan against his broad chest, Wortham released a shuddering, frustrated sigh. k' Ádhá and Saint Kóráhm might look favorably on Kavan Cliáth, but the events of his life were rarely simple, regardless.

While such happenings, such a lifestyle, did little for the captain's nerves, it prevented his life from becoming boring.

Kavan moaned and grimaced as he shifted in Wortham's arms to press his face to the man's chest. How could this be? Not Ártur. Kavan had wanted a brief mental contact with the cousin he had not seen in many months, wanted to know the source of Ártur's sudden vexation, but he had not expected this. There was too much pain, burning through every muscle, pulsing through his blood, crawling across his skin. He was trapped in it, powerless to push past it to formulate clear thought or make any effort to undo whatever had been done. Unable to break the link between them, uncertain he would if he could, Kavan could only share whatever torment his cousin was suffering. He had been through a very similar pain not long ago; those memories of torture seared him like quicksilver and made every nerve, especially those in his hands, throb and sting in recollection. But there were more assailants facing the healer, it seemed, and Ártur was ill-equipped to stand against them. He was a physician, not a warrior. He could not survive such an attack alone.

"My Lord? Kavan? What about Ártur? What has happened?"

Lifting his head to face the throaty voice, the bard did not see him. All he saw was crimson pain. Ártur should not be in the streets of Rhidam alone in the middle of the night. This attack should not be happening. Kavan should be there to protect his cousin…or someone should be. Killing was not something Kavan favored, but it was something he could do, something he had done more than once in his life. It was something Ártur could not do, however. He lacked the training and his Oaths would not permit it.

There would be no one to punish him or strip him of status if he did so, but his conscience would surely suffer.

The thought of death, of killing, sparked an idea. Could he be of such use from so far away? Would any effort he could make succeed, or would he damage…possibly kill… Ártur in the attempt?

The familiar sensation of a blade slicing into his flesh made him convulse. Biting his lip, he buried his head in the crook of Wortham's neck, the man's dark curls and beard serving as an emotionally secure shelter. Despite the pain, despite his distaste for death, he knew he had no choice. If he did nothing, Ártur would die painfully. At least if Kavan failed, his cousin's end would be mercifully quick.

He reached into his center, gathered as much energy from within and without as he could harness, focused it through the mental link binding him to the man several thousand miles away…and let it go.

❧3❧

∾Chapter 2∾

Gaelán had given no thought to his actions, but he intuitively knew that pursuing the older healer was something someone had to do…and he was in the best position to do it. Nor had he given thought to what he would do when he reached the destination pulling him across the sleeping city. As he and Asta fled past one dark home and shop after another, the feeling of terror deepened in his belly. No one else knew where Ártur was heading, no one else, as far as he knew, was aware of the threats on the healer's life. If Gaelán could not find him, no one would find him until it was too late.

He stopped abruptly mid-stride, bringing Asta to a halt since her small hand was clutched in his, and then, without a word, turned down an unlit side street.

"The Boar's Garden is this way," Asta started.

"I know where I'm going."

It was partially true. He knew where Ártur had been heading, but something was leading him in a different direction. He did not know where he would end up, or what he would find when he got there. The sounds of chaos, a brawl in progress, resonated where there had been silence moments before, and the sense of fear he carried grew nearer, deeper, until he stopped. There was, as he stared at the sight in front of him, a hot, hard knot in his middle where his stomach should be.

He could not count the number of assailants; there were too many. They weaved about too much in the shadows and it was too dim to distinguish their dark-clothed figures clearly. But there was only one victim. It was Ártur's healer's bag thrown away from the skirmish as if a discarded bit of rubbish. Gaelán knew he should intervene, but what could he do? He was a child; any delusions of adulthood he had carried before were gone. He could not hope to confront so many armed attackers. Though he opened his mouth to shout, in the vain hope of distracting them from their assault, perhaps draw them away into a chase, no sound emerged from his constricted throat.

Asta's hand slipped free. Before he could stop her, she disappeared into the shadows of the alley ahead. A second, unexpected, form followed her, larger but no less stealthy. k'Ádhá, Gaelán thought with horror. We were followed! Asta's life was now in danger too. Too terrified to take a step, he listened to the screams of confusion in front of him and the running steps behind him. Thinking the screams to be Asta's finally propelled him into action, but he went only a few steps before a violent surge of energy erupted from the midst of the melee, radiating outward in a powerful psychic wave, knocking Gaelán and others off their feet as a hand caught his shoulder.

There was silence. Everything ceased to exist at that moment except for Gaelán's psychic senses. His head began to pound but his focus on the energy at his center felt stronger than it ever had, allowing his mind to withstand the worst of that burst. More footsteps thundered up the path, running past him towards where the melee had been.

Lachlan guards.

But there was no more movement where there had been fighting. Gaelán pushed stiffly to his feet, grateful to be by the man who had grasped his shoulder. Justice Corbin, as it turned out.

Once steady, the young man started forward again.

"Master Cáner…"

"I'm a healer; Ártur needs me…" He had to hope it was true, that the older healer could be treated, was not dead from whatever had just thrown Gaelán off his feet.

Having reached the same conclusion as the words were spoken, the Justice had already released him.

Though his feet no longer felt leaden, Gaelán found it more difficult to close the distance of the alley than expected. His stomach churned, alternating between fire and ice, with fear. Fear for Asta, fear for Ártur. But Asta stood beside her father, wiping her bloodied knife on the black trousers she wore. His relief that she was safe allowed Gaelán to turn his focus to where it was needed the most.

When he saw Ártur's twisted, bloody form on the ground in the middle of several exploded corpses barely recognizable as men, he knew what had happened. Not just to Ártur, but to his attackers as well. And he knew what he had to do.

But there were too many injuries, more than he, as a novice thought he could heal in time to save Ártur's life. Broken bones, lacerations, internal bleeding, and cranial damage of a sort outside of his experience. His young hands shook as he swallowed the bile at the back of his throat. It was too much for an apprentice, perhaps too much for any healer to fully tend before death came. And Ártur was slipping. There was a powerful third presence that Gaelán could feel when he put his hands on his mentor, a presence keeping the healer from death, a presence Gaelán did not have time to identify or recognize. He was certain, however, that presence was the only hope Ártur had.

He divided his attention long enough to say, "I can't…I need Syl…I will do what I can…then we carry him, get him to the keep…but there's too much. I cannot do this alone."

He turned his focus to healing, losing track of those around him, trusting them to act, to protect healer and patient, without instruction.

❧ * ❧

There was no simple, immediately available explanation for the sensation of searing heat inside his skull, that spread down his neck, along his stooped shoulders, and into the muscles of his back. It was something that had never happened to him in all of the centuries of his life. There had been a mind-numbing surge of power in the eye-blink before the heat came, and a building discomfort and weakness shortly before that, the culmination of which left him psychically blind for the span of several gulped breaths. Thankfully, that blindness, and those sensations, subsided quickly and were gone now, leaving this uncomfortable throbbing in his head and overall weakness in his body that frightened him.

Balancing on the nearest stool lest he fall, he shuffled to the side, collapsed at his desk, and took up a quill from the inkwell. On the nearest blank sheet of parchment he found, he began to write of this event, to record it for posterity. bhydáni Tíbhyan did not know what this experience meant, but he knew it was important.

He wondered if anyone else, anywhere in the world, had felt it too.

❧ * ❧

The bard had grown still long ago, a stiff calm that might have been mistaken for death if not for the shallow rise and fall of his chest and the pounding heart that Wortham could feel against his breast. The captain continued to hold him, afraid of losing him, hoping that his mortal, Teren strength was enough to pull Kavan through whatever he was enduring. The smoky gray crystal the bard wore about his neck had glowed as if lit from within for several moments before the bard's collapse into stillness, but Wortham did not know what it meant. It no longer glowed, and other than a faint redness on Kavan's chest where the crystal rested against his skin, there was no visible indicator that anything unusual had happened.

When he did release Kavan, it was to reassure himself that the Elyri was breathing. He wiped blood from Kavan's lower lip, where it appeared he had bitten himself, wrapped the man in the sheets with the hope that it would prevent shock, and then settled back to keep watch, with one milky white hand clasped in one of his rough, battle-scarred ones.

That something had happened to Ártur, Wortham had no doubt; the bard had muttered the healer's name repeatedly before lapsing into silence. That Kavan's state hinged on that, the captain also did not doubt. Whatever had occurred had not been good, and he prayed the healer was alive, that this would pass. But would it pass soon enough? They had a ship to catch in the morning, if the encroaching storm did not delay their departure. Wortham knew they needed to reach home as quickly as possible; they could not afford delays. If Kavan did not regain consciousness by morning, what were they to do then?

That question Wortham answered for himself once the flood of doubt and panic were banished from his thoughts. His lord had a duty. Kavan would return to Rhidam, would cleanse that ancient chapel and reset Enesfel onto its proper path, even if Wortham had to carry him the entire way home.

⤙*⤚

Something jolted Syl abruptly from her sleep. A quick check on the children revealed that Chethá was awake sucking contentedly on her fingers. Llucás was curled around his pillow, sleeping soundly, though the corners of his mouth and eyes and his fingers were twitching as though in a dream. She could not dismiss the waking premonition of trouble, of danger, and as it did not fade after rising, she made the rounds of her home. Elyriá was safe. Her doors and windows were closed. Bhen slept on the divan in the sitting room with a book across his chest, breathing deep though even his expression was restless and uneasy. There was no storm outside, the wind was calm, and she could see no movement in Bhryell's pre-dawn streets.

Yet none of the seeming calm, none of the reassuring rightness of things, displaced the disquiet that gnawed at her nerves. Wrapping her pale beige wool shawl around her shoulders, she leaned on the sill in her infant daughter's room, trying to focus on the source of alarm.

It was not the first time she wished she possessed some small measure of Kavan's incredible gifts. If she did, she might be able to uncover the answers she sought.

Tonight, she could only wait and worry.

❧*❧

The young man's hands fell away from his patient and he collapsed back against the sturdy legs of Caol Dugan. He was grateful, for his own sake as well as Asta's, that the inquisitor was there.

His healing efforts were far from complete; he had barely succeeded in staunching the life-threatening internal bleeding. There was still so much damage to his mentor's body that he could still feel though his hands were no longer splayed over the man's torso. Despite his previous focus, the boost of power that eruptive burst had provided, his pool of energy was again too quickly spent. There was nothing more he could do until he rested and replenished his strength.

The Healer's fate was no longer in Gaelán's hands.

He nodded to the nearest guards who lifted Ártur on a cloak between them and started carrying him to the castle as quickly as they were able. Supported by Asta and her father, Gaelán intended to follow, hanging his head as he struggled to his feet, to stay upright so that he could walk on his own. He grabbed the discarded healer's bag, refusing to leave it behind, but the weight of it seemed a terrible burden to bear. Tears streamed down his now dusty cheeks despite his attempts to wipe them away, stop them from falling. Ártur would die and it was his fault.

"I have matters in hand here, Lord Dugan," said Darius Corbin with a wave. "Send General Agis; I will keep trespassers out of the area until you have the chance to look it over.

The inquisitor grunted, not expecting to find anything that would tell him more than he already knew. No one seemed suspicious of his early arrival at the crime scene, no one yet aware of what he had been doing this night, and Caol intended it to remain that way. The Justice shrugged off the non-committal sound as he circled the scene, seeking clues and evidence beneath the flickering light of the torch he carried.

Shifting most of Gaelán's weight away from his daughter as they began the long walk back, Caol said, "You have done what you can…"

"But it isn't enough…"

"If you hadn't followed him, no one would have found him until it was too late." Pulling a kerchief from her pocket, Asta gave it to him as she spoke, not finding his crying to be unmanly or improper. When she noticed her father's questioning glance over Gaelán's head, she shrugged. "You gave him a chance to live. It is better than no chance. By the time we get back, you'll be able to do more."

His tone puzzled and pensive, Caol asked, "That wasn't you, was it? Did you have anything to do with what happened to those men?"

The younger man lifted his teary face. "You mean the ones who exploded?" He briefly considered that perhaps the inquisitor was implicating him in the attack. "No, sir. I felt it happen…I mean, I felt the power of it…but I didn't cause it. I can't do anything like that."

"Ártur?"

"I don't think so. His oaths wouldn't allow it."

Asta interrupted with a tug on her father's arm, eagerly trying to interpret the confusion on his face. "Do you think it's important?"

"Could be…"

"I've seen this before…one other time…back home…"

Caol's breath caught. Gaelán's words brought back the memory of decimated corpses in Levonne, after the attack on Kavan. He shook his head. "But Kavan wasn't here…" he muttered. Not Kavan, perhaps, but someone else. Perhaps someone else had been present both times.

Gaelán shook his head, guessing at the man's train of thought. "No one else was there…no one who could have done…that…" Caol's mention of Kavan's name confirmed something that Gaelán had not recognized in his rush to save Ártur's life. He knew that power signature now. He knew who was keeping Ártur alive.

In the distance, the bailey walls loomed into view. Caol stopped walking, his expression thoughtful. "Can you make it the rest of the way?" If they were further away from the keep, if it was anyone other than his daughter, he would have stayed with them the entire way. But his daughter had proven her merit tonight, and child or not, she would make sure both were safe. "I want to get back…"

He had an idea and wanted to pursue it, while it, and the evidence, was still fresh.

Asta nodded, her chest puffed with pride as she pulled Gaelan's weight against her. "We will be alright, father. The sun is coming up…and it's not that far."

"Straight there…nowhere else…and wait for me," he warned, watching the two stumble and stagger towards the castle. If either was to be a target, it would likely be Duke Cáner's half-Elyri, half-Teren healer son. But he trusted his daughter's instincts, now more than ever. She had entered that fight unprompted, emerged unscathed after killing two of the nine assailants, which spoke volumes about her skill. Asta still had much to learn, but he believed he had chosen his successor wisely.

Turning back towards the scene of the crime, he hoped Healer MacLyr had done likewise.

❧Chapter 3❧

Waves slapped the wooden sides of the single-masted cog, a sound that soothed the captain's agitation as he took another moist towel from Zelenka's hand and replaced the now warm one on the bard's forehead. The woman's brown eyes were sad, her expression scared, but after the initial glance at her once they had Kavan settled, Wortham had not been able to look into her face again.

He should, he knew. She had given up her familial home because of a cultural superstition that seemed like nonsense to him, but she had left the southern lands, the world she knew, chosen to be on this boat now, to follow him. There was as much courage in that action, stepping off into the unknown, as there was the fear of being alone. It was courage similar in nature to Wortham's own blind willingness to follow Kavan wherever the bard traveled. It would be considerate of him to show sympathy, understanding, and gratitude, to try to explain their situation to her better than he had, but his attention, his concern, were focused wholly on the comatose Elyri.

When Zelenka came before dawn to tell him that their chartered boat was prepared to depart as soon as the worst of the night's storm passed, Wortham was forced to carry Kavan and most of their belongings to it. Urian, the blind monk who had traveled with them during Kavan's southern pilgrimage, could not carry such a burden, though he did his best to help, and while Zelenka too carried more than was her share, she could not manage more and there were few coins left with which to hire help. The Elyri's condition had not changed since slipping into this trance-like state. He breathed, occasionally twitched and muttered unintelligible syllables, but his eyes did not open and he did not shift in his apparent sleep. He could not carry anything. The choice was for Wortham to do it, making multiple trips, or else to miss their boat and await a change in Kavan's condition.

Wortham would rather die than fail Kavan that way.

The cog pushed away from the dock not long after the four were settled. It was a merchant vessel, not meant for passengers. A corner of the cargo hold was cleared for the four and their belongings, and hammocks had been strung for them, but that was all. No luxuries, no beds. Passengers meant fewer goods that could be carried, hence the significant fee the cog's captain had charged.

It had been necessary to sell the horses and the mule, which had to be done anyhow, and now Wortham fretted about how they would proceed once they disembarked in the port town of Yashir. He could not carry everything they owned. Particularly if Kavan failed to awaken. Urian, however, was confident that they would find what they needed, that k'Ádhá would provide for Kavan's needs, whatever those were, as he always did.

Yes, Wortham thought glumly, listening to Zelenka move away as he toyed with the damp strands of the Elyri's hair; k'Ádhá would provide for Kavan. But would he provide for the rest of them?

❧*❧

Try as he did, Gaelán could not stop weeping. He did so in silence, but the tears continued to fall until his eyes burned and his nose hurt from wiping it. By the time he reached the room where Ártur had been taken, he had recovered enough strength to heal the multiple fractures in the man's skull, but that was all. Any more effort would have to wait until he had the opportunity of a good night's rest. One of the Lachlan guards had been sent to gdhededhá Tusánt to bring Syl from Elyriá before it was too late to save her husband. Before Ártur died.

She had come, as Gaelán had known she would, and had been in that room ever since. He had been unable to look her in the eye.

The thought of his uncle's death brought a renewed outpouring of tears, the weeping expending the energy he was trying to gather. Not even Asta's arm around his shoulders helped. The King stood at the end of the corridor outside of the Healer's room with his sister, the two speaking in hushed tones. Why were they not yelling at him, Gaelán wondered, demanding to know what had happened? Why did no one ask why Gaelán and Asta were out of the castle in the night? Why did no one inquire about why Ártur had left the grounds unguarded and alone?

"They're too worried about Lord MacLyr's life to ask questions, Asta whispered. Gaelán looked at her in sorrowful surprise, knowing that he had not voiced those questions aloud. The girl's shoulders shrugged as if to say she did not know why she had said those words, before looking at the Healer's closed door. "What is taking so long?"

Feeling another rush of tears, Gaelán wiped his face again on his long-ago soaked sleeve. "There was much damage…and it can take a long time to find some of the smallest…I should have told them…this is…I did this…"

"Told who what, Gaelán?" He met the princess' worried and yet somehow stony gaze before hurriedly looking away. He was spared the need of responding by the opening of the chamber door.

Syl, her pale features more ashen than usual, stepped through the arched doorway, followed by the gdhededhá, her expression as weary as Gaelán felt. Princess Diona turned towards the sound, not waiting for the door to close again before asking, "Will he live?"

The King left his doorway sentry post to hear the conversation more fully.

"I…cannot…it is too early to say." Syl's voice was small as she wiped her hands on her healer-yellow smock. "I've repaired as much as I can…as much as I found. There is swelling in his brain…which will either diminish and heal or…" She swallowed hard, unable to continue. "He must not be moved until he is stable, to give the head trauma time to heal. I will stay with him until I am certain he'll live."

"Thank you," began Diona.

Pressing on, Syl tried to hide her frown as she continued. "I humbly request, Your Majesty, that he be released from service, to return to Bhryell where he will be safe. His life is not worth this…"

"Of course," King Hagan replied hastily, unable to deny the woman who had raised him, after his mother's untimely death, anything she wanted. The royal house needed physicians, but putting Ártur at further risk was not what the King wanted either. "Please do not hold me responsible for this, Lady MacLyr. I have encouraged him numerous times to go to Elyriá, to get out of Rhidam before something like this happened…"

She nodded grimly. "But he would not go. I know, My Liege…but I think he may change his mind after this…if he survives. He has children to think about…a family…" Pausing again for breath in an effort to level her emotions, she murmured, "How did this happen? Why was he out in the city at…?"

"My fault…" Gaelán stuttered, bracing for a backlash of negative words and emotions.

"Your fault?" By her tone, he knew she found his claim difficult to believe.

But Asta interrupted protectively and put her hand on Gaelán's knee. "It is not his fault. He…there was a written threat…that Lord MacLyr ordered him not to speak of…"

Believing she understood his guilt now, Diona squeezed his shoulder gently. "He told us about it, Gaelán. None of this is…"

Footsteps undercut her words as a soldier strode towards them from the nearest stairwell, a familiar face that was comforting to see.

"What is it, Yorick?" asked the King.

The soldier bowed and then straightened. "Lords Dugan, Corbin, and Agis are on their way to the Stateroom if you desire a briefing on the matter of last night's event. They sent me ahead to tell you…"

"Good. Excellent. Tell them I shall join them shortly." The King looked at each of those around him. "Gaelán, Asta…since you both seem to know something of this matter, you will attend as well. I want to hear what you have to say." They were his friends, despite his jealousy over the relationship building between the two, but he could not extinguish the small sliver of hope that whatever part Gaelán feared he had played in this might be enough, not to punish him, but to prompt the apprentice healer out of Rhidam so that Hagan might have Asta to himself. "Lady MacLyr, I will share the details with you later, if you prefer to remain here with…"

Tusánt touched her arm gently. "Go with them, if you wish, my lady. You said yourself there is little more to do than wait now. I will stay with him until your return. Go…hear what is said first hand. It will give you a moment's rest."

And perhaps, his words went unfinished, prove some degree of comfort or peace of mind as well.

Taking her fussing infant daughter from the dedhá, cradling Chethá against her shoulder, Syl accepted the hand of the Boy-King to accompany him to the Stateroom. There was blood on Asta's clothes, as well as Gaelán's. Neither had taken time to change or eat. Syl did not question them yet; the story would come out soon enough. But the vision the two made as they rose from the hall bench, hand in hand, Gaelán refusing to lift his gaze from the floor, strengthened the feeling that despite Tusánt's hope for peace of mind, Syl was not going to like what she learned.

❧*☙

"Why have you invited me to your palatial home, cousin? Or," Prince Kjell set down his cup of wine and wiped his mouth on his napkin, a habit most of the de Cormick line did not share, "is it something we should not discuss in the company of your guest?"

Prince Harcourt of Hatu raised one brow but did not address the question. It was not his to answer. He had not come to Prince Owain's home with any expectations and had certainly not anticipated meeting the Nethite heir-apparent, a name barely heard outside of Neth's border, a man rumored, when he was spoken of, to be a simpleton. This man before him was no simpleton. Prince Espen was not confident in his position as a statesman in this place; if Owain asked for privacy to speak with his cousin, Espen would not be offended. But Prince Kjell's boldness in bringing up some covert matter in his company gave Espen hope that he would be included.

"Prince Espen is here on behalf of Princess Diona; it is she who will be most interested in the outcome of our meeting. Including Espen will remove messy communication problems." Owain lay his fork down and studied his kinsman evenly. "Unless you feel that his presence might jeopardize your safety?"

Both men knew, if Kjell feared that risk, he would not have brought up the possibility of including Espen in their dialogue. Kjell leaned back in his chair, pushing his plate away, and folded his arms across his chest. "Little Prince Harcourt can do that could put me in any more jeopardy than I am already in. Unless," he eyed the dark-haired prince curiously, "you have some direct access to my brother I do not know about and intend to inform him of my visit here?"

If there was a threat or challenge in that question, Espen chose not to take the bait. "There is no need, or wish, for that, I assure you. Nor can I imagine having a direct connection to Merkar and not having already made use of it. Please dispense with formality; Espen will suffice."

"I shall, if you do likewise, Espen."

Motioning for his guests to follow him from the dining room, Owain sighed with relief. When he had invited Kjell to Fiara, he had not expected him to come. Hoped, yes, but not expected. Nor had he expected any discussion between them to include anyone else…just two kinsmen talking hypotheticals by the fire over glasses of brandy.

But Espen's arrival at this time was fortuitous and Owain wondered if he should invite the Valdis King or heir, Renfrid or

Govert, the High Mother, and Gabrielle, to join them. Such summit talks would be an ambitious undertaking but it was too early to press that advantage. He needed to gauge Kjell's standing and intent before including anyone else in a united stance…against Merkar, against anti-Elyri violence, against certain leaders of the Faith.

He smiled as they stepped onto the back promenade. If this conference was the success he hoped for, he would see to such a meeting of like minds that included the other rulers at a future time.

"Foremost, Kjell, I offer assurance that I did not invite you here to place your life in danger. Nor did I do so on behalf of King Hagan. What I seek comes from myself. My proposition could be of great benefit to all of us, but what we say here stays between us, unless…until…we jointly decide to include others. As such, Espen, I ask you to swear you will not share this with Diona, and definitely not Hagan, until we three decide upon a course of action."

While Espen did not want to hold secrets from Diona, he understood the diplomatic necessity of doing so at this moment. He nodded, settling on a bench as the others chose seating nearby. "Diplomats in negotiation. Nothing more. I cannot speak on Diona's behalf, nor on Noreis', but I offer what assurances I may. Nothing leaves the table of this deal until we are certain of its arrangement."

"A schooled diplomat," grinned Kjell. "I like you Espen. I welcome you to hear these negotiations…such as they are. Whatever you wish to say, continue, cousin. I will hear you out."

Owain nodded with a long measured breath. "I must stress, though I do not speak on the Crown's behalf, that I assure you the Lachlans have no desire to destroy Neth's sovereignty. We desire peace, desire for things to stand strong and fair between us, and I believe that is your desire as well, Kjell. A diplomatic accord that can guarantee continued peace would be to the good of all kingdoms."

"You are aware that peace for Neth…with Neth…could result in our increased might, if things stand as they are. That might not prove to be so beneficial to Enesfel or Cordash…"

It was the one thing, perhaps, that had kept Neth from overrunning their neighbors to the west and south. As long as the country was subjugated by a tyrant and kept from thriving, Neth posed no significant threat to anyone outside of its borders. He did not believe Owain was suggesting that particular status quo remain in place.

"I do not believe renewed hostilities would have to be a necessary result. It has been many generations since the people of Neth have known stability…freedom from fear. The man who could deliver that would not be easily dismissed…or challenged," Owain said pointedly. "I don't think most would be interested or eager to leave that behind. If we…the three of us here, do our duty properly, there should be no reason for our kingdoms to be at odds any longer."

"A lofty goal…but you are assuming that Neth's ruler is open to negotiations…and is a reasonable man. Peace is the farthest thing from Merkar's mind…as it was for generations of de Cormick kings before him. Or are you suggesting I claim the throne?"

"Have you any interest in it?" countered Owain.

Grinning, Kjell slid from the bench onto the grassy ground. He did not object to looking up at his cousin, felt no need to be at eye level to be on equal standing with him. "Would I be a de Cormick if I didn't? If there was a way to overthrow Merkar without being responsible for his death…literally or in part…I would take it without hesitation. I do not want his blood on my hands. I do not want to be that sort of king. It's the only reason I endure his unchecked nonsense and stupidity. I try to temper his actions without giving myself away…without letting him know I understand much more than he believes I do…"

Espen fingered the edge of his tunic. "It cannot be easy to play the fool," he murmured, hoping Kjell did not find the comment offensive.

Kjell shrugged. It was precisely what he did in the company of his family or anyone else at home. It had worked thus far. "Worth the effort if it keeps me alive. I wonder sometimes why General Glucke does not prompt me to action or has not tried to kill Merkar on my behalf with the expectation of controlling me on the throne. I doubt he believes I have a master plan to act when the time comes…most believe me too simple for planning. Maybe he is waiting for Merkar to kill me, so that he, in turn, can murder Merkar and take the throne. It is an uneasy truce, but I doubt it will last much longer. Disliked kings rarely last long here…and Glucke is an old man. With his second, a fellow named Barre, firmly in my control, fortunes will swing in my favor…but perhaps not quickly enough."

"Never quickly enough, not while he sends spies into Enesfel. What does Merkar want? I have executed three of his elite agents and turned away countless others at the border. Elyriá is fending off military units braving the mountain crossings. What is he after?"

"I do not know." There was undeniable honesty in Kjell's tone. "I know he is interested in the nature of your internal unrest. Perhaps he is hoping to take advantage of it. It would explain the spies. As for military exercises against Elyriá, only Merkar knows. Gluck says he wants a path into Enesfel at any cost, but will not tell me why. Yet even I know that trying to pass through the mountains is expensive, tedious, and ultimately futile. If there is a reason beyond typical de Cormick mulishness, Merkar has not disclosed it to me…or to Glucke."

For Neth's top general to be intentionally excluded from the planning and purpose behind a royal command of the men beneath his leadership, it was not a good thing. For Neth, or for Glucke.

"Not quite any cost, or he would simply throw troops at Enesfel or Cordash and attempt to force his way in."

Espen nodded in agreement with Owain's words. "He may assume that Elyriá is easiest because they lack a standing militia and thus are unlikely to produce trained soldiers? I would think that failing to find them such an easy target must be humiliating…"

"Which fuels his eagerness to succeed. He blames failures on the usual excuses…collusion with evil powers, the incompetence of his soldiers, his generals…" Kjell shrugged again.

"Which feeds directly into our current troubles," muttered Owain.

"Then the rumors are true?"

Espen smoothed his beard as he sighed. "Anti-Elyri violence is rampant…throughout Enesfel. The King is working tirelessly to rectify the situation, but I do not know how he can be successful against prejudice and fear."

"Hence our need for peace…at least between our kingdoms. Enesfel needs it. We have the capacity to protect ourselves, should Merkar's efforts continue…and perhaps having a common, external enemy would distract the public from their current bent long enough for it to die down. No one wants war…except maybe Merkar…"

Running footsteps interrupted his words moments before Owain's son Piran erupted around the edge of the hedges. "Father, I heard that…" The boy stopped at his father's stern expression and bowed his head after quickly looking at first one guest and then the other. "I am sorry, Father. I did not know you had business."

Owain motioned the child closer, the apology gaining the boy immunity from immediate chastisement. "You know Prince Espen, Piran." He paused, wondering how best to introduce Kjell, but the Nethite resolved the issue for him.

"I am Madron. It is a pleasure to meet you, Prince Piran."

The little boy laughed. "I am not a prince…am I, Father?"

"Your father is a prince," Espen answered for Owain. "That makes you one too. My lord, if you need to tend your son, we can resume this business later…if Madron has the time to remain for it."

Eyeing both men skeptically, not wanting to detain either to humor his son, Owain asked, "Are you certain it is not an imposition?"

"A boy needs his father, and a father should give his attention when he can," Kjell replied, with a melancholy note of longing. "If it is acceptable, perhaps Espen can show me your grounds and we can…talk…" Time alone to familiarize himself with the Hatu prince would be a benefit regardless of their topic of discussion. He wanted to know who he was preparing an alliance with, what sort of man his cousin trusted.

Owain, relieved, smiled. "Of course it is. Shall we gather for the noon meal?"

"I will be here," agreed Espen.

"As shall I." Kjell bowed and waited to speak again until after Owain departed with his hand gently, but firmly, on Piran's shoulder. "Madron is my mother's family name, and my middle name, common in central Neth," he added, addressing the question he would have asked if he was in Espen's shoes. A false claim, even a necessary one, needed to be addressed before it established an unfortunate pattern. "It could be traced to me if Merkar wished to dig, but it would take more time than he would care to give me, I'm sure. My mother's family is quite prolific I am told."

With so many Madrons to choose from, uncovering Kjell's subterfuge would not be an easy task.

"Will you accompany me on a tour of my cousin's home, Espen?"

Espen bowed his head and clasped Kjell's extended hand, amazed at how much trust the Nethite was willing to extend to him. "I would be honored to welcome your company. There is much we can learn from one another…that I think will be to both our benefits."

Kjell smiled. "I agree."

❧*❧

If there had been any inkling of what lay in store for her and her brother, Princess Diona would not have sent Espen to Fiara. Without him, she had no one to confide in, leaving her anxious and uneasy. Kavan had fled Rhidam because of her impetuousness, Espen had been chased away by her inability to commit to what she wanted most, k'gdhededhá Tythilius was dead, and Ártur MacLyr was hovering on the brink behind him. Too much to bear alone, and yet not a burden she could easily share with her brother, the King. There had been a time when they had served as confidante to one another, a simpler time when their father was still alive, but that had evaporated with Hagan's ascension to the throne. Nervously twisting her long black hair around her fingers, a habit carried over from childhood, she watched Gaelán's distracted face on the opposite side of the Stateroom, Asta's smaller hand clutched in his, both blood-splattered and dark-eyed and trying not to yawn. They had been awake too long, but at least it appeared that the novice healer had reined in his unchecked tears.

The story had come out in bits and pieces, at least as much of it as could be revealed to the King. The healer had received a message claiming Kavan was in need of healing at the Boar's Garden on the northwest outskirts of Rhidam. No one at the table questioned why Ártur would risk going alone to aid his cousin in the dead of night without considering the dangers. Gaelán had found the message in Ártur's room, and aware of the previously made threat on the healer's life, deduced the letter to be a ruse and went after him, leading Justice Corbin and the guards on their search for the missing healer. Without Gaelán, they would not have found Ártur until he was abandoned, dead. Without Gaelán, the man's internal bleeding would have been too long untreated and he would have no chance of survival. Gaelán was the hero of the night, even if he did not feel as though he was.

There were unanswered questions, however, as no attackers lived to give useful clues. Caol had killed one, Asta had killed two others, and the rest had been obliterated. The three bodies they had would be identified if possible, but the inquisitor had little hope of learning much about them, particularly since King Hagan demanded that the Association be kept out of the matter. Caol left the room in an angry huff, much to Hagan's astonishment, but the young king did not have the nerve or experience or will to demand his uncle's return.

The King, his sister, Justice Corbin, General Agis, Gaelán and Asta remained in the Stateroom after the others departed, Syl returning to her husband's bedside. Hagan discussed at length what should be done with the Justice and General after sending a messenger to Levonne requesting Bhríd's hasty return. The two youngest people, not yet dismissed, were ignored as if forgotten.

Taking pity on them, the princess rounded the table and joined the pair on the bench where they had been seated for the entire conference.

"Gaelán?"

"My lady?" he mumbled, trying agai not to yawn.

"Always the gentleman like your father." Diona forced a light smile though she felt no lightness within. "You look weary. You should sleep."

He shook his head, his stubborn expression looking much the way his father's did. "I cannot…Ártur might need me…"

She resisted stroking his hair. That was a gesture for a child and he had proven that he was not that. "Lady MacLyr is with him; she will summon you when you are needed, I'm certain. You will be of no use if you are exhausted. Come, I will escort you to your room. Asta, will you fetch a tray for him, please?"

Happy to have some way to help, though she did not want to leave Gaelán, Asta nodded and chirped. "Of course."

There was an unspoken exchange between her and Gaelán before she hurried out of the Stateroom at an unladylike run. Once she had shared her affections evenly between Gaelán, his brother Tayte, and Hagan, but Diona could see that, after last night's adventure, the pair had bonded in a way unlikely to be easily broken. With a wave to her brother and a bow when she received his acknowledgment, Diona guided Gaelán out and up the stairs. They did not speak the entire way up, and when he paused in front of the healer's door, trembling, his gaze riveted on the barrier between him and Ártur, it took force for the princess to steer him gently towards his room.

"It is little comfort to say that you have done everything you can for now, that you are a hero for giving him the opportunity to survive," she murmured warmly, "but if he lives, he will owe you a great debt."

"And if he dies…"

"You did not do this to him, Gaelán…"

"But I did not do enough. And I think…" He sighed and glanced over his shoulder, "if he lives, it will be someone else who deserves the credit."

Thinking he meant Syl, she nodded. "Of course Lady MacLyr will be credited…"

"I don't mean k'aene. Someone else. Someone intervened, stopped the attack; someone is protecting him, keeping him alive."

With her hand on the latch to his chamber door, Diona paused with a sharp breath. His expression revealed his beliefs and his apparent certainty, visible even if his words were less confident, made her knees tremble. "You believe Kavan is…?"

"I do not know how it could be possible…he is too far away…but I am certain it is true…he is there…inside of Ártur."

"He caused those men to…?" She had not seen the carnage, but Caol's description of the scene was vivid enough for her to imagine it.

Gaelán shrugged, his eyes troubled and mournful as Asta appeared with a tray of food faster than any servant could have brought it up. He might not have answered Diona's question, but the princess knew what he had not said.

Asta followed Gaelán into the room and closed the door behind them after a half-curtsey to her cousin.

Diona did not know how Kavan could have done anything, how he could know Ártur needed him. But if Gaelán believed it, that meant it might be true. There was an embarrassed, anxious pain in her chest; perhaps this attack, and Ártur's condition, would bring the bard home.

She wondered what she would do if she ever saw the harper again.

➮*➮

"Any change, Captain?"

The burly man sighed, barely lifting his gaze from the rise and fall of the bard's chest to look at the blind man who had stumbled back into their traveling corner. "None. He mutters in his sleep, but there have been no changes. He neither wakes nor moves."

"Is he dying?"

Wortham choked at the thought and clutched Kavan's hand tighter. "I do not believe so, but I am not Elyri and my knowledge of them is limited to him. I have no idea what his condition truly is."

From deep inside the haze of his mind, from across the thin threads that bound him to Ártur and tethered him to his body, Kavan heard the words, heard the emotion in Wortham's rough voice. He disliked causing his dearest friend pain, but feared that pulling his focus away from his cousin for even a moment while Ártur's hold on life was so fragile, would be an irreversible mistake. He knew the results of his previous efforts from those who touched Ártur's skin, his mind. He knew that many men had met a mysteriously grisly death, knew that his efforts, in combination with Gaelán's and Syl's, were keeping the healer alive. And though the physical injuries had been treated, there was still significant danger. The power Kavan had forced through the psychic link into Ártur's unsuspecting mind, while driving off the attack, had also done its share of damage and compounded the head trauma. Maybe there was other damage too that Syl had yet to heal, but Kavan feared if Ártur died now, it would be his doing.

He could not accept that. Given enough time, the healer's internal rhythms would recover from the shock of power and regain their proper balance. It was the Elyri way. Kavan intended to maintain his connection with his cousin until that balance was struck, holding death at bay. Or he would hold it until his center of energy was depleted, which would cause the link between them to fail.

He did not know which would come first.

But he also felt a strong need to reassure Wortham. This man, more than anyone else, remained faithful through intervals when any lesser man would have turned away. Kavan had behaved abominably during their journey south, had caused the captain unspeakable anguish and frustration, and still Wortham's love remained strong, steadfast, and pure. Kavan owed him this…and so much more.

Though it was difficult to split his attention, he did so for the briefest of moments, long enough to force his hand to contract and squeeze the one that clung to his.

Wortham felt it, felt the shiver it produced that traveled along every nerve ending in his body. Grateful, he kissed the man's fingertips, feeling a shudder at the intimate gesture though he was not certain it was real or imaginary. He looked over his shoulder at Urian with a faint smile. The dedhá could not see Kavan's small gesture, could not see that smile, but Wortham suspected he did not need to.

"I think dedhá, he is going to be fine."

The squeezing hand was reassurance enough.

Once Syl resumed watch over her husband, gdhededhá Tusánt returned to Hes á Redh Náós, wringing his hands the entire way. The King would not allow him to leave the castle without several soldiers, for which Tusánt was deeply grateful., but once they reached the náós gate, Tusánt sent the men back. He was safe here, without Claide to trouble him, and he wanted to be alone. Restless and ill at ease, he spent hours pacing the length of the náós, praying for everyone he could think of, everyone touched by the long, grueling night that had just passed. Everyone except gdhededhá Claide, and he felt no remorse for leaving that man out of his prayers. Claide may not have traveled to Fiara as he asserted, but at least he was not present to be a distraction, to worry Tusánt with trifling matters that paled in comparison to what they had just endured.

"Is it true?" dedhá Rankin's strained voice echoed against the walls of the náós from the far end where he burst in at an almost run. Sweaty and red-faced, having been out on some errand that Tusánt had given no thought to, he stumbled to a stop at the altar steps and gasped, "Has Lord MacLyr been killed?"

The Elyri rubbed his aching eyes, wondering who had started that rumor and when. It had only been a matter of hours. How quickly the truth became distorted, he thought bitterly, particularly when it came to anything Elyri. "He is not dead…or he was not when I left him with his wife. But his condition is not good. Whoever his attackers were, they meant to kill him."

Hands thrown up in a gesture of frustration and despair, Rankin collapsed onto the nearest bench. The hem of his robes was dusty, his boots scuffed from his outing, and his untonsured mouse-brown hair was disheveled and swept haphazardly out of his eyes. "This is absurd. Why must the innocent be abused…for what? A matter of race?"

Tusánt made no effort to hide his surprise. "I did not know…this issue…troubled you…"

"Of course it troubles me! The Faith teaches love, tolerance, peace…we preach it every day…and yet this violence springs from where our words fall and spreads despite our efforts. It is ludicrous. Despite our differences, I do not believe any one of us is more or less equal in the eyes of divinity…except perhaps Lord Cliáth…"

The insult in his tone melted when Tusánt embraced him and held him to his breast for many moments. After his initial surprise, Rankin returned the embrace without hesitation. "You feared I dislike you?"

"I feared our differences were cause for discord, yes…or apathy at the best. We can never assume our allies…and we cannot have too many…cannot be too careful…"

Rankin pulled back to look into his fellow dedhá's face, clasping Tusánt's arms in friendly reassurance. "Please count me among those allies, Tusánt. I have always been thus. I would have it no other way."

"Thank you." It was a touching relief to know that he was not alone within the walls of his Faith. "I…feel I must pray…and I fear I have left the Royal House alone too long as it is, but I must also draft word of these things to Claide…wherever he is. If you are available…would you be willing to offer Lady MacLyr…and the others…a sympathetic ear while I tend these duties?"

"I will go at once." Not a vain man, he felt no need to make himself presentable for the doing of duty, not even when attending nobility. "Is there anything you require before I go?"

"Not unless you know of some way to ensure my safety in this time of day to day violence…"

"There is but one thing I can do." His square face set with determination. "I will make certain that Claide continues to believe I am as apathetic to anti-Elyri violence as you believed I was and serve as your eyes and ears in his presence as much as I can…act as a buffer between you until we find the k'dedhá and this matter is put right."

Find the k'dedhá. Tusánt had almost forgotten about that other grisly subterfuge he held secret. How much longer would that take, to find Jermyn, to make the truth known, to reveal the inevitable that might make Rankin's promises mute?

Until then, he thought with a nod and a murmured word of gratitude, accepting Rankin's offer, and taking up Princess Diona's offer of a guard or two, might be his wisest course of action.

"What is it, Lord Justice?"

After being kept awake most of the night by the unexpected chaos, the King was aggravated to be roused from his afternoon nap for some purpose other than dinner. From the look that passed between his Justice and Inquisitor, he suspected that whatever news they were bringing, it was not going to improve his mood.

"Have you learned something about the attack? Or…" The words stuck in Hagan's throat but he forced himself to ask, "Is Ártur dead?"

"Not to my knowledge, My Lord. The men have discovered…"

"What?"

The King's impatient interruptions, justified in their worry as they were, chafed on Caol's already raw nerves but when he opened his mouth to continue, his annoyance gnawing at the back of his throat, the Justice spoke first. It spared Caol the indignity of uttering some remark he would later regret.

"The men have uncovered a basement door in the storage building where the trunk of…" The Justice shuddered at the unpleasant memory of those dismembered children. "Where the trunk was found. Lord Dugan aided in gaining access. There is a room there, below the building. What we found…we thought you should know of it before the news becomes public." He paused, cast a sidelong glance at Caol in the hopes that the Inquisitor would be the one to speak the words, but when he said nothing, Darius continued, "We discovered the body of k'dedhá Tythilius and have taken him to the náós for burial."

The King's face paled. "The body? His body? He is…dead?"

"With the condition of his corpse, there is no way any man or woman could live through the brutality of the torture he must have endured, My Liege. He is barely recognizable as anything other than a man. It is not a pleasant sight." The strangled, sickened measure of the Justice's voice supported his words.

"Barely recog…then how do you know it is him? Perhaps it is someone else…" The King hoped it was anyone else. The murder of k'dedhá Tythilius, if murder and torture it had been, would be a crippling blow to the Faith, to Rhidam, and the stability of Enesfel.

"This was on his finger." Caol held the ecclesiastical ring of the man's office in the palm of his hand, the ring the portly clergyman had worn during his entire tenure in Rhidam. King Hagan reached to touch it but jerked his hand away before contact was made, bumping Caol's hand, knocking the ring to the floor, where it clattered before coming to a silent stop, its crystal blue stone popping from its setting and cracking upon impact. The inquisitor retrieved both the ring and the stone with a grunt as the King lurched to his feet.

"I want to see him at once."

Knowing his nephew's weak constitution well, Caol asked, "My Liege, is that wise? He is…as Justice Corbin says, a gruesome sight."

With a dismissive wave, the King replied, "How bad can it be?" He had seen a man beheaded, had seen the dismembered bodies of children, had seen his father's corpse. Though his stomach churned at each of those memories, how could anything, he mused, be worse than that. "Besides, he is…was…the k'gdhededhá of Enesfel's Faith. As King, I should tend him…and see that it is as you claim."

"The ring is not proof enough?" the Justice asked.

But Caol knew the answer to that question, and he followed the King and Justice from the keep without saying anything more. Hagan was prone to demanding concrete proof, and frequently would accept nothing less. When he saw the princess in an open doorway as they passed, he nodded, doing his best to ignore the knot in his stomach.

Thus far, their plan was proceeding as intended.

The King needed but a short glimpse of the corpse to flee the thóres, sick to his stomach. He did not remain long enough to take in the details, but the bloody, hairless, twisted form that he would swear no longer bore a bit of skin, was enough. He could not imagine how anyone could determine that thing was a man, let alone the k'dedhá.

"It was not easy, My Lord," Tusánt was saying with a hand on his shoulder as the King's hearing began to return, "but I read him…as much as I could stomach. It is…or rather was…k'dedhá Jermyn."

"He…he must be buried…at once…before anyone else sees…"

Tusánt could not agree more. "His wishes were to be buried in Alberni, where he was born. Perhaps the dedhá at Saint Kóráhm's will permit his burial there. Unless you insist that his burial be in Rhidam."

"I don't care where you bury that thing. I want it gone," the King spat. Seeing Tusánt's pained, dismayed reaction, Hagan regained his composure and bowed his head. "My apologies, dedhá…but that…is not…the k'dedhá. He is gone. Bury that wherever you think best. We will have a service here…for him…and you will get word to dedhá Claide? He must be summoned back to Rhidam at once."

It took great effort for the Elyri to keep his expression neutral at the mention of Claide. "He did not tell me his schedule, where he will be, but I will do my utmost to see he is informed and summoned home. May I have leave in the interim to take k'gdhededhá to Alberni?"

"Tonight? Oh…yes…I suppose you should see to those details before anyone sees him here. I should return to the castle and break this news to my sister…to Lady MacLyr…they will want to know."

"I can do that," Caol offered, attempting to relieve the King of this unpleasant duty.

Hagan shook his head. "No…I think this is something I should do. Your job…you and Justice Corbin, is to find whoever did this and make them pay for their crimes. Do whatever it takes to find those responsible…but leave the Association out of it."

Mouth puckered, Caol turned back to look at his nephew, making no effort to disguise his annoyance. "My Liege, how do you suggest I do my job without the resources? It is not possible."

"Make it possible, Lord Dugan. That is final." Knowing his uncle was angry without seeing his inquisitor's expression, the King was thankful he could not look the man in the eye. Despite what his uncle said to the contrary, Hagan no longer trusted the Association contacts Caol utilized on the Crown's behalf. He felt certain those contacts were part of a much bigger problem.

It was time for that connection between the Lachlans and the Association to end.

❧Chapter 4❧

Watching the ship pull away from Pháne, Prince Muir wondered if he was doing the right thing by remaining behind with the second shift of soldiers recruited to staff his outpost. With the barracks reduced to smoldering rubble, the men would be forced to sleep in the open, forced to live sparsely, until the next ship arrived with food, water, and enough supplies to begin rebuilding the charred fortification. Nothing remained of the structure except the foundation; the attacking ship's fire had done its work.

So, Muir noted with grim satisfaction, have we. The vessel that had come upon the island during the night could be seen several hundred yards out to sea, half-submerged with wisps of white smoke curling up from those portions not yet swallowed beneath the water. What had become of her crew, he wondered? Had any survived or had the waves claimed them all? If so, it was a terrible way to die, a fate the prince did not wish on anyone. But that ship and its crew had been the aggressor, and Muir's men had the right to defend themselves. He did not feel guilty about the deaths of strangers, and intended to send men to scour the island's coastline in case anyone, dead or alive, washed up on its craggy shore.

As further precaution, he organized a second search team to row out to the wreckage to scavenge either salvageable supplies or survivors. He and the men remaining on Pháne had the responsibility of clearing away rubble and debris and preparing for the next attack since the Prince felt certain it would come. It did not seem likely that last night's assault would be the last.

❧*❧

Balint Gabersdon hesitated at the gate of Saint Kóráhm's, his horse's reins in his hand, anxious to be gone back to Rhidam yet not wanting to leave. Dhybhé was stronger, her health returning under the care of the women and men in this place, and he knew he would see her again. He had never been one to mourn parting company with anyone, not even his parents; he saw mourning as an unproductive waste of effort. But he readily admitted he would miss her more than he had anticipated, and that realization, as well as the other events during his time in Alberni, troubled him.

Having witnessed the gdhededhá late that first night in the burial plot, presuming that someone had died, he was confused to find no marker on the plot, no trace of anything more than the freshly turned earth. It was likely, if the death had been a sudden one, that an appropriate marker had not yet been crafted, but questioning gdhededhá Garrett as to the individual's identity gained him only grim faced silence, something that, to Balint, indicated either intense mourning or subterfuge. He had thought little more about it until late last evening, when gdhededhá Tusánt arrived from Rhidam with the mutilated body of the lake k'gdhededhá of Enesfel, asking that the man be buried in Saint Kóráhm's burial ground. A handful of the residents showed little surprise at the request, as it should be since the revered man hailed from Alberni. But even fewer faces expressed a lack of surprise at the man's death.

He was buried, as requested, in a prominent location in Saint Kóráhm's plot, not in the hidden corner of recently turned earth, and then Tusánt departed to oversee a memorial service for the patriarch in Rhidam. Tusánt, after a melancholy greeting and explanation given to the knight, asked Balint to join him in his return, but Balint would not, under any circumstances, leave his beloved horse behind.

Besides, he continued to hope he might learn something about that first grave.

But he gained nothing, and whatever the brothers and sisters of Saint Kóráhm's knew about the k'gdhededhá's demise, they were not forthcoming with the details. Deciding that Tusánt would be a more forthcoming source of information, and hoping he would reach Rhidam in time for the service, Balint was starting for Rhidam with the rising of the sun, his horse as eager as he was to be away. Whether he reached Rhidam in time for the service or not, he would have the truth, and he would offer his continuing sympathy and sword to those who had known the patriarch best.

And he hoped, for the sake of clear-headedness, that the long ride would give him the opportunity to sort out why Dhybhé's absence from his life felt so peculiarly troublesome.

❧*❧

Bhryell was unusually still that morning in the bhydáni's opinion, wrapped in a pall that none of those people passing in the street outside of his home noticed. They seemed ignorant of the cloud of gloom, seem unconcerned, unaware, and unaffected by the disquiet that plagued Tíbhyan. He rested on a stool near his open door, watching the townsfolk go by, knowing each by name, clicking his walking stick against the wall as if ticking off each person he counted. The pain and discomfort of last night's episode were gone, finally allowing him to sleep, but an unfitful rest and the dawning of a new day had left him feeling no better, particularly since it seemed that no one else in the village had experienced anything out of the ordinary.

Then he noted the familiar figure of Bhen MacLyr running towards him, red-faced, disheveled, with an expression that bordered on distraught. Something had happened. It had not been Tíbhyan's imagination. Perhaps Kavan had returned and was injured or ailing. That could, depending on the nature of injury or ailment, explain what had occurred. The ancient man leveraged himself up with his cane, to greet the young man on unsteady legs and receive the news he brought.

"It is Ártur…" Bhen started, dispensing with pleasantries in his breathless haste. During the years the sage had known Kavan, he had grown to know the bard's family as well, and any news pertaining to his favorite student was of interest. Healer MacLyr was one of those closest to Kavan; if something unfortunate had befallen Ártur, Tíbhyan wanted to know that too. "He was attacked…last night…in Rhidam. Syl is with him. I do not know how he…I am on my way to tell gdhededhá Kesábhá and gdhededhá Bhílári…"

"Go then," the sage gestured, voice small, wobbling on legs that threatened to give way beneath the weight of that news. "Thank you."

Bhen nodded and continued across the village to the náós.

Ártur. Attacked. Nearly killed if Bhen's tone and expression were any measure. It explained the pall Tíbhyan could taste in the air, the disquiet in his soul…and it explained something else.

That eruption of power experienced during the night now had a source. The draining he had felt just before it had been neither arbitrary nor malicious. He knew of only one man possibly capable of such a feat, who might be able to tap into his power and use it in defense of another, in defense of Ártur. With a ghost of a smile on his lips but sadness in his eyes, colored by his concern for both healer and the bard who had endeavored to save his life, Tíbhyan settled back on his stool and closed his eyes.

It was good to know Kavan was still alive. Not knowing either man's condition, however, was a worrisome thing.

❧*❧

Princess Diona allowed the dice to fall from her hand without looking at them, her attention turned towards the window though she could see nothing through it except the cloudless blue sky. Her heart was not in the game, nor were her thoughts as she glanced at her brother across the table where they played, at his suggestion. He had seen the k'gdhededhá's body, something she had been unable to bring herself to do, and from his subdued demeanor since, she knew her reluctance was justified. Why see the man's face as it had become? Why mar what she remembered with the horror that would forever replace it if she viewed the truth?

Every citizen in Rhidam would soon know the secret she had lived with for the last several weeks. It would be a relief to discuss the prelate's death openly, perhaps, to share her grief and horror, but what she had learned about her brother through this disaster did not ease her suffering or her mind.

She could not offer a single reason why anyone might want to kidnap the k'gdhededhá without subsequently demanding a ransom, a single reason anyone might choose to inflict such tortures on the man, a single reason that would not implicate dedhá Claide or give away her suspicions. k'dedhá Jermyn had been pro-Elyri, had spent half of his life living in Elyriá, and many of his closest acquaintances were Elyri. Diona believed that to be a significant portion of the reason for Jermyn's death. Other than that, no one, as far as she knew, had cause to hate the man enough to be so brutal. To her knowledge, most of Rhidam, most of Enesfel, nearly everyone Jermyn had met, had adored him…except for the man who wanted the power Jermyn's office held.

Hagan had scoffed at her. He proclaimed the anti-Elyri violence had nothing to do with Jermyn's death. He had been abducted as a by-product of it, perhaps, but Hagan believed the guilty must surely be someone with a grudge who had taken advantage of the chaos, not an anti-Elyri zealot. Despite his entrenchment in that belief, he could not offer a reason or example of such a grudge, or who might hold one, that did not, in some way, tie back into the violent scourge devouring Enesfel from within.

The princess bit her lip and refused to speak about it further, dismayed at her brother's stance. Perhaps clinging to that belief made him feel better, safer, more secure. Either that, or believing the k'dedhá had no enemies because of his political beliefs, thinking some other matter of animosity was the cause, thinking that anti-Elyri posturing was limited to the common and the uneducated, was an indicator of just how naïve her brother was.

The violence would touch the Lachlans directly in time, more directly than the death of k'dedhá Jermyn or the attack on Ártur. Next time it would be someone closer, and not necessarily one of the Elyri they employed.

It was conceivable that she or Hagan could be targets, a frightening possibility that the King refused to acknowledge.

"I have a delivery for you, Your Majesty." The soldier Denyan, once one of Káliel's elite but now part of the Lachlan guard since long before Diona and Hagan were born, stopped in the doorway of the dayroom and bowed.

"A delivery?" The King looked at his sister. "I am not expecting anything."

"A large trunk delivered on a wagon, My Lord. The driver said he was paid by two men on the docks to bring it to you, but he does not know what the trunk contains or who sent it."

"From Lady Dilyn, perhaps," Hagan said with a smile as he offered his arm to his sister. Anything arriving by ship had likely come from Káliel or Hatu, and a delivery from Hatu would likely have come via Prince Harcourt.

Denyan continued. "After the recent discoveries, Justice Corbin thought it wise to detain the driver and show caution when opening it until you arrived."

"Of course. Thank you. Shall we inspect our gift, Diona?"

More out of concern for her brother's welfare than any curiosity, she took his offered arm and replied, "If you wish it."

The trunk in the courtyard was indeed large, the width of the wagon bed from which it had been unloaded and nearly a third of its breadth. It was of expensive construction, oak and iron, with gold leaf insets, newly made and showing little wear from its travels. There were several latches held closed with a heavy chain and a single lock, but there was no visible key and the wagon's driver did not have it.

The King circled the trunk several times, admiring the craftsmanship, more certain than before, judging by both its construction and the heavy aroma wafting from it, that the Prime Magistrate of Káliel must have been the one to send such a costly gift. They waited for Caol to arrive to open the lock, as the King was hesitant to break it and knew that his inquisitor had the skill necessary to slip the mechanism. If the lock was of workmanship comparable to the trunk, it could be used for some other purpose so long as it was not damaged.

When the inquisitor arrived, he did not look at his nephew or speak to him. The page who fetched him had told him the purpose for the summons so there was no need to ask, and Caol was beyond small talk with the monarch who demanded he do his job but stripped him of the tools he needed to do it. After his own slow circle around the trunk, visually inspecting it for clues as to how it opened, and what it might contain, judging by the peculiar mix of aromas coming from within, he squatted to examine the lock, expecting some manner of trap. When he was satisfied there was none, he picked the lock with the tools in his breast pocket without offering a word or explanation.

Despite its visible quality, its mechanism was a simple one that required little effort to open. As a final precaution, however, once the lock and chain were removed and the latches popped open one by one with the blade of his knife, Caol stepped back, motioning everyone else back as well, and used one foot to kick the lid open, ignoring the King's aborted exclamation of disgust over such a seemingly callous, unwarranted action.

"Bags?"

"Spice," Caol muttered as if the King should know what the tightly woven cloth bags contained simply by the variety of aromas perfuming the air as the trunk opened. Removing them one by one, he opened each and handed them to whoever happened to be closest.

"Cinnamon. Cloves. Dill. Fennel. Seems they sent everything…"

"No need to identify them, Uncle. I'm sure the cooks will know what they are," Hagan quipped in amusement, missing his uncle's irritation or choosing to ignore it.

Hoping to avoid the unpleasant confrontation simmering around them, Diona asked, "Why send this without a message? This is an expensive collection."

"Perhaps there is a message at the bottom." The King drew closer as the last bag was removed from the trunk, but there was nothing there to see. Caol squatted again, keeping his back to the King, this time studying the wooden bottom with eyes and fingertips, rapping it occasionally with the hilt of his knife. To his eye, the interior bottom was too high from the exterior. Holding his breath, hands trembling as he worried about what he might uncover, he slid the knife blade along one inner edge to pry the bottom lose, to lift it up…

…and immediately dropped the knife into the contents of the hidden compartment. The words of annoyance the King had been about to utter regarding Caol's wanton destruction of such an expensive gift, were lost behind his sister's gasp as she fainted against him. Hagan, retching now with his back to the trunk, failed to catch her. His face was discolored and moist, hidden behind his hands from the soldiers who came to assist both him and the princess.

"How many?" Justice Corbin asked in an uncomfortable tone as he tried to rouse Diona.

"Seven." The six missing children, Caol thought with disgust. The six children whose torsos and severed limbs had already been buried in the Lachlan crypt against the King's wishes, he was certain, and one other. The inquisitor was willing to swear to it without the proof of an Elyri here to identify them. Those six children and his little informant.

Though he had no connection to the first six, the seventh child's death was his personal burden to bear because he had been the one to pay her for information when she could not have known the risks of speaking with him. Caol may not have killed her, but her blood was on his hands. The sight of severed heads would not normally have affected him much, but these were children, each under ten years of age, and one of them he knew.

He felt sick.

But at least, due to her inclusion, he had a suspect.

"Should they be buried with…?"

Caol did not need to finish. The King did not know where the others were buried, but he nodded vigorously in agreement, refusing to look back until the inquisitor closed the trunk. "I will see to it…and have a talk with the delivery agent." Again the King nodded. If Hagan considered that his inquisitor would take this matter up with his Association contacts, he for once made no mention of it and did not forbid Caol to make use of them. Not forbidding him was as good as sanctioning their use. Both the King and Caol wanted answers.

❧*❧

With Owain called away, this time to intervene in a fight in Fiara's square, Kjell was left to his private pursuits this morning while Espen wrote a letter to the Lachlan princess. Kjell spent several hours wandering the halls of his cousin's home before settling in the library, his thoughts uncharacteristically scattered and disjointed. He hoped that reading would clear his head and allow him to tackle the topic of recent discussion from some other angle. He could read, all de Cormicks could, but censorship was prevalent in Neth and to Kjell, there was little left worth reading. Any documents of import or interest had been confiscated, locked away or destroyed by the monarchy's paranoid effort to control what their subjects knew.

But Owain's library contained many histories, religious works, and a large number of volumes written by Elyri authors, works that intrigued Kjell enough to prompt him to pull a religious text written by an Elyri from the shelf. Such a work would bring execution if it was discovered in Neth, but in Fiara, Kjell felt safe. This might be his sole exposure to such materials, and wanting to make the most of the opportunity, he sat near the window to read.

Kjell did not doubt his capacity to rule, nor did he doubt his ability to hold the throne once he had it. If it came to pass, such censorship would be lifted. The military backed him and he knew how to manipulate people to his advantage. Unlike most de Cormicks before him, he despised needless bloodshed or he would have ousted his inept, blood-thirsty brother long ago. If he ever did rule, Kjell wanted to be remembered in the historical chronicles, those that told the truth that was and not some distorted, state-sanctioned version of it, as an honest man who lived morally, justly, and did right by his people.

Rubbing his fingers across his brow and cheekbone, he closed the book without reading more than a few sentences. If he were honest with Owain and himself, he would admit there was one obstacle keeping him from demanding his place as King. Fear. He had known since before King Loris' death that he was different from the rest of the de Cormick bloodline. No one had told him, and he suspected that his mother had been the sole holder of the truth, but Kjell felt certain that the late King Loris was not his father. Not that it should matter; more than one de Cormick king had been a bastard child, their lineage overlooked so long as they retained the de Cormick name. But Kjell suspected that, whoever his father had been, he had been no ordinary Nethite. There was potential in that unrevealed secret to damage Kjell, to turn his life upside down, thus he neither pursued the truth nor placed himself in a position where anyone might be interested in finding something to use against him. He would allow history to pave his path rather than actively carve out a future for himself.

Whatever would be, would be.

But he was beginning to think it was time for that fear to be set aside. That it was time for action. But what action, he mused with his hand stroking the cover of the book, did he want to take?

❧*❧

"You feel it too…when you touch him. Don't you?"

"Feel what?" Syl felt many things when she touched her husband's immobile, silent form, but she did not think most of them concerned her brother's son. The unconscious man looked better than he had, color returning to his cheeks, his muscles relaxing as the trauma bled out of them, but he had not yet shown signs of waking and both healers were worried about what that could mean.

Gaelán perched on the edge of the bed and stared at Ártur for many minutes before speaking again, certain his aunt would ridicule him, or not believe him, for what he wanted to say. "There is someone else with him," he murmured. "Someone keeping him alive. It is like…two minds inside of his. Here…I will show you…"

He took her hand to point out the traces of power he felt, the power he believed she had not noticed. It was fainter now, as he struggled to point her in the right direction, and then it disappeared altogether as if retreating from his efforts to find it. Ártur was alone in his own body; his breathing stabilized, his pulse eased into a normal rhythm, and the tense set of his mouth relaxed.

Syl stared at the young man. "What did you do?"

Gaelán shook his head. "I did nothing, aene. I wanted to show you the other, but it is gone now. I did nothing else." He watched as she closed her eyes and placed a hand on the rise and fall of Ártur's chest.

"He is out of danger." Her voice carried deep relief. "Whatever was holding him back…"

Exasperated, Gaelán snorted, "It was not holding him back! It was keeping him alive until he could survive alone. I am not speaking false, aene; it is true! I felt it, even if you did not!"

"Gaelán," she said to the petulant youth. "There is no need to…"

Her scolding was interrupted by a knock on the door and both looked up as Gaelán's father entered the room.

"I came as soon as I received word." The black-haired Elyri offered a hand to each, feeling the tension in the room and hoping to act as a bridge to ease it. "How is he? Is there anything I can do?"

"He is out of danger, due to our collective efforts." Syl squeezed Gaelán's other hand, acknowledging his contribution, and though he did not withdraw from the gesture of gratitude, he was still annoyed. "If you want to do something, tágdhá, convince him to come home."

Gaelán crossed his arms, his patience running thinner. "Who will train me? Who will be the Lachlans' healer? I can't do it! He can't go! He needs to be here when k'aendhá Kavan…"

"Enough, son." Bhríd clasped the young man's shoulder, failing to understand the changes that had come over his son in the last several months. It was more than discovering he was a healer, or of approaching adulthood. There seemed something more at play and Bhríd intended to find out what it was. "This is not the time for this. You and I will talk later."

"If you are going to lecture me about going out of the castle alone, don't. I was not alone, and if I had not gone, he would be dead," Gaelán grumbled pulling away from both hands and getting up from the bed to put distance between himself and the adults.

Bhríd scowled and cleared his throat. "Since you seem to know so much about what has happened, you will tell me the story. Then we are going to talk about decorum, comportment, and adulthood. Is that clear, Gaelán? And I will talk with you later, sister."

"I will be here," she sighed apologetically. She was not straying far from her husband's side until he opened his eyes. "Please excuse my absence from the memorial to the king…" Hagan would understand her fear of leaving Ártur, her fear of putting herself and her daughter at risk. They were fears Bhríd understood as well.

Gaelán trudged after his father, his expression angry instead of chastised or concerned about punishment. He had never been prone to fantasy or dishonesty. If he was giving in to either, then both Syl and Bhríd knew something was wrong.

But if, as Syl suspected, he was telling the truth, he might require more training then Ártur could give him. Syl had been reluctant to read her nephew, reluctant to learn the truth. She did not want to admit that Gaelán might possess gifts she did not, that he had been right in his assessment that it was not her healing, or his, that had saved Ártur's life, brought Ártur back. If it had been someone else, if it had been Kavan as Gaelán implied, such news might be enough to convince

Ártur to remain in Rhidam awaiting his savior, and Syl was as afraid of that possibility as she was of his death.

❧*❧

Despite his efforts to maintain a constant vigil, Wortham jerked awake when his head lolled awkwardly to one side. He wiped the moisture from the corners of his mouth as he glanced quickly around, hoping no one had been witness to his undignified state. He judged it to be late evening since Zelenka was asleep and gdhededhá Urian had ceased whittling in favor of his bedtime prayers. Wortham had been asleep long enough for the day's end to pass unnoticed. There was a hungry twist in his stomach, and though he knew where their rations were stored, he did not want anything. It required moving, which he did not want to do.

A salty breeze swirled through the open hatch nearby, making him shiver, but rather than close it or find a blanket to warm himself, his first thought was to adjust Kavan's coverings, to see to the bard's comfort before his own. During that short passing of time, the Elyri had slipped out of his rigid trance into a seemingly comfortable repose. His breathing was that of shallow weakness and fatigue, but if his life had been in danger before, it seemed that danger was behind them.

Wortham smiled with relief. He could rest without worry now. Perhaps tomorrow, if the bard awoke, he would share what had happened. If he chose not to talk about it, Wortham would be content with that too. For tonight, the captain closed the porthole window and lay down beside his friend, one hand crooked around the Elyri's arm, lending the bard his warmth as he fell swiftly into a welcome sleep.

❧Chapter 5❧

It appeared as if everyone in Rhidam had crowded into the expansive Gathering Hall of Hes á Redh Náós, filling the benches, congregating in the aisles, massing around the doorways and overflowing into the yard beyond. It was a testament to the late k'gdhededhá's generosity and faith. For a man as self-effacing as Jermyn had been, humble to the end of his days, a display of such devotion would have moved him to tears if he had been alive to witness it. Jermyn Tythilius had never believed himself greatly loved or respected, had believed himself to be a forgettable sort of man, and the manner in which he had died had likely reinforced those beliefs in his final hours. Maybe he had believed no one would ever find his body, ever learn the truth, would miss him when he was gone. Or perhaps, shuddered Tusánt as he stepped away from the pulpit to allow gdhededhá Rankin to speak, something good could come from the man's death. If the unity expressed by those gathered in his name today could hold, perhaps there would be peace in Enesfel again.

He was partially glad, partially disappointed, that Claide was not present to witness this. If the senior Teren clergyman saw this devotion and solidarity, he would likely gnash his teeth in annoyance that the Elyri-sympathetic man should have garnished such a following. It would also likely have angered him to the point of taking action, initiating another surge of violence more deadly than before. For that reason alone, because he believed Rhidam needed peace more than he needed to make a point to Claide, Tusánt thought it best that Claide was far away from Rhidam today.

The aroma of rose and amber incense drew his attention from Rankin's words, causing them to fade into a buzzing stream of sound. He had read what Rankin intended to say; he already knew the words. When Tusánt came to Rhidam twenty-two years ago, it had been the example of k'dedhá Tythilius that had drawn him. He had mistakenly believed the man's presence would make Elyri safe in Enesfel, and hence it would be safe for Tusánt. Seven years into his tenure, he was disavowed of that notion by a string of attempts on his life that left him warier and more cynical. Yet life had gone on and the danger had passed, and over time he had again settled into a routine without constantly peeping over his shoulder for threats in the shadows. But that danger had never truly gone, had instead buried deep in Enesfel's gut to fester unseen. The harder Jermyn and Tusánt and others tried to foster harmony between Teren and Elyri, the more resentful Claide had become, the more the darkness in the land had grown.

The wound was now a raw, open thing, oozing with the pus of violence and anger. Jermyn could no longer apply the salve in the hopes of healing the one-sided rivalry, and anything Tusánt felt he could do might only make matters worse. Was there anyone, anything, that could bring peace to Enesfel, he wondered, or must every Elyri die or be driven out of the lands before the Teren were satisfied?

The chords of a brass-strung harp brought Tusánt back to the ceremony and caused his heart to flutter and pound in his throat. Could it be? But it was only the harpist in the choir loft, joined by the voices of the eight children, indicating the end of the two-hour High Gathering. Shakily, the Elyri gdhededhá rose to give the benediction. He did not know precisely why he felt such a powerful instant of joy with that sound, why the thought of Lord Cliáth's presence should fill him with hope. But he was too much a believer in intuition and premonition to dismiss the feeling. Though he did not know what the hope in his soul meant, it did not mean it was meaningless.

General Agis wiped his hands on his black trousers before pushing the stone slab into place over the crypt. Burying those heads with their tiny dismembered bodies was not a task that should have fallen to the Lord High General of Enesfel, but the King had been unable to make any commands regarding their disposition, his revulsion too great, and the only other man willing to take up the task was the inquisitor. The general did not think Lord Dugan should be expected to do the job alone, so after dedhá Rankin blessed the grisly new additions, Agis stayed to assist the inquisitor in laying the children to rest properly. The task was mostly complete by the time Agis sent Caol away to attend the High Gathering in the náós. The nomad was not one for large gatherings of people, and had not been as close to the holy man as Caol had been, although he had held deep respect for him. Caol, on the other hand, had been one of that core few who had come to Rhidam together to make Arlan Lachlan the king so many years ago. The dedhá had been part of that too. It was proper for the inquisitor to pay his final respects with those who had begun that journey together.

Besides, there had been something eating at the general, something he wanted to investigate before these unfortunate children were interred forever in the Lachlan family crypt. When he was alone with them, before the stone was sealed, Agis untied the bag and removed a single head. Examining the stump of the child's neck confirmed what he had suspected after his first glimpse at the dismembered torsos. The angle of the cut, the direction it had fallen, the slight saw-toothed edge of the impact, were details only a Cíbhóló, or one familiar with their culture, might recognize. It was the mark of the waji, the weapon of execution and sacrifice amongst his people. Warriors of great distinction, or a tribal shaman, could possess the waji, and such a man or woman would give up their life before parting with their blade. To protect one's tribe from great danger, to repeatedly survive against staggering odds, for distinguished performance in combat, or to kill a warrior who already carried it, any of those deeds could earn someone the waji, if their tribe thought them worthy of it. Agis had not gained such personal distinction before he left the desert to serve King Arlan. While he did not regret his choice, he did often wish to return to his people long enough to win the honor of the waji for himself.

But it appeared, from what he saw, that the waji had come to him. This mark indicated that Asta Dugan's claims were accurate. There was a Cíbhóló connected to the people calling themselves Corylliens, a man calling himself Narn after the greatest warrior in Cíbhóló oral history…a man stooping low enough to execute, sacrifice, innocent children. But to what end?

Agis had come to Enesfel for the adventure of serving a prince in a foreign land and had stayed out of respect for that prince. In return, Agis had become a general, a leader, a position and title he might not have gained in the desert with four older brothers to claim the head of the family and the tribe. But Narn was a name usually given to the oldest male child, and the waji made this stranger someone of eminence and power amongst the tribesmen. He should have had everything a tribesman could want, so what, Agis wondered, had brought him out of the desert, into Enesfel, to kill children?

Once the crypt was closed and sealed, the general strode to his quarters, deep in thought. *You think none will know the mark, that perhaps I will not see,* he mused. *Or perhaps you do not know I am here. I am Cíbhóló. I know. I can find you. I will find you. By the breath and blood of my forefathers, I will hunt you to the ends of the land. Your reign of terror and insult will cease. The waji will be mine.*

❧*❦

Fingering the blue cord which held his hair at the nape of his neck, Bhríd stood beside his sister, looking at Ártur's sleeping form as he quietly murmured, "I apologize for Gaelán…"

She squeezed his free hand between hers. There were dark circles beneath her brother's eyes, but he had dismissed her earlier efforts at doctoring him. Once upon a time, it had been easier to take care of her older brother. It seemed maturity and the burdens of life had brought an end to that intimacy. When she released his hand, he sank into the chair beside hers. "There is no need or excuse for…"

He brushed away her words with a gesture but did not immediately speak until his visual appraisal of the healer was complete.

"Perhaps…but I feel I must explain. Not excuse but…" He shrugged. "He is maturing, of course…and after what he has endured recently, he is beginning to wonder if becoming an adult is worth the trouble. And he feels bound to Kavan…indebted…perhaps because he saved his life. Kavan's absence has affected him more acutely then I expected and I am at a loss to offer reassurance or advice. Mostly, I believe his outbursts of attitude stem from learning how different he is from his brother, that even though they share the same parentage, he is Elyri in the ways that mark us most, whereas Tayte is not. Not only power…but physically…his hair…his younger appearance. Being so different in this time of hatred is undoubtedly frightening, even if he will not say so. He might not even see it as fear, but fear is what I sense when we speak."

The slight lines around Syl's mouth and eyes tightened. "He should be afraid. So should you."

Bhríd snorted. "I am the King's Champion, the finest knight in Enesfel." There was no boasting in his statement; it was a fact known through Enesfel and beyond. "I am always on guard…"

"But you are one man. If a large group…and you were unarmed…or someone has a bow…or poison."

Still studying Ártur's face, he clasped his sister's arm lovingly. The healer had not yet opened his eyes, but if Syl proclaimed him to be out of danger, it was likely true.

"I am always armed, Syl. Even when I sleep, my sword and dagger are within reach. I must think about Madalyn and the boys. Tayte has every appearance of being Teren, but those who know him, or know his family history, know the truth. He is vulnerable, even if he thinks he is not. And Madalyn…I will not leave her during these troubling times, no matter the price to myself unless we determine it to be in her, their, best interest. For now, I stay in Enesfel for my family."

"What price must Ártur pay? Or our children?" She glanced into the cradle where Chethá slept. "She does not know her father." Wiping her eyes on the back of her hand, she bit her lip. "He insists he is in no danger here, that he is protected and must stay for the Lachlans…for Kavan…but what good is he to any of them if he is dead?"

And how protected was he if he flaunted those protections at the smallest provocations?

"Kavan would not want him to lose his life on his account," Bhríd conceded. Anyone who knew Kavan would admit that. "Perhaps this brush with death will convince him it is time to go home."

From the tone of his voice, however, Syl knew her brother did not believe that would happen any more than she did.

❧ * ❧

Closing the wooden shutters of his home, it took effort for Bhendhámyn MacLyr to resist rushing to Rhidam as he longed to do. If Ártur had died, he trusted he would know by now. If he was still in danger, his life still in the balance, he believed he would know that too. But still, he worried. Since neither case appeared to be true, then something else was preventing Syl from returning home, and not knowing what that was made Bhen anxious. He was a man who thrived on action and information, being called a gossip by some and overly talkative by others. But Ártur was his uncle, and Bhen felt he had the right to know what was happening, particularly since Llucás continuously asked questions for which Bhen had no answers. When were his mother and sister coming home? Had something bad happened? Was his father okay?

This morning, Bhen had been at the náós bidding farewell to k'gdhededhá Kesábhá, wishing him a safe and productive journey.

Before the man's arrival, Bhen had not been aware of how apathetic the leader of the Faith was to the plight of Elyri outside of their homeland. It was, after all, a common enough belief that Elyri should not be in Enesfel, in any Teren land, even during times of peace. Yet k'gdhededhá Dórímyr had been informed of the current dangers existing abroad, had been told of the fate of k'gdhededhá Tythilius, and had so far done nothing. No words of support for the murdered clergyman, no proclamations made, no attempts to caution Elyri further against the hazards they might face, and no attempts made to summon home any Elyri traveling outside of Elyriá. Dórímyr was not interested in his own peoples' welfare, it appeared, or in the upcoming election of a leader to take Jermyn's place.

Khwílen Kesábhá was not going to tolerate such apathy. Neither, it seemed, were many of their fellow countrymen. Bhen volunteered to confront the k'gdhededhá in Clarys, as he was not a man to avoid confrontation if he felt it justified. If Dórímyr chose to threaten him, to punish him with excommunication, Bhen was willing to accept that price on behalf of all Elyri if it meant keeping those he loved safe. But Khwílen dissuaded him from hasty action. The time was not yet right to take such direct steps. When that time did come, however, when enough ammunition was prepared and enough support gathered to request Dórímyr's removal from his post, if Bhen was still interested in the confrontation, Khwílen would be honored to accept his support.

Until Syl returned to Bhryell, with or without Ártur, Bhen would have to wait. He was not needed in the shop today, and had time on his hands, time that ate at his peace of mind the way a beaver devoured trees. Then, unexpectedly, he smiled. He could take his young charge to visit Bhydáni Tíbhyan. The old sage would have numerous ways to occupy their time, their minds. Perhaps he would even have some way to belay Bhen's fears.

❧*❧

The letter in her hand should not have surprised her. Princess Diona did not know why she felt shocked to learn that the Corylliens, whoever they were, claimed responsibility for the attack on the Court Healer. But it did surprise her that anyone would brashly assault someone in the royal employ, claim responsibility for it, and then make themselves known, albeit anonymously behind the name of a dead man. It was an act of folly and arrogance. There were any number of messages they could be trying to convey to the King with their brutal act, but the most obvious was simple: Elyri were not welcome in Enesfel, even those in the kingdom at the Lachlans' request.

There was nothing to be done about the attack now, however. No way to undo what had been done. There was no trace of the author or the deliverer, Bhríd had not read anything from the parchment to indicate who wrote it and the healer's assailants were all dead. Syl refused to touch it to try, and the King did not consider asking Gaelán to do so. If the inquisitor was allowed to do his job, pursue his investigation while the incident was fresh in the peoples' minds, perhaps something could be learned.

But the King continued to demand that Caol keep the Association out of royal affairs, and without the Association's network of informants and spies, Caol felt helpless. He was paying for those he could from his own resources, and Princess Diona was supplementing that fund with as much coin as she could without raising her brother's suspicions, but both believed there had to be a better way.

King Hagan, however, was currently more interested in the gala he was organizing, a grand event that Diona assumed was his way of avoiding the tediousness of daily drudgery and kingdom-wide mayhem, as well as an effort to erase the reason painful events from their collective memories. Still a child, she mused, folding the letter and tucking it inside her bodice. He was too young to be Enesfel's ruler, too young to shoulder so much responsibility, but by the accident of his gender at birth, he was Enesfel's king. Diona's sole recourse was to make him see the realities of the world while there was still time. Before someone else they loved died.

❧*❦

He was alone in a dark, swaying world when he opened his eyes, but alone was as it should be. The danger had passed. Ártur would live. And though Kavan had no clear idea of how long he had slept, it had been long enough to recover his physical capacities and the majority of the energy stored in his center. Wortham had gotten them to sea somehow, for which Kavan was grateful, as it meant that they were likely, by now, several days closer to their next destination. Pushing up on one elbow, he suppressed a yawn and stared at his hands in the dim light that pierced through the small cracks in the wooden planking above his head. The single porthole nearby was closed.

The healing of his hands was recent enough that it still filled him with awe when he looked at what had been the source of his livelihood throughout his adult life. It would be many years, if ever, before the vivid memories of their disfiguration at the hands of thugs, and those agonizing months of self-flagellation afterward, would fade from Kavan's mind. As he studied them, flexing his fingers, noting the lack of stiffness or any other reminder of the injuries taken from him, he made the silent vow never to forget. He could live without the memory of pain and without recalling the events which preceded that attack, but to forget the hell he had put himself through afterward would leave him open to making those same foolish mistakes again. The agony suffered had been ultimately worth it, however, because it had brought him a deeper understanding of his own nature; in tádóbhmátá, the place of eternal anger and suffering, he had found who he truly was. He had no desire to go back to before, to relearn all that his suffering had taught him. Experiencing it once was enough.

After many days of immobility, his legs were stiff and unsteady, but he climbed from the boat's hold to discover the sun setting over the coastline to the west. The watercraft in these lands always traveled within sight of the shore, and others could be seen both before and behind them. Orynn had told him how sea-trade worked here, and he was satisfied to see that it was as she had explained, though he had no reason to doubt her. She had never lied to him.

He closed his eyes at the thought of her, a response to the pain her absence left. It had been but a few weeks since he had seen her last, yet it felt like an eternity. In some ways, it seemed she had been a dream, a part of something lost upon waking that could not be recaptured, a part of his life he would never be able to return to. She was not of his world, could never be a part of it. And yet she was more a part of him than anyone had ever been because she had revealed to him in her very being that there was no sin in love, that he was a man capable of that emotion, capable of receiving it from others, that there was no shame in it. And now she was gone.

The memory would remain and perhaps the pain of her loss would as well. But it would lessen in time. All pain did.

At the prow, Wortham stood with one arm around Zelenka, his other hand steadying Urian who, though he could not see the purple and gold in the fading day's sky, faced it with a smile. It was good, the bard thought, that Wortham had returned his attention to her and had not remained with him until waking. He feared losing Wortham's affections to a woman, but the captain's care and concern, felt through the touch of his tender hands, had remained steadfast over the last several days. He had seen Kavan through the danger, and then, when Kavan's need had waned, he had refocused on Zelenka. She needed him too, not only as a translator and a friend but something more. Kavan did not need the Sight to know that the two would remain together. He regretted only that such a destiny did not appear to be within his grasp.

Rather than interrupt them, Kavan went astern to watch the churning waves in the boat's wake rather than the sunset. He wondered if he could manipulate the currents enough to hasten the boat on its journey north. Perhaps in the morning, when he was more rested, he would try. His thoughts circled back to the other he had left behind, creating a reluctance to move too quickly away from his dark twin. What was Myreth doing now? Had the cloister opened or had they returned to their daily routine as if Kavan had never been there? Had Myreth been freed of the bonds that had kept him in that place far longer than the Teren around him lived? Did he miss Kavan, the bard wondered, as much as Kavan missed him?

He was humming without realizing, the tune that he and Myreth had composed together, until the footsteps behind made him aware of the sound of his own voice. He did not stop or move until big hands clasped his shoulders lovingly. The captain turned Kavan to face him and pulled him into his embrace. Though normally one to avoid such intimacy, Kavan did not resist. With Wortham, as always, such embraces felt welcome and right.

"Praise k'Ádhá and Kóráhm," Wortham said in a low enough voice that no one but Kavan heard him. Urian had returned below deck and Zelenka held back, giving the men privacy as she watched with uncertainty. The captain coughed to cover the husky emotion in his tone, embarrassed that Kavan might think him close to tears.

He was, but he did not want the bard to see it.

From the place where his head pressed against the side of Wortham's face, breathing in the familiar scent of security and protection the man provided, Kavan murmured, "I was in no danger, Wortham, but I thank you for your concern and care. You have carried on without my guidance…I am grateful to you."

Shrugging, Wortham smiled, shivering at Kavan's breath on his skin, and released the bard to allow enough distance so that they could each regain their composures. "You have a duty, my lord. I could not let anything interfere. Someone had to see that we continued north as planned. It was never a burden. Is everything…is Lord MacLyr…?"

Though Kavan had not been aware of speaking his cousin's name, it did not surprise him either. "He is out of danger. He was…" An involuntary shudder passed through him at the memories he carried of those two separate attacks and he touched the point within him that was Ártur to reassure himself the man was still well. "He was accosted by several assailants…an anti-Elyri attack."

Wortham snorted but said no more as he leaned on the rail, their arms pressed against one another as if to share the burdens of which they spoke through the contact. He had been with Kavan long enough to know what the bard was not saying. The healer had nearly died. Kavan had, in some way, saved his life. Not a miracle, but rather Kavan's awesome, incredible power. Miracles were not always needed; Kavan's own power was often enough. The captain glanced over his shoulder and motioned for Zelenka to join them but she shook her head and would come no closer.

Though he frowned with the disappointment he imagined Kavan felt, he understood the woman's choice and nodded. "Forgive her, my lord. She feels that you do not want her with us…and your condition frightened her. She says you are dhesádhá…"

"Touched by k'Ádhá…or by the gods…" Kavan said, translating for his friend, for once feeling neither sick, offended, or alarmed by her choice of epitaphs. Nor, he realized, was he as seasick as he normally would be after many days at sea. Perhaps he would be spared that torment this time.

Both realizations and the hope of easy travel made him smile. "Perhaps I am. I have no way of debating the issue convincingly on either side. Go to her, Wortham, offer what assurance you can. Tell her I mean her no ill will and welcome her into our companionship."

"Truly?" Wortham did not know why he was asking. Kavan would not have said it if it were not true, and the sincerity in his voice and on his face was almost tangible. Yet he had not expected the Elyri to wholeheartedly welcome this rival for the captain's affections.

"Truly. Go. I wish to be alone with the sea and my prayers. I am not weary. My own company will suffice."

"As you wish," he murmured, kissing the bard's forehead in affection and relief that he was well. "Would you like anything to eat? Are you up for that? You have not…"

"I am fine, Wortham. Set something aside if you wish; perhaps I will eat when I come down. For now, I have no desires."

In the near darkness, he did not watch Wortham and Zelenka go. He was too engrossed in contemplating the uncustomary calm in his soul. He could let Wortham go and knew the man would still be there. He no longer doubted the man's loyalty.

❧*❦

It was Tusánt's habit, when he was unable to sleep, to kneel with his prayer beads at his private altar to settle his soul with the words of any devotion that sprang to mind. Though Claide objected to his having a private altar, the late k'gdhededhá had allowed Tusánt to continue a practice common and popular throughout Elyriá. He suspected it was not the practice itself that bothered Claide, but rather the practitioner. With Jermyn gone, Claide would likely call a halt to the practice if he could, and if Claide was elected the new k'gdhededhá of Enesfel, Tusánt was sure he would.

Fumbling through his drawer in the dark, he tried to locate the simple fabric pouch that contained his beads. A presence, something sinister in the prickle it sent up his spine, made itself known, someone outside of the window. He turned slowly, hand still in the drawer, expecting to see someone watching him there, an assassin perhaps. It would not have surprised him, with the amount of anti-Elyri violence that had spiked throughout Rhidam since the Feast of Saint Kóráhm. It surprised him more that he had not yet received an attack or threat.

He doubted his religious status was protecting him; it certainly had not protected Jermyn.

By the time he faced the window, however, the presence was fading and there was no one to be seen. But there was movement beneath his hand that caused him to jerk away from the drawer, smacking the back of his hand against the upper edge of the dresser. There was something alive inside the bag with his prayer beads. He would swear to it. He gingerly lifted the bag by its drawstring and set the pouch on his nightstand before lighting a candle and gingerly using the handle of the candle snuffer and a nearby stylus to loosen the string so that the pouch would open, not trusting to do it with his fingers. Nothing happened at first, beyond the cessation of movement within the pouch. A little prodding with the stylus, however, drove the intruders out, a pair of small yellow scorpions. Their combined sting would likely have killed him. Pulse quickening, he grabbed his tin water cup and trapped them both beneath it before sinking onto the edge of the bed to catch his racing breath.

The first attempt on his life had come. He was certain the creatures had not come to be in that closed pouch accidentally. Though he wondered what he should do now, particularly with the scorpions, he wiped his brow and frowned. Whatever he did tonight, he knew what he would do first thing in the morning.

He would approach Princess Diona on her suggestion for acquiring personal guards. If done correctly, right under Claide's nose, all the better. It had to be done. He had no desire to be a martyr too.

Tusánt wanted to live.

❧Chapter 6❧

Sir Balint Gabersdon, Duke of the southern city of Nelori, pulled his horse up short, assessing the rabble in front of the merchant shop. They were peaceful but tense, frightened, an indication that something was amiss and that they were there to gawk at it as people often did. It was barely dawn when he reached Rhidam, and he had not expected to be met by anything more than silent streets or other early morning travelers. Dismounting, the knight decided it was his place to investigate since there were no Lachlan guards or Rhidam patrol present to disband the mob before it grew any larger.

They were peaceful now, but that did not mean they would remain so. Fear had a bad habit of breeding chaos.

On the wall near the open establishment door, where it appeared the merchant had been interrupted in his set up for the day's business, a Kílyn cross was painted in red, still glistening as it dripped onto the stone and dirt below. Balint was not sure what the symbol was meant to convey, but he suspected it was intended as a warning.

"Who did this?" he demanded, seeing the merchant beyond the open awning, unsettled and afraid as if hiding from those gathered outside. Balint received no reply but he had not expected one. By the time he pushed to the front of the gathering, he saw something he had not seen from the back; there was a hand on the ground below the defacement, red with blood, the object hacked from the limb it had once been part of and obviously used to paint the symbol.

Not paint then, but blood.

"You." He gestured to the nearest man who clutched a wool cap in his shaky hands. "Summon the Justice and Inquisitor at once. The rest of you, if you cannot tell me who did this or why, go your way."

Rather than touch anything, and wanting to discourage others from doing likewise though he doubted they would dare, Balint stayed near the door, near the defacement, his sword in his hand, staring down any who seemed prone to continue to linger. He motioned for the merchant to approach once the crowd began to hesitantly disperse, some only as far as the other side of the street. With the diminished size of the curious crowd, and the knight's presence lending to a sense of safety, the quaking man reluctantly shuffled closer.

"This is your shop? What do you know of this?"

Unable to look at the severed hand at the knight's feet, the man shook his head and stammered, "I know nothing, my lord…I did not know it was there…until I opened the awning and saw them all…and peeped out to see what they…" He choked on rising bile in his throat and turned his head away.

"Do you have enemies that might target you like this? Has anyone threatened you recently?" The merchant did not appear to be Elyri, given the length of his scraggly beard and his dark brown eyes, but there were other reasons someone might have made him a target.

Again the elderly fellow shook his head. "My lord, what man does not have enemies…business rivals…unhappy customers? But to do something like this? I do not think so."

Rubbing his chin, Balint grunted. Discovering motive was not going to be an easy task, any more than finding the guilty party would be. As the old man suggested, a squabble between merchants was no cause for such an act of vandalism, for leaving a severed hand at the site as part of the message.

"You sell leather goods?" he asked. His attention had been focused on those gathered around the door, seeking signs of guilt or trouble, and he had taken little time to inspect the items set out on the awning shelf for display or sale.

"Shoes, my lord…best in Rhidam…and we sometimes take in boarders since my daughters are all grown and married…when the inns are full and there is nowhere else for travelers to go."

The Duke scowled. "Any Elyri boarders recently? Any Elyri buy shoes?" Given the symbol left behind, the grizzly nature of the message, it was plausible that some dealing with Elyri had prompted this act, though a pair of shoes or an overnight bed hardly seemed to warrant this manner of retaliation.

After scanning up and down the street and straining his eyes to see through the windows of the shops across the road, the cobbler eventually replied, "Aye…there was a boy…a child…all alone. He stayed two nights ago…hungry little mite…needing a bath. My wife gave him shoes because he did not have any. He did not stay, departed during the night after cleaning up the shop while we slept. He took a wheel of cheese…but it was not a theft worth reporting…and we have not seen him since. You don't think he…?"

Balint's scowl turned into a disapproving frown. "Not him." He could not imagine any child cutting off someone's hand and doing something like this…not after having gone to the trouble of thanking his hosts for their generosity by cleaning their shop. Nor could he imagine an Elyri ever doing such a thing. "Likely someone who thinks you need to be discouraged from harboring or helping Elyri." That was far more likely.

He squatted to examine the hand without touching it. It was not the hand of a child; the thick fingers with wide, calloused knuckles and dirty nails looked to be the hand of an older man, someone who toiled in the dirt for a living. Given the number of missing peasants, the hand could belong to anyone. It meant that the Elyri child, wherever he might be now, had not been caught and used for this expression of disdain. "You are fortunate they did no more."

People had died at the hands of the Corylliens for less offense.

"You do not think…would they kill a man for showing kindness to an orphan?" the cobbler asked incredulously, either unaware of the stories, the rumors, or else he had never believed them to be true. At the very least, he appeared to have believed that anti-Elyri violence, if real, would never touch him and his wife directly.

"Only if that orphan is Elyri." It puzzled Balint why this message had come now if the boy had come and gone days ago, but perhaps it had taken that long for the perpetrator to find a usable hand for the job.

The cobbler growled, indignant and afraid. "Do they think to dictate how I run my business?" His tirade was cut short by the small woman with a long gray braid who tugged on his arm anxiously. "The fear of death alone…it is not fair to them…that we should have to turn a child away…"

"You are right; it is not fair." There was too much blood for him to tell if the hand was Teren or Elyri, but he guessed Teren, and fretted over who had needed to lose their hand so that someone else might be warned. "If any come to you in the future…send them to the castle…or to the náos. Have them ask for me or for dedhá Tusánt…no one else." He would rather keep Elyri in Rhidam, feeling their continuing presence was more of a benefit and a blessing to Enesfel then a curse, but not at the expense of their lives or anyone else's. "Find something to remove this. Once the Justice and Inquisitor have seen it, I will assist in cleaning it away."

It was the woman who gaped in surprise and croaked, "You, my lord? Such a menial task is…"

"I am hardly above this, ma'am." If whoever had left this mark was continuing to watch the cobbler, to determine the effectiveness of their warning, Balint wanted them to see his contribution, wanted them, and all of Rhidam, to know that this was a problem that affected each of them. He wanted them to see in his actions that it was the duty of all, equally, to rectify such villainy, to expose it and change it. "You will not be in my debt, I swear it. I offer my assistance freely."

The cobbler and his wife stared, nodding mutely in surprise and gratitude. Balint managed to smile, but it was a strained one. He was willing to do this to make a point, despite the distastefulness of the task, and he was going to make sure that anyone who passed saw him there. Then he was going to lend his sword and his influence to the Crown in whatever ways might bring this madness to an end.

❧*❧

It felt good to be so exhausted, to know the joy of making music for the sake of others, to be empty and open to the peace Kavan could find nowhere else except in music. Zelenka had grown progressively more seasick as the hours passed, and was unable to sleep restfully. As a salve, Kavan sang, longing for a harp he had not played in months but making do with the only instrument he had. It was enough to give the woman the sleep she needed, and enough to bring a smile to Urian's face and tears to Wortham's eyes and dampen his cheeks and beard when they spilled free. Rather than speak when his voice fell silent, not yet ready to sleep himself, Kavan squeezed the captain's hand and went up to the prow, wondering how long this newfound comfort with his voice would last.

Focusing on the water below, as soon as the day crew slept, he was able to push the ship through the current until his energy began to dwindle. In the darkness, without the shoreline clearly visible, it was impossible to tell how much further, how fast, they had traveled. Come the dawn, the crew would fix their position with visible landmarks and realize they were ahead of schedule without guessing why. Kavan had no intention of raising suspicions by being here at the prow when that moment came. Let them think they had caught a strong current or favorable wind.

Hastening their journey was the sole compensation Kavan desired.

"You have been awake all night," Wortham commented when Kavan finally returned below, his hair damp from sea mist and his skin cold to the touch.

The bard cocked his head and murmured, "As have you." Wortham sat on the floor at Zelenka's side, whetstone in hand in the service of sharpening the dagger he always carried in addition to his sword. It was where Kavan had left him.

Wortham shrugged, not trying to mask his grin. "I slept, but not well. I heard you go up. Our movement felt too…swift…I have been trying to gauge our progress." His grin grew as the bard lay down on his pallet, his ringed hand reflexively coming to rest against his trunk of belongings, his expression one of feigned innocence. "If you can get us to land sooner, I am sure Zelenka will appreciate the effort." The woman had never been to sea, had never traveled for so long, had never been so far away from home. Wortham was certain her seasickness was compounded by a good deal of homesickness.

He listened to Kavan's breathing, the knife blade humming against the stone, both men lost in thoughts that denied them sleep. Wondering if it would help Kavan to speak his troubles, Wortham asked, "Are you prepared for what awaits in Rhidam?"

In the darkness, Kavan scowled, taking his time to consider a response before speaking. "I have not considered that far ahead, to be honest. I dread the day…but it will come." It was unavoidable. Rather than dwell on it, building up nervous expectations, he had settled on pushing it from his thoughts and letting events play out as they would. "If I could return…cleanse the chapel…" the ring on his hand tingled as a pulse of power raced up his arm from the trunk beneath his palm, "and be gone without anyone knowing I was there, it would be preferable…but I do not think that is my path."

"There are many who need to see you, my lord." Wortham sympathized with his friend's predicament and wished he could help. "The princess included," he added gently.

Kavan's scowl deepened and his hands flexed into fists he did not think Wortham could see. "You have forgiven her?" The words ground out as if rolling over broken glass.

"You have not?" Kavan did not reply and the captain turned in an effort to look at him. "It was not me she has wronged. I was angry for the pain she caused you, for her disregard and disrespect. I may not choose to serve her, or the Lachlan House, but I have less to forgive than you do."

"Not serve? What shall you do? Return to Káliel?" It had not occurred to Kavan that Wortham's choice to leave Lachlan service might be permanent, even if the bard decided to return to Rhidam.

The captain chuckled as he lay the dagger and stone with his belongings. "I will serve you as I always have. I wish to serve no other master. I do as you command. If you order me to reclaim my position to the King, I shall…but I would rather remain your man."

Kavan's skin flushed. Wortham knew it, even though he could not see it in a room lit only by the moon and starlight squeezing in between the wooden planks above them. "I am not your master, Wortham…but I am honored to call you my friend."

"And I am honored to be yours and will serve you as a loyal comrade who has no other need in life. That is enough for me, if you will continue to allow it."

Across the short distance between them, Kavan reached a hand towards Wortham and was grateful to find the captain reaching back. Their hands clasped tight. There was comfort in that bonding gesture in which Kavan found unexpected strength and reassurance. "Let us first reach Rhidam," he murmured. "There will be time enough to consider our future once we are there."

❧*❧

The widow's home looked no different than any other in Rhidam. It was a single dwelling above an unused tanner's shop at the northern edge of town, a single room that housed everything a lone individual could need in a living space. After receiving his third unofficial report that Claide had been seen in Rhidam when he was supposed to be in Fiara, this time supposedly having taken lodging in the widow's home, Caol no longer thought these sightings to be insignificant coincidences of a man similar in appearance. He, like several others, had not believed Claide had traveled to Fiara, but he had not believed the dedhá was foolish enough to remain in Rhidam where he might be spotted and recognized. Then again, Caol doubted the dedhá knew much about subterfuge. Eventually, if he was in Rhidam, the inquisitor would discover what he was up to.

While pensive and sullen, ill-tempered and seemingly put out by her unexpected visitor, the widow showed Caol around her home as if she had nothing to hide, answering questions without hesitation with words and tone that sounded rehearsed to him. She had an answer or explanation for everything…except why the senior Teren dedhá would be repeatedly seen near her home when it was proven by the neighbors that Claide had never made purchases in the nearby shops.

Caol couched his questions not with suspicion, but with the guise of needing to get word to him about k'gdhededhá Jermyn's death. But the widow, who admitted that she had known Claide for many years, since his coming to Rhidam, who admitted that he sometimes called on her to see to her welfare since she had no living family to do so, steadfastly insisted she had not seen him, had no knowledge of his whereabouts, nor had any idea when he might be returning to Rhidam.

There was no sign of Claide, or anyone else, in her home. Short of tearing the place apart board by board from top to bottom, Caol saw nowhere the man could be easily hidden. If Claide had been there, he must not have stayed long, and was not here now.

Caol did believe, however, from years of experience with people, that this woman was willing to lie for Claide, that he was more to her than a caring leader of the Faith come to see to her well-being.

Thanking her for her time, asking that she summon Claide back to Rhidam if she should hear from him, Caol left her home, feeling the bindings on his hands grow tighter. The paranoid young king was making it more and more difficult for him to do his duty. With fewer resources, less useful information, and less time to spare before someone else died, Caol had come up with only one viable solution.

And no one was going to like it.

❧*❦

Early in the third month of Adar, Fiara was still haunted by the cold of fading winter, but it was hunting weather, weather that Owain enjoyed whenever he had the opportunity. Any outing in the early spring or fall was invigorating, even when he was not hunting, and today was no exception. He enjoyed Espen's company here in the outdoors, and it was exhilarating to have Kjell with him. Piran liked Kjell, and it had been Piran's suggestion that they undertake this outing before Kjell departed for home. Despite the potential risk, Kjell had eagerly agreed to the proposition.

They had ridden at dawn on oft-used trails, alert for prey they might bring home for the evening meal as well as for threats hidden amongst the trees. There had been no kills thus far, and now they had paused to take their midday meal in a sunny clearing with a good view of the road in either direction and the forest's edge a good distance away to discourage an easy ambush.

"Will you ever marry?" Owain asked Kjell though his attention was on Piran. The boy was enthralled with Espen's saber and had begged to try it, but it was not the sort of blade he was accustomed to holding and he was having difficulty mastering its weight.

Kjell stretched his legs out before him and shrugged. "I do not know. It is not that I do not want to marry…but there are few eligible women of my station available who are not in some way already related to me by birth or marriage," he said with a laugh. "Those few that are available are, sadly, not worth my time…and Merkar is in no hurry to use me for any sort of political matchmaking alliance. I have yet to meet anyone who would not be a liability…"

"Or who can match your wits," Owain chuckled. "I know of one, but I do not believe Espen would appreciate a rival."

"Princess Diona? I have heard much of her strengths…though of course, most of what I hear portrays her in a less than flattering light…much like the rumors spread about her brother…"

Aware that Kjell was fishing for information, and feeling that providing factual information was better than allowing Kjell to believe the worst, Owain offered, "King Hagan is not yet fifteen, still a child in some ways it is true. But he is hardly the first young king in the Sovereignties. He is doing a fair job, given the state of affairs he faces. If you were to meet them both, I have no doubt your opinions would be much better informed…that neither of them are what your rumors paint them to be. I may be able to arrange it, if you wish?"

"Meet the Lachlans?" Such an offer was a tempting surprise. "A truly dangerous undertaking…but perhaps worth the effort. It would be interesting, I do not doubt. I will need to give the idea careful consideration…and planning." More complicated than a visit to Fiara, but now that he was presented with the possibility, it was one Kjell knew he would continue to dwell on until he could make it happen.

"There is one other I have long been interested in meeting…if you could guarantee that, perhaps I can be enticed to take the risk."

He grinned at his cousin's perplexed expression.

Pondering who that individual could be, Owain asked, "Lord Dugan?"

"Lord…? I do not know that name. Clearly, my brother's spies are less than efficient."

"They must be not to know the name of the man married to King Arlan's sister." Not that it mattered any longer. Both Arlan and Deidre were gone. "Who then? General Agis? General Zarkosta?" Both were logical choices for a man of Neth's military mindset and noble background to desire to meet.

"Lord Cliáth."

Choking, Owain stared, not knowing what to say or what to think of that admission. There was a tug of fear in his belly; most Nethites avoided anything to do with Elyri. Why in the name of Ethenae would Kjell want to meet the bard?

"You think me insincere…or perhaps suspect my motives. I assure you, I have none. The only other man, beyond King Arlan, of whom such a volume of tales is told is the late General McHador. Even in Neth, that one Elyri is raised to an almost god-like…or monster-like…status. Despite our ingrained hatred and fear of all things Elyri, this one man gnaws at the fringes of our consciousness, challenging our beliefs, on one hand said to be powerful beyond imagination and respected, revered because of it…or reviled and loathed and feared for those unnatural evils. Gentle, benevolent, gifted, or else a cursed thing to be avoided. I have never heard his music…none of us have. I would like to. I want to know how one man inspires such divergent claims, what he is truly like, which claims are true."

Though he knew Kavan would be grieved to hear such high praise or such brutal accusation, Owain relaxed with Kjell's honesty. "He is all of those good things…and so much more. Any who despise or distrust him…revile or ridicule him…are fools. He has more cause than most to hate me and yet he considers me his friend. I dare say he trusts me, though I often wonder why as I gave him few reasons for it. There is no man I trust more."

"You know him intimately then?" It had not occurred to Kjell that his cousin might be close friends with the White Bard of Bhryell. The best he had hoped for was Owain knowing the bard in passing, enough for a polite introduction.

"As well as he will allow anyone to know him. He is guarded with his thoughts…for the same reasons he is well known. When he…I will endeavor to arrange for you to meet him, but you may not hear his music…at least not from his hands."

"Why not?"

The older man's expression grew sad. "He was attacked, mauled by anti-Elyri extremists. His hands were mutilated I am told; nothing short of a miracle will allow him to play again, I fear."

Untying the cord at the back of his neck, Kjell allowed his unruly blonde hair to fall free around his face. He reminded Owain of Farrell Lachlan at that moment, a memory that caused Owain to swallow back those memories as he watched his cousin twist the cord around his fingers. The younger prince stared into the distance and his lips moved silently; Owain wondered if he was praying. Religion of all sorts was frowned on in Neth, as it served as a means of bringing people together under some banner other than the de Cormick's. It was irregularly persecuted, always discouraged, but Kjell had proven that he did not fear his brother the king and would do as he wished.

And thus far, he had played the fool enough that Merkar found no threat in letting Kjell do as he pleased.

"I would settle for meeting him. I will ask for the miracle he requires, though k'Ádhá is not likely to listen to the prayers of a heathen like me." He chuckled with melancholy disappointment and changed the subject. "I will leave it to you to decide what to share of our talks with your King and his sister. Now I fear I must head back. I have packing to do before daybreak if I am to return north before my brother realizes I'm gone."

Owain nodded with reluctant agreement. Their hunt may have been unproductive but the company had been good, making the outing a success on its own. "I have arranged an escort of sorts for you…at least as far as Fiara's outer limits. I have a…friend…who does not ask unnecessary questions and will be certain to guard you with her life when it is known you are my guest."

"Her?" Kjell chuckled again. "I hope your trust in her is justified. I made it to you on my own, after all…"

"I know you did." He motioned to his son and Espen to mount their horses. "But I will feel better knowing you cross out of my lands safely. I would never forgive myself if you do not."

They rode back in silence, each wrapped in their own thoughts. Even Piran, tired from the day of hunting, riding, and sword practice, was quieter than normal. Espen had been a remarkably obliging guest in Owain's opinion, allowing he and Kjell their privacy, entertaining Piran, spending a significant amount of his time in the streets of Fiara alone looking for the information he had come for. Thus far, no one he had spoken with had seen gdhededhá Claide and none of the naós

"Espen and I will see to this one." Kjell shoved the prisoner in the back hard enough to make the man stumble. "What of the others?"

"Leave them for the carrion," muttered Owain, "or for their friends. I do not care. I am taking Piran home."

In his arms, face buried against his father's chest, Piran murmured, "I want mother."

It was a knife in Owain's heart.

"Yes, we will go to mother," he promised. "I am sorry, Piran."

But the boy, holding on to his father's neck in a way that indicated his total trust, said nothing more. His glassy gaze grew distant, his body shaking in shock and fear. If not for Espen and Kjell, Piran might have been taken from his own lands. Or he might be dead. Owain realized he had waited too long. Piran had to go to Káliel until this nightmare was behind them. While not without its own dangers, Owain believed the islands had to be safer than Enesfel. Anywhere, except Neth, had to be safer than Enesfel.

❧*❦

The world hurt. Not the world, he realized, turning his head slowly without opening his eyes, but his entire body. Every muscle ached, every nerve end burned as if too long exposed to the sun. He felt raw. There was an empty, unbalanced feeling inside, his healing sense jumbled and unfocused. There was something else there too, a residual trace of power, a presence…

"Kavan!" Ártur jerked up, his body screaming at the abuse of long-unused muscles but all of his thoughts and senses were focused on a single goal, a single word. The name he had uttered.

"You felt him too."

It was not Kavan with him in the nearly dark room, but rather Gaelán in the chair beside the bed, looking at him with concern on his tired face. The apprentice healer adjusted the pillows and helped him settle back into them, but he said nothing else. Ártur, unsure what his nephew meant, turned his unfocused healing senses inward to assess his physical condition and Gaelán, understanding his need to judge his own welfare, did not interfere.

"He was here…" the elder healer finally murmured. Everything he gauged from inside his own skin attested to the bard's presence.

Gaelán shook his head. "In power only. What do you remember?"

Ártur closed his eyes and tried to think. It hurt, caused a throbbing in the back of his skull and between his eyes, but he finally replied in a sick, shaky voice, "There was a message…I was attacked…"

"Yes."

His brows furrowed. "But Kavan. he has been here…he was…"

"No. He saved your life, though I don't know how, but I knew it was not me or aene Syl. It had to be him. Just like it had to be him who killed most of your attackers. No one else could do that." His foot swung and kicked the bed frame in frustration. "But no one believes me except Asta and her father. aene did not feel it…the presence in you, keeping you alive…but I did. It was…I know he was there."

If it were anyone else but Kavan, Ártur might not have believed it either. But what he felt inside, the power signature that remained, was specific to his cousin and Ártur had no doubt that Gaelán was telling the truth as he understood it. "I feel him; he has been with me. I do recall the burst…"

"They exploded…like the ones that attacked him in Levonne. That's how I know it was him." Swallowing the sigh, feeling a little better for being believed at last, he turned his attention to the physical needs of his patient. "Are you hungry? Thirsty? Shall I bring aene…?"

"No." The vehemence of the command prevented Gaelán from rising. "We will fight when she comes…I know what she will say."

"She wants you to return to Bhryell."

It was obvious to Ártur that Gaelán did not want him to go. Tonight, however, Ártur did not want to think about the future, or the past. "I am not up for discussion tonight…and I definitely do not want to fight. I'm not hungry…but I could use a drink before I sleep. You will stay? You will not tell anyone I…"

"If you wish it," the young man promised hastily as he filled a cup with water from the bedside pitcher. He would promise anything, he realized selfishly, to keep Ártur with him.

The healer gave him an affectionate smile, not missing the desperation in his voice and actions. "Thank you." He drank the entire glass of water, returned it to Gaelán's hand, and fell asleep before Gaelán looked back at him.

Smugly, the young healer got up to stand at the window, to stare into the distance across the roofs of the sleeping city. Let everyone call him a liar. He knew the truth. Kavan had been with them, in power and in spirit. Gaelán knew it. And Ártur knew it too.

ॐChapter 7ॐ

Rain was falling from the mist when Kavan decided it was time to go below deck. His internal clock indicated the hour was nearing dawn, though heavy fog made it difficult to judge. The merchant cog was making excellent time, the ship's captain had commented, though he did not know how it was possible with the thickening haze and near dead calm wind. It would not be much longer, at this pace, before they docked. Kavan was that much nearer to Rhidam, to redemption, to hoped-for peace of mind.

A shimmer in the fog, movement further out to sea, kept him on deck despite the rain's attempt to drive him below. He detected nothing there, felt no presences, no signs of life, no trace of energy, and for many minutes he believed he had imagined that faint visual trace of…something…or that some sea beast had breached the surface only to dive again before he could get a closer look. A whale, perhaps, blowing its breath into the air, stirring the fog, allowing enough of a shift to let the moonlight or birthing dawn through the fog.

He would have liked to see a whale.

But then the shimmer appeared again, the image ghostly through the vapor, though real enough to be deemed more than a trick of light and air. A ship, long and sleek like no vessel Kavan could recall seeing before, either on the sea or in the books and paintings he had spent hours studying. Her three white sails were full to billowing despite the lack of wind, but she was not approaching the vessel on which Kavan stood. Rather, she appeared to be traveling beside them, parallel, keeping pace despite the lack of current beneath their hulls or wind to fill the sails.

The emerald on Kavan's hand throbbed as the ship's image became clearer, as did the crystal that hung about his neck, but Kavan could detect no hint of life or power, saw no lights, heard no sound beyond the soft spattering of rain on the deck at his feet and on the almost glassy sea that sloshed gently against the sides of the cog. Then the ship's image began to fade, disappearing into the mist and clouds as if part of them; he shook his head, blinked the rain from his eyes, and then she was gone, making him question whether she had been there at all. Perhaps it had been some manner of hallucination, or the Sight. But he had never been prone to hallucinations and had consumed nothing that might have caused them, and there were none of the usual symptoms which accompanied episodes of the Sight.

He was certain, however, that he was not dreaming. He was certain he was awake.

Brushing wet strands of silver-white from his face, he continued to wait, hoping the vision would reappear. A fleeting memory rose to the surface as he stared at the horizon, a painting of a fleet of ships that hung in Kyne Mórne's palatial home, a painting he had seen several times during the occasions he had been invited to play there as a younger man. No one had been able to tell him the artist and the painting bore no signature or claiming mark. Nor did anyone know where the work had originated. It's unusual canvas and pigments were purported to be ancient, and the painting had been in the palace since the building's constructions many generations ago. Where the painting had come from before that, or if it had been commissioned for the new Elyri palace, no one knew. Those painted ships, however, had seemed no ordinary ones to Kavan, unfamiliar in size and design, and as he recalled them now, their image bore many similarities in line and design to the visage in the fog.

Another thought pushed into his head, a snatch of a tale recently learned. A ship from across the sea. The same sort, he mused, that had brought Kóráhm's parents to this land? The same vessel, or type of vessel, that might have come later and taken the Heretic-Saint's mother away? Where, Kavan wondered with excitement, had it come from? What land could possibly lie beyond the sea and what connection, if any, did it bear to Kóráhm's history…and to his own?

He shivered with breathless awe at this close brush with the past and secrets he had yet to uncover.

"I often wonder where she went."

Kavan's surprise was brief but his heart continued to thunder in his chest at the unexpected jolt of power in the presence beside him. He had not seen his patron in many weeks and it was an exhilarating relief to be in his company again. "My lord Kóráhm," he murmured to the auburn-haired man beside him, said to be dead and clearly was not. The saint's arm pressed against his was as real and solid as if it were

Wortham standing there. "She did not tell you where she was going? That she was leaving?" There were other questions he could ask, answers he could have demanded, but it was easy to fall into the conversation Kóráhm had initiated, to follow his lead. If the saint wanted to discuss his life, Kavan was eager to hear it.

Saint Kóráhm the Heretic lowered the hood of his cloak, caring little about the rain. The dampness glistened in his coppery hair, causing it to cling to his gently chiseled features. "I do not think she had the opportunity," he admitted. "He came for her…and she left."

"You were their son. They should have taken you with them…or at least allowed you the chance to meet the man who gave you life."

"To what end? I spent my childhood not knowing him, and I was a grown man when she departed. I had my own life by then, my own path. I would have liked to have known the truth…but it would have changed little, I suspect. For me, at least." How it might have affected his half-brother, and the history that unfolded from that day, he could not guess. "If I had gone with her…with them…history would have been different. Perhaps I would not have been responsible for the unfortunate events that came after…but that speculation is of no use. I made my choices…just as she made hers. It is all any of us can do."

Hearing the deep sorrow in the saint's voice and longing to heal it, knowing how difficult it was for Kóráhm to reveal that private detail, Kavan longed to put his hand on the other man's arm, cover his hand with his own. But he dared not; his fear of Kóráhm retreating from him was stronger than Kavan's desire for that moment of contact.

He could try to heal with words, however, and said, "You were not responsible for your brother's actions. A man does what he can…what he thinks he must in a given moment…and life goes on around him. Others are responsible for their own actions. Dawid was responsible for the path he chose, not you."

Kóráhm smiled sadly. "It warms me to hear you say so, that you have learned that lesson at last, kyag. If you learn to apply those words to your own life, you will be truly wise."

Neither spoke for many minutes as Kavan pondered that statement, and his own, letting the truth of the words sink in. Eventually, Kóráhm spoke again, the melancholy in his tone unchanged as he stared into the water. "It is also possible that the stories are wrong…that she simply left Ergoth, perhaps to trade as she sometimes did, and decided not to return…or met her death on the road. The romance of a returned true love from across the sea could be nothing more than fabrication."

"You do not believe that," Kavan said with a shake of his head. There was a touch of the romantic in Kóráhm, Kavan had seen that side to him in the man's journals. It was a side, he admitted secretly to himself, that the two men shared.

Kóráhm chuckled and clasped Kavan's hand, and though the bard knew what to expect, again felt the thrill of amazement at the touch of a man who should have been dead for thousands of years and yet was solid, warm, flesh. "You know me well."

"Not as well as I should, given the amount of study I have invested in your life and words." It was easy to chide himself for what seemed like foolishness now. That there still seemed so much more to learn, that each new morsel of knowledge surprised him when it was uncovered, was a source of frustration and wonder.

"Ah, but you know what is available to know from the sources you have had…and you read between the lines clearly when you allow yourself to. This journey you have undertaken has filled in some of your gaps I believe. As with anyone in our lives, there is more, of course, but I shall leave it to you to discover on your own." His small grin carried a hint of both mischievousness and worry. "It is better for us both that way."

Kavan could not attest to that, but nor could he argue the point or pressure Kóráhm into revealing anything he was reluctant to speak of. Thus far, the various portions of Kóráhm's stories had come to Kavan when he was mature enough, emotionally tested enough, to know them, and he suspected further revelations, if there were any, would come in similar ways, at similar times.

"Why have you come to me tonight, my lord…if I might ask? Has something happened? Has someone died?" He did not think it would be Ártur, for he believed he would feel that death if that day ever came.

"Must my arrival always herald bad tidings?"

"No…but lately when you come it has been with news or information, good or bad."

Kóráhm's head cocked as he stared thoughtfully across the horizon, into the mist where the ghostly ship had been, and Kavan wondered if that was the matter the saint wished to speak of. Instead, Kóráhm said, "True…but it is not so every time. I recall times spent with you when you played, simply for the pleasure of your company. Have you forgotten?"

"Never; those are treasures carried in my heart for comfort. Many of those times…you came in response to petitions for peace of mind." Or he had believed that had been the reason. Maybe, he realized, he had been wrong. "And frequently you did provide information in those times as well. This time there was no summons…"

"Could you accept that for once I came because I desire your company? Or does that confuse you…that someone like me…could desire your companionship…you who still consider yourself unworthy of so much?" He covered Kavan's hand with his. "I was aware of your thoughts; I wanted to be near you. Is that good enough?"

"I have no harp to entertain you," Kavan stammered. He welcomed the saint's company and hoped the man knew that, but he still felt as if he owed something in exchange for the camaraderie.

"You can sing, kyag. More beautifully than I ever could. But I did not come seeking entertainment…unless you wish to offer it. I came only to stand with you until dawn comes and the others rise."

Kavan thought Kóráhm looked tremendously sad, tormented by deep thoughts and the possibility that Kavan might ask him to leave. That Kavan could ever deny him anything. "lásánai…Kóráhm…if it were possible, I would keep you with me at all times. There are few who understand me as you do, few who are willing to try or who are willing to tolerate my…sometimes insufferable arrogance. Those who have done so, who do so still, are dearer to me than my life. Stay. Stay as long as you wish. I welcome you here.

The saint did not release his hand and remained beside him at the rail, staring through the lifting fog and falling rain to the place where the ship had been. Kavan wondered what he was thinking, what thoughts a saint could have in those private moments of silence, what regrets or hopes. He wondered if Kóráhm too had seen the ship, if he had known it was there, if he could reassure Kavan of its reality. But he did not ask. When the first of the day crew came to relieve the skeletal night watch, Kóráhm faded into the remaining mist as that ship had done, though the sensation of his scarred hand on Kavan's remained even after the bard left the prow to sleep.

❧*❦

"You wish to accompany me to Rhidam?"

Espen had not considered the possibility that Owain might choose to ride with him, despite the decision to take Piran to Káliel. Much of what Owain and the Lachlans did, however, surprised him, as they rarely acted in ways the Hatu prince expected royalty to act. The attack they had endured had not been against Espen, but he could see how Owain might feel obligated to offer protection in the aftermath. Espen had come to Fiara with neither guards, nor escorts, nor retainers, and while he had not considered the possibility of danger before, he could admit that he worried now for his return to Rhidam. He had requested an escort, but instead of sending his men, the Lachlan prince chose to be that escort himself. The need to remove Piran from Fiara coincided with Espen's need to travel.

He supposed there was safety to be found in the midst of numbers between Owain and the men he would bring with him.

Owain yanked off his boots and placed them by the fire to dry. There had finally been rain last night, not enough to make the spring planting promising, but it was moisture nonetheless and it made for a muddy, damp early morning survey around his estate. He had given instructions to his groundskeepers, his grooms, his hound master, preparing them for his absence. He was soaked to the skin and cold. Duty was done. He had only to get warm and wait for daybreak.

Pulling off his wet tunic he replied, "As you said, there is nothing more to learn here of dedhá Claide, no indication that he was, or is here, and you are right to take your findings to Diona…and I must take Piran to his mother. I should have taken him as soon as this nonsense reared its head, but I did not think it would reach Fiara…believed I could keep him safe. He does not deserve to be caught in the middle of this…and yesterday was too close. Unless Káliel is likewise infected, it will be safer for him there. Traveling together makes sense…and I must speak with Diona…"

"About Prince Kjell? Did he agree to include her in our dialogue?"

"He said to use my best judgment. He trusts me…though k'Ádhá knows why. It is not in the de Cormick blood to trust anyone, particularly other family members. I suspect he wants something in return for his trust…even if it's nothing more than my trust of him…and the opportunity to meet Kavan, if that opportunity arises."

"He does not seem duplicitous," Espen agreed, but he knew that appearances, especially amongst nobility, could be deceiving. It was what those in power often did best.

"When he needs to be…like any other man I suppose. It is an art necessary to hone if one is to live in the de Cormick house…to have survived as long as he has. I watched him when he was a boy, and though he has grown, matured, he is much the same. He is a survivor. I do not think he has been lying…"

"But you could be wrong?"

Rubbing his bare arms, Owain inhaled the first words he started to say then exhaled them into the heat rising from the fire. "I could be. It would not be the first time I misjudged a man. If I am wrong, then I will certainly deserve the fate Arlan once intended for me."

❧*❧

Though he had been awake for many hours, listening to the sounds of the day, Ártur had remained still, eyes closed, alone except for Gaelán's comings and goings. He wondered where Syl was, why she was not here, keeping vigil when Gaelán was not. He doubted she had returned to Bhryell unless the welfare of their children required it. Perhaps someone else required her medical care. He had been tempted several times to question Gaelán, to ask about his wife, but each time he decided against it. She would come soon enough. He did not want the argument he knew would come with her.

Despite his wishes, however, perhaps in response to his musings about her whereabouts, the door opened and stayed that way in silence for many moments. He knew it was his wife without opening his eyes, her presence, the sound of her footsteps, the sound of her breathing, the smell of her skin and hair, all intimately familiar and greatly missed. He knew there was no use in pretending to be asleep. She knew him as well as he knew her. Reluctantly opening his eyes, watching her stare at him with tears on her cheeks, their daughter in her arms, he struggled for something to say. He did not need to speak, however, since she ran to him with a stifled sob as soon as their gazes met, placed the child on the bed where she would not fall, and clung to him as if she would never let him go.

"I am forever in debt to the miracle that saved your life," she cried.

Her yielding form felt good against him, her pale red hair soft beneath his fingers and against the side of his face. "Your hands and Gaelán's repaired the injuries…" He stopped there, not wanting to speak the other name that hung between them, out of fear of the backlash that would come, not trusting his voice further until he had his own impulse to weep under control. "I am sorry…it was foolish of me…I should not have…but I thought…"

She finished his sentence for him, the underlying bitterness beneath her words impossible to hide. "You thought Kavan needed you. He is your strength, kyá, but also your weakness. I hope you see that now. Even if he were dying, he would not want you to risk yourself on his account…"

Stung by that thought, he pulled back to stare at her, using one thumb to wipe away the tears beneath her eye. "I would risk anything for him…I must…" He partially regretted his words the moment he said them, as he read the undisguised hurt and anger on his wife's face.

"And you did…your life…your family…me. Do we mean nothing to you?"

"Syl…"

"You must come home." She clung to his hands, wringing them tightly. "You told me you would come home if it appeared you were in danger…"

"I am no longer…"

"You did not even tell me about the threat! You hid it…lied about it…are you so callous of my feelings? What of our children? The danger is real, Ártur. You know it. You were threatened…lured out in the night…attacked…nearly killed. The King has set you free. He releases you from duty to save your life."

"Releases me?" He blanched, appalled by the thought, not ready to hear her words. Part of him knew her arguments were valid and true, but he felt his own were equally important and valid, and no one seemed inclined to hear him. "Who will serve them? Gaelán is not yet fully trained; he needs me to…"

Eyes narrowed with frustration, Syl challenged, "As do Llucás and Chethá. As do I. Bhríd has agreed to send Gaelán to Bhryell, to live with us while he is trained…"

Ártur shook his head stubbornly, hating to hurt her, hating that she could not understand his needs, his fears, his desires. "I cannot leave the Lachlans without a healer in these troublesome times; it was my sworn duty…"

"To Arlan…one Hagan has released you from…"

"Against my wishes! I won't leave them. I won't leave Kavan."

This was an argument he had not wanted, and he had thought he had known how it would end. He believed Syl would give in and accept his choice the way she most often did. His words were final and he expected her to be resigned to his decision. Thus the fury on her face was unexpected as she pulled free from his touch, picked up their daughter, and stepped away from the bed.

"You do not know if he will return. What will he think if he does and finds you have been killed while waiting for him? He, more than anyone else, would tell you to come to Bhryell…to be safe…to protect your family. He would not want you to…"

The thought of Kavan never returning to his life tore at Ártur's heart, made his eyes tear, and made him more determined to do whatever he could to make his cousin's homecoming happen. "He will come back. He must. I need to be here, to see him when he arrives, to thank him for saving…"

She shuddered and he saw it. "Gaelán told you?" she whispered in both disgust and disbelief. "You believe his fantastic tale…"

"It is no tale, Syl…he has told me nothing. It is what I felt in here," he thumped his chest, "the moment I awoke. It is what I felt in the last conscious moment of the attack. I do not know what happened…how it could be true…but I know I would have been killed if not for him…"

"If not for him! Exactly! For him, you risked everything…for him, you nearly died. He should have been the one to save your life! He owes you that. He owes me! He should be the one to save you now by urging you to come home!"

"Syl," Ártur began again.

Her loud, distressed voice was making Chethá squirm and fuss and chew on her fist in a frustrated effort not to cry. Patting the girl on the back before tucking her own hair behind her ears, Syl's expression hardened as she challenged, "Come home with me." There was to be no resignation, no compromise. She was not going to back down. "Come back to Bhryell with me…or do not come back at all."

Stunned by her words, his face losing color, he opened his mouth to say something, anything, that would sway her choice, make her see reason, but words failed him.

She shook her head, stopping him from speaking. "We do not need the grief or worry of a sometimes present husband and father. It will be easier for the children if I tell them you are never coming home."

Ártur made no attempt to hold back his tears, though he knew she would interpret them as a desperate ploy to manipulate her. He was unable to accept, or believe, that his marriage would come to this. Something felt to rip within his chest, as if trying to tear his heart out between his ribs, and his nostrils flared as he fought to catch his fleeting, rapid breath. Never to see her. Never to touch her. Never to talk to her. Never to see his children again. She must change her mind, had to change her mind. Surely if he remained firm in his convictions, she would have to. Would she not?

Because he saw no other choices available, no other future except the one the Lachlans laid out for him when he had come to serve King Innis decades ago. The Lachlan court was the only life he had known how to enjoy; Rhidam was the only place he had ever felt as if he belonged, save for the few brief years spent with Kavan in Bhryell. His loyalty to the House he had served for so long, to his beloved cousin, were too intense to be merely abandoned, but so too was his love for his family.

Wherever Kavan went, Ártur could follow, could be content, but he could not imagine giving up his family for his cousin…or vice versa. He could not give up the family he had built, could not give up the generations of Lachlans he so willingly served, could not willingly abandon the one person he had ever felt able to call sínréc.

His long, uncomfortable struggling silence was answer enough for his wife though for Ártur it had been no answer at all. Without a word, Syl left the room without looking back, and he watched her dumbly, unable to think of any way to make her stay.

When Gaelán opened the door later with the evening meal in hand, Ártur realized how much time had passed, how long he had stared at the door hoping she would come through it and retract her ultimatum.

She had not.

He swallowed hard, unable to look Gaelán in the eye. "Is she…?"

The young man set the tray on the bedside stand. It was unclear from his blank expression how much he knew about the argument, but he shrugged and replied, "She went to Bhryell. She told father Chethá needs to be safe…that no one here…" Watching his uncle collapse into the pillows in defeat, he whispered, "I am sorry…if it is my fault. I told her you had to stay, to train me, that the King needs you. I know you are not an Enesfel citizen and that you have no reason to feel such loyalty to them…or me…"

Still not looking at him, Ártur squeezed Gaelán's arm. "I did this, Gaelán; you have no fault here. A marriage is a union of compromise." In this instance, however, he did not know if compromise was possible, if there was any to be offered, any to be made. "I have not given up trying. I will find a way."

"I hope so…it will break k'aendhá's heart to think he was the cause of the dissolution of your marriage."

It was not until the young man left with those parting words lingering in the air where he had been that Ártur rolled onto his stomach, wrapped his arms around his pillow, and wept. Breaking anyone's heart, Syl's, his children's, or Kavan's, was the last thing he wanted. But he did not think he could have it both ways. Some choice must be made between his employers, his family, and his cousin, and as conflicted as he was, he could not abandon Kavan. If he could not make his wife understand, he risked losing her, and his family, forever.

"It is not my field of knowledge…even the King knows it. And Darius has his angles in investigations to work…his own problems. We have learned nothing new since the King gave this matter into our hands; we don't even know where to begin. You should be the one investigating the vandalism, the death behind it, the guilty party."

Biting back the acerbic words that crossed his mind, the inquisitor instead directed his annoyance and exasperation towards the document he had begun writing, crumpling it in one fist and throwing it across the room towards the fire. He would have to rewrite it, which only added to his frustration, although he had barely gotten one line written before the chamberlain entered the room. "How? How can I do anything? He has forbidden me to use any of my contacts…"

The dark-haired Elyri smirked. "A command you have, of course, obeyed to the letter since it was given."

Caol shifted in his seat, uncomfortable under Bhríd's gaze. If anyone else had said that, he would have worried that his activities had been betrayed to the King. He knew his secrets were safe with Bhríd, but still they caused him a few moments of anxiety. "I have never claimed to be without fault, Lord Chamberlain," he said with a forced chuckle. "I know of no other way to achieve results…and imagine every inquisitor before me has had their own similar network of informants. My network happens to come with the name Association attached. But I have been trying to find ways of complying with the King's demands. It leaves me less fruitful then I care to be…and I do not believe Enesfel can afford my inaction much longer. If this Narn, whoever he is, is there…one would think it should be easy to find a Cíbhóló with an unusual sword in Rhidam. I know Agis is seeking him too…but if he is in any way connected to the vandalism…"

He shrugged. "Agis did want a word with me, but our duties have not yet permitted it."

Hands clasped behind his back, Bhríd nodded. He understood the demands and restrictions of duties all too well. "You know I am the strongest voice for following the words and wishes of the sovereign. It is my nature. But I think, given the state of things, the threats we face, the lives at risk if we do nothing, we are justified to act in the best interest of Enesfel…of the Crown…even if the King does not realize the dangers of this unchecked violence. He must not understand the threat, for I refuse to believe Arlan could have raised his son to be uncaring about those he rules. If you decide you must act against his wishes," he finished solemnly, "I will support you."

"One vote of confidence…or make that three. But there is little I can do without funding to reimburse my informants, and I have stretched my personal funds as far as I can." Thanks to his marriage to Deidre Lachlan, he had been granted lands and a title and the income that came with that, but those lands required upkeep as well, and the income they provided could only do so much.

Bhríd clasped his shoulder affectionately. "I will see what can be done. Flannery might be able to aid us if approached properly." Flannery McGranis had once been Bhríd's squire. If anyone could wring a favor out of the other man, it would be Bhríd.

"Then it appears I have work to do." Starting, Caol decided, with tracking down Agis. "Will you excuse me, Lord Chamberlain?"

Bhríd bowed, a habit continued from the earliest days of his acquaintance with Prince Arlan. Anyone of status got a bow from him, whether they were higher ranked or not. "I will not detain you. Go…and find us the answers we need."

"I will try." It was the only promise Caol could make.

It could not be over. Bhen refused to believe that one of the most solid institutions in his life might be ending. Ártur and Syl had been husband and wife since before he had been born. How could that have changed? Such relationships were not supposed to crumble. His grandparents had their differences, and yet they had managed to remain married for over one hundred years. Surely, he thought, Ártur and Syl's differences were not insurmountable.

But Syl, he knew, was a stronger woman than Dháná in many ways, unwilling to be treated as inconsequential, and Ártur was as stubborn as his father, though more forgiving and compassionate. That Ártur loved Kavan to the point of risking death for him was an unchangeable fact. Bhen knew it. Syl had known it since before they were wed. Anyone who knew the cousins knew it. Though he barely knew Kavan himself, Bhen believed he understood, from the stories he had been told, how the bard would feel to discover what had happened during his absence. Kavan, like Bhen, would be devastated. Ártur must see that as well.

If he did not, Bhen decided he would make him see it. He would do everything in his power to undo the damage that had been done, even if he had to return to Rhidam in the midst of danger to do it.

❧Chapter 8❧

That Gaelán chose to remain in the room rather than flee the impending argument gave Ártur the fortitude to hold his ground, to face his parents and nephew when his impulse was to retreat. Having no real relationship with either his older brother Sámel, or his nephew Aleski, it did not surprise him that neither man was present at this gathering, opting instead to be about the family business. But he had expected, had hoped, that Syl would be here. Instead, she refused to see or speak to him, or to allow him to see his children when he came to Bhryell that morning. She chose not to support him against his family now. As if she had believed he would come to persuade her, she escaped to her parents' home with the children beyond the outskirts of Bhryell, leaving instruction with Bhen that her husband was not to follow her. Ártur had gone first to Kavan's home, where he knew she had been staying, and then to Bhen's, and finally to his parents' home in the hopes of finding her there.

That was where he stepped into the ambush.

It was no surprise that they were largely united against him; they had every reason to be. gdhededhá Khwílen's visit to Bhryell had enlightened many to the dangers lurking beyond Elyriá's borders, and everyone in the family knew of his near-death experience now. Yet he chose to stay in Rhidam for Kavan's sake, when the man had not been seen in many months, amidst the dangers, a risk that was incomprehensible to his parents, even his mother who had raised Kavan as though he was her third son and had doted on him as much as her husband would allow. Ártur's pallid features worried her and she chided him for being unable to take care of others if he would not take care of himself. Bhen, though not pleased with his uncle's choices, was doing his best to remain outside of the conflict, not speaking though his tortured expression revealed how he felt. It seemed to Ártur that no one but Gaelán understood his need to remain in Rhidam, his need to be there when Kavan returned…not if. And Gaelán was the youngest of them all.

Ártur refused to sit despite the lingering physical weakness, refused to accept the accusations leveled against him passively. If he could not make them approve, he wanted them at least to understand. He read Gaelán's concern for his health every time he glanced at the boy, and realized that was part of the young healer's reason for remaining near him. He might have had a late start in training, but he had a healer's heart.

"I've made my choice, bhydhá. I am staying in Rhidam for now. You are the man who taught us not to avoid our responsibilities…"

His father grunted. "Your family is your responsibility…not the Teren you stubbornly, flippantly serve." Tám made no mention of Kavan. "If you were not prepared to assume the responsibility of family, you should not have married. You should not have left your…"

Feeling the back of his neck grow hot, Ártur knew his face was crimson. He took one step towards his father, the first time he could recall ever confronting him in that fashion, aware of his mother's distress as he held his ground. "I did not leave my family. They left me. They came here to safety, which is where they should be. If I did not care about them, their safety, I would demand Syl and the children stay in Rhidam. Rhidam is no place for our children; we both know it. She wanted to bring them here, and I agreed with that. I do not stay in Rhidam to spite her, to spite anyone. I am staying out of duty to those I serve. I stay for Kavan."

Tám took a matching step forward, a man never afraid of a fight though he had never struck his sons. As he snarled, "That man has nothing to do with this," Ártur wondered if he would come to blows with his father.

"Even now you refuse to speak his name as if he were dead!"

Bhen, to Ártur's relief, chose that moment to step between them, preventing the confrontation from becoming physically violent. "k'aendhá, this is not the time…"

"I believe it is, Bhen. Kavan is family! I will not turn my back on him as you have done." He glowered at his father. "We have familial responsibility to him too. If you were not prepared to accept responsibility for your brother's son, bhydhá, you should not have brought him into your house, into our family! I would gladly have taken him to Rhidam with me when he was an infant, if you both had not convinced me otherwise…and I now take the responsibility for him I should have taken then. It was my fear for his welfare, my love for him, that put me at risk that night; it is true I acted irrationally, foolishly, ignoring precautions put in place for my well-being, but I believed he needed me. I am a healer; it is my duty…and he is kin whether you acknowledge that or not. Each of you, Syl included, would rather allow him to die than offer him aid!"

There were angry tears on his cheeks, the resentment towards his father, in particular, kept inside too long. He knew that including them all was inaccurate, and could feel their reactions pushing at his already raw nerves. Gaelán's pride at knowing he was excluded from the accusation, his mother's wilting guilt, his father's fury at being condemned with the truth, Bhen's inner conflict, as he turned towards the window, the younger man having no desire to see Kavan suffer and yet not knowing if he would have the fortitude, the courage, to take such a risk on his kinsman's behalf.

Swallowing hard, Ártur continued. "I have been the one person in this family to remain loyal to him, love him unconditionally, the way family should. I would lay down my life for him as I would for any of you…as he would do for any of us. He deserves far better than we have given him. You turned him out, made him unwelcome in his home…his town. He sought refuge outside of Elyriá and I followed. If he is forced to remain apart, I will follow him still."

Pausing for breath, the healer swallowed and wiped his face, allowing a long enough pause for Bhen to find his voice. "You speak the truth, k'aendhá, though some of us are loath to admit it. Even I, who desire to share his company and know him better, must admit that fear keeps me here, away from him…and might have kept me from doing what you have done. But you must also acknowledge that it is unfair to condemn Syl to solitude for loving you and wanting you safe. Not all of us can be so noble. Perhaps there is a compromise that might be acceptable…if you are both willing to hear and consider it."

The healer held his breath, almost afraid of what his nephew might suggest. Having missed so much of Bhen and Aleski's childhood, he did not know Bhen well enough to guess at the workings of his mind. Ártur had failed to think of any option Syl might be willing to consider, and could not reach out to her if he had. Could young, unmarried Bhen have a workable solution?

Beside Ártur, his mother wrung her hands, her eyes down and, he thought, too intensely focused on her husband's foul mood to be listening to her son any longer. In a gesture of support for his uncle,

Gaelán shuffled in front of Ártur and allowed the man to wrap his arms around him. Ártur allowed his gratitude to pass through the connection the contact provided and murmured, "What do you suggest?"

"You say you will not leave Rhidam permanently and want to retain your post as court healer. As you say, there are no Teren doctors who can fully replace an Elyri healer and you feel they need you in this time of crisis. Gaelán is not yet trained. You are not averse to traveling by Gate and have one accessible…"

"Bhen…"

"Hear me out. Why could you not spend your days in Rhidam and return to Bhryell at night? aendhá Bhríd is present in Rhidam much of the time, or thus says Syl, and will see to Gaelán's safety if he remains. You fulfill your duty and train Gaelán during the day, and if there are minor incidences at night, Gaelán gains the experience of tending them." Bhen smiled at Gaelán encouragingly. "If the medical need is more acute, Bhríd comes for you. For the night hours, when Elyri are most vulnerable, you would be safe in Bhryell, and during the day you would be protected by the heavier guard activity."

He shrugged, realizing as he rambled that he was, perhaps, speaking out of turn by advising his elders, but he was eager to help Ártur and Syl find a resolution. "You would be as safe as you could be…and if Bhríd must be absent from Rhidam, you could agree to remain in Rhidam overnight under the condition that you never again leave the castle without an escort. Such an arrangement might relieve Syl's mind enough to allow you to fulfill your obligations to the Lachlans, k'aendhá Kavan, and your conscience."

Now that the idea was spelled out, contingent on both Syl's agreement and Bhríd's cooperation, Ártur was surprised he had not thought of it himself. Perhaps he was too close to the situation to have considered that solution. He did not know if Bhen had already suggested it to Syl or if it was Syl's idea. Was she willing to negotiate?

Was it worth a try to suggest it?

He nodded, agreeing to try, his relief easing some of the tension from his shoulders. "It could work, if she is agreeable."

"Good." Bhen offered his hand, ignoring Tám's exasperated expression. "I will present it to aene Syl, and you will discuss it with aendhá Bhríd. Will you be staying in Rhidam a little longer?"

"The King has given me leave to recuperate here; I will be staying at Kavan's for the next several days. Gaelán is staying with me." They had a meeting with bhydáni Tíbhyan tomorrow." It was a long-overdue appointment that Gaelán was eagerly looking forward to.

Ártur continued to ignore his parents, though he was aware his mother was squeezing her husband's hand, either for strength and comfort or to keep him quiet. Ártur did not expect to spend any time here in his childhood home, not until the air was cleared between him and his parents. Directing Gaelán towards the door, he nodded to Bhen, eager to escape, not wanting to face his family any longer. As conflicted as his feelings were at that moment, he was tempted to wish he never saw them again.

❧*❧

"See that everything on this list is obtained promptly. Take as much extra as you can fit onto the fleet. I am sending three additional ships with you to carry the goods and I want them filled to capacity. Head out as quickly as manageable, today if possible. No delays. Oh…and be sure there is room for passengers; you will have two physicians traveling with you, to see to their welfare…"

Clianthe entered the villa office to find her mother giving stern orders to a collection of men around her desk. She had not overheard all of what was said, but she recognized a few of the faces in the room, men Muir had handpicked for his mission on Pháne. Her hands began to tremble and she clasped them together to steady them. Gabrielle Dilyn-Lachlan motioned her daughter into the room as the men bowed and retreated, each intent on the duty they were given. Before Clianthe could ask what had happened, her mother sighed and said, "The outpost was attacked."

Clianthe deserved the truth. There was no use in hiding it from her or couching it in delicate terms.

"Attacked?" The younger woman's voice was a small squeak, her head filled with too many horrifying scenarios for her to keep calm.

Gabrielle embraced her daughter sympathetically. "Muir is well; no one was killed. There were injuries and the outpost requires repair, but everyone is safe. Those scheduled for leave came as intended, but many will return with the supply ships. Muir stayed to oversee cleanup and reconstruction. So long as the weather holds, he felt staying would be better for his men's' morale…"

"I want to go to him."

Gabrielle's embrace tightened around her daughter. Despite their differences in age, they were similar enough in stature and appearance to have been sisters rather than mother and daughter. "Where would you sleep? What would you do? There is no place for you while the repairs are in progress; you would be in the way and the men would feel inclined to cater to you rather than work."

She let Clianthe go when the younger woman was about to protest and scooped up a scroll from the desk to hand to her. "Here is Muir's letter; he says the same thing. He will return to you as soon as he is able. For our part, it is up to us to see that the Council better equips the outpost, that they do not end the work we have begun. If someone is willing to declare war on the islands, even an island not normally inhabited, we must do what we can to stop it."

Trying not to crush the scroll in her hand, Clianthe sighed and bit the inside of her cheek. This was not the way she had envisioned spending the first months of her marriage, but she was powerless against the hands of fate. The realities of life did not often make way for dreams, not even hers.

"Very well," she muttered. With her features set into a stern, focused, frustrated expression, she asked," Shall I call the Council to emergency session this evening?"

Thankful she had been able to redirect her stubborn daughter from running off to Pháne, Gabrielle nodded. "That is a splendid suggestion. I am going to the docks to oversee the loading progress, see what else is needed, so please inform me when the Council is scheduled. I suggest you reply to Muir's message first, if you intend to; the ships will leave as soon as they are loaded and they will not want to wait."

Clianthe's head bobbed once as she sank into her mother's chair behind the desk. Gabrielle left her to it. This was Clianthe's first real taste of political responsibility, something she had been sheltered from by her mother's tight grip on political dealings and her own disinterest in it. Gabrielle had made few efforts to engage Clianthe in political matters after Clianthe's first handful of refusals. She could see in the young woman's face that, if forced to the task as the absence of her husband had thrust upon her, Clianthe could fulfill the role of Prime Magistrate, but she had no desire to do so. What Clianthe wanted was to be a wife and mother…if only she was given the chance.

❧Chapter 9❧

The gauzy outline of the woman on the shore appeared to have her back to him when Kavan first saw her. A gust of arid wind blew across the dry land, lifting her auburn hair from her shoulders, waving it in flutters towards him. Without seeing her face, he knew her. There was no mistaking her aura, the scent of her, the shape of her that he recalled too vividly in his dreams every time he closed his eyes to sleep. To be near her after so long, even though she was beyond his reach and looked to be too far away to hear him, was torture. He had believed his heart had begun to heal from the loss of her, but now that he saw her again, he believed it no longer.

"Orynn."

She turned her head slightly, not looking directly at him but enough to indicate she had heard her whispered name on the wind, or had sensed him there. He groaned in frustration that he could not touch her, the distance between shore and ship too vast to easily bridge.

"Orynn…look at me…speak to me…" He had never thought he would see her again after the way they had parted. If she had come back, there was a reason for it, a reason, he suspected, more important than missing his company.

Her voice, distant and gentle like birdsong on the night breeze, tickled his ears. "I should not be here, my lord…I do not wish to hurt you…but I had to come." Still, she would not look at him or turn to face him. "I have come only to ask one question. Can you swim?"

"My lord!"

Waking with a start, Kavan bolted upright, his hammock swaying and bumping something solid on one side, Wortham's big hands on his shoulders and his bearded face creased with distress. The monk was clasping the railing of the steps out of the hold and Zelenka clung to him. There was no visible shoreline, as they were below deck on the merchant's cog, and Orynn was not there. But as his eyes adjusted to the dark and sleep left him, Kavan was sure of one thing: her appearance had been no dream. Her scent, her aura, lingered still and in those waking moments, he understood her words to be a warning.

His hammock bumped against the side of the hold as the vessel listed heavily to one side.

He did not need to ask Wortham what was wrong.

"How bad?"

"Lower hold is filling. She's going down."

The bard swallowed his panic as Wortham helped him out of the displaced hammock. "Are the crew evacuating?"

"There is no crew…it seems they have already abandoned ship."

Abandoned ship and left their passengers to drown? That was disconcerting and made no sense. Where could they have gone?

"I've been up top," Wortham continued. "Saw no one in the twilight and fog, no other ships to offer aid. I found no transports we can use. If they are overboard…in the water or in rafts, I did not see or hear them. With the angle…the rate we're taking on water, if we do not hurry, we will go down with the ship. We will drown."

Kavan shuddered. That was not the sort of death he wished for or envisioned…and he still had a duty to perform. With Orynn's question in mind, he staggered as the wooden sides of the cog groaned under the strain of the water's weight and he squared his shoulders. "We are not drowning. Can it be repaired? Can we bale her?"

"There's too much…and I don't know where the breach is," the captain replied. "We've either been rammed or she's been taking on water for many hours."

Certain he would have felt it if the cog had been struck, or had struck something else, it meant the latter was likely the case. They had few options available. "Can you swim?"

Wortham, already gathering the belongings he could reach, snorted. "I'm from Káliel. I'll have to leave the armor." but that was of little consequence compared to losing his life. "Zelenka cannot."

"Nor can I," interjected Urian, patting Zelenka's trembling hand on his arm, doing his best to soothe her. "Rather…I know how, but finding my way to shore will be a problem."

"It's not far; we can make it there if I help Zelenka and you aid Urian." Wortham did not need to ask if Kavan could swim.

"The trunk…"

Wortham nodded, his expression grim. Many of their belongings could be replaced. The contents of the trunk, however, were priceless.

"How long?"

"Til she sinks?" The captain shrugged. "An hour…maybe more, maybe less if we hit a strong undercurrent or the wood buckles."

"Can you make it to shore and back…for both of them? I can maneuver the ship nearer…lessen the distance…" There was no reason to doubt he could, but he risked the hold filling with water faster in doing so. "Or I can swim the distance myself…"

Wortham scowled. "Without light on the shore, it'll be difficult…I do not know if I could find my way back," he reluctantly admitted.

As the cog lurched again, Urian pulled Zelenka up the steps. "Knew there was a reason I rarely travel by sea," he muttered. "I can get there…if someone directs me." He was willing to try.

Feeling wetness around his boots, Kavan looked to see a thin sheet of water trickling over the angled boards. There was no time to waste in debate. "Wortham, find a rope…bind Urian to you. Guide them both. The three of you must get to shore."

Catching Kavan's arm as the bard hoisted the treasured trunk, Wortham grunted, "My lord, you cannot swim with that." He knew how heavy it was, how awkward. Without a raft or someone's aid, he could not imagine the bard making it to shore with so much weight.

Kavan sighed and shrugged. He had the strength to carry it, but did he have the strength to swim with it? "I must try…but I will see you safely to shore first…and then…" He shrugged again and pulled free. "We pray k'Ádhá is with us."

The view from the deck when they emerged from the hold was worse than anticipated. The cog was rapidly approaching the point where the middle level would take on water as well. Once that occurred, complete submersion would not be far behind. With the trunk at his feet, Kavan secured the ends of the rope Wortham had cut free from the sails, around Urian and around the captain. He refused to listen to Wortham's protests, and Wortham, realizing the effort was fruitless now that they were quickly running out of time, gave up trying to convince Kavan of some different path. Side by side, hand in hand, the soldier and monk jumped into the water, the monk's heavy robes left on the listing deck with Wortham's armor. Once the two men bobbed to the surface and were calmly treading water, Wortham called up to the woman on the deck to join him.

Zelenka shook her head and screamed terrified words down to the captain that Kavan could not understand. It seemed that no amount of reassurance from Wortham would convince her to jump.

"Zelenka." Kavan touched her elbow, channeling as much soothing energy through the touch as he could. "You do not understand me…but if you stay here, you invite death. If you wish to survive…to live…you must jump. Wortham will keep you safe."

He hoped that his tone and touch would persuade her, but she refused to move. Briefly, he toyed with the thought of pushing her in; she would be afraid and angry, but she would, at least, live. Yet fate had something else in mind for the reluctant woman. The ship bucked as the water level inside continued to rise and Zelenka was tossed into the sea without Kavan having to do anything. He grabbed the rail and clung to it, hoping to avoid falling as well, as he was not yet prepared to join them. He listened to several minutes of splashing and screaming as he steadied himself, before both Urian and Wortham caught Zelenka between them with her head above water.

"Follow the light, Wortham…it will guide you to shore."

"You will have no time to…" began the captain as a silver-blue glow appeared several inches from his face, dancing on the surface of the water in the mist, pointing him towards the distant beach.

"Go."

The bard said no more as he pushed the glow in the desired direction while simultaneously struggling to affect the tide, trying to ease his companions and the sinking boat nearer to land. The fog continued to thicken, making it difficult to see either the trio in the water or the coastline, but Kavan trusted his instincts. When they disappeared from view and the sounds of Zelenka struggling had stopped, Kavan prayed they remained safe. He sought their auras and sucked in a relieved breath when he found them.

As long as he could feel them, they were alive.

The sinking vessel pitched again. The trunk he had been steadfastly guarding slid from between his feet and he scrambled to catch it without losing his grip on the slippery rail. But the cog was nearly on her side and maintaining his footing was no longer possible. He landed in a jumble, one hand catching a length of anchor chain, the fingers of his other hand curled around one trunk handle. He could not hold either grip for long. If he did not let go of one, he would be forced to let go of the other.

With his focus shifted to survival and not losing the items he had struggled so long to gather, the beacon leading the others was snuffed out. The current slowed. Kavan, hoping the others were near enough to shore to be safe, heard his name shouted in panic but he did not know by whom. There was no time to answer. He had to take to the water while the trunk was still in his possession.

Reluctantly, he released the anchor chain and slid into the sea where he was pulled beneath the waves by the weight of the trunk. The air was forced from his lungs as his body recoiled from the impact with the water, as though he had been slammed into a wall, but the sensation passed quickly. As Wortham had predicted, even his Elyri strength could not swim with the full burden of the trunk; its shape was cumbersome and he could neither hold it with both hands and swim or pull it along with one hand behind him. Struggling beneath the waves to pull it back to the surface proved futile. The trunk was like a boulder tied around his body. He could not rise to the surface for air without letting go.

Dismayed, horrified, and angry, Kavan was forced to abandon the trunk by the necessity of survival.

When he broke the surface, he gasped for breath, saltwater stinging his eyes so that he could not see beyond the bulk of the ship. That meant the shore was behind him. There was pain from the fight for oxygen, compounded by the overpowering panic and despair that tried to drown him as well. He could not lose that trunk. It contained his future, his and Enesfel's. Without it, he might as well be dead. He could not have come this far to have the necessity of duty die here.

After another gulp of air, he dove, frantically searching for the trunk in the depths through the oxygen bubbles the ship belched as it was dragged towards the ocean floor. He dove again and again without success. The emerald on his hand pulsed stronger as he swam deeper, but he could not see either his hand or the trunk, could not find the seabed. And the current, while not strong enough to carry the trunk far, could have sent it northward, or towards the shore, or it could have been pulled down with the wreckage to be buried beneath it when the splintering cog found its resting place. Surfacing again, aware that he was running out of strength too quickly because of his panic, Kavan was torn between saving himself and continuing his search. Desperately, his thoughts cried, "Kóráhm! k'Ádhá! Help me!"

"Kavan!"

That cry was Wortham's, but it was too far away for Kavan to locate without effort. He wondered if the others had made it to shore, if they were safe. Little of the cog remained above the water now, only splintered planks and lengths of mast and bubbles of sailcloth like blisters on the sea where the air was trapped beneath the waxy canvas.

The air and thick fog felt colder against his overtaxed muscles, but the water temperature was bearable and he did not think he would die of exposure.

Wishing his companions well, since there was nothing else he could do for them, Kavan let out a long breath. One more dive, he thought with desperate determination. Perhaps if senses other than his eyes led him, he would find what he sought.

He followed the pulse of the ring on his hand, the strength of the power drawing him a little north and further out to sea than he had expected the trunk to travel. The current was stronger here, more difficult to swim against, and would not make retrieving the trunk easy, but Kavan was determined to try. Another breath, deeper than before, and he dove, fighting the current, fighting the pressure of the water bearing down on him, fighting the need for air in his straining lungs. His eyes were closed this time; they had misled him before, brought him no closer to finding what he sought. So he trusted the connection between Kóráhm's ring and the contents of the trunk.

The water pressure increased the pain in his head, in his ears, in his chest. When he believed he could go no deeper, his hand touched something solid and a static pop shot up his arm, through the ring into his head. Frantically seeking a hold as it felt he and the trunk were being ejected to the surface like a cork released from the bottom of a barrel, he found the handle, closed his fingers around it, but the press of water sent a flash of searing pain through his body and he lost consciousness.

"I don't see him." Wortham rubbed his arms to warm them as he paced the sea's edge, seeking some sign of his best friend through the fog. He was thankful he had left his armor, although it annoyed him to have lost it and his sword. His trunk of supplies was gone too, as were Zelenka's few belongings and Urian's robes and whittling tools. Disappeared to the depths of the ocean to serve as food and shelter for the fish. But at least three of them had avoided drowning. Those things, as useful as they might have been, were replaceable.

Gathering potential firewood as he paced, he could not help worrying about Kavan. The bard's power beacon had led them half the distance to shore and the incoming tide had pushed them the remainder of the distance. No one was injured, only weary and waterlogged, but they were cold in the night air without dry clothes or blankets to warm themselves. Urian was trying to light a fire but was having little success. Zelenka was huddled against him, shivering from cold and the trauma of her first experience at sea. Without a fire, they could not get dry, could not get warm, and Wortham worried how they would fare the remainder of the night.

And Kavan was gone. The fog thinned enough that Wortham could see that their ship was nearly devoured by the sea now, but there was no sight of Kavan, and with each passing moment Wortham feared it had been too long. Kavan should have come ashore by now, with or without that trunk. It appeared that trying to save the important collection of relics had cost the bard his life and Wortham could barely refrain from cursing fate for its cruelty.

"Captain?"

He turned reluctantly from his watch at the dedhá's words and took over the task of starting a fire. His throat burned, though whether from grief or too much swallowed seawater he did not know. He should not have left Kavan alone, should have demanded the bard come with them. Trunk be damned. If its contents were necessary for his success, k'Ádhá and Saint Kóráhm could have seen to its safety. Wortham should have seen to Kavan's. To lose him now, to the sea where there would be little chance of finding his body, was one of the worst possible ends to the bard's life the captain could imagine.

When the fire finally roared and crackled, he stripped off his shirt and boots, lay them beside the heat to dry, and returned to the water's edge where the surf lapped at his feet, stubborn to the last.

Perhaps there was still hope. The captain did not want to give up, especially where Kavan was concerned. The bard had survived so much; surely he could survive this. Come the dawn, if there was still no sign of him, then it might be time to consider what the future held. But not before daybreak…and perhaps not even then.

Music. Faint, unfamiliar, but it was music. Tinkling bells and soft, melodic strings. There were voices too, three male voices, unfamiliar words that struck an uncomfortable chord within, as if he should know those words, those voices, when he did not. He wanted to open his eyes, to look about him, but he was unable to do so. He lacked the strength, or perhaps they were somehow preventing him from seeing them. Perhaps this was a dream. Perhaps he was dead. He remembered nothing, felt nothing, except a ringing tingle of pain in his ears and a thrumming within his head that ached of power used and lost.

But he knew when something touched his forehead, warm and soft and smelling of spiced ointment. The sensation was as real as the pain. A hand, he believed, applying treatment, offering health. It offered comfort, it offered peace, and then there was nothing.

How many hours had passed? With darkness and fog clinging to the sea, Wortham was not certain. He heard Zelenka rise many times, gathering driftwood and dried sea flora for the fire, and once she had stopped beside him with her arm hooked around his and her head on his shoulder. A sigh and a kiss to the top of her head were the sole acknowledgments she received and then she left him alone as silently as she had come. Though still weak from seasickness, she was making an effort to attend to the needs of the men, her duty as she saw it given the cultural upbringing she had known. Wortham wished she would not cater to him as if she was a slave or servant. She needed to rest, to conserve her strength for the journey ahead…whenever Wortham decided to resume it. Instead, she was doing what he would not, seeing to the fire and Urian's care. It made Wortham feel guilty, although not guilty enough yet to compel him to act. Urian was speaking to her in low, quiet words Wortham could not hear, but he did not care to know.

He only cared about one thing.

Dawn was not far off; he could feel it before he realized the sky was growing brighter behind the mist. They should be on their way soon, in search of proper shelter, clothing, food, and water, and he was beginning to despair the inevitable. His debate was about whether he should return to Rhidam to inform those who had loved the bard of his loss, or whether to go elsewhere, never look back, build a life here in this foreign land with Zelenka and Urian as companions. How could he face those in Rhidam if he failed at the only duty in his life that mattered, failed to keep Kavan safe as he had sworn to do?

Zelenka's second touch on his arm jolted him back to his surroundings to notice that the fog had lifted more with the advent of morning, and out to sea, much further out then their sunken vessel, a second ship sat unmoving against the horizon haze. Or Wortham thought it was a ship. Taller than any sailing vessel he was familiar with, he believed it to be an illusion as it came and went in the fog, except that Zelenka saw it too, had been the one to point it out to him with excited fervor. During his youth on Káliel, he had never seen any ship like this one at the islands' docks. She had too many sails, was too long and graceful, to match anything he could remember. The way she hovered motionless on the glassy sea, her sails slack, silent without lights on her deck, was more like a ghost than any solid ship.

"Sósáná saeitá gaetió!" Zelenka repeated the phrase several times but Wortham was unable to translate it. She was both excited and frightened it seemed. Tugging at his hand, shifting as though uncertain if she should step closer to the water, or retreat from it, she repeated the words again.

"I do not understand," he muttered, rubbing his eyes to see if the mirage disappeared when his weariness was wiped away. It did not. "What are you telling me? Are we in danger?" He had no sword with which to protect them if they were. All he had was his fists, and the fire that was nearly out.

Frustrated, she stomped her foot and struggled to find the words she had been learning from Wortham and Urian to explain. "Legends. Dead ship. When she returns from the sea…when someone sees her…it is a good thing. Good sign. She helps those in the sea of need."

"Dead ship? You mean…ghost?" Ghost indeed. The vessel was gone now, disappearing over the horizon beyond their line of sight. He shivered as his eyes strained to find it. "Those in the sea of…do you think…?" Perhaps she believed Kavan was not dead.

But her face grew sad and she looked down at her hand around his arm. "I do not know. What can the dead do to help the living? I know the story. I have known no one who has seen it that could say."

But there was a chance, however slim, that Kavan was on that ship, that he might be taken to the next port for care and Wortham would find him there. He refused to be led to the fire. All myths held some kernel of truth, he had believed that since he was a child. And years of acquaintance with Kavan had further proven that to be true. He was exhausted and should get a few hours of sleep if they were to start away, but now that he had hope, he felt compelled to continue his vigil until that ship reappeared. If that ship was the key to their deliverance, to Kavan's salvation, Wortham would not be caught asleep and miss their chance.

For as long as his hazy memory could recall, he had been embraced in a gentle rocking motion and the soothing sound of water sloshing against wood. He had not known where he was, as his eyes refused to do his bidding, but he was certain the sensations were real. He now swam towards consciousness, and though the sounds of the sea remained, it was different. Distant, free of the impediment of wooden walls.

Instead of being surrounded by the sweet pungent aroma of incense, it was the stickiness of sea salt that clung to him and filled his nostrils. He was cold and damp instead of warm and dry, and water lapped at his toes. The soothing rocking of the sea had been replaced by the unforgiving grit of sand. It was troubling that he could not recall anything else, not even how he had gotten here, as he cracked his lids open and stared into the reassuring, powder-blue early morning sky.

He did not want to move. His head throbbed as if a hundred tiny horses were racing inside his skull, his entire body carried the aching burn of overexertion, and he felt exhausted despite the certainty that he had already slept for an unknown number of hours, long enough for night to have become day. His ears were ringing and the taste in his mouth was metallic and stale. Seabirds danced overhead; he recognized their silhouettes and harsh voices though he could not see or hear them clearly. His senses confirmed he was near the sea, knowledge that brought back the memory of the sinking ship, the lost trunk, the unfamiliar music and voices.

Panic sank deep, clawing at his heart, wringing from him the desperate need to find that trunk. But as he rolled to his side, intending to rise, to search in the light of day, the movement made his stomach spasm with agonizing nausea. Pulling into a ball as his muscles cramped, his empty stomach retched for several moments, expelling the saltwater he had swallowed and whatever bile there was to follow. Pain jolted through him with each convulsion, causing him to lie motionless when it was over and fall quickly asleep.

⮫*⮨

"That's right. Hold the focus longer. More…"

Gaelán sank back into the chair with a pout, away from the bhydáni's hands, refusing to allow the tears at the corners of his eyes to fall but visibly frustrated. "I cannot, bhydáni. No matter what I do…I lack the ability…"

The ancient man shook his head with a scolding scoff. "It is not ability you lack, little Cáner, it is faith in yourself. I read much power in you. If you learn to focus it…"

But again the young man interrupted, unable to believe the sage's words. "How can I focus when everything around me is chaos? k'aendhá Ártur and aene Syl…Rhidam…the Corylliens…Kavan…"

A gnarled hand on his head silenced him and Tíbhyan sighed. "You care much about Kavan; I read in you. But tell me why you feel this need to continually dwell upon him?" Such worry about anything was inappropriate for such a young man.

"Because no one else does." Gaelán frowned as he squirmed beneath that touch. He was sure the sage was poking around inside his head, learning secrets he did not want to be known. Fidgeting, he stared. "It is as if he died…as if he was never here. No one will talk about him; they are caught up in affairs of state or their own troubles. When…if he comes back, I want him to know that one person stayed true to him, that one of us kept him in their thoughts, their prayers."

"Commendable…but you think we do not? Do you believe that driving yourself into madness would please him more than learning you have made the most of the talent his tragedy revealed to you?" When Gaelán did not reply, he continued. "He was my dearest student; the dearest friend an old man can have. I have learned as much from him, I dare say, as he ever learned from me…perhaps more…and I tell you this: his deepest wish is to be treated the same as any other person. He wants our love, yes, but not crazed devotion. Do not treat him like a god, like a saint, little Cáner, or you will achieve the opposite of what you wish for."

"I did what I could to save his life…because he is kin and he needed my help…because I love him…and he left anyhow." Sniffing, Gaelán wiped his eyes and added bitterly, "He did not even say thank you…or farewell."

"From what I was told, he bid few farewell, so I do not think he singled you out to be overlooked. A man under duress does things he would not normally do…and often fails to do things he normally would. You think he loves you less because he left without a goodbye? That you failed him in some way and need to atone for your lapse to gain his affection? Believe me…such self-torment is not worth it. In those moments when he left, he thought of none but himself. When he finds the will to return, you will see. He will be more pleased by your progress then by any fanatical devotion."

The sage refused to use 'if'. He chose to believe Kavan would return when he was ready. Kavan always did.

"You think so?"

He patted Gaelán's hand. "Would he have placed such trust in me if I was a dishonest man?"

He rose from his stool and tottered about the room, pouring a cup of tea, closing a book on the desk, pushing his window open to allow in the breeze while he gave Gaelán a chance to ponder his words.

Eventually, Gaelán held forth his hands.

"If you believe I have potential, bhydáni, then I know he would say the same. Teach me to master it so he will be impressed…and happy to see me."

❧*❧

From the bench in the garden behind Kavan's house, Ártur studied the white roses that, until recently had spent years largely untended. They were pruned and shaped this year, done by the lady healer's hands, and the small two-story stone house had recovered the feeling of home that had filled it when Kavan had lived here. Ártur liked it on this bench, the bench where he and Kavan once sat on the night Donal Lachlan died. There had been many changes in the years since, but this house was not one of them. This house, his cousin's house, remained constant, even when Kavan did not reside in it.

The healer sighed and stared at his nephew, his fingers rubbing the place where an attacker's knife had cut him, as Bhen murmured. "I am sorry, k'aendhá. It is the best I could arrange this time."

It was too soon, Ártur knew. Syl was too angry to accept a compromise. Her fire, passion, and tenacity had been some of the traits he had first grown to love about her. She did not take slights easily and was able and willing to be strong for her family when she felt the need. His first fiancée, Elys, had been the same way, both women so different from his mother. Syl considered it a personal insult that he would choose Rhidam over her, the Teren over his children, and Kavan over everything else. Nothing except time was going to change anything, unless he capitulated entirely to her terms. To do so, however, would drive a different wedge between them because, in time, Ártur would come to resent her for making him abandon Kavan.

Eventually, he believed Syl would see that too.

The best he could offer was the compromise Bhen suggested. Pursuant to King Hagan's agreement, and Bhríd's, the healer would spend his days in the Rhidam keep and his nights in Bhryell unless summoned by Bhríd or Tusánt or some other Elyri messenger. Syl would not take him back, but she did agree to give him access to his children, allowing him to visit when he chose, allowing them to stay with him each night if he wished.

But his wife would not see him.

He closed his eyes. "This is not your fault. You've done your best. There is nothing…it is the most I can give, the most she can give. I must accept it, as she must." Accept it, yes, but neither had to like it.

"I will tell her you agree." After a single bob of Ártur's head, Bhen asked, "When do you go back?"

"Tomorrow, I think. Rhidam has been too long without a healer. Gaelán…we must go back." Particularly since Ártur was fighting the strong compulsion to know if there had been any news from Kavan. "I will be right here until then."

"Not on this bench, I hope."

Though he did not intend to stay on that bench the entire time, the healer snorted at Bhen's mirth and said, "This bench is as good a place as anywhere else to be."

The younger Elyri nodded, pressed his open palm to the carved stone, and murmured, "Because it is his."

Ártur closed his eyes and gave a single long, forlorn breath.

When Kavan's senses stirred again, rousing him to full waking, it was to find himself in the embrace of strong arms, with tears dampening his shoulders and thick hands twisted in his still moist, sandy hair. He did not have the strength to pull away and had no will to try, particularly after his initial confusion and distress subsided and he realized who was holding him. Dearest Wortham, he thought, his raw throat refusing to allow words to pass. After hours in the sea, after losing the trunk and nearly his life, Kavan wanted comfort and serenity, and he knew Wortham would give him both. Wortham would give him anything he wanted…just not those things lost to the ocean.

He shivered and gave a small, involuntary whimper.

Wortham pulled back enough to look into the bard's face. "Praise be you are alive!" Then he again crushed the slender man to his chest, more tightly than before.

Kavan was still unable to speak, this time because his face was buried in the big man's shoulder. Without the strength to stay upright, when Wortham eventually released him, Kavan collapsed onto the ground. Tall grass of pale green and gold surrounded them, and though he could not see the water, he could hear the surf and smell the salt in the air. There were the remains of a fire nearby, giving off no heat now that the embers had died. He believed he had been nearer to the water when he had awakened before, and concluded Wortham must have found him and brought him here. The sun was higher, nearly noon, and though he did not feel normal, he no longer felt sick, his ears no longer rang, and some of the physical pain had lessened.

Without turning his head, his eyes shifted focus to Zelenka, who brought a handful of red berries and offered them to him with a hesitant hand. The captain cradled Kavan against his side and helped him to eat. Though the berries were firmer than expected, perhaps not yet ripe, and sour on his dry tongue, they were not unpleasant and the tang prompted his mouth and throat to begin working. She watched as he ate, her eyes mirroring the captain's concern and expressed a degree of excitement Kavan did not understand. Her tunic was tattered and dirty but it was dry, as was her unkempt hair, suggesting they had been safe by their now-dead fire for some time. He tried to touch her, wanting to assure himself of her reality and her wellness, but she was beyond his reach. With a soft sound of frustration, he closed his eyes and let his hand drop.

"Rest, my lord. I have seen many men survive the sea; it will take time to regain your bearings and strength. I have no water to offer, and little food, but a period of rest will help. dedhá Urian believes we will find a village or caravan if we find the north road, perhaps new supplies and proper beds. When you are ready, we will start north."

He settled the bard into the grass and covered him with his own dry tunic. "No use in getting sunburned," he murmured. "I am darker skinned. We must make do without extra clothes, but at least ours are serviceable. We lost much to the sea…but we still have these."

Wortham pointed and for the first time, Kavan noticed the two trunks on the other side of the fire. One he did not recognize, appeared bigger than anything they'd had before, but the other he had thought never to see again. With a strangled sound, he tried to sit, to reach it, but Wortham pushed him back down.

"Yes, I do not know if you saved it or…but Zelenka found you and both trunks further up the beach. k'Ádhá spared you and the relics…and saw fit to provide us with other items…"

He presented the dagger he had found in the second trunk, something expensive that Wortham had fastened to his hip and refused to relinquish. There had been a robe passable for Urian's needs, four empty water skins, and a few items that Orynn had left with Wortham that he had believed lost. How they had come to be in that second trunk, the captain could only guess. "I do not know how we will carry them, but we will worry about that in the morning."

Finding his voice, eyes alight with anticipation, Kavan rasped, "Tonight."

Wortham shook his head. "You are weak. So is Zelenka. We are not fit to travel. Tomorrow is soon enough."

"Night will be cooler; it will be better." Kavan believed it to be true, though he could not explain the feeling behind that belief. "We must…go home."

Feeling the certainty in his friend's voice, Wortham patted his shoulder. A few hours, he thought, would not harm anything, and might mean all of the difference between Kavan walking on his own or being carried. "Sleep. I will seek fresh water…something more to eat. We will see what evening brings, fair enough?"

Eyes closed, the bard nodded. Or perhaps he dropped off to sleep instead of nodding his agreement, since he appeared to be asleep the moment his eyes closed. Though hesitant to leave him, Wortham was bolstered by the fact that Kavan lived. If he hoped for it to stay that way, he needed to find water, otherwise, the joy of their reunion, their survival, was going to be short-lived.

⁊Chapter 10

Settled on the back of his bulky roan, having ridden so long today that his backside was growing numb, Owain had seen the shrouded figure at the side of the road long before he and Espen were close enough to assess its threat level. The person had been traveling with quick steps, turning their head frequently as if watching the riders' approach, and then veered off the path into a copse of tangled trees. Unable to tell if the individual was a criminal, a fugitive, or merely someone fearful of strangers, Espen agreed that the person's actions warranted investigation. If they meant to cause mischief, Owain and Espen could prevent it. If it was some poor, frightened soul traveling alone in Enesfel's climate of violence, perhaps they could offer protection for however far he wished to travel.

Or her.

Owain brought his horse to a halt when he was still several yards from where the person had disappeared at the side of the road, and called, "Stranger? Are you in need of aid? We wish you no harm." He dismounted, leaving his sword sheathed, but Espen, prepared for an ambush, prepared to protect the boy who rode with him, drew his sabre and waited for the first hint of trouble.

The brush rustled, twigs snapped, and slowly the figure emerged with his hand resting on his hip, likely where a weapon waited beneath his cloak. Owain doubted this was an ambush, as the stranger made too much noise to remain effectively hidden, and gave every indication of wanting to flee. Instead of attempting to do so, however, he lowered the hood of his cloak and remained resolutely stationary as if staring into the face of expected death.

Elyri.

Espen and Owain relaxed. Being Elyri explained the traveler's anxiety and his furtive behavior. That he chose to face Owain, face potential execution, when he could have stayed hidden, spoke either of naiveté or else great courage. As the light breeze tugged the gentle waves of pale blonde from his face, he shifted his weight and tightened his grip on his hip.

"Of what assistance could you be to me?" The challenge was laced with a note of fear.

Liking the sound of the man's voice, his accent slightly different than Kavan's suggesting he was from some different part of Elyriá, Owain chuckled softly in the hopes of putting the man at ease. "These days, few travel alone in Enesfel…particularly on foot. Elyri in Enesfel are especially at risk."

He imagined the stranger already knew that.

Sadness undercut his hardened expression. "I am aware of the dangers. If you wish to kill me, be done with it. I am on a pilgrimage only; I will not fight you."

"Which is why your hand is on your weapon?" Espen asked. Piran, sleeping against his arm, turned a little with the cessation of travel and the voices, but he did not open his eyes.

"This?" The Elyri threw back his cloak. It was no blade at his hip, but rather a recorder of pale polished wood. "If you think I can kill you with this, I will try if you insist."

Owain laughed, hoping he did not offend the man in doing so, and offered his hand. "You believe we wish to kill you?"

The stranger did not accept the offered handshake. "As you say, Enesfel is not the safest place for my people."

"I cannot say your precaution is unjustified, but I assure you not all of us are out for Elyri blood. We intend no harm. We are on our way to Rhidam; may I inquire about your pilgrimage?" Owain was not aware of holy sites in this region, but he had never made a study of them either.

"I heard of the attack on Harper Cliáth and wish to offer my support, my prayers for him in Saint Kóráhm's if he will accept my company." Noting the look that passed between Owain and Espen, he frowned. "Has the náós been destroyed? Harper Cliáth killed?"

"I sincerely pray not," replied Owain, choking on the words.

Espen continued. "Lord Cliáth left Enesfel shortly after the attack; the last we were in Rhidam he had not returned, though perhaps he has by now. You risk your life on a journey that might be for naught."

There was disappointment on the Elyri's face but his determination lingered. "If I can offer consolation to his kin, that will be enough. I will continue on to Saint Kóráhm's regardless…unless you tell me it has been destroyed."

Shaking his head, Owain climbed back onto his horse. "Not that I know of. Why do you risk the road? Why not travel by Gate?"

The blonde man's eyes widened and he took several steps backward. It was, for most Elyri, policy to never reveal the knowledge of Gates to Teren. Such knowledge would be too dangerous to let out. Teren could not operate the Gates, but knowing about them meant an increased danger from frightened Teren who could guard such places and kill any who attempted to use them. "You know of the…"

Owain realized he had not introduced himself, and may have misspoken in revealing his knowledge of the Gates. "Apologies for not…I am Owain Lachlan," he started, as if that explained how he had come by such a secret. "This is Prince Espen Harcourt of Hatu…and my son Piran." He motioned to the other riders who lingered further back, too far back to have heard his question about the Gates, watchfully awaiting his instructions. "My retainers. Lord Cliáth is a dear friend; I have traveled by Gate with him many times. It is a privilege I do not take lightly."

Glancing at the riders behind them, then back at the man on foot, Owain asked, "Would you…if you will allow me the honor, we can escort you as far as Rhidam and bring you directly to Healer MacLyr, Lord Cliáth's kinsman. I offer our protection as best we can."

"You are not likely to encounter safer traveling companions," interjected Espen, his sword now back in its sheath.

When the Elyri again hesitated, Owain offered his hand, this time removing his glove. "Read me if you wish. Test the honesty of what we say." The offer was a risk, but one that seemed worth taking.

And one that paid off as the Elyri's boyish features softened. "You know our ways well if you are willing to make such an offer. Perhaps that should be enough to win my trust…but forgive me if I accept…"

He reached for Owain's hand and Owain swallowed hard. "Your life is at stake…" He expected nothing else. If he judged this man wrongly, the Elyri could easily kill him…or so said every myth and story Nethite children were indoctrinated with. But Owain did his best to disbelieve those tales, and with so many armed men nearby, he did not believe the stranger would risk attacking him. The Elyri closed his eyes as their hands clasped; Owain barely had time to notice how much the man's hands reminded him of Kavan's before the touch was gone.

"You speak true…and the tale you tell of Harper Cliáth…is a great shame. I will ride with you, if I may, and repay your hospitality however I am able."

"Come…mount up with me."

The Elyri was astride the horse in one swift movement, marking him as an expert horseman as well as a bard. "Welcome to Enesfel."

He let the words hang, the final note prompting the stranger for an introduction he had not yet made. The Elyri smiled and chuckled, a sound that again reminded Owain of Kavan. This man's company would be all the more welcome for those reminders.

"Bhyrhán Bhíncári."

❧*❧

At this hour of the day, before the early morning Gathering, the náós was quiet and dark, Tusánt's favorite hour for reflection and prayer. He felt more in need of both of late, and he treasured any time he could get alone as he struggled to feel at peace in a world that offered so little of it to men of his race. Today, however, the footsteps that approached his room announced the end of his moments of solitude before he had the opportunity to enjoy them. He did not look up until the familiar steps stopped in his open doorway.

That was a mistake, he realized. Anyone could kill him in that moment of seeming inattention.

"dedhá?"

The Elyri clergyman turned on his knees to look at his visitor. "Yes, Valgis?" Since his arrival in Rhidam earlier in the year, no one except Claide had succeeded in convincing Valgis to call them by name. He continued to use titles, as if the youngster still considered the others to be his superiors rather than his equals.

"There is a young man here to speak with you about the requirements for the priesthood." Valgis looked as if he wanted to say more, but a dark-haired young man appeared behind him and Valgis shuffled awkwardly to one side. Tusánt got to his feet, looking the young man over, thinking he looked more awake and alert than most at this early hour.

It seemed, as Tusánt took the newcomer's hand, that Valgis did not want to leave the two alone, but as he sensed no danger in the arrival, Tusánt waved Valgis away and the young dedhá reluctantly left. To be certain their conversation would not be overheard, Tusánt closed the door. He did not think this man's arrival was a coincidence.

"How old are you?" he started, thinking the young man looked of age to make a solid choice about entering the service of the Faith but wanting to be certain. Young men and women came to dedhá with requests to serve often enough. The only oddity about this request was the hour at which it was being made.

"Twenty-two."

"Good age…though a late one for the path you seek. You desire to join the gdhededhá…?"

"I have a strong sense of faith and commitment, dedhá, but I admit that this path was not my idea."

Tusánt almost asked why this man felt compelled to enter the Faith at someone else's request. He was old enough to make his own choices, and only some obligation of duty might override his free will. Something in his stance struck Tusánt, his broad shoulders, muscular arms, his rigid comportment. A soldier by vocation, no doubt, or someone who had trained for soldiering.

He sucked in a breath. "Her Majesty sent you." The early hour, when others might not know of his coming here, made sense now.

The young man nodded and spoke in a low voice as if he too feared being overheard. "My family is from Alberni; I came to Rhidam to serve in the royal guard as my father and uncles have done before me. I came with Lord Gabersdon after learning of the death of k'dedhá Tythilius. I wish to serve justice, to end the violence. Duke Cliáth has brought prosperity to Alberni and has done much for my family, and as far as I can see, the Elyri have wrought nothing but benefits for Enesfel. None of you deserve the mistreatment you receive. When Her Majesty learned of my position and view from Lord Gabersdon, she spoke to me of your need for protection…and the need for secrecy and care…"

"You realize this could be…"

"Dangerous? Permanent?" He nodded grimly. "Yes. As the youngest son in my family, my parents will not be displeased if I follow the path of Faith. I have given the Princess' request serious consideration and am prepared to make this commitment…to Faith, to your service, for as long as necessary, until my dying breath. There will be no dishonesty in my apprenticeship, dedhá. I will follow every tenet to the end…and protect you with my life if necessary."

Unwavering loyalty and commitment, not to the Faith but to his safety, was something Tusánt never thought he would see from a Teren. He opened his mouth to say something but no words came out. He did not know what to say.

The younger man offered his hand. "I am older than most novices, but I am not the first to enter the Path late in life. I believe this is my destiny; it is what I want, if you will accept me."

"What is your name?" Tusánt asked in a quavering voice, clasping the offered hand as if sealing a pact.

"Saul Peado. My family are dye and ink makers…and soldiers." He grinned and squeezed the dedhá's hand.

"Well…Saul…" Tusánt wiped his hand across his face as if wiping away sweat, but it was actually to wipe away the tears in the corners of his eyes. Elyri did not normally sweat, but tears came to anyone. "Let me give you a tour of Hes á Redh, find you a room, and introduce you to the others. We cannot waste time. If it is satisfactory, you shall begin your training at once."

Before Claide came back to Rhidam.

Saul smiled. "That suits me well, dedhá. I am at your service."

❧*❦

The hour was early enough that Ártur knew he was unlikely to encounter anyone but servants when he returned to Rhidam. Gaelán went directly to Asta's room, which meant that soon enough the entire staff would know the healer had returned. For now, however, he remained in the chapel, pondering the state of his life, but mainly wondering what had become of Kavan. What if Syl was right? What if Kavan never returned? How long had he been gone? Five months? Ártur had been separated from his cousin for longer periods, particularly when Kavan had been a child, but those absences had been the healer's choice. Kavan had never left him before, it had always been Ártur doing the leaving, and he wondered if the emptiness he felt was the same Kavan experienced all those years ago when his cousin seemed to have abandoned him. For Ártur, now, without Kavan in his life, the world made little sense.

He wanted him home.

Touching the feet of the form of Dhágdhuán the Intercessor, he remembered each time that figure had bled, each miraculous event that had occurred within these hallowed walls. If the outside world ever learned of those sacred moments, Rhidam's keep would become another pilgrimage site for the faithful, as Bhryell's náós had become long ago. The Faith might not have dubbed Kavan a saint, but with people already flocking to the sites of some of the major events in the bard's life after the attempt to kill him, it seemed likely that would eventually come to pass.

Perhaps it was better for Kavan not to come back to see what had become of the places he knew so well.

"Lord MacLyr."

The princess was the last person Ártur expected to seek him out so soon. His heart fluttered with the hope that perhaps there had been news about Kavan after all and he turned to look at her with undisguised hope. "My Lady?"

Princess Diona looked nervous as she took a few more steps into the chapel, sniffing the air as if she expected to detect something worth noticing. She felt Kavan in this place, as she knew he must, and the sense of him made her uncomfortable.

"I saw Gaelán and assumed you would be here. There has been no news during your absence, no event of import…I thought you would want to know that." If she was in his position, she would want to hear the news, good or bad. She would want to know if Kavan was home. Her eyes shifted nervously away, unable to meet his gaze, and she murmured, "I wish he would come back."

Sighing, refusing to allow his shoulders to slump under the weight of what felt like defeat, he said, "As do I."

"Does your return mean you are resuming your post…or have you come to say goodbye?"

She sounded both worried and hopeful, and he guessed she, like Gaelán, wanted him to stay as the anchor that might bring Kavan home. "I am…uncertain. I must discuss the matter with Bhríd and the King. I cannot remain in Rhidam full time, as Syl…it is obviously not safe here. But there is a compromise to be made if your brother and Bhríd are willing."

"Your safety is paramount. I think Hagan will hear your suggestion and will gladly agree to a compromise that will best serve everyone. He is currently in chambers with Lord Gabersdon and Lord Cáner; shall I let him know you are here and wish to speak with him?"

"There is no need to interrupt them." He was in no hurry for what could be an awkward discussion if Hagan did not wish to accept his proposal. "I will speak with them at their discretion. If there is no pressing need for my services now, I ask to be alone to pray."

He could have asked for time to rest, but he was not weary. He was too anxious to be weary. He had no bags to unpack. What he really desired was to seek Kavan within, and seek answers from Kóráhm and k'Ádhá, that might draw Kavan back.

The princess nodded, finding no offense in his request. "Of course…and welcome back, Lord Healer."

ॐ*ॐ

She would not tell him what she wanted to mark the day of her birth. Like her father, Asta did not find any need to celebrate the day beyond simple words and generally did not accept tokens from anyone except the late King Arlan and her mother when her mother had been alive. But both were gone this year, and Gaelán was determined that she would accept something from him in their place. If it were something practical, it would be less of an issue, but things like lock tools or new boots did not seem appropriate. The gold locket he had found in Bhryell, with some of the most beautiful filigree work he had ever seen, while hardly practical, had made him think of her as soon as he saw it, and he bought it without thinking…until after his return to Rhidam. After their recent adventures, he felt strongly she deserved it, and if she would not request something from him, she would, he hoped, accept this small token.

But something she had said today sparked his curiosity. Instead of her usual refusal to discuss gifts, Asta told him she would tell him what she wanted tomorrow. Tomorrow was her fourteenth birthday. There was a precocious twinkle in her eyes as she skipped away that made his belly do little flip-flops. It would be too late to buy a gift by then, perhaps too late to make something, but he doubted it was that sort of gift she alluded to. At least, for once, she did want something, and whatever it was, she was asking it from him.

As he went in search of his father, to tell him of his return, Gaelán wondered what it would be…and whether it was something he would be able to give.

ॐ*ॐ

Cold to the bone, wet through and through, and abjectly miserable, Prince Muir daydreamed about the warm comfort of his wife's arms rather than concentrating on the horizon as he should be. He and the three men standing with him had the watch; without shelter and proper supplies and equipment, they could not afford to be caught off guard. They could not survive another attack. The early spring rain was an uncomfortable annoyance but it was the smallest of their worries.

The ship sent to the main island would have reached port, his message delivered to Gabrielle and the Council. With luck, more supplies would arrive within a few days'. There were food and drink and arrows available, but they had nothing left to rebuild and he did not think there was enough to ward off attackers. With the tools that remained, the men had some success felling the largest trees within reach of their location, which allowed them to start rebuilding their sleeping quarters and provided wood for cook fires.

Most of the men were complaining; there were few on Káliel, other than sailors and vineyard workers and farmers, who were prepared to live in these conditions. Few were trained for it. Warfare was a foreign concept to the islanders, even to the highly trained Káliel guards, but it was something they were being forced to face. Muir believed it was coming. Gabrielle believed it too. This latest incident supported that belief. Despite Káliel's isolationist policies, or perhaps in support of it, the Prime Magistrate had known there would come a time when the islands would need to defend themselves without necessarily relying on others.

That time was now.

But there were no ships on the horizon, and there had been no survivors of the sunken vessel found on Pháne's rocky coastline. The cave Muir had come to protect was devoid of any signs of life except for barnacles, crabs, and seabirds. The first attack had been successfully repelled. With luck, the next one would be too.

But how long would it be before these new attackers looked for some other route to their destination? How many more outposts would Káliel have to build…and would the Council approve?

❧*❧

"A boy? Looking for me?" Bhríd rose from the desk where he had been perusing expense reports and adjusted his tunic. "Did he give his name? Say what he wants?"

The soldier shook his head. "No, sir. He came for the last three days, always during my watch. He asked…demanded…to see you…"

The chamberlain scowled. "And you did not bring him in? Did not tell me of this before?"

Stammering, red-faced, the soldier replied, "Lord Corbin's instructions were to allow no one into the keep without permission…"

"But a boy…"

"Could still cause trouble." The soldier understood the chamberlain's point of view, but as he had followed orders, he hoped the Elyri knight would not seek to punish him. "We thought we had scared him off the first day, then explained to him the second that you do not have time for idle conversation. He seemed offended and departed and we thought that would be the end of it. The third day…yesterday…he seemed mightily disheartened, begged us to let him see you…but we could not…and he has not yet come today…"

Grumbling, Bhríd muttered, "So why bring this to me now? You followed orders…drove him away…" He might not agree with the actions, but he did understand them.

The soldier looked more nervous than before and fidgeted awkwardly. "I…don't know, my lord. I thought yesterday…we were wrong to send him away. I thought when I went on duty today, that if he came again, I might give in to his request. When I saw Master Cáner earlier…I realized how young that boy was…how dirty…always alone…and I think he was Elyri."

Bhríd straightened his shoulders. Keeping unnecessary and unauthorized people out of the castle since the attack on Ártur had become the standing order, and the fellow had been correct to follow it. The possibility of threats to anyone in the keep was high, and Bhríd's daily duties would not permit him to entertain everyone who wished to have words with him. But an Elyri boy, alone in Rhidam, was different. Bhríd would never turn one of his people away.

"What did he look like? How old? Did he say anything?"

"He only asked to see you, would say nothing else. I guessed him to be perhaps ten or twelve…not older than your sons. He was tall…as tall as the king, with dark hair touched with red…nearly violet eyes…blue but not blue…if you understand what I mean…"

The chamberlain's head bobbed as he made written notes of the boy's description. He had seen eyes like those before, though rarely. In the right light, his own blue eyes reflected a hint of violet as well.

He did not know what genetic peculiarity led to those Elyri with features such as his, but most considered them to be a sign.

But none could say a sign of what.

"Tell Justice Corbin what you have told me…and then tell General Zarkosta and Agis. If this boy returns, if anyone sees him, bring him to me immediately, no matter what I am doing."

"Yes, sir," the soldier agreed with a nod before scurrying out of the room, relieved to have gotten free with no more than a side-handed reprimand of disappointment from the chamberlain.

Bhríd's hands were shaking. That description was similar to the one the cobbler had given Sir Gabersdon of the Elyri boy who had stayed in his home, to whom he had provided shoes. It was hard enough to be an Elyri in Rhidam now. To be a child, alone in the streets, must be a nightmare. Perhaps he had come seeking aid for his family, or else seeking shelter or protection as Sir Gabersdon had advised. Being turned away from one of the safest places in the city left the boy with nowhere else to go.

What would he do now?

Bhríd had to find him. The best way, the fastest way, would be to set the Association on the lookout for an Elyri boy of that description. The chamberlain decided he would put Caol and all of his resources on the task at once, with or without the King's approval. He would pay for the expense of it himself. He would not allow a child to suffer a day longer than necessary, nor allow him to die out there alone. Not if he could find him.

It was a relief to know that the King accepted the compromise to his duties without argument. Ártur's safety was one of the King's primary considerations, and making Syl happy was always high on Hagan's list of priorities. If it meant that the Lachlan house must hire a Teren physician in the interim, to delegate the responsibilities in order that Ártur could remain safe, King Hagan was willing to do so. Ártur would spend his nights in Bhryell and his days in Rhidam, unless the Chamberlain was called away by duty or by family.

The decision elevated Gaelán to the status of Court Healer, at least during the night, and though Bhríd worried about the effect such additional responsibilities might have on his already volatile son, he could offer no other suggestion and agreed that something of this nature was necessary for the welfare of all concerned and for the sake of his sister's marriage.

Though the compromise should have relieved him, made him feel better knowing that he retained his position, Ártur found it difficult to leave when evening came…even with the lure of his children waiting in Bhryell. He knew Bhríd would come for him if he was needed, but would it be quickly enough to save a life? Would someone die because he was too far away to aid them in time? Ártur was left no choice, however, but to have faith in his mostly untrained nephew and trust that k'Ádhá would watch over those he loved.

Touching the altar reverently one more time, longing for the sound of harp strings, the healer entered the Purification Chamber alone. The children would be with Bhen tonight, waiting for him in Kavan's home, and Ártur had no doubt that Llucás, at least, would be eager to see him, just as he was eager to see his son again. His children were the only things that made leaving duty in Rhidam possible to bear.

❧Chapter 11❧

They had not started north from their beach camp come evening as Kavan hoped, nor had they traveled come the morning. He was too weak, too sick. He had barely enough strength to shuffle a few feet away from the fire and there was no way Wortham could carry two trunks and Kavan as well. Instead, the bard slept much of the time, drinking water Wortham had found from a narrow creek some distance away from their position, eating berries and clams Zelenka and Wortham found along the shore. Food did not stay in him long, but it was enough to slowly renew his strength.

During those periods when Kavan slept, Urian fabricated three cloth packs from the heavy cloak found in one of the trunks. Between them and the basket Zelenka wove from the drying beach grass, they were able to carry the contents of the second trunk in a more efficient manner. There was one large, canvas bundle which Wortham kept from Kavan's view as he distributed the weight between the three packs. Both trunks had proven to be watertight, preserving the contents within, more a miracle at Kóráhm's hand, Wortham believed, than any feat of craftsmanship or luck.

Even the collection of books and journals was undamaged.

By dusk the second night, however, Kavan refused to remain camped. It disappointed him to leave the second well-made trunk behind for someone else's use, but they simply could not carry it. With Zelenka carrying her basket and guiding Urian, who had one pack slung over his shoulder, Kavan carrying the second pack as he leaned on Wortham's arm, and the captain carrying the third pack and the trunk with the relics and journal, they started their slow trudge north. A cool breeze wafted from the sea, softening the toll of their exertion, but they stopped frequently to rest because neither Zelenka nor Kavan could maintain the quick pace the bard tried to set, and despite his resolve to be confident and positive, the fact that he was hindering their progress made the Elyri irritable. Not that he said it, and he hummed much of the time to hide it. But Wortham could read the emotion in the bard's tight grip on his arm, in the way his eyes tracked the horizon, in the way he tensed every time he stumbled.

Eventually, Wortham cleared his throat and spoke, hoping to offer a diversion from pestilent thoughts. "My lord, may I ask something?"

"An attempt to distract me?" Kavan asked with a tilt of his head.

The captain grinned. "Would it matter? I am curious how you got the trunks to shore. I watched for you but could not see you…"

It was a reasonable question. "I did not do it." At least he had no memory of having brought them to shore. His shock at seeing them safe and undamaged, the contents intact, had been, he believed, greater than Wortham's. "I lost ours to the sea and tried to recover it." He was quiet for a few minutes before asking, "Where did you find them?"

"Beside you, when Zelenka found you. They were too heavy to float…and I do not think the current was strong enough to drive them to shore, so I thought you had…" It made no sense, however, not for one trunk and definitely not for two.

"The last thing I recall was diving to find it…after losing it. I caught the handle but it felt as if I was bursting, as if I would explode if I did not breathe…as if I was being propelled to the surface…and then I woke up on the shore. I recall snatches of sounds…smells…but nothing is clear…like a dream that flees when your eyes open."

Wortham nodded. "I…we saw a ship and wondered if perhaps…"

"A ship?" Kavan shuddered and the ring on his hand throbbed.

"Zelenka pointed it out. I did not think it real, believed it an image in the fog, but…" He glanced at her, said a few words in her language, and she excitedly repeated what she had said to Wortham that night.

"Sósáná saeitá gaetió."

With a start, Kavan realized he needed no translator to understand her. "High Elyri," he whispered to Wortham's unspoken question. "In trade…it would translate as the ghost ship of Sósáná; in Elyri it would be more precise to say the ship of Sósáná's ghost. Was it tall, with three large masts, longer than the Cordashian schooners?"

"Aye," Wortham replied. "You have seen it too?"

"One morning in the fog; or I thought I saw it as we sailed, briefly before Kóráhm…" He stopped walking, causing Wortham to stumble and nearly drop the trunk.

"My lord?"

Kavan nodded. "Sósáná…the name of Kóráhm's mother." He swallowed hard. "It is said his father came from across the sea, from a land no one now knows. He left her here before Kóráhm was born…and when she disappeared many years later it was said her husband had returned and took her away with him."

What were the odds, he wondered, of such a name in Kóráhm's stories emerging twice? Could the ghost on the ship be the same woman who had given birth to a saint?

Wortham translated the bard's words to Zelenka, and then spoke again to Kavan after she eagerly responded. "The legend she knows says that a princess, one of the k'elyryhánag…" He stumbled on the word but Kavan understood his intent, "that she went to sea aboard one and never returned, is thought to have been lost to the storm it left in. Many traders and travelers have claimed to see the ship during their time of need, in tempests or foul weather, and it is said she will return one day for those she left behind…"

Though there was no mention of Kóráhm or children left in Zelenka's recounting, the overall tale was consistent with Kóráhm's story…if his mother was indeed a princess. That unfamiliar word k'elyryhánag, used a second time, gnawed at Kavan, seeking definition and origin, demanding to be known. That Kóráhm was Elyri, Kavan had no doubt, thus the word applied to the Heretic Saint…and hence to Kavan as well.

"Were you on that ship, my lord?"

"I…" Wortham's words interrupted his thoughts and he blinked. "I cannot say. Possibly. I recall men's' voices…the movement of a ship on the water…strange, unfamiliar music…but nothing is clear except waking on the beach. Someone may have rescued me…the trunk…left us the other…but I could not say who."

"It is doubly unfortunate then that we were forced to leave it behind." They had not traveled far, and Wortham wondered if he should leave his companions to rest and retrace their path to retrieve the abandoned trunk. Carrying it was still impractical, however, and he regretted the fates that had forced them into this position.

The ring on Kavan's hand pulsed and tingled, much the way it had when that ship first appeared, the way it had during those barely conscious moments surrounded by the unfamiliar. The ring that was said to belong to Kóráhm. It was a connection beyond coincidence between the ring and the ship, but Kavan had no proof other than what he felt. He doubted Kóráhm would tell him if he asked, doubted the Saint knew the answer. Perhaps someday, after the chapel was cleansed and peace was restored to the Sovereignties, Kavan would be able to pursue the mystery of that ship.

Now there was no time.

The brief conversation and the puzzle to ponder distracted Kavan from his own weakness, enabling him to grow steady and calm again without effort. He stumbled less as they continued, until they found a road winding along the shoreline, the packed nature of the dirt and the cutting of ruts into its surface suggesting it was well and frequently traveled. Taking that road eased their journey, enabled them to quicken their pace and cover more distance as darkness began to wane. Sometime near dawn, as they debated where and when to make camp, the clatter of wagon wheels rattled from some distance behind them, announcing the first other people they had seen in days. The group moved to the side of the road to allow the two wagons to pass, but the lead wagon came to a halt after rolling past them a short distance, allowing the other sufficient time to do likewise.

The fellow seated on the first wagon, dressed in florid yellow and red paisley trimmed in black velvet and bleached leather tassels, called to them in greeting and uttered a loud, long burst of rapid, boisterous conversation. When Zelenka began to respond, he dismissed her in favor of her male companions. Her tone reflected her apology as she continued, explaining that the men did not speak the language and that she was their interpreter. Wortham tried to sort out the words he knew, hoping to communicate directly, but the stranger spoke too quickly, with too heavy an accent, for him to understand without effort.

"I think they are asking if we would care to travel with them. We are…how did he put it…a pitiful sight, not equipped for journeying even as pilgrims," Wortham chuckled.

"We are pilgrims," Urian laughed too, his eagerness to accept the offered hospitality an easy thing to recognize.

Kavan wanted to refuse. The strangers seemed innocent enough. Six individuals, all riding within the wagons. Two men, three women, and one small child. One wagon was empty but smelled of spiced meat and fruit, suggesting that the roving traders had come from business elsewhere. They had food, water, and transportation, things Kavan knew he and his companions needed, and they were traveling as far as the town of Yashir, where the sunken cog had intended to take them. It was almost too convenient. Riding in the wagons would be faster, easier, and more comfortable than walking, but the expediency of the wagon's arrival, the timing of it, and the uncomfortable prickle at the back of Kavan's neck warned him that all was not as it seemed.

In the end, however, because he could not explain his discomfort, could not see any danger in these people, he allowed Urian and Zelenka's desire for comfort to sway his concession. The pace he set was hardest on them. He owed it to them to be accommodating when he could be.

Reluctantly he allowed the captain to help him into the empty wagon with the others. Zelenka, and then Urian, were asleep quickly towards the front of the covered wagon bed. Wortham was intent on keeping watch at the back hatch so that Kavan could rest as well, but Kavan found sleep to be an elusive thing and he sat at the other side of the opening, watching the receding road behind them.

Something was following him. He had carried the nagging feeling during the night as they walked and was aware now that he had felt the same irksome sense on the cog the night it went down. The wagons rolled on, allowing faster progress, and though he thought it would leave that following thing behind, it instead matched pace though it never came nearer. No one else seemed to feel it. No one else was aware of the vaguely malicious, wary thing that wanted him…and only him. Thus far it kept its distance as if waiting for him to lower his guard. But he knew it would not wait forever. Sooner or later it would come.

Because he had to sleep. If he did not, he would be unable to confront whatever it was when it caught up with him. He doubted Wortham would know when it was near, doubted the captain could combat it. Wortham might be keeping watch but this enemy, Kavan was sure it was an enemy, could get past the captain. And it would.

He fought sleep as long as he was able. Even Wortham dozed before Kavan did, the company of the others and the security of the moving room around them, allowing him to drop his guard and rest. The feeling of being followed faded as the sun climbed higher, and by noon Kavan could no longer feel it. Perhaps it had given up.

But it was not until the wagons stopped and the camp was laid for the night that Kavan felt secure enough to sleep while the others ate and enjoyed the music and hospitality of the traders' fire. The feeling, that distant hunter, had not returned.

❧*❦

"Are you going to tell me what you want?" Gaelán followed Asta to the stables, a nervous bounce in his step, aware that if his father learned he was outside in the twilight he was likely to be reprimanded. Still, he wanted a private place to bestow the gift that had been burning in his pocket all day, and when Asta suggested this excursion after berating him for buying her anything, he had been unable to refuse. He realized more every day that he would do anything for her, anything she asked, regardless of the consequences. That realization was both frightening and exhilarating. "The day's almost over."

"You should give me what you have first." She stopped in the smoky glare of a lantern that hung near the stable door. Inside, he could hear kittens mewling and he wondered if the kittens were what Asta had brought him here to see. Did she want a cat of her own?

The fingers of light combed through the gold in her hair, taking his breath away. He loved the color of her hair. Unconsciously, he tried to touch it; she laughed nervously but did not move away, although her laughter caused his hand to fall.

"I thought I might cut it."

The sound of her voice jarred him back to the moment and he blinked. "What?"

"My hair. It is such a nuisance being this long. It is not conducive to disguises and it gets in the way."

"Why should you want to…"

She shrugged. "Practicality. Too much like my father, I suppose, and too little like my mother. Would you object? If I cut it?"

He was fond of her long hair, would rather she kept it, but decided that, ultimately, the length of her hair was unimportant. Fumbling for words, he stammered, "I think you will be pretty either way."

Being alone with a girl had never left him tongue-tied before. This felt new and he could not explain why. "I…here." He thrust the small pouch into her hand, nervous about touching her when such contact had never bothered him before either, and said, "I found this in Bhryell. It made me think of you. I want you to have it."

She took the velvet sack, hesitated long enough to look at him, and then tugged the braided drawstring to open it. He heard her choke as the gift dropped into her hand, and out of fear and concern, he murmured, "You don't like it? I can find something else…"

Tracing the finely tooled surface, she lifted the locket from her palm. "This is perfect," she whispered. She was young, but thanks to her father's keen appraising eye and his teaching, as well as her kinship with Princess Diona, Asta recognized expensive jewelry when she saw it. "Mother wore one on a ribbon…she said I could have it someday, but it was lost." It would have been one of the few mementos of her mother she had, and she was devastated at its loss. To be honest, as the first piece of jewelry from someone other than her father, she found this to be worth more than all of those items combined. "I will find a red ribbon tomorrow…and keep it near my heart always. Is there anything inside?"

Gaelán took her at her word without thinking she could be lying. She never lied to him. As well as he knew her, he believed he would know if she was. "You can put whatever you want in it…or nothing."

"It is beautiful. I like it very much. Thank you." She tucked it back into its pouch and down into the front of her bodice, making sure it would not fall out and be lost, and giggled at the relief on his face.

"What else do you want? You never ask…so it must be big. I don't know if I can give you whatever it is, but I will do my best…"

"Of course you can give me what I want; it's not that big." She smiled, this time with an awkward blush, and said, "I want a kiss."

Mouth falling open, throat shrinking around his airways, he was unable to speak at first as she stared at him hopefully. "Me?"

"I like you. You are honorable…and I trust you. A girl has to get her first kiss from someone…and I want it to be you. Surely you have kissed a girl before? The way Tayte talks…"

Flustered and annoyed with his brother, he shook his head in denial and said, "I sneak out a lot, like to visit girls, but I have not…"

Her gaze fell, though Gaelán could not tell if she was disappointed or if she was relieved that she might be his first too. "If it is too much to ask…" The corners of her mouth set in a familiar expression of defiance and she looked back up at him with challenge in her eyes. "I can find someone else. I will not wait until I am as old as Diona to…"

Heart jumping at that challenge, he shot back, "She has kissed people…" At least he knew she had kissed Kavan. Or she had tried to. He had never really thought about the princess kissing anyone.

"Not a man…not like that…not someone she loves. I heard her talking to Belda once. I am not looking for something like…just a small one…and I was hoping you would be first."

Deciding then that, despite her threats to find someone else to be first, she did not want to share that moment with anyone other than Gaelán. "We can wait if you're not ready…"

Gaelán continued to stare at her in the lantern light, seeing her in a way he never had before. She was his best friend, had been his best friend all of his life. He had daydreamed often about sharing something more with her without knowing what that something more should entail. Her words spoken about Diona, about a kiss from someone she loves, made his heart hammer louder. Was Asta saying she loved him? Was she old enough for that? Was he?

Suddenly kissing her seemed the right thing to do, though he had no idea how to go about it without embarrassing them both.

As if reading his thoughts, the girl rose on her toes, leaning forward slightly until her mouth touched his. She lingered there for a few moments and then drew back. His lips tingled, his skin flushed, and every corner of him inside felt to be on fire. He touched his mouth with his fingertips and realized he was shaking.

"It wasn't bad was it?" she whispered, a touch of fear in her voice that perhaps it felt less…right…and good…to him than it did to her.

He started to shake his head, but she grabbed his hand and yanked him into the shadows with a hand clamped over his mouth. Moments later, a serving girl and one of the stable hands passed and disappeared into one of the stalls at the rear of the stable. Asta pulled his hand and they slunk away, hurrying back towards the castle before they were discovered by the amorous pair. Halfway there, she burst into relieved laughter. With his blood pounding fast and hard, feeling more alive than he had ever felt, Gaelán laughed too.

❦*❧

Everyone was gone.

Not everyone, Kavan admitted, as he rolled and pushed stiffly upright. Wortham snored loudly nearby, one arm protectively across Zelenka's side, and not far from them, Urian sprawled on the ground like a drunken man where he had last been awake the evening before. But the rovers and their wagons were gone, without Kavan or the others having heard them leave. Worse still, the few possessions they owned, the basket, the packs, the trunk, were missing as well. Stolen. If Kavan had known the words to use, he would have cursed himself for falling asleep, for not obeying the instincts that told him those people were not what they appeared to be, were not to be trusted. Instead, he could only struggle not to weep as a hole of despair opened within. His journey, his hard work, the suffering, had been for nothing.

Movement behind told him Wortham was awake, roused by the bard's movement or perhaps by the strangled sounds of controlled grieving. The captain noticed abruptly that something was amiss; he sat, glancing around them frantically, muttering, "Where…?"

"Gone," Kavan whispered.

"Just like the ship's crew," the captain said with a scowl. "Do you think someone seeks to prevent us from reaching Rhidam…doing what you intend? Did they take…?"

"Everything. Everything we own…even the water."

The morning sun caught the emerald on Kavan's hand and something in that green glimmer made Kavan pause long enough to reassess their situation. He still had the ring, and with it, he could find that trunk. It might not be a simple task, might not be quickly accomplished, but it could be done.

"We will find it." He wiped his face and brushed his hair back from his eyes. "Something or someone wishes to stop us…but I will not let that happen." Regardless of the strengths of his adversary, he had k'Ádhá and Kóráhm on his side. He was certain he could prevail.

He felt assured of that truth the moment he spoke it, and was surprised at the confidence that replaced the despair. The ancient chapel had been defiled by the evil of a single man and persisted to this day. If Kavan was meant to rectify that wrong, then he needed to be strong. He would follow his path or die trying.

Rousing the others and explaining their situation, the group gathered what little there was of use around the snuffed out campfire, Wortham's knife, a discarded tin cup, an unwrapped hunk of bread growing stale but suitable enough for a meager breakfast, and a cloak someone had dropped in the roadside brush which they wrapped around Zelenka's shoulders to ward off the early morning chill. Kavan followed instincts that rarely failed him, instincts he should have trusted before, following the pulse of the emerald. It was a bitter pill, a hard lesson to learn, but one he hoped he had learned at last.

The malicious force returned, taunting him from where it lingered at the fringes of his perceptions, where it had first been noted not long after the decision was made to press on. Kavan believed it would have left him alone if he had given up, if he had chosen to allow his failure to win. At a split in the road, he paused, gauging the power's location, judging which path he should take. The one to the right followed the shore and seemed to be the road most likely to take them directly into Yashir. The road most traveled. If the rovers in their brightly painted wagons hoped to lose those they had robbed, they might have gone left, expecting Kavan to continue on the shore path.

The second route would, he thought, also take them to Yashir, but it would take longer, be less direct. It could also, he assumed, be a ruse or trap. They might expect him to travel the inland road, expect him to think they had gone that way in the hopes of confusing him.

The choice was his. The ring pointed him east, closer to the sea. The shore road was the path he took.

A rumble of silent anger behind them confirmed his confidence in the path chosen. The thing that followed did not want him to go that way. It surged forward, rushing through and past him, overtaking him and rearing up as if to attack. Kavan stopped as he felt the wave rush over him, every mental shield and discipline he possessed instinctively coming up against the strength of this confrontation. But the push of power that rammed through him created momentary pain, bringing back the ringing ache in his ears, and he inhaled sharply, choking on the sudden sensation of smoke and sulfur in his throat. He thrust out a wave of power, hoping to drive the negative shift away long enough for him to regain his bearings, and the others continued walking, pulling ahead, not yet aware that he had stopped.

He did not fear for them. Whatever this was, it only wanted him.

The wave turned like a tornado and flew back, hitting him with the force of a wall of water slamming into his body, engulfing him as if to drown him. It recoiled in its own pain, however, as Kavan pushed back. He had never done this sort of battle before; there was no need in Elyriá for it thus Tíbhyan had been able to teach him none but the most rudimentary aspects of psychic combat, offering small tastes based on legends and myths that existed from the days when Elyri had first come to these lands. Kavan acted out of instinct rather than experience, his lack of that a disadvantage.

After the brief retreat, it returned, and Kavan suspected it was toying with him, testing his limits, looking for weaknesses that it could exploit in order to dominate him. *You think I will show you my limits, Kavan* thought defiantly. *I will never give you that satisfaction. They are my secrets.*

He had to believe that he could outlast, outmatch, whatever this thing was. Not knowing what it was, he had little desire to destroy it. But he did want to drive it away, incapacitate it, force it to leave him and his companions alone. Another burst of hot energy sent the other reeling away, enough force used that Kavan was soon unable to detect it within reach of his senses. Devote enough power to complete a task but do not expend all you have; that had been Tíbhyan's earliest advice to the boy he had mentored. Learn how to expend as little energy as possible to achieve the maximum results. This time Kavan had been successful, but he did not know if he would be when it happened again.

That force would be back. It might be wounded, but it had not been stopped.

"My lord?" Wortham was kneeling beside Kavan in the empty road, gripping his arms to hold him upright where Kavan had not realized he had fallen. "Do you need to rest?"

"No." Kavan allowed Wortham to help him to his feet but then gripped the man's arm tightly to keep him near. "Be diligent, Wortham; you cannot detect or battle the enemy we face." Something had been unleashed, something they might not be able to conquer. "If I am incapacitated, if I am unable to continue, you must do it for me. Kóráhm will guide and instruct you, I swear it. He will protect you and tell you what you must do."

Wortham frowned, wondering why the saint would protect and guide him to do these things if he would not do likewise for Kavan, but he did not speak his doubts. He did not understand Kavan's words, did not know what the bard alluded to, but he accepted the truth of them as he did everything else Kavan had ever asked of him. He would obey simply because the Elyri bade it, no matter what was to come.

Caol no longer harbored lingering doubts that dedhá Claide had remained in Rhidam rather than travel to Fiara as he claimed. He had proof enough that it was so to erase those doubts. One of his contacts, a young boy whom he had spoken with regarding the whereabouts of the Elyri orphan mentioned having seen a man who looked like the senior Teren gdhededhá coming out of the Boar's Garden the night before. Of course, no one in the tavern could, or would, confirm it when he asked, but six separate sightings of the man since his alleged departure from the city, was damning enough to the inquisitor.

Finding him, however, was a more difficult matter. He had to be hiding somewhere Caol had not looked, in the home of some wealthy patron most likely. Caol could not get permission from the King to conduct a door to door search of every home in the city, not without raising the King's suspicions further and revealing what Caol and a handful of others knew or suspected. Unless the Association was moving the dedhá, or he was somehow using and manipulating them to cover his whereabouts and business, there was nowhere else in Rhidam the man could be hiding.

Caol prayed the Association was not involved, even though it would tidily explain why his usual contacts were unable to provide much information of worth. He did not want the King's beliefs to be validated. Caol did not want to be proven wrong. He wanted the King to be mistaken about the people who worked for him. Thus he would continue to use the Association for a little while longer and see what he could shake loose from its many branches. Before the King made good on his threat to shake branches of his own.

❧*❧

Bricks and mortar. Not wood. Peat for fires. Rations and barrels of water and wine. Muir could not have been happier unless Clianthe had stepped off the supply ships too. That Gabrielle and the Council opted to send bricks to rebuild the outpost meant they considered this to be a more permanent structure after the attack. It would not easily burn a second time. Craftsmen had come to aid in the construction, and with luck, they could have the foundation and part of the walls set in place by the time subsequent ships returned with more bricks.

And bows and arrows, javelins and spears. Weapons designed to fight from a distance. Gabrielle was lobbying for a ship to be permanently docked on Pháne, the islands' first warship which could be used to drive away attackers rather than allow the outpost to sit helplessly under fire. For once in her history, Káliel had something akin to a standing navy, even if it consisted of a single ship, its crew, and Muir's twenty-six soldiers in training. And Prince Muir Lachlan, for all of his military inexperience, was Káliel's first General by default. He had no intention of failing that responsibility or the people who had given it to him.

❧*❧

"Nothing happened while you were gone," Gaelán said, perched on the edge of the older healer's bed, swinging his feet. Though he had not seen Asta yesterday, and had yet to see her today, he had been unable to wipe the grin from his face or suppress the bubbling delight in his belly. It had been a single kiss, not much of one at that, but it had changed everything, causing him to look at the world differently, causing him to wonder if he was too young to consider marriage. Asta was not. In most Teren kingdoms, her fourteenth birthday made her eligible for marriage, though her father had made no effort yet to seek a husband for her. And betrothal to Gaelán, not yet considered a man, sounded like some sort of punishment to him. He wanted to talk with her about it, wanted to know if she was displeased with their kiss and what she thought about the possibility of binding their lives together.

Ártur noticed his nephew's distraction but did not comment on it. He had distractions of his own. A wife who would not speak to or see him, a son who did not understand why his parents were apart, a family he could not come to terms with. No matter what choices he made, it seemed someone would be angered by them. In the end, he could only make choices to satisfy his conscience, yet even that was getting harder to do. Was this the frustration Kavan so often voiced, the need to be what everyone else expected, the inability to be true to himself?

"I did not think it would." Thankfully, life in the castle seemed calm and normal in the aftermath of the attempt on his life, minus the presence of his cousin of course. "Has the King found a physician?"

Gaelán shook his head. "Not to my knowledge. I do not think he has been looking." That pleased Gaelán, as it meant that Hagan trusted his medical skills, as new as they were. At the same time, however, Gaelán worried that some serious crisis might arise that he would be ill-equipped to handle, that someone would die because he was not able to save them.

"I will talk to him." Ártur, too, worried about what could happen during his absence. Knowing that the boy would take his saying so as an insult, he continued. "bhydáni Tíbhyan asked when you would come again, and I cannot take you until another physician is installed. I will discuss it with the King before I start painting."

"Painting?" Gaelán asked, bouncing off the bed and following his uncle to the door. Ártur often painted during his spare time, but it seemed an unusual thing to do when he had just come to Rhidam. "What are you going to paint?"

The healer's response was a grin before he turned down the corridor in search of the King. A pout played on Gaelán's face briefly but it did not last. The prospect of another visit to Bhryell was exciting for a boy who rarely traveled anywhere other than between Levonne and Rhidam, and more training meant becoming a better healer.

Perhaps he could take Asta with him next time, if she was willing to go. He wondered if her father would allow it.

❧*❧

They discovered the wagons as the sun reached its zenith in the cloudless blue sky. The horses lingered at the side of the road, untied, grazing on scrub grass, calm but watchful. There was no sign of anyone at first glance, no hint of why the wagons had stopped or why the horses had been turned loose. Zelenka explained that rovers never abandoned their wagons, that their wagons were a symbol of the family who owned them, painted with imagery specific to that family. Kavan assumed then that the owners were nearby, though he could not hear them and heard no trace of rushing water or any other lure that might have compelled them to stop. Their absence allowed Wortham the opportunity to search for what had been stolen from them, something he began to do as soon as Zelenka spoke. Leaving Urian seated on one of the folded down steps that Wortham used to climb into the first wagon, Kavan swallowed the unpleasant, unbidden taste in his mouth and began a slow, wide circle around them, not knowing what he expected to find.

He was some yards away, following the edge of the road where cracked earth suggested water sometimes ran, before he finally saw the bodies strewn across the road several dozen feet in front of the foremost wagon. All six, even the child. Dead. In their midst, the reliquary which Qol had given to Kavan, the box containing both the Chalice of Llyr and the crown of the Staff of Drebhoti. The box was open, its contents, if still inside, exposed.

Qol had warned Kavan not to open the box until it was time to use the items inside, and he wondered, as he cautiously approached, if these peoples' deaths were the result of having curiously opened the box to look. Given their distance from the wagon, the way their bodies were positioned, he suspected there had been something else at work here. Had the malevolent force caught up with them, prompting them to try to flee with the box, only to kill them as they ran? Had the lid popped open on its own when it hit the packed earthen road, or did that force possess the ability to open it and take what was inside after making certain that those who possessed it paid the price?

Had that force taken, destroyed, or otherwise defiled those things Kavan needed to succeed?

Not knowing if he dared to look or if he should avert his gaze as he approached, he opted for the faith that had been required so many other times during his months away from Rhidam. Closing his eyes, he followed his senses, picking a slow trail between the bodies until he bumped the box with his toes. He squatted, reached out carefully, and shut it with one hand. There was a stinging static pop when the ring touched the box, a sensation of closure that assured him, without seeing it, that the relics were safe, still housed inside.

Then he turned his attention to the rovers.

There was no blood, no sign of a struggle except that each one's eyes were open and they appeared to have dropped to the ground mid-run. He saw no apparent agony or pain, but he was no healer. He could touch them, read how they died, but that did not seem necessary or right. It was enough to see that they had. Enough that the stolen relics were back in his possession, though he was grieved that anyone, innocent or guilty alike, had paid for that theft this way.

"I found…my lord!" Wortham stopped short, disgust, dismay and surprise in his voice. "What has happened?"

Relieved there was no accusation in the captain's tone, that his friend did not think him responsible for the carnage, Kavan replied, "I do not know. I could speculate…but it appears they each died at the same time…of the same cause." He did not want to talk about those possible causes. He did not even want to think about them. "Do we bury them before we go on?" He had what he needed, was still slightly bitter about the theft and his own failure to prevent it, but he could not simply leave the dead in the road to the carrion. The child, in particular, deserved more respect than that.

Zelenka approached with Urian holding her arm, glanced at the bodies callously, seemingly not bothered by so much death although she grew more nervous and uncomfortable as she noted that each person's eyes were still open. A glance around as if for evil spirits she could not see, and then she tugged on Wortham's arm as she spoke.

"She recommends we do not stay here. She says we can take the horses, but if we take the wagons we will be accused of their deaths. No one takes a rover's wagon…not even another rover. The horses, however, are fair game, as is the food and water. And, my lord," Wortham added, feeling uncomfortable with the thought of taking everything the rovers had owned after their misfortune, simply because the rovers had earlier robbed them, "It seems they have traveled the road we walked…for they have the second trunk you were given…the one we left behind."

"Good." Horses would make their trip to Yashir easier. They could secure the trunks and other items, take just enough food and water to get them there, and be on their way. "But we will bury these people first. I will not leave the dead in the road."

There were still many hours of light in which to work and be away. Kavan, like Zelenka, wanted to put as much distance between them and the dead as they could…but for entirely different reasons.

☙Chapter 12❧

Gdhededhá Tusánt made note of the peculiar expression on Valgis' face but pretended not to see it as he went about his business. Edward Lindunn, a local merchant's son, was the second to seek apprenticeship to the Faith from the Elyri dedhá. Unlike Saul, however, Edward's arrival drew few questions. Young, enthusiastic, and bright, he had served his stint as altar attendant, had sung in the choir under Tusánt's direction, and had spent many hours over the years following the Elyri around the náos, asking questions about the Faith, about Elyriá, about Elyri. k'gdhededhá Tythilius once commented that Edward, a boy at the time, was destined for the priesthood, but Edward had been out of Rhidam for more than a year and many had assumed he had married out of familial obligation or had fallen ill and died. Valgis did not know him due to that absence, but most others in the náos did. His return to Rhidam was a surprise, but his readiness to serve as gdhededhá was not.

Edward, now sixteen, had spent his last year in Cordash, training in their military. His father's family were Cordashians which required Edward to serve a seven-year contract in King Renfrid's military. For reasons Tusánt did not know, Edward had been released from that duty to return to Enesfel as soon as his father died. Tusánt suspected there had been a conflict between his faith and being a soldier, a conflict King Renfrid chose to honor rather than quash. Once free of that obligation, with his older brother to take the family business, Edward was free to follow his heart's calling. He came to Tusánt not through Princess Diona, but because he wished it, and offered his protection willingly to the man he knew was at risk.

Honest of commitment, capable of protecting him, there was no reason Tusánt could think of to deny Edward's vocation. No one except Valgis thought it unusual that Edward asked Tusánt to train him, and no one knew of the secondary duties asked of both Edward and Saul. With both starting their novitiate so close together, they swiftly became friends. Claide could, when he returned, demand that Tusánt turn one of the novices over to him or to Rankin, but Tusánt did not believe Claide would be so bold. Such an action would raise questions about his motive at a turbulent time when the náós was understaffed. Tusánt was the senior dedhá; it was his right to train them, unless for some reason he felt he could not, unless there were too many to manage, or unless a novice requested a different mentor.

There would be others Claide could train. Tusánt believed that, with the death of Jermyn, Claide was going to occupy himself with other things besides the training of apprentices.

The two newcomers were housed in the small room next to Tusánt's. Since the room where novices typically lodged was under repair, and the room next to Tusánt's had been vacant for some time, the decision did not raise suspicions either. But something had obviously roused Valgis' ire. Tusánt saw it every time he saw the newest dedhá. Perhaps Valgis felt he was being displaced, or had some personal reason not to like the two men. But Tusánt hoped that once he saw the novices at work, participated in their training, he would feel less threatened and stop looking for faults where there were none.

Hopefully before Claide returned to Rhidam.

࠾*࠾

"Uncle!"

Diona had not felt so pleased to see anyone since Espen had come to Enesfel last. That happiness was magnified when the Hatu prince entered the room on Owain's heels, Piran sleeping against his shoulder, and though she wanted to throw herself into Espen's arms, she settled for hugging Owain in an effort to hide the shard of disappointment that Espen was not available for the same greeting.

"What brings you to Rhidam? We were not expecting you. Does Hagan know you are here?"

"I did receive the invitation to his gala," Owain chuckled.

"You wrote you could not come."

He shrugged and released her. "Circumstances changed. I am taking Piran to Káliel and chose to escort Espen at the same time." He beckoned the third man forward, a blonde Elyri that Diona had only marginally noticed until that moment. "It is fortunate for our friend that we chose to travel when we did. Princess Diona, may I introduce Bhyrhán Bhíncári."

"Bhíncári," the princess said with surprise to the man who took a few graceful steps closer, took her offered hand, and bowed deep, the regal bow of Elyriá's elite, before kissing her knuckles reverently. His actions, more than his manner of dress or the brightness in his eyes as he assessed her appearance and then demurely lowered his gaze, made her flush and smile. "Related to the High Mother?"

There was no mistaking his lineage, either by his mannerisms or his name. Though she had never met the High Mother, she had seen portraits. Never in her lifetime, or her father's, had an Elyri dignitary traveled to the Lachlan court in Rhidam. Her grandfather had met the High Mother more than once, but that had been long ago, and he had traveled to Elyriá to see her. A Bhíncári choosing to come to Enesfel had to have some unexpected significance.

Embarrassed, Owain glanced at Espen to assess if the Prince shared his discomfiture. Espen, however, having noted Diona's reaction to the Elyri, nobility or not, was fussing over Piran and pretending not to pay attention to the discourse. Owain realized he should have recognized that name but it had not occurred to him that he could be escorting a foreign dignitary. The man's on-foot pilgrimage in no way suggested his station.

The young Elyri remained bowed but appeared less affected by the fuss the princess was making than by the woman herself. "One of many grandsons, Your Majesty; hardly a dignitary. Only a bard. I heard about Lord Cliáth's attack and hoped to offer my support but am told he is unavailable."

Diona sighed, some of her enthusiasm subverted by those memories. She glanced at Owain, wishing she had better news. "He has not yet returned to Rhidam, I fear."

Though Bhyrhán's eyes showed disappointment he asked, "Is Healer MacLyr still here?"

"He is still in our service, but away until morning. You are welcome to remain until his return if you wish." Even if only a grandson of the High Mother, a visiting Bhíncári was worth the effort to entertain, and protect. It was also, reluctantly worth alerting him to the dangers of his choice. She wanted him to stay, an Elyri bard of any sort would be a welcome guest, a welcome diversion to soothe the emptiness where Kavan belonged, but she also wanted him to be safe. He reminded her of Kavan when he smiled and rose from his bowed position. She felt no shame in wanting him here, in wanting him to fill the gap left in her life by Kavan's absence.

"You should be aware, my lord, that while you may stay where you wish, here or in the city, your safety may be in question anywhere in Rhidam. We offer as secure shelter as we are able, we will afford you every luxury and defense, but if your identity is discovered…"

"I would be honored to stay, at least long enough to speak to Lord MacLyr before journeying to Saint Kóráhm's…and I trust my safety in your hands." He had no plan beyond that visit, however. Since entering the room, he had a strong feeling his life was about to change in some significant way and he wanted to leave himself open to that.

Elated, Diona barely refrained from clapping like a happy child. "Wonderful. Uncle, your room is prepared of course, and Espen, yours is likewise maintained." Her gaze lingered on Espen long enough to realize he was avoiding looking at her, and then she stoically forced her attention to her guest. "I will see that a room is made available to you as well, Lord Bhíncári. Is there anything any of you require?"

"Not tonight," Owain assured her. "It is late and Piran should be in bed. But there are matters I must discuss with you at your leisure, tomorrow if you will."

Guessing they were matters of a sensitive political nature, ones that did not involve her brother, she nodded, anxious to hear them, and then since Espen still had his arms full of the sleeping boy, she offered her arm to Bhyrhán. "My lord, will you accompany me to my brother? I am sure he is still awake and will be delighted to meet you."

The bard glanced at his traveling companions with nervous expectation, and since no one seemed inclined to detain him, he said, "I would like that, Your Majesty. Thank you." He took her arm and followed her and her gaggle of retainers out of the Hall.

As soon as they were gone, Owain took Piran out of Espen's arms and muttered, "You're a fool."

"Pardon?" With the friendship they were forging, such words from Owain were a surprise, although they mirrored exactly the way Espen felt about himself.

Piran stirred long enough to recognize his father's jawline and wrap his arms around the man's neck and fell asleep again. Owain patted his back until he settled and then said quietly, "If you wish to convince her to marry you, such coldness after weeks of separation will not help…nor will using my son as a shield." He cut off the prince's retort with a shake of his head. "I don't care if she's fawning over Bhíncári…you know it means nothing…unless you let it. She may not have given your proposal the definitive answer it deserves, but she will…and I believe she will marry you. But not if you punish her like a misbehaving child."

Prince Harcourt's response was a quiet grunting huff as he strode out of the Hall. He wished he carried the same belief that Owain and others shared about Diona's intentions. He doubted that belief would come until the day they wed…and might not fully take root even then.

❧*❧

It was a peculiar gathering Ártur found in the Stateroom when he entered. Most of those present were Hagan's advisors. The princess was at the Boy-King's side as she often was. Ártur wondered for a moment if there had been some requested conference that he had forgotten, particularly since Prince Espen and Owain were present as well. With them was a young Elyri man and the sight made Ártur wither inside. A healer? One without the encumbrances of family?

He bowed to the King, doing his best to pretend that thought had not crossed his mind. "Pardon the intrusion, My Liege. I wished to announce my arrival. Gaelán said you wished to see me but not that you were in discussion…"

"No formal discussion, Lord Healer." The King motioned him towards an empty chair. "We were discussing the ball…and the need to find a resident Teren physician."

Not a healer then? It would have been a minor relief if he was certain. "What do you require of me?"

"When applicants arrive, you and Lord Chamberlain will screen them. I will not have anti-Elyri sentiment under this roof if we can avoid it, particularly in one with whom we entrust our lives."

"Of course."

"Will you attend the ball?"

"As much as I would like to be here…I cannot." Not without risking his wife's wrath. "Unless you demand my attendance…"

For once the young King showed common sense. "I want you to be safe…and I do not want Lady MacLyr to be angry with me. Since you cannot attend, I want you to meet…"

The door opened, causing the King's face to crease with irritation. A soldier, red-faced from running, bowed and said breathlessly, "Pardon my intrusion. I have come with a message for Lord Dugan."

There was silence in the room as everyone waited for whoever was to speak next. The soldier expecting permission to speak, Caol expecting permission to leave the room to hear the report, and the King waiting for the intruder to continue. Finally, Hagan rolled his eyes in exasperation and snorted, "Well, get on with it. Give him the message so we can get back to business."

The soldier bowed his head, but instead of delivering a verbal message, he handed a folded scrap of paper to the inquisitor. "The man who delivered it said it was urgent."

Caol read it hastily and let out a whoop of excitement. "We've got him!" Or they would have, if they acted quickly.

"Who?" asked Agis with a tingle of anticipation that raced over his skin and sparked in his eyes. "Narn?"

"Yes!"

The King was out of his chair, annoyed still with the interruption, annoyed that he had no idea what Caol and Agis were talking about, annoyed with his own presumptions of who the messenger had been.

"I told you to have no further dealings with the Association."

"My Liege," Caol began to protest. No one had mentioned the Association, no one had said that the messenger was Association, even though Caol suspected the message had come through those channels.

The paper was ripped from the inquisitor's hand, and after hastily reading the few lines of script, the King turned his accusing eyes onto the chamberlain. "I gave this investigation to you."

Undaunted, Bhríd said, "Aye, you did, My Liege. But I was having no success and deemed the investigation too important to leave idle while I see to the other matters you have asked me to tend to." Chiefly the ball. "I asked Lord Dugan for assistance…"

Feeling no need to listen to the tirade he knew was coming when there was work to be done, and knowing he would say something unsuitable if he stayed, Caol stood up, intending to leave the room.

"Where are you going, Lord Inquisitor?" the King snapped, causing Caol to stop when he reached the delivering soldier's side.

"You can read, Your Mightiness." His tone and choice of words were not lost on those present, and if he risked the King's wrath, he no longer cared. If he was going to be prevented from doing his duty at every turn, he had few choices left to him. "Narn s cornered. If we want him, we must take him at once."

Agis climbed quickly to his feet. "He is Cíbhóló; it is my duty."

Caol gestured to the general to follow as the King barked, "Cíbhóló? How do you know…?"

But his inquisitor and general were already leaving and his aborted question went unanswered. Hagan might be little more than a boy, but he was smart enough to see that his image, his control as King, was slipping from his grasp, and he had no desire or strength to resort to tyrannical measures to enforce his wishes. In an attempt to save face, he returned his focus to the others, pretending to ignore the men who had left and the matter of a man named Narn.

"Lord Chamberlain, please see to it that everything is in place for the ball, and let me know when there are any candidates for Court Healer. Prince Espen, Uncle…will you join me in the gardens? I want to hear how things are in Fiara."

Ártur did not move or speak during the entire awkward exchange. He felt like an outsider, as if he had not been in the room, did not belong in it. Not that most of the dialogue had involved him, but the King's planned words to him had been swept away in favor of escape from the unpleasant tension in the air. The princess touched his shoulder sympathetically as she passed, and he stared at his hands as the room emptied. Thinking he was alone, he too began to rise, and quickly realized that the blonde Elyri still sat where he had been when Ártur entered, his expression neutral, his hands folded in his lap, as forgotten by the Teren as Ártur was.

"Is the Lachlan court always this interesting?" the blonde asked.

"Only since…" He wanted to say since Kavan left, but the words would not come out past the knot in his throat.

"Since the violence began?"

"Yes…that would be accurate."

The blonde frowned at the healer's clipped, cool tone. "You do not remember me, do you?" he asked without insult or surprise.

"Should I?" He had met many over the years, but he could think of no healer he had met who matched this man's features.

"We met twice…though I have met Lord Cliáth several times."

Thinking the stranger was a messenger from his cousin, his face brightened and Ártur slid to the edge of his seat and eagerly leaned forward. "You know Kavan? Have you seen him? How is he?"

The other shook his head reluctantly, dashing the healer's hopes. "Sadly no; I have not seen him since the last time he played in Clarys."

"That was…" Ártur sagged against the back of his chair.

"Over thirty years ago. I was a child myself then. He probably will not remember me either, but when I heard of the attack…what happened to his hands…" He shook his head again, this time with great sorrow on his face. "His artistry has been the biggest influence on my life, perhaps to my parents' consternation. I began a pilgrimage from Clarys, walking much of the way here, contemplating his life, his words, his pain, his sacrifices…his courage and his faith. I came hoping for the opportunity to offer my support. I encountered Lord Lachlan and Prince Harcourt on the road and found respectable protection for the remainder of my journey through Enesfel. Since I am unable to offer him my support, I extend the same to you, if there is anything I can do that might be of assistance or comfort?"

Sweeping his hand through his short reddish hair, the healer groaned. "Not unless you can find him and bring him home safely and quickly. Or if you can guarantee that he will, indeed, return to us."

"I will continue to offer prayers for those things; may k'Ádhá hear them and grant our petitions," he murmured with a bowed head.

No longer feeling the bitterness towards the stranger, Ártur sighed. Even if he was a healer, he knew, or had known, Kavan, and that made him welcome. "Are you remaining in Rhidam for long?"

"I intended to leave for Saint Kóráhm's in a day or two, complete my pilgrimage, but King Hagan has asked that I provide entertainment for his gala."

The last of Ártur's tension bled away. "A bard then." He should have known, particularly after the stranger admitted the influence Kavan had been on his life.

"I play recorder and flute…sometimes I sing…though none of it is as eloquent as the harp in Kavan's hands. But each has its charms and they are my best friends. They are what I excel at."

"Kavan would extend his welcome if he was here. With his exceptional memory, he might surprise you by recalling your name at first sight." He chuckled. "I am not so fortunate."

The blonde rose and offered his hand. "Bhyrhán Bhíncári."

"Grandson?" The healer could see the similarities between the man and Kyne Mórne as soon as he spoke his name. Most Bhíncári had a similar high-arching brow and gently up-sloped eyes, and such pale blonde hair adorned many in the noble Elyri family. Ártur should have recognized the younger man sooner, but it had been many years since he had been to Clarys, many years since he had seen the High Mother or any other member of the Bhíncári family.

"Yes, I was present at your cousin's first performance at the Festival of Candles. I was six."

Six. No wonder Ártur had not recognized him. A man changed a lot between childhood and adulthood, even when that man was Elyri.

"Then you and he are kin." Bhyrhán got to his feet as well. "His mother was Bhíncári."

"Truly?" The revelation was a surprise. During Kavan's visits to the royal Elyri court, Bhyrhán thought someone would have made mention of their kinship, no matter how distant. He wondered if there was some reason it had not been revealed. "Then I have further cause to meet him and shall endeavor to do so as soon as I may. Perhaps, if we are fortunate, he will return to Rhidam while I am here."

"I pray, Ártur said in a melancholy tone, "that we are so blessed."

❧*৶

It took Balint several minutes to calm the angry merchant, by the time he succeeded, the offender was gone. After his smooth handling of the vandalism incident, King Hagan had asked the Duke if he would patrol Rhidam in an effort to keep the peace, a public relations gesture intended to boost the King's image. Balint had an easy, confident rapport with the common people that was often difficult to find in a man of his station, which made him well-received by the majority of people he met. And his status as knight of the realm made him respected by many others. The handsome Duke accepted the appointment without the hesitation many in his station would have shown. Most of his peers would have balked at the seemingly menial task and would have sought any excuse to avoid it in favor of some action perceived as more glamorous and noble. But the Duke who had once held the title of the youngest knight in Enesfel was not like his peers. The King knew it. The people knew it.

Rhidam had seen relatively few incidents since the Duke's return from Alberni. There had been a handful of drunken arguments, some stone-throwing at gdhededhá Tusánt after one of the man's visits to the castle, and one fight in the market between women wanting the same bolt of cloth. That there were few Elyri remaining in Rhidam undoubtedly lent itself to a calmer atmosphere, but Balint, like others, suspected that would change when people learned that the grandson of the Elyri High Mother was in Rhidam.

He was patrolling on foot when he heard the cries of "Thief!" erupting further down the street from where he stopped to speak with a group of young men eager to make his acquaintance. It took more time than he liked to escape his admirers and push his way towards the crowded storefront of the bakery, but he did not hurt anyone by elbowing through the throng. No anti-Elyri violence today, but rather a case of theft by a hungry boy, of which there were plenty crawling around Rhidam like fleas on the underbelly of a dog. Balint had not gotten a look at the culprit as he disappeared into the crowd, but from the comments made by the baker and those gathered there, he thought this boy might be the one Chamberlain Cáner was seeking. If the boy was Elyri, he would know he could not safely enter most establishments in search of food or shelter, not when Elyri were hunted like animals. Any Elyri not employed or arriving without coin in their pocket would be forced to theft in order to survive.

The Duke paid for the stolen items, a loaf of bread and two sweet cakes. Barely enough to feed a growing boy for a day. Afterward, the baker satisfied and the commotion dispelled, Balint decided to start his own search for the boy in the vicinity of the baker's stall. If he could not offer him safety or comfort, Balint might at least be able to provide him enough coins so that he would not starve.

❧*❦

No one had yet come out of the dilapidated riverside tavern; Caol had made certain of that as soon as he, Agis, and a dozen palace guards arrived. Mid-day, it was the sort of place that would be nearly empty, and the sort of place Caol knew he should have looked at more closely. But none of his handful of clues had brought him here, and he was personally spread too thin. If the Association had been the ones to find his quarry here, Caol hoped it would be a point in his, and their, favor with the King.

If not, his parting remarks to his nephew, and the way he had ungraciously charged from the Stateroom, would be another nail in the inquisitor's coffin.

The lower floor of the establishment was devoid of patrons as expected. Behind the counter, a bent, wrinkled man of unknown age motioned the inquisitor and general towards the staircase with a fearful expression. Not sure who the fellow was afraid of, Caol fingered his knife but kept it sheathed as he motioned towards the stairs. Without discussing the matter, the inquisitor was satisfied with allowing Agis this capture as a matter of tribal and personal honor. And the general was satisfied allowing Caol the prestige of the find, of going first.

Besides, the inquisitor's experience made him more adept at stealth and they did not want to risk their prey escaping. Agis knew Caol's life and position with the King were at stake.

Most of the doors on the second floor were open, the rooms unused at this hour of the day. There was banter near the end of the corridor, a woman's dull, bored voice and a man's rough laughter. It came from behind a closed door, the room the message to Caol had indicated. Fortunately, the door opened with barely a creek, allowing Caol and Agis to watch the dark-skinned man wrestle the woman on the thin, stained mattress. He was clothed. She was not.

What little sound the door made, however, was enough to cause the man to pause his tussle and look up. Composed, not startled as Caol expected, the man did not speak or move. He knew his weapon was beyond his reach, laying across a chair too far away to be easily retrieved. With Agis' bulky frame filling the doorway behind the inquisitor, the man on the bed was at a disadvantage. He stood. While taller than the general, he had less mass; Caol assumed he must judge it an unfair fight since he gave no effort or objection when Agis took the waji from the pile of belongings on the chair and shoved it through his belt. The woman retreated to the far corner of the bed wisely keeping silent, looking frightened enough that she might have been surprised at the interruption.

Or she might have been the one to tip Caol off.

While the inquisitor picked up the rest of the man's belongings, two knives, a pouch of coins, a pair of well-worn boots and a bag that clattered when he lifted it, Agis took Narn by the arm and pulled him out of the room towards the stairs where the Lachlan guards waited at the bottom. Caol gave the woman one last look, and when her customer was out of sight, she nodded and smiled in a way that suggested she would expect her reward for this favor later.

Definitely Association.

Caol remained alert and cautious during the tense return to the castle through the late morning streets of Rhidam. He could not shake the feeling that this capture had been too simply, cleanly, executed. Every story he had heard about the Cíbhóló as a boy in Durham, every dealing his family had ever had with them, even his association with Agis over the years, had led him to believe the desert-dwelling nomads were a violent, passionate people. Rather than fight with Agis, however, the man had capitulated without protest. Caol wanted answers, but suspected that Narn, if that was who this was, would not give him any. Agis would have to do the talking, and Caol had doubts that even he would gain answers from their stoic captive.

"A cell," grunted the general, leading the way to the dungeon. It was not customary to question captives in their cells. Normally they were questioned before incarceration, to determine some level of guilt or innocence first. But Narn had eluded them too long, and if Agis suggested a cell, for whatever reason, Caol was not going to second guess the general. Agis unceremoniously shoved their prisoner into the first empty cell he reached, closed and locked the door, turned his back and stalked away.

Confused, Caol followed and waited until they were out of Narn's hearing range before speaking. "We should question him…"

The general shrugged. "To what end? He is Cíbhóló. He had the waji, the weapon which has killed many children. He is Narn. We know enough."

"You know, but we don't. There could be other Cíbhóló in Rhidam, others with this…"

"Waji." Agis drew the curved, jagged-toothed blade from his belt for the inquisitor to inspect. "This is that weapon. Only a Cíbhóló would know this…would use it. Few carry it; few are permitted. Few are honored enough to win the right. It is unlikely there is more than one in Rhidam. It is how I know."

"The King will want answers…more than a sword as proof, unless you want one of the Elyri to read it…"

"Elyri are not necessary; I know. He will not answer. He will show no respect to an authority he does not recognize. He may speak to me, if I approach him with honor, but even that is unlikely. A man who would commit such acts as he has done has no honor. But perhaps…"

He rubbed his chin as they entered the Great Hall.

"What? Perhaps what?"

Decision made in that few brief seconds, Agis grunted. "I will give him time to contemplate what he has done and then I will challenge him. Tell me what you need to know and I will ask. Be specific. You may act as mediator to hear his answers, and if I am killed, you will know what must be done.

The inquisitor snorted. "The King will never approve of a duel to the death." Caol did not approve either. Not in this case at least. Agis was too valuable to Enesfel and the Lachlans. King Arlan might have agreed, but his young son never would. "He will ask Ártur or Bhríd…"

"He will not know. We do this…you and I…and no one else. It is the way of the waji…there will be no honor without it and he will not talk otherwise. He will take his own life before he will allow anyone to force information from him. Come with me and we may shortly have our answers."

Caol frowned, considering his options, considering the nature of the man who stood before him. He did not like it but had to trust that Agis knew what he was talking about. Trust that the general would win any fight if that came to pass. "Then I suggest we find somewhere private to talk," he grunted, "before the King discovers we have returned with our prisoner. Quickly, otherwise you will not have the opportunity to be honorable."

If they did not act swiftly, the King would take the choice out of Agis' hands.

❧*❦

Ártur had not anticipated liking the first Teren candidate for court healer that came through the castle doors. Nor had he expected the first candidate to meet each of his, and the King's, expectations and requirements. He had talked with the ash-haired man for nearly an hour before the King interviewed him as well, and then waited as the man was returned to the library by Justice Corbin, the man who had recommended his appointment. This particular physician seemed to be everything they could want, and experienced enough to be a man Ártur would feel comfortable placing the Lachlans care into. If he had to leave their care to someone else overnight, he doubted he would find a better Teren candidate.

He stood as the Justice left them alone again, welcoming their guest back into the room. "You do understand that, at least during the daylight hours, there will be three of us here and you might have more free time then you are bargaining for."

"Three?" I was under the impression it would be you and me…"

"And Gaelán, my apprentice. Not fully trained, but capable enough. He does not know medical practices, however, has not been exposed to many of the more common Teren methods of treatment, and as they are practices he should learn, if you accept this position you will be expected to participate in his training."

Flustered, the doctor nodded. "I will gladly share everything I know. I do not have an apprentice…and that should keep me busy enough." Not busy healers meant everyone was in good health, and he did not see that as a bad thing. "The King said you will read me?"

Surprised that the physician showed little fear at the notion, the healer nodded. "A necessary precaution. There are a number of Elyri employed here, and the King deems it important and necessary that anyone hired by the Crown is willing and able to co-exist peacefully."

"Of course. I am a passive person by nature; sadly, I did kill a man once, in self-defense. I would take that death back if I could, but I do not regret it. Please," he held out his hands, "read me if you wish."

The gesture suggested that the man had dealt with Elyri before. Rather than take those hands, however, Ártur lay his hand on the man's shoulder. Contact with his thoughts took longer to establish that way, but it was less intimate and took no longer than clasping a friend's shoulder in support or sympathy would.

"You know Kavan?" He read it in the man's thoughts, but his surprise demanded he voice the question, seeking confirmation. His world was suddenly filling with people who had known and liked his cousin and he shivered, wondering if this was k'Ádhá's way of letting him know that he was not alone in his support, that there were others who cared about Kavan even if most of his kin did not appear to.

"He did not speak of me?" The physician's face sagged in disappointment.

"He speaks little of that time. He does not want the reminder of what we lost…the prince…Lord McHador…"

"The young prince; yes, I see. He is not one to dwell on the past; I should not be surprised." Not being talked about did not mean he had been forgotten. It only meant the private Elyri bard had kept some things to himself. "When shall I hear regarding the position?"

Unable to fault his eagerness, as a full-time appointment to the Crown meant a reliable income, Ártur replied, "I cannot speak for the King, but I believe you are ideal for our needs. I know he wants the post filled at once. I will speak to him directly and we will let you know as soon as possible. Where shall I contact you?"

"Justice Corbin knows where I live." He had lived in Rhidam most of his life and had known the Justice for many years, since the events precipitating the young prince's death.

"Then I shall send word as soon as I know the king's wishes."

Rouvyn Talis nodded and bowed and was escorted from the keep by the man who had brought him in. This was the best candidate they would find; Ártur was sure of it. Not only because of his skills, talents, or experience, but because he had known Kavan…and Kavan had liked him. Another Elyri supporter in the castle was what Ártur, and the bard, needed. Fill the keep with love, he thought, and perhaps Kavan would come home.

❧*❧

Through the bars of the dungeon cell, Caol watched the general place the curved blade on the stone floor at his feet midway between himself and the one called Narn, a line to cross, a challenge. Agis had not explained the process, but Caol understood that gesture. Both Cíbhóló folded their arms across their chests as though shielding themselves and stared at one another.

"Narn."

"General."

Agis did not react. So this man had known he was in Rhidam, knew who he was, and yet had dared such defiant acts. The prisoner did not speak in the Trade tongue, either because he could not or because he was confident he would win the fight ahead and was hoping no one else would know of what he spoke. But he understood Agis when the general asked, "Children?" in the Trade tongue, telling Agis more of what he wanted to know about his adversary.

Narn did not shrug, made no shifts that would expend energy. His was being reserved for what awaited. "Pawns. Means to an end. Unfortunate but necessary."

"Dishonorable." Narn nodded his agreement and Agis, not having expected that, asked, "Why?"

"Promise."

A promise? To whom? But Agis knew he was not going to receive that explanation. Promises were sacred to the Cíbhóló and when it came to a battle between a promise and honor, it was often a difficult choice. The sort of promise that could compel a man to kill children, commit a crime against his honor, was a thing Agis could not fathom. Even if King Arlan or Hagan had commanded something similar from him, Agis knew he would never be able to carry it out. There was something in Narn's eyes then that had not been there before, or if it had been, Agis had not seen it. Shame and regret. At being captured, the general wondered, or for what he had done? "Names?"

Narn spoke words that Caol could not understand. Possibly names, possibly more. But the word Jolgier was likely a name. Heward certainly was. Anri Heward again. Balling his fists, the inquisitor forced himself not to grin, not to let Narn know he understood any of his conversation. One notch closer, Heward, he thought. I am keeping score and I will win.

Inside the cell, Agis slowly, deliberately, turned his back on Narn. Caol, not knowing what was happening but not liking the risk Agis was taking, fumbled with the keys in his hand, found the one he wanted, and slid it back into the door lock. It was enough time for Narn to act, for him to kill the general without Caol being able to stop him, but Caol would kill him in return if that happened. But in those tense moments, Narn did not move, weighing his options, and Agis warned Caol from entering the cell with a look. The general steeled himself. If he had misread his enemy, he would die. His death would be on him, not on the inquisitor.

He heard movement behind him, but he did not look and did not look at Caol to gauge what was happening. His eyes remained fixed on a point across the corridor in the opposite cell. Moments dragged by. Metal scraped stone. Bound by the general's command, the only thing Caol could do was utter a strangled sound and watch. But Agis trusted the code of the waji. It would not condone the death of a man from behind, any more than it welcomed the shedding of innocent blood. Already carrying the weight of the children's deaths, it was Narn's choice now, the path of the waji or a path of deeper dishonor. Agis was gambling that a Cíbhóló would take the former path.

It was not until the thud of great weight hit the floor that Agis turned. Narn had, as Agis expected, chosen the waji. He had done the only honorable thing left to him, chosen to take his life freely rather than have it taken from him. He had quietly, without fanfare, slit his stomach in an inverted U from left to right. The inquisitor, more astonished by the act than disgusted by the mess left upon the floor, stared while Agis retrieved the waji and wiped its blood on his hands.

"Custom?" Caol asked with a cough, thankful the general's bloody hands gave him something less grizzly to focus on.

Agis nodded. "I require two teeth to place in the pommel, but I will retrieve those later."

Caol wiped the back of his hand across his mouth as if to see that his teeth were intact. "I don't think the King will approve of the death of our prisoner before he had the opportunity to speak with him…"

"I will explain it, Lord Dugan. This burden is not yours. By his self-death, his deeds of dishonor have been erased. To deny him the chance to reclaim what he lost would have been an indication of my cowardice. The wrongness of his deeds stands, but his personal honor has been restored."

"I don't care if he died now or later, so long as he told us something useful, his capture was not in vain. Did I hear Heward?"

"In vain? He cannot kill another; that is reward enough. He confirmed that he killed the children, and others, as part of a promise, but he would not elaborate on what sort of promise it was or to whom it was made. He was mostly responsible for passing messages. Instructions were delivered to him from someone named Heward."

"Our Anri, no doubt."

"Likely. The other is called Jolgier."

"Is that a Cíbhóló name? Man? Woman?"

"He did not meet either of them, never spoke with them to know, but the name is not Cíbhóló as far as I know. He received instructions and passed them to another messenger, who in turn delivered them to individuals meant to carry out orders. He did not know the connection between Heward and Jolgier, whether the two knew each other or not, but he did indicate that sometimes their instructions conflicted with one another. It is likely the two are working at odds. I presume his promise was to one of them, but that is speculation."

Rubbing the back of his neck, Caol stared at the dead man's face. "Not common in Cordash or Enesfel either…and it doesn't sound like an Elyri name. I'll speak with Prince Owain and Prince Espen, see if they recognize the roots. It's not much, but at least we have learned something…and took out a link in the Coryllien network. Finding Heward is our top priority. We remove him, there will be immediate progress towards peace."

"Agreed. I will speak with the young man he mentioned delivering messages too if I can locate him, and I will take up these deeds with the King while you pursue your contacts. You do not need to come with me. You cannot tell the king any more than what you witnessed, whereas this is on my hands. If anyone is to be reprimanded for misconduct, it will be me.

Caol nodded, acknowledging that he liked this man, unable to imagine Hagan reprimanding someone of Agis' size and strength. The inquisitor left the cell and the dead man to Agis, almost wishing he could see the look on the King's face when he saw the smear of blood across Agis' hands and clothing. But Caol had duties to see to. It would not suffice for the Association to bring messages directly to him any longer. It served to make the King angry, even when the results were positive and beneficial. But there was another way, a means he did not think the King would suspect, and it was time to put it into action, even though the risks made him queasy. The King, however, was leaving him few other choices.

❮*❯

From the edge of the promenade path, Prince Espen watched Diona stare at the stars for a long time. She did not seem to know he was there. Even when Owain joined her on the bench amidst the spring flowers, she failed to notice him. It angered him at first, that she had invited him to Rhidam, seemed eager and pleased to see him, and then turned her mind to other matters almost immediately. But he knew that, if this had been Hatu, she there visiting him, circumstances would have been similar. Duty might have kept him away from her when he would rather have been by her side. And in Hatu, because she was a woman, she might have been forced apart from him for the duration of her visit, unable to speak with him except perhaps through a curtain or small window by virtue of her gender. She would not tolerate that. And neither, he knew, would he.

She could not be faulted for the political state of Enesfel. She was doing the best she could with the hand she had been given.

Enesfel was changing him. Had changed him. Growing up, he had not understood the need to keep women apart from men, and his time in Enesfel had led him to further question his country's long-held practices. He believed in equality, in sharing, in spending as much time as desired with the woman he loved without cultural convention coming between them.

Or perhaps it was his feelings for her that made him believe this.

He should speak to her. Tell her he loved her, words too long left unsaid. But he suspected this was not the time. He had wasted time in watching her, and Owain might be discussing Prince Kjell with her. That matter required her full attention. Perhaps tomorrow, if he could find a moment alone with her. Or at Hagan's banquet. He smiled at the thought of that night, of dancing with her before the eyes of every lord and lady of the realm. That would be the ideal opportunity to proclaim his love and put his proposal to her one more time. He would make the moment perfect and she would be unable to refuse.

Hearing footsteps on the path, Diona looked away from Owain in time to catch a glimpse of Espen's retreating back. She did not know what he might have seen or heard, how long he might have been there, but as she had nothing to hide from him, she did not understand why he was departing, why he did not approach.

"Are all men…are they all afraid of me?"

"Afraid of you?" Owain was unaware of anyone being afraid of the princess.

She nodded, her expression pensive. "Most my age are married, I know…I suppose I should be as well. I would be…if I could commit. Men tell me I am beautiful, intelligent…a princess. Yet how many suitors have I had? One. Even Flannery and Kavan…I have pursued both to varying degrees, yes, but neither is interested. Espen alone has tried to court me…and though I think he loves me, sometimes I catch him looking at me like he does not know who I am."

Owain gave the question serious thought before speaking; she deserved an honest answer, if he could formulate one into words. "I believe Flannery is daunted by you, yes…he is a meek man, quiet and thoughtful, while you are bold, decisive, determined. As for Kavan…if he ever marries, if he ever loves anyone that way, I doubt I will be alive to see it. His lack of romantic interest has little to do with you and everything to do with his own nature. As for any others…you know that men, particularly noblemen, do not appreciate the idea of a wife who knows what she wants, who speaks her mind, who wields power and strength. Most of the men with notions of marrying you are those with dreams of sitting on Enesfel's throne, and they know that, should you rise to position of Queen, you would not share your power with anyone."

She frowned deeper. "Do you think that is why he wants to marry me? Because he wants to be king?" Espen was in line for the throne of Hatu, but he would not rule unless his brother died without an heir. It was unlikely Espen would ever rule from the Hatu throne but she had never considered that he might have his eye on Enesfel's instead.

"I do not know him well enough to say. I believe he knows you will not be bullied, and I think he would not have spent so many years pursuing you if he was not interested in you as a woman. If power was his goal, he would seek it some other way instead of waiting for you to accept his proposal. When will you give him an answer, Diona? It is cruel to make a suitor wait so long."

Diona looked as if she might hang her head but she did not. "I do not hesitate out of cruelty. I do not know why I do. The time Lord Cliáth has been away has taught me many hard lessons. I miss him; I want him home. But it is solely for the purpose of seeing him, speaking with him, listening to his music, seeking his advice. I sought something from him he cannot give, but I know that marriage is not what I need from him. I do want to marry Espen. I need him beside me. But every time I try to say it to him, something separates us and the words will not come out."

Owain nodded, relieved to hear the confirmation of his suspicions. "I will not tell him what you have said; that is for you to do. But may I encourage him to keep faith, encourage him not to give up hope?"

She nodded with a small, hopeful smile. "I wish you would. I do not want him to leave Enesfel and not come back. If Kavan does not return…while I will forever ache for what I have done, I know I can live without seeing him again if I must. Not so Espen. I cannot imagine life without him."

Owain swallowed over the painful lump lodged in his throat. Never see Kavan again. He did not think he could live that way. But for Espen's sake, it was good to know that the princess had chosen the Hatu prince over the bard. It would be good for Kavan's sake as well. Not being pursued by Diona Lachlan might encourage the bard to stay, if he ever found the courage to come back.

❧Chapter 13❧

Alone finally, Gaelán leaned on his windowsill, watching the birds in the courtyard pecking at crumbs a kitchen maid had tossed out for them. He was trying to decide why he felt exhausted when it was barely past noon. He was not even hungry as he normally was at this hour. Too many things had happened today for which he had been unprepared, too many changes, and the day was but half over.

Bhyrhán Bhíncári was a wonder to him, the only Elyri musician Gaelán had ever met besides Kavan. They talked about music briefly, but though it was something Gaelán loved, he had no talent for it, and so the topic had shifted quickly to something they both shared a passion for. Horses. They had spent nearly an hour in the stables until a servant summoned Gaelán away…to Ártur who had the second surprise of Gaelán's day.

He had known there was a plan in place to hire a Teren Court physician as it was part of Ártur's agreement with Syl. Hiring one was both in Ártur's, and the Lachlans, best interest. He had not expected to like the chosen individual, however, not expected there could be any physician in Rhidam who would know Kavan.

It had also not occurred to him that this newcomer would assist in his schooling. Ártur could teach him everything he knew, herbs and poultices and the best ways to bandage wounds or splint broken bones, but Ártur believed that a second mentor would be to Gaelán's benefit. It might speed up the learning process, reinforce the lessons in a different way. The novice healer's instruction increased from three hours a day to five, not including the hours he spent with his father practicing swordsmanship or horsemanship, or the hours spent discussing diplomacy, etiquette, history, and philosophy with Asta's tutor. On top of that, there were two hours he spent each week discussing topics of Faith with whichever dedhá was chosen to come, teachings his father made sure he attended whether he wished to or not.

The thought of so much studying made him groan. He wanted to ask if this was what it was like to be an adult, no time for riding or spending time with Asta, no time for the diversion of doing nothing. But he knew how much Ártur had endured as a novice healer, far more than he faced. Ártur had not had to learn diplomacy and swordsmanship but he had spent many hours learning to utilize his Elyri gifts to their fullest, healing gifts and others. If Gaelán wanted to be the sort of healer his uncle was, he needed to know those things. He would not, however, need to know diplomacy and swordsmanship and was trying to find a way out of both paths of study. He wanted to know what other Elyri gifts he possessed, would rather have spent time exploring those, but he was afraid to ask Ártur, afraid that the healer would think he was not putting enough focus into healing.

That was the advantage of Bhyrhán's arrival. The bard might not be in Rhidam for long, but he might be there long enough to teach Gaelán a trick or two…if he ever found the time to be alone with him.

He also longed to be alone with Asta. They had talked briefly in passing about the upcoming banquet, which Asta was looking forward to with great excitement. Her fourteenth birthday seemed to have changed her. Changed the way he looked at her, the way she looked at him. The way others looked at her too. There also seemed to be a slowly widening gap between them that he could not help but worry about. He had become too busy with his studies and the responsibilities as secondary court healer, and could scarcely find the time to sleep. Likewise, Asta spent more time with her father than usual though no one, other than Gaelán, seemed to notice. He wondered what new things her father was teaching her.

This morning he had seen a stranger with Asta, a girl he did not recognize. He knew the children around the grounds and knew this girl was not one of the servants. She was pale, with freckles across her button nose and hair the same color as Syl's, that pale rose-blond color that Tayte also had. The girl was almost painfully thin, and laughed and giggled with Asta as if the two had been friends their entire lives. If she was unhealthy, however, there was no other sign of it.

Perhaps they had been friends and Gaelán had somehow missed her. Perhaps she was another Dugan, come from Durham. Gaelán did not know. He knew that the sight of Asta on such intimate terms with anyone else hurt him when it should not. He was not accustomed to such a feeling and did not understand it.

He yawned as he turned from the window, shoulders slumped. The thing that bothered him most, however, was something that had yet to happen. His mother and Tayte were due to arrive soon for the King's ball. He felt distanced from them, as if they were not part of his life any longer. His life had become that of an Elyri healer at court; everyone in Rhidam treated him as if he were Elyri. Having his mother here would remind everyone that he was not what he was pretending to be and he imagined that his mother would be hurt by the ways he had changed. Tayte would make a point of driving home their differences, ridiculing him. Gaelán did not want to face either of them, which was why he had refused to go back to Levonne after accepting Ártur as his mentor. He did not belong in his mother's world any longer and saw no way to make her, or his brother, fit into his.

His bedchamber was the one place in the castle Caol felt he was guaranteed privacy. The servants might come to clean, to bring water, to leave an occasional meal, but beyond that, no one except Asta came unless they needed him, and such people always knocked and waited to be summoned inside. It made it the ideal place to school his daughter in the lifestyle she had chosen. It was not the sort of life he, or her mother, would have selected for her, but he had recognized early where her talents and interests lay and he had known she was too stubborn to be dissuaded. He agreed to school her with the understanding that she might someday be skilled enough to fill his shoes as inquisitor but that she might never, because of her gender, have that opportunity.

He had not, however, planned for her to need these skills so early in her life.

"You understand what you are to do?" he repeated. Only the desperation of making certain she was prepared for this duty made him ask the questions a second time, in different words, when he already knew the answer.

"Father, I am not a fool," Asta griped, rolling her eyes with more annoyance than she felt.

Chuckling, a sound of relief and apology, he tousled her hair. "I know you are not. I also know that despite your royal blood and upbringing, you are equipped to live on the street if you have to. But you are still young and this is your first…assignment. It is no longer a game or a test, and I have every right to be concerned. No one, especially me, will blame you if you have doubts or questions."

Most born into the Association were performing more dangerous feats at a much younger age, the necessity of street life forcing them to excel at theft, subterfuge, stealth, even murder, while still children. Asta, a woman now according to the custom of the land, would have been immersed in her chosen craft for years if she was not also of royal blood. Training had prepared her, but training was different than life experience, and any failure now could mean her death at the hands of her king and cousin, or could mean Caol's death. While not a matter of day to day survival, this was no game either. Rather it was a matter of kingdom security that could not be taken lightly. It was a wise precaution to be certain she understood what was required, what was at stake, but until she had the opportunity to put her skills to the test, her word was the only gauge by which to measure her readiness.

"It is not a difficult thing." The way she wrapped her arms around his neck showed that she appreciated his concern. "Marta gets information from outside, gives it to me, and I give it to you. You give information to me and I pass it to her to send elsewhere. Accuracy is crucial, secrecy essential. I can do this."

He nodded. It was not a difficult duty, as she said, but that did not mean it was not dangerous. "If you can carry this out, there may soon be more for you to see to, particularly if I…"

"If you what?"

Shaking his head, he grinned. "It is of no consequence now. When the time comes…if it comes…I will explain. For now, let it rest. Do you have plans for today?"

"Diona Is helping me select a dress for the banquet," she bubbled and her father sighed in mock annoyance.

"I should have known. Women and their clothes. Promise me you will not embarrass me and I will let you go about your business."

"Me?" Asta giggled. "Embarrass you? Father, I did not think that was possible." She laughed as she hugged him tighter and skipped out of his room. Caol leaned back in his desk chair, wondering if Deidre had been like this as a child or if it was the Dugan blood that made his daughter irresistibly precocious.

❧*☙

According to Cíbhóló custom, Agis took Narn's body out of Rhidam, wrapped in a wool blanket, seeking an appropriate place to dispose of the corpse. He was alone, although many had volunteered to accompany him. But this was not the same as paying respects to the late King Arlan. Narn had not been a leader. Narn had been a man who had made regrettable choices, but his end was still dictated by custom.

If he had been able, Agis would have taken the body back to the desert, found Narn's family, given them the choice of final rites. Instead, the best he could do was send Narn's few possessions, minus the waji, with a messenger in the hopes of finding any kin the man had. Whether the messenger succeeded or not was not Agis' concern. He had the waji. No more children would be butchered by the man's blade. And Narn was at peace with himself.

In a fallow field, far from inhabitation, the general stopped his four horses. Two pulled a cart of wood and the supplies needed to create a pyre for the deceased, while another carried the body and a large clay jug for the ashes. It took several hours to build the pyre to his expectations, and many more, into the early morning hours of the following day, for the body to be consumed by the flames. Then the ashes had to be gathered and buried deep, since there were no desert winds here to disperse them.

But he had made all necessary arrangements with the King so it was known that the general would be away from Rhidam for an unspecified length of time. This was a Cíbhóló's final moment and it must be carried out properly. Even if the man had been a child killer.

"Lady McPhelan." Hagan bowed nervously and kissed the young woman's jeweled hand. His own were clammy, his stomach tied into a tangle of knots. He knew her, had no reason for his reaction to her company, but perhaps, he realized, admiring her amber and green gown, knowing what lay ahead, the intent of choosing a wife, had made him nervous in her company. "Welcome to Rhidam. I am pleased you are able to be here."

"You beckoned, I came." The sparkle in her blue eyes was not lost on the Boy-King, and he found it difficult not to flee the room as instincts bid him. He had arranged this event solely for the purpose of beginning to select Enesfel's queen. He did not want to marry, did not feel ready for such a commitment, but he believed it was necessary. It was his duty to secure Enesfel's future, after all, which meant marriage and children. Jilletta McPhelan was three years his senior, and had been pursuing him for that long. She was pretty enough, aristocratic, with her blonde hair twisted into a braid high atop her head, her face made up like one of the finely painted dolls in Diona's collection, but the King could not help but feel that her interest was in the status such a marriage could afford her and her family, not in him. It was likely her father's hope as well, to marry his daughter into the royal family, hence the only reason she was not yet betrothed or wed. She would likely do anything Hagan asked if he bestowed on her that honor, her father likewise, but Hagan had few doubts that she would grow bored of him before long, and he of her.

The door to the Hall reopened as more guests began to arrive. The celebration banquet was two days away, but he knew from experience that many guests would arrive early. It was the nature of such events, nobles coming either in the hopes of a few minutes of the King's time, to curry favor with one or another of the royal advisors, or coming to leech off the royal house for as long as the King allowed. In most cases, it had to be tolerated. He did not want to be considered inhospitable and did not have the courage to deny most requests made of him. Fortunately, he thought, Diona did, and spared him often of the absurdities presented to him.

It was also to his fortune that those guests needed his attention too, drawing him away from Jilletta. He knew she would not feel slighted; she did not care how much time he spent with her as long as she gained what she sought. The banquet had not yet begun and the King felt he had already eliminated one of his most likely candidates. Jilletta McPhelan would likely be his absolute last choice.

Bhríd did not know how to reassure his wife of his safety in Rhidam, although Madalyn was not as fretful over him as Syl was with Ártur. Bhríd was the King's Champion and still early in his Elyri prime; age had in no way dulled his reflexes or lessened his strength. He had no doubts about his ability to defend the King, nor did Hagan. And unlike Ártur, he did not feel immune to the anti-Elyri violence plaguing the kingdom. He had already been involved in one incident and come out alive, though until today his wife had not known about that. But she did not doubt his ability to protect himself either, and her sense of duty to the Lachlans was perhaps stronger than his. If he wished to remain in Rhidam, Madalyn supported his decision. It would not, however, stop her from worrying.

It was not her husband she was primarily concerned about, however, despite having learned of the attack he had endured and the subsequent attack on Ártur. Her concern was for her youngest son. Bhríd watched her pace the entire length of the library in the gathering twilight, listening to her, wanting to disavow her of her worry but knowing it was well-founded.

"I know he is more like you," she said, "more Elyri than Teren. I thought I was ready to allow him to pursue healing as far as he could."

"But we could not anticipate how it might divide the family." He had anticipated it, being Elyri and knowing what that could be like in the public eye, but he was not going to lay blame for their situation at his wife's feet. He stubbornly clung to the belief that his family would be mostly immune to such problems, that they could and would weather any storm that blew across their paths. "I feel it with Tayte, when he looks at me like I am not his father, or in a way that suggests he wishes I was not. Perhaps he resents what he does not have…or fears it. Although he will not say it, I suspect Gaelán fears it too."

"Fears that he can…?"

"Not what he can do, but what it makes him. Tayte can declare to be Teren, can live as a Teren. I have seen no one question that right or assertion. Gaelán's path marks him as Elyri, whether he chooses to heal or not, and that makes him dangerous to some."

"He could give it up." Even when saying it, Madalyn knew it would not happen. Her youngest son was too stubborn, too much like both of his parents, to give up something he wanted. And giving it up now was too late. The world had already seen who and what he was. He was forever marked.

"What would he gain? Too many know what he is capable of, and he feels that to not heal when he is able would be a grave sin. Healing is the first thing in his life he has shown interest in, other than horses and girls, and he has been studying hard to achieve it. He has never put this much focus into anything. But it puts us all in a precarious position. To deny him may cause him to hate us. To encourage him and ignore the risk would be callous. I believe the best we can do is make sure he is aware of the ramifications of his choices, let him make his decision, and support him in what he does."

Madalyn slid her arms around his broad waist, reminded again how un-Elyri like he was. Taller, more muscular, darker. In some ways, he did not look Elyri, save for the youthfulness of his features that belied his age. How many more years, she wondered, before their sons looked older than their father. "Do you know why I love you?"

He shook his head with a chuckle. Her professions of love never failed to lift his spirits, and the easement of the burdens he faced was a welcome thing.

"You always have an answer...a solution...even when you are uncertain of the course to take or choice to make, you produce a workable answer to our problems. That, and of course you are the most handsome man in Enesfel."

"Only Enesfel?" he asked before kissing her mouth.

She laughed warmly. "I have not been anywhere else to make comparisons, but Enesfel is enough." Resting her head on his chest, she asked, "What do we do about Tayte?"

His breath caught and she heard his pulse quicken beneath her ear. "I...though I hate to suggest it, it might be in both their best interests if we keep them apart as much as possible."

"Apart?" She drew back enough to look at him.

"You saw it when you arrived; I know you did. The two of them alone in the same room is asking for trouble. Gaelán has not mastered the finer arts of Elyri power...and Tayte has become antagonistic. If he pushes, there is no knowing what Gaelán might do, accidentally or not. And Tayte has mastered the finer points of weaponry. If Gaelán gets it into his head to challenge his brother to a duel, or accepts such a challenge from Tayte..."

Madalyn groaned, seeing his point. It seemed incomprehensible to her that the brothers should have come to this, brothers who had once been so close as little boys. They had loved and respected each other, and their father. It was impossible to believe that Tayte could have grown to despise those he once loved. "What will that mean for us? You here, me in Levonne?"

The chamberlain sighed, not knowing how to resolve the situation equitably. When Madalyn had proposed to him years ago, they had discussed the potential of living apart because they had barely known each other and accepted that duty and circumstance might place such a demand on them. Now he loved her, and the thought of being apart from her more than they already were was not a future he wanted to ponder too deeply. "They are of an age where they do not require constant supervision." Even Gaelán, he thought reluctantly, despite the boy's mutable rashness. But he was now in the tutelage of many others; he was rarely without guidance. There was little reason Bhríd and Madalyn could not travel to and fro without their sons.

"I suppose we should find the boys," she sighed knowing he had no further answer to give her. If, when, he developed a solution, he would tell her. In the meantime, there were other matters to tend to.

"Yes…I think we should."

Stomping her foot on the straw-covered stable floor, Asta was tempted to stamp on Tayte's toes to make him listen. She had been as fond of him as she had been of Hagan and Gaelán in their years growing up together, but like much else lately, Tayte had changed too much for her to comprehend his actions any longer. Perhaps because he was nearing his fifteenth birthday, and hence was considered to be a man, he still considered them to be children, beneath him somehow. Whatever the reason for the difference, Asta did not like his behavior or his attitude and she hoped he still thought enough of her and their friendship to listen.

"You are being a bully, Tayte Cáner." She allowed Gaelán to get up from the ground himself; there was no point in encouraging Tayte to think his brother needed a woman's help. In the dark of the stables, she could not see Gaelán's face without looking down at him, but she knew he was upset. "What has he done to you? He's your brother!"

"He's one of them," Tayte sneered, emphasizing the final word as he glared at Gaelán.

"So are you!" Gaelán retorted. "We have the same parents…"

"I do not practice sorcery!"

"Healing is not sorcery," Asta spat, pushing Tayte backward before Gaelán could speak. Tayte wanted to strike her, she knew, but he did not. She wished he would; it would give her an excuse to knock him to the ground the way she wanted. He would never see it coming. "It is an art! It saves lives!"

Drawing back his shoulders, Tayte snarled, "It is evil and I hope they kill you for it!"

"Tayte!"

Madalyn's jaw was slack, her eyes wide in horror as she stared at the young man she believed she had raised better than that. Beside her, Bhríd clenched his jaw to keep from saying something he would regret. His eldest son needed to be taught a lesson, but at the moment the chamberlain was beyond rational thinking. His child hated him for what he was. Wanted his brother dead. Most likely wished his father dead too. Unable to believe what he had heard, he could think of nothing suitable to say that would not estrange them further.

Resisting the impulse to run to his father for protection, Gaelán instead clutched Asta's hand, trying not to let the tears in his eyes break free. There were several minutes of awkward silence before Tayte stalked from the stable, ignoring both of his parents, his brother, and his one-time friend. After a nod from her husband, Madalyn pursued their eldest son, the one most likely to speak sense into the young man, the one he was most likely to listen to. Bhríd did not need to point out how correct he had been in reading their sons' characters and relationship. Madalyn now saw it for herself.

He wanted to have words with Gaelán, reassure him, and might have sent Asta away to do so, but the grip Gaelán had on her hand made Bhríd decide against it. If he found comfort in her company, Bhríd was not going to take that away.

"I could say this will not happen again, but we both know it would be a lie. But I promise you I will protect you, Gaelán. You are my son. I will do everything in my power to see that harm does not befall you."

Gaelán did not nod or try to speak. He watched his father depart after placing a loving hand on his son's head, presumably to find and talk to Tayte as well, punish him, perhaps, for what he had said. When the man was out of sight, Gaelán let go of Asta's hand, kicked at the nearest bale of straw, and ran.

She did not try to stop him. Not knowing where he might go, but knowing he wanted to be alone, she scuffed her toes in the dust and straw on the floor, feeling awkward and confused, until she decided to find her father. If anyone could make sense of what had happened, she hoped he could.

Kavan doubted they would find a room when they finally reached Yashir long after the sun had set, but Zelenka and Urian insisted they try. Though the brothers of Saint Bhenádíctus were missionaries by nature and traveled constantly through most of their lives, as long as their health permitted, Kavan suspected the blind man had traveled more in the last few months than he had throughout the rest of his life. Not that Urian complained. True to his calling of Faith, he remained annoyingly cheerful, even when doing his utmost to influence the group to seek proper beds and meals each time they reached a town. Zelenka, on the other hand, had not left her village since birth and was now hundreds of miles away from everything she knew. Neither riding a horse for hours at a time nor walking day after day were activities she was accustomed to. Nor did she enjoy them. They stopped too often, rested too long, as Kavan tried to accommodate her needs.

But he needed to return to Rhidam. Soon. The malignant force had not been felt since he had confronted it, and he feared that the longer they spent on the road, the sooner it would return for him…or that it had moved on to Rhidam to wreak havoc and destruction while he was too far away to stop it. He did not know how long he had before the cleansing must be done, but these delays could not be good. Having been told he would know the day when it arrived, he worried he would miss the deadline and be forced to wait another year before he could make the attempt. If the attack on Ártur was any indication, Enesfel could not afford to wait another year.

Tomorrow, while Urian and Zelenka gathered food, water, and supplies from the local monks, Kavan intended to search Yashir for a Gate while Wortham sold the horses. It was a difficult choice to make, but with the money gained from their sale, Wortham could replace his armor and sword, things deemed more important to their survival, and a pack animal to carry the rest of their belongings. They might even be able to replace their lost clothing and Urian's whittling tools. If they were lucky, perhaps they would have enough left to replenish their supplies once they reached Enda.

From there, they had little enough distance to travel before they were home.

Or Kavan could sing. He had not performed before an audience since leaving Myreth and he wanted it, badly. Music and lyrics crowded his thoughts, demanding an escape. There had been a bound ledger in the rover's wagon, mostly blank, and a quill and ink. When they camped each evening, Kavan wrote his days' worth of creativity on the empty pages, purging his soul, only to find that by the next evening there was more to set down. He did not consider himself a lyricist or poet; before the tragedy with his hands, he had not composed many musical works for voice that were not prayers written by Kóráhm and others or sacred passages. Without his harp, however, after many months without creating music, his soul had a backlog of emotion to release. Wortham asked often what he was writing. Kavan smiled at him and shook his head, intending to share those songs only when the time was right. If they ran out of money and the kindness of strangers, the White Bard of Bhryell would be able to perform for their room and board as he had in times past, only this time with his voice, not his harp.

Not tonight, however. Not in Yashir where the late hour meant the town was silent and most except for a few street patrols and fishermen were asleep. They tried to return to the inn where they had stayed during their last visit here, but the doors were locked, the lamps extinguished. Even the temple was shut for the night. They were forced to make camp at the city's edge, and when Zelenka again complained, Wortham did his best to gently remind her that if she had not insisted on frequent stops throughout the day, they could have arrived at a timelier hour and found the lodging they sought.

She glowered at him, pouting, and turned away to sleep.

Urian fell asleep quickly, while Kavan poured out the latest collection of words in his head. There was no listening to Wortham teaching Trade to Zelenka tonight, only the sound of Wortham's knife blade against his whetstone until he too lay down to sleep. Kavan's was the first watch of the night, the hour he normally took as he had grown accustomed to spending the late evening hours in prayer as a boy and had continued that practice into adulthood. When he was finally empty of the day's creativity, he lay back and stared at the starry sky, senses tuned to the approach of danger, his thoughts tangling around his cousin and those likely waiting for him in Rhidam.

The sun was beginning to brighten the eastern sky but Gaelán had not returned to his room. After the confrontation with his brother, he had spent the entire night wandering the grounds, dodging sentries and servants, trying to be alone with his troubled thoughts. There was a hole inside where the concept of family had been, a hole he was unable to fill with the flurry of thoughts and feelings that spun in his head. Having watched those people he lived and worked with, he had grown up believing that family was the one thing in the world that could not be destroyed except by external forces such as death. But he was a spectator now to Ártur and Syl struggling with their marriage, to Ártur combatting his family's prejudices and fears, and his own brother wanting him dead. Where was the stability of family in that?

His father sided with him, promised to protect him, but his mother had said nothing. She had not chastised Tayte, to Gaelan's knowledge, despite her obvious horror at his words. Gaelán suspected that, regardless of what her private words had been to his brother, they would not change anything. Others might believe this would pass, once Tayte adjusted to his brother's abrupt differences, but Gaelán did not. Perhaps the Elyri in his blood sensed that Tayte's words burned deep with jealousy. Or perhaps he was being pessimistic and paranoid. But Gaelán could believe neither of those things. His brother spoke what he believed, and that scared him.

There had been despair at first, and then anger as his shattered illusions of family failed to reform. By the first hint of dawn, Gaelán had made his choices. His mother might not be pleased, his father might not approve, but it was his life, his future, and he did not believe there was any other option open to him. Healing made him different. The Teren he met each day did not see him as Teren as they did his brother. They saw him as Elyri. Some accepted him, some did not. But he could not play the role of half any longer. He could not pretend to be something he was not. He might not share their longevity, or many other traits, but in every way that mattered, he was Elyri.

Decision made, he snuck back to his room, eluding the staff, and crawled into bed in the hopes of a few hours of sleep before Ártur came. As he dozed, he knew that from this day forward, his life would change. He was no longer the son of Bhríd Cáner, the Elyri, and Madalyn Dubuais, the Teren. He was the child of Bhríd Cáner. He was Elyri, purely, completely, forever. The Teren in him shriveled and fell away during the night; only the Elyri remained and he embraced it.

ৎChapter 14ৎ

There were no Gates in the city of Yashir. If there ever had been, they had been too long disused and no longer radiated any power Kavan could detect. He searched the places most likely to contain one, the temple, the oldest structures in the area, spaces which might lend themselves to that secretive sort of travel. He tried shops, public areas, the docks, and though he did not enter homes, he had used each of his senses to scan for what he hoped to find. As scarce as Gates were, however, he had not expected to find one here, but he was still disappointed that he did not. A Gate might have meant no more traveling on foot, or at least very little of it, provided the Chalice and the staff crown did not conflict with the Gate's usage.

Unable to do anything more as the hour came to meet his friends, he went to the inn where they had previously stayed, expecting only to regroup and share a meal but discovering that their rooms had been held for them since their previous visit to the city. A costly loss for the innkeeper, if he had held the rooms vacant all of this time, or else Orynn had recently arranged the rooms for them. If k'ílshwythnec asked for something, it was given, whether the innkeeper was aware of her identity or not, and Kavan marveled that she had so much faith in his getting this far as to reserve them rooms ahead of time. The man refused payment, saying the charge had been covered for as long as the group needed to stay.

The resurrection of Orynn in his thoughts brought a melancholy clutching in his chest, as he left his belongings in the room he would sleep in, aware that Wortham had already been here to deposit the trunks in that same room, and returned to the downstairs tavern to await the others. He stared into the empty fireplace with the fleeting hope that the flames would burn the memories away for the night. He did not want to think about her; it brought pain to remember and pain brought despair, but to push those thoughts away felt like disloyalty, an affront to her memory and thus something he must bear. When he

ৎ167ৎ

saw her next, if he saw her, he did not wish to say she had been forgotten. Yet he knew he would never forget. When he closed his eyes, he believed her there, her hand on his, the smell of her, the sound of her breathing, were as real as if she was seated beside him now.

"Lord Cliáth!"

Kavan's eyes flew open, his ears playing tricks on him, half expecting the speaker to be Orynn. Instead, it was Zelenka, speaking his name for the first time since they had met. It was past the hour they were supposed to have gathered, and Kavan realized his daydreaming had lasted longer than intended. He did not understand the rest of her hasty words, except for Wortham's name, and yet from the sinking twist in his stomach created by her distress, he knew something bad had happened. Taking her hand between his to calm her, not daring to open his mind to her distraught thoughts, he looked at the blind man for answers, Urian's face dark with the same obvious concern.

"gdhededhá, what has happened?"

"Captain Delamo has been arrested."

"Arrested?" Kavan could scarcely say the word. Wortham was the most obedient, law-abiding person he knew. But they were in a strange land and it was possible the captain had unknowingly offended someone or broken a local ordinance without knowing it.

"I do not know why," Urian continued, sounding offended. "No one will tell us. They would not talk to Zelenka and they ridiculed me as a foreigner." Zelenka interrupted with another tirade and the monk translated with a growing frown. "She thinks maybe they recognized the horses, though why that should matter she does not know. Maybe they think the captain stole them…or worse. All of his purchases were confiscated. I am on my way to speak with the local priests in the hopes they can assist. We cannot continue on without the captain."

Kavan emphatically agreed. The man's physical and emotional strength, his companionship, were needed if Kavan was to make it to Rhidam. He would never be able to guide a blind monk and the frustratingly displaced woman to Enesfel without Wortham beside him. "I would never abandon him. One of us should stay to watch our belongings." The trunks and packs were stowed upstairs, but having had them stolen once, Kavan did not feel secure in leaving them, particularly if someone wanted to confiscate everything they owned as those who had arrested Wortham had done.

"You should do that, my lord. No offense, but I may need Zelenka to translate…and if someone wishes us harm, to delay us or steal what we own, I suspect you can protect them better than Zelenka or I can. Succeed or fail, I will let you know immediately."

Heart in his throat, Kavan murmured, "I will pray for that success." Remaining idle, not going to Wortham's side, went against everything Kavan was, everything Wortham was to him, but Urian was right. He was the best one to protect the treasures they possessed.

He was not good at waiting. He was a man of action when action was needed. When there was a problem, particularly with his friends, Kavan would do anything he could to correct it. He tended to procrastinate and avoided actively making corrections and changes in his own life, yet for those dear to him, he rushed to do whatever he could, hating helplessness. But the last time they had been in Yashir, it had been Urian who had gotten what they needed from the local monks, and it might hold true this time as well.

So Kavan prayed. And paced. He composed his prayers into beseeching hymns without consciously trying to do so. In the room where he intended to sleep, where the trunks sat at the foot of his bed with the cloth packs on top of them, he was soon singing out loud, and then louder still, as if begging anyone to hear him. k'Ádhá. Dhágdhuán. Kóráhm. Anyone. Wortham had to be freed or Kavan would be forced to do it himself. He had broken a man out of a dungeon before. He would easily and willingly do so again without a thought for his personal welfare.

There was a quiet knock on his door that interrupted his song, and he turned as it opened. Urian's expression said enough.

"I am sorry, my lord," the monk muttered, flustered, ashamed, mortified by his failure. "I tried all I could think of, even begging and bribery. While the k'dedhá spoke to the headman, to learn the nature of the captain's offense, he would not, could not, win his release. Involving themselves in domestic affairs is not allowed, he said. Even if a man is about to die, I asked, but he said they could only pray."

"About to die?" The strength left Kavan's legs and he collapsed into the nearest chair, clutching the arms of it until his knuckles hurt.

Urian could not see the bard but he could hear the distress in his voice. "Someone took offense to the captain selling the horses, as Zelenka feared; she thinks perhaps he should have bartered them instead…or kept them… and we might have been safe. The guards at the gaol would not tell us more. It was enough of an offense to someone that they demanded his execution, and whoever that accuser is, they seem to have enough influence that, unless someone steps forward to by the captain's freedom before sunset tomorrow, he will be executed at dawn two days hence. They are asking for more than we can pay. Six hundred krips, the k'dedhá said. Even the sale of the horses had not gained us that much. Selling the Diwi and Orec and everything else we possess would not be enough. I do not know how we can help him, my lord, short of begging for a miracle."

"Executed." Kavan's voice faded into a choked silence and he closed his eyes. Miracles occurred in his life. That Kavan lived could be considered a miracle by many, given the events he had endured. But as Wortham had pointed out to him long ago, it was most often the miracles Kavan did not actively seek that were granted. The times when Kavan prayed hardest for divine intervention, none came.

This would certainly be one of those times of prayer, for Kavan could not in good conscience keep prayers silent on his friend's behalf, but would that mean Wortham was doomed to die? What was he to do? Chest aching, stomach twisting in sickening knots, he only knew he could not allow the man dearest to him to be executed.

"What should we do?"

Kavan looked at Urian with an effort to put on a brave, determined face that he knew the man could not see. Zelenka cowered behind the monk in the open doorway, her heartbroken expression of guilt, the belief that maybe she had caused this by her allowance to take the horses, was enough to steel the bard's resolve.

"If we cannot buy his release, I will see to it myself. Perhaps if I speak to the headman…"

"You do not know the language…"

"There are other ways to communicate. I will do whatever necessary, anything to get Wortham out of that place. Will you stay here with our belongings? I must try, must speak to Wortham and assure him that we are not abandoning him.

Zelenka said something to Urian with a tug on the sleeve of his robe and the dedhá said, "She thinks they will not allow you to see him at this hour."

"I will see him. That is one thing I promise." He rose from the chair with resolve, though the wobble in his knees reminded him that he was less confident than he appeared. "I may not return until late, but I will see him. Is there anything either of you wish to tell him?"

"That my prayers are with him," Urian replied as Zelenka, understanding enough of Kavan's words to know he would find a way to see Wortham, pushed something into the bard's hand. It was the first time she had touched him voluntarily and he offered her a gentle, sympathetic smile. In his palm was a flat, smooth, clear, pale pink stone. A charm for luck, the bard guessed without her explaining. "We will stay here until you return…and we will pray that the captain is with you when you do."

Kavan nodded, choked by emotion, and left the inn. Any other end did not bear consideration. It was not difficult to follow the beacon in his soul that was Wortham's heart and soul, to the building that served as the city's prison. He stood outside for many minutes, studying the auras within, assessing the situation. While perplexed, Wortham did not seem fearful. Either he did not know he was facing execution for some unspecified crime or he believed beyond doubt that Kavan would prevent such a thing. The man had such faith in him; Kavan could not let him down.

The guard at the door did not prevent Kavan from entering the building, but the man who waited inside behind a roughly built, shoddy desk rose as Kavan entered. The bard could not understand what the man said, and knew the fellow would not be able to understand him either. Grasping the man's wrist without speaking, as if in greeting, Kavan allowed for a brief mental exchange without the man knowing what was happening. Then Kavan released him, head bowed, swallowing the sigh that rose in the back of his throat and retreated from the room back into the twilight.

They would not permit him to visit his friend. He could persuade them to permit it, but should the headman return, those guards would suffer punishment for disobedience, and Kavan did not want that. Besides, there were other ways of getting inside, just as there were ways of getting Wortham out should the expected legal recourses fail.

For the moment, however, Kavan pondered the situation from the early evening shade of a tree across the street from the building. The story Urian had gotten out of the guards was all there was to know it seemed. The exact nature of the captive's crimes had not been revealed to the guards either, only the price of the requested bond and the time frame given to receive it. Kavan would seek to learn who had orchestrated Wortham's imprisonment when morning came, and he would do what he could to convince that person to release the captain into his custody. If he was unsuccessful and they could not raise the freedom price, Kavan would be left with one option.

"You cannot free him, kyag."

Kavan had heard the approaching footsteps but his mind had been too focused on finding a solution to this problem to recognize his companion until the man spoke. He did not look up but rather closed his eyes as if it would erase the words the saint had spoken. "I must, my lord. To leave him there is to let him die…and I cannot do that."

Kóráhm sighed. "You must accept his death. He is Teren. It is inevitable."

With a shudder, Kavan whispered, "Someday, perhaps…when he is old and has lived a long, full life. But not yet. I need him."

"Yes," the auburn-haired man agreed, "you do. He is not destined to die yet."

"Then I will succeed in winning his freedom?" The thought brought tentative joy back into Kavan's heart.

"I did not say that." Kóráhm leaned on the tree without looking at him. "I said it is not his time to die. Whatever happens, you must not free him from this. You will not like the consequences if you do."

"I will not like the consequences if I don't."

"Have faith when I say all will be well, Kavan."

"But how…?"

The Saint would not elaborate. In fact, he was gone as quickly as he had appeared, causing Kavan to scowl in frustration. Kóráhm's words forbid him to act, binding the bard in a way that he did not think he could obey. He might not be able to break Wortham free, but Kóráhm had not forbidden him from visiting, and this was the time to do it. Before he did something far worse.

The white rat slid between the bars of Wortham's cell window and waited on the ledge, watching and listening. The guard in the corridor and the one at the desk were asleep through no doing of Kavan's, but it was to his benefit as long as they did not wake. Wortham huddled in one corner to absorb the warmth from the clay walls, whistling a song in the dark that Kavan recognized as one of his. The captain did not notice the rat until it leaped from the ledge onto the floor beside him. He started to shoo it away, the ghostly coloring of the creature not striking him as familiar, but as he scooped up pebbles from the stony floor to throw at the creature, to chase it away, the rat disappeared and Kavan sat in its place.

"My lord Cliáth!" Kavan placed his fingers to the man's lips but it did not stop Wortham from adding, "You frightened me."

"I apologize for that." He could have touched Wortham's mind, announced his nearness and intention, but in his haste to see Wortham again, he had not considered it. He dropped his hand and looked the man over for any sign of injury or abuse. "They will not allow us to visit you; I had to gain access any way I could."

"I am grateful you came; perhaps you can tell me what is happening. None of my keepers will speak to me."

Sliding nearer, getting as comfortable as the hard ground would permit, Kavan asked, "Can you tell me what happened today? Everything you remember?" It might help him piece together what had gone wrong to place the captain in this precarious position.

"See for yourself." He took one of the bard's hands in his, his mind open to Kavan without hesitation, an indicator of trust that Kavan found with few others. Wortham had found a man trading in livestock, horses, goats, and cattle. He sold the horses to the fellow without difficulty, fine, sturdy animals that they were, and had gone off to find the supplies on his list. While looking for a set of whittling tools for Urian, several of the town's guards entered the shop, grabbed him without word or accusation, took all of his purchases and the coins in his pouch, and brought him here. Wortham knew nothing more, had seen nothing that might have alerted him to trouble, and nothing Kavan could see or hear in those memories explained what had happened. Wortham had been in this cell since mid-morning, wondering if his companions were aware of his predicament. He was thankful Kavan had found him.

The bard leaned back, his lips pursed into a frown. While not a rare expression, Wortham knew that something was more wrong than usual. "What is it? What did you see?"

"Nothing…" That was the problem. He shook his head. "Zelenka and Urian learned that someone took affront to the sale of the horses…but we do not know who. She thinks perhaps someone recognized them and considered you a thief, a murderer, or both. The accuser has enough influence to demand your arrest, and enough to ensure that, unless bail is paid by sunset tomorrow, you will be executed the following dawn." His final words died into sadness.

"Executed?" Wortham's frown mirrored Kavan's. "For selling horses? Don't I get a trial?"

"This is not our land…we cannot expect our customs to hold here. Urian asked the monks to intercede, but the religious cannot interfere in secular matters it seems. Nor can we afford to pay. Even the Diwi and Orec will not provide enough coin, nor selling all we own, but I will sell it all if I must."

Wortham squeezed Kavan's hands tightly. "No. You will not. You need those things to cleanse the chapel…"

"I need you, Wortham." Kavan stared at their joined hands before continuing. "Those are commodities. I will find a way to replace them. You, I cannot replace. I cannot allow you to die."

"You will free me." He knew Kavan had done it with Caol, long ago. It was logical to expect it now.

Kavan's voice caught. "I wish I could."

"Wish…why…?"

"Kóráhm has forbidden it; he told me I must not…" His voice choked in his throat, strangling around the small sob that came with it.

"Then I will die." It was not the sort of death he had imagined for himself, he had always assumed he would die in battle, in service to Kavan, protecting his life, but he was determined to meet his end with dignity, no matter how it came.

Kavan shook his head. "You will not."

"But you said…"

"Kóráhm said not to release you…but he also said this is not your time to die."

Sighing with strained relief, feeling little of the doubt he could hear in Kavan's voice, Wortham said, "Then we shall have faith and believe his words."

Sounds from outside in the street caused both men to jump, but it was only a passerby dropping something that created a loud, metallic clatter. We must have faith, Kavan thought, but Kóráhm is not infallible. He was not as a man, and whatever he was now, a small part of Kavan latched onto the possibility that there was a chance that Kóráhm could be wrong. Faith would carry the bard as long as it could, but when it came to it, he would risk setting Wortham free regardless of the consequences.

"You should go, my lord. The others are waiting for you…and it would not do for anyone to find you here."

Though Kavan knew it to be true, he did not want to leave. The captain, however, to encourage cooperation, pulled him to his feet. "Here…Zelenka asked me to give you this. For luck, I believe. And gdhededhá Urian asked me to tell you he is praying for you."

The captain nodded, clasping the stone in his hand as if it were a holy relic meant to save his soul. "I hope you are as well, Kavan."

"Always, Wortham."

"Then all will be well."

The bard nodded and faded from sight, the rat reappearing in his place at Wortham's feet. Lifting the animal to the window, rubbing his thumb along its furry back, Wortham watched when it leaped to the ground outside and scurried away into the darkness. Rather than lying down to sleep, he remained where he was, watching the stars, wondering how many more nights he would have to enjoy their perfection.

❧Chapter 15❦

"Claide!"

Tusánt dropped his stylus and knocked over the inkwell when the senior gdhededhá appeared in his doorway without preamble or warning or announcement of his return. The young man seated beside him looked up, blinking in surprise, but there was no hint of distress in his reaction as there was in Tusánt's, despite the Elyri's effort to temper it. "When did you return? We received no word you were back."

The thin man looked down the length of his angular nose with an expression that suggested he would prefer not to talk to Tusánt if he could avoid it. "Late last night. Everyone was asleep, though I did see dedhá Hazen in the chapel."

For Tusánt, that meant the man had come in near midnight, as Hazen was often found in prayer in the thol at that hour. Not many people would travel that late into the night, and it made him wonder if Claide had tried to hide his return. Seeing the way Claide was looking at his companion, Tusánt cleared his throat and said, "You remember Edward Lindunn…" He considered welcoming Claide home, but as he felt no welcome for the man, he left the sentiment unspoken.

Edward rose and offered his hand, a gesture of greeting he knew was expected even if the man was looking at him with unhidden disdain. "I am here to follow my desired calling to be gdhededhá, sir. I begged dedhá Tusánt to accept my instruction, as he was the most senior dedhá here…"

A logical reason, as novices usually sought training from the most senior clergy, and neither Jermyn nor Claide had been here. There was no need for Claide to be suspicious, and little need for Edward to explain himself. Now that he knew Edward's name, he recognized the young man who had served as altar attendant for many years but had matured significantly since last in Rhidam.

"Rankin and I both interviewed him," Tusánt interjected. "His path is clear and well-chosen…and there is another…"

"Another novice?" Under Jermyn, there had been many novices pass through Hes á Redh Náós. Tusánt had trained some of them, as had Rankin, and Claide. The majority had been trained by the k'gdhededhá, however, as was expected, a fact that had greatly irritated Claide despite the normalcy.

"Saul Peado, from Alberni. He arrived several days before Edward; his family wishes for him to enter the Faith." Not entirely accurate, but it was true enough for Claide's ears. "I accepted his apprenticeship as well, but of course, we will have to see how true his calling is." There was no doubt about Edward's. "If you demand it, of course, I will turn Saul's instruction over to you…"

It was the last thing Tusánt wanted, but the offer had to be made.

"No…no need for that." Tusánt was surprised at how quickly Claide rejected the idea, and just as quickly disavowed of that surprise as Claide continued, "With the state of things, I may not have the time to train novices; it is best they remain under your instruction for the time being. I never understood how Jermyn found the time for those he taught."

The Elyri tensed. He understood, or thought he did, the implications of those words better than Claide realized. His speaking of Jermyn in the past tense did not go unnoticed. Perhaps Claide did not want novices in order to keep others from learning his plans and intentions.

Although Claide spoke of Jermyn in the past tense, understandable if he had heard of the k'gdhededhá's death, Tusánt dared to presume he did not know and murmured, "The k'gdhededhá should train them…but now that he is dead…"

"Dead? He was found? When? Where? What happened?"

Despite their suspicions about Claide and his motives, the man's shock seemed genuine if superficial. Tusánt bowed his head and swallowed hard before answering. "Lord Dugan found his body in an abandoned building. He was badly tortured…I saw him myself. It was…horrific. There was a message in his death, I am sure of it. No one does something like that for sport." If he was expecting Claide to confirm it, he was disappointed, but there was a look of confusion in Claide's eyes, as if something Tusánt had said made no sense. "As per his wishes, his remains were taken to his home town for disposition, the gdhededhásur of Saint Kóráhm's permitted him to be buried in their plot; it seemed fitting…"

"Yes…certainly…a perfect place." His tone sounded distracted. "It would have done no good to bury him here."

Tusánt wondered what that meant. "I sent word to k'gdhededhá Dórímyr, but there has been no response yet. He may have only recently received the news, or the messenger has yet to reach him."

Claide paced the width of the small room, his hands flexing at his back as if he was nervous or perhaps wanting to lash out in violence. Tusánt wanted him to leave, wanted to speak with Edward about what he saw and heard, but Claide showed no sign that he was going anywhere. "Continue with the novices. It appears I may have elections to organize if Dórímyr fails to respond. Any others that come, pass some along to Rankin. I do not believe Valgis is prepared to take on novices." He paused, rubbing his chin as he continued pacing, and then asked, "Has there been any other news during my absence?" as if Jermyn's death was not news enough.

Hearing no remorse or sympathy over the death of his superior, Tusánt bit back the words he wanted to say and instead answered the question. "The King is having a banquet tomorrow eve. The Crown has taken on a Teren physician…"

"Lord MacLyr was released? Or has something happened to him?"

Claide seemed more interested in the healer than in Jermyn's death, a realization that made the Elyri bristle. "A precaution." He decided the attack on the healer was none of Claide's business, that if he heard the news, it would not be from Tusánt. Nor did he think Claide needed to know about Ártur's arrangement with his wife or that Gaelán Cáner had become part of the Royal House's medical entourage. "His name is Rouvyn Talis."

"Interesting." Claide did not sound interested at all. He sounded pensive and distracted. "If there is nothing more, I am off to breakfast and to speak with Rankin and Valgis. Afterward, I shall visit the Lachlans and offer my condolences; I know the royal family was fond of the k'dedhá. I shall offer my services in his place, of course, and later today I will interview our novices. Be sure they are available."

He departed without another word. Comfort the Lachlans? Offer his services? Tusánt decided he had best make his own visit to the palace before Claide had a chance to go there. He had to warn the princess that the man had returned, and tell her that Claide had his sights set on the Enesfel k'gdhededhá's seat. It was as they had expected. Expected and feared. The man who had shown no remorse over Jermyn's death, who may have had a hand in it, had to be stopped.

❧*❧

"You must go to Rhidam, Your Grace. It is your duty."

The k'gdhededhá of Clarys, the head of the Faith in the Five Sovereignties, lowered his water glass, his hard gaze tearing up from the papers on his desk to stare at his aide. With his pale blue robes spread around his feet, he looked more like royalty than the head of the Faith, but such attire had become commonplace for the k'gdhededhá centuries ago and few thought little of the opulence, if they noticed it at all. "It is not your place to instruct me on duty, Hwensen," he growled, the haughtiness of his tone mirroring the self-importance of his dress.

Though the younger aide was normally easily cowed by the man he served, preferring to keep the peace rather than make waves, today he felt compelled to stand his ground. "Someone must. If what they say is true, to allow gdhededhá Claide uncontested free reign in Enesfel will be disastrous for the Faith and our relations with…"

"We are the Faith. We are not a political entity."

"You know that is not true…not in practice at least. We have our own politics…and I was not referring to secular relations. If a k'gdhededhá is chosen who can turn Enesfel against us, turn all of the Teren Sovereignties against us, it will fracture the Faith and be a danger to Elyriá. You must meet the candidates, appoint a new k'gdhededhá. It is the only way to keep the peace…"

Dórímyr set his glass down with a heavy-handed thud. He had held this post longer than any of his predecessors and he was used to the control, to getting his way. Those who crossed him, or lectured him, often found themselves relieved of their position, and as he stared at Hwensen, he was debating a similar fate for this particular aide. Dórímyr hesitated, however, because Hwensen was the most efficient and capable aide to serve him to date and because he owed the man's brother a hefty debt that he did not yet feel was settled.

"Would you have me place my life in danger? What good would it be if I was murdered abroad? If they killed the k'gdhededhá, another Teren, what makes you think someone would hesitate to kill me?"

It was a strong argument, a valid point, but Hwensen pressed, "dedhá Tusánt is there; no one has harmed him. Take your guards.

Demand that the Lachlans provide you with an army if that would assure you. But you must do something; to do nothing is…"

Hwensen could not continue. Dórímyr's face was red and his eyes flashed angrily. "Is what?"

With a shivering sigh, Hwensen finally found his voice. "To do nothing is to tell all Elyri that you do not care about their welfare." He left the room, not wanting to bear the backlash from the man's anger any longer. Fortunately, Dórímyr did not summon him back.

Gaelán had assembled everyone he wanted to speak to in the dayroom, where he anxiously awaited their arrival. Ártur, Asta, Bhyrhán, his mother and father. He wished Kavan could be there, but it was best his brother was not included. And this was not something the King needed to hear. Bhyrhán was there in Kavan's place, a moral support surrogate. What he intended to say, he wanted to say only once because he did not think he would have the courage to explain it again. Others would learn of it when it was important for them to know.

When everyone was assembled and seated, his parents clasping their hands and watching him with concern, the young man cleared his throat and got up from the bench where he had forced himself to wait without fidgeting. Refusing to pace though he wanted to, he faced his mother, barely able to maintain eye contact; she would be the one most hurt by his words, but he hoped he could make her understand that this was for the best.

"I…please forgive me, mother. I have done a lot of thinking during the night. After what occurred," how many knew about Tayte's words, he did not know, "I do not think I will be going back to Levonne. Rhidam is my home now, with father." He swallowed as his mother nodded sadly and Bhríd squeezed her hand. It seemed they were less surprised by his choice than he expected, and looked as if they had assumed they would hear something much worse.

But he was not done speaking. "I also want each of you to know something…as I know it. I understand that I am different. I can never be full Elyri, but nor can I be Teren. In the eyes of those who know me, I am more Elyri than Teren. Some are afraid of me. I don't want them to be, but they are. I could cease training, go back to Levonne, pretend I'm something I'm not…but the truth is always there. I look Elyri. I have Elyri gifts. I will be treated as one regardless."

"Gaelán…"

"Please, mother…let me finish. What I am, what Tayte is not, is not your fault. Or father's. I don't blame anyone. That would be foolish. But I cannot deny destiny. I am a healer, for however long the ability persists. k'aendhá explained that the power, the abilities, may fade with time…because of my blood, but should that day come, I will have been trained as any Teren physician as well. I will still be a healer. It is an honorable profession that will bring the family no shame, and perhaps by helping people, they will be less afraid of me."

Bhríd leaned back in his chair, letting out a breath he had not known he was holding. This was Gaelán stating residency and a chosen profession, nothing more. This was acknowledging truths of blood he could not avoid. He had feared something else. "There is no shame in such a profession, as you say, and we honor your decision. We have faith you will be a good and just healer. And we agree," he looked at his wife to gauge if that agreement stood, "that you remaining in Rhidam, with me, is in your best interest."

"There is more." Gaelán looked at Ártur, trying to see Kavan there, but since the older healer's recovery, Kavan's presence had been absent. There had been no more episodes of seizures, no pain or blackouts, and Gaelán felt a deep hole in his life where Kavan had once been. If Kavan had been here for this, everything would have felt so much simpler.

"For the sake of sanity and simplicity…I am Elyri. I cannot be Teren. I cannot live as both, or as Teren, because no one will permit it. By the necessity of what others see in me, and my own choice, I will be Elyri from this day on. Completely, or as completely as I am able to be."

"I am your mother."

He sighed and looked at his feet, a response to her dejected pain. Feeling it surround him like a smothering embrace made It difficult to continue. "I cannot deny it…nor do I wish to. In my heart, you will always be loved as my mother. But don't you see? When people discuss who I am, it is 'Bhríd Cáner's son'…not the son of Madalyn Dubuais. Tayte is the only one referred to as your son…the Teren son…never me. The world marked us, separated us as far back as my memory serves. I've decided to accept that, and am letting you know. I must shed the things I am not and devote myself to what I am. There is no other way to protect you, mother…or my brother."

Madalyn reached for him but he was beyond her grasp and her hand fell limply away. "You will be in such danger."

"I am already in danger. When I considered myself half Teren, there was a sense that the world would see it too and not hate me or wish me harm. But you heard Tayte. It will never be true and it's foolish for me to cling to that hope. At least, by embracing the truth, I can be better prepared…or at least not surprised at the insults."

He watched his father rise, half-fearing what the man would say. Bhyrhán's face was unreadable. Asta was grinning, though he did not know why, and Ártur was staring at his hands. If Gaelán wanted support, it did not appear he was receiving much of it. Bhríd placed his hands on his son's shoulders and squeezed gently.

"Not long ago I said that you were still a child, that you did not possess the wisdom of an adult. That appears to have changed. There is wisdom in what you say that not many would admit to, and there is courage in your choice. We cannot deter your path, nor should we, but let me remind you of one thing. You are young. The future can change and you may one day find that you must change your mind. There is no shame in that either. Remember that, though you have chosen the Elyri path, you do not need to deny your mother your love to do so."

Gaelán embraced his father, knowing the gesture might not be adult-like, but not caring. He had spoken his heart and it seemed his parents loved him still. Even his mother's eyes shown with pride behind the sorrow. He wondered fleetingly if Ártur's parents had ever loved him enough to accept him and let him go.

"Would it be improper to inquire as to the details surrounding the k'dedhá's death?

Improper, no, but if the inquisitor had his way, or the princess had hers, dedhá Claide would be told nothing. But they knew the King would reveal the details as he knew them because that was his way. He trusted all dedhá unfailingly. At least Caol could relax in the knowledge that Claide would never know the full story because the most important details had been kept from Hagan. Much of the public story Claide already knew, details the princess suspected her uncle had not yet proven. She was grateful she and Caol were here, with her brother, when Claide came to call.

"Lord Corbin's men found the body in an abandoned warehouse," the King began.

"I was told Lord Dugan discovered it…"

The inquisitor bristled, wondering who had told him that and how he could explain a discrepancy in the story should the King ask. But the monarch seemed not to hear anything unusual and continued, "Well, yes. Technically, Justice Corbin's men found the warehouse and Lord Dugan helped them gain access and thus was the first one to see the corpse. It was a terrible sight. He was brutally tortured, mutilated; if not for the ring on his hand and dedhá Tusánt reading him, we might not know who he was. The warehouse owner took his life before we could learn much from him, but apparently, he had no direct knowledge of the k'dedhá' demise, but he did give us a name…"

"Which," interrupted the inquisitor, "is better left unmentioned. We do not want the suspect to learn we are on to them until we are prepared to make an arrest."

Nodding, Claide pursed his lips in frustration. "Of course; that is wise. It is unfortunate no one was able to locate Jermyn while he lived…to save his life. This puts the Faith in a quandary, Your Majesty. Enesfel is without a k'gdhededhá. Tusánt has sent word to k'gdhededhá Dórímyr, but it may take overly long to reach him. He should come, appoint a new k'gdhededhá; it is the way it is done, but who knows when that might occur, or if it will. His plans to visit Enesfel have never come to pass before."

The King straightened on his throne and frowned. "Surely he will come now; it is his duty."

"Duty, yes," muttered Claide in a bored tone, "but who would blame him for hesitating given the dangerous conditions? His safety and security would be a prime concern…and we cannot wait indefinitely. It may become necessary for the Enesfel Faithful to elect their own k'gdhededhá."

"Can we do that?" asked the King. Caol kept Diona from interrupting with a hand on her arm, and though her expression eased back to neutral, she did not relax.

Claide shrugged. "It is not standard protocol, but there are provisions for such a measure in the ecclesiastical annals. Shall I investigate the matter and make preparations?"

Caol read the eagerness in that question and believed the hawkish man had already done all of the investigation into the matter he needed. He was tempted to interrupt too, but for once, whether because he heard the eagerness too and found it suspect or because he was not yet prepared to let Jermyn go, the King chose a more sensible approach. "We will wait. The k'gdhededhá must have time to be notified, time to consider the matter, respond, make plans to travel…and to travel if that's what he chooses. The Faithful can function for a time without a k'dedhá; they have already been doing so. When I think we have waited long enough, or k'dedhá Dórímyr tells us he will not come, then we shall see about elections."

The corners of Claide's eyes and mouth twitched as he stood to depart. "Very well, Your Majesty. I pray your choice is the wisest."

Hagan frowned at the man's seeming dissention but quickly pushed the feeling away as Diona spoke, interrupting the dedhá mid-bow. "Oh, dedhá, how was your trip? Did you see Father Loefel? He is such a dear old man; I grew quite fond of him when he was here and intend to travel north to see him again."

Expression puzzled but as bored as before, Claide replied, "dedhá Loefel is good, as mischievous as ever. He did inquire about you, My Lady, and I was pleased to tell him you are in good health."

She smiled gratefully and asked. "And dedhá Eleza? Is Fiara's naós in satisfactory condition? Lord Lachlan wrote to me that he thought it is in need of repairs?"

"It is?" asked the King. "He never mentioned it to me…"

"Nor have I heard it," Claide remarked. "We did not discuss many details we should have, I'm afraid. There are many small naós there that required my attention, but sadly my time was too short to cover all of the business I should have. I would have remained in the north longer to see to it, but with k'gdhededhá Jermyn missing, I felt it wiser not to stay away from Rhidam any longer. There are matters here that needed my attention, whether he was found or not."

"Yes, there are." The King got to his feet. "You will need to shoulder his duties until a replacement is appointed. Or elected. Shall I see you out, dedhá?"

Though it vexed him to leave the King alone with Claide, Caol chose not to accompany them. He waited until they were out of hearing range before turning to Diona with a curious frown.

"Small talk?"

She laughed at his suspiciousness but there was a hollow note of seriousness to the sound. "Information. Owain and Espen contacted each of the naós in and around Fiara; none had seen Claide or expected to see him. None except Shepherd's Heart in Fiara were expecting a visit from k'dedhá Jermyn either. He was to inspect facilities, after the request for repair funds, to see what needed to be done."

Caol snorted. "And Claide is not even aware that repairs are needed. And dedhá Loefel?"

"Died two weeks prior to Claide's trip. The news of his passing reached dedhá Tusánt a few days ago, but I learned of it earlier, as one of the women who saw to his dietary needs knew I was fond of him and sent word on the day of his death. If he inquired about my health, if Claide saw him…"

"Then either dedhá Loefel should be canonized or Claide is speaking with the dead. You know I received seven separate reports of Claide being seen in Rhidam…that we were likely correct and Claide did not leave the city. It's possible he knows a great deal more about what we have done than we want him to know."

The princess chewed her lip. "We will have to pray that we are in a position to act before he does. I wonder if Hagan would execute his sister for treason."

"I don't know," the inquisitor said with an offered hand, "but I suspect he would execute me…unless Asta could stop him."

❭*❬

It took too long for Kavan to locate the headman in a decrepit tavern on the north edge of Yashir, a wasted effort since the man had nothing to say to Kavan over the lip of his mug of spirits. Forcing mental contact revealed what little Kavan already knew: a young man, a messenger had come to the headman with money and the demand to have the bearlike foreigner arrested. Who had sent the messenger, however, the headman did not know. Nor did he care.

Frustrated, Kavan spent the remainder of his morning in search of that messenger, or for the livestock seller the captain had sold the horses to, but neither was found. The livestock seller had traveled on to his next destination, and no one was able to direct Kavan to a man matching the courier's description. It was as if the whole of Yashir had been sworn to secrecy, but Kavan's touch on those minds he suspected of lying revealed that not one person knew who he was seeking.

The sun had slid past its zenith when Kavan went to the dock, not expecting to find anything of use there but hoping the one place he had not searched might yield an unexpected answer. There was a large ship anchored offshore, not as large as the ghost ship but larger than the typical trading transports that roamed up and down this southern coast. Its gilded sides and the three deep crimson and yellow sails marked her as a vessel of wealth that he deemed to be a personal vessel of someone of note, someone familiar enough with the ghost ship's description to model their ship after it. He watched her for some time, wondering where she had come from, why the sight of her filled him with hope. She was being unloaded into several small skiffs and by the time it was necessary to meet with the magistrate, the ship appeared to be empty as the skiffs ceased their trips.

What was their cargo, he wondered, turning back to the duty at hand, swallowing the nervous bile at the back of his throat. Why did her crew not come ashore themselves?

Rarely one to give up hope, he was beginning to despair of finding the answers to Wortham's freedom. His last avenue required a mid-afternoon appointment, at the cusp of the day's end, when the remaining hours might be too few to allow action if he failed. Unable to place his faith entirely in Kóráhm's words, however, there was still time. Until the headman took Wortham away from him, there was time, a chance, and Kavan intended to make use of it.

The magistrate's home was as sparse as everything else in Yashir, as barren as the lands around her inland perimeter. The slight, handsome man escorted Kavan into the garden terrace that shaded his front door. He spoke quickly, as if in a hurry, and though Kavan had begun to learn some of the words of the languages in this land, he could make no sense of the man's hasty speech. He offered a hand as if in greeting, or to thank the magistrate for his time, and only in doing so was Kavan able to learn what he needed to, his questions fed through their contact, answers gleaned the same way.

It was another dead end. The man knew less about Wortham's arrest then Kavan did. He promised to look into the matter, discover the cause of arrest and work for his release if his arrest appeared to be in error. But if the accusations held, there would be little he could do. And at this late hour, he might not, Kavan knew, be able to act swiftly enough to see justice done. But he promised he would try as he ushered Kavan back to the garden gate and deposited him in the street.

Promise. The offer was sincere, but there was a nagging sense that the man had no intention of following through on that promise. Even if he did, the avenues of information would be much the same as those Kavan had followed, meaning he would learn very little of use in the hours Wortham had left. The sun would set soon. If the release fee was not paid quickly, Wortham would run out of time.

Holding back his anger and the sinking, sick feeling in his belly, Kavan returned to the tavern, hoping for promising news from Urian. At the door, not paying any particular attention to the people he passed in the street, he was stopped by a hand on his arm, a nondescript, plainly dressed middle-aged man in attire that marked him as a foreigner as well, looking at him expectantly.

"Pardon, my lord," he said in a stilted, heavily accented attempt at the Trade Tongue. Not the messenger Kavan had been seeking, but a messenger nonetheless. The fact that he spoke in a language Kavan understood was enough to gain the bard's full attention. "I am sent to inquire what you might need for your journey."

"Might need…? Journey?"

The man bowed and placed a parchment and writing stick in Kavan's hand. "Pardon if my meaning is unclear. If you will list the items you need to travel and have it ready for me within the hour, my patron will see to your needs."

The unexpected offer made Kavan suspicious of someone wanting to be rid of him before the hour of Wortham's execution, wanting to fill his time with some matter other than Wortham's release. "Who is your patron? Why do they wish this? I am traveling nowhere without my companions…including the one falsely accused and awaiting execution." If this was some plan to divide his party, it would fail.

The man shrugged. "I know nothing of that, my lord…but I will see that my patron is aware of the matter. I was instructed to make inquiry and report back, nothing more. I will return in one hour, when my other errands are complete."

He slipped away, leaving Kavan, perplexed, to enter the tavern alone. Urian and Zelenka were sharing a platter, the dedhá eating heartily of a decent meal for a change while Zelenka only picked at it. Kavan had no appetite, had not had one all day. If he spent his evening eating and compiling this list, he would certainly fail his friend.

Perhaps the official was the patron. Or Kóráhm. Or even Orynn.

Regardless of who it was, he was not leaving without Wortham.

But there was no way to raise the necessary money now, unless he stole it. Not even playing in the city square would gain him the price he was expected to pay. If he put the price at the top of his list, he might gain the sum from this mysterious patron. It was worth the attempt. An hour for the messenger's return, and perhaps an hour back, would leave the bare minimum time to get the price paid.

There was no more time to waste.

Zelenka lowered her gaze, her hands clasped on her lap, when Kavan joined them at the table, alone. There was no need for Kavan to state the obvious.

"There is still time for a miracle," Urian said.

"Perhaps…" The only miracles Kavan could hope for now was a reversal of the charges, the magistrate's intervention on Wortham's behalf, or the aid of this potential patron. He spread the page on the table "I have been instructed to make a list of what we require to continue our journey…"

"List?" Zelenka understood that word but not the rest fully.

"I do not know who…if they are friend or foe, but if someone wishes to be of aid, it might be a mistake to reject the offer. Wortham's release, or the price to be paid swiftly, is at the top of the list and I am praying that will be enough. I will not leave him here…not like this…whatever happens, I will take him with us…"

"You think he will die?" Urian's voice was heavy.

"I pray not, gdhededhá. It would…I would…"

The blind man reached across the table and clasped Kavan's wrist. "Go to him; perhaps they will allow him to see you. Perhaps that will be enough to sway them."

Intending to do that much later, Kavan shook his head. "First," he said in a small voice, "we make this list. Once it is on its way…"

The longer he waited, the deeper the night, the more likely he could get the captain away. He had every intention of doing just that if this list failed to succeed.

❧*❦

Asta turned before the mirror, trying to see her reflection from every angle. Having little experience with gowns of this sort, only now permitted by her father and social mores to graduate from the attire of a girl into something befitting a woman, she could not decide if she liked what she saw or not. She would much rather have worn trousers, but tonight, she had a mission, and a gown such as this was more fitting. Smoothing the red velvet with her hands, she frowned and then adjusted the ribbon at her throat, from which hung the locket Gaelán had given her.

"You don't think this dress is…?" Diona looked gorgeous in such gowns, refined and elegant, at home in velvet and lace and satin, jewels at her throat, tiny pearl buttons and expensive embroidered accents. Asta had dreamed of the day she would wear such gowns, but seeing herself in one was discomfiting.

"Inappropriate?" asked the older woman with a laugh as she finished nesting ivory combs in her hair. "I felt that way my first time."

"I am not as…mature…as you." She did not feel like a child, she was of legal age to be a wife and mother, and had seen and done things in recent weeks that had yanked her from the realm of childish things, but she hardly had Diona's fuller figure or height, and felt that the rouge on her powdered cheeks looked unflattering and out of place.

Diona moved behind her and made adjustments to the way the dress hung. "Fourteen is hardly a child. Are you hoping to impress someone in particular? Gaelán perhaps?"

With her cheeks crimson, Asta tried to shrug and seem nonchalant. "I like him. He is not like anyone else…and I trust him, even if he is still a boy…"

"Only for a short while…he will be a legal man soon enough, a handsome one. Trust and honesty are important…as is respect." Her tone was thoughtful.

"He looks like his father…except for his hair."

"Yes, he does."

Turning from side to side to again inspect as much of herself as she could see, Asta murmured, "Can you keep a secret?"

"Of course." She was keeping many now. Another was not a burden. "What sort of secret?" She pointed to the bed, and when Asta was seated, Diona helped her lace her slippers.

"A girl secret…between cousins."

Mildly amused by Asta's embarrassment, finding it had been a long time since she had shared a girl to girl talk with anyone, even her chambermaids, Diona nodded. Asta giggled, leaned forward and whispered, "I kissed him." At Diona's grin, Asta hurriedly added, "Only a small one…on my birthday. Please don't tell my father."

"It was a kiss. Nothing more. I doubt your father would mind."

"But I'm his baby! And a girl! Fathers worry about that sort of thing, at least Gaelán says so. He does not want to dishonor me."

That was good to hear…and more than Diona had given Kavan, much to her shame and embarrassment. "Then he is a man to hold on to. I promise this is our secret. Now…let me dress your hair." There were chambermaids for this sort of thing, but Diona had wanted time with her cousin and sent them away. "If we do not hurry, the banquet will begin without us and Gaelán will be disappointed."

"As will Prince Espen."

About to protest, Diona picked up the hairbrush, noting Asta's impish smile in the mirror. "As will Prince Espen," she agreed, smiling in return.

❧*❧

There was no moonlight, no stars visible behind the clouds that rolled off the restless sea. Somewhere to the east, a storm brewed, but there was no indication yet that it might make landfall before dawn. With no torches or lanterns in range, the lack of moonlight meant Wortham's cell was darker than it had been the night before, a pall that reflected the shadows that felt to be strangling Kavan as he arrived. He again entered through the window, not trusting himself to face the guards, not wanting to be denied or have his visit with his friend hindered. The captain rose to greet him with a scowl, experience telling him the bard's thoughts without Kavan saying anything. He had not bathed, had not eaten, and from the looks of it, he had not slept either. Every detail made Wortham fret.

"You should not have come." He did not want his last memory of the bard to be the pale man suffering.

Touching the captain's face, Kavan struggled to restrain the sob choking him. "I could not stay away. I tried, Wortham…I truly did…"

"I know, my lord. I trust you. None of this is your fault."

"There must be something…I cannot leave you here to…"

Gripping Kavan's shoulders, Wortham grunted, "You will not do it, Kavan. I will not come with you willingly if Kóráhm says I must not." He wanted to do the exact opposite, leave with Kavan now, but neither the bard nor the saint had ever failed Wortham before. He did not believe either would now. "You would have to render me unconscious and carry me."

"I can do that." Kavan could break down the cell door, render the guards asleep, walk out with Wortham in his arms with very little effort. Only Kóráhm's admonition was keeping him from doing so, but he did not know how long he could fight that particular battle. "You would rather die than…?"

"I would rather trust k'Ádhá that Saint Kóráhm was honest. As should you."

Kavan sagged in the man's grasp, remaining on his feet only because Wortham held him there. "Then you are a better man than I." The thought of Wortham's death was an unbearable torment. Acutely aware of the press of each of the man's large fingers into his flesh, the strength of the man's arms and body, the scent of him, the sound of his breathing, Kavan made sure to imprint each of those things into his memory, anchors meant to keep Wortham with him for all eternity.

"That is why you should not have come; I knew when the sun set you had not..." Wortham paused to clear his throat of the emotion lodged there. "I made peace with my fate. If you had not come, you would not need to bear this burden..."

"I bear this burden whether here with you or not. To not come...I had to tell you...I love you, sínréc..."

It was an endearment Wortham had heard Ártur use with Kavan often, some form of special bond that, as Wortham understood it, was mostly used between kin or couples. But he did not know its precise meaning, and had never heard Kavan speak it to anyone, not even his cousin. To be given this place of honor in the Elyri's heart brought tears to the burly captain's brown eyes.

"I would know it whether you spoke the words or not. You are always with me." He pressed one hand to his own chest and then to Kavan's. "And I am always with you. Now...I beg you, my lord. Do not come at dawn. I will face what is to be alone. It will be easier for us both if I do not have to see your grief...and if you do not have to witness my fate. I do not ask for a promise, for it could be a promise broken and I do not want that to be the lasting legacy between us...but I do beg you. And I ask one last thing..."

"Wortham..."

The captain pressed his lips to Kavan's forehead and whispered, "A song. Words to comfort me at the end. A hymn to accompany me to Ethenae if that is to be my fate."

The hymn was fresh in his mind when Kavan, at last, collapsed onto his bed with his arm over his eyes, a mask shielding him from the world. He and Wortham had clung to each other as Kavan sang softly, both men weeping though trying not to for the sake of the other. The captain's fingers had tangled in Kavan's hair tightly enough that his scalp tingled still, and the bard's fingers and the skin of his neck prickled from the roughness of the man's beard. They had remained that way until Wortham pushed Kavan away, turned his back, and demanded the Elyri leave, and Kavan knew it was the most difficult thing both had ever done. Reluctantly he returned to this room, the parting too fresh, too raw, to allow sleep.

He knew he might never see Wortham alive again, no matter what Kóráhm said. The dawn might leave him alone in a way he had never been, and Kóráhm's words or not, Kavan could not bear the possibility that maybe the saint was wrong. As time crept past, he wondered how the saint could expect him to stay away, how Wortham could expect the same, if there was even the smallest chance he might win the man's freedom…or when he could certainly gain it on his own.

Visions of Wortham enduring one painful execution after another dragged through his mind, carving furrows of pain, reminding Kavan that he did not know how Wortham was destined to die. Quick and painless? Would he be tortured first? Would it be a public spectacle or a private affair? Kavan had not asked because he was afraid to know. Thus his imagination was gaining ground on his sanity, bringing with it panic and deepening misery. Even the hymn he had created, which he tried repeatedly to focus on since singing it to Wortham, was unable to compete with or still the horrors in his head.

Regardless of the penalty, Kavan decided at last, that it was a price he would gladly pay for all of eternity, Wortham had to live. Kavan needed him. He could endure anything as long as the beloved man lived.

He began to rise from the bed, determined to set Wortham free, only to be forcefully thrust back by sharp pains in his wrists and ankles, familiar pain that elicited a shriek of agony before he could bite the sound back. With his hands held over his head, pinned awkwardly against the wooden headboard, held immobile as he was, he knew without seeing the proof that there was blood, knew it before the wetness of it slid from his skin to soak the pillows and the sheets beneath him. The sensation of something sharp biting into his side, a hot, slicing pain he had experienced before, was expected but no less painful for it. Head tossing from side to side, he gasped, teary eyes unable to focus on anything as he struggled to remain conscious.

Humbled, humiliated, he understood, and his soul begged for mercy and forgiveness. He had given in to temptation, refused to trust Kóráhm's admonition, and k'Ádhá had sent a sign, a reminder. Why else was he experiencing this again after so long without it, the bedding growing slick and sticky beneath him? The last time had been with Myreth. He had thought it gone from his life, thought the bloodletting had served its purpose.

But this pain, the blood, the humiliation of it reminded him what he was rebelling against in his arrogance. To be pinned this way made it certain that he could not go to Wortham's aid, that he could not free his friend from the clutches of death because he could not free himself.

He was bound to an invisible pyre, bound the way Dhágdhuán had been bound and he could not escape his destiny.

"Wortham…" he moaned, the sound absorbed into the darkness. "Farewell." He could do nothing, through his suffering, except pray for the man's soul.

❧*❦

King Hagan smiled wearily as he watched his sister leave Owain's arms and return to Prince Espen's. She spared few dances for anyone other than the Hatu prince, only Owain and Caol and a single dance with Gaelán before Asta arrived. There was promise in the air between Diona and Espen, and the King hoped they would marry at last. In the eyes and opinions of many, that union was long overdue.

Asta's entrance into the Hall took Hagan's breath away. Her red velvet gown was more feminine and grown-up than anything he had seen her wear before, and he could see that no one was treating her as a child tonight, particularly not Gaelán. Though she danced three times with her King-cousin, and sometimes with her father or the chamberlain, she focused her energy on the apprentice healer much the way Diona focused on Espen. The King was smart enough to know that nothing except force would convince Asta to marry him now.

But there were others of interest amongst the flurry of colorful gowns. He had expected there to be three young women to select from, and instead, he was surprised by the number of eligible ladies who had turned out in response to his invitation, as if they all knew his intentions. Most he had never met before, a few he knew by name or had seen from a distance only. Not having advertised his purpose, it seemed that, with his ascent to the throne, his eligibility had brought every possible young noblewoman to him in the hopes of winning his attention and affection. Some were nice, a few were beautiful. Jilletta McPhelan demanded the most dances from him, as if it was her right and his obligation, and he reluctantly relented to her persistence because he did not have the stomach for public confrontation. Her efforts, however, further proved to him that she would not be his first choice for a queen. He had no desire to be tied to someone he might spend most of his time afraid of. It was difficult enough to stand up to his strong-willed, opinionated sister. He did not need a wife who would likewise intimidate him in every aspect of his life.

Still, he was left enough time to speak with, and dance with, many of the others. He had a lovely conversation with Ordelia Cornell, catching up on the months since they had seen each other last, but he felt no compulsion to marry her. She had been a friend, like Asta, since they were very young, and from appearances, as he watched the dancers move on and off the floor, his closest friend, Dayly Niall, had his sights set on her…and she on him.

All the better, he admitted with a sigh. Her grandfather, Minos Cornell, had been one of the earliest casualties of the anti-Elyri violence when news had leaked that he potentially carried traces of Elyri in his familial history. That meant that, as diluted as it was, Ordelia did too. Hagan knew that if he was to bring Elyri into the Lachlan bloodline, it might spell the end of a royal dynasty that had lasted for generations.

Which meant that by mid-evening, after picking his way through the uncomfortable process, he was faced with the two most promising candidates. Lira Brocke was not of noble birth, but her family was one of the wealthiest in Enesfel. She had an exotic, adult air though she was weeks younger than the King, and she was an excellent dancer. She was intelligent too, much like Diona, and pious. Not yet betrothed, there was talk by some that she was destined for a life of service in the Faith…unless her father, who was actively screening suitors, found what he deemed to be a suitable husband for her. She exhibited none of the quest for power and privilege Jilletta did, and enjoyed conversation and books. He did not know if protocol would permit such a marriage, but Hagan intended to look into the matter.

The other candidate was Dayly's sister Sigrid. Her beauty was not like Lira's or Asta's. She was delicate, refined, and simple in her style. She was also demure, quiet like Hagan, and considerably shyer than the King was forcing himself to behave this evening. She was not yet betrothed either, but according to Dayly, it was expected by her father that she would be married by the next Solstice Gathering.

On the dais at the side of the Hall, Bhyrhán was persuaded to play another round of songs by the boisterous collection of guests. The enthusiasm with which they greeted the Elyri minstrel was nearly enough to convince Hagan that the day to day anti-Elyri violence was little more than a nightmare, an aberration in a larger tapestry of peace. It was enough to remind him that he needed a new court musician. Lord Cliáth was not here, and unlike some others, the King did not think the bard was coming back, at least not for a very long time.

Perhaps Bhyrhán would stay if Hagan asked. Why the grandson of the High Mother would wish to, beyond some kinship it seemed he shared with the Healer and his not so hidden interest in Diona, Hagan could not say, but it would not hurt to inquire.

A commotion arose in the midst of the dancers, bringing Hagan to his feet. He pushed through the gathering, half-anticipating a fight between suitors, as often happened when men had too much to drink and were involved in the pursuit of women, or when noblemen brought their personal differences to bear in this inappropriate setting. Instead, it was Gaelán collapsed on the floor, limp, flushed, unconscious with Asta kneeling over him, trying to wake him up. Hagan sighed, and though he knew it was wrong and shallow to feel it, he could not help but think how it was just like Gaelán to interrupt the King's banquet by drawing attention to himself.

Though she showed no panic, Asta's eyes betrayed her fear, and Hagan hoped perhaps the situation was not as serious as it appeared. In the stifling air of a banquet hall, fainting was not uncommon. As long as no one had tried to poison Gaelán, how bad could it be? For someone to poison a boy, Elyri or otherwise, would be disastrous for the banquet, for his reign.

Madalyn, on the other hand, was gasping, squeaking in hysteria, asking for Tayte, though no one had seen him, asking why no one was trying to help her son. Hagan could not recall having seen Tayte all evening. Bhríd held his wife, trying to still and console her as the new Teren physician Rouvyn squeezed his way through the crowd, picked Gaelán up and started out of the Hall without a word. Asta and Gaelán's parents followed.

Whatever was wrong, tending him elsewhere was, the King agreed, the best thing to do, but by then, the damage had been done. Where there had been revelry, there was silence punctuated by hushed murmured rumors. The King bit the inside of his lip, wondering what he should do, what he should say? Did he send everyone away? Did he speak words of reassurance or pretend that nothing had happened? The rumblings of poison suggested he had to do something.

"He has fainted," Diona spoke to the guests nearest to her and the King, her smile easy and sincere, poised and diplomatic in a way Hagan's never felt to be. "The heat of the Hall. Open the doors…let in the air…and please…enjoy yourselves."

Thankful she had spoken, taken command of the situation though he knew he should have been the one to do so, Hagan pushed back to his chair, hoping he appeared unruffled and relaxed as he sat again.

Bhyrhán, as doubtful of those words as Diona was in the speaking of them, nodded to the princess, then to the King, and resumed playing. None of the guests moved, some staring in the direction the physician had gone, some at the King, some at each other as the whispers continued. It was Owain who turned to the woman next to him, older than himself but regal and stately in appearance, and drew her into another dance, caring little for who she was. Espen and Diona followed suit. From somewhere unnoticed, Lira reached the King's side, took his hand, and offered without words to dance. Taking the cue from his sister, knowing that he had to appear unworried, he smiled at Lira gratefully hoping that Gaelán was well, that his ball could be salvaged, and that the fears and rumors would not be true.

Rouvyn bent over the bed, rechecking Gaelán's pulse, monitoring his breathing, checking for fever or anything else that might explain what was wrong. He too might have believed Gaelán had fainted, as there were no obvious signs of illness or poison, but he would not wake up when the smelling salts were waved beneath his nose.

"What happened, Princess?" he asked, not looking at her as he spoke. No one had talked on their way from the Hall, and no one except Madalyn had interrupted him with unnecessary fussing.

Still maintaining her composure as best she could, Asta replied, "We were dancing…then he clutched his head, doubled over, and collapsed." She made note of the odd discoloration points on Gaelán's wrists as the physician did, a single one on each, nearly identical, but had no explanation for them. Bhríd continued to try to console his wife while Caol, who had followed them far enough back to warn off the curious who might have thought to join them, lingered in the doorway in the hopes of helping if he was needed.

If nothing else, his daughter might want him there.

"Poison?" asked Bhríd, voicing the fears of many in the room.

Rouvyn shook his head. "I see no indication…he seems to have fainted but…I do not know." He was already producing purgatives from his healing bag, looking for the one that might work best.

After a glance at her father, Asta cleared her throat and said, "Not poison. This has happened before." Curious looks urged her to continue. "Not this precisely…he has had…something. The one time I saw it, he said something about headaches…about dreams…about needing Healer MacLyr…I thought maybe it's the Sight…"

Looks were exchanged, particularly between the young man's parents who understood what that might mean for their son and feared it. Caol stepped into the room and used one hand to pull Bhríd away from his wife. "If Ártur knows of this…"

"I will bring him at once," the chamberlain agreed. If Ártur could reveal what this was…he could reassure them of what it was not."

Rouvyn hastily agreed. "Yes, please. This is nothing I have ever encountered." If the healer knew what was happening, then the healer should be present.

Madalyn tried to cling to her husband's arms, but he shrugged her off with a kiss to her forehead and hurried out of the room.

"What else can you tell me, Princess?"

"I know he has fainted before…but I have not seen it. Whatever it is, he says it makes his head hurt, sometimes his wrists and ankles…sometimes his side…" She pressed her hand against her own body to indicate the location. "He does not know the cause though." He had confided in her that he feared it was a product of his mixed blood, but Asta thought it best not to say so in Madalyn's company when the woman was clearly frightened for his life.

The purgatives made Gaelán retch until there could be nothing left in his stomach to eliminate. To Asta, he was smaller, frailer, in a way that began to frighten her. But apart from the bruises, darker now, tinged blood red and dead-skin black, his unwaking state, and the pallor left by the purgative, Gaelán was, by Rouvyn's assessment, as healthy as ever. But the physician was apprehensive, afraid that his inability to diagnose or cure whatever was wrong would fail both his employer and Gaelán. He liked Gaelán. He liked these people. He liked his new position. He did not want to fail.

He was relieved when Bhríd returned to the room with Healer MacLyr in tow, though he worried that so much time had passed that the young man would be lost. The Elyri healer sat on the edge of the bed and placed his hands on the smaller chest, healing threads seeking a source that no Teren would be able to detect. From what Bhríd had told him when he burst from the Gate in Kavan's home rather than waste unnecessary time running across town, Ártur knew what he expected to find.

He did not understand it, but he was not disappointed.

"Kavan."

So much power had been thrust into the younger healer that Gaelán's body had shut down in defense of itself. Some reoccurring condition in Kavan was manifesting through Gaelán. Ártur's senses traced the paths of pain to the bruises on his ankles, his wrists, his side, but there were no injuries there, only phantom pain and bruises.

What sort of injury, he wondered as his hands faltered in their search, could Kavan suffer repeatedly in those simultaneous locations that could cause Kavan enough distress that he might lash out with power to stop it?

"kyag k'Ádhá," he murmured, looking at the deep burgundy bruises now with his eyes rather than his healing senses, stung by the turn his thoughts had taken. He could not accept that irrational conclusion, did not want to accept it, and if he was even close to correct, he knew that Kavan would not accept it either.

"Ártur?"

He shook his head, choosing not to reveal that suspicion. "Nothing to be done, Bhríd…but I swear to you Gaelán is in no danger. He will suffer quite a headache when he wakes, but there will be no lasting harm done." At least he did not think there would be. He could not imagine Kavan knowingly hurting Gaelán, or anyone, this way.

Still wringing her hands, Madalyn choked, "Poison?" Though Rouvyn had already ruled out toxins, it remained the root of her fears. The possibility that her eldest son might have harmed the younger one would not leave her now that she was aware of the divide and animosity between them.

"No." Ártur ran his hand through his hair. "It is Kavan. Somehow, though I am at a loss to explain how, Kavan is projecting through Gaelán. I do not know if he is aware of it, but Gaelán mentioned before that these episodes bring a heightened sense of Kavan's presence…and I feel him there. It seems that Kavan is projecting the pain of some injury outwards and Gaelán has served as a conduit for it, a gatherer of the pain and power into his center. When there is too much of it…he collapses as his mind shuts down.

The explanation did not appease Madalyn, who frowned as if wanting to be angry at Kavan for this, but at least it was a relief to hear that Gaelán was not in danger of dying.

"Lord Cliáth is being tortured?" Not knowing where the bard was, Caol's first concern was the ramifications this could have for Enesfel.

"I do not know. It is reoccurring… same symptoms, same pain. Something residual from the attack he endured, perhaps. I don't know how he could be doing this…but Gaelán will be fine. He should not require monitoring, but you may if you wish, Doctor Talis. You may give him something for the headache if he wakes before I return."

"You will not stay?" Asta asked. She wanted to believe every word Ártur said, believed Rouvyn to be a good doctor or else the King would not have appointed him, but she wanted Gaelán to have the best possible care. And that was, to her and many others, Healer MacLyr.

"I wish I could…but he does not need me now. He is safe…."

"And of course I will stay with him," Rouvyn accepted with a bow. "If someone will stay while I fetch a few more items…I will remain with him for the night."

Asta and Madalyn both volunteered. Bhríd did not need to accompany Ártur back to Bhryell, but he did go with him as far as the chapel, suspecting there were details Ártur was holding back, knowing the King would want a full report. Perhaps Caol would be him to that, as the inquisitor was already striding down the hall towards the stairs, leaving the chamberlain to get answers from the healer.

"You would rather stay, wouldn't you?" Bhríd murmured. "Touch Kavan through Gaelán…be certain of what you read…"

"You believe me?" The Teren in the room would not have known what to believe, how what Ártur suggested could be real. Ártur did not know that either. He would not have been surprised if Bhríd had doubted him too.

"I know of no reason for you to lie; I saw your reluctance to pull away…and I know you well enough."

Sighing, Ártur put his hand on the oratory door. "I would give nearly anything to stay, to understand, except for my family…and I doubt Syl will be as understanding as you. If he wakes before morning, let him know I was here, that I will speak to him when I return."

Bhríd nodded as his cousin disappeared into the dark chapel. Though concerned about Kavan's welfare, and Gaelán's, it was a relief to know that his elder son had not poisoned the younger.

That did not, however, explain where Tayte was tonight.

❧Chapter 16

Halting in the doorway of the room he was directed to by the bony woman serving bread and fat porridge to guests downstairs, Wortham felt his breath strangled from him, wrenched away by the gruesome, unexpected sight. The white-skinned man on the bed lay with his arms stretched over his head, which was cocked at an awkward angle to one side as though he had collapsed mid convulsion or someone had snapped his neck and left him where he had fallen. The bedding beneath him was soaked in blood, his nude body covered in it, though at a cursory glance Wortham saw no wounds that could account for so much blood. No man could lose that much and still be alive. Suicide? Not Kavan. Surely the Elyri could not have committed such a grave act over the thought of Wortham's death.

The big man rushed to the bed and felt for a pulse at the side of Kavan's neck, noting as he did so that the bleeding appeared to have come from Kavan's wrists, his bare ankles, his side. Not suicide then. His stomach clenched into a nauseated knot. rósádhá. That knowledge made the captain feel no better. Kavan had been forced not only to endure the looming loss of his best friend, but the torment of this…physical, emotional, and mental…alone. If the blood loss had not killed him, the heartbreak certainly could have.

It took Wortham several minutes, and the movement of his fingers over multiple places on the man's body, to find a point that yielded a feeble, slow pulse. But at least it was a pulse, and Kavan's chest rose and fell in sporadic, shallow breaths, showing he was alive, offering hope that he might live if properly tended. Wortham could not send for a physician or healer for there would be questions regarding what had happened that the captain could not answer. If anyone guessed at the cause and nature of it, the bard would know no peace for the rest of his days. The bleeding had ceased some time ago, it appeared, and since Kavan seemed likely to live, Wortham set about bathing the blood from Kavan's skin, his nudity partially covered with a portion of the sheet that hung on the floor, wondering what he should do next.

It was dawn. Or near to it. Kavan knew this as his senses came back to him. There was light in the room that he could detect beyond his closed lids, and the warmth of a fire, and sounds in the distance which seemed like birds and people passing in the street, on foot, in carts, on horseback. There were nearer sounds as well, breathing and the gentle sloshing of water in a bowl, followed by a cool, damp cloth on his fevered skin. Someone bathing him, if he judged correctly. It took many moments to recognize the touch of those large hands. Wortham's hands. Emitting a whimpering moan, Kavan was certain he had died and was now in the same afterlife the captain had found.

"My lord?"

The voice, the strain in it, sounded too real, too near, to be a dream. So were the aches in his wrists and ankles, and the throbbing below his ribcage. Afraid of what he would see, Kavan slowly opened his eyes. The walls were the same dull amber he recalled from the evening before, the scents of clay and whitewash a reminder that he was in the same room he remembered. Not dead then…and Wortham was with him, leaning over him, flesh and blood. Hesitantly he touched the captain's face, half expecting his effort to meet empty air, and when his fingers met the resistance of physical form, he lurched up and clung around Wortham's neck, weeping with relief.

"Praise k'Ádhá…"

Wortham chuckled, the sound an effort to keep from weeping too. "Kóráhm told you I would live…although until the final moments I did not think I could be spared. I prayed you would come, rescue me, regardless of what I asked before, but I see you could not."

Desiring not to think about the night's torment, not yet having seen the blood he had spilled, Kavan whispered, "What happened?"

"I was to be beheaded…" When Kavan stiffened in his arms, Wortham held him tighter. "As hideous as that might be, it would have been swift and painless at least. My neck was on the block…I closed my eyes…and then I heard voices, a middle-aged man speaking to the headman and giving him a bag of coin. There was some discussion, angry words I could not understand, but in the end, I was released. I thought maybe you had sent him…"

Kavan shook his head. If he had been able to raise the bail payment, he would have delivered it in person. "Perhaps…a man came to me last evening, asking for our requirements for our journey. Your release was at the top of the list we provided…or the coin to secure it ourselves. He was middle-aged…" He dared not peer into Wortham's mind to see the intercessor's face. It would have opened Kavan up to Wortham's final despairing moments and he did not want to endure that. "He would not say who had sent him…why a benefactor might wish to…I thought maybe Orynn had…"

"It is fortuitous that someone took your request seriously." He pulled back and smoothed Kavan's hair from his face. He had not washed the blood from the bard's white locks yet and they were still matted. "Lady Orynn…Kóráhm…or someone else. I am grateful."

As was Kavan.

"May I fetch more water? I have not completed what I began."

Kavan turned to look in the mirror and was shocked by what he saw. He was more shocked to note, out of the corner of his eye, the condition of the bedding. "Aye…it appears bathing is in order…and additional payment to our host for this…" He gestured towards the bed in dismay without finishing his sentence.

"I will tend to that while I…" He did not know how, as he had no coin, but he could barter his services in exchange if necessary. He was interrupted by a knock on the door, and assuming it would be Urian or Zelenka, he hastened to keep either from witnessing the condition of the room, or Kavan.

But when he opened it, it was to reveal the messenger Kavan had spoken with the previous evening. From the expression on Wortham's face, it was the same courier who had paid for his freedom.

The stranger bowed. "Pardon my intrusion at this early hour." He smiled at Wortham with a nod. "I am pleased to see you free, sir. My lord, everything you requested is waiting, if you will come with me…"

"I must tend to…" Kavan's hands caught in his blood-matted hair.

The man bowed again. "Yes…of course…" To do anything else, to appear in public in the state Kavan was in, would invite questions and troubles they did not need. If the stranger was curious or appalled about what had happened, he did not ask. "Bathe…but do not be concerned for the room, the bed. I will see to any fines. But I beseech you to hurry…lingering would not be…wise…"

Kavan did not ask why. If there was some technicality that might prompt Wortham's arrest a second time, or some reason a mob might form and turn against them, the bard did not want to remain in Yashir long enough to learn of it. "Wortham…summon the others…but stay out of sight if you can. Tell them to save discussion about your release until we are on our way."

"Aye, my lord." The captain was not happy about leaving Kavan alone, not happy about following the messenger out or risking anyone else seeing him, but he understood duty and was eager to be away from this miserable town before he unknowingly broke some other ordinance and was killed outright without the benefit of arrest.

Nearly thirty minutes later, Kavan shakily emerged from the tavern to a wagon awaiting them, pulled by two large gray horses, with feathered hair growing over their hooves. It was stocked with food, water, their personal belongings, and all of the confiscated items Wortham had purchased days before. Despite the abundance, there was room for two to travel in the rear, room enough to lay down and sleep, and room enough on the wagon bench for two or three to sit as well. A quick perusal through the supplies revealed a collection of kindling, tinder, flint and steel, blankets and waxed canvas to serve as protection from the sun or the rain should they need it. The wagon was sturdy and solid, larger than the rover wagon had been and of new construction, a gift, along with the horses, of obvious expense. Neither wagon nor beast of burden had been part of Kavan's list.

Someone had anticipated everything they might need for the remainder of their journey. Someone with more foresight than Kavan.

Wortham helped Zelenka into the back of the wagon and Urian had already been assisted onto the seat at the front. The captain was securing the trunks he had brought down from their rooms as Kavan turned to the courier.

With his head clearer now, he was able to study the man more closely. He appeared to be Elyri, felt to be Elyri, but there was something different about him, different enough that Kavan decided he must be of mixed parentage like Orynn and Myreth. The thought of them both brought a pang of longing, but he pushed the emotions away. "Whom shall I thank for this abundance? I can never repay such generosity, nor for sparing Wortham's life, but I must try…"

The courier shook his head and interrupted, his unfamiliar accent thick and strange as he spoke, his use of the Trade tongue stilted and formal. "Repayment is not necessary; none will be asked or accepted. I am not given leave to speak my patron's name…but I shall relay your gratitude. That will suffice. It is time for you to be on your way. Part of the condition of your man's release was that he leaves Yashir as quickly as possible…and I fear your time runs short. If I might recommend, it would be wise if he does not return here for many weeks at least."

"I have no intention of doing so," Wortham muttered bitterly, though he was happily smiling at Zelenka as he settled in the wagon bed beside her. Now that they were heading once more to Rhidam, he did not believe he would ever have a reason to travel these lands again.

Stomach clenching with unwelcomed jealousy, Kavan clasped the stranger's hand, careful not to breach his privacy by reading him in spite of his curiosity. He mounted the front of the wagon, joining Urian there, because he believed Wortham wanted time alone with the woman and knew the monk could not guide the horses.

This time, however, instead of dwelling on his inner conflict, he acknowledged his possessiveness and stowed it away. Wortham was alive, and for that, Kavan would endure as much time as the captain wanted to spend with her, so long as he spared some for Kavan as well.

With everyone settled, he said again, "Thank you," with a bowed head to the messenger, who returned the gesture with a formal bow. The wagon rattled north. To Enda. The southernmost city in the Five Sovereignties. And from there home. Rhidam was but a few weeks away. Despite the bedeviling disquiet at the thought of seeing the princess, Kavan yearned to be home. Weary of adversities, weary of travel, weak in body and mind, his heart was in the return at last.

"By all means, go, Lord Gabersdon," the King said gravely as he walked with the older men on the promenade. With the spring's continuing warmth, he enjoyed spending more time outdoors. He could no longer cavort and enjoy his friends' company the way he had last year, when horse races through the country, meals spread on open fields of grass, or romping with new hunting pups had been ideal ways to spend his leisure time. Now he had to appreciate what relaxation he could get, even if it was nothing more than a stroll through the gardens in the sun, despite the too early hour of it this day. "Someone should oversee the matter, and I would rather keep General Agis in Rhidam. Take General Zarkosta with you, if you think it prudent, and as many men as you think you will need to put down the unrest."

"I will join you, Lord Gabersdon, if I may."

Both the Duke and King were surprised by Prince Espen's offer. The report had arrived of disorder in a village west of Rhidam. People had fallen victim to an unknown ailment, after which several graves were found open and empty, prompting rampant rumors of demons and witchery. Fear of the dead living again, in the wake of Enesfel's other ongoing problems, was a troublesome prospect. It seemed wises to put an end to the matter, and the rumors, before someone blamed this new mischief on the Elyri too. But the matter was King Hagan's problem, not Prince Espen's, and after last night's ball, the King had expected the prince and his sister to be inseparable. "Why?"

Espen shrugged. "I would like to be of assistance. I came to Enesfel to help, not to remain idle. I can take my forces, which will reduce the strain on your resources…and we have no fear of the undead, of open graves, or other grizzly matters. We heard enough such tales as children to doubt the veracity of such rumors. Seeing to this will provide an interesting diversion…and should you have need of me and my men, you have but to send for us and we will return to Rhidam at once.

The proposal was given a few moments of thought, none of which dwelled on the King's sister. "You are no subject of mine to be commanded to do this, but if you wish to provide aid, it is welcome. Lord Gabersdon, take Prince Harcourt and his men and settle this business swiftly. I want to hear no more of this nonsense."

It was clear in his voice that one crisis after another with barely a break between them was making the young King irritable and alarmed. As the Duke bowed, he admitted that, like the King, many were weary of the state of things in Enesfel. All any of them wanted was peace.

If only they could agree on what that meant.

Gaelán awoke in a soft down bed to the worst headache he had ever felt. There was such pain behind his eyes that he was afraid to open them. Instead, he lay quietly for a long while, wondering where he was and how he had gotten there. He remembered dancing with Asta, and then there had been pain and that overwhelming sense of Kavan that robbed him of strength and coherency.

So that was it. It had happened again. He shivered involuntarily, causing movement behind him. Someone else was in the room. With a grimace, he rolled onto his back and forced his eyes open, surprised to see not Rouvyn or Ártur there, nor his parents, but Asta, still in the red velvet she had worn the night before. She was rubbing her sleepy eyes and he guessed he had awakened her.

"Have you been here all night?" he asked in a cracked whisper.

She blinked and said, "What do you think?" to cover her alarm at being startled. She did not like to show such weakness.

Hand wiping his face, he muttered, "I think my head hurts…a lot."

Asta climbed onto the bed and gently rubbed his temples the way her father used to do with her mother, when the woman had suffered so in the months before her death. "Lord MacLyr says it has something to do with Lord Cliáth."

"I think so." There was comfort in her touch, even if it did not take away the pain.

"How odd it must be to feel someone inside of your head. I think it would be frightening."

"If it was someone I didn't know…maybe. But this is not scary; it just hurts. I hope I did not ruin the banquet."

"I did not go back but it continued for several more hours, so you're safe."

"I apologize for spoiling…"

"It was a ball; there will be others. It is not like you caused this…and we got to dance." She grinned sheepishly. "Others will ask what happened, of course. I think they believe you were poisoned."

"An ailment, something I ate, the heat. I will think of something." He opened his eyes and his gaze lingered on her neck. He had noticed last night, but had not said so before his collapse. "You wore it."

"It's not the red ribbon I wanted, but this will do for now. I told you I would wear it always. And it's no longer empty. Want to see?" He nodded and wiggled closer as she snapped the locket open and leaned nearer so that his face was inches away from her throat.

Tearing his eyes from hers, his gaze traveled to her mouth and then down to the locket. The tiny portrait inside was exquisite in detail and likeness. He swallowed hard and knew he was blushing.

"Me?"

She giggled and closed it. "Lord MacLyr did it for me. It's a gift from you; you should be in it. This way, you are forever near my…"

The door creaked open and Asta quickly backed away. Ártur pretended not to notice, not even their mutual embarrassment. Without speaking, he placed one hand on Gaelán's forehead and when he removed it, much of Gaelán's pain was gone.

"Can you teach me how to do that so the next time this happens, I can heal my own headache?" Gaelán asked in relief.

"You anticipate this will continue?" Though it had happened before, the older healer had not given thought to the experience continuing…or what that might mean for Kavan.

"Don't you? Until he comes home…I think it will. I don't think he knows he's doing it, whatever it is, but when he sees…"

When. Not if. Gaelán's conviction that Kavan would return made Ártur's heart swell with both hope and loneliness. Blinking away the emotions that brought tears to his eyes, he cleared his throat and asked, "How do you feel?"

"Embarrassed." He looked at Asta. "Everyone had to see it." He frowned. "It was the same, wasn't it? I did not do anything inappropriate did I?"

"It was not quite the same, but I assure you, from what I was told, they only saw you faint. You have been asleep longer this time, and there were bruises…"

Gaelán's brows knit together as he looked at his arms. Where there had been dark marks before, there was only a faint yellowish stain. "Did I hit something? How did I get them?"

"You did not hit anything," Asta promised.

"Perhaps Kavan can explain it." If he will, the healer thought. If his guess was accurate, Kavan might never admit such a thing, even if there were witnesses.

Trusting the healer's words, and that he would later show him how to combat his headaches, when his head and body stopped hurting enough for him to focus on power, Gaelán looked between Asta and Ártur and asked, "Must I remain in bed?"

"Only if you want to. I do not think study in your condition would be productive so we will postpone until tomorrow. You should rest, however, and while you do," he looked at Asta, "will you keep an eye on him, Healer Dugan? Find me if he needs anything?"

Asta giggled and clapped her hands, more girlish then she had seemed last night. "I will take care of everything," she promised enthusiastically. Gaelán flushed and sank into his pillow to hide from his embarrassment.

The healer did his best not to laugh.

❧*❧

Though Piran scampered out of the office the moment they arrived in his second home, Owain remained where he was, looking over the back terrace through the glass-plated windows, admiring the island foliage. After time away from Rhidam, spent in Fiara, he had been amazed at how much everything had changed, the atmosphere, the routines, the people. Becoming King had forced Hagan to mature somewhat, Diona had grown more grounded and focused on duty, and Gaelán, barely more than a boy, was becoming a healer. And Rouvyn Talis, a man Owain had not seen since the death of Prince Bertram, was now part of the Lachlan court, something that could not have happened under Arlan's reign. Ártur, haunted by Kavan's absence, by violence at every turn, and a crumbling family he was attempting to save had become a shadow, as faded and weary as the memories of Kavan that seemed to grow fainter in the hearts and minds of his employers with each day he was gone. It felt to Owain that Kavan was being replaced by the Elyri newcomer, and the discomfort of that made Owain relieved he was able to escape to Káliel.

"You came." He clutched at the arms that encircled him and narrowly resisted turning and burying his face in the hair of the woman who spoke. "It has been months."

"And I am deeply sorry for that. Believe me when I say being away from you is never happily by choice."

Gabrielle slid around to the front of him without releasing her hold around his body. "Duty is a burden we both bear…and I am as much to blame as you. But it is good to see you…to have you here." She pressed her lips to his and smiled. "To what do I owe the pleasure?"

"Piran wanted to come." His tone indicated that their son was not his sole reason, and her face lit with both expectation and concern. "Yes, there is more." More that he did not want to share. He knew his wife, however, and she was not going to allow him a moment of peace until he spoke the truth.

"The violence has spread to Fiara. I've had spies, riots, murders. Brigands waylaid us when Piran was with me…" It seemed prudent not to mention that they had attempted to kidnap his son. That attack was bad enough. He knew she appreciated the blunt truth, but from the shock and worry on her face, he believed holding that detail back was wisest. "I intended to bring him sooner, when the first incident arose, but I could not get away. He will be safer here."

Frowning, Gabrielle stepped back and entwined her fingers with his. "For now, perhaps…but Pháne too has been attacked…a single ship. Muir and his forces destroyed it, but the outpost was lost, and he believes they will come again…whoever they are."

It was Owain's turn to show concern for the son he barely knew but loved as deeply as he loved Piran. Gabrielle kissed his fingertips. "He was in good health and spirits when his message came, uninjured but cold with the spring storms. He drives Clianthe to distraction, of course, as he remains there to oversee reconstruction and bolster the men's' morale. You will not likely see him during your visit…"

"I will if I go to Pháne." He wanted to see for himself that Muir was well, wanted to hear what had happened with the ears of a soldier and see if there was anything he could do to help.

Gabrielle smacked his chest playfully. "And here I believed you came to see me."

Smoothing his hands down over her hips he rumbled, "I came to see my family… Muir included. Do not fear, you will not be forgotten or abandoned, beautiful lady." It had taken half a lifetime to find her, and Owain would not risk losing her to negligence.

She nestled her head against his shoulder with a contented sigh. "I pray not." No man until Owain had been able to help her get over Kavan. Kavan had been a fantasy, a wish, the impossible dream of a young girl. Owain, and his love for her, were real. "Any news of Kavan?" she asked as those musings passed through her.

He grunted and held her more tightly. "No. King Hagan hosted a banquet last night…and I got the impression that there is little hope of him ever coming home. Ártur…Gaelán…myself…a few others perhaps. His place as Court Bard is filled…and few are comfortable talking about him. It was as if he is dead…"

He choked on the last word, the possibility clawing at his insides. Grateful that Gabrielle could not see his face, he squeezed his eyes shut and fought the overpowering sadness.

"He will come back," she assured him. "Regardless of what has happened…there is unshakable strength in him. He knows where he belongs…where he is needed."

"I marvel at your faith in him. You should go to Rhidam and remind them."

"Perhaps I keep faith because no matter how many times he has gone out of my life, he always returns. No matter how long he is away, I always see him one more time. Perhaps that time is now…but I do not believe so. Trust him."

"I am trying."

"Good. Now," she smiled, the tiny lines around her eyes creasing with relief as his sorrowful mood lifted a little. "If you wish to go to Pháne tomorrow, we must charter a vessel. Once we do that, you will have the remainder of the day to spend with your wife, daughter-in-law, and youngest son."

That thought peeled back the edges of his depression further. "That sounds like the tonic I seek. Thank you."

❧*❦

Hands shaking, the inquisitor fingered the message received from his daughter minutes before. After months of dead ends, questionable leads, and a crushing lack of progress, he had something he believed he could use. Not just any sort of lead, but the name of someone within the organization that called itself Corylliens, and the date and location of an upcoming meeting of members. This was the sort of lead the King should know about, the sort he once would have taken directly to Arlan, proof that his business with the Association was not in vain, even when the flow of information was slow or non-existent.

But King Hagan could not know. Arlan had trusted his inquisitor's judgment, Hagan did not. The information had to be verified, of course, and there was but one way to do that. Someone had to go to that meeting. This was one time, however, when Caol did not trust his spies to do the work. Enesfel could afford no more wasted time. The swiftest, most certain way to infiltrate the organization and learn what he needed to know to bring it down was to do it from the inside. He was going to have to do it himself.

He did not doubt his ability to do the job. If allowed to proceed without restraints, it would be a simple thing. But the King would not make the process easy, if he allowed it at all. If King Hagan agreed to listen, Caol suspected he would instead send royal soldiers to arrest everyone attending that meeting, destroying any chance they might have of delving deeper and uprooting its core, its leader. Either that or the King would demand some lesser man be sent to do the job, someone expendable. Then, if something went wrong, the inquisitor would be left to pick up the pieces and proceed without interruption through anything that remained of the trust built with his contacts.

Expendable men were not what Enesfel needed. The Kingdom needed someone who could do this job right the first time. Caol suspected that, if they failed at this opportunity, they might not get another.

He knew how to solve the dilemma. He knew what needed to be done. The first step was to write two letters, the first to his son Wilred, the second to Onea Pantel, the leader of Fiara's branch of the Association and someone Caol trusted. If he failed, it would be up to her to uncover the truth. If he failed, he would die, either at the hands of the Corylliens or at the command of his nephew, and Onea would be the only one capable of picking up the investigation and following it to its conclusion. Asta for all of her growing skill, was not yet ready for that responsibility. While he would prefer that his death, if it came, be at the hands of the Corylliens, he had no illusions about his status with the King he had helped to raise.

◈*◈

Diona wanted to scream, berate someone, hit someone if anyone had been near enough, but she held enough respect for Belda to refrain from taking out her frustration on her. She had sworn, on the day she learned what her position entitled her to, that she would never abuse that privilege by mistreating any of those who served her. To date, she had kept that promise to everyone except Kavan. She had abused his trust in the worst possible manner, driven him away, and had to live every day with that knowledge. It had, thus far, kept her from making further mistakes.

She had made her decision, after a sleepless night and a path worn in the carpet between the window and the bed, and had intended to share it with Espen as soon as she awoke. After laboring over the pros and cons as darkness crept by, after hours of short prayers and arguments with herself and the ghost of Bertram she carried in her heart, she concluded that she was ready to marry Espen. There was no one better suited, nothing she wanted more than her need for him in her life, and it was well past time to tell him.

And he was not in Rhidam to hear it. She looked everywhere she could think of, only to learn from General Agis that the Prince had left shortly after breakfast with Duke Gabersdon to put down unrest in a nearby village. He had left without saying goodbye, without leaving a message, without any hint about his return.

The perceived rejection hurt and she imagined it was how he often felt when she would not give him an answer. Perhaps he had expected an answer during the banquet. Undoubtedly she had waited too long. Likely, she thought bitterly, he no longer wanted to marry her, though the way he had danced with her seemed at odds with that. She wept, wishing her father was here to give advice, or that Kavan was here to give her direction. Both would tell her the same thing they had told her for many years. Marry Espen.

But it might be too late.

Spinning out of the library, Diona decided not to give up yet. Espen's belongings were still here, which meant that he had to return to Rhidam for them, or send someone else to retrieve them. She would have them taken to her chamber and instruct the servants that no one was to remove anything from her room, not even Hagan or Espen. He would have to talk to her if he wanted what she had. He would have to come to her once more before leaving Rhidam altogether, if that was his intention. Then she would ask him if it was too late to give the answer too long in coming. If she could break through to his heart, if he loved her still, it was time to end the stalemate.

He asked both Lira and Sigrid to linger in Rhidam, but Lira regrettably had to decline. Her mother was ill and she was needed at home to care for her siblings. It seemed a flimsy excuse to Hagan, as surely the family had servants for such duties. It caused him to wonder whether her father disapproved of a match with the King, but he decided not to force the issue. Lira's family were not nobility. They likely did not have the servants at their disposal that the King and noble houses would have. Her explanation, and the regret expressed with it, seemed honest.

Sigrid, however, did agree to remain, along with her brother and father, which took the sting out of Lira's perceived rejection. After dealing with the unpleasant business of grave robbing, the King shared a leisurely stroll through the castle with Sigrid, Dayly along for propriety's sake. She seemed to suspect nothing; they had been friends before the paths of their genders took them in opposite directions, and Dayly was still his closest friend. Her unassuming manner appealed to him. She treated him as both king and friend, but more as a friend, which he felt desperately in need of as his life grew more stressful. In her simple gown of pale lavender, he thought she was more beautiful than she had been the night before.

He was not in love with her. He did not know what being in love was like. But he did like her and by noon he decided that he could find no objections to having her here all the time. He chose not to rush his decision, wanted to wait a few more days to be certain, but if she did not find the atmosphere of royal court life unbearable, and he did not find anything objectionable between them, he made the preliminary choice to ask her to be his queen. If nothing else, it meant having Dayly around more often, and Hagan could find no fault with that.

❧*❧

After so many weeks of incessant travel mostly on foot, having the wagon was a welcome blessing. Sometimes, as they jostled and bounced through the ruts and pits of the packed dirt road, Kavan wondered if his party would have had this luxury if he had been the one to rescue Wortham from execution. But he chose not to dwell on those events, wanting to keep that morsel of past in the past. Wortham was averse to discussing his near-death experience and Kavan respected his wishes. Yet he could see that something troubled the captain even after the third day since departing Yashir, and Kavan felt compelled to find out what was wrong.

When they stopped the wagon to prepare meals, Urian whittled at a furious pace, making up for lost time it seemed while Wortham continued teaching Zelenka the Trade language over whatever was simmering on their fire. Neither Urian nor Zelenka knew about the bloody mess Kavan had left behind, as Kavan was sure the woman would be more afraid of him than before and the dedhá would make the occurrence into more than it was. Zelenka was beginning to smile at Kavan, tried to engage him in conversation when they were alone or in the group together, likely, Kavan thought, because she believed he had some hand in securing Wortham's freedom. But with Wortham's seeming efforts to avoid being alone with him, the bard wondered if he was troubled by what he had seen in that room, or if his failure to free Wortham had somehow hurt or offended him.

Unable to carry on decent conversations with Zelenka, feeling little need for discourse with the dedhá, and with Wortham unwilling to talk to him privately, Kavan spent most of his time singing. Or writing. Or asleep as he recovered his strength after that massive blood-letting. There had been two empty journals in the goods stowed on the wagon and Kavan claimed both for his use. He was filling one with the personal odyssey he had endured over the past several months, chronicling the events for whatever posterity he might leave behind. The gaps in Kóráhm's story had taught Kavan that, while he might consider his life unimportant in the overall annals of history, someone in the future might require the knowledge of his peculiar life, of the events he witnessed and participated in, the history he uncovered during his travels into these unfamiliar lands. Once he recorded the most recent events, he would turn to his origins, his childhood, everything he could remember, everything he knew of the occurrences he had been part of. And he would write down everything he knew about Kóráhm and historical events he uncovered.

He wanted the world to have as much truth as he could leave behind.

Thanks to the wagon, they were making excellent progress. They made up for the days lost at sea, lost on the road, lost in Yashir. If they could not find a usable Gate along the route, they would at least reach Rhidam quicker than they could on foot. The wagon also meant they could travel for a time after sunset, as they did not need to be concerned with predators. Kavan's handlight could light their way, but it was cumbersome to focus on it when he also had to steer the horses. It was either him or Wortham, and the captain had not ridden with him on the driving seat since leaving Yashir.

Rhidam was growing steadily nearer and Kavan looked forward to being home…but not without Wortham's support.

Seated on the opposite side of the fire this morning, the journal in his hand, there was no one to catch him when the wave of nausea washed over him, causing him to drop the journal and pitch forward as his vision blurred. The Sight had not come to him in some time but he recognized the accompanying signs. There was a boy, an Elyri, alone in the rafters of Hes á Redh Náós, huddled beneath a tattered blanket, crying in his sleep. His hair was black with highlights that shown red in the candlelight, indicating he bore k'kairá blood. He looked too young to be there alone, though from the debris scattered around him, it seemed he had been in that place for many days.

As quickly as it had come, Kavan's eyesight cleared and the vision left him. Not one of his nephews. He would recognize Tayte or Gaelán. Of what significance was this boy? The details of his hideout were too dark to be clear, but the boy's face stayed with Kavan as the rest faded. Not a man. Barely ten. Kavan felt very close to the boy at that moment, as if the child was waiting for him, needed him.

Believing that no one else knew the child was there, that sense of need felt all the more potent.

Wortham was too far away to help him up, and had not moved from where he sat when Kavan straightened and retrieved the fallen journal. Unsettled, Kavan retreated to the back of the wagon to write where he would not be seen by the others. It was Wortham's turn to drive the team, and the Elyri knew he was not wanted there. He would turn his thoughts to prayer for the orphan as he wrote…and ponder whether he should reach out to Ártur for help or leave the child be.

❧*❧

After a calm sea journey to Pháne, Owain was relieved to grip Muir's hand and astounded at how mature his oldest son seemed. Muir had been a man since the two had met, but seeing him in armor, his skin browned and blonde hair bleached by the sun, with his features haggard from fatigue and several weeks' worth of growth on his square jaw, made Owain see him in a new light and made him again regret everything he had missed when Muir was a child.

"I cannot stay long," he said contritely, his grasp remaining firm around Muir's hand. "The ship returns to Káliel in the morning, and Ártur will expect me. But I could not pass up the opportunity to see you and assess your situation."

"I am pleased you came." Muir squeezed the other man's hand, happy to see him. "Not much left of the damage," he added, indicating the structure behind him that men were busy building. "We've worked continuously to get her done before it rains again. I hope to be better prepared for the next ship that crosses us."

"They want the cave?"

Lowering his voice to match his father's, Muir grunted, "There is nothing else here they could want, except a launching point with proximity to Káliel, and each possibility is equally bad. I have found men trying to get in there, so there is no other assumption to make. It would be insane for anyone else to consider building a fortress so near to Káliel, so it must be the cave. We found no survivors from the ship to ask, but I'm glad their efforts to drive us away failed."

"They likely did not expect to meet resistance."

"Perhaps. I doubt they will be so easy to dispatch next time."

"You will be careful?"

❧216❧

Smiling at his father's concern, though his eyes continued to convey the seriousness of the situation, Muir replied, "Of course. I have a wife waiting for me and have no intention of dying before I see her. Or before I see Kavan again."

"He has not yet come home," was all Owain could say.

Muir's smile melted into a pout of disappointment. "I have never known him to…I know Diona hurt him, but I do not think she will…"

"I doubt she…whether he can forgive her or not may be irrelevant. I suspect, if he returns, it will not be until he has made peace with the loss of his hands."

Both men knew the likelihood of that was slim. His hands were his life, without them, Kavan would believe himself to be no one, worthless. Choosing to change the subject, not wanting his father to associate his visit with gloom, Muir asked, "Shall I show you my humble domain? It is not as grand as Fiara, but it is mine. Perhaps you can recommend improvements."

Owain smiled gratefully and clasped his shoulders. "It appears you have everything in hand without my aid, but I would like a tour."

The gardens stretched between the castle walls and the bailey had an unusual eeriness at dusk as the sun crept lower in the sky, creating long, shadow fingers through the branches and vines. As a boy, the King had found the gardens disturbing at this hour, perhaps because the entrance to the royal crypt was nearby. Though he was older now, he still chose to avoid the fragrant pathways as soon as the sun began to set, meaning that Diona could meet her uncle here without fear of being heard by her brother, and the inquisitor made sure they were alone before joining her on the stone and iron bench.

"I've sent a letter to Wilred explaining my plans and his part in them. Few will know what I am doing…Wilred, Asta, you and Onea. I cannot risk any more…unless you think I am forgetting someone?"

It was a sad state of affairs that there was no one else they could trust. "I can think of no one at this time." She would regret keeping such a secret from Owain, from Espen, but there was no need for them to know, and knowing might put them both in peril. "You realize the risks, Uncle…do you feel it worth it? Necessary?"

Caol grunted. "To end this? You expect anything less of me?"

The princess shook her head, both already knowing her answer. "Can you do it? Infiltrate them? I can cover you, feign ignorance easily enough, but you have a more difficult task ahead."

"Do not concern yourself with how but trust that I will. The less you know, the better. I will approach your brother about a visit to Durham tonight. I do not think he will object, but if he does…" His voice trailed off and he stared into the darkening sky. "If, after the grief he has caused me of late, the way he hinders my duty, he refuses to allow me a visit to my first grandchild, I will be forced to resign."

Lamely, Diona asked, "Must you?" But she understood there might be no other way to go forward. On some level, she was surprised that Caol had continued as inquisitor as long as he had, with both his wife and King Arlan gone and the new King refusing to trust him to do the job he had been doing for decades.

"If it allows me to hunt the Corylliens, then yes. I will regret it, of course, but there may be no other way."

"What if they ask you to do something…?"

"Like kill someone?" It was a possibility he was trying not to think about. "I will deal with that if it arises. For now, all I want is to get into that meeting, see what I can learn about the people in it, the organization, their plans…and who is funding their efforts." He expected that to be Claide, but it was possible there were many supporters paying for the Corylliens' crimes. He could not know the truth from the outside.

"Then you should go to Hagan." She covered his hand with hers, hoping to remember the feel of it when he was not in Rhidam to continue to offer her support. "Whatever he says, please let me know what you will do…when you will leave. I will have one less supporter against Claide…and though I understand the importance of this, I expect you to at least extend me the courtesy of a farewell."

"You know I will, Diona. I apologize that this solution is not ideal. Asta will continue to function as Association informant and has been instructed to bring anything she learns to you. It will make you and her acting-inquisitors while I am on the outside; if you need me, send word through Asta."

"You have worked out all the angles, haven't you?" It made Diona feel better about his plan, but she was still anxious.

"I hope so. If not, this could be a short exercise in stupidity." He helped her to her feet and kissed her knuckles.

"Good luck, Uncle. I will be praying for your safety and success and your return to us." She did not envy his choice and admired him for being able to make it in spite of the cost. She did not believe she would have the same courage if she was in his position.

"Thank you," he said with a nod as he released her and left to find the King. He was going to need as much luck as he could get if he was going to bring down the Corylliens and return to his daughter.

❧*❧

The voice on the other side of the Purification Chamber curtain was young. It was unusual only because Tusánt had heard no concessions from any of the younger Faithful in the three hours he had been at this post today. With Adhár four days away, the chambers had been fully utilized every waking hour of the last two days. The year had passed quickly; Tusánt could barely believe they were into the fourth month. The King's birthday was imminent, preparations needed to be made to honor that, and he doubted Claide had given any thought to it despite his interest in currying the King's favor. The man's mind was too focused on the need to replace k'dedhá Jermyn as promptly as possible. Preferably, Tusánt was sure, with himself.

The voice beyond the curtain came back to him, jarring him from his distraction. "dedhá?"

Tusánt could not tell if the speaker was male or female.

"Forgive me. I am easily distracted of late," he admitted softly.

"It is not easy being Elyri in Enesfel," the speaker sighed as if talking from experience, giving the first clue to their identity. Tusánt had not seen any Elyri, beyond those in the keep, in several weeks.

"Are you alone? Are your parents with you?"

He did not receive an answer. There was no chance to finish the question. The chamber door opened; he turned to see who was there, expecting it to be one of the other dedhá, but was blinded by the glare of a burning rag tossed in before the door banged closed again. The reflexive shielding of his face with his hands kept the flames from burning his cheek and hair and the rag fell to the floor where he ground out the fire beneath his boot. His hand, however, was stinging.

"dedhá? I smell fire…"

"It is nothing. I hurt my hand on the sconce." The explanation did not excuse the scent of burning cloth and flesh, but it was the best Tusánt could offer.

"May I see, dedhá?"

Gaelán Cáner. Tusánt sighed with relief and slid his burned hand beneath the grate that separated them. Fingers brushed lightly over his skin, taking away both pain and injury. When he drew his hand back, every trace of the burn was gone.

"You should go to the castle, have the healer examine you. I may have missed something."

"I do not think you have. What about your concession?"

But the youth was already gone; Tusánt could no longer feel him behind the drawn curtain and grate. He sat in the chamber, wondering if he should tell someone about this incident, and who he could tell?

It was too late, as someone else had already taken the youth's place in the chamber, and there was little chance of apprehending whoever had attacked him without adequate description. He chose to remain where he was until Claide shooed the parishioners out of the náós for the night. Afterward would be soon enough to ask Saul and Edward to escort him to the castle to speak with the princess and, he hoped, allow him to thank Gaelán for what he had done.

He would have to give serious thought to keeping himself safe in moments like this when his guardians could not be with him.

❧*❦

Owain clasped the healer's hand after coming into the entrance hall of the villa to find the Elyri there. "I did not mean to keep you, Ártur. The seas were rough; we made reasonable time but docking proved a greater than expected challenge."

"I understand." Ártur bowed with a fretful smile directed at Muir. "I am glad you made it safely…and it is good to see you, Muir. Your sister will be pleased to hear you are in good health and spirits."

Ignoring protocol, Muir embraced the healer warmly. Growing up, the healer, Kavan, and Guthrie McHador had exerted more impact on Muir than King Arlan or any other men. "It is good to see you too."

"I know you have recently returned, my lord," the healer murmured, eyes on Owain in that brief embrace, "but we must hasten our return…if you wish to return tonight? I am expected in Bhryell…and shall be late as it is."

Understanding the healer's unfortunate quandary, Owain replied, "Of course, I will get my things. Muir…will you help me?"

Ártur shuffled uneasily, worried about explaining his tardiness to Syl, worried about whether she would accept any explanation, reasonable or not, that he could give. He was not in Rhidam, in the danger zone, and his lateness was not of his doing, but he doubted Syl would be forgiving of those excuses. His talk with Gabrielle as they waited had been pleasant, and it was good to see Muir again, but he was an hour late as it was. He had to leave at once.

"Tell Syl you were under my protection," offered Gabrielle.

"I shall." He did not, however, think it would do him any good.

❧*❧

"You should consider returning to Elyriá." As if in response to Tusánt's unspoken protest, the senior Teren dedhá continued in as neutral a tone as he could manage. "Not that you are not needed here. Of course you are. But if someone is trying to kill you, I certainly do not want another of our number to meet an untimely end. The loss of Jermyn was unfortunate enough."

Particularly if such a death occurred on náós grounds, Tusánt thought, his face blank although he was not entirely convinced that Claide had not had some hand in that attempt on his life. He did not know how Claide had heard about the Purification Chamber incident, but he was not going to deny it, now that it had been brought up. Better for Claide to condemn himself.

"A burning rag hardly makes a murder attempt. It could have been a boy's prank. I have no intention of going anywhere."

He thought for a moment that Claide looked disappointed by his response. "If you will not tend to your own safety, I will be forced to."

"Meaning?" He did not hide his suspicion. If Claide wanted an excuse to monitor his activities, this would be it. Then again, perhaps he intended to order Tusánt out of Rhidam. As senior gdhededhá and temporary acting k'gdhededhá, he could do it, if he chose, but it would raise questions Tusánt suspected the man did not want to answer.

Claide paused, seemed to mentally retrace his steps, took the time to look at Edward and Saul, both of whom were taking this incident more seriously than Tusánt appeared to be. "As novices under his instruction, I expect you both to keep an eye on him. Report anything suspicious to me at once. Have you shared this with the King?"

Tusánt shook his head, surprised that Claide would recommend the novices already there to protect him. He feared for a moment that this had been the plan all along, that the two were already loyal to Claide. But he knew Edward better than that, and he had sensed no dishonesty in Saul, so he dismissed the idea as something borne of paranoia. Perhaps Claide hoped that 'anything suspicious' would include day to day details Tusánt did not want to share.

"No, I have not," he admitted, finally answering the question. He had told the princess about the rag incident, but not the King.

"It is too late tonight to go out; it is not safe. But I want you to do it first thing in the morning and I want both of you to go with him."

"Yes, dedhá," Saul nodded.

Edward agreed. "We will see that no harm comes to him."

Satisfied, thinking he had their compliance, Claide grunted, "Good. One of you stay, with him…and all of you, get some sleep."

Tusánt snorted. "I can sleep alone, your grace. I am not afraid."

Claide's parting expression, brief as it was, gave Tusánt every reason to think that perhaps he should be. It was enough for him to decide to allow one of the novices to remain in his room after all.

❧*❦

Ártur had known his wife would be angry, but he had not expected her to come to Kavan's home to seek him out when Bhen had been enlisted to take their son back and forth between them. That arrangement had been Syl's idea to avoid her husband. Whether she had come tonight to see him, or simply because he was detained, he had known there would be a price to pay for his lateness.

Bhen shrugged apologetically as he took Llucás into the house.

"I know I am late, but I swear to you I was not in Rhidam, not in danger…and it was not my…"

"Anywhere but Elyriá is dangerous," she spat furiously.

"Even Káliel?" That disrupted her anger momentarily as she swallowed her initial tirade. He hastily continued. "I had to retrieve Prince Owain, and though I left before sunset, his ship to Pháne, to visit Muir, was delayed by rough seas. I could have left him for another night…but Gabrielle begged me wait. We were talking…"

"About Kavan."

The hostility with which she said the bard's name made Ártur flush angrily. "About how Hagan is faring as King and about Bhyrhán Bhíncári. By the time Owain returned and was ready, it was after sundown. I delivered him to Rhidam and came straight here without leaving the Gate. I never set foot outside the chamber in Rhidam. I was under Gabrielle's protection. I am sorry. Please do not be angry."

Her expression was still dark with irritation, but she said nothing as she stormed off the porch. She knew he was being truthful, knew that he had not purposefully broken their arrangement. In truth, he had not broken it at all; he was not to be in the Rhidam keep after sunset unless it was an emergency and he had not been there beyond the moments necessary to deliver Owain. He had come to Bhryell straight away as promised. She knew this, but she was not prepared to admit that she was wrong.

❧Chapter 17❧

Tusánt was beginning to question if he was meant to stay away from the Purification Chamber. He had heard some unusual things there over the years, but nothing that stood out as the strangest. Within the span of a few days, he had spoken briefly to an Elyri youth he had determined had not been Gaelán…which meant it might have been the orphan the chamberlain was seeking, he had someone throw burning cloth at him, presumably to frighten or maybe kill him, and now this.

"Have you told anyone?"

The other voice timidly replied, "I have been afraid to do so, dedhá. I don't want to die. But I cannot live with this any longer. I needed to tell someone…so that the King can be told…"

Tusánt shook his head, though the fellow on the other side of the curtain and screen could not see him. "I cannot tell him. Your words to me cannot pass beyond these walls; I cannot break the Faith."

"Not even to protect your people? Protect yourself?"

The Elyri rubbed his face. "It is forbidden. You know this." The wish to do so, however, in this instance, was compellingly strong.

"But the King must know! Shall I write a letter?"

"Perhaps…but anonymity might not be best, for a witness willing to speak freely is more credible and the King can protect you. If you feel it necessary, come to me afterward and I will grant asylum at Saint Kóráhm's. No one can touch you there. But only you can make this decision. k'Ádhá forgives you for the fear that has kept you silent. Let Him guide you."

There was a shuffling sound behind the curtain and a groaning sigh. "Thank you, dedhá; I will think about what you say."

Listening to the man depart, Tusánt could not hold back the shiver. His suspicions, the princess' suspicions, were confirmed, at least in part, and he was powerless to tell anyone. He could only pray that the man would do the right thing and that Claide never learned of it.

∾*∾

Grinning, Kjell sank into the chair after General Glucke left the library where the prince spent much of his time when his brother had no need of him or when some political function did not require his attendance. None of those advisors or people he associated with suspected that he had been in Enesfel. They believed he had gone hunting alone, something he often did, without the King's knowledge or consent, despite the extended duration of this particular trip. Hunting was a past time Kjell had cultivated specifically for the purpose of hiding other activities when he needed to. That he brought home several pheasants, three deer, a dozen rabbits and a handful of quail supported his claim and attested to his known prowess.

What amused the prince, however, was that King Merkar had not even realized he was gone. Kjell wondered how long he could be away before his brother noticed. Long enough, he suspected, to leak secrets to the Lachlans or anyone else, long enough to defect and bring back an army. His brother, he thought, was truly a fool.

General Gluck was unable to tell him anything about the King's plans, despite Kjell's casual wheedling for anything 'exciting' he might have missed while away. The general believed his lack of information was because the King had no motive or strategy, that he was merely curious about Enesfel's troubles and was inept enough to try to use his entire army in a quest for truth. What the general's lack of knowledge told Kjell, however, was that Glucke had fallen out of the King's favor. Perhaps Merkar had decided Glucke was a threat. More likely, there was someone else, a new advisor in place that the prince had not yet noticed or met. It gave Kjell a mission to cautiously pursue without drawing attention.

He had seen his brother briefly as he passed the dining hall. The King had been eating, engaged in conversation with one of his usual advisors, and had not seen Kjell pass. Loathing filled the prince, confirming the resolve that grew inside. His brother must be dethroned. If he could find a way to imprison Merkar for treason, it would be best. Kjell did not want to kill him. If he was to become king, he did not want to do so by bloodying his hands. But Owain was right. Merkar, like so many de Cormick's before him, had to be brought down if Neth was to thrive. One way or another.

❧*❦

There were so many scrolls and parchments piled on Jermyn's desk Claide had doubts about ever finding time to sift through them. He had been tending the man's duties since his initial disappearance, but had left more personal documents and matters on the man's desk so that he could tend them when he returned, or so that someone else would choose to tend to them first. Of course, nothing had been done with any of it, and it fell to Claide to sort through it all at once. He should have done this from the start, he thought bitterly. He should have foreseen this tedious task.

He began to paw through it, creating three separate piles according to subject matter and urgency. Some would be given to Rankin to take care of, some would be given to Tusánt, and some he would see to himself. Most of those that required actual effort, however, he was shoveling onto Tusánt in the hopes that the Elyri would complain about his workload and perhaps ask to be transferred out of Rhidam, or better still, out of Enesfel, to somewhere with less to do.

It would solve a problem Claide had yet to resolve.

Fingering the sealed document he had just picked up, he studied the front and frowned. Witsom. He opened it and his frowned deepened. dedhá Loefel of Witsom was dead, had died over a month previous. He had not been alive during Claide's absence from Rhidam, and he had told the princess the old man had asked about her. Had she known of his death, Claide wondered, or had it been an innocent query? With her, it was difficult to tell. He knew she held no affection for him, did not trust him, but he had seen nothing in her demeanor or behavior that suggested she hated him outright or that she knew too much about matters she should not.

Best to drop the topic of dedhá Loefel. If she inquired again, Claide would inform her of his death. To say anything else, to raise unanswerable questions, would be an unfortunate mistake.

❧*❦

"Your announcement…" Caol did not know what else to call it. "This is no whim? You intend to marry Lady Niall?"

He could not read the King's face but he thought the young man looked trapped and scared of the vow he had publically made during dinner. The Niall's were not present, which made the declaration even more unusual, and Caol thought it best to seek the truth.

"A king must have a queen," Hagan squeaked. "And an heir. It is expected."

In theory, Caol agreed, but in this instance, he felt the betrothal was somehow wrong. Hagan was young still, little older than Asta, and barely able to manage the responsibilities placed on him by the crown he wore. The additional duty of family would surely tax his already stretched nerves. "It is not expected of you to marry if you are not ready for the obligation and commitment of a wife and children. There is no need to rush a hasty decision."

Squaring his shoulders, offended that his judgment was being questioned despite the fact that Caol was speaking the very same arguments Hagan was wrestling with, he said, "I do not see how marriage could be any more of a responsibility than being king. It should be easy compared to that." He wondered, from the look in his uncle's eyes, if there was something about marriage and family that he had not taken into consideration. But his resolve did not waver. This had to be done.

Caol bowed to mask his expression. He believed it was a mistake, but this was not the time to argue or offer frank advice he did not think the King wanted to hear. Caol had enough problems without prying in the King's romantic endeavors. "I hope you will wait until my return from Durham. I want to be here for your wedding…but I think it is important I see my granddaughter before she is grown."

The King chuckled. "It has hardly been that long since her birth, Uncle, but of course I will await your return. It will take a month or more to make preparations I am told. You do not plan to be gone longer than that, do you?"

Not knowing how long he might be away, he knew there was a high probability that he would miss the King's wedding unless he was extraordinarily lucky, but he replied, "A few weeks at most. It will take time to journey there and back, and I plan to spend more than a day or two with Wilred and his family. Lord Corbin and Chamberlain Cáner have been briefed with everything I know, with everything I have been doing. They will have everything in hand, but of course, if you need me, you may summon me."

"I will," Hagan said in a tone that struck Caol as a promise. "I have gifts for you to take. You will tell Wilred and Bianca I say hello? Give them my blessing? Extend an invitation to my wedding?"

"Of course. They will feel honored to be invited and to be here. If you have no further need of me, My Liege, I must prepare for my journey." He thought it wise to escape while he and Hagan were on relaxed speaking terms.

"Best speed, Uncle."

Caol thought he detected a note of apology in the King's voice but he chose not to acknowledge it or ask about it. He could not afford to.

❧*❧

External pressure, like a boot pushing down on his skull, brought Kavan abruptly awake. His eyes shot open but he could see nothing around him that could create that sensation, and an attempt to grasp at the weight with his hand produced only a fist full of air. Awake and aware now, the pressure increased until he thought his skull would split under the force. This was no physical attack, he realized, but rather the effect of that presence from before, surrounding him, cutting off the air into his lungs, working to incapacitate his body on the dry, cracked soil where they camped.

Throwing up every defense he had ever learned, Kavan struggled for many minutes to shut the thing out. Eventually, Kavan's body aching with exertion, the entity was forced to withdraw but continued to linger nearby, waiting for another opportunity. Or perhaps it waited to see what Kavan would do, if he would pursue or strike out and leave his friends vulnerable. Keeping his senses tuned to its location, he sat, wiping the unexpected blood from his nose and upper lip, feeling as though he had spent the night wrestling when he had barely moved from the position he had fallen asleep in. Wortham was poking at the fire, stirring it to life, and after looking at the bard and frowning at the blood on the man's face, he resumed preparing breakfast.

Neither spoke.

Because Kavan chose not to attack, only monitor the presence as he went about his morning routine, it grew bored and departed. Or Kavan assumed it was bored. The presence showed no coherent thought pattern; it was a swirl of energetic anger and determination focused on only one thing. Kavan. Or the relics the bard carried.

They had ceased traveling for this holy day, at both Urian's and Kavan's insistence, despite Kavan's eagerness to press on. It seemed fitting, by the bard's reckoning that their mission, holy in purpose, should pause to commemorate holy days in accordance with the teachings of the tenets. They were to remain camped for four days, during which time Urian made a more determined effort to indoctrinate Zelenka in the ways of the Faith, while Wortham spent his hours away from the camp, away from Kavan, hunting the portly rodents that dotted the patchy, scrubby landscape and seeking out berries, mushrooms, and any other edible commodities they could find. The animals did not provide much meat, but by roasting and drying what they did provide, it would supplement their travel rations. Kavan had aided the hunt the day before, the kestrel's sharp eye and sharper talons proving beneficial, but still, the men had exchanged nothing more than necessary instruction and small talk.

Frustrated and melancholy, Kavan turned his attention away from hunting and onto the composition of a hymn, something both Kóráhm and Myreth would be proud of…and thus perhaps Wortham as well.

Not merely a hymn, he decided, leaning against the boulder at his back. He wanted something more elaborate, more ambitious, a three-part anthem to commemorate the cycle of life, death, and rebirth that these festival days were meant to celebrate as well as the ascension of Dhágdhuán into the ranks of an after-life that, before him, had been unobtainable to the living.

There were no words at first, only a melody forming in his heart. As the others awoke and began their day, the counter-melody emerged. Then the harmony. He realized he was thinking in terms of four voices, his and Myreth's being two of them. Odd, he thought, since he had never attempted to compose anything of this nature before. But as no one seemed inclined to interrupt him in his perceived prayers, he chose to commit the work to paper for later use. Perhaps next year he would be among people who could share the joy of this work, if only Myreth could be there to sing it with him.

Perhaps Wortham would enjoy it too. Perhaps by then, the awkwardness between them would have passed.

❧*❧

Having bid Owain farewell, the King was alone in the dayroom, pondering his next matter of business. He hated the weeks that immediately followed major palace events. As the guests departed and the castle staff and life, in general, returned to normalcy, depression invariably followed. He had hoped Owain would stay longer, as conversing with his uncle would have given him something to do, but with problems awaiting in Fiara, Owain could afford to linger no more and Hagan reluctantly permitted him to leave. Duty came first, and the kingdom's welfare was of top priority, even if Hagan sometimes wished it was not.

At least, he thought, Sigrid and Dayly would return soon from their short trip home. Hagan was elated that she, and her father, accepted his proposal, and happy that Dayly too approved. Many had been surprised by his announcement as none had realized marriage was under consideration and he had not been actively courting anyone. This marriage, however, was more about political stability than courtship, and if they disapproved, none but his uncle questioned it. As the oldest man in Hagan's family, Hagan accepted that it was Caol's right to question his intentions, but the inquisitor had not advised against the marriage, even if he thought it was a mistake.

For Hagan, not being advised against it was the only approval he needed.

Thinking about Sigrid made him smile. He would prepare a welcome for her, a private meal during which they would begin to discuss the details of their marriage ceremony as soon as she returned. Afterward, if Sigrid was not too weary from her travels, he would ask her to ride with him; perhaps he would invite Asta and Gaelán as well. With no other pressing matters, both diversions sounded ideal.

"My Liege?"

Groaning, suspecting his beautiful fantasy plans were about to be dashed, the King turned from the window to face the open door behind him. "Yes, Lord McGranis?

The chancellor bowed. "There is a gentleman here who wishes to make an appointment to speak with you…"

"Now?"

Unable to guess the source of the King's irritation, the other man replied, "He said appointment…which does not mean now…if you are busy. He asked to see you at your convenience on an urgent matter."

How urgent could it be if he was willing to wait? Hagan frowned and said, "This afternoon. Mid-hour. I have plans until then." He knew the chancellor was aware of Dayly and Sigrid's impending return. "If he will return then, I will speak with him" He would forego a ride if he must, since Sigrid would not likely be up for that after her morning's travel, but he would not pass on the opportunity to dine with her. "Did he say what he wanted."

"No, My Liege…only that it is important."

The King hesitated. Perhaps it was information about the Corylliens, or about any of the missing individuals. Perhaps he had a name or identity of someone that Caol's Association network had thus far failed to offer. Or it might be nothing. Little was likely to change in the next few hours; whatever the man wanted would wait.

"Very well. This afternoon then. Take him to the Stateroom when he returns and let me know when he is here." He strode from the room without waiting for the chancellor to say anything more that might derail his plans.

❧*❧

It did not take Balint long to decide that Espen returning to Rhidam would be for the best. There was little the prince could do and the man's sulkiness had worsened with every passing hour. The prince had surprisingly not protested the suggestion to return to Rhidam, did not try to use his royal status to stay. Espen understood that it was best to allow the duke and general to complete the work they had begun while he attended to personal matters that were eating at him with ravenous abandon.

The tales of the dead emerging from the grave, causing mysterious deaths in the village, had been solved quickly. The Hatu soldiers had caught three young grave robbers hiding the unearthed bodies in the butcher's basement. The location had masked the smell of death initially, but a thorough search of the village had revealed the eleven decomposing corpses hidden there.

The seven deaths from a mysterious ailment, while more difficult to unravel, turned out to be the result of snake bites. General Zarkosta had seen such deaths before, and while the snakes used were never found, one of those three grave robbers confessed to having used a snake to kill his victims, a host of people who had, in some fashion, caused the killer trouble over the years.

The other two men, knowing nothing about the snake induced deaths, were given stiff penalties to pay and spent several days in the public stockades, shamed by their neighbors. The third, guilty of seven counts of murder, was sentenced to death.

It solved the village disturbance, although a fire erupted the morning of the execution which delayed the prince's departure. A single structure was destroyed, the one in which the condemned man had been detained, and he turned out to be the sole casualty of the day.

It eliminated the need for execution, but it raised suspicion about what else the fellow might have known, a matter the general and duke decided to remain to investigate. Twelve of the Hatu soldiers remained with them, as much to assist in rebuilding the burned structure as it was to investigate the fire and the victim's connections. Prince Espen and the remainder started back to Rhidam.

❧*❧

"I am honored you agreed to see me, Your Royalness," the tiny man said as he groveled and bowed with exaggerated respect. "I did not think you would."

The King motioned to a chair, already wondering why he had agreed to this meeting. The fellow who entered the room smelled foul, was missing most of his teeth, and though it appeared he had tried to bathe before coming to the castle, his efforts had done little to remove what was likely a lifetime of filth. Hagan struggled not to grimace in distaste. There were two guards in the room, and a page lingering in the corner, not in an effort to intimidate the already quaking visitor but as a precaution for the King's protection. Though the man had been searched for weapons and did not look to be a threat, Hagan was taking no chances.

"Normally I would not," he admitted, "but circumstances of late require a certain amount of…flexibility. What brings you here today?"

The man looked even more nervous and began twisting his battered felt cap in his hands. "I have information…proof…regarding several people who've been…" He glanced furtively at the others in the room as if afraid for them to hear.

"Speak freely, sir. None here will repeat what you say to me."

"The warehouse…where k'dedhá was found…belongs to my sister's husband. He lent the place to several unsavory sorts before the k'dedhá's disappearance. I don't know why, what it was for, but I saw them go in and out many times; I work nearby…I'm a tanner, My Liege. When I heard the good k'dedhá was tortured…found in his basement…I suspected the worst. I can give you names…my brother in law…his family…his friends…if you agree to give protection…"

The King leaned forward, interested. "What makes you believe these men of whom you speak are linked to the k'dedhá's death?"

The small man continued to fidget. "Unsavory sorts, like I said. They paid…but never enough…and made threats when they didn't want to pay...or could not. They were rude, surly...brutal and cruel. Like their station makes them better than us. One was Cíbhóló but I have not seen him in days. The others I still see...though never near the warehouse. And there's another out of place...not like the rest."

The mentioning of men of class, and the Cíbhóló, was noteworthy. While desert traders were not common in Rhidam, they did come on occasion, and one constantly mentioned in connection with the Corylliens led the King to believe it was likely the same man Agis had executed. "Out of place how? The nomad?"

"Not the nomad. He spoke little, and I saw him there before the k'dedhá was taken." He grimaced and began to shake more violently and finally muttered, "I saw dedhá Claide go into..."

Gripping the arms of his seat, the King growled, "dedhá...are you certain it was...?

"I saw him myself. I recognize him...though he was not wearing Faith robes...but rather a plain..."

"Then it could have been anyone!" The King's anger prompted him to rise and made the other man slide his chair back to do the same. "You are accusing a man of the Faith of murder..."

"My Liege...we are all men of Faith..." the fellow whimpered, "and I never said..."

"This is a serious accusation. No dedhá would consort with murderers or participate in killing his..."

Sticking to his story, on his feet now, the little man interrupted out of fear and dismay, "I don't know why he was there, My Liege...I could not guess...but he was there! I know his voice. dedhá Tusánt said you could prove my statement..."

"We shall see. Guards, take this man below until I can get to the bottom of this," Hagan snarled with a wave of his hand.

"Your Royalness!" It took only one guard to subdue the small man who was too terrified to struggle as he was dragged from the room. "Please! Speak to dedhá Tusánt!"

Visibly shaking with anger, the King pointed at the other guard in the Stateroom and barked, "Bring me dedhá Claide! I want the truth!"

❦*❦

Young Hagan? To marry? The concept seemed peculiar to Kavan. When he left Rhidam, Hagan had seemed a child still, despite being of legal adult age. Though it had been nearly six months since that day, and in the interim Hagan had become a king now nearing his fifteenth birthday, he did not seem old enough to marry. But the vision of a familiar girl trying on gowns, discussing her betrothal with her maids, had not been a dream and the Sight was never wrong. Incomplete, yes, but never wrong.

He scowled. He should be there for Hagan's wedding. He owed it to Arlan to be there for his son and Enesfel's king. But he had no idea how soon Hagan was planning to wed, and even at the wagon's fastest pace, Kavan knew he might not arrive in time.

It reinforced the need for a Gate, but so far he had detected none they could use.

The second image came no less clear, although it was vaguer in meaning than the first vision. A man in prison, a common Teren, begging for Tusánt, seeking validation of some claim he had made. The image meant nothing specific to the bard, but the aura of foreboding that accompanied it made Kavan sad.

"My lord?"

Wortham dropped beside him, the first time he had done so since Yashir, concern on his face that was red with exertion. He had been gathering firewood and had either returned by chance at the moment of the two visions, or else Kavan's consternation had drawn him back.

"Our King is planning to marry," Kavan said, rubbing his face with both hands. The revelation did not explain his sadness, however, and the captain scowled.

"Pr…King Hagan?" Kavan nodded, noting that Zelenka was still bathing in the nearby stream while Urian, unable to see her, kept watch enough that he could shout for aid if it was needed.

Wortham, also finding the notion of the boy marrying to be an odd one, muttered, "It is necessary, I presume; there must be an heir after all. Shall we not arrive in time to attend?"

"I do not know."

When Kavan did not look up, Wortham scowled and asked, "What are you not telling me?"

While not surprised by the captain's intuition, the timing of his choice to talk was unexpected. "The other I saw…is unclear. I do not know what it means…who he is…only that dedhá Tusánt knows him."

"Someone is in danger?"

Kavan had no answers, only guesses based on what he felt. His piercing gaze lifted to cut through his friend at last, wanting answers but uncertain how to seek them. Rather than reply, he said, "I should be the one questioning you."

Perplexed by the shift in topic but not by the bard's tone, Wortham glanced away long enough to put another piece of wood into their fire. "My lord?"

"What are you not telling me? What have I…something has troubled you since leaving Yashir. I thought it might be a matter of your brush with death…or else…" He swallowed but refused to shift his own gaze. "Or did my…did the blood…?"

Never before had any miracle unsettled the captain. He had always taken such things in stride and never treated Kavan any differently. But something had happened in Yashir to come between them and though he feared the answer, Kavan wanted to know the truth.

"No…never that. The amount of blood was…unsettling…and my momentary fear that you had taken your own life…" Wortham sighed and shrugged. "But you did not…you lived…and what happened was not at your hand. You have done nothing wrong, my lord."

"Then it is the other?"

"I have faced death before…for you, for others…it was closer this time, sobering…but that is not what has been on my mind."

Wortham wiped his sweat-soaked face on his sleeve, thinking he too should take the opportunity the nearby creek presented. It had been too long, and in Kavan's presence, he felt particularly unclean and ashamed that his tension and distraction had hurt his friend.

"It is illogical, I know, to blame myself for what almost happened…to blame myself that you might not have been able to complete your quest…because I sold horses…but I do. We are on our way home, yet still I struggle with how I almost failed you…"

"You could never fail me."

"So you say…" He glanced in Zelenka's direction, hearing her humming to herself though he could not see her, "but you know that isn't true. I have failed you many times…and may yet fail you again, despite my best intentions."

"You are only a man, Wortham…as am I. We fail…but I shall never blame you for any of it."

Though not yet prepared to absolve himself, Wortham felt less guilty for hearing Kavan say so. "I have also been perplexed by our…my…benefactor…and I admit it has been a sore distraction. I might have believed Lady Orynn was responsible for my freedom, for the many gifts we were given, as she has been of great service to us in the past. But there is something…I do not believe it was her…which I admit I find disappointing." He grunted, knowing his discontent at her absence was likely less than Kavan's and he regretted, after seeing the pained flicker in the bard's eyes, that he had spoken her name.

"There was something…as we were leaving…I saw a woman's face briefly in a window…a stranger…and yet I swear I have seen her before. Not knowing who…or why I recognize her…why I feel…threatened by her…is unsettling. She could have been our benefactor, but that does not coincide with this feeling of…dread…or perhaps I saw her in Yashir before and her face stayed with me…"

"Perhaps your feeling of dread is for what is ahead of us, not what is behind," offered Kavan.

"Perhaps," Wortham agreed, though why that dread and that face had inspired a jolt of fear he could not guess. "Will we go soon? Zelenka is weary of sleeping in the wagon…though she prefers it to the ground. She understands our delay is of religious import, but she does not understand why…since her faith is not our own. Perhaps if you explain it in song. I think you could teach anyone easier that way than Urian can with sermons and parables."

He clasped the bard's wrist affectionately, the first bridging of the gap that had been between them since Yashir, and Kavan felt a flush of excitement rush through him. He covered the man's big hand with his, knowing Wortham would feel the trembling there but not desiring to hide his joy that they seemed to be on speaking terms once more. "Anything to hear me sing, Wortham?"

"Anything to hear your music…which has been too long absent." The hours since leaving Yashir had been too still. His contributions to generating that stillness cause the captain too long to rectify it. "It will help pass the time, will make the occasion solemn and joyous at once…and give you the chance to sing. You have not done so in too long, my lord…and I apologize for my part in that. If not for Zelenka, do it for me."

"No need to beg, Wortham…for you, I shall do anything…"

"Likewise, Kavan." Especially, Wortham thought, if it would atone for his recent withdrawn silence.

❧*❧

Claide stood before the throne, his hands clasped contritely in front of him as he bowed to the young man seated there. "I humbly request that you release this man, My Liege," he murmured, relieved that his face was not visible in that position for the King to read.

"He has slandered your name," Hagan protested.

Face unreadable as he straightened from his bow, Claide shrugged as if he did not care what anyone. "Only to you. No one else has heard his claims." He did not know that Tusánt had previously heard them and had been the one to send the fellow to the King. "He may be misguided and delusional, a sick man with a brain fever perhaps, but he is not dangerous to me. The Faithful know me. His claims will be unheeded if he utters them to anyone. I am prepared to ignore this and forgive him, but if you feel he will persist in his delusions and it might cause further unrest, send him to Saint Bhílycá's. He can cause no harm to anyone there."

The dedhá's calm, kind words and air soothed the King's ruffled nerves. "I suppose you are right, dedhá. I had hoped he had something useful to offer, but he is clearly a man not to be believed. After this, anything else he might say will be suspect. I will do as you suggest and let him know if he continues to pursue these slanderous fantasies, he will be sent to Saint Bhílycá's. Thank you."

The dedhá bowed again and kissed the King's offered hand. "I should thank you, My Liege, for thinking highly enough of the Faith to bring this to my attention. I hope our combined efforts can continue; we might yet bring an end to the unfortunate times and situations in which Enesfel finds itself."

The possibility made the King smile. "I hope so, dedhá."

As soon as Claide was gone, Hagan ventured into the dungeon, to show his benevolence by freeing the man with his own hand. He had never been into the dungeon as he imagined it to be full of the sounds of torture and the smell of death. And though the level was dimly lit, stale smelling, and eerily quiet, it was not as frightening as he had imagined it would be. Bolstered by his own bravery in confronting his fears, Hagan found the prisoner, with the help of one of the attending sentries, and unlocked the man's chains.

"My Liege?" the man stammered hopefully.

"You are free to leave here."

Instead of rising to his feet, the man prostrated himself and kissed the King's shoes. "You are most benevolent, Your Royalness. I knew you'd believe…"

Shaken by the unexpected gesture, the sort of reverence none of his subjects had ever shown before, Hagan put his hand on the man's shoulder and tried to draw him to his feet. "dedhá Claide has chosen not to hold you accountable for your words," he began.

The small man jerked back and stared at him with horror. "dedhá…you spoke with him?"

Not understanding his captive's reactions or fears, the King said, "Of course. It is his name you sully with your slander. But he chooses to forgive you, and bid me set you free…on the condition that, if you speak of this to anyone else, you will be sent to Saint Bhílycá's…"

Hagan did not know what he expected, but the small man's next actions and words were not it. He scurried back to the wall where he had been chained and cowered there, quaking in terror. "Please, I beg you; do not make me leave this place."

"Do not…?" The fellow must be truly mad; no sane man would choose to remain in a dungeon.

"If I leave here, I'll die. I have spoken against him; he'll kill me."

With a cynical snort, Hagan said, "dedhá Claide will kill no one."

"He will kill me," the fellow wailed. "Or he will have someone else do it! Please, Your Royalness…be merciful…"

Firm in his belief that releasing the man was the most merciful thing he could do, the king pulled him gently but firmly to his feet. "You cannot stay here. There is no life for you here."

"Then call for dedhá Tusánt; he offered sanctuary. He promised!"

Hagan shook his head with a bemused chuckle. "You will be given a decent meal and sent on your way." A meal seemed the least the King could do. "This man," he indicated the sentry beside him, "will escort you home, if you are concerned with your safety, but remember what I have said, sir. Further slander will not be tolerated"

He left the dirty man with the sentry, trusting the soldier to see to his welfare. Once he was free, Hagan was sure he would be alright. Any man who begged to remain in a dungeon was delusional indeed.

❧*❧

Diona entered the morning room, book in hand, expecting it to be empty at this hour. It was too dark within to read, except by candlelight, and of the palace residents, none but the chamberlain sometimes came to read here. Years of experience and familiarity with the people around her had taught her which rooms were most likely to allow solitude at any hour of the day, thus finding Espen there, looking out the window with his back to the door, his clothes dusty and disheveled as if he had just returned, was a welcome shock. She took a few hesitant steps, setting the candle she carried on the nearest flat surface, her heart thundering in her breast, feeling a strength of emotion that was entirely new and unfamiliar. As he turned to face her, she stopped moving, until the moment their eyes met. His expression was tormented, his dark eyes heavy with sadness. Out of the sheer exhilaration of seeing him, and perhaps to prevent him from speaking and saying what she feared he might, she dropped the book and dashed forward to throw her arms around his neck.

Without thinking, she kissed him. Kissed him the way she had wanted Kavan to kiss her, the way she had never kissed a man in her life. Temporarily taken aback, Espen froze, but when he did respond, it was with more ardor than she had hoped for, more of the fury of passion she had hoped to arouse in Kavan.

But she was not thinking about the bard. She thought of nothing but Espen, his firm shoulders beneath her hand, his dark curls tangled around her fingers, his hands on her waist that drew their bodies together. Dizzy with emotion and physical responses she had never imagined, she could not think at all. This was what she wanted, the way she believed love should be, the way she had known it would be with Espen when she gave in to what her heart wanted rather than listening to her troubled thoughts.

But footsteps running in the corridor interrupted them and she stepped back abruptly, fighting to regain composure, in appearance at least, more quickly than Espen expected after the passion of that kiss. The page in the doorway breathed heavily and looked, to both prince and princess, to be frightened.

"Pardon the intrusion, My Lady…My Prince…but I thought it best to find you at once…"

"What is it, Peter?" He was her favorite amongst her brother's pages and she often sent him on errands when she thought Hagan would not notice.

"You told me if I ever saw or heard anything…I should report to you at once."

"Of course."

"I was with the King. A man came…after the noon meal…a man from town. He said he was…that his wife's brother owned the warehouse…where k'dedhá Jermyn was found."

Eager to hear the tale too, Espen came to Diona's side. The potential importance of this message erased his disappointment over the interrupted kiss. "Easy young sir…catch your breath and then continue." Espen looked at Diona, hoping he had not overstepped any boundaries, but she nodded to encourage him. Anything that would prompt Peter to talk was welcome.

The boy nodded and pushed his raven hair from his black eyes. "He claimed to know names of those who rented the space, prior to the k'dedhá's abduction…a Cíbhóló…men of class…and said…" He shuffled his feet. He was eleven but seemed much older and younger at the same time. "One of those he saw there…was dedhá Claide."

He did not miss the hopeful glances shared between the princess and prince. "The King was angry and cast the man in the dungeon until he could…"

"Dungeon?"

Peter nodded. "I think he wanted to confirm the story. The man begged him to seek out dedhá Tusánt, but instead, he summoned dedhá Claide. I know you wanted me to tell you when he comes, when he is in audience with the King…" He did not know why, but he was bright enough to know the princess suspected the dedhá of something, "but I thought it better to stay, to learn what they said, what would happen."

Although she would have liked to witness the exchange herself, Peter staying not to miss anything had merits too. "And he came?"

"Aye. He asked for the man to be released, said the fellow was mad…though he did not seem that way to me. He did not seek charges or sentence, and so the King went to the dungeon straight away. I followed as far as I could. The man begged to remain, claimed he was in danger, but the King forbid him to stay. He was to be given a meal and then set free…"

"Perhaps he is still here; dinner is not yet served," Diona said hopefully as she fumbled in the desk drawer for a quill and parchment on which she set down a hurried letter. "Give this to whoever is on dungeon watch and have the fellow brought to me at once."

Dutifully, Peter bowed and ran from the room, message in hand. Diona stared after him, trying to calm her thoughts, clenching and unclenching her fists for many moments. "Hagan is a fool."

Though Espen was inclined to agree, he was also inclined to give the King the benefit of the doubt. "To be fair, he does not know he should be suspicious of dedhá Claide."

"Perhaps not," Diona snorted, "but he should have enough sense to learn the truth of accusations before jumping to conclusions that could get a man killed. He could have asked Bhríd, or one of the others, to read the poor man…then there would be proof. We might have names. Advising Claide that someone is implicating him before seeking the truth gives him the chance to hide his involvement."

Espen reached for her but she edged away from him in her frustrated distraction and he frowned. "If we question him ourselves, we can gain the names and have him read," Espen reminded her. "It will be something to pass on to Lord Dugan when he…"

But Peter was already returning with a soldier in tow, and both Diona and Espen wondered if the page had kept the other man waiting at the end of the corridor in case she wanted to see him. The soldier bowed, barely disguising his worry as he said, "Master Peter says you wish to speak with the man we held today…but he is not here…has been released…"

"He was to eat before…"

"I know, My Lady. Peter speaks true…but he opted for a hasty departure and has already been escorted home."

"Then find him and fetch him back. Bring him directly to me. Wherever he is, I want all of Rhidam searched until he is found."

The soldier bowed, his expression indicating that he respected and perhaps even feared the power the princess wielded. "I will do so at once, My Lady." He departed to obey, running when he was out of her sight in the corridor, but Peter remained in the doorway.

"If you wish to speak with the King, he is going to be on the promenade until the meal is served," he offered hoping to be helpful.

"Not now…thank you, Peter." She would see that his loyalty was rewarded, but not until that man was found. With a wave of her hand, she dismissed him.

The lone stub of a candle on the desk sputtered and flickered out. In the silence of the dark room, she became more acutely aware of Espen's presence. It amazed her how quickly thoughts of duty fled at that moment when her senses filled with the memory of his kiss, his taste, his smell, the touch of his hands. His slow steps were like thunder and she tensed as he stopped behind her, his hands finding an anchor against her hips. Conflicting desires warred within, to run, to say something, to kiss him again and summon back the force which engulfed her senses before they had been interrupted.

Instead of doing any of those things, she froze in unexplainable, and unexpected fear. The strength of her longing frightened her, as did the way he held her against him. It did not hurt, it was no threat, was actually something she wanted more of, but still, she was afraid.

Intellectually she understood the union she wanted as much as she believed he did, but something made her pull away before she could succumb to that desire.

"Diona…"

"We…I…cannot…"

Espen's dark eyes bore confusion at first and then shifted with a spark of insult. "You think I would dishonor you? Make demands on your chastity? After this many years, do you believe me to be a barbarian who would do such a thing?"

"No, I do not…I mean…" They were the sort of demands she had made of Kavan, and realizing that brought up her shame all over again.

He shrugged and strode towards the light of the still open door. "Do not think I will apologize for a kiss. There is no shame or dishonor in it. Perhaps I took advantage of you…but I think not. I think you desire it as much as I. But if this is not what you wish, then it is the cruelest game to offer yourself and then turn me away heartlessly." Maybe it was the way of courtship in lands outside of Hatu. If so Espen wanted no part of it.

In the darkness, alone and trembling, confused about the tangle of emotions and feelings within, Princess Diona sobbed.

❧*❧

Refusing to pace, Tusánt looked from the window where he had stared into the darkening city for too long to the man who entered his office with worry in his eyes. "No sign?"

Saul shook his head, his brow furrowed, his mouth twisted into a frown. "None. Are you sure he will come?"

The Elyri groaned. "I'm not certain of anything. I thought he would…but perhaps he changed his mind about going to the King…or has decided our help is not needed. Perhaps the King is protecting him." Or perhaps, he grimaced, it is too late to help him.

"I will wait longer if you wish? Shall I send Edward to you?"

"Good lad…but no. I think it is too late tonight…and Edward will already be asleep. If he were coming, I suspect he would be here by now. You might as well sleep."

Saul shrugged and grinned. "I can sleep on a pew. Such discomforts are good for the soul occasionally." He chuckled. "If someone comes, I will hear them…and Edward is near enough that you have only to call for him if you need him."

"Your devotion to the unfortunate souls we tend is admirable, Saul. Thank you." It that fellow survived the night, made it into their safe custody, it would be Saul who deserved the credit.

"You're welcome, dedhá. Goodnight."

❧*❧

If, as the soldier claimed, the formerly imprisoned townsman had been escorted to his home, he had not arrived there. The man's wife had seen no sign of him since he left the house for the náós early that morning. A quick search of the tanner's home indicated that some of his belongings were missing, but his wife could not account for them, as if he had been back to take them without her knowledge. The soldier assigned to escort him swore he had left the man at his front door, but could not say if he had gone inside.

It was only certain he was not there now.

Fretting, Diona tapped her fingers on the sill in her sitting chamber. If only Hagan had talked to her first. Before he had become king, and even in those first early weeks of ruling, she had been one of his primary advisors. But he seemed to resent her intrusion and advice now, as if wearing the crown was all that was needed for a man to make a sound decision. She did not claim to be perfect or wise or all-knowing, but she did believe she had more experience than Hagan.

But as Kavan pointed out many years ago, in matters of state, she would always be powerless unless she held the throne. Because she was a Teren woman, her thoughts and opinions might not be taken seriously by those in command. As unfair as it was, there was little she could do to change it. Her brother's advisors, except perhaps for Chancellor McGranis, showed trust and interest in her opinions, but in truth, she had no say in matters of state if as her brother ignored her.

She had not left her room today. She was avoiding Hagan, avoiding Espen. What she wanted to do was find the prince, kiss him again, be assured that she would feel that same desire and that he did not hate her for her inconsistency. Little had ever frightened her, but she was afraid now and it made no sense. If she knew what it was she feared, she could at least discuss it with him, help him understand. But there was no one to talk to except her servants, to whom she did not want to show such weakness. Perhaps she should invite Muir to Rhidam. He had proven helpful to her in the past. He was the only one she could think of who might listen to her now.

"You sent for me, Princess?"

Turning from the window, she forced herself to smile but her eyes conveyed her darker emotions. "Thank you for coming, dedhá. I hope you did not come alone." Other than her brothers or her uncles, he was, perhaps, the only man she could invite alone into this room without causing scandalous talk, but an Elyri traveling alone in Rhidam was a risk.

"Both Edward and Saul accompanied me…at Claide's insistence no less…though he does not know I was summoned. They are visiting friends in the barracks. What might I do for you?"

"Please…sit." Tusánt obeyed, guessing from the lines around her mouth and eyes that what she wanted to say would be bad news. "Someone came to Hagan yesterday with information about dedhá Jermyn's murder. I was told he asked for you. Do you know anything about this? About him? Where he might be?"

The Elyri shifted uncomfortably. "He came here?" She nodded and he rubbed his face with his hands. "He came to me in the Chamber…and I cannot reveal what he said. I encouraged him to come here, to share what he knows so that the King could make an arrest…"

"You should have sent him to me." Diona did not mean to chastise the dedhá, but she was annoyed with the way events had unfolded. "He told Hagan he had names…but before he provided any, he spoke of Claide's involvement, and Hagan threw him in the dungeon for slander. Rather than summoning you…or asking someone to read him, he sent for Claide."

Tusánt's face lost color. "kyag k'Ádhá…"

"Claide forgave him, convinced Hagan to let him go, but the fellow begged not to be released. I learned all of this too late, after Hagan sent him on his way. He did not return home it appears, or at least he did not stay there, and now he is missing. We have no names…and Claide knows there is someone who suspects him. If he thinks you or I…"

"There could be dire consequences…for all of us." Tusánt felt like a fool, but he had not thought the King would act the way he had. "I told him to come to me after he spoke to the King, if he did speak to the King, and I would take him to Saint Kóráhm's. Saul waited in the sanctuary all night, but he did not come."

"Then he is either hiding or has gone to Saint Kóráhm's on his own, or else Claide has intervened. If only he had given us names…"

"He gave me none other than Claide's." Tusánt did not feel he was breaking any confidence in divulging that, since the fellow had already spoken to the King. "I am sorry. I did not think the King would…if I see him, I will make sure he is safe, and let you know at once."

"I do not blame you, dedhá…and would appreciate anything you can do…as I am sure he will. I have men searching Rhidam and hope he is found before Claide finds him. I am also overdue," she grunted, "for a talk with my brother."

"Can you do that without giving our suspicions away?"

"Of course." Or at least she was determined to try. "He does not suspect me of anything…and he knows I dislike Claide. If I can prompt him to be more cautious with sources, with Claide, everyone will be better for it."

"I pray so, Princess. You will have my prayers." As would the man whose life he might inadvertently have put at risk.

⁂*⁖

With k'dedhá Tythilius' death, there came a shift of ecclesiastical burdens, and in Claide's efforts to push his Elyri partner too far, much of that burden fell on Tusánt's shoulders. Now that there were two novices under his direction, however, capable young men with good heads and better hearts, Tusánt was able to shift some responsibilities onto them, allowing them to do the work while he oversaw their progress. Given his experience with the náós choir, placing the weekly musical matters into Edward's proficient hands made sense. It pleased Edward as well; he had enjoyed his years in the choir, loved to sing, and thus directing the children and adults who participated in the musical contributions in every Gathering was an honor he did not take lightly. Saul's talents lay elsewhere, in day to day administrative matters and in spiritual outreach with the sick and the needy. Edward in no way saw his assignment as lesser, and with the King's upcoming birthday, he would have the opportunity to prove his merit with the Lachlans as well as the gdhededhá who trained and guided him.

Alone in the loft, he looked across the sanctuary, pondering what musical selections he should make. He was no composer or instrumentalist, but he could sight-read music and had a good memory for lyrics and tunes. The children had not yet arrived. Six came from within the boundaries of Rhidam, another three were under the care of the gdhededhásur within the náós, while two were brought from the city orphanage. None were extraordinarily gifted, but they had adequate talent and most importantly had interest and enthusiasm. With their help, Edward was determined to turn the King's day into a memorable event. He hoped to enlist the aid of the Lachlans' new bard as well. His talent would be of considerable help and would, Edward hoped, overshadow any ability the children lacked.

The clatter of something above startled him. There was nothing to be seen from where he stood so he assumed something had fallen in the rafters. Was there a hole in the roof? Damage from the winter storms? Collapsing tiles or rats? It should be looked into. dedhá Claide would want to know if repairs were needed prior to the King's day.

But the first of the children began to arrive and Edward decided he would investigate the noise later, when there was enough light to see by, so that he could make a proper report of what he found.

❧*❧

"kyag."

Her hands were on his face, brushing aside his pale hair as she traced the line of his jaw with the light touch of her fingertips. There was someone else with her, a presence…no two…he could not identify but partially recognized though he could see no one beneath the weight of his heavy lids. He could not even see her. It was instinct that told him she was there, and that was enough. He wanted to look at her, but was incapable of doing so. He must be dreaming of dreaming, or else dreaming of being awakened by her. The soft touch of her lips brushed across his forehead, eliciting a shiver, pulling long-buried passion to the surface. It was enough to wake him, but she was not there, if she had ever been. Dawn was still a long way off and the others in his party continued to sleep, Urian and Wortham by the dwindling fire, Zelenka in the bed of the wagon behind Kavan. The presence of Orynn in his dream was gone and he was alone on the wagon's seat where he had fallen asleep.

Swallowing his disappointment, Kavan wrapped his arms around himself. He wondered how he would ever get over the pain of losing her if these dreams would not stop. The sensations of her touch, her lips, her breath on his skin felt too real and lingered still, making the memories seem not like a dream at all.

It was nearing dawn. The morning of Adhár, the New Spring. Though he was grateful for the renewal of life and his part in the cycle, he was also vaguely disturbed that the rósádhá that had plagued him for so long had not manifested itself on the eve of Dhágdhuán's recorded sacrifice. He had braced for the possibility, thinking it the logical thing to do, climbing onto the wagon's seat to be away from the others if it should come. But the night passed uneventfully and dawn brought no trace of blood or suffering. He wondered if this manifestation was similar in that regard to the passing of other miracles, if he expected it, it would not come, or if the Faith had gotten this date wrong as it had gotten so many other things wrong.

The day was far from over, just beginning, and he might well suffer before the sun set, in a way that the others might witness. The notion horrified him, but if it came that way, it could not be helped.

Laying down on the empty bench, his foot struck something heavy. A wooden chest, and not one of the two they already owned. This one was smaller, but of solid construction, and when he touched it, he choked with emotion and pulled back in surprise. Orynn had been there. It had been her touch he had felt. She had left this for him, whatever it was, and had not stayed long enough for him to wake.

Maybe she could not…or did not want to risk the inevitable pain of parting again.

Within the trunk nestled in a bed of deep blue velvet, was a silver weight scale, the sort merchants used for weighing products or tax collectors used for counting coins. It was an unusual item to be left as a gift and so he guessed it was something he would need later. He withdrew it from the box long enough to examine its craftsmanship and test its slight weight. Beneath it rested another velvet pouch, this one a pale peridot green, barely big enough to contain anything at all. His hands shook as he replaced the scale with one and removed the pouch with the other.

The contents were emptied into his palm.

Kóráhm's Cross. Similar enough to the one he had previously worn to cause him to fear that harm had befallen Myreth and Orynn had returned the pendant to its original owner. But this cross was slightly smaller and lighter, though both were made of the same mysterious silvery metal. He raised it to his mouth reflexively, pressing the coldness to his lips. Though he did not regret giving his pendant to Myreth, he had felt uncomfortable without it around his neck where it had hung for sixteen years. This gift would not only take its place, but it would also remind him of he who wore the other…and of the woman who had brought it to him now, as well as help re-establish his connection to the Heretic Saint who was his patron.

Orynn, he mused as he closed and locked the box. You bring me gifts…but what am I to do with them? When will I see you again?

The pondering of those elusive questions, he knew would deny him any hope of sleeping for the rest of the night.

❧*❧

The day of Rebirth already. gdhededhá Kesábhá had many more villages and towns to visit before he felt he would be ready to confront the k'gdhededhá, and yet he felt his time to do so was running short. He had traveled as far as Cyllyá, the town which had been his most difficult challenge thus far. Though the parish Faithful invited him to celebrate their Gathering with them, they were far from pleased with his accusations against the leader of their Faith. It was no surprise, no offense taken, for this was Dórímyr's birthplace. Khwílen had believed if he could sway any of those in Cyllyá, he would be able to convert anyone to the rightness of his cause.

But he could only do so if given the chance. He convinced one or two of the Cyllyá leaders of the truth of his position, and knew it was not necessary to convince each of them. Still, he had wanted to try in the remaining time he had here. After that, it would be time to move on and allow the truth to grow, to spread, on its own.

Leaving Cyllyá introduced a higher likelihood of someone taking word of his efforts to Clarys, which might open up an inquiry against him and prevent him from going any further. The ecclesiastical head of the Faith could defrock him, excommunicate him, possibly demand his execution though Kyne Mórne would have a say in that. He knew Dórímyr would do something, however. To ignore the accusations was to invite trouble, while reacting too harshly might be seen as an admission of guilt and raise questions throughout the land regarding his fitness for a post many thought he had held too long.

Khwílen almost hoped it happened. If he was to be a martyr for a cause, he could think of none better.

For now, he must hurry, and pray the k'dedhá did not yet know of his efforts. He wanted to finish his circuit of Elyriá before death or expulsion from the Faith were delivered. He had been away from Enesfel too long to know the order of things, but he did not believe anything could have improved during his absence. The attack on

Healer MacLyr supported that. Something had to be done, the carnage had to stop. Khwílen was prepared to do his part to make it happen.

❧*❧

It was to be the final Gathering for which Tusánt would lead the choir for some time to come, and Edward had asked to sing with the children. His baritone voice sounded a little out of place with the blended trebles, but Tusánt's tenor helped even out the balance, creating a pleasing Adhár choir. Edward was happy to have the opportunity to sing under Tusánt's direction once more, and hoped it would not be his last.

During the entire Gathering, whether singing or listening to the dedhá below, Edward felt a wary prickle up the back of his neck, as if someone was watching him, someone other than the children he sat with. At times he thought he heard noises above him, or off to one side, and at the edge of the choir loft he thought he heard singing reverberating through the plaster wall. What he thought he heard was a high voice, youthful and clear. It had to be a trick of acoustics, however, of those singing on his other side, their voices shivering off of the walls around them.

But still, it troubled him. He was not Elyri, had no way to determine why he thought he was hearing a voice where one could not be, why he felt he was being watched, and Tusánt, it seemed, sensed nothing. The Elyri's lack of notice and concern should have reassured Edward, but it did not. Something unusual was happening, and in his capacity as protector for dedhá Tusánt, Edward was the man to determine what that unusual was. It would not happen again today, however. He and the other dedhá were invited to an Adhár feast in the keep, and if Tusánt was going, Edward and Saul were going too.

❧*❧

"You realize, Mister Alty, that not just anyone is suitable. I was told you're interested in our cause, that you're potentially a valuable asset, but there are precautions I have to take before you can be trusted. I will need to talk to you more, get to know you somewhere more private, do some checking, and we will see if membership is a good fit. If you don't check out…"

The dusky-haired man nodded, rubbing the scar which trailed from the edge of his faint mustache almost to his ear. "Of course…I'd expect it. You never know who might try to get in, what sort of trouble they might cause. I want the monster that did this to pay, him and all his cursed race. But I'm a patient man, within reason. I can bide my time if the payoff is revenge…and if you can't help me…" he shrugged, "I'll find some way to do it myself."

Chuckling, the other offered his hand. "I believe you've come to the right place, Alty. I'll be in touch. Do I reach you the same way?"

Alty nodded. "Yeah…best for both of us. Don't want any unnecessary questions from the authorities…or anyone else."

The stoop-shoulder man nodded and shuffled away from the lamp post into the early evening shadows of the alley behind them. The one with the scar wanted to smile as he listened to him depart, but he did not. Someone might be watching.

He seemed to have passed the first test, as this fellow did not know that Johann Alty was actually Lord High Inquisitor to the Lachlan court. The man was cautious, as expected, but he was not intending to harm Caol. The Elyri were that man's targets, along with those unfortunate Teren who either got in his way or consorted with the pale-skinned demons. Johann Alty had been born this day and had taken his first steps into his new life. All Caol could do now was wait.

❧Chapter 18❧

Though he had been reasonably certain he was hearing noises from the náós rafters, Edward was not expecting to find evidence of someone living there. Crumbs of bread littered the wood panel flooring beside the tattered remains of a threadbare blanket. Given the drafts here and the lack of any sort of insulating features, this flimsy article would not provide much warmth. There was a water flask, a shirt and trousers hanging over a beam, and a leather pouch that jangled when he lifted it. Coins? Why would anyone with money be staying here?

Unless…

He opened the pouch and looked within.

Elyri bhelts.

Edward placed the pouch exactly where he had found it and glanced around one more time. There was no sign of whoever was making their home here, but he was confident the squatter was Elyri and would know his hiding place had been invaded. The upper reaches of Hes á Redh provided a safe, though not the most comfortable, haven, and he wondered how the person had found their way here. He had no wish to evict the tenant, however, as long as the person was not using fire here, and as there was no trace of either candle or lamp, he chose to leave them be.

But how, he wondered, was the person surviving? This was a likely explanation for the food that gdhededhá Hazen repeatedly reported missing from the kitchen in recent days. Poor fellow must be hungry. At least he assumed it was a man, a boy judging by the size of the clothing hanging nearby. Forced to hide, forced to steal, and apparently living alone. Regardless of their station of birth, Edward had never met an Elyri who seemed anything other than noble. To be forced to live in this way must be barely tolerable.

Yet there were ways Edward could aid him, foremost of which was keeping his presence here a secret. He might mention it to Tusánt so that the boy could be moved, if he wished, to Saint Kóráhm's, but in the meantime, he would find ways to provide for the boy's needs. A proper bedroll and blankets. Clothing. Food and drink. It would take time to gain his trust, particularly when he learned he had been discovered here, but Edward needed to try. An Elyri child being alone in Rhidam had to be the worst possible fate in the world.

❧*❧

The outpost looked no different than when he had left it, no further damage, a few more repairs on the outside completed, no loss of life incurred. But each man relayed the same tale, another ship had come to Pháne during his absence, similar in size and design to the first. It had attacked before dawn on the morning of Adhár, the day Muir had set sail to come back, but thanks to the ship and crew that the Prime Magistrate had ordered stationed here, the attacker had been driven away, badly damaged but not sunk. At least, she had not sunk in sight of the island, but the captain of Káliel's vessel had thought it wiser not to pursue lest another come in behind him, cut him off from the island, and attack the outpost.

Muir wanted a second ship, one to patrol close, another to pursue attackers and trespassers. He wanted captives, hostages, people he could question who might be able to explain why that cave was important…and who it was important to. He recalled nothing there of interest, although he remembered that Bertram's killer had expected to find treasure within. Was there a treasure they had not taken time to find? What had Kavan discovered in the back room that no one else but Wortham had seen? They had brought something out with them, but Muir had never asked what it was. It had not seemed important before, as Bertram lay dying and the world fell apart.

But it seemed important now, and Muir wanted to know. If Kavan had what these people wanted, he needed to know. He needed to know what people were willing to fight and die for.

He wondered if it might be better to allow someone to gain entry, to prove that there was nothing there worth having. Perhaps he should take men and look into the matter himself. Kavan's warning had been stern, however, that no one should go into that cave for any reason, and after the earthquake and the collapse of some of the walls, that seemed a prudent idea. Regardless of the reason, Kavan would not have given such instruction frivolously. And if there was still a treasure there, coin, knowledge, or a weapon, could Muir risk anyone finding it, taking it, using it against him…or someone else? If the treasure was the danger Kavan eluded to, Muir thought not.

Stuffing the letter into the leather tube, he gave it to the sailor who would deliver it to Gabrielle. Then he resumed scanning the horizon for any trace of intruding ships. There was no sign of trouble. He hoped Gabrielle could talk the Council into a second ship. He wanted to be ready for the next assault and would not be able to approach the Council himself for the foreseeable future. He was needed here. Trips home would have to wait.

He hoped Clianthe would understand.

❧*❦

There was a message from Kjell awaiting when Owain arrived home. The de Cormick heir had suffered no incidents on his return to Neth's capital and no one suspected the truth behind his absence from court. His brother had not even realized he was gone. Which meant, to Owain, that Kjell was more resourceful and cunning then claimed and had a better hand on the pulse of Neth's political power than anyone knew. Owain felt confident that, once they discovered a flaw in Merkar's infrastructure, found his weakness, it would be a simple thing for Kjell to overthrow him and step into the seat of power without the bloodshed he was reluctant to permit.

But there was no easily identified indication of what Merkar wanted, what his interests in Enesfel were. That would take more time and investigation. Kjell believed that, if they learned it, he might have what was needed to confront his brother, perhaps force him to abdicate the throne, though even that would not be easily accomplished. Owain was less confident of the possibility, but Kjell knew the Nethite King better so Owain had to take him at his word. Just as Kjell was taking him at his, that he would have Enesfel's full support when the time was right to act. Diona's support did not guarantee the King's, but Owain had to believe that, when the moment came, Hagan would see reason and logic and the benefits that action against Merkar would have for everyone in the Five Sovereignties.

The danger of such a tentative belief clawed at Owain every night, during every waking hour. And there was not a single person he could discuss it with.

❧*❧

Surviving the rutty roads and thirsty heat, the wagon passed into Hatu near midnight on the day after Adhár. They could have stopped to set camp earlier, as Urian and Zelenka wished, but Kavan, feeling the pull towards Rhidam more strongly the closer they came to familiar territory, had pushed on until Wortham demanded they stopped. Kavan itched to continue. As he had the first watch that night, he kept the wagon rolling longer than the others hoped, but once it was Wortham's turn for the watch, the captain refused to bump along any further. As he pointed out, he did not have Kavan's heightened senses and the others were weary of trying to sleep as the wagon groaned and tossed along the cracked, parched road of yellow clay.

But at least they had entered the Five Sovereignties, which for Kavan's morale and resolve made a great difference.

Wortham surrendered the third watch back to Kavan and slept in the wagon because there had been no opportunity to build a fire when they stopped. With everyone onboard, Kavan started them moving again. When Wortham was jostled awake before dawn by an unavoidable furrow in the road, he was annoyed but not especially angry, though he wanted to be. If there was a reason for this increased urgency, if their time to reach Rhidam was running out, Wortham would oblige him as much as he could.

But he would not drive the wagon in the dark.

Due to the bard's persistence, they caught sight of the outskirts of Enda after three hours of daylight travel, and after pushing the horses as much as they dared, they reached the sprawling city nearly an hour later. Zelenka stared slack-jawed at the biggest city she had ever seen, patch-worked though it was from centuries of conflict and conquest, and she bombarded Wortham and Urian with an endless stream of questions about everything she saw and much of what could not be seen. Kavan shut the questions and chatter out in exchange for a focus on details he hoped to find, anything that spoke of the dangers he suspected lay ahead, any small details that might give him a warning, or at least give him hope.

When the horses stopped and the wagon bumped to a halt in front of the náós they had passed through months earlier, Kavan helped Urian disembark as the Faithful poured into the street to greet them, astonished that they had returned alive, amazed that Kavan's hands were no longer mangled and deformed. Uncomfortable with the recognition he knew he should have expected, that he knew he would face more and more the further north they traveled, Kavan spoke little, leaving the telling of their tale to Wortham, and reluctantly to the more talkative Urian, those two men just as capable of speaking the truth as Kavan, though Urian's truth was considerably more embellished than it needed to be. They were welcomed as if they belonged there, as if they had never left. Some of the gdhededhá took the wagon to the rear of the building where the horses would be tended and his companions followed the gdhededhá into the shade of the náós, but Kavan remained in the street, hoping to avoid the discomfort of reliving his ordeal through an unending barrage of questions.

He knew instead where he needed to go. He recognized the pull he felt and favored addressing before leaving Enda. He owed the old sage a debt he could never sufficiently repay. Assuming Wortham would guess his destination, the bard set out through the city streets without informing the others of his intentions. Zelenka needed the captain, and Kavan needed Wortham to stand in his place, speak for him, when he, comfortably, could not.

This was a pilgrimage Kavan needed to make alone.

Bhóité's disjointed hovel had not changed in the months since Kavan had been there. The bucket of pitch Wortham had used to repair the man's roof, dried now from exposure to the air and warm weather, still rested at the base of the rickety ladder which leaned against the wall where Wortham had stood on it. The fire ring they had enjoyed together was cold, filled with soot though the ash of its last fire had long since blown away. There had not been a fire here in many weeks.

Squatting, Kavan laid his hand on the black earth and listened to the sounds of the day. Heat-spurred insects chirped and buzzed, laying a constant blanket of sound beneath the others, distant barking dogs, bird song, the braying of sheep and goats in the surrounding open fields. All distant noises, none of them emanating from the area immediately encircling the dilapidated hovel. It was as if a bubble of air, impervious to sound, surrounded him, making the crunch of his feet in the soil, his heartbeat, even the sound of the dust shifting beneath his hand, seem louder than it should. Something at the fringes of the fire pit caught his eye and he shifted his weight to reach for it. The wooden figure Urian had made, the figure Kavan had given Bhóité in partial payment for the information he had needed to make his journey south. It lay face down on the dry earth, its crevices dusty with the effects of extended weather exposure. Closing his eyes,

Kavan tried to read anything from the object that would tell him when it had been dropped here, but nothing came. It was a cold, dead piece of wood.

With a shuddering moan of suspicion, fueled by the muted silence and heavy weight that unexpectedly pressed upon his chest and stole his breath, the bard approached the front door. It was ajar, as it had been when he was last here, but he hesitated to enter. The old man had feared no one, had felt no need to bar his door just as Tíbhyan did, but the atmosphere felt different, and even before entering Kavan knew what he was likely to find. When he had left here, it had been with the impression that he would not see the sage again. In the hopes he had been wrong, he knocked on the doorframe, eager for an answer he knew would not come.

"bhydáni?" It was not an official title belonging to the ancient man, as far as Kavan knew, but it seemed to apply now as much as it had before. When no answer came, he pushed the door open far enough to enter and stepped inside.

The man's home was tidier than it had been, as if someone had cleaned it with the intention of being gone for a long time, or of leaving and not returning. There was uneaten food in the pantry, grain infested with maggots, cheese withered by the air, fruit moldy and shriveled into a hardened lump. An empty pitcher on the table bore rings around the inside, left as its contents evaporated. On the table near the man's bed was the bottle of wine Kavan had given him, empty and uncorked, and an open book.

He was afraid to touch that book afraid to read it, although he guessed it had been left there for him, left open to a page he was intended to see. If, as he suspected, this was the same Bhóité of whom Kóráhm had spoken in his journals, this man would have been more than three thousand years old when Kavan met him. Such a lifespan was not something Kavan wished to consider. Elyri lived a long time, longer than any Teren; bhydáni Tíbhyan was four hundred and sixty-six years old. The oldest Elyri Kavan had ever heard of had been nearly six hundred before his disappearance. But three thousand years? It was inconceivable.

Disappearance. Not death. The graveyards in Elyriá held no Elyri who had died of age. The old ones left their homes and families and did not return. No one knew what became of them, or if they knew, it was not discussed. When Kavan, as a boy, brought the topic up with his elders, others around him, particularly the clergy, seemed uncomfortable, almost terrified, and refused to talk about what those disappearances meant. It was difficult to preach the immortality of the soul in an unending afterlife when it was unclear what became of an Elyri's mortal shell.

Kavan often pondered the fact that perhaps he could not die. Be killed, yes. Fall ill and die, of course. But he might not succumb to age as Teren did. Bhóité's absence gave every sign of fitting into the classic Elyri end of life pattern. Bhóité had turned his back on life, it seemed, called to whatever end awaited their kind, and had not returned. Would never return. Kavan knew this and believed the book had been left as a farewell gift. It might contain answers, but they might be answers Kavan did not want. He did not want to know if he was immortal, did not want to know how long he might live among Teren, watching those he loved be born, wither, and die around him.

Closing his mind against any images that might emanate from the book, he picked it up and perched on the edge of the bed long enough to take several calming breaths. No brooding. Brooding would lead to the pitfall of melancholy, and he had chosen, after the healing of his hands, to avoid those dark, dangerous places as best he could. Instead, he would look around the man's home for anything else he and his companions might use, anything of import Bhóité had left behind, and then he would compose a song in the sage's memory. Before that, however, the loss of the sage gave him the impetus to do one other thing first. Back against the wall, he closed his eyes, sought the energy within, and reached out with a sigh.

Tíbhyan stopped mid-step, barely believing what his senses told him. He closed his eyes to focus on the strength of the sensation, leaning heavily on the strong arm supporting him.

There was no imagining that presence, that touch. The force of power was as strong as if his favorite student stood beside him, although he could sense that the bard was still very far away. How far, he wanted to know. What are the limits of your strengths?

But the questions were ignored as the younger Elyri sought reassurance that the sage who had given him much as a child was still in the world. In return for that reassurance, Kavan offered his, proof that he was alive and safe. Someday, the sage might receive the answers he craved. Perhaps then he would be able to supply Kavan with a few in return.

"bhydáni? Are you unwell?"

Focusing on Bhen, the old man's face spread with the widest smile the harp maker had ever seen on his face. "When your uncle returns, tell him I have a message."

It did not take a large leap of logic for Bhen to guess the bhydáni's meaning. "Kavan spoke to you? Just now? How? What did he say?"

Tíbhyan chuckled, little surprised that Bhen would reach that conclusion so quickly. Though largely untrained, Bhen was an intuitive sort that knew enough about Kavan, and Tíbhyan, to connect the truths with very little visible evidence. "How is not so simple to explain…especially given the distance between us. There is no specific message, just the knowledge that he is alive, safe, and…"

"Perhaps he is coming home!"

The sage did not have the heart to undercut the joyful, wistful expression on the young man's face. Having no way of knowing if that hopeful declaration was accurate, he prayed it was true. But whether Kavan returned or not, Tíbhyan was happy knowing he was alive.

❧*❧

Asta wanted to see the letter, to know what her father had written, but since the message was addressed to the older princess, Asta obediently refrained from opening it. She had taken on many of her father's duties without raising questions from the King or his royal advisors. With those duties being performed as efficiently as ever, no one appeared to think about, or notice, who was addressing them or how they were being fulfilled. Diona alone knew the truth, although Asta suspected Gaelán was growing suspicious. Sooner or later, Asta would have to tell him the truth, but not today.

"What does Father say?" she asked, giving her cousin adequate time to read the message.

"He has been asked to a meeting…the Corylliens are inviting him to join them. It appears he is in." Diona was both relieved and worried, because although everything had gone according to his plan thus far, the hard part for Caol still lay ahead.

"Not in." Asta turned from her cousin. What her father was doing was exciting, and she was eager to be there with him, but she was also aware of how deadly this could be. Worry outweighed her excitement. "Gaining their trust now…the first meeting could be a trap…"

"You are afraid for him," Diona murmured as if realizing it for the first time. "He knows what he is doing."

"I know. I have faith in him but I know, whatever happens, I might not see him again."

There was nothing Diona could say to reassure her. Would it be any worse for Asta to know her father might be gone than it had been for Diona to wake up one morning to discover her father was dead? She wanted to tell Asta that everything would be fine, that Caol would come back, but regardless of how deeply she believed it, life experience had taught her that belief did not necessarily match reality.

"We must hope for the best," she finally said, burning the letter as she had promised Caol she would do, leaving no record of their contact, no trail to follow to connect them. "This stays between us."

"Of course it does." She would fail her father if she began giving away state secrets. Fingering the locket at her throat which she had not taken off since Hagan's ball, she tried to smile. "May I be excused?"

Thinking it best that Asta had a friendly distraction, one Diona wished she had, she replied, "Go…and say good day to Gaelán for me." As Asta hurried out of the room, Diona watched the remnants of Caol's letter turn to ash.

❧*❦

He was sulking, he knew, but the knowledge did not change anything. Bhríd was leaving for Levonne today. It was not his father's departure that upset him, but rather the realization that Tayte's birthday was three days away…and Gaelán could not be there to celebrate it with him for the first time. He could have demanded to go, but what was the point? Why go and face Tayte's hatred? Why ruin his brother's day? And why remind his mother of the pain of unchangeable things?

The one good thing to come of it was that Ártur would remain in Rhidam rather than go to Bhryell at night, because there was no one to fetch him should the Lachlans require his aide. There was a comforting bond between him, Ártur, Rouvyn, and Bhyrhán. Perhaps it was an Elyri thing, though Rouvyn was not Elyri, or perhaps it was a healer thing, though Bhyrhán was no healer. Why no one considered that Bhyrhán could summon Ártur from Bhryell, Gaelán did not care. He much preferred having Ártur here. It helped Rhidam feel normal.

"Master Cáner?"

He recognized the man in the novice robes of the Faith, but Gaelán did not know him. He sat straighter in his chair, hoping that someone had come to him for healing. He needed something to do. "Yes?"

Edward stepped into the room, shuffling his feet. It was not facing an Elyri that made him uneasy, but rather being inside the castle, facing a young man of noble blood. And asking for favors from a stranger was always unsettling for him. "This may be an odd request...but...do you have...?" Although Gaelán did not appear annoyed or inconvenienced by the interruption, Edward feared this was a bad idea.

"Go on, dedhá."

"Lindunn...Edward Lindunn. I found an orphan...your height...I thought first of you and wondered...if you might have any clothing to spare?" He could have rummaged through the collection stored in the náós, donations from the people to be given to the less fortunate, but Edward felt that would take too long. He had no money to buy decent, new clothing, but something had compelled him to come here, to ask a young man nearest to the orphan in size.

Gaelán skewed his face in confusion. "Why should it bother you to ask? I would be happy to help. I may have some items; anything in particular?"

"He has nothing...so anything would help." He watched the young healer open his armoire and begin to rummage through it. "I am hardly of your station...this is...akin to begging."

"You are dedhá, and this is asking for a donation for the needy. Not begging. Worst I could do is say no. As long," he added as he began to pile clothing on the top of the dresser, "as the user does not know the donor is Elyri..." Gaelán did not have to stretch his imagination to know how that knowledge might affect the recipient's willingness to accept the donation, the backlash that might come to Edward if it was known.

"That will hardly matter, my lord. I promise your name will not be mentioned. I am sure he will be grateful for anything he can get."

❮*❯

"You could have extended the courtesy of saying you were leaving us. You could have told me where you were going."

Taken aback by the angry edge to Wortham's voice, not understanding it, Kavan felt appropriately chastised. He also felt unexpectedly annoyed. "You were occupied, eager as I recall for a real meal, and Zelenka needed you. I had to see him…Bhóité…to know if he…you should have known I would go there, that I would seek a Gate You should have trusted me."

That was the crux of it for Kavan, that for some reason, the captain had not trusted him after all of their time together and the years they had known one another. It made no sense to Kavan and it hurt.

Wortham leaned into the wagon, securing the supplies he had obtained from the gdhededhá, using the work to avoid eye contact. "Of course, I knew. Of course I trust you. But the stories, my lord…the violence in the north…the dangers…"

His voice trailed off before it broke. Every person he had spoken with since arriving in Enda told of Elyri persecution in Enesfel, violence bleeding south with the passage of time. There had been no episodes in Enda, but there were no Elyri here, beyond the old man, as far as anyone knew, giving few reasons to be prompted into negative actions. Their arrival, Kavan's presence here, could, Wortham feared, change that. And it could have been the reason that no one had seen Bhóité in a long time. His anger stemmed not from mistrust but from the fear that his friend could have been hurt, or killed, and the captain would not have been there to prevent it.

Eventually, when Kavan did not speak, he continued. "There have been no incidents here, praise be, and no one seems inclined to violence. There are few Elyri to test the climate in Hatu…to know for certain…and now you are here. It could happen. You will certainly face danger the further north we travel…and I will never forgive myself if I allow harm to come to you…or am unable to prevent it because I fail in my duty to be at your side."

Sighing, Kavan swallowed his pain and acknowledged Wortham's right to fear. "I likely will face danger; I cannot deny it. It will require me to be always on guard, but I cannot allow it to hinder me…even when it takes me away from you. If I can find a Gate we can use, it will relieve us of worrisome travel through Enesfel. That is my hope. The few I have discovered have failed me; the power in the Chalice and staff interfere with their use. If such continues to be the case, we are resigned to travel by land and sea…"

The captain grunted. "Precisely so, my lord, which is why I fear for your safety. You can fend for yourself, I know…but to not fault me my concern and my love…"

"Wortham." Kavan's hand covered Wortham's on the edge of the wagon's bed, contact that calmed them both. "I do not fault you for anything. Your strength and devotion are beyond reproach and I thank k'Ádhá for you every day…even if I fail to thank you. But please remember, there may be duties that I must see to alone. They are not meant to cause you worry. I will endeavor to be more considerate of your concerns and your wishes, to inform you my whereabouts and intentions…if you will likewise endeavor to trust me."

Knowing Kavan was right did not remove his worry. Wortham could not help it. He stared at the hand upon his for several still moments before swallowing, looking into Kavan's eyes, and murmuring, "I will try. Trying is the best I can promise. The old man…is he dead? The people here seem to think he is, as no one has seen him or his fires since one more…after our visit here."

So long, Kavan mused. He had been gone so long. "He has departed this life." Wortham would interpret that as the man having died, without Kavan specifying it. It was better that way, for Kavan could offer no explanation for where Bhóité had gone. "I see the wagon has been loaded."

"Nearly so. There is food and water still, which will be added at our departure. Might I request leaving in the morning, my lord, instead of today…unless you have reasons not to? A delay gives the dedhá more time to ready food, and Zelenka has asked to see more of Enda. Besides, there are merchants in town who have asked if you will perform while you are here. The White Bard has never done so…and though I explained you have no harp, they believe your hands still injured…they believe that such an injury should not prevent you from making music. They are most eager to hear you." He gave a crooked grin and dropped his hand to his side, breaking the contact between them. "I told them I would present the request but made no promises. Perhaps in doing so, we will gain something in return…"

At first, Kavan said nothing. He had not considered that the closer they came to Rhidam, the more people might seek out his music. Nor had he considered that they would see his hands and know he had been healed. Perhaps he could offer music, though not in the form they expected, but would they approve? Would they ridicule his voice? Would they flock to the miracle that had made him whole again?

There had been no derision in the south, no flocking to the man some called the Bhryell Saint, but those people had no preconceived notions about who and what he was.

"Do you fear their disapproval, my lord, even after the praise you have received…?"

Kavan sighed as the old feelings of self-doubt attempted to take root and busied himself with tightening a rope that did not need it. "You know me too well"

"These people believe you a cripple who cannot play…and yet they seek your music. They must believe you capable…"

"Or they seek to mock me."

Having been shunned enough in his life for differences he had not asked for, it was difficult to think this would be any different. If he was to try, however, if he was to plant seeds that could grow before him as he traveled so that those ahead would know what to expect, then beginning again in this place was the smartest thing to do.

At least these people who had never heard him play would have nothing to compare him to. They were more likely to be honest in their assessment for it.

Wrestling with the possibility as the day wore on brought him to stand on a makeshift platform in the nearest tavern before a room crowded to overflowing with people from all across Enda. Kavan sensed no anti-Elyri sentiment among them, only the anticipation of people waiting to hear what they had only ever heard about. It felt like the first time he had performed in a tavern in Enesfel, when he first took his talent to people who had no idea what to expect. Now, as then, he knew he could perform; his fear, however, was for what they might think of a man with the voice of a child…or a woman.

But there was no room for timidity. With a deep breath, he opened his mouth and sang from his soul. Song after song, until the tavern needed to close. Even then, as he made his way back to the náós for a night's rest, there were people gathered around him, asking for stories, a short song, a poem or prayer, or for nothing more than his touch, until Wortham pulled him inside the náós and ordered him to bed.

But the emotional high that left him drained also left him elated, depriving him of sleep. They loved him. He knew it, even though he found it difficult to believe or accept. His voice, as unique as it was, was as welcome in this place as his harp had once been…or would have been if he had ever traveled this far south to play. He had feared the loss of public adoration, all while feeling ashamed of needing it, and now it seemed his fear was groundless. That people still wanted his touch in the hopes of miracles, that they believed his prayers somehow carried more weight with k'Ádhá then their own, still troubled him. Yet he could not prevent that short of pushing people away, hiding from the world, and he unabashedly admitted to himself, admitted to those listening to his prayers, that he needed their love too much to do either. He had been cut off from people too long as it was.

And since he could not know whether such miracles occurred, as people claimed, who was he to deny what k'Ádhá might give them?

When he arose before dawn, it was to a large gathering flocked around the náós, flocking around the wagon as the gdhededhá brought it out and Wortham hitched the horses. The enthusiastic greeting of the crowd followed them to the northern limits of Enda, and some continued on with them, a larger gathering of pilgrims than Kavan expected. Crowds had always followed him, but he had never witnessed anything like this. He spoke to them as they journeyed, sang for them, and when his voice grew rough and weary, the night's lack of sleep catching up to him at last, the blind dedhá took up the task.

It took little time to realize this was no ordinary crowd. The White Bard of Bhryell had been healed of his deformity. He was a man favored and blessed by k'Ádhá, by Dhágdhuán, by all that was holy. Some of Hatu's beliefs differed from those in Elyriá and Enesfel, but if this Elyri was favored by the heart of the divine, they wanted to know why. They wanted that which made him blessed.

Dozing as Wortham drove the wagon north, Kavan knew that his life, his image in the public eye, was shifting dramatically. Or perhaps his own perception had shifted enough to see something that had been there all along. Whichever was the case, Kavan was at peace with it. And with himself.

❧*❧

They were going to burn down a peasant's farmhouse because an Elyri had slept there.

It seemed a drastic measure, though thankfully those who resided there were to be spared, in order that they might be taught a lesson at the expense of their home, everything they owned, any food they had stored, any animals trapped inside, their livelihood. Such warnings were of little use if the perpetrators did not live to learn the lesson, though sometimes the organization deemed it necessary to kill to get the message across to everyone else. Caol did not know where the farmhouse was or when the fiery purge would take place, nor could he be certain the farmer and his family would be spared despite the assurances that they would be. He was informed of the event, allowed to listen to most of the planning, but this time was forbidden to know more and forbidden to attend the burning. Since no lives were to be lost, in theory, Caol was content to let the burning happen without a word of complaint or protest.

To stop it, to interfere at this early stage, could blow his cover and lose him the trust of the men he was attempting to join. Afterward, when he learned more about what had happened, either through the organization of from Asta, he would do his best, covertly, to provide for the unfortunate family, to help them rebuild or relocate, whatever they thought would benefit them most.

There were no women in the organization that he had seen. Every person in attendance that night was male. If there were women involved, he had not heard them mentioned. He made notes of the names he learned, committing as much as he knew about each participant to memory to be written down later. He was storing his list in a place known only to him and Onea. If he failed to survive this, if it became evident that he was never coming out, everything he learned would be there for the Lachlans to use. It might not destroy the Coryllien organization, but it would hopefully be enough to prune the Rhidam branch and incapacitate the rest. After two meetings, Caol had nearly forty names. He intended to live long enough to get many more, as well as the head of Anri Heward. He owed it to the late King Arlan and all of those still living he cherished.

The matter had been given consideration long enough. Prince Kjell was the best means of learning what was transpiring in King Merkar's court. It was a bold step, to ask the Lachlans to place their trust in Neth's heir-apparent, but Owain was willing to take the blame should his faith in Kjell prove misplaced. He was the link between the Lachlans and Kjell, between Enesfel and Neth, and arranging this, playing the role of intermediary, would make Owain feel useful to the Crown in its struggle against their current troubles. If his efforts provided the Crown with anything they could use, encouraged amity between the two kingdoms, he was willing to accept a minor role, a footnote, in the history of peace. He would have the satisfaction, or the guilt, of knowing what he had wrought for the kingdom he had been raised to love. That was enough. Enesfel and the Lachlans had taken much away from him, but it had given back too, and Owain held no resentment. Kavan had taken all of the resentment away and replaced it with forgiveness, forgiveness Owain now felt he could repay by negotiating peace with Neth.

He sat at his desk to draft the letter, planning to address the matter to Princess Diona and allow her to judge when, and if, the matter should be divulged to her brother. Owain trusted her judgment more than he did the King's, although he would never admit that to Hagan. It was hardly Hagan's fault that he did not share his sister's years of experience, nor the years of experience Owain shouldered. Nor was it the King's fault he was not adequately prepared for the weight of rule.

Hagan had only what knowledge and wisdom Kavan and his other tutors had been able to foster, and Owain prayed that Hagan made the most of what he had been given.

☙*☙

The nearer they drew to Enesfel's borders, the edgier, more alert, and more irritable Wortham became, hyper-vigilant and barely sleeping. It was something Kavan understood, something Urian could empathize with as he too slept restlessly and listened more intently to those traveling with them for any out of place sound. Zelenka, however, inexperienced with violence of the sort they were anticipating, understood neither the danger nor Wortham's distracted behavior. She hovered too close now, following behind him no matter what he was doing, often in his way but unwilling to step away. She talked incessantly, tried to engage him in conversation by tugging on his sleeve, doing more than her share of duties to assist him, gave him every favor she could as if it would make him happy and relaxed again. He was given the first of the food and drink at mealtime, provided with the prime sleeping place even if she had to wheedle it away from Kavan or Urian, made sure he was the first to go anywhere, do anything. Her behavior was tolerated, but more and more his responses to her questions were given absently, or sometimes not given at all.

Increasingly dissatisfied with his unresponsiveness as the wagon pulled away from the village of Avarrou, she turned her attention to Kavan.

Her grasp of the language was improving, although Kavan was still unable to communicate with her as easily as either of them would like. He understood that she felt she had somehow displeased

Wortham, that she felt she was being punished for some unknown slight, and was desperate to know what she had done and how she could correct it. Kavan was unable to successfully convey to her that she had done nothing wrong; she simply could not understand, or perhaps her upbringing would not allow her to believe that the captain's mood was something beyond her control. Eventually, she gave up seeking answers and instead hunched in the corner of the wagon, watching the dirt road pass beneath them over the wooden edge of the wagon bed, brooding and pouting, no longer making an effort to speak to anyone.

The silence allowed Kavan to direct his thoughts back to his journals, but the awkwardness would not permit him to focus and his thoughts would gradually stray back to the images the Sight had shown him over the past few nights every time he tried to sleep. Myreth in the open gateway of the cloister, looking at the outside world as if he had not seen anything beyond the walls in which he had lived his entire life. The man's handsome face vivid enough that Kavan felt as if he could touch him. His dark eyes aglow with wonder and fear at the world awaiting him. Then, though no sounds came, no shift in the light or the scenery around him, disappointment settled on his features, a pout marred the seductive press of his lips that Kavan recognized before his hand slid from the edge of the gate and he turned back towards the cloister's halls. Each time, Kavan tried to lure Myreth out, urge him with everything the vision permitted, willing his dark twin to come to him. Myreth would pause as if listening, but in the end, he reluctantly turned away, seeking instead the voice of leadership he had followed for too long.

Would he venture forth, Kavan wondered, or would his fear and Qol's desires hinder him, hold him back? Or would he wait for Kavan's return, as Kavan had bid him to do? Kavan had urged Myreth to do what he must when they had last been face to face, and he had pleaded with Qol to give Myreth the freedom to make his own choice. But Kavan did not know if that would be enough. If Myreth was still there when Kavan returned the Chalice and staff, assuming he was able to do so, the bard intended to bring the man out with him, regardless of Qol's protests.

Yet there was no guarantee Kavan would ever see either man, or the cloister, again. All of that was still somewhere far in the future. Avarrou had been a replay of the events in Enda. No usable Gate was found. People asked him to sing, to talk, and lavished attention on him and his companions afterward, providing everything they could want for their travels. They continued to follow, many still with them from Enda, such that the size of their gathering grew larger every day. There were converts among them, men and women Urian blessed and welcomed into the Faith, a few who sought instruction to join the blind man in the Order of St. Bhenádíctus, and Kavan believed that there would be many more by the time they reached and departed Palil. The size of the throng both worried and reassured Wortham, for the more protective and devoted the people around them were, the more difficult it would be for any harm to come to Kavan. But it also meant that it might be too easy to lose an attacker in a panicky crowd if someone did strike at the bard.

Such worries about crowds and the possibility of assassination would be moot if a Gate was found with which the relics' power did not interfere, but it was looking more and more that their journey would continue as it had from the beginning.

There was talk of taking a ship from Kílyn to Levonne, despite Kavan's general aversion to sea travel and the likelihood that Zelenka would resist it after her first experience at sea. However unpleasant it might be, however much Zelenka might fight it, sea travel would be faster and they could avoid potential delays due to violence in Enesfel or the drag on their pace the burgeoning gaggle of disciples created. Avoiding the dangers of overland travel through Rhidam, if the rumors they heard were true, made a short stint at sea worth the discomfort.

Kavan sighed and rubbed his temples as he listened to Urian whittling beside him, voices silent for the night as sleep stretched across their host of followers. Many of his countrymen had died in the violence in Enesfel. He had no exact number, no one did, but for every story he and Wortham heard, he knew there was at least one other they knew nothing about. Ártur's suffering had nearly been one of that burdensome statistic. There could not be many Elyri left in Enesfel now; surely they had either been killed or had the wisdom to flee. Except for those in the Lachlan court who steadfastly refused to be intimidated, members of the Faith scattered across the kingdom, and the boy Kavan had seen. Kavan wondered if those who served Saint Kóráhm's remained or if they too had fled to Elyriá. He would not fault anyone who chose to leave. He did not want his grand endeavor to become a tomb for the Elyri in Enesfel.

The more tales of horror he heard, the more convinced he became that the items he carried were the salve required to heal Enesfel's wounds. He could take no unnecessary risks with his life; he had to live long enough to initiate that cure. After that was done, whether he lived or died, whether he saw Myreth again, would not matter. He would have fulfilled the purpose he believed was intended for his life.

No man could ask for more.

The attempt would be futile, but Tusánt felt he must try. Refusing to fidget or express the discomfort he felt in the other man's presence, he took a breath and squared his shoulders, grateful the other dedhá was not looking at him. "The k'gdhededhá might not have received our messages…" he began.

Claide dismissed him with a wave. Without looking up from his writing, he snorted, "Both of them? I sent one. You sent one. He must have received at least one."

Tusánt guessed he was recording the names of his allies and opponents, but he could not read anything from where he stood.

"With the amount of unrest and violence of late, there are high odds that any messengers on the road to Elyriá have been killed," Saul remarked, deciding not to leave all of the arguing up to Tusánt. "Particularly if someone learned that they carried messages for the k'gdhededhá. If I was an anti-Elyri supporter, I certainly would not want messages reaching Clarys."

Edward leaned forward, nodding with an innocent expression as if he were neutral in the topic of their discussion. "Although, if I was anti-Elyri, I think I would want to encourage the k'dedhá to come in order to kill him." He noted the dark shadow that fell across Claide's face and shrugged. "That is, if I was anti-Elyri, of course. I have no interest in killing anyone, or having them killed. Killing goes against every tenet of the Faith."

Tusánt did not think he was the only one holding his breath as they waited for Claide to speak, waited for his reaction to Edward's not-so-innocent words. The Teren dedhá had been very vocal over the last few days about the looming need to replace Enesfel's k'gdhededhá as quickly as they could, and they had heard his complaints about how the King refused to press for an election, preferring to wait instead for some word from k'gdhededhá Dórímyr.

That was the reason this meeting of Rhidam's gdhededhá had been called. Perhaps he was seeking voices in agreement for a rushed election. Perhaps he was hoping that, if enough of Rhidam's Faithful thought Dórímyr had been given enough time to respond, they would demand the King allow an election to proceed. He was disappointed, however, as nearly everyone gathered had voiced in favor of continuing to wait. Valgis and one of the female dedhá had voted for a prompt election, and as Tusánt watched her, surprised by her unexpected support of Claide, he wondered what was in it for her.

"We shall wait a while longer," Claide finally relented with a grunt as if he had no choice, when in truth he could have sent out the edict for election any time he chose. Tusánt could think of any number of political reasons he did not. "I see no harm in it. But I think you are all blind to his disinterest in the matters of Enesfel's Faith. He and the Elyri establishment have shown nothing but apathy for our troubles and have allowed us to do as we see fit until now…"

"…as long as it does not interfere with the function and tenets of the Faith," commented someone at the rear of the gathered group. Tusánt could feel Claide's eyes on him, wondered if those words were addressed at him, but he did not turn to see who had spoken.

"Yes…well…I see no reason for him to change his pattern now, to behave any differently. We merely wish to take care of our own…"

His voice trailed off, the thought left unfinished. Then he cleared his throat and straightened in his chair, closing the journal within which he had been writing. "I will draft another letter and send it tomorrow. If you think he will be more inclined to respond to you, Tusánt, I encourage you to do likewise. As for the rest of you, return to your duties. See to it that they are kept current, done properly and promptly, in case he comes. Without an anointed k'dedhá…there is much to do and it falls on all of us to see it is done. You are dismissed."

Tusánt did not rise; it was his office they had met in and he felt no need to cater to Claide. He did not fail to notice Claide's annoyance at having been outnumbered in his vote, and he noticed something else for the first time.

Some of the gdhededhá were moved by Claide's words.

Though the disinterest of the Elyri Faith leaders in the Teren church was perpetually obvious, it seemed more so when the attention of the k'gdhededhá was most needed. Having it pointed out to them, driven home by the continuing seriousness of Enesfel's troubles, which should have drawn the Patriarch's attention, at least a letter, underscored the truth of Claide's assertion. Enesfel needed to see to their own future if k'gdhededhá Dórímyr would not.

It was not only the Faithful that were included in that statement, Tusánt knew. He suspected Claide was implying much more by saying that the Teren must take care of their own. At any price.

Tusánt groaned in frustration and lay his head on his desk, feeling utterly alone.

❧273❧

❧Chapter 19❧

Reports of a disturbance in Hangman's Grove brought Agis thundering, a unit of thirty soldiers behind him, to subdue any chaos before an angry mob set its sights on Rhidam. Yet it was obvious something was amiss as he approached the infamous grove and heard nothing but the sounds of nature. No shouts, no clash of swords, no screams or evidence of combat, nothing that indicated an outbreak of violence. Suspecting a trap, he held his men at a distance, selected the nimblest of his followers, and sent the fellow forward alone on foot to investigate. Agis continued to listen, but heard nothing as his scout crept dutifully into the brush. When he was slow to return, the general, suspecting trouble, swung down from his mount and proceeded into the grove, his sword in hand.

He was not as stealthy as his scout, but he was not trying to be. If there was trouble, he wanted everyone to know the Lord High General had arrived to take care of it. When he stepped into the clearing, however, he stopped in shock, not believing the sight that greeted him.

There were few people in the clearing, the smallest of which should have been his scout. Instead, it was the Lord Inquisitor's daughter who appeared to be inspecting the gruesome find with less disgust then the scout was. Her horse was tethered to the scrub at the edge of the clearing. Agis did not waste the time in questioning her, but instead approached the nightmare they had been led to, the three crucifixes adorned with the graying bodies of the dead. The one in front of Asta had no hands or feet and his head was twisted awkwardly to one side, hopefully a break that had occurred before the torture of dismemberment and crucifixion were inflicted.

"Elyri," Asta said quietly, her voice steady, though barely so. "Two dead and…"

Movement turned her head and caught the general's attention too. One of the three unfortunates was alive. She had known it but she had been unable to help him down on her own. Agis summoned one of his men with a whistle and shouted, "We could use a healer…"

"I can ride back to…"

Agis snorted. "No, you shall not. You should not even be here." This was not her doing, there was no blood on her hands and no way a girl of her age and size could have carried this out. It would have taken multiple people, multiple men, to perform these particular executions. He and his dumbstruck scout began to lower the crucifix as carefully as possible in the hopes of removing the living victim.

"He's not likely to live long enough for that" With the number of visible contusions across his thin torso, there was a great deal of internal bleeding. That he still lived was incredible.

"We should at least try," protested the girl, wanting the man to live not only for the information he could give but because the thought of this Elyri being the first to die on her watch as acting inquisitor, to see him die before her eyes, was not a burden she felt ready to carry.

Annoyed with the interruption and the distraction she was providing, Agis glanced at the arriving soldiers. "Denyan, take this fellow and Lady Dugan back to…"

Asta crossed her arms with a glare. Just because she was arguing to save a man's life did not mean she should be treated as a child. "Do you think I should not perform the duties of inquisitor because of my age or because of my gender, Lord General?"

Duties of inquisitor? Is that what she was doing? Did her father know? Agis began to speak, more frustrated by her attitude than angered by it, but the dying Elyri had one hand free of the rope that bound him to the crucifix and was able to grasp Asta's ankle with all the strength he could muster. She froze, eyes wide as she dropped to her knees beside him as if to hear him, though he spoke no audible words. She brushed his hair, wet with blood from a head wound, the only external bleeding being where a patch of pale blonde hair had been torn from his scalp. She was more composed and businesslike than some of those soldiers around them, despite the blood and gore and death, and Agis mused how much like her father she was.

"I will do my best to see justice done," she murmured, prying his hand from her leg, squeezing it reassuringly, trying not to squint in response to the pain now throbbing behind her eyes.

When the words were heard, the dying man's arm went slack and his eyes rolled back into his head as his breath gave out. Asta, shaken from what had happened, her mind reeling from the force of information that had been thrust through that physical contact, pushed to her feet and took a few unsteady steps as if to make an investigative circle of the grove or to escape the man who had died right in front of her. She could do nothing with what she had been given; there was too much of it and it was a jumbled, undecipherable mess inside of her skull, but she believed that any of the Elyri in Rhidam could help her sort it, make sense of it, find something useful. When they had names or faces or any other detail worth having, she would be able to determine how to proceed.

Agis, unaware of the silent communication between the princess and dead man, thinking her words had been meant to reassure him in his last moments of life, steadied her as she swayed although he did not look up from the body he was still inspecting for clues. She nodded gratefully, extracted herself from his grasp when she felt steady again, and began her own investigation of the grove.

The clearing presented no useable evidence. There had been no riot here. The only violence that had occurred here had been inflicted on these three Elyri, the places of beating, of dismemberment marked, examined, the undisturbed earth noted where the crucifixes had been assembled then dragged into place to have the men secured to them. The report Agis received had been a ruse meant to bring the general to find this, the agents of death likely having expected their victims to be dead by the time anyone arrived.

Maybe they thought in doing so that there would be nothing left to expose them to the authorities.

This had been a warning to the Crown, the general decided, a treasonous act he would not allow to go unpunished. Only he, Asta and the scout at his side knew that one of the three had lived, only they had touched him, but that ought to be enough for any of the palace Elyri to use. Something here ought to offer evidence. Something here had to be enough to damn the guilty.

As the other bodies were being lowered to the ground and all three were secured to horses while Asta made her circuit around the clearing, she wondered if her father had been here, if he had been forced to participate in this vile crime, if this was the work of the Corylliens or someone else. There was no hint of him in what the Elyri had shown her, and Asta could not imagine her father stomaching such an act. But had he known? Was he the one who had sent her word? Had he sought any means of stopping it?

If she could get a message to him, perhaps she would act, but as she rejoined the soldiers with her horse to accompany them back to Rhidam, she decided it might be better if she did not know just what her father was capable of.

❧*❧

It took several days of delivering food to the site of the bedroll in the attic, hearty portions saved from his own meals, until eventually, when Edward came again, he could see that the food had been accepted. The tray was empty of every trace except crumbs. The clothing given by Gaelán and the bedding collected from the store of donations for the needy were accepted much more readily. He suspected the squatter feared being poisoned but it seemed that hunger eventually won him over. That the orphan remained in the rafters rather than flee after his hideout was discovered please Edward, while also making him wonder if the boy did not flee because he had nowhere else to go. Perhaps the presence of Elyri living below was enough to offer security.

Edward did not see him; he either hid when Edward came or else he came here only long enough to sleep and eat whatever was left. The novice would not risk climbing here in the dark. It did not matter to him if he ever met the unfortunate youngster…he was satisfied knowing he was helping, satisfied knowing that the boy would not starve or freeze. He hoped, however, that sooner or later they would meet, that he could find other ways to help.

❧*❧

"I have not spoken to Hagan of this," Asta fidgeted, her gaze darting from the healer to her cousin. Having grown up with the King, she was one of the few people who still referred to him by name when not in a formal setting, though his change in status meant that there was little friendly interaction between them anymore. "I don't know what General Agis will have told him, but I'm sure there will be questions about why I was there."

"What will you tell him if he does?" asked Diona, watching the healer rapidly sketch face after face as the dim light of sunset faded from the back garden. The realism of the images was startling, even though she had seen the healer's work before.

❧278❧

Asta shrugged with a nervous smirk. "That I was curious…and bored…inherent Dugan traits that don't necessarily mix with the demands of nobility. That's one thing about men, present company excepted of course," she added with a winning smile at Ártur who did not see it. "Many of them think women have no ability, or very little, to think for themselves. Makes it easy for us to hide the truth by feigning ignorance or foolishness. Shall I present this to…"

"Once Lord MacLyr is through, yes. You should send word to your father…and the images…if you believe he can use them."

"I'm sure he can." Maybe Caol already knew who the criminals were. If he did not, getting the sketches into his hand was necessary. "How long, Lord MacLyr?"

"With another nineteen faces…perhaps an hour…and if you desire additional copies, it will take longer of course. I would say by morning I should have them ready." It would mean little sleep, but this was a matter he deemed too important to set aside for something as selfish as sleep. Three Elyri had been slaughtered. The healer owed it to them to facilitate the apprehension of the killers.

Asta nodded, relieved that he did not ask sensitive questions. He would not know that Caol had not traveled to Durham as he claimed, that he was still in Rhidam. He accepted that delivery of these images to the inquisitor was an expected duty. "A second copy would be appropriate…perhaps more…as I think we should keep one here and I know my father will want one.

The healer bowed his head and continued to sketch.

"I will return to help you," Asta promised, her drawing ability lacking but her ability to copy sufficient enough that she might be able to duplicate some of the healer's work. "I should first speak to Hagan." She giggled to cover the underlying anxiety. Fortunately, the King was rarely angry with her for long.

❧*❦

Kavan's thoughts wandered more frequently to the late King Arlan as the wagon rolled nearer to the city of Palil. The last time Kavan had been here had been the night of Arlan's passing and at the time he had never thought to be here again. The man's death had hit him harder than any other had before, and the pain of it had been buried and disguised as something else beneath the bard's personal hell, after the loss of his hands, set aside during his quest for peace, healing, and some sort of acceptance of himself. Even when that torment had fallen away, after the healing of his hands, as he began on the return path towards redemption, Arlan's death had seemed a thing of dreams, a cloud in his distant memories that could not possibly be real. On the surface, it was as if it had never happened.

Palil's encroaching boundaries peeled back the layers of his heart and memory and unearthed the ignored grief. He had met Arlan on the day the Lachlan prince had been born, and befriended him some ten years later by some miracle of accident or fate. Doing so had brought Kavan out of Elyriá on a quest to make Arlan king, and had kept Kavan in Enesfel when most Elyri refused to travel there. The years had been good, despite the heartaches of lost children and loved ones, but now Arlan was gone. Enesfel was no longer the welcoming place for Elyri it had been during his reign, and Rhidam no longer felt like home. Kavan did not feel the same connection to Arlan's children as he had felt to Arlan, though he had once, in her early childhood, felt close to the princess. Diona had destroyed that closeness, driven it far down within him, with her unthinking acts, and he did not know if that previous affinity and affection were retrievable.

They were not with Arlan. Arlan was gone.

Without that loyalty to bind him, Kavan did not know if he would stay in Rhidam after his return, after the cleansing he intended, after he did what it seemed he was destined to do. He believed Ártur would stay with the Lachlans for as long as he lived, or as long as they allowed, because Ártur's loyalty to them was different. Kavan's loyalty was not to oaths or family names, but rather to something else he had never found a name for. The individual, perhaps, or some intangible ideal. He imagined he might stay if he was needed, either as advisor or tutor to any royal children produced by Hagan's upcoming marriage. Otherwise, he would go somewhere else.

He had no idea where.

Losing Arlan had cost him part of his soul. He did not want that sort of bond with any other Teren. Yet it existed already with Prince Muir and Prince Owain, and more intensely still with Wortham. There existed bonds with Orynn and Myreth too, but both had been taken from his life before their ties grew unbreakable. Watching those other three beloved Teren friends die might kill him if nothing else did.

He was composing a melody in Arlan's memory when they reached Palil near noon. Their first stop was the great stone circle on the outskirts of town, the circle Kavan had been led to before, with the

Gate that had taken him to Arlan on the King's final night. As with every other Gate found and tested, however, this one failed to function with the relics in his possession, the conflict of power too strong for him to manipulate. Frustrated, the bard sent Wortham to gain water for the next day's journey. Yd Haszafni was larger than Palil, better equipped for replenishing their supplies. Some of those following them had continued on towards there already. For now, they had enough provisions to hold them overnight, and as there was no inn in Palil, they were forced to set camp within view of the stone circle. With the weather warm and the sky clear, they were in no danger from the elements or the crowd around them.

Kavan remained apart from the others, seated in the center of the stone ring which many were reluctant to approach, the reliquary on his lap, open to the energy around him that his followers seemed to sense and fear. Or perhaps they feared the circle itself. He poured his power into the circle over the course of the night, reserving enough to operate the Gate should it grant him access. Having the power within unused for too long, the draining was a relief, if unproductive otherwise, but even more welcome was the release of grief into the song for Arlan that he sang over and over long into the night.

As dawn came, his face wet with tears and his chest aching with the echoes of grief in the crevices and corners where Arlan resided, Kavan prayed the late King had heard it and knew how heartfelt every note and word was.

❧*❦

"Kavan…" Ártur tried to think of words to say, but he could not find his voice as his heart stretched and swelled in response to the news he had received. As agreed, as soon as Bhríd returned from Levonne, Ártur went back to Bhryell at sunset to spend his night with his son. Kavan's house was dark and quiet, no one had been expecting him. He was building a fire to take the chill out of the empty evening air when his nephew arrived and as soon as his son had hugged him, the boy shot up the stairs to see what treasures his father had brought. His youthful greeting might have been short, but it was heartfelt.

Bhen leaned against the doorframe, tempted to take a seat but deciding not to. After he gave Ártur the news, he knew the man would want to spend the evening with his son. Bhen did not need to be here for that. "If anyone but bhydáni Tíbhyan had said it, I would have thought them mad; I do not see how such can be possible…"

"It is very possible," Ártur breathed, excitement in his voice and his nervous posture. "I know from experience that he can communicate at least as far as Hatu to Rhidam. Reaching Bhryell…for him…is probably just as easy. Did he say anything? Ask anything? Give any message?"

The younger Elyri shook his head. "Apparently not. bhydáni said it was a brief moment of mutual reassurance that both were well. He did say he detected joy…and thinks perhaps Kavan is coming home."

Coming home. It was the one thing Ártur had waited months to hear, but did he dare hope it was true? As difficult as it was to admit, he had been nearly out of hope for too long. What hope he had clung to hinged on that peculiar contact his cousin occasionally had with Gaelán. He did not know if he dared put faith in this new morsel of hope, as he did not think he could survive if his expectations were dashed or continued to be stretched too thin.

"Thank you…for telling me…" he murmured as the thunder of Llucás' footsteps descended the stairs.

Bhen smiled in reassurance and bid him goodnight, the boy's excited cry of "Father!" following him out the door.

Kavan. Coming home. k'Ádhá, thought the healer as he got to his feet. Let it be true.

❧*❧

He was not surprised to learn that Owain had divulged their discussions and preliminary planning to the Enesfel princess. He had agreed to that possibility when he left Fiara. Owain spoke highly of the princess, as did Prince Espen, and by weeding through the various rumors circulating Neth, Kjell knew there was substance behind those men's' flattering words. Nor was he surprised that Owain chose not to reveal those same details to King Hagan. Though a man was king, it did not make him wise or trustworthy. Neth's long history of murderous, ineffectual kings was proof of that.

And Kjell trusted Owain.

He chuckled and smirked at the again fleeting idea of a union between himself and Princess Diona. He had never met her, never seen her, but he suspected they would be a well-matched pair, the likes of which the Five Sovereignties had never seen. Such a union had the potential to either bring a peaceful merger between their lands and the establishment of a new order for generations to come, or else it would result in war and the destruction of much of what the two were separately striving to save. As entertaining as the idea was, it was not one Kjell took seriously. Having an ally, not a wife, in the Lachlan court was what was needed, and thanks to Owain, Kjell was beginning to believe he had found it.

In Rhidam, Diona was thinking much the same when Owain's letter reached her. Prince Kjell de Cormick? An ally of Enesfel? As implausible as it sounded, she had no reason to think Owain was lying or that he was mad. If Prince Kjell was willing to act as an informant in King Merkar's court, was capable of discovering his brother's intentions and plans, the benefits to both kingdoms would be invaluable. It took no great wisdom or thought to know that a treaty to aid Prince Kjell in the gaining of Neth's throne might be in their mutual best interests…and likely Cordash, Elyriá and Hatu's as well.

Under no circumstance would she reveal this discussion to her brother, however, until such time as Prince Kjell needed Enesfel's aid and had proven his intentions beyond a verbal agreement with his cousin. She suspected her brother would put little faith in Prince Kjell's intention, particularly if he sought advice from Claide before doing so, and the possibility that Claide might have access to King Merkar was still one Diona did not discount. There would be no gesture of good faith from Hagan to Kjell without some significant gesture on the Prince's part…such as the assassination of his brother. As much as Hagan loved Owain, she knew he also harbored a twinge of suspicion, just as their father had done, that Owain might still be inclined to reclaim Enesfel's throne.

It did not matter that Owain had voiced no such ambition before Arlan's death, nor after it. Hagan, with his low confidence, feared it could still be true. Something Kavan had once said to Muir, a secret never fully divulged, led Diona to feel that Owain would never make that attempt. If it was true that Owain was not the son of King Innis, or of King Bowen, as was rumored, then he had no right to the throne and never once had she heard him mention a desire for it.

For now, it was best to keep their talks with Prince Kjell private. Espen knew of the agreement, according to Owain, had been present during the deliberation, but Diona could not even discuss it with him. When she attempted to approach him, he avoided her, and when he tried to come to her, she seemed always to have some other duty at hand. There was a sinking, growing hole between them that convinced her that marriage was no longer a possibility. She had waited too long. The relationship they shared was beyond repair.

Perhaps she should consider a union with Prince Kjell.

Despite everything, she loved Espen and was not ready to give up. Perhaps if she told him that, it would help. Not once, in the years she had known him, could she recall speaking those words aloud. If she was ever to say them, she knew she was running out of time.

🙂*🙂

When he first saw that face it had been for a single brief moment, too brief to be certain of what he had seen. One face in the midst of the crowd in Yd Haszafni where he felt he had once been shunned. As his voice now rang over the heads of his audience, an audience that seemed not to recall that distant day or the way they had treated him, Kavan was sure that for those short initial seconds he had seen the young bard Eridel in the crowd. His heart and hopes sored with his voice. Perhaps the man had not died. Perhaps it had been Kavan's melancholia, as Orynn had tried to convince him, which had led him to believe the mangled form he buried in the southern scrub had been the blonde harper when in fact the man might have returned north, to familiar lands, and lived still.

The crowd swallowed the stranger before Kavan learned the truth.

When the multitude eventually began to thin and disperse for the night, Kavan saw him again, a man at the rear of the tavern, laughing with four young women as Eridel would have done if he had been here. With less distraction between them, fewer bodies, less muddle in the air, Kavan could identify now that this man's aura did not match Eridel's. They might look similar but they were different men.

Kavan sank onto a stool at the bar, delightfully exhausted by the effort of his performance, pleased with the welcome the people gave, but that realization, and the dashed hopes about Eridel, brought sadness too. If he was honest, he had to admit that people only wanted him, needed him, for his music, for what he could give them. He loved to give it, needed to give it, to see their faces rapt with attention, to feel the adoration. But he wanted something more, wanted acceptance and love beyond the confines of the White Bard of Bhryell.

"Pardon, my lord." He had not noticed the man approaching. Up close, the fellow looked less like Eridel than expected. "I noticed your gaze…your disappointment. Do I somehow trouble you?"

It was bold of a stranger to ask such things; Kavan had not realized his scrutiny, or his disappointment, were obvious to anyone else. He shook his head no but said, "You remind me of a bard I once knew; I thought perhaps you were him. You share a similar build…a similar fashion of hair…but I can see you are not the same man."

"Was he a friend?" He sat on the nearest stool and motioned for the woman behind the bar to bring him a drink. She scowled, the hour late enough that she wanted her guests to be away, but because Kavan had brought so much coin into her establishment tonight, she obliged the Elyri's companion without a word, setting a mug of frothy ale in front of the second man. He put coins on the counter, more coins then were necessary, and she nodded approvingly. That was worth a few more minutes of inconvenience.

Was Eridel a friend? Kavan had not taken the time to find out if they could have been friends. "He…we did not know each other long enough to become so, but we traveled together for a time. He was killed by animals on the road." Or by my own callousness and cruelty.

The newcomer drank half of his mug of ale before speaking again. "I am sorry to hear it. Had he talent?"

"Enough." Enough that he might have had a good career if Kavan had given him encouragement instead of hostility.

After wiping his mouth on the back of his sleeve, he said, "I too am a bard. I have no specialty like you, and not your talent. I sing a little, play the lute, violin, trumpet, shawm, harp…anything I can get my hands on. I tell stories, juggle, perform slights of hand, have even been known for a puppet play or two. And I know you, of course." Nearly every bard in the Sovereignties knew the White Bard by reputation and description, whether they had ever heard him perform or not. "I heard about your hands…" He finished his drink and pushed the mug away, "and am pleased to see that rumor was false."

"It was no rumor, but things…changed." Kavan felt awkward talking about it, but he did not want lies to spread by his denial.

The stranger stared at the Elyri's hands. "Then it is a miracle and I will be sure that every bard in the Sovereignties knows about it." Seeing Kavan's face darken, he continued. "No offense, my lord. Your voice is beautiful and I am honored to be among the first to hear that you have branched out…but when the news of your tragedy reached us, we all mourned your loss. Elyri or not, you are first among us, the light so many of us aspire to be. The loss of your talent caused considerable grief for those I know. How much greater will be the joy to know you can resume your place? If you forbid mentioning it, of course, I shall."

Unable to fathom having that sort of influence over anyone, let alone every bard in the lands, though he knew his name and reputation were widespread, Kavan shook his head. "Who am I to forbid you anything?" However pure the other bard's intentions, eventually the tales of miracles and healing would become disproportionate to the event. It was something Kavan had endured all his life. He did not like it, but he could not alter the reality of it.

And it had been a miracle he was healed. Denying it would be a greater sin then hiding his hands from the world.

The bard with the dark blonde hair nodded, his eyes expressing understanding of what Kavan did not say. "I will use every discretion, my lord…but they need to know. It will heal many wounds to hear it."

Would it, Kavan wondered. Would it aid in the healing he was returning to Enesfel to bring? Perhaps even this was necessary to restore peace to the Sovereignties.

"Your harp?"

"I did not bring it south with me…I feared losing it in my travels." Having been unable to play it with mangled fingers, he had also not wanted that constant reminder of loss. But he missed her dearly.

"Indeed."

Brushing his hair from his eyes, Kavan studied the man's slender face, the tavern now nearly empty, only Wortham lingering at the base of the stairs in a protective, yet seemingly bored, stance. The man on the other stool was not as boyish as Eridel, several years older it seemed with a less playful expression as if the years and trials of his life had begun to etch their weight on him. He did not look much like Eridel now, but he still looked familiar. "May I ask your name?"

The man offered his hand sheepishly. "How rude of me," he chuckled. "Cedric O'Grady. From Cordash, my lord."

Though he wished Cedric would cease calling him lord, Kavan did not feel like making an issue of the title. He clasped the offered hand. "Related to Sir Paul O'Grady of Eleva?"

Cedric smiled wider. "You have a good mind for names. He is my uncle, my father's brother. I am the youngest of five sons…my father the middle of three brothers. It limited my opportunities. I will not gain much of an inheritance, and found I was better suited to this life than to the military or the Faith…and the family name can be useful in certain situations." When he winked and Kavan smiled he added, "Pleased I can offer mirth and lift your spirits. I can retire now. I am bound for Natrona in the morn, you may join me if you wish."

He had seen the crowd that followed Kavan into the tavern but had not, it seemed, seen the mass of them that had followed him into the city. Kavan did not think Cedric would want to be joined by the horde. "I am bound for Kílyn," Kavan replied, having decided that course without saying so to Wortham. "Then to Levonne, by sea if we can find a ship."

"Do you travel alone?"

Kavan inclined his head towards the man at the foot of the stairs. "The other two are likely asleep." Urian and Zelenka had been in the tavern for his performance, but had retired earlier, just as the crowd began to dwindle. "We have been traveling too long and I cannot blame them for seeking beds when such can be had. We will depart in the morning as well."

"Then I wish you safe travels and leave you a warning. Enesfel is unsafe. I am sure you know this. There has been a spillover of troubles into Hatu but nothing like you will find in the north. Please, be careful."

"I shall be. And when you are in Rhidam next, please come to the castle. I should like to see you again. Likewise, if you are ever in Alberni and in need of lodging or supplies, do not hesitate to come to my home. Whether I am there or not, if you mention my name, and our acquaintance, your needs will be tended. Musicians are welcome wherever I call home."

"Your offer is generous. Thank you." He shook Kavan's hand again and, after a bow, disappeared up the stairs, giving a smile to Wortham as he passed. The captain remained where he was for several minutes until the barkeep began to put the lights out in the room. Determining that Kavan was not yet ready to sleep, Wortham left him alone there, instead following Cedric up the stairs to the rooms they had rented for the night.

Pleased with how easy the conversation with Cedric had been, ease he rarely felt with anyone other than musicians, Kavan rose from the stool and smoothed his tunic with his slightly trembling hands. The energy of the night had not yet drained, leaving him unable to sleep. He chose to walk, careful to be alert for danger in the dark streets, wondering if he had changed so much during his months away from Rhidam or if there was something about Cedric that made him so comfortable. The night air soothed him, the silence calmed him, until eventually he felt ready to settle for what remained of the night. Dawn would come soon.

Before going inside, he went around to the rear of the tavern to check on the horses and the wagon, wanting to reassure himself that they could be on their way at dawn without delays. Their most important belongings had been brought into the tavern overnight, but everything else had been secured in the wagon, with promises made by the stable staff that everything would be safe until morning.

But such was not the case, and when Kavan realized it, his heart caught in his throat and his hands clenched at his sides. The wagon was not where they had left it. The horses were stabled, munching quietly on oats, but the wagon was gone.

Stopping beside Kavan, having already seen their loss and walked entirely around the stable facilities in the hopes that the wagon had been moved elsewhere, Wortham put his hand on the bard's shoulder. "We resume on foot," he muttered with obvious annoyance. "I have spoken to the staff…to others…but unless it's housed in another building, the wagon's now far away from here it seems." No one had seen or heard anything, or if they had, they would not admit to it. "I am beginning to believe you when you say someone does not want us to return to Rhidam."

Kavan grunted with a nod. For every step of progress they made, it seemed that something happened to deter them time after time. "There are three Gates in Kílyn," he said, the first mention of where he planned to go next. "It is not many days from here. On foot will suffice." It would have to, regardless of Zelenka's anticipated complaints. If the Gates failed, the next leg of their journey would be by sea, and from Levonne, he was certain Bhríd and Madalyn would provide them anything they needed. Regardless of the setbacks, they would reach Rhidam soon.

"The others will not be pleased."

"Perhaps gdhededhá Urian will decide he has traveled far enough. I do not wish to burden him with further discomfort." Kavan was surprised the blind man had remained with them as long as he had. "As for Zelenka…we will continue to accommodate her as best we can. Please stress to her that we do not press on out of cruelty or a wish to make her uncomfortable."

"I will try," the captain snorted. The woman did not understand the importance of Kavan's mission, and had no concept of how far they had already come from the village she called home, how far they still had to travel before they reached the journey's end. As sheltered as her life had been, residing with her mother in the same village, the same home, her entire life, there was no way she could have known what she was agreeing to when she chose to follow Wortham across the world. She had no idea how big the world really was beyond the border of her village and its fields.

"Rest, Wortham; at least we have horses to carry our effects. That will be enough."

The captain, not ready to look on the positive side of their predicament, still angry about the theft of the wagon, muttered. "Unless someone steals them too."

"They won't," Kavan promised. No one was stealing anything more from them…even if he had to sleep the remainder of the night in the stable to see to it.

Caol studied the faces of the men gathered without being obvious about it. He had mastered the art of feigned boredom, of feigned ignorance, so that no one was aware of what he was truly doing. Some were familiar from previous meetings; many he had not met before. From the two groupings, there were some he recognized from the drawings which had come into his hands earlier that day, drawings sent by his daughter. He read her brief account of how she had come by them and, pleased with her accomplishment without any prompting from him, he wished he could congratulate her in person.

And warn her to be careful, now that he saw some of the shady murderers for himself.

As usual, he did not speak as the meeting was called to order. Such gatherings rarely lasted long, barely long enough to make mention of new members, the loss of previous ones, and to share news of Elyri movements around Rhidam. With the death of so many, and most Elyri wise enough not to travel into Enesfel or careful enough to avoid capture, there was typically little news to share. When a sighting was reported, it became an open debate as to what to do about it, and when there were no sightings, the discussions turned to ways to discourage collaboration between Teren and Elyri and how to garner support and recruits for their cause. Most of the actual planning, it seemed, happened in dark corners and alleys outside of these gatherings, and how he was to learn anything that way was a dilemma.

The more of these meetings he attended, the more Caol wondered how the Association had failed to uncover the cell. He saw no faces he recognized as Association, but he did not know them all. There were too many Corylliens to have easily passed unnoticed, some of them prominent Rhidam citizens. The Association cell he had grown up in kept its finger on the pulse of a city's life. They thrived on gossip and news. How could Rhidam's cell have missed something that seemed so obvious?

"You seen anything, Alty?"

Caol blinked, jarred out of his musings, and stared at the man who had spoken. He covered his faux pas with a yawn as if he had been dozing off instead of paying attention and shrugged. "Haven't seen any Elyri other than the chamberlain…but I won't take him on, thank you. He's twice my size." There were chuckles around the room. Most of these men might fear and hate Bhríd Cáner because he was Elyri, but none of them doubted or disrespected his battle prowess. "I did learn something though."

He had debated whether he should mention it, if he should say anything about his daughter's revelation or not. He had not heard about the slaughter of the Elyri beforehand, had not been included in that project's planning. He had, however, been angered by the audacity of crucifying three men, three Elyri, in a public place and then summoning the Lachlan Guard to the scene. The whole act might have been intended to send a message, but it might also backfire. Alerting the Corylliens to their failure might mean harsher repercussions to Elyri in the future, but at least the victims would not be forced to suffer lingering deaths.

"Lachlan guards got information. I don't know what kind, but I heard some soldiers talking at the Eagle's Nest. They found some crucified Elyri…but one of them wasn't dead. He lived long enough to say something to General Agis, something they think they can use. It's just a thought…but if anyone knows who's responsible, they might want to get a message to them, have them lay low for a while."

He spoke as nonchalantly as possible, as if he was passing on words that held no meaning to him, and the spokesman, the stooped man named Layton who had brought Caol into the group, folded his arms across his chest and stared at him. Caol could not tell what the man was thinking, if he was suspicious or not, but Caol remained calm under the scrutiny and did not react to it. He did not want Layton to know he had anything to hide.

When Layton finally spoke, it was to agree with Caol's sentiment. "They should have been dead. I'll find out who was responsible and make sure such mistakes do not happen again." If he knew others in the room were connected to the crucifixions, he did not look at them. "As for lying low…what could the guards have gotten that could threaten anyone? We're cautious…"

"But what can they do? The Elyri I mean. If one lived when he should have died…perhaps he had some secret way? A spell? Maybe he's still alive?" Caol hated the words as he spoke them, but he had to maintain his charade. How long could he spout such slander, he wondered, before he began to believe it?

Layton grunted. "I see your point. I'll get the warning out." His shifty eyes fell on another man, someone who had attended every meeting Caol had been to but who had not been in any of the images Asta had delivered. The man nodded back as if giving permission and then the meeting was adjourned, with Layton signaling for Caol to remain as the others shuffled out of the room. There had been no discussion this time of between meeting plans, no mention of when they would meet again. Caol assumed he would learn those things later, that no mention meant they intended to kill someone, as killing was never publically discussed.

Having no idea what Layton wanted and being in no hurry to leave, Caol continued to sprawl in his seat until Layton pulled another chair in front of him, turned it around and straddled it to face him.

"I think, Alty, it's time for you to take the next step."

"Next step?" His palms began to sweat, but with them tucked beneath his arms, Layton could not see it. He was hoping for something more, some deeper involvement to ferret out the strongest links which needed breaking, but he hoped he was not about to be asked to kill someone to prove his worth. He was not ready for that.

"I'm organizing a little party by the river…few people there who need some reminding about Elyri treachery."

Caol scowled. "We're not killing anyone…"

Laughing, the stooped man shook his head no. "Would it matter?"

"Killing Elyri is one thing…they have no souls." He swallowed his disgust at the words, hoping his expression tilted his distaste towards those he slandered. "But killing Teren…before they have a chance to repent…that's different."

"Ah." There were others in the organization who felt similarly, working alongside those with considerably fewer scruples. To each their strengths. So long as they did not betray one another, all men, no matter their principles, were welcome. It kept the membership high, allowed the Corylliens to accomplish multiple hits at once.

"Nothing like that, I assure you. Just a reminder. I don't have the details yet, but when I do, I want you there…with me and the others. You listen, you share…you seem to have a good head. Time to put that to use, if you're interested."

If Caol was honest, vandalism and thuggery were not interesting. But such things were necessary if he wanted in deeper. If he could prevent at least a few deaths here and there, it would soothe his conscience about this otherwise distasteful work.

"Tell me where and when and I'll be there."

He would be there and hope it was not a trap.

❦*❧

The girls huddled on a bench in front of the castle, seemingly engrossed in the kittens on their laps. Marta came to the castle every other day with a man who delivered milk, cheese, eggs or other foods to the kitchen staff, giving the appearance that she was merely a peasant girl or merchant's daughter helping her father. Because of Asta's independent streak, no one thought it unusual for her to befriend a girl beneath her station, even if there were some who looked down their nose at her doing so. The King did not notice their friendship and if her father allowed it, no one was about to speak ill of the stranger. What Marta did outside the castle walls, however, was something none of them could ever know about.

The tiny girl leaned forward until her button nose was inches from Asta's. "It's a woman," she said with a conspiratorial whisper.

Catching a kitten as it tried to squirm off her knees, Asta asked, "How do you know?"

Marta shrugged. "There are ways. It comes from Neth, some sort of upper-class name that's gone out of fashion in recent years…some sort of connection to a mythological queen of winter.

Asta's eyes darkened with displeasure. If the name had mythological connotations, how come no one had recognized it before? Or was it linked to some far north mythology that was not popular anywhere except its home region? "Wonderful…a Nethite with a heart of ice…"

"Maybe. It also has Hatuish roots…very old ones…but it isn't much used there. I talked to someone who claims to have seen her. Not up close enough to describe her, as she was hiding in her cloak…but they swear Jolgier is a woman. They're willing to testify to that if given protection."

"Given the vagueness of description, I doubt the King would offer it, but I'll see what I can do. Can you get this information to…?"

"Already on its way. He should have it by end of day." Marta stretched her legs and then let her bare feet swing freely as she put the kitten she held on the ground. Asta wished she had the freedom to dress so casually. Her father permitted her the rare luxury of wearing men's breeches, but even in doing that she was forced to maintain a degree of propriety befitting royalty.

The last kitten was placed with the others and they turned to wrestling with themselves and ignoring the girls. "Good," Asta nodded. "Maybe he will have some idea of how to find her. Thank you, Marta."

"My pleasure, princess." It was a good-hearted, friendly jab, but Asta wondered if the use of her title was meant to be insulting. Regardless of her opinion of royalty and nobility, however, Marta was proving to be good at what she had been asked to do, and that was what mattered. Marta did not have to like her; they only had to work together for the betterment of Enesfel.

❧*❧

The crowd of followers numbering almost a hundred when they departed Yd Haszafni had dwindled to thirty-five before they reached the halfway point of the deserted road to Kílyn. The weather had turned unexpectedly cold and drizzly, which encouraged many to seek shelter or turn back. Today, as Kavan and the group drew nearer to the holy site, the weather shifted again, the shining sun bringing back the much-missed warmth to the day. Word of the White Bard's arrival traveled before them, causing the ranks of supporters to swell again. He tried to count them when they stopped for the mid-day meal after an extended push across Hatu, but the mass moved about too much, people meeting others, speaking excitedly about the adventure they had embarked on, to get an accurate assessment of their numbers. Now that they had reached the Kílyn shrine, with the next destination intended to be reached either by Gate or by sea, he wondered what would become of the group then but it was not his concern. He could not take them with him; they were safe with each other. Kóráhm, he trusted, would see to that.

Zelenka had not complained about their hurried, extended pace today. She had been silent for much of the way, and only seemed excited when Kavan explained that they were destined for Saint Kóráhm's shrine. She knew the name Kóráhm. She understood the term shrine, and she seemed eager to be there. She walked quicker, with more determined steps, then she had since leaving her village. No one asked her why.

"Shall we leave an offering when we arrive?" Wortham asked when Kavan rejoined him at the front of the procession of pilgrims. Kavan had walked among them for a time, speaking matters of Faith to them, singing as he felt compelled, but now his voice was weary as darkness began to descend and his nerves were raw from the press of so many attentive souls.

Wortham did not ask if they would rest with the darkness. They were close now. He knew the bard would not want to stop until he reached Kílyn.

Falling into a comfortable stride at his side, Kavan replied, "I know of nothing Kóráhm might want except my gratitude and friendship, which he knows he has."

"Music?"

Kavan did not reply to the captain's teasing; Kóráhm always appreciated music, and of course, Kavan would give it whether vocally or in the prayers that left his heart in silent song. As rough as his voice had become after a day of singing, Kavan did not know if he had it in him to offer more. As for offerings, he suspected Kóráhm was beyond the need for the usual offerings of food, drink, and coin.

He glanced back at the blind monk supported by two strangers as they walked hastily along the packed dirt road. Urian had been silent today, not even filling the lapses in Kavan's speech and song. For the duration of their time together, when Kavan had been at his worst, when his world had been bleakest, the blind man had been full of advice, encouragement, wisdom, and joviality. Since the healing of Kavan's hands, however, Urian's sagely comments had grown fewer, except when it came to preaching to following crowds, village gatherings, or when teaching Zelenka the Trade tongue. He looked thinner, wearier, and Kavan wondered often why he continued to travel with them to the point of exhaustion, if the man knew something he did not about the days ahead…or something they had left behind.

Still, Kavan was grateful for his continuing company, as his presence served as a reminder of so many things the bard did not want to forget. It felt fitting that Urian remained, perhaps followed their journey back to Levonne where they had started, and he was sure that, without Urian's determined efforts, Zelenka would not have mastered as much of the language as she had.

"I think," the blind man said, speaking for the first time that day as if aware of Kavan's gaze on him, "that he would be more pleased with the offerings made to the others. We have…you have, my lord, brought many souls to the Faith. Presenting them at the foot of his shrine…I cannot think of any offering more fitting."

Lights on the distant horizon prevented Kavan from making any awkward, self-deprecating rejoinders to his involvement in converting anyone. He could not refute Urian's words, even though it was his first reflex to do so. These people were here to follow him, but beyond that, it opened them to the possibility of hearing the gdhededhá preach. In that way, Kavan felt that Urian was much more responsible and influential in the path to conversion. Rather than deny something he felt it would be too prideful to claim, he chose to focus on Kílyn's glow and say nothing.

Besides, whoever was ultimately the most influential, Urian was right. There was nothing better that Kavan could give to Kóráhm than the opening of souls to the Faith.

Home of the supposed sight of Kóráhm's martyrdom, Kílyn was one of the few cities in Hatu to house inns and taverns open late into the night to accommodate pilgrims and travelers. Many in Kavan's company peeled off towards those establishments as the group passed through the streets at the city's fringe. Despite Kóráhm's status as both heretic and saint in Elyriá, hundreds of people came to the shrine every year, most of them Teren. Until his music had been ripped from his life, Kavan had never been here. He had been remiss in his duty and devotion to his patron and he was determined now to make this pilgrimage once a year. The Gates would make that a simple thing.

He chose that path not for Kóráhm's sake as much as for his own, lest he forget the trauma, the agony, the enlightenment and the healing he had been fortunate enough to find with Kóráhm's aide over the last year. The saint was not merely his patron and his role model. Kóráhm was also his friend.

Like Wortham had done before, Zelenka would not approach the shrine, though she did stare at it through lowered lashes with unquestionable reverence. Her upbringing demanded that women could not approach such places but she could respect and revere them. She knew little about Kóráhm beyond the old stories learned as a little girl, nothing about the religious significance he eventually grew to encompass, or the heretic status with which he had been later encumbered, but she had come to understand that the three men with her revered Kóráhm for a host of reasons and thus he had become important to her too.

Unlike the last time they had been here, Wortham stopped at the foot of the T-shaped monument, constructed of marble to resemble lengths of wood secured together, put his hands on it, and remained long enough to offer his own silent prayer of gratitude and petition for success and protection, and then he returned to Zelenka and stretched out on the ground with a groan and a sigh. They had no fire and were not in Enesfel yet, but they were near enough that he imagined he could smell it. Near enough that he could consider himself to be home.

Others among their followers were less reserved in their reverence and pressed around Kavan and Urian at the base of the shrine, eager to touch, to hear, simply to be in the presence of the nearest thing to divinity any of them would ever know. Some lay down there to sleep, others prayed and chanted into the night, while others silently watched and waited for some clue from their Elyri leader.

"Sing for us," a woman called from the darkness.

Despite the late hour and his fatigue, Kavan felt compelled to oblige by the nature of where they were. With his back against the marble, a tingle of power real or imagined coursing through him, he sang his way through his repertoire of every prayer of Kóráhm's he knew and then began to put others he had memorized to music as well. Focusing on his own inner peace rather than the near-ecstatic state of his audience, he sang with his eyes closed, and for the first time since leaving Myreth and the cloister, the presences, the beings of energy and light and power encountered since his early childhood joined him there, gathering thickly around him, caressing his skin, his thoughts, his soul. He shuddered to realize that others felt them too, particularly Urian. Not only were they feeling the nearness of those holy entities, some were seeing them as well.

Yet they were not afraid. Someone touched his hand in awe, someone other than Urian, and through their eyes, he saw the záryph gathered around the shrine, their wings of storm-cloud grey and silver fluttering and wrapping around him as if in an embrace.

It was one more aspect of his life, his Faith, that at times he wished he could deny, but the earliest Faith teachings he knew of spoke of záryph gathered around the Faithful to guard and comfort them in times of need. If it was true for each person, why not for him as well? The only thing that made him different was that his music in some way lifted the veil between realms and enabled him to feel them there, to see them at times, sometimes enabling others to feel and see them too. Until tonight, he had not known for certain what it was that came to him in such moments of prayer and reflection. Until tonight he had been afraid, reluctant, to look, to know the truth.

Though the crowd either did not see the stranger in the gray cloak, or did not recognize him if they did, Kóráhm was there too. Kavan could feel him as he wove through the gathering, laying hands on heads and shoulders as he passed. Sometimes Kavan watched him through barely open eyes, the rest of the time he kept them closed, losing himself to the Saint's comforting nearness, continuing to sing until the first rays of sunlight broke over the eastern horizon. By then his voice had grown ragged and weak with effort and thirst. When he opened his heavy lids fully at last, it was to see that most of his followers were asleep with expressions of contentment. The only person still awake sat cross-legged directly in front of him.

"You have been here all night."

Kóráhm chuckled and lowered his hood. "As have you." His auburn hair caught the morning rays and shown almost with a light of its own, the sunlight seeming to cast a golden crown around his head.

For a moment Kavan was mesmerized by the beauty, longing to touch it but not daring to try. "I felt I owed you that much," he whispered, as if speaking any louder might rouse the rest of the group. "Without you, I would be a different man." He might not even be alive, and that gift alone was worth a night of song.

Kóráhm smiled and laid his hand on Kavan's head. The warmth of flesh, accompanied by a surge of power and affection, sent a flush through Kavan's body. "I am pleased to have helped you. I can stay no longer, but…" He pressed a kiss to the top of Kavan's head as he got to his feet, "you have honored my humble words. They have never sounded better, not even when falling from my lips. k'Ádhá has heard your prayers tonight. Keep the Faith, Kavan; rest and remain strong. Your trials will not be in vain."

Wortham awoke to see the cloaked figure sitting with Kavan but paid little attention; there had been such a throng around them for days that the captain was hard-pressed to recognize any of them. He had listened to Kavan sing for several hours, bore witness to the záryph at the shrine, and shortly thereafter had fallen into the most restful sleep he had experienced in months. Kavan was still singing when Wortham opened his eyes again, telling the captain there would be no traveling this day. It was just as well. There was no luxury in remaining still while there was work to be done. He could seek a ship bound for Levonne or at least Káliel and arrange potential passage for them, if it proved to be needed. His status as captain in the Lachlan guard, though a position he had resigned to follow Kavan, might gain them favor and passage, otherwise he would sell the horses and make what arrangements he could. If the Gates again failed, he wanted to have another plan in place and waste no more time in their travels.

He was also determined to learn what he could about the state of affairs in Enesfel, now that they would be venturing beyond Hatu's borders. Kílyn was no more than a four-day ride from Enesfel, making it likely that there was a plethora of information to be had here. Kavan's well-being, his life, were in the captain's hands; he had promised Ártur he would take care of Kavan, and being this close to home, if any harm befell the bard, those in Rhidam would learn of his failure. He did not want to be a failure. He did not want to fail Kavan.

Kílyn's docks were bustling with the comings and goings of fishing skiffs bringing in early morning catches and others heading out for their first trip of the day. The merchant vessels Wortham sought were rarer, but after speaking with multiple sailors and fishermen, Wortham found a promising craft. She was not journeying to Levonne, but she was going as far as Káliel to trade in spices for silks. Wortham knew that Gabrielle would provide them passage to Levonne. It would be good, he believed, for Kavan to see Prince Muir before facing those in Rhidam, no matter the possible awkwardness of being in Gabrielle's company.

He sold the horses for a higher price than expected, giving him funds to reserve passage for four, with the remainder to be paid when they boarded. There was enough left that he realized he might end up with more coin than he had started with. He already knew what he intended to do with it.

When he returned to the shrine hill, it was to a much thinner crowd of pilgrims, as many had wandered into the city for meals and the purchase of goods they could not easily obtain in the south. The man in the gray cloak was gone and Kavan slept in the monument's shadow, while Urian was where Wortham had left him, whittling as if he had never stopped. To Wortham's surprise, however, Zelenka was not there, and Urian claimed only that she had gone in search of a secluded place to tend to her private needs. Wortham searched the remainder of the crowd and a small collection of buildings meant as water closets, not thinking her daring enough to wander very far on her own. Most had not seen her, looked at him with blank expressions of ignorance, until eventually a small group of monkish looking fellows claimed that they had seen a woman of her description leave the shrine camp and head into the heart of Kílyn.

Thinking she had tried to follow him, Wortham chastised himself for not waking her before setting about his duties, to either bid her stay and wait or else come with him. He had thought she needed the rest most, after the previous day's forced march, thought she would be well and content to wait for his return. He had never thought she might try to find him. In this unfamiliar place, she had probably gotten lost.

An afternoon of searching produced no success and he grew more concerned. What she knew of the local language was stilted and awkward, enough for a basic conversation but little else. She carried no money, had left her few belongings at the camp, and carried no means of defending herself. He did not even think she knew how to. If anything happened to her, while he was trying to do his duty by his lord, he would never forgive himself.

Thinking he should return to the shrine, that perhaps she had found her way back by now, that he would have more success if he enlisted Kavan's aid in the search, the sun was nearly set when he finally spotted her solitary figure on the docks overlooking the vast, glassy bay. The sight of her, recognizable from a distance without seeing her face, brought such a rush of relief that he gasped and ran towards her.

"Zelenka!" She turned with a start. "I've been so afraid." When he reached her, he drew her into his bear-like arms, barely noticing that she stiffened in his embrace. "I've been looking all over for you. Come back with me…let us eat…"

"No."

Her gaze, her features, were timid when Wortham pulled back to look at her, but her voice was firm with conviction.

"You must. It is not safe for you here alone."

With her broken use of Trade, she shook her head and said, "I will find a way. I will…be alright."

Though the dock was steady, sturdy and still, Wortham felt as if it rolled beneath his feet as shock rocked through him. "Have I…what have…you believe I no longer want you with me?" That had to be it. As wrong as that conclusion was, he knew how she had come to it. He had been less than cordial and attentive, had been moody and distant with everyone, and though he believed she should know him better than that after so many months, she had been brought up in a world of subservience to men. It was likely easy for her to conclude that if he did not want her there, she would leave, even though it obviously hurt and frightened her to do so.

"I have angered you and k'elyryhánag. Each day you are angrier; I will go and anger you no more."

"Zelenka." He pulled her down to sit beside him at the edge of the dock. She did not resist but he could feel her reluctance, as if she thought he might cast her into the shallow water. The tide was low and their feet did not reach the surface.

"You breathe life into my heart and make my burdens lighter. I am not angry. With you or with anyone. I am worried for Lord Cliáth. The closer we get to home, the more danger he faces…and the rest of us with him. Some people fear Elyri…want them dead…because they are different. I hear tales of terrible dangers, and though I would stop him from going on if I could, he has a duty to perform…and his family is there. He will go whether I follow or not, and I swore I would be with him…protect him. He tells me not to worry, but I do. Constantly."

He squeezed her hand, pleased to see a spark of understanding in her eyes, though she was not ready to believe he wanted her to stay. It had taken several attempts to explain the situation, to bring her to this moment, and though he did not know what he had said differently to help her understand, he was thankful she was beginning to.

"I cannot make you stay. You are free to do as you desire. I do not possess you or control you. I will worry if you go…would rather you stay. I will be happier if you do." His expression softened and he kissed her hand as he pressed the pink stone she had given him, drawn from his breast pocket, into her palm. "If you wish to go, at least allow me to provide you with coin, let me find somewhere safe for you."

Shyly, she looked up from their joined hands, from the reminder that he carried with him, and murmured. "I would rather stay with you." If he treasured this simple gift she had given him, then he must still treasure her as well.

Her words, her tone, caused Wortham to impulsively kiss her mouth for the first time. Her eyes grew round, and though she neither protested nor encouraged him in her shock, there was something in her eyes and a flushed glow on her cheeks that proved she did not object. He stood and offered his hand. "Let us go back. The others will be worried…and you must be as hungry as I am."

As expected, the Gates Kavan knew of in Kílyn refused to be used in proximity to the staff and Chalice. He left the blind man to protect their belongings, trusting that Kóráhm would keep both safe, trusting that Wortham and Zelenka were making purchases and preparations for whatever step of their journey came next. He made an investigative circle of the city; determined to make one of the Gates work, Kavan tried one without the box or the emerald ring, a Gate in an abandoned náós built long before Kóráhm's shrine was erected. He successfully gated to the first recognizable point he found, Káliel, and then back again to where Urian waited for him. He tried again, this time with the ring on his hand, and was again unhindered.

But as soon as he lifted the reliquary and stepped into the ring of power that was the gate, the combination of power between himself, the ring, the Chalice and the staff canceled out any hope of using that particular means of transportation.

Irritated, his power stretched thin to the point of causing his head to throb, he returned to the shrine to find that Wortham and Zelenka had come back with a warm meal they had purchased somewhere in town. The captain looked at him expectantly but Kavan shook his head. Wortham sighed.

"I think I must accept that Gates are of no use to us," Kavan muttered as he sat.

"I feared as much. I sold the horses and chartered a ship. It will not go to Levonne, but I am sure Prince Muir will be pleased to see you."

He watched Kavan's face to gauge his reaction, hoping he had done right by the man he dearly loved. He was relieved to see that, after a brief flash of panic, the bard nodded his acceptance, his distress at the potential of sea travel, of seeing familiar faces again…and them seeing what had become of him during his months away, set aside.

"I would like to see Muir," Kavan murmured. The prince would show no judgment, no condemnation, no unnecessary adulation. It might help ease Kavan's transition back into the Lachlan world. Wortham did not need to add that there would be ships to take them from Káliel to Levonne. That was a given.

"She sails before dawn. I hoped to find one willing to make a delay, in case you were not prepared to leave, but tomorrow is the best I could do. We may board tonight, if we wish, after we eat. The ship's captain has permitted us overnight lodging so as not to delay their departure in the morning."

"I have longed to see Rhidam," Urian interjected, inviting himself not only as far as Káliel or Levonne, but all of the way to the end of Kavan's journey.

Kavan glanced at him, wondering if that had been the dedhá's ongoing intention, to see Kavan through to the end. Since there was no reason to deny him, he bobbed his head. "Then visit you shall."

They would eat and be on their way. Káliel. Two steps away from home. Kavan wondered as he wrapped his portion of warm bread in the cloth napkin he had been given, unable to eat any more now, if he was ready for what was to come.

Clianthe stared out the tall window at the rear of the villa, watching the moonlight dance on the stone tiles as it filtered through the spring growth of the trees around the courtyard. Something had caused her to wake, brought her to this room, although she wondered now if it had been nothing more than her unsettled stomach.

"Clianthe?"

She looked over her shoulder at her mother, whose weary face looked older in the midnight hours. "I don't know, Mother. It's…" She looked out the window again and shrugged. "I think he was here."

"He?" Gabrielle expected her daughter to say Muir, as it would be natural for her to dream about her absent husband and to think him here upon waking.

"I felt it twice, for a moment." Clianthe paused, wishing she knew how to explain what she felt, wishing she understood why she believed it to be real as strongly as she did. Her mother said nothing but waited for her to continue. "Lord Cliáth was here. Tonight. I know it."

Gabrielle's breath caught as she touched the younger woman's auburn hair. She had never told her daughter the truth of her heritage; Clianthe did not know she carried Elyri blood. If she were anyone else, Gabrielle would have attributed those words to a dream or imagination. Knowing what she did, however, about her daughter, about Kavan, about what was hidden in this room behind a storage closet door, she knew it was possible, even likely, that Clianthe had not imagined it at all.

Kavan could well have been there. But why?

"Perhaps he was," was all she chose to say as she put her arm around Clianthe's shoulder and steered her from the room, pausing in her step long enough to glance at the closet that housed Káliel's Gate. She prayed it would open, that Kavan would step out of it, that she would see him again. It would be the only proof necessary to know that he lived and was well, the only proof needed to suggest that maybe he was coming home.

<h1 style="text-align:center">❧Chapter 20❧</h1>

Alone with Kavan in the ship's hold for the first time since leaving Kílyn's port, Urian fumbled through his pack, muttering to himself. "I have something for you, Lord Cliáth." Kavan looked up from the journal he had been trying to write in, despite the muttering and rustling the blind man was creating and his own distraction as he faced the upcoming reunions. "There is no need," he began, closing the journal and tucking it back into his pack, deciding the effort was in vain even without the dedhá's interruption.

"No need, perhaps, but it is something I meant to give you since we first met. This," he said with a triumphant grin as he found the treasure he sought and held out a cloth drawstring back, "is a gift… repayment for any hardship and hindrance my handicap has been."

"You have hardly been a…"

"I thought I lost it, but Captain Delamo kept it safe, even when our belongings were thought to be swallowed by the sea," he continued, ignoring Kavan's interruption.

"I should be repaying you for tolerating my often insufferable behavior." He took the pouch but was hesitant to open it. Carvings, he suspected, the lightness of the wood within laying easy in his hand.

Urian patted his arm. "You had cause, given all that you suffered, and, in the end, it has brought you deeper faith and brought me insight into the nature of men's souls, hearts, and faith. Without you, I would have never ventured so far south, nor won as many converts. If I ever return to the mother náós, I will have quite the tale to tell. I have enjoyed all of it, my lord…please; accept this with my thanks."

The leather drawstrings of the pouch were tugged and the bag opened to deposit two objects onto Kavan's lap with a gentle clatter. Both were nearly six inches in height, larger than those Urian usually produced but not so large that they were difficult to store. One was a familiar image of Dhágdhuán on the pyre, flames snaking upwards around his lower body, his mournful eyes upturned towards Ethenae.

It was the same basic image that appeared in holy places throughout the Five Sovereignties, and though Urian might not have seen those images since he lost his sight, he had undoubtedly done so as a child and had likely laid his hands on at least one in recent memory.

The other figure, which Kavan caressed longer, bore a detailed likeness of the man Kóráhm he knew, and Kavan would have believed the dedhá had seen the Saint too if he was not blind. With the shepherd's staff in the crook of his arm, a harp in one hand and the other outstretched in a gesture of friendship and welcome, the image looked so much like the saint that Kavan longed to see Kóráhm again.

"He is much with you," Urian was saying, though how he knew which image Kavan was studying, the bard did not know. The statement could have applied to either figure. "I thought you would treasure such reminders of our journey."

"I could never forget," Kavan whispered. "Thank you."

"You are welcome." The dedhá closed the pack and used his hands to guide him to sit beside Kavan on the edge of the swaying cot. "You are troubled? Are you concerned about our safety at sea or something else?" For a man who could not see and could barely swim, another incident at sea after their first one was certainly cause for anxiety.

"No storm is due; we dock in the morning and there is no reason to believe the weather will not hold." He was not sea-sick either, but something was not right. "Yet…I cannot sleep."

He did not try to explain his apprehension. The nearer they drew to Káliel, the more intensely the reliquary radiated with the power of the items within. The emerald on his hand drew that power into him, which was exhausting and caused his head to ache. The malicious force continued to follow, even across the sea, although it kept enough distance between them that Kavan could not easily affect it or vice versa. The only connection he could make was that between the objects he carried and Pháne. Dawid Coryllien had been on those islands, had possessed a piece of the Staff of Drebhoti, and had defiled both the Pháne altar and the one Kavan intended to cleanse and reclaim. Pháne was awash with the negative presence of Coryllien and Kavan suspected that the reliquary items were reacting with that negativity.

The force and strength of that clash, the constant sparking of power, troubled him.

"Something your arrival in Káliel will rectify, I have no doubt.

Kavan, however, was less certain. That uncertainty was followed by a distant rumble, and having expressed confidence in the weather, having seen nothing but blue sky when he was on deck at noon, Kavan frowned. Rain would not be a problem, but lightning could be.

Excusing himself with a reassuring clasp of the dedhá's shoulder, Kavan went up top to assess their situation. The clouds on the horizon before them were steel gray now, the air growing colder as the wind pushed against them as if to hold them back. Lightning crackled through the billowy layers and the thunder it birthed rippled across the increasingly choppy water, reminding Kavan of his first storm on this very same sea. Whether inspired by nature's angry energy and hoping to take advantage of it, or creating the storm to do the same, the spiteful entity had drawn closer. If the latter was true, Kavan did not know how he could combat such power and drive the storm away.

Wortham nodded in passing as he escorted Zelenka below. She was pale, frightened by a storm of the sort she had never experienced. As sea travel agreed less with her than it did with Kavan; there was no need for her to be on deck to watch what they were heading into. Listening to the churning waves slapping against the side of the ship, feeling the vessel lurch and pitch, would be bad enough.

The ship felt seaworthy. Kavan did not think the building waves, like great watery hands, would succeed in pulling her beneath the surface. This boat would not sink the way the last one had.

Wortham rejoined Kavan at the rail several minutes later, leaning there, prepared to help the ship's crew if he needed to in order to keep them afloat. "This'll slow us, I wager." As near as the hour was to dawn, the sun's evidence of that obscured by the clouds, they would be lucky to dock by daybreak.

"As long as we reach port alive, I do not care where we sleep…or how long it takes," the bard said. "I'll sleep in the streets if I must."

The thought made Wortham chuckle, his mirth reassuring to hear in the face of the storm. "Do you want Lady Dilyn to take offense? I would not want to hear it, my lord. She would sooner be awakened by your arrival at midnight than learn that you made your bed in an alley so as not to wake her." The ship rolled from side to side, and as Wortham's footing threatened to leave him, Kavan caught his wrist with one hand. "It may not be safe for us to remain here…" He had intended to offer the scurrying crew his assistance, but for the moment it appeared he and Kavan would only be in the way if they stayed.

"Come below…sing for us. It will take Zelenka's mind off of the storm…help time to pass."

Whether he meant it figuratively or literally, he did not look back to see if the bard was following. He knew Kavan was right behind him.

❧*❧

k'dedhá Dórímyr did not look at his aide in the red robe of his office as he dictated the expected reply, did not see the darkening air on Hwensen's face. He did not need to, to know it was there.

"Tell them I cannot possibly come to Rhidam at this time. Preparations are underway for Kyne's celebration day and I must be there. I have too many gdhededhá to ordain…"

Hwensen muttered. "Two, Your Grace. The numbers continue to fall, and many have left the calling since…"

"So pessimistic, Hwensen. It is a temporary matter. There will be more." Noting the man's tone, however, the older Elyri finally looked at him with a challenging, bitter expression. "Is there a problem?"

It took several moments for the aide to muster the nerve to speak. They had discussed this matter multiple times and each time it seemed that Dórímyr was surprised by Hwensen's words and views. There were problems aplenty in Hwensen's eyes, and the k'gdhededhá was choosing to ignore every one of them. "You should go to Rhidam, Your Grace, and appoint the new k'gdhededhá. There are ways to ensure your safety. Everything here can wait. That is your duty too, and it is in everyone's interest…"

Dórímyr's pinched face flushed with annoyance. "I am the ecclesiastical authority, Hwensen. Not you. I decide what is in the best interest of the Faith, which duties are most pressing…and I say that to travel to Rhidam would be the worst possible thing that could be done. Tell them that, urge them to have elections as quickly as possible so this is behind us, and inform me of the outcome when there is one."

He stalked from the room, insulted, as he usually was, when anyone second-guessed his decision, but no more insulted than he was by any of the other numerous things he disdained. Hwensen looked at the notes he had taken, wanting to throw them into the fire and pretend he had sent the letter instead of actually sending it as the k'gdhededhá asked. He knew he could get away with it; the tone of both Claide and Tusánt's letters indicated they would not be surprised if the k'gdhededhá failed to respond. It would force them to hold the election

❧308❧

on their own. Then, regardless of its outcome, the k'gdhededhá would not have verbally sanctioned it and could not be blamed if the situation outside of Elyriá continued to deteriorate.

Hwensen also knew Dórímyr was not expecting the results of such an election for quite some time. No one but Tusánt would likely send word, and only then if he was not killed in the interim. Hwensen begged the k'gdhededhá to summon Tusánt back to Elyriá to protect his life, knowing it was safer here than where he was. Putting forth that summons would show people, the Elyri at least, that their religious figurehead cared. Rumors had been circulating for some time, and Hwensen believed he had heard every one of them. He did not think Dórímyr blind and deaf to the lack of trust the people were beginning to have in him, and yet the man who had held the k'gdhededhá seat for almost two hundred years did nothing. No summons were given, no effort made to offer assurance, a blind eye turned.

He would send the letter, however. Hwensen was too devoted to duty to disobey, and he was beginning to feel that, if Dórímyr wanted to condemn himself, his aide should let him. He would write two copies, have both of them sealed by the k'gdhededhá when he sought his seal for the other letters he was to send. One would be kept as evidence. He would wait to send the second as long as he felt he could, claim it was lost amongst other documents on his desk. Claim the messenger was delayed. He would do anything he could that might allow enough time to change the k'gdhededhá's mind.

The storm was not as frightening as he had feared. Though the wind howled and the force of the waves was powerful enough to hinder the ship's progress, the lightning had subsided by the time the rain began to fall and the strength of the current continued to carry them forward. They dared not draw too near to Káliel, for fear of ramming the docks or beaching on the shoals, but by mid-morning, the rain had slowed and the clouds cleared enough that the ship's helmsman and captain were able to correct their course and point them towards their destination. Passengers and cargo alike were kept on board as the island dock workers inspected the vessel; by the time they finished, by the time Zelenka had her legs under her and Urian no longer felt as if every slight movement would wrench his stomach from his body, it was mid-afternoon.

With one arm guiding the monk, as Wortham steadied Zelenka and oversaw the unloading of their belongings, Kavan stepped off of the ship onto the more stable surface of the dock with a long breath of relief. The harbor patrol, perhaps due to the roughness of the seas, had not questioned their ship's arrival nor their right to disembark as was normally the case. They might have believed the crew and passengers were in need of respite, or else Wortham's presence afforded them respect. Judging by the way many of the workers looked at Kavan as he disembarked, he could have been the cause as well. They could not have been expecting Kavan's arrival, unless Gabrielle had left standing orders for their welcome any time he required it.

Though seasickness had not plagued him during this journey, his legs were tremulous as he slowly made his way through the city streets and up the familiar path to the Magistrate's villa, their belongings towed on a small, wheeled cart that clattered and rattled as Wortham pulled it behind them. Each step made Kavan's heart pound harder, stole his breath, ate at the quiet in his mind until, by the time he caught sight of the home on the hillock outside of the city's edge, his head was pounding, his chest aching with an effort to breathe normally, and he stumbled more than he liked. Wortham's presence at his side steadied him enough to keep him moving forward, but it did not soothe his disquieted soul.

He had not seen any of these people after the attack, but they would know about the mutilation of his hands. Ártur would have told Muir and Gabrielle, and either or both would have shared the news with Clianthe. Muir might even have endeavored to talk sense into his sister and thus learned far more, including awkward details Kavan would rather not have shared. Now they would see him for the first time, see his hands, and know the truth. He did not have to fear for their acceptance or love; those were things he knew Muir and Gabrielle held regardless of his circumstance. But still, he worried.

The front door of the villa opened as he passed through the gate and started up the path. Clianthe stood as if scanning the garden for something unspecified, and Kavan felt, rather than heard, her excitement when she saw him and his companions. Her welcoming smile was weary but sincere.

He should have known she would be the first to sense his arrival.

Running along the path, she came straight to him and wrapped her arms possessively around his neck. He put the reliquary on top of their other goods on Wortham's cart and returned the embrace uneasily, touched by her enthusiasm. "I knew you were coming," she gushed. "Mother did not believe me…thought I was mad to have the harbor guard keep vigil all week…but I knew you would come."

A week-long vigil meant she had likely sensed his efforts to Gate from Kílyn to Káliel; he should have considered she would be sensitive enough to feel his attempts. Before he could respond, Clianthe sidestepped to embrace Wortham. "And Captain, welcome. Mother will be delighted to see you both…and will welcome your companions." Her hands reached simultaneously for Urian and Zelenka, and though there were no embraces, there were handshakes of greeting. "Mother is in Council but will return this evening."

She took Kavan's hand then and squeezed it, acknowledging his healing but not speaking of it the way others would. Some of the concern he had shouldered dissipated.

"Muir will regret missing you, but I will send him word that you are in good health and safe…unless you intend an extended stay?"

"I…" Muir's absence unsettled him after the snippet of vision seen the night of Ártur's attack., and it troubled him that he had given little thought to the young man's well-being since then, that he had assumed the prince was well, assumed he would know if Muir was not. But the arrival of servants coming to take their belongings into the villa interrupted him, and then came the gleeful sound of a child, Piran he presumed, laughing in the back garden.

As if reading his thoughts, Clianthe continued, "Owain is not here either. Do you require rooms? Will you be here long enough to need them? You can rest and refresh until Mother returns. I'm sure after that storm, you could use a decent rest."

"We would appreciate the generosity, your ladyship," Urian said with a smile and an exaggerated bow.

"I'm sure Zelenka will too," added Wortham with a warm glance down at the woman clinging to his arm.

Zelenka, more comfortable with another woman, even if that woman seemed of a higher station, curtsied and said, "Too much sea."

Clianthe grinned. "You're not the first to suffer from that affliction. Come." She took the blind man by the arm, motioning for the others to follow. They passed into the entrance hall, the room looking no different than Kavan remembered from his first visit here. For a moment he imagined he would see Gabrielle in riding attire coming down the stairs as Clianthe led them to the base of the staircase, but it was only Delia herding page boys with empty buckets down the steps.

"I had baths drawn as soon as I saw you," the young woman said. "Your room is prepared as always, Captain, as is yours, Lord Cliáth."

The other three went upstairs with her, but a glance over her shoulder showed that Kavan had veered away from the group towards her mother's office. She trusted Kavan there and did not call him back.

The large plate windows of the Prime Magistrate's office afforded the best view of the back terrace, where Piran played with toy boats in the fountain. Kavan felt little Elyri in the boy; with his blonde curls and stocky build he carried more of his father than he did his mother. He looked very much the way Kavan remembered Owain looking the first time they had met as children. Only the shape of his eyes and mouth and the shape of his hands resembled Gabrielle. In this time of open hostility, Piran being primarily Teren was for the best. Like Gaelán, Piran might someday exhibit Elyri abilities, but it was more likely he would not. It might keep him safe.

It was the same reason Gabrielle had never told Clianthe the truth.

When Piran ran out of Kavan's sight, the boats abandoned in favor of chasing a blue and yellow butterfly, Kavan sank into the Magistrate's chair, content to rest there rather than go upstairs. He wanted a bath, wanted sleep that was not on a rocking boat, but his nerves were taut with emotion and he needed to know what was happening with Muir. He would not rest well until he knew Muir's whereabouts, knew he was well. He listened to the footsteps and voices that ventured up and down the stairs until they ceased; not long after, he felt Clianthe stop in the doorway behind him, apparently content to look at the back of his head or else respecting his need for silence and awaiting permission to speak.

He waved her into the room with one hand without looking away from the window.

"You've lost your robes," she murmured with warmth in her voice. He glanced at the black breeches he wore, at first finding it odd that she would so quickly notice that detail. Yet after spending so many years in the same white robes, he supposed a change would be noticeable to those who had known him longest. "And your hands?"

"Fully usable, my lady." There was no reason to hide or deny it now that they were alone.

"You will play for us?"

"I do not have my harp with me…and have not played in many months. Tonight…I am too weary." There was a large harp in the villa, however, that Gabrielle had once tried to give him. It was not his preferred instrument. When he picked up a harp again, he felt it should be his own, but he no longer needed his harp to make music. He could sing. "Perhaps tomorrow."

"You will stay?" she asked giddily.

"If your mother permits. A few days at least. Zelenka and Urian need a respite before we press towards Rhidam." He turned to look at her at last. "How is Muir? Where is he?"

Scowling with annoyance that was clearly not aimed at the bard, she scooted one of the chairs on the other side of the desk and sank into it with a frustrated sound. "On Pháne. There have been at least three attempts by someone to gain access to the islands. We, the Council that is, have established an armed outpost there under Muir's command to discourage trespassers, to police the strait. We don't know what they want, and the Council is debating the need for outposts on the other islands as well now, but so far Muir and his men have kept everyone away."

The bard knew what someone might want from Pháne, and he frowned at the prickle that clawed up his spine. The negative entity following him was not likely here by chance, might take advantage of Kavan's leading it here, making it more imperative he see Muir, make certain the prince was safe.

"He should not be there."

"Someone has to be, and no one else has the experience." Muir had little military experience, but surrounded by more practiced sailors and the Káliel guard, Muir had the head for leadership. She knew that, despite the islands long-standing isolationist tendencies, they boasted some of the most skilled soldiers in the Sovereignties. Wortham's prowess was proof of it. To Clianthe, however, her husband was the most qualified man for any duty put to him.

"Last time he was here he confided that he believes the attacks are connected to the violence in Enesfel, though I don't know how they could be, or why. There's nothing on Pháne worth having, not even enough trees to build with. But if Muir says it, I believe him. He's not due home for several more days. Unless he returns early or you wait longer than you anticipate, you will likely not see him."

The disappointment in her voice mirrored the earlier scowl, the separation from her new husband the cause of her frustration. "And your mother will be out for a few more hours still?"

"That's up to the Council. Muir requested more ships…and like I said, they're debating now the need for additional outposts. Mother presented his request this morning. Debating it could take weeks…or they might reach a decision today."

As much as Kavan admired Káliel's representative form of government, he also felt that there were times when a decision needed to be made quickly and not delayed by bureaucracy. Having raised Muir and taught him as much as he could before the young man moved forward with his life, Kavan believed Muir would not have made that request if he did not believe additional ships were necessary.

"I think then," he said as he stood, "that I shall accept your offer of rest and refreshment if that is agreeable." He was tempted to go to Muir but was also reminded that leading whatever followed him to the prince might be detrimental to all of them. Rest might clear his head and give him answers about what he should do.

Clianthe chuckled as she got to her feet. She did not know Kavan as well as some, but she knew him well enough. "You fear you are being rude if you do not stay and answer my questions? Mother will undoubtedly want many of the same answers, those you can provide at least, so why should I make you answer them twice? I'll see your bath is refreshed and have a tray sent up."

"The water will be warm enough." They had not been speaking together that long. However warm the water was now would be satisfying. "You are a treasure, Clianthe. Muir has chosen well."

His compliment made her smile. "Muir chooses his companions and friends as wisely as you, my lord. Would you expect him to do any less in picking a wife?"

Kavan smiled too. "I would have been surprised if he had.

≊*≋

Hidden behind the thick attic beam, hewn centuries ago when the náós was built and reinforced a handful of times since then, the boy held his breath. He had known it was a gdhededhá coming here, bringing food and drink, clothes and bedding, but he had not known which one. This was the first time, since he had felt ill this day and had not yet ventured out of the loft, that he had seen his benefactor.

Not a gdhededhá, though, but one of the novices, the youngest of the newcomers. He arrived with another plate of food as he did once every day since discovering evidence of someone living here. Not just bread and water, as he could have brought, but a full meal, just as he had brought nearly every other time. The plate came every day, in the evening, and contained a collection of foods gathered from meals throughout the day. Bread, cheese, meat. Sometimes gruel or stew, fruits or vegetables, puddings or soups. Sometimes even sweets and boiled eggs. There were rarely large portions of any one item, but there was an ample selection put together so that the boy was not likely to go hungry. He saved what morsels he could to get him through the following day and ate the rest in a single sitting. The offering meant he did not have to steal to eat, meant he no longer lived with a constant growl in his belly, and though he was reluctant to rely on the tray being there each evening, he had begun to expect it.

Tonight the novice left the plate beside the bed where he usually left it, an inverted bowl covering it, as usual, to keep away the rats and flies. He paused and looked around, his hand still on the tray. The boy held his breath.

Did he know he was not alone?

He did not move until after the novice smiled to himself and then went out. Once certain the man would not be immediately returning to catch him, the boy scurried from his hiding place to examine tonight's offering, one eye kept on the hatchway used for coming and going.

Lamb and potatoes with heavy gravy. A small cup of milk and an apple. Dabbing his finger into the cup, he was relieved to find no alcohol. No trap again tonight, just food for a hungry boy. He sat cross-legged on the collection of blankets that was his bed, pulled the plate into his lap, and dug into the first full meal he had enjoyed today.

Though he tried to sleep, his effort was not as restful as he hoped, plagued by dreams he could not hold on to every time his eyes opened to stare at the ceiling above. His head and ringed finger ached as if he was being bombarded with too much power and his ears hummed as if bees were burrowing into his brain. The sun was setting now, but it felt as if it had been doing so every time he peered out from beneath heavy lids. This time, however, he sensed he was not alone and, rather than ignore the sensation in favor of continuing to seek sleep, he forced himself to sit without looking at his guest.

"Have you been here long?"

"Would it matter?"

Adjusting the sheet over his lower body for decency as it slipped away from his white shoulders, Kavan replied, "It would mean I failed to recognize or sense your arrival." That rarely happened, although perhaps that was why he had been unable to sleep.

In the tall-backed chair beside the bed, Kóráhm sighed. "There is too much here vying for your attention. You followed your instincts to Káliel; it is good you are here."

"There was little choice. The Gates do not work with the reliquary, and Wortham found no other ships sailing north."

"Sometimes fate directs us to where we need to be as surely as our hearts do. But your first step is here; there is no one but you who can see it done." There was regret in the saint's voice and he looked away.

"Pháne." Kóráhm nodded. Kavan looked at the ring upon his hand. What began in this place, with Kavan finding the cave, had to be ended here. "What must I do?"

"You are so eager?"

Thinking Kóráhm expected resistance, the bard shook his head. "No…but I am resigned. And determined. I've resisted the thought of going there, bringing danger to Muir…tell me what I must do.'

"Enter the cave. Destroy it."

Kavan blinked with surprise. Always before Kóráhm's instructions had been vague references to Kavan knowing what would be needed when the time was right. He had not expected such bluntness. "How? I cannot…"

Predictably, however, the saint was gone, giving him no more than that single tantalizing command. The seed had been planted, Kóráhm as always the planter and nothing more, and Kavan was left to riddle out his purpose. He got out of bed, frowning, and dressed without lighting the lamp, seeing no point in alerting anyone to his being awake. He considered if he should linger long enough to learn if Gabrielle was home, to speak with her first, but decided against it. It would delay the inevitable and if anyone suspected his intentions, they would try to deter him, particularly Wortham who would not want him venturing near that cave alone.

But Kóráhm had directed him and he would deny the saint nothing. He would not put anyone else in danger, and the swiftest means of travel at his disposal would only permit transport of himself.

He opened the window and gazed at the darkening sky for several minutes, smelling the night, the intoxicating mixture of garden flowers, sea, and the smoke of an island's worth of cooking fires. In those scents, he found reminders of Alberni, memories that tugged his heart in the direction of home. But home, be it Alberni, Rhidam, or Bhryell, would have to wait. Focus turned from remembrance, he directed it into flight, claiming the white kestrel form he had not assumed in too long and taking to the sky.

"Kavan?" Gabrielle knocked on the chamber door but received no answer. Behind her, Wortham shrugged when she looked at him.

"He is likely sleeping. None of us have slept well of late." Urian and Zelenka had not yet emerged from their rooms either, thus the captain was not concerned about Kavan. The Elyri might not have expressed or exhibited fatigue, but he was capable of pushing himself beyond what other men might endure, and then when the time came, falling into a sleep that might last for days. He was not worried.

Gabrielle, however, was not easily assuaged. "I would feel more at ease seeing him…seeing that he is here and truly well." After the horrific tales she had been told, she felt the need for proof that her faith in his return had been rewarded.

"You think I would be here if he was not?" asked Wortham with a touch of indignation as she pushed open the door.

"Of course not, but…" With the door opened further, the light of the lamp in her hand spilling into the room, they could see that the bed had been slept in but was empty now. As was the room.

And the window was open.

Hoping to disavow Gabrielle of any distressing conclusions he knew she would jump to, conclusions that pushed through his mind as well, Wortham said, "He may be in the gardens…or your daughter told him where he could find Prince Muir and he has gone to see him." The prince was a large part of Kavan's decision to come to Káliel; it made sense for the bard to seek him out.

"Muir is on Pháne."

Despite Wortham's words, however, Gabrielle knew him to be equally worried, even though he had not known the prince's whereabouts. That revelation increased his concern.

"You don't think he would have gone there…without seeing me first…without telling you?"

Since it appeared that Kavan may have done just that Wortham leaned against the doorframe and shrugged. "He has done many things in recent months that he would not before. He has changed…for the better, I believe…but there is much expected of him when he returns to Rhidam. I do not know what is required, but the knowledge of some greater destiny lies heavy upon him. If he feels the need to see the prince before he continues on, or if he desires solitude or something more, I must accept his wishes…"

Few others would be so forgiving or accommodating. Gabrielle herself was one of those pushed to be less patient with Kavan's choices despite her love for him. She wanted to give him those things, but she knew she failed more than succeeded. "I am thankful I chose to send you to Enesfel, Wortham…that you have become…"

"His friend. Anything he wants and needs me to be."

He moved past her into the room, remembering the first time he had met Kavan on the deck of a supply ship. He did not know what Kavan's thoughts had been that night, but Wortham had looked at the beautiful, white-skinned man and had known he would follow him anywhere, not out of duty to Gabrielle, but because something in Kavan begged that of him without the bard saying a word. "I will wait for him, if it pleases you, and inform you when he returns."

"No need to do that…unless he needs something you cannot supply. If you are with him, I will have to be content with his well-being. I will send up dinner shortly. If I do not see you until morning, goodnight, Captain."

Wortham nodded, slid off his boots, and lay back on the bard's bed, knowing that the woman was more worried than she expressed. He was glad she had not asked what destiny Kavan faced, that he had not had to explain how entangled the bard's fate was with the history of a man called Coryllien. Any mention of Pháne, Coryllien, that cave or the violence in Enesfel would only foster panic.

He would rather focus on the positive and pretend that panic did not exist. Kavan would come back safely. The future of Elyri in Enesfel demanded it.

❧*❧

The outer door which opened into the island's mountainous interior was closed, though Kavan knew he had not closed it fourteen years ago when last in this place. Perhaps it had closed on its own, the rise and fall of the sea having drawn it shut. Perhaps Muir had done so. Or perhaps Kóráhm had closed it. It was high tide now, meaning that the water lapped at the ledge on which Kavan balanced as he sprung the latch the way Caol had once done and peered into the dark passage with unexpected apprehension. His heart pounded in time with the throbbing in his skull, the effect of both making concentration difficult. He did not need the Chalice or staff crown in hand to know that the energy of this place was stronger than it had been when he had left the cave behind. The emerald ring on his hand pulsed and glowed faintly, dimming in the moments of peak negative energy and brightening when Kavan fought back against it.

Nothing would be accomplished on the ledge. He needed to go inside, no matter how uncomfortable it made him.

He opted not to use a light source as he started up the slippery path. The heat of it would create fog in the tunnel as the moisture on the walls and floor evaporated, and the light might alert anyone ahead of his arrival. He sensed no one, but the pervasive negativity that surrounded him might be hiding someone. There was no doubt he would have to confront that thing before the sun rose.

Should he have brought the Chalice? The staff crown? Anything at all? Should he not have come alone? Kóráhm had not instructed him to bring anyone, had left him to trust his instincts in knowing what to do, thus he had to hope his faith and strength would be enough.

Several times before he reached the double doors, his feet slipped out from under him. Each stumble made the knees of his trousers wet and his sleeves were damp where they brushed the sides of the passage. His hands were scraped, from the walls and the floor, but he avoided any other injury and encountered no one until he reached the moisture slickened doors that barred him from the chamber. Though he could not recall closing this door either, someone had done so. It was just as well. Keeping others out of this chamber was in the best interest of every man, woman, and child in the Sovereignties and beyond.

He had not thought to bring the Káliel Serpents, and even if he had, he did not have the Coryllien dagger with him, all of which had been necessary to open the door before. The pulse and itch across the back of his hand, however, birthed by the power in Kóráhm's emerald, suggested an answer to the absence of keys. Thinking the ring to be the answer, he began to remove it from his hand just as his vision blurred and went black. He doubled over with a groan at that moment, just before Myreth appeared in his mind's eye, asleep on his pallet, his expression innocent and peaceful. It was a warning, surely; the ring had belonged to Myreth for so long that whatever Kavan was about to do seemed likely to affect the dark-haired man.

It was possible the negative power had forced that image, that premonition, into his head to prevent him from proceeding. Inaction was a risk he could not take, however, and when his hand shot out to keep him from falling beneath the assault of pain and nausea, the ring touched the stone door and his body went rigid.

Needles of pain shot up his arm, into his back and head, down his legs, and the heavy dead air around him refused to be drawn into his lungs. He thought he heard screaming, Myreth's he believed, and as he struggled to remain upright, an apologetic rush of power traveled back along the route he had taken since leaving the cloister.

He hoped it reached its target. He could not be sure of anything except the crushing weight and the fire in the nerves of his arm.

The door hinges popped and the latch released, allowing the door to retract as if pulled violently away from his hand. The negative power was stronger behind the door, as if waiting in ambush, and it rushed over him, around him, seeking to press into his core and drown him. But Kavan held his ground, mental shields strengthening automatically against the force that buffeted him like the Kármár against boarded windows. As his hand dropped, contact no longer maintained between the ring and the door, the needle pain subsided quickly, leaving only a lingering ache in its wake.

The screaming loitered in the back of his skull, joined by the persistent shadows of Myreth sitting upright in his bed, his head between his hands. Though Kavan did not want to be the cause of the other man's pain, if indeed the image was real, he could not turn back. Real or not, he could not afford to dwell on it. The sooner he did what he had come to do, the sooner that vision, Myreth's pain, would end.

Thrusting a wave of power before him drove the negativity back and allowed him to take slow, steady steps towards the altar at the center of the room, resisting every attack, every effort it made to hinder him. He molded the energy into a bubble of protection that required little effort to maintain. For the moment, as his assailant sought to harm him through the impenetrable shield, Kavan was safe.

Much of the upper ledge around the cave's perimeter had collapsed fourteen years ago, leaving rubble strewn across the stone floor in a haphazard pattern. Gray dust covered everything, the footprints of those who had been here that day were no longer visible. In spite of that and the near darkness, the only light coming from the popping crackle of energy where positive and negative collided and the glow of the ring on his hand, he was able to pinpoint the place where Prince Bertram had been robbed of his young life. It was unreachable from where he stood, and he did not need to touch that spot for the grief to try to overwhelm him. The thing coming at him was struggling with ever-growing frustration. If Kavan allowed grief to distract him, all would be lost.

Not knowing what he was searching for, believing he would know it when he found it, he began a slow circle of the room, examining the walls, the floor, and as much of the ceiling as he could make out. He wanted to be certain there was nothing he and his companions had missed that day, nothing of worth that someone might be searching for in this place. But there were no rooms, no panels, no hidden objects or secret messages. No symbols carved into walls, no traces of those who had once used this cave as a temple and secret meeting place.

But when he reached the entrance to the alcove where Coryllien's corpse had laid undisturbed for hundreds of years, the negative force raced inside, pushing past with enough power to halt his movement and with enough strength to do everything it could to drive him back, keep him out.

Defiler. Traitor. Brother. Words Kavan had heard fourteen years ago, words that echoed and swirled within the stone room struck back at him, bringing with them an understanding he had not had then. And he understood something else for the first time. The malicious force that had been following him resided here, was rooted in this place as if it had sprung from the earth beneath his feet. It had been in this room when Kavan had entered the first time, and it had been Kavan who had unleashed it on the world.

Or rather, it had been Wortham who had done so, when he smote the mummified corpse's head from its body and allowed it to crumble to dust. There was something of Coryllien in that negativity, or perhaps, as Kóráhm continued to exist long after his supposed death, the troublesome energy was what remained of Coryllien. A thing denied a body. A thing seeking the vengeance it failed to find in life.

Kavan's faith in his ability to proceed, to succeed, wavered for the first time. He believed that each person contained a spirit, a soul, something of them that lived on after the physical body went into the earth. Perhaps Elyri took the physical with them, but that little piece of life was, by the tenets of the Faith, believed to be immortal, indestructible, the piece that journeyed into eternity in Ethenae with the spirits of all who had gone before.

If this force, this entity that pursued him, was Coryllien's immortal soul, could it be destroyed? Should it be destroyed? What would become of it if Kavan succeeded? And who was he, of all people of the world, to be the destroyer of souls?

More frightening still, could Kóráhm's soul be harmed in a similar fashion? Could Kavan's?

Or was he meant to restrain it, trap him again as he had once been trapped within the decaying prison of his body, to prevent him from further acts of harm against the living?

If Kóráhm or anyone else heard his unspoken questions, they did not offer an answer.

It took effort, but Kavan pushed into the room, feeling his protective shield buckling and shrinking around him as he struggled. The room was empty of everything except rubble and dust, dust from the exploded rock, dust from the disintegrated corpse. A screeching, different from Myreth's now silent scream, took root in Kavan's head, a sound he could not quell in spite of his efforts to do so. He began to consider retreating, finding a solution in the main room rather than here where he was not wanted, but then he noticed the faint tickle of something he had not noticed fourteen years earlier.

The residual energy of a Gate.

It had not been used in centuries, perhaps since before Coryllien's body was put to rest in this place, but the barely-there signature energy was unmistakable. It was possible that Coryllien's followers had brought him to his final resting place through this Gate, rather than by sea. If true, it implied that at least one of those in the vile man's inner circle had shared Elyri blood.

Needing time to think, Kavan returned to the central room, where the screeching in his skull faded as he had hoped. At the altar, he studied the faded stains, the remains of innumerable sacrifices Teren, Elyri, and animal. These sacrifices were similar to those below Rhidam's castle, but his instructions for this space were different. He had not been asked to cleanse it but to destroy it. He did not think

Kóráhm's request stemmed merely from a desire for it to be erased from the world. Destruction here, Kavan believed, broke a link between the chapels and would make the required cleansing easier to accomplish.

But he could think of only one way to do it, the way Kóráhm himself had wanted to destroy it. He could pull the walls in upon themselves until the entire structure collapsed, but if he was not very careful, very quick, he would be crushed in the attempt. He had faith in his own survival, for he had another duty beyond this room to perform, and his death here would make that impossible. But that did not mean he could be reckless and foolish.

Testing himself, he focused on the altar, its destruction an easy enough thing. With one hand on it, he sought the center of its stony heart, gathered energy in his core, held it long enough to embrace the altar in its own shield so that the blast to follow would be contained. The ball of energy was released down his arm, through his hand, resulting in the explosion of stone within its power bubble. Infuriated, the negative entity beat upon Kavan's mental shields, demanding he stop, promising retribution if he did not, but Kavan ignored it and instead strengthened his protections hoping that, when he took the next step, that shield would be enough to keep falling stone from trapping and killing him.

Rather than look back at the alcove, he stared at the doorway that had been his entrance into this chamber. He could attempt the destruction of this place from there, and risk the rock coming down around him, trapping him in the passage with no certain way out if he could not run down the path fast enough. Or he could confront the screeching thing in the alcove and hope there was enough power within the Gate, hope that his necessarily divided concentration, would allow him to use it. The risk was the same either way, the possibility of being crushed, buried alive, something he might be condemned to regardless.

But he trusted his abilities, trusted his mastery of power and Gates, to think escape the more certain option. Once his mind was made up, he entered the alcove without giving in to the negativity's assault.

He stepped onto the Gate, sensing at once that it had but a single destination, one he did not recognize. He did not know where it would leave him, what his fate might be on the other side, but with few other choices available, he intended to make this work.

Maintaining the shields around both his mind and body, he reached out with another bubble of energy, pushing further and further, deep into the rock, until the cave temple and everything within it were enveloped in power. The aggressor, focused as it was on driving Kavan out of the alcove, failed to realize what was happening until it was too late, until it too was trapped inside the outer bubble just as Kavan was. Then it began to fight against him in earnest.

Dividing his attention was difficult but not impossible. Even as a child, Tíbhyan had marveled at how Kavan could perform a myriad of psychic tasks at one time. Keeping the Gate open required the least amount of focus, followed by tending his defensive shields to maintain them at an adequate strength. Feeding energy into the bubble, was more difficult, and it left only a marginal amount of focus with which to beat back his attacker. It allowed the malignant thing to perceive a glimpse of the possible limits of Kavan's power.

But it could not be helped.

With a great focus of strength and will, Kavan pulled the outer bubble back to him, sucking the energy into himself, controlling it, redirecting it into protection against his attacker. There was a crack and shudder, the breaking of roots, dissolving rock, fracturing earth. The inner bubble of power was drawn back to create a second skin; it might not save his life, but it allowed him a better chance of surviving while allowing more energy and focus to go where it was needed. The ground beneath his feet began to quake and the tunnel entrance became the first to collapse, the weakest point in the cave.

If Kavan failed to do anything else, at least no one would ever be able to enter through that passage.

The alcove where he stood was the second weakest point and it too began to crumble, even though his effort to pull the walls inward was directed into the central altar room. The closeness of his energy skin meant that he felt the jarring impact of every bit of rock that fell against him; if one struck his head, it might break his concentration long enough for the falling debris to kill him if his attacker did not. The room was filling with dust and dirt, depleting the breathable air, and he did his best to protect his head, his mouth, his nose, as he doubled his efforts to collapse the primary room.

When the moment came, when he could feel the stone begin its final collapse beneath his tightening grip on power, there was a thunderous rumble, a blast of dust exploding through the alcove archway, and a gush of putrid air. He could not see, could not breathe, but he could not leave, not yet, not until he was certain of success. The energy engulfing the stone slipped, his energy depleting too fast as he reined it back in. In desperation to complete what he had begun, he gave up his hold on the Gate and turned everything he had into drawing more energy from the room. The emerald on his hand hummed, shooting power up his arm, filtering the negative energy from that which he was attempting to utilize. As the walls buckled, the entity bellowed and grasped at him, trying to attach to the tendrils of power in the hopes of avoiding destruction or captivity.

No longer able to afford a delay as the world crashed around him, Kavan tapped into the Gate's energy, there, where he stood, and with a panicked grasp at the exit point of light somewhere beyond the cave, he pulled hard.

The spot where he stood filled with rocks and earth and dust.

Struggling to breathe, gasping, his body cut and bruised by falling stone, Kavan emerged in a heap into the open air on a stony slope with the rolling sea to the north and the ground shaking and shuddering below him. Some of the points of earth around him had collapsed into themselves, forming craters and pits, uprooting trees, sucking brush and mossy grass into the fallen places that belched dirt and debris. He stayed still where he was, poised to take to the air if the ground sank beneath him, but fortunately, it did not and after several more moments of shaking, the world settled and was still.

A study of the horizons revealed Káliel to the west, which meant he was still on Pháne, somewhere on the rim of the mountain face that had once served as the temple's roof. Power still emanated from the Gate below his feet, but anyone attempting to use it would materialize amidst of broken rock and collapsed dirt. Such an attempt would kill any user. If he had the knowledge to create and destroy Gates, he would have destroyed this too, but he did not expect that anyone would ever try to use this one.

No one was likely to ever know it was here.

Too tired, physically and mentally, for flight, and glad he had not had to try, it would be some time before he would be able to return to Káliel. The position of the stars announced that dawn was a few hours away. The chaos of men scrambling, shouting in the aftermath of the earthquake told him the direction of Muir's outpost and reminded him that those on the main island would likely have felt it too.

Few, if any, would ever know he was the cause.

He chose to rest where he was. Once he determined the state of the cave, and was recovered enough to walk, he would make his way to the outpost. By the time he felt strong enough for that, the ruckus of men would have ceased and he felt sure Muir would be relieved to know that the cave he was trying to protect was no longer a threat.

Dust and power burped from the sunken ground and for a moment, Kavan wondered what had become of Coryllien's energy. He had lost contact with it as he Gated from the collapsing room. Had it been trapped, he wondered. Destroyed? Or had it found a way out with him?

At the moment, he had no way of knowing.

Kóráhm, he sighed, staring wearily at the moon. I hope I have done as you wished. I hope it was enough.

∾*∾

With a violent fit of seizures, the woman collapsed on the granite floor in the dark room in which she had taken shelter that day. She looked dead, or unconscious, but she was keenly aware of everything around her, and of things too far away to see.

The defiler had returned. She could feel him in her bones, in the corners and crevices that made her who she was. He had destroyed everything she had struggled so long to find. Of what use were her fleets, her fortunes, if there was nothing left to retrieve?

But there were some things, things which would restore her if she could gain them, and she knew they were in the defiler's possession. If they were not to be had, she would at least take her revenge on him as she should have done long ago.

It was her duty.

It was her birthright.

❧Chapter 21❧

By the time Muir clambered around toppled furniture and staggering bodies to make it outside of the shuddering outpost, the ground movement had subsided to an occasional rumbling tremor. He had heard stories of earthquakes since coming to Káliel, as they were relatively common on the islands, but he had never lived through one. His blood was driving hard enough through his veins that his body ached as if it would explode.

As his gaze swept the vicinity for damage, he listened to the men around him talk. While not the strongest shaking some had lived through, many believed it had originated nearby, possibly beneath them, and they spoke with concern about aftershocks and the large waves that could be upon them soon. A portion of the rear wall had collapsed, leaving the kitchen and dining area exposed to the elements, but the majority of the structure had suffered only minor damage that was easily repaired. As long as the sea did not turn on them and the weather held, the prince felt they had little to fear. The ship he would take back to Káliel had come and he would be on it in the morning. He would ask for more bricks to repair the unexpected damage then.

Most of the inspection was complete as Muir examined the fallen rear wall, attempting to gauge how many bricks would be needed there. Movement in the darkness beyond, on the steep hill behind the outpost, caught his eye, something too large, its movement too erratic, to be any of the rodents and other small creatures native to Pháne. It could have been one of his men scouting the perimeter to look for further hazards, but since he had not sent anyone out into falling dusk, he worried that someone had taken advantage of the chaos to find another way onto the island with the intent of sneaking up on them. He drew his sword, held his ground, and called, "Drop your weapons and show yourself."

The figure that appeared from between the scrubby trees after several tense moments wore torn black trousers, ripped and soiled now, and a once white shirt. There was too much distance between them for Muir to recognize anything else until the form moved into the moonlight, exposing silver-white hair and snowy white skin.

The sword dropped from Muir's hand.

"Kavan!" Forgetting age, rank, and his surroundings, Muir leaped over the lowest part of the collapsed wall, scurried up the rocky terrain, and was rewarded by pulling his former tutor into a powerful embrace. He could find no voice, no words, and would not have trusted either if he had. His relief at seeing the bard again meant all he could do was cling to the man the way he had as a child when seeking comfort from the one person guaranteed to give it. The returned embrace, while less exuberant, was equal in sincerity and emotion.

Muir was alright.

"I prayed you would come…that everything would be better…the way it was…that you would be…" Muir pulled back, clutched the Elyri's hands, and brought them up where he could see them. "Praise be! You do not know how much I…"

"I think I do," Kavan murmured, stopping the man's excited rambling. "Please…" No words were required and hearing them would make the bard uncomfortable, no matter how honest and true they were. "I apologize for not arriving in a more proper…"

"Proper? I don't care how you got here. It is enough you came. Come inside. We don't have much, but do you want food? Drink?"

"Do not trouble yourself; I want only to rest…and talk with you for a little while."

Sensing a degree of fragility in the bard that was not normally there, Muir carefully guided him through the hole in the wall and then motioned for him to sit at one of the nearest tables. He brought a lamp from elsewhere in the room, set it in front of Kavan, then brought a pitcher of water and cup before digging through their food stores for something the man could eat.

"Our situation doesn't lend itself to feasting," he said as he returned with his offerings, bread and dried fish and a morsel of fruit he had saved for himself. "You look exhausted.'

Ignoring his concern for the moment, Kavan broke off a piece of bread. "Compared to what I have dined on for the past several months, this is acceptable, my prince."

Muir glanced to the side as a bit of broken brick tumbled from its precarious position down to the floor. His eyes widened and he looked back at the slowly eating bard. "Any connection between your arrival and…that?"

"Why would there be?" The two things could have been purely coincidental, but Muir knew him too well.

"No reason…just a hunch. Since you singlehandedly scared at least one life out of me by appearing out there, would you at least be kind enough to enlighten me?"

The corners of Kavan's mouth twisted into the beginnings of a grin, but the expression failed to fully blossom. "You do not need to concern yourself with the cave any longer," he murmured. "It has been destroyed. No one may enter now."

The prince looked skeptical. "Destroyed?"

"Collapsed. Filled with debris. Impossible to enter."

Muir stared at him for many minutes, studying the way the muscles in his jaw flexed as he ate while pondering what he had said, and what he had not. If he was inclined to doubt Kavan's involvement at first, he was no longer. Such use of power as would have been necessary to destroy a cave would account for Kavan's weariness.

"Perhaps…but I want this outpost to remain as insurance. Those seeking entrance will not stop trying unless they see the destruction themselves, and I have no intention of letting anyone get that close. It would be difficult to explain to the Council that all of this," he gestured around them, "is no longer necessary after the effort it took to gain permission…and after the attacks we've already endured."

"Indeed…I do not think anyone will stop trying to get in there for the foreseeable future…but I assure you they will not." The possibility that those who had attacked the outpost might turn their attention to Káliel was one Kavan wanted Muir, Gabrielle, and the Káliel Council to continue to take seriously. At least until the Rhidam temple was cleansed, the threats to all, Teren and Elyri alike, remained.

"You have been to see Gabrielle? And Clianthe? Is the captain with you?"

"I spoke to Clianthe when our ship arrived; Wortham and the others were given rooms. Gabrielle was in Council, and though I intended to dine with them before coming to see you, Kóráhm bid me tend to business first."

"She'll be furious…temporarily," the prince said with a grin. "Having you back and whole, however, I doubt her fury will last. When will you go back?"

Until that moment, Kavan had not realized how much he had missed the young man's smile. "As soon as I'm rested enough to make the return…" A pair of soldiers entered and spoke with Muir about repairs, eyeing the stranger as they did so, a man they had not seen disembark the supply ship when it arrived. From their curious back glances as they went out, Kavan suspected they knew who he was, even without introductions. "I should like to stay longer, but there are things I must do and I do not know how long I have to do them."

"You are going to Rhidam."

It was not a question. Kavan involuntarily shuddered and his embarrassed gaze dropped to the uneaten remnants of his meal. "You have spoken to your sister."

"You cannot speak her name." It was telling, and to be expected, but still it, and the man's discomfiture, made Muir sad. "I am sorry, Kavan. For all of it…though it isn't my fault. What she did was reprehensible and I, and others, have rebuked her for it. None would blame you if you do not forgive her…even she will not. She is contrite, and I believe she has learned a valuable lesson from the price she…and you…paid for her mistake. But sorry is not enough to warrant forgiveness. I've not seen or spoken to her since Arlan…"

"Died." Kavan squeezed the young man's hand, offering and receiving comfort in the touch. "You may say it, Muir. Not saying it does not make it hurt any less, or make it any less true. But yes…I will go to Rhidam soon. It is my burden to put an end to the violence."

"Can you?" Muir could not imagine how. "Your return, your proximity to the Lachlans…do you know what happened to Ártur?" He had heard the report from Owain. The danger, especially to one of Kavan's prominence, seemed particularly high.

"I know. And I'm aware that my return will be divisive…but it must be done. I cannot explain it…but it is something I must do. Tomorrow…a day or two…" He had yet to decide when the final leg of his journey would begin, but he knew he needed to go soon.

"I will be in Rhidam for Hagan's celebration day; you can travel with us. Perhaps we can avoid days of tedious sea travel?" His voice was hopeful as he joined Kavan on his feet.

"I do not know if I can wait that long, but for you, I will do so if I can." He had not considered how near it was to the King's celebration, how long he had been gone. The reminder was disturbing.

A clanging bell interrupted and Muir inclined his head towards the Pháne dock. "My ship. You may join me if you wish…"

"I will leave the way I arrived." It was tempting to take the short sea ride, to spend time with Muir, but it felt as if it would take too much time. There was a nagging sense of urgency that bid him fly and rejoin his companions. "It is good to see you well, Muir…I was worried you would not be."

"And yet I am." Muir embraced him again, less like a child and more like the friend he considered himself to be. "I am overjoyed to know you are well and whole, Kavan. We, many of us, have been so afraid we would never see you again…"

"I shared those fears during much of my travels. I regret I did not offer you a proper farewell, but you are the first, other than your wife, to know of my return."

"And I am blessed for that." He released the Elyri and watched him step through the hole in the collapsed wall into the first hints of dawn. His skin tingled pleasantly everywhere the bard had touched him, making him want to cry in relief, but like Kavan, he knew there were things he needed to do if he wanted to be on that boat. If he was lucky, he might make it to the villa before Kavan departed for Rhidam. If not, he would eagerly await his half-brother's celebration for the chance to see the bard again.

❧*❧

Gaelán understood the import of the surge of power as soon as it forced him awake. There was no pain, no strange bruising, no passing out. Glancing at the predawn sky through his window, there was nothing unusual about the morning save for the residual power and the strong undeniable sense of Kavan all around him. Rather than shut out the intrusion the way Ártur had been teaching him to do, Gaelán chose to welcome it, embrace it, and try to decipher where it originated and why he felt it so strongly. It felt nearer this time.

There were shouts outside, filtering in through the open window, originating near the river, but he could see nothing from his room. Thinking the shouts could be connected to the sense of Kavan that would not leave him, the young healer ran to Ártur's room in the hopes of a better view. He could see fire at the river's edge, a glow in the dissipating darkness, but he could not tell how big the fire was or what was burning. Any fire within the city was a threat to all of them, however, as fires could spread quickly through the narrow streets, and so guards scurried out of the castle as soon as the gates opened, with

General Zarkosta and Justice Corbin leading the way. If the General was involved, it might be something important.

Rather than returning to bed, thinking his healing might be needed if the fire spread, Gaelán remained at the window, watching, until the flames dwindled to smoke and the smoke dissipated into the light of the sun which had crested the horizon. His hopes of being summoned went unheeded, and not even Physician Talis was called for. Gradually the soldiers began to trickle back through the castle grounds, two of them escorting a bound individual. The arsonist, perhaps.

He decided to find Asta. She would know what had happened, what was happening. Somehow, she always knew. He prayed, as he left his uncle's room long enough to dress before seeking her out, that no more Elyri had been killed.

❧*❦

Though he refused the tray Delia prepared, having little appetite beneath his overpowering weariness, Kavan accepted the chair Gabrielle offered, aware that all eyes were on him, each person for different reasons. Each wanted to ask questions, but no one wanted to be the first to assault him with words. Taking a peculiar pleasure in the uneasy silence, Kavan drank from the glass of juice the servant left and chose to meet Wortham's gaze first.

"I apologize for my absence; it was not planned…but there was something I needed to do."

"You went to Pháne." The earthquake had reached the main island too, and Wortham quickly correlated it to the bard's absence without knowing what it meant.

"Did you see Muir?"

Overlapping her daughter's question, Gabrielle began, "You said no one should go there." Muir might be there, and others, but though her daughter assumed Kavan's primary interest in the rocky island was her husband, Gabrielle knew it was not his only interest.

Rather than deny any truth Gabrielle suspected, Kavan said, "It was the necessary first step in eradicating what Wortham and I unleashed all those years ago." The captain hung his head, knowing what the bard meant, but Kavan touched his shoulder affectionately. "There is no blame; we did what was necessary at the time…" And they had not been the ones to set this particular wheel of action into motion. That had begun long ago when both Kóráhm and Coryllien had been alive. "It would have come to pass one way or another, I suspect, but it was necessary I deal with it before I return to Rhidam. I did speak to Muir," he added with a glance at Clianthe, "to let him know I am well and safe. He will be here shortly…"

"Safe for now," Gabrielle grunted. "If you go back to Rhidam…"

The lines on her face were something Kavan had not noticed before, and facing her mortality for the first time troubled him. He had known her for so long that, as with Arlan, he had never given thought to her dying before him. If her comment was meant to prompt him to reveal his purpose on Pháne, he instead said, "Return is inevitable. I know the dangers, the risks, but I must go back."

"dedhá Urian said the same," Gabrielle continued with a scowl, "but no one will elaborate on why you are the one liable for the security of the Sovereignties." From her tone, it was clear she was worried, perhaps even angry for whatever suffering the fates had in store for him, and she wanted him to explain it.

But there was little explanation he could give when he had yet to know that future himself. "I do not know what the end is to be, what part I will play, my lady. Suffice it to say that there is history that must be made right if there is to be peace, and I am the one destined to do it. Whatever is required will be revealed to me in its right time…and I must return to Rhidam to see it done."

"Like a prophet?" whispered Clianthe, having never seen Kavan as a man of prophecy. He had always been a wise man, a bard, a pious man, but never a prophet. She knew the stories of the Bhryell Prophet, Bhryell Saint, they were impossible to avoid, but her experience of him was limited to his comings and goings through the Gate.

She did not even know what Elyri abilities he possessed.

"Or," Kavan countered, uncomfortable with her words and the way she looked at him, "one who must fulfill it, nothing more."

Unsatisfied with his answers but knowing from experience she would get no more from him than he was willing to give, Gabrielle asked, "How long will you stay?"

"If Zelenka and Urian are prepared to travel, I would like to depart for Levonne in the morning. That is…I carry something which may not allow my usual means of transportation, thus I must request a ship if that again proves true."

As close as he was to Rhidam, and as eager as he was to be back, he did not feel ready to Gate into the castle. If the Gate worked, he would take it as far as Levonne where something else awaited doing.

Otherwise, it would mean a few more days of travel by sea, time to meditate and reflect, time enough, he hoped, to prepare for the inevitability of facing Princess Diona.

"You may request anything of me, Kavan." Her fingers brushed over the back of his hand but he neither flinched nor pulled away from her touch and his gaze remained uncharacteristically steady. "I will request a ship at standby, should you need it. You will play for us, while you are here, won't you?"

Predictable disquiet lit his eyes and he murmured, "I think not."

Though disappointed by his choice, Gabrielle accepted it. Many put demands on him, and normally he was willing to meet them. Given everything he must have endured in recent months and how weary he appeared to be, it was no surprise that he refused her request. "You are exhausted, of course. Your room is still ready for you and I will see that a bath is drawn. Dinner will be served at its usual hour." He was dusty, dirty, and needed clean clothes, and Gabrielle was eager for the chance to serve him. "Come, Clianthe, let us prepare."

The women left the three men there at the table, Urian near the window with the sun on his face, eyes closed as if he had heard none of the conversation. Piran and Zelenka's voices could be heard from the rear garden, where Kavan had seen the boy showing off his boats when he flew over on his arrival. The moment of stillness with Wortham was privacy of a sort, and Kavan welcomed it.

"Why do you hesitate to play, my lord?" the captain asked with worry in his eyes, fearing there was something the bard was not saying. "You are amongst friends."

"It is not that, Wortham. I will not touch a harp until I hold my own, that is all."

Wortham nodded, satisfied with that choice. The black kestrel harp was the closest thing Kavan had ever had to a lover, and the drive to be loyal to that particular mistress made sense to him. But he was not ready to give up. "You could…"

"Sing." Kavan had not said he would not sing, only that he would not play. Gabrielle had heard him sing long ago when he had been barely more than a boy, but never without his harp. Still, she had heard him; only Clianthe had not. Kavan did not know if he had the courage to try, but he was considering it. "It has been a long time since she…my voice has become more polished but I…"

"You mean you have become more confident and freer with your natural gifts. Polish has little to do with it."

Appreciating the gentle teasing, Kavan began his retort, only to double over the edge of the table so that his forehead struck the wooden surface. Wortham caught him before he slid from the chair.

"My lord?" Wortham knew what those sudden onset symptoms meant but until Kavan could speak, the captain could only hold him and provide calm, steady comfort.

"It was…is…gdhededhá…"

The man turned from the window. He might not have been paying attention, might have been dosing, but he was less distracted than he appeared. "Me?" Kavan had not spoken a name, but Urian felt that incomplete sentence as if it was a weight on his chest. During their months together, he had learned that sometimes Kavan Saw things and that most of those things came to pass, one way or another.

Kavan's eyes opened, newly bloodshot with physical and emotional strain and he stared at the monk with alarm. "I beseech you…do not travel to Enesfel. It is in your best interest not to go to…" He had never been able to stay a man's fate by warning them of what he Saw, but as before, he had to try.

"I am going to Rhidam," the blind man said stubbornly.

"This is no fancy, no effort to be rid of you. Please, believe…"

"Am I to die?" The Elyri did not reply but the silence held all of the answer Urian needed. "If what you See comes to be…I will not evade the fate k'Ádhá has in store for me…"

"A warning of doom should be heeded," interjected the captain. "Premonitions are but warnings; you should heed him and…"

But Urian continued to shake his head. "You are a prophet, my lord, whether you choose to be or not. I will not stay here like a coward; death will find me wherever I am. It is inevitable. I have accomplished all in my life I set out to do…have lived more than many men combined, journeyed to lands of unimaginable uniqueness and beauty. If it is my time, I will meet death as k'Ádhá intends. Besides, perhaps what you see is incomplete. I will return to Levonne, where we started our journey…and from there, fate will deal my hand."

Sensing the bard about to protest, Urian chuckled with a stern look on his face. "You can forbid me from following…leave without me…bid the Prime Magistrate chain me and hold me here…but sooner or later I will be free and I will go to Enesfel. If death intends to find me there, how do you know it will not do so when I travel there alone rather than with you? If I am to die on familiar soil, allow me to do so at your side, if it is k'Ádhá's desire. Will you deny me that?"

Kavan did not hear the dedhá's entire plea as he fled from the room before the words were spoken. He knew what the blind man would say without hearing it. Urian was right; Kavan did not know if his death would come on this journey or some other, only that it would occur on the road to Rhidam. He also knew that, in spite of his misgivings, he would take Urian as far as Levonne. They had met there, they would part there. Kavan, too, was not one to run from fate. He would take Urian with him and do his best to keep the man alive.

᷇*᷄

Asta would tell him nothing, claiming to be too busy to spend time with him today while instead spending her hours, every time he saw her, with either Princess Diona or the girl Marta. While he suspected it was duty, that something was afoot, Gaelán was beginning to resent Marta more than he did his brother. In spiteful annoyance he made the conscious decision to avoid Asta the next time she looked for him, to claim as she was that he had no time for her…regardless of whether it was true. If she was able to shut him out of her life, he was going to do the same to her. Or he was going to try.

But through eavesdropping, he learned a little about the early morning events as his father spoke to the general, his father who had gone to fight the fire despite the dangers to Elyri in the streets. There had been a group of men at the docks, tormenting another by dunking him repeatedly into the river. Though the victim lived, he refused to reveal what his tormentors wanted and since the culprits had fled the scene, leaving their victim as soon as the knocked over lantern started the fire, none of them were available either. Only one, who foolishly remained to help with the fire and was apprehended as soon as the blaze was under control. Though brought back to the dungeon where the victim was cared for by one of Rhidam's physicians, the fellow would not speak, but he did not need to.

His guilt, if not for this crime, was spelled out in the collection of drawings Ártur had done for the murders in Hangman's Grove. That was evidence enough to hold him, to call for his execution, but King Hagan would not have it. He wanted the man alive, wanted him to answer questions without the use of Elyri reading or torture. His staff, those men familiar with people of this man's ilk, advised against it, but the King chose to follow his own counsel and gave the captive the opportunity to recant and save himself. He wanted to have faith, and he did not want torture or execution to take place so near to his birth celebration which might detract from the festivities.

The thought of those crucifixions, which he had not seen but had heard about from Asta, made Gaelán's wrists tingle and burn. He had not thought deaths of that nature would occur in his lifetime when there had been no crucifixions in decades. Dhágdhuán had been crucified and burned alive, and Kóráhm as well but those had been a long time ago. It should not be, but after forcing the images out of General Agis' head when Asta would not share them, Gaelán at once regretted doing so. The images made him sick, worse than seeing Ártur's injuries, worse than seeing Kavan's. He did not know why. He only knew that the one thing they all had in common was shared blood.

And those three were dead because of it.

He had been dreaming again of Orynn. Or rather, he dreamt of her nearness and a heavy brooding sense of anxiety. As with before, he could not see her, could not touch her, but the scent of her, the sense of her proximity, were real enough that, when it was gone and he awoke with a start, he rose from the bed, arms wrapped around himself, feeling undeniably alone, feeling as if he had eaten something that his stomach refused to digest.

There had been a quiet meal with Gabrielle, her son and her daughter, earlier in the evening, the mood of it more somber than he liked but he did not have the heart to draw life from the full-scale Cliáthan harp she owned in the hopes of lightening their evening. He could feel their concern for him, that perhaps his previous injuries were not as healed as they appeared, or that perhaps he had given up music now that he had suffered for it. Yet still, they loved him. Gabrielle, he knew would continue to love him in a way few others did. She had given up waiting for what he could not give, had married Owain and built a happy life, but there was a part of her that would forever belong to Kavan.

He knew it, though he refused to think about it.

It was for her, and for Wortham, that he finally pushed his plate away, waited until the rest were engaged in conversation or private thoughts without looking at him, and began to sing. It was a soft hymn of gratitude and blessing and as expected, Wortham was the first to notice, to look at him with a spark of delight in his eyes. The other heads turned one by one until he had every eye upon him, and with his audience now captive, he opened into a song of full-fledged praise that filled the Prime Magistrate's dining hall with a remarkable fullness of sound and emotion. Gabrielle held her breath each time the notes soared, gasped at each crescendo, sighed at each emotional dip, and when he finished that one song, words having been sung in High Elyri so that none except possibly Zelenka understood them, Gabrielle collapsed against Kavan's shoulder and held him in a tight embrace while the others awarded his gift with applause and smiles. As the ovation died and Wortham encouraged the others to retire for the night, to give Kavan and Gabrielle privacy, she continued to cling to him. Only when they were alone in the room did she draw back enough to kiss him, a mere press of her lips against his.

She did not need to feel his disquiet to know it was there. She rose as she released him, straightened her dress, and tenderly touched his cheek. "Consider it a gift in kind. Owain will understand." She smiled warmly and left him alone to the comings and goings of the serving staff who arrived to clear the table of the last of the meal's remnants.

Yes, Owain would understand. He would know that kiss in no way reflected on the state of his marriage and would know Kavan had no intention of coming between him and his wife. Owain knew Kavan had that powerful effect on many people, and Kavan suspected that, if Owain was a woman, he likely would have done the same long ago.

What perplexed Kavan was that the kiss did not trouble him as much as it once had. He felt no pull towards dismay, despair, or distress. Tonight it left only a glow of acceptance and trust that she remained steadfast in his life when many others might not have.

He slept then, but his nerves had been too jangled to allow it to be a night of restful sleep, and now that the dream, or the Sight, had brought Orynn to mind, a response to that kiss perhaps, he knew he would not sleep again. The hour was late, the moon halfway through its nighttime journey but dawn would not be far away. There was no point in trying to sleep again. He would stand at the window until the others stirred.

He was three or four days, a week at most if he was forced to travel by sea and did not linger in Levonne, away from Rhidam. He was sure Madalyn would supply horses if asked. Before that final leg of his odyssey, however, there was something he needed to do in Levonne, someone he needed to see, though even thinking about it made him ashamed and threatened to drown him in those troublesome emotions he had struggled to put behind. The only way he was going to put that behind him, however, was to confront it. Doing so would give him the courage he needed to return to Rhidam.

Either that or Kavan would demand as much of Wortham's strength to do so as the captain could spare.

❧Chapter 22❧

Inspired by the bard's song of praise the night before, Urian's last-minute pilgrimage to the shrine of Saint Bhenádíctus, which Kavan had been unable to deny after the premonition the Sight had given him, delayed their departure longer than Kavan liked. Zelenka's late rising and Gabrielle's fussing over him as she worried for his safety, were further delays. In a way, it might have been for the best, as the ship Gabrielle arranged would not be ready to depart until mid-afternoon and there would have been nothing for Kavan to do in the interim except fret and pace and worry about what was to come. He debated with Wortham the possibility of taking the captain, the woman, and the dedhá through the Gate to Levonne, where they could room and wait for him if the reliquary forced Kavan to travel by sea. But as with every other time Kavan suggested it, Wortham rejected the offer and refused to leave the bard's side. After so many months of traveling together, he refused to leave the Elyri alone now.

"Would you care to stay for the noon meal?

"My lady," Kavan said warmly, raising her hand to his lips and kissing her knuckles. "I know you fear for my welfare. I cannot tell you not to…but Enesfel is where I need to be. If this does not work, we will share it with you. If it does, you will see me soon enough."

Those words were as good as a promise and she stepped back as his companions joined them in her office. "I will hold you to that."

With a pack slung over his back and one trunk in his arms, the captain asked, "Can we use the Gate?"

"I am about to find out. Have you explained this to Zelenka?" He did not expect the woman to understand, but the process would be easier if she was less fearful of it.

The explanation, however, was likely to be moot.

He set the trunk he carried next to the other. "As much as I am able. She would rather cease traveling, but she understands that we are nearly at the end of the journey and has agreed to proceed so that it can be done."

"If this works, she can spend the remainder of the day at her leisure. Lady Madalyn will grant us sanctuary I am sure, and Zelenka may rest there while I tend to duty before we start for Rhidam."

Wondering what Kavan intended to do, Wortham looked at him curiously while relaying the message to Zelenka, who nodded wearily and tried not to appeared dismayed at more travel. She did not understand why they were meeting in this room, why the closet door was open, but since she assumed travel meant horses, foot or ship, she guessed this was a waiting area.

"Wortham, if you please." Reluctantly, not certain that Wortham would be safe from the power of the reliquary, he placed the box in his friend's hands. Though the man grimaced and seemed to strain to hold it, as if it was a burden nearly too heavy for him, he did not drop it and waited with silent resolve.

It could be killing him and he would have endured it.

"I do not know if this will work…" For all of his other attempts to use the Gate, Kavan had been carrying the reliquary, the joint power of the ring on his hand against the reliquary conflicting with his own. It had occurred to him as he watched the night give way to day, that breaking that connection, allowing someone else to carry the box, might allow him just enough leeway to manipulate a Gate's energy. The worst the effort could do was fail…as long as the reliquary would not harm the holder.

"I will take you…if I can…and come back for the others." If the Gate failed after transporting the reliquary through it, at least Wortham and the box would be in Enesfel, and Kavan would have to find some way to transport Urian and Zelenka.

Understanding that he must protect what he carried with his life, the captain steadied himself for travel as he had done numerous times before. This time, however, he felt uncomfortable, as if held to the ground by roots that clawed from deep in the earth, through the stone floor, into his boots. When Kavan's hands closed around his wrists, he jerked, startled by the powerful vibrations that erupted between his hands and he stared at Kavan apologetically.

"You are afraid." Wortham had never expressed this fear before and sensing it now surprised and disappointed the bard.

Wortham pouted and shook his head. "It is not the Gate, not you. It is this box…what I sense in it…the power I sense here drives home the gravity of what we face…"

Taking the explanation at face value, understanding those things while finding them peculiar at the same time, Kavan nodded and asked, "Shall I continue?" He had already located the point of energy for the destination he desired, the sparkle of light that represented Levonne within the power web of the Gate system, and he could feel the pulse of it in his center. With Wortham's hands between himself and the reliquary, the conflict was less troublesome, and Kavan believed he could do this, but if Wortham refused, he would not try.

The captain's response was to swallow loudly, relax his shoulders, and open his mind as much as any Teren could to the contact with an Elyri. He surrendered to the bard's will, to the invasion of power in his center, allowing Kavan to do as he would with him.

Awed again at Wortham's willingness to trust, Kavan reached through the haze of conflicting powers, and firmly grasped that familiar point of destination. It was the most success he had made since leaving the cloister. But making the connection was the easiest part; he had done it for the first time when he was not yet seven. The remainder of the process had never been difficult for him either, but with the reliquary objects crowding his concentration as if they possessed lives of their own, it took his focus away from his intention.

As he had done in the cave, he threw up his mental shields against it, shutting the power's intrusion out of his head while still remaining aware of it humming loudly against his efforts. Determined to avoid the ship, to avoid further delays, deciding that he would be in Levonne today, regardless of the interference, he concentrated everything he had on forming a solid connection to Levonne.

To his amazement, the power in the reliquary withdrew, allowing him to proceed without further interference.

Wondering if exhibiting a mastery of power and readiness to face destiny was all that he had needed all along, he held his breath and allowed the gentle rise and fall of power waves to wrap around them, the warm mist that embraced them both like the tender arms of a lover. And when it was passed, when his feet felt steady beneath him and the warmth had trickled away, he dared to open his eyes and meet Wortham's gaze.

"I believe you have done it, my lord." The captain's voice was thin, stretched, an uncomfortable tone of awe as he pushed open the door of the Purification Chamber and stepped into St. Poul's Náós in Levonne. He recognized the lofty, expensive decor, the marble carvings, polished wood, iron and gold etchings, and the pictures of stained glass that made the building feel more palatial then holy. Like Kavan, Wortham had never been comfortable here, but he suspected he would be asked to wait for the others to join him.

When it seemed safe, as he could sense no one about, Kavan motioned Wortham out of the chamber, refusing to acknowledge the awe in the other man's voice. He had only been in St. Poul's a few times, had felt as uncomfortable here as he felt in Clarys' seat of Faith, but it was the most accessible Gate for their purposes. "Wait for me, and do not leave this unattended or unguarded." It was an unnecessary instruction, but he felt it necessary to speak the words. "If I am not back within fifteen minutes, you will know that there is some reason I am unable to return."

Bringing Urian through he did not think would be a problem. Convincing Zelenka to enter the closet without knowing what was happening would be more challenging.

"Fifteen minutes. I will go to Lady Cáner if you are not here."

Trusting Wortham but still reluctant to leave the reliquary somewhere beyond his control, Kavan stepped back into the chamber and emerged alone from the closet in Gabrielle's office, cheeks flushed with the effort and relief of having finally moved the reliquary through the Gate. Zelenka pushed past him to look inside, to see where Wortham had gone, and she was visibly shocked and frightened to find the small space empty, to find that Wortham was no longer there.

"He has not been harmed…I swear it on my life. Nor will you be. I can take you to him now…or I can take dedhá Urian so you can watch and see what happens…"

The woman backed out of the closet with stumbling steps but could not pass Gabrielle to flee the room.

"Travel through a closet?" Urian relied on his intrigue to subdue his apprehension. "Show me how it is done, my lord…I want to know." After adjusting the pack that was slung over his shoulder, he struggled to pick up the trunk that Wortham had exchanged for the reliquary and let Kavan guide him into the tight space with his awkward burden. "What must I do?"

"Relax as if you are praying or meditating. Do not be afraid…it will be only a moment…"

Kavan had barely uttered the words, with his hands around the blind man's wrists, before the dedhá's mind was entirely emptied of all distractions save for a repetitive mantra Kavan had often heard him pray before sleeping. His ability to pray to purge himself of fear, worry and doubt came to Urian as readily as breathing, and within moments, the creaking of a door made the dedhá turn his head to the sound.

He could not see the changes, but he could smell them, the exchange of scrolls and books and stored fabric for wood polish, lamp oil, and incense. "My lord…" Wherever they were now smelled like a Gathering Hall. It smelled like Faith. And he smiled.

Wortham took Urian's hand and escorted him out of the chamber, the reliquary tucked beneath his arm. Urian side-waddled from the little room with the trunk, allowing Kavan to retreat back into it.

"Wait…my lord…" Kavan looked back after Wortham left Urian at the end of one prayer bench; the captain pressed something warm and smooth into his palm. "Give this to Zelenka; show her I am unharmed and that there is no danger in trusting you. This protected me…it will protect her too."

The pink stone that the woman had given to Wortham the night he had faced death had been carried in the captain's tunic pocket ever since, near his heart, and he periodically showed her that he kept it there when she seemed weary and full of doubt. Of any token Wortham could use to coax her, this seemed the best one. When Kavan emerged back into the Prime Magistrate's office, the three women were as he had left them.

Gabrielle shook her head, having been ineffective in convincing Zelenka not to be afraid, and Kavan sighed. He could use force, the way he had once done with Guthrie McHador, but he did not want to.

"Zelenka…" He offered the stone to her in his outstretched palm. "Wortham is safe. He says this will keep you safe too."

Skeptically, Zelenka took the stone and studied it as Kavan addressed his host. "You have blessed me with your generosity yet again; thank you, my lady."

"There is no need for that, Kavan; you bless me every time you come. Stay safe…k'Ádhá protect and keep you…because I intend to see you again."

"You shall," Kavan promised, as Clianthe offered her hand too. Having witnessed his coming and going through the Gate now, having felt the energy of each exchange, he knew the younger woman had questions. He suspected she might even be able to use the Gate, if shown how, but it was not his responsibility to teach her. That choice was between mother and daughter. "Look after Muir for me, Clianthe…I shall see you both soon as well."

"I will do both," she promised.

Little by little, Zelenka inched towards the closet, her eyes wide, her chest heaving with each anxious breath, as her hand clenched white-knuckled around the stone. With the farewells exchanged, Kavan stepped into the closet, dragging the second trunk inside with one hand, and waited for Zelenka to make her choice, to push him into making his. When he held out his hand to her, she swallowed hard and put hers into it, taking one last steely step into the closet.

He did not need to take her other hand to work the Gate. No longer did he have to physically subdue and unwilling individual and his command of power was just as strong through the touch of one hand as it was through two. Two hands typically made for a more intimate experience, but intimacy was not necessary. The door had barely closed behind her when another opened, presenting her with Wortham's embrace and Urian's smile on the other side as her knees buckled in shock. In the captain's arms, however, she did not fall, and her gasp of relief at seeing him again, being unharmed by whatever Kavan had done, was Kavan's reward for success.

A long exhaled breath echoed in the empty chamber around the sounds of relief Zelenka made. The bard closed his eyes, breathed in the peace of Faith to be found in this uncomfortably ornate náós and the lingering perfume of incense that hung in the air.

Enesfel. At last.

He was nearly home.

He was unable to move from the Purification Chamber doorway, overwhelmed by the weight of what awaited him a mere three days ride to the north. It had been a long time since he had stood upon this soil, basked in the presence of a náós. Most often during those months in the south, he had believed he would never be here again. Yet in spite of his fears, in spite of everything, he was here. He pulled up the courage to cross the room, to kneel on altar steps as he had not done in too long, to genuflect with his eyes on Dhágdhuán's form above them, and offered prayers of gratitude for that safe return…and requests to any power listening that he would remain safe long enough to fulfill whatever purpose Kóráhm had in store.

Behind him, Wortham too offered his own prayers for those same things as he tucked the reliquary into one of the larger trunks but he knew that what he felt was but a small measure of the things Kavan must be feeling. He did not begrudge the bard his time on those steps. They were in Enesfel now. He would stand watch over the Elyri for as long as it took to satisfy Kavan's soul.

When Kavan rose and left the security of the náós for Levonne's streets, it was without saying a word. The others followed. Beneath the bright sun, he paused long enough to survey his immediate surroundings, seeking threats, trying to gain some sense of where he had been that fateful night so many months ago. Nothing looked the way he remembered, even though he had passed through these doors, these streets, numerous times before. He could barely remember coming here that night; the escape from Rhidam had been reflex, and as numb as his mind had been, he could as easily have ended up in Fiara, Clarys or any number of other places in the Sovereignties.

Perhaps, he decided as he adjusted the trunk in his grip, starting the trek towards the Dubuais-Cáner estate, Kóráhm had led him to Levonne to facilitate his quest for the Chalice and staff crown. But that suggested that Kóráhm had led him into suffering, as ultimately advantageous to Kavan as that had been, or that k'Ádhá had led him to it, and Kavan refused to believe that either possibility was true.

It was more satisfying to believe that everything that had come to pass was a matter of coincidence, not fate.

His suffering had been a result of his own choices, choices made in response to words and accusations he should not have given heed to. The princess was responsible for her words, but there was no one for Kavan to blame for his reaction to them except himself. k'Ádhá and Kóráhm had made the best of those fateful choices and directed Kavan towards the healing, physical, spiritual, and mental, he had desperately needed and the duty he had been destined for.

Eyes followed him as he passed through the streets. How many knew about the attack? How many knew about his hands? How many knew of his extended absence? Unwilling to know the truth, Kavan made no effort to touch those minds to seek it. He sensed no hostility, which was his primary concern, but by the time the Dubuais-Cáner home came into view, his nerves were raw as if someone had rubbed them repeatedly with sandpaper.

It would be good to get indoors away from those abrasive gazes.

The Levonne estate was more impressive than his own Alberni estate, larger and newer in construction. It was situated on the edge of the city with its sprawl of vineyards and fluted columned pathways. It had an air of urban charm that was absent in Alberni and Kavan knew that inside was considerably more opulent than he preferred. But it was a display of Dubuais wealth that stretched back generations, and it was not his place to determine how those long gone had lived, nor how his kinsman and his wife chose to live as well.

Bhríd enjoyed the regal, the noble. It was fitting he had married into it.

The front gates at the bottom of a low hillock, separated from the city by a moat with water redirected from the Tegid, overlooked the rooftops of Levonne. The rear oversaw vast acres of grapes and the sea to the south. Family guards and laborers eyed them, stepped aside to allow them passage or bowed when they went by, but no one spoke, offered welcome or assistance, or moved to announce their arrival to the residents of the house. The oddity of that further agitated Kavan but he refrained from pointing it out so as not to trigger the overprotective captain at his side.

It was possible Bhríd and Madalyn were in Rhidam, or on duties in the vineyard. They might not be here to receive an announcement. Despite evidence on which to base a conclusion, someone was clearly watching from the house, for the double doors opened as they reached the raised portico and a quiet servant, an unfamiliar face Kavan did not remember from previous visits, bowed and bid them enter the main hall with a nervous bow.

"Is Lord or Lady Cáner here?" Kavan asked politely.

The woman curtsied low, recognizing him now, and recognizing too that his hands were not as they had been when she and the house staff had last tended him. He might not remember her, but the joyous rapture in her hazel eyes indicated that she remembered him. "The lady is on the grounds but will return by evening. If you wish to…"

"Who is here?"

Kavan turned towards the clipped question and met the young man's gaze. He was taken aback by how much Tayte had changed in the past months, taller, broader, sterner. How much he looked like the men on his mother's side of the family. Kavan noticed something else as well, a trace of something sinister that flashed across Tayte's face. But then the young man bowed in a stately manner and Kavan dismissed that impression as surprise at seeing Kavan again, or else a trick of the mid-afternoon light that came through the hall windows.

"It has been a long time since you were here last, my lord." There was a touch of contempt in Tayte's voice that suggested Kavan's first impression might not be in error, but Kavan did not want to believe the evidence of his ears. It was noteworthy as well that the young man, standing regal and proud as any lord, did not acknowledge their kinship. "To what do we owe the privilege of your visit?"

Something was wrong. Perhaps Tayte had taken offense at the manner of Kavan's previous departure. That seemed petty to Kavan, but his ungracious behavior could have sparked some hard feelings. Or something else may have happened during his absence, perhaps to Bhríd or Gaelán, that prompted such anger and contempt. Choosing his words carefully as he continued to seek an explanation for Tayte's stilted behavior, Kavan bowed and said, "I have returned from my travels. I apologize for any previous inconsiderate behavior on my part…leaving as I did after all your family provided, and I humbly ask forgiveness and an audience with your mother…"

Tayte squared his shoulders but his expression did not change. "There is nothing for me to forgive; it was not me you slighted. And you were free to come and go as you wished; this house is not a prison." His words suggested welcome, but his tone and his too-stiff stance did not. Kavan judged that it was Madalyn he had previously offended by leaving the way he had, and because of Tayte's affection for his mother, it made sense to believe that his cool welcome was on his mother's behalf. "You seek lodging or…"

"The náós will provide us sanctuary," muttered Urian, apparently liking the undertones of the youthful voice less than Kavan did. "If cordial welcome from kin is inopportune, we shall…"

"It has been a tedious journey," Kavan gently interrupted, finding the blind man's tone as unsettling as he did Tayte's. He was indeed weary and in no mood for conflict. If they were not welcome here, he would go with the others back to the náós and bid them wait for him there while he did what he had come to Levonne to do. Assuming the Gate worked for them again, they could be in Rhidam tonight. "I thought it appropriate to thank your mother and brother and staff for their previous courtesy." When Tayte bristled at the word brother, Kavan made note that the seeds of the peculiar hostility might be there. "If you will give them word that I have returned and will be starting for Rhidam soon, I would appreciate it."

Beside him, also sensing the unusual enmity in a young man he had known his whole life, Wortham inched forward with his hand on the hilt of his sword. Tayte made note of the gesture and backed casually away, although there was nothing casual about his demeanor.

"Please…forgive my inhospitality." He bowed and when he straightened, his expression and stance were more neutral, though still far from what Kavan expected from the friendly boy he had once been. "dedhá is right; you are my father's kin, and I would be remiss to not offer you respite until my mother returns. Enesfel has not been a friendly place of late." He eyed Kavan and then Wortham's sword and when the captain's hand tightened around it, Tayte continued, "We cannot be too cautious, even with family and friends, but one should be welcoming to a leader of the Faith. I was not expecting your arrival after what I have heard and…"

"No one is expecting us and we intend for it to stay that way," Wortham grunted, a warning in his tone and in the dark shadow that fell over his face, a shadow Kavan had rarely seen there since the night Arlan had become king.

Doing his best to appear unaffected by Wortham's show of force, Tayte gestured to the servant who had answered the door and said, "Give our guests rooms, and see that their needs are attended…"

"it is not necessary…"

"But appreciated," Wortham finished the sentence for Kavan, interrupting him with a hand on his arm.

The servant bowed and led them to the second floor, and by coincidence or not, deposited Kavan in the room he had used the last time he was here. The others were taken elsewhere. With his stomach sinking to his knees as he closed the door behind him, struggling not to think about the array of memories this room contained, he leaned against it with his eyes closed. Those swarming recollections, his twisted hands, the emotional mire he had sunk himself into compounded the emotional battery he had endured in Tayte's presence and he did not know if he would be able to sleep in this place.

But he could rest here, or try to. After placing the trunk containing the reliquary next to the bed where he trusted it would be safe, he crossed the room to open the window, trying to determine from that view where Gaelán had found him, where the Merry Sow was. The memory of that sign had dogged him as he crossed town, but he had not seen it. Given how hazy most of his memories of that night were, he was not sure his remembrance of the sign was accurate, but he was certain about the name. For some reason, those two words had stuck with him over all of those months and miles he had fled to escape it.

The door opened behind him and the floorboards creaked. "Pursuing ghosts?"

Not looking at Wortham, Kavan rested his forearms on the sill. "Preparing to. Tomorrow."

"Would company be welcome?" He doubted Kavan would want to be followed on his personal demon hunt, but he was concerned for the Elyri's safety. And his sanity.

"Do you fear that memories will drive me into hiding, or that my safety will be compromised if I go alone? Or is your curiosity begging to be appeased?"

The last question stung the captain's pride. "I admit part of me fears the weight of memory will be nearly unbearable for you…but I also believe you are strong and will not falter beneath them. And of course, your safety is my concern. I swore to Ártur, to Dhágdhuán, to you, that I would allow no preventable harm from befalling you. I did not feel hostility as we crossed the city, but and Elyri alone anywhere in Enesfel is a risk. I would prefer to accompany you as your protector. As for curiosity…you know I will retain a respectable distance and speak not at all unless I must. I do not need to know what you are doing or why, I only wish you to be safe."

Kavan covered Wortham's hand on the ledge. "Apologies. Your loyalty is admirable and appreciated." Of course the man had questions. He had carried those questions in silence the majority of their journey together. Curiosity was a natural thing. "You know," he murmured, "I would tell you anything if you but ask."

Head shaking emphatically, Wortham snorted. "I cannot do that, my lord. Knowing is not my place. Whatever brought you back here, whatever happened, it caused great torment and despair. I would never ask you to relive those things for my own satisfaction."

But for the first time since that night, here in the comfort of Wortham's company in the place their journey had begun, Kavan wanted to talk. He hoped that speaking of it now would take some of the fear out of tomorrow and what lay ahead after that. As loyal as the captain had been during all of those grueling months, Kavan felt he owed the man something.

He swallowed hard without looking at the man's bearded face and began in a small, nervous voice. "The princess wanted…"

Yes, he felt stronger now, but that strength made the telling of memory no easier.

"I awoke to find her in my bed…words were said…she kissed me. When I would not give her what she wanted…to share a bed as husband or lover…she…"

His stilted speech and the topic made the captain shift awkwardly. He had guessed at enough of that night to have painted a likely image in his mind. He did not need the details spread before him. "Enough, my lord. There is no need…"

"She pulled away the sheet I held over myself," the Elyri forced himself to continue, "called me nothing…less than a man, cold, dead." Those particular memories brought tears to his eyes, though he knew they were not true, and he drew comfort from the hand now resting on his shoulder. "All my life…the one thing I sought, to be a man like any other…to know I am not an aberration…or monster."

"You are no monster."

Rather than surrender to the urge to collapse against Wortham's shoulder in weeping, Kavan shivered and drew away from the captain's hand, not in rejection but in an effort to remain strong. Wortham, accepting this, let him go.

"I fled…came here. I drank too much. I tried, unsuccessfully, to bed a prostitute. In the end, I could not even do that…proof, at the time, that the princess' words were true. I was sick in body, mind…heart and soul…when they found me, beat me. I had no ability or desire to defend myself, would have let myself die if not for…"

If not for Orynn, but those words would have made less sense to Wortham than they still did to Kavan. His voice now barely audible, he finished with, 'The rest, you know."

Wortham allowed Kavan to retreat from him. The man he had spent a lifetime knowing would never have gotten drunk to the point of inebriation, never risked that sort of death, would never try to bed a whore. He could scarcely imagine Kavan doing so even under the most extreme emotional duress. He understood it, yet he did not. What he did understand was something Kavan had not said.

"You wish to face this woman?"

The bard blinked, shuddered, and fought against the denial that rose immediately to his lips. "I used her abysmally. I was neither a gentleman…nor a client. She offered kindness and I mistreated her, and did not even reimburse her for her time. I must face her, apologize, for my own peace of mind and to clear my conscience. I also believe that seeing her will drive home the end of this nightmare…as will finding the alley where they…where my hands were…"

The captain bowed his head. "As much as I will worry about your safety, I will allow you to walk these paths alone, do what you need to do to be whole again, as long as you swear to be on your guard."

Kavan returned to the window, near enough that his arm was pressed to Wortham's, an anchoring in distress that he sorely needed. "I must do these things…but I dread them. Whether I can…perhaps, if you were with me I would be unable to back out."

"Whatever you need, Kavan. I give you whatever you need."

Several servants entered the room then after a curt knock, carrying pails of steaming water to pour into the washtub behind a folded curtain near the water closet. There was an uneasy air about them that made both men uncomfortable. Only after they departed with silent bows did Kavan notice the captain's frown. "What is it?" he asked as he drew his tunic off over his head.

"Would you take offense if I stay in your room with you, while we are here?"

Kavan shrugged as he removed his boots and breeches and stepped into the tub. If it had been anyone other than Ártur in the room, he would have been too self-conscious for that. "Why?"

"Perhaps I am paranoid; after so many rumors, after…everything. I do not think you are safe here."

"In my own kin's home?"

"He shares your blood, but I do not trust him. Call it a soldier's sense, but Master Tayte has changed…and not in your favor. I pray I am wrong, that there is adequate cause for the nature of his greeting, or lack of it. But if not him, there are servants, and any one of them might not want you here.

Choosing to give his nephew the benefit of the doubt, choosing to believe that Bhríd had selected staff who would not be hostile to his children, himself, his kin, Kavan shook his head. "I appreciate your concern, but I do not think it necessary. We shall be safe here. Go and rest. Entertain Zelenka, show her the vineyards…show her Levonne. You can leave me for a few hours without fear."

The captain was not convinced, but he bowed and went out, allowing Kavan the privacy of a leisurely bath. Kavan listened to his movements, followed the sense of him until Wortham, as Kavan suggested, took Urian and Zelenka onto a balcony that overlooked the Dubuais vineyards, and then relaxed into the hot water in the hopes it would wash away any stain that might still linger on his soul.

Long after the water cooled to room temperature, he chose to emerge from it, drying and dressing to the sounds of the city beyond the estate's walls. He considered going out alone, but since he had no pressing need to do so and did not want Wortham to chastise him if he returned to find the Elyri gone, he chose solitude over socializing, chose to reread Kóráhm's journal in the comfort of a cushioned chair while there was still light to read by. He hoped it would offer him some clue or guidance into the path that stretched ahead of him. The proper course of action, perhaps, would be to approach Tayte, talk to him, learn what had changed or affected him so.

But as it seemed that Tayte viewed their arrival as an inconvenience, as it seemed that the bard, or perhaps no one, was welcome here, Kavan decided it was best to await Madalyn's return. Maybe he feared what harm Kavan's presence might bring his mother or his House. An understandable concern, and since he had not yet heard or sensed Madalyn's arrival, Kavan decided to wait.

Until something clattered at his feet, having come in through the open window, Kavan had little sense or belief that he could be at risk in Bhríd's home. It was evening by then, barely enough light to see the pages, the lengthening shadows bringing with them a flow of footsteps into and out of the house. Thinking that such a gesture seemed more the prank of a quarrelsome child, he reached for the item that bumped his boot, expecting a stone but finding, instead, a small dagger with a slip of parchment curled around the hilt and held there by a dirty strip of leather. He read the words there, and reread them a second time, his blood running colder with each repeated reading, unable to accept what his eyes were telling him.

A knock at the door startled him enough that he jerked up with the dagger in his hand as if he might need it for self-defense. A female voice from the other side of the closed barrier called, "My lord, Lady Cáner has returned and is serving dinner in the dining hall. She asks if you will join her or if you wish to dine in your room."

Not wanting the servant to see the dagger if she chose to come into the room, Kavan quickly got to his feet and stuffed the blade into the bedside dresser. The curled note was still in his hand. Eat, he thought with a sickening twist in his belly? After what he had read? But he had to go down; Madalyn would expect it and he did want to see her. "I shall be there momentarily, thank you."

He waited for her steps to retreat, long enough to recover his poise and tuck the paper into his shirt pocket, long enough to pull his boots on and close and lock the window. He would have done the same to the bedroom door upon leaving if he had been able to do so.

Dinner was a small, private matter, a modest spread at a dining table meant for a much larger collection of guests. His traveling companions already sat around the offering of pork and spring potatoes, roasted apples and dried grapes, a fit meal that smelled especially enticing after so many months of traveling rations. Tayte, however, was not there, and after the dagger incident, the bard felt ill at ease as he entered the dining hall. Madalyn rose to greet him with a warm smile and welcoming, familial embrace. "Welcome, Lord Cliáth…it is good to see you home and well."

"Kavan, please, my lady. We have known each other too long to continue formalities."

She laughed as she admired his change from his previously customary attire, and gestured to the empty chair between her and Wortham. "Yet you persist in addressing me as 'my lady'. Hardly a fair standard, wouldn't you agree."

"True. But you are the wife of my kinsman, a lady of rank and noble birth. I may not address you by name…but nor do I address you as Lady Cáner," he challenged with a force of mirth that he hoped masked the uneasiness inside.

"Aye, your point is well made. I was told you were here…that your hands are…"

When she seemed unable to say the word, Kavan finished her thought for her. "I will play the harp again. Do not fear for that." Only death would keep him from it now…a death he realized he had to be more vigilant against than he wanted to admit. "k'Ádhá saw fit to restore them and I would be remiss in not making use of the blessing I was given. I thank you for the care and generosity you offered when I was last here, and apologize if my hasty departure caused offense…"

"Nonsense. No offense was taken," she assured him as the platters and trays of food were served to each of her guests. "I regret I could not do more…but that you have returned is gratitude enough."

Since everyone was being served from the same dishes, and the staff looked to be doing nothing suspicious, Kavan should have been at ease with the meal. But he was unable to do more than pick at his food, eating what he saw others eat but only in small quantities. The others drank wine, to no ill effect, but Kavan refused to touch his water glass despite his thirst. Wortham plied their host with questions about events in Enesfel during their absence, offered a few details of their own travels, and Kavan listened, his ears trying to detect something he could not identify. When Zelenka hesitantly took her leave of the table to escort the groggy, slightly inebriated Urian to his room with the help of some of the staff, Kavan pushed his plate back as if he had eaten his fill.

Wortham noted how little the bard consumed and asked in a low voice, "My lord?" The Elyri rarely ate large meals, but the captain had expected him to eat more than he had. It was possible his nervousness about tomorrow, about going to Rhidam, had robbed him of his appetite, but if he was not feeling well, Wortham wanted to know.

Though Kavan shook his head rather than reply, not wanting to draw Madalyn's attention, she had already taken note of both his barely touched plate and the concern in Wortham's voice. "Kavan?"

He could lie. Or at least he could skirt the truth and blame his disinterest in food on fatigue and anxiety. Both would be true. But it was unfair to hide this particular truth from the duchess, and Wortham would ferret the information out of him before the night was over.

"I did not wish to speak of it…and I certainly do not believe it reflects on you…"

"The meal is not to your liking." She shrugged, taking no offense in it. "Your unexpected arrival did not permit me time to…"

"It is not the meal. It is excellent. It is…" He sighed and removed the rolled note from his pocket in order to offer it to her in his visibly trembling hand. "This."

Madalyn read the short message hastily, her face turning crimson with indignation. "Who gave this to you? When?"

"It was affixed to a dagger thrown through my window, just before the summons to dinner." When she held it back to him, Wortham snatched it away to read it as well.

Kavan wished he would not.

"No wonder! I would not eat after that either! I am appalled that this should happen here, in my house, but I cannot say I am surprised." She folded her cloth napkin and set it on the table beside her plate. "Levonne has had its share of violence since your attack…as has all of Enesfel…as I am sure you know. Both Elyri and Teren have been killed, the same as everywhere else. Even my House has been infected by this toxin. I am sure you noticed the changes in Tayte."

"Yes, but I did not think…"

"He hates you. Or more precisely he hates the Elyri blood he carries and those he shares it with…especially his father and brother. Sometimes I think he hates me too…for doing this to him…making him what he is. It seems so sudden; I do not know what has caused it.

Bhríd thinks Tayte is jealous that Gaelán is a healer and he is not. You should see Gaelán…"

Her words trailed off and she stared into her wine glass. "He is more…like you. You would never know they are brothers. He shares Bhríd's physical, and apparently mental traits, while Tayte is as much Elyri as I am. He told Gaelán he wishes all Elyri were dead. Not in those exact words…but it is what he meant. I heard him. We both did."

She closed her eyes to shut out the associated memories as well as Kavan's surprised, sympathetic stare. "I have discussed it with him as much as he is willing. While he lives in this house, while I live here, I will not tolerate such talk, and he knows that any Elyri who come to our doors are welcome…particularly family. But the damage is done. Gaelán will not come back home and Bhríd feels obligated to remain with him more than we would like, at least until Gaelán is legally an adult and surer of himself."

"Would it be easier for you if we take lodging at St. Poul's?" Wortham voiced the question because Kavan would not. The Elyri's face looked washed out, pinched, and miserable.

Madalyn shook her head. "That would be giving in to the madness of those seeking to run, or ruin, our lives. Given the state of affairs, you would not necessarily be better protected there. I will set guards if you wish…"

"No offense," Wortham grunted, "but I will be my lord's guard."

"Kavan?"

The bard nodded, accepting Wortham's protection and already feeling safer for it.

"So be it. But I will talk to my staff nonetheless and if one of them is responsible for that…or knows who is…there will be consequences, I promise you. How long do you intend to be in Levonne?"

"Through tomorrow night." Kavan found forming words to be difficult in the back of his tight throat. "I have things I must see to here and our arrival was too late today to tend them." He could have done so, perhaps, but he had not been in the right frame of mind to try. "Wortham will accompany me outside of your home, of course." The decision was taken out of his hands; with a death threat looming over him, taking Wortham with him was the wisest recourse.

"Try to stop me," muttered the captain.

"You are welcome for as long as you choose to be here. You will then go to Rhidam? Will you require horses? Supplies?"

"They would be appreciated but not required." He had wanted to request them, but now, with this threat he had brought into the duchess' home, he felt awkward in asking for anything. Anything more than two nights' shelter felt inappropriate and unimportant.

But Madalyn did not agree and scoffed at his reluctance. "Nonsense. You are family and though Rhidam is not far, I suspect you have endured more walking than any man should. I will have horses ready when you choose to depart, and Bhríd will see to their return. It is the least I can do." Especially now. After everything else Kavan had endured, whatever that had been, he had come home to a death threat. In her home.

When they parted company for the evening, Madalyn set off to make sure that her personal guards were in place, aware of the threat, and would double their efforts to keep the household safe for the night. Wortham did not doubt her efforts, but he followed Kavan closely up the stairs, bid him wait in the corridor long enough for him to retrieve his belongings and a blanket, and then entered Kavan's room first to make sure it was empty, safe, and undisturbed.

"Do not worry about me, my lord. Sleeping in a chair is hardly beneath me, but I will need a blanket if you plan to leave your window open." Except during the worst rain or winter storms, Kavan was prone to leaving his window open. Tonight, Wortham wanted to advise against it, but he doubted his efforts would be profitable.

"I'm not certain it would be wise," Kavan admitted with a reluctant sigh as Wortham pushed the door closed with his foot, "but I cannot sleep with it closed." Doing so made him feel trapped, and trapped was something he did not want to feel tonight.

The captain nodded with a grunt, set down the trunk next to the chair and shook out the blanket he had pealed from his bed. "Perhaps," he said after dropping it over the back of the stuffed chair and kneeling to open the trunk, "this would help you sleep. I wanted to give it to you sooner, but Lady Orynn bid me wait until the time was right." For Wortham, that time was now.

Without removing the supple leather case, without touching it, Kavan knew what was in the bundle Wortham offered. It was Eridel's redwood quarterscale kestrel Cliáthan harp, the sister to the harp Kavan had abandoned in Rhidam. When he did not take it, feeling unworthy of possessing it after the way he had treated the young harper, Wortham put it directly into his hands. "I know you will not play it. You may not play it ever…but it is fitting that you have it. Eridel would have wanted it."

Kavan did not agree. Eridel would have wanted to keep the instrument…if he had not been prompted to flee by Kavan's cruelty, if he had not met his death at the hands of wild beasts or bandits on that southern road. Relishing the feel of the wood beneath his fingers, he whispered, "I thought it destroyed…"

"The lady caught it before the fire could do it harm. The gut strings were burned, but nothing more. We carried it in the hopes of returning it to Eridel…but when we were unable to do so, she instructed me to keep it for you. I considered giving it to you sooner…but thought you should have the chance to find faith in your voice first." He grinned impishly, knowing that at least in that choice, he had been correct.

Wortham sank into the chair that he had pulled around so he could prop his feet on the bed, adjusted the blanket around him, and closed his eyes. There was no need to monitor Kavan's actions. Though he dozed lightly, he was aware of the bard's movements when, nearly an hour or more later, he laid the harp on the nightstand, undressed, and blew out the lamp. It was later still when the bard lay down, his restless mind and heavy heart ready at last to sleep. Whatever memories came with that harp, they proved enough to take the Elryi's mind off of unfortunately timed threats of death.

❧*❧

Ártur dreamed of music that night, of a harp's brass strings, of a choir high in a Gathering Hall's loft, of a voice not heard in so long that, when he awoke to silent darkness, there were tears on his face and pillow. But they were not tears of misery and emptiness. They were tears of ecstasy, of joy at the rapture of music inside his head. The tunes, new and unfamiliar, were with him still, and something in their unfamiliarity gave him hope where for too long there had been none. Clutching his pillow to his chest as if embracing it, he stood at the window of Kavan's Bhryell home, staring in the direction of Rhidam.

❧Chapter 23❦

Ithout much effort, he located the alley where he had been beaten. It was near enough to the Cáner mansion that surely the guards must have heard the fight if Kavan had struggled or cried out for assistance. Surely they must have heard the drunken slurs and shouted taunts of his assailants. Perhaps they had not known it was him; there was no reason for them to since Kavan, to everyone's knowledge, had been in Rhidam for Princess Diona's birth day celebration. If their orders had been to remain on duty at the gate despite what they heard elsewhere, there was no reason to believe they should have come to his aid.

Thank Ethenae someone had. Though he had little proof, he believed, from things she had said, the large cat he remembered being there had been Orynn…or perhaps Kóráhm. There was no one else, to his knowledge, it could have been. She had brought Gaelán to him, taught the young man to heal, so the likelihood was that she had saved his life many times over. He would never be able to thank her enough.

Wortham remained at the head of the alley, blocking the entrance, watching nearby doors and side paths for movement that might prove hostile as Kavan took one step after another into his memories. With his eyes closed and senses tuned, it would take little effort for the bard to find the places where his tormentors had died, but it would also be easy for him to be taken unaware in that trancelike state; not, however, if Wortham could help it.

Eventually, Kavan found the focal point as well, the center of the chaos, the place where he had fallen, though there was no blood there now, no physical evidence of the events of that night. With his fingers pressed to the dirt of the unpaved alley, he swallowed and allowed every second of that terror to wash over him, reliving all of it without the actual corporeal trauma, seeking anything about that night that he should know but had either forgotten or had not noticed before.

It proved harder than anticipated to withdraw from the memories, from the emotional pain and depths of self-loathing that had been so strong that night. Despite his resolve to change, to become a stronger, different man, there was a part of him that continued to teeter on that brink, a part that would always find it too easy to slip into self-deprecation until the day he drew his last breath. Even in his happiest moments there existed the fear of worthlessness, the fear that his differences somehow made him less than other men, unwanted and useless. It would be easy to go back, to give in to the taunting darkness, to believe the negative and hurtful things others said.

This time, however, he overcame those things, partially due to the support of the man who appeared beside him at the moment when he needed reassurance the most. Wortham pulled Kavan to his feet, steadied him until the bard was ready to walk, and then followed without voicing platitudes or questions.

Inquiries made of people on the streets brought them to the Merry Sow in time for the noon meal. The sign was just as Kavan remembered it, but he was perplexed about how he had come to be in that particular alley. The path between them was convoluted and long, doubling back on itself, meandering as any drunk's path might be.

That, at least, made sense.

They ordered drinks so as not to raise questions about their business in the establishment, and Wortham insisted on sampling Kavan's water to be certain it was not poisoned, despite Kavan's protest. There was a woman tending the counter this day, not the man Kavan hazily remembered. The table where his attackers had been seated that night was empty when they entered, but did not stay that way. Glances were made in his direction by each person who came in, causing Kavan to shudder and try to push away the memories and the prickling curiosity of others.

Somewhere over his head was her room. Was she there? Should he ask for her?

"What was her name?"

For a moment, Kavan's expression suggested he either had not heard or did not understand the question. In truth, in his efforts to forget so much of that night, it took him time to remember her name. "Cora. She was heavy, dark hair, too much paint and rouge, approximately Zelenka's height."

The captain nodded as he got up from their table, and casually approached the barkeep to strike up a friendly conversation. Within minutes he gained a free drink and a laugh out of her. Kavan watched, fascinated by the interplay and how easily some men approached women. The very thought of trying terrified him.

His thoughts turned towards Orynn just as the tender's expression shifted to something disappointed and less friendly. She tried to move away from Wortham, making a show of reaching for a cleaning rag, but the captain caught her wrist and would not release her until she spoke to him. After a glance around the tavern, perhaps gauging the proximity and moods of the other patrons, perhaps looking for someone she knew who might defend her if the conversation turned violent, she decided to civilly answer his queries without raising a fuss. Kavan suspected Wortham had pulled rank, as few people chose to anger a captain of the Lachlan Guard. She gestured up the stairs, looking at Wortham with fascination and disdain, and put something in his hand before he released her and she went back to work. Wortham remained at the counter long enough to consume the drink she had given him, remaining nonchalant as he did so, and then he rejoined Kavan at the table.

"I am sorry, my lord." He had not given Kavan's name, had been careful to frame his questions so that no mention of the bard was made, as if he was seeking Cora for himself, but with the way the situation had turned, he felt as if he needed to apologize for all of it. "It appears the search ends here. Miss Cora was beaten and strangled about six months ago, found in her room, killed by a client…"

Six months ago had been approximately when Kavan had last seen her. "She is dead?" If she was, then it was likely because of him, he realized glumly. Though most of his attacker's exact words he could not recall, he did remember someone saying that the woman should have known better than to be tempted by an Elyri's pretty face, saying that she would be taken care of, that she would never make that mistake again.

And now she was dead.

Tears spilled despite his efforts to contain them. Wortham began to rise, thinking to shield Kavan from the view of others, but the bard clutched his hand and prevented his friend from moving.

"If I had not accepted her offer…had not followed her upstairs…she might still live…"

Turning his hand in Kavan's, Wortham squeezed tenderly. "You are not to blame for the actions of those who murdered her. A man cannot be blamed for what he does in a state of delirium…and you would have helped her if you could. You did not cause this, my lord."

Kavan nodded once, knowing the words were true even though he could not feel or believe that truth through his grief.

"I have the key to her room…if you wish to go up. No one has used it since her death." The captain did not tell him that it remained unused because superstition suggested the final Elyri customer had cursed or defiled it. The bard did not need that burden too.

"She owned little…at least I remember little in the room…I do not know if she lived there." He swallowed hard and dried his face with his free hand. "I cannot beg her forgiveness or make restitution…"

Though the captain believed Kavan should let the matter rest, he understood that the bard was not ready to do that. "If you ask, dedhá Urian will provide proper penance I am sure. We can return to the house and ask him, if you do not wish to go upstairs."

A rowdy gaggle of young men came through the door and almost at once focused on the only Elyri in the room as they gathered around a distant table. "Is there anything else you wish to do? Anywhere you wish to go?" Wortham thought it best that he encouraged Kavan to leave this place, to escape both the memories and a potential fight with the newcomers.

"St. Poul's," the bard whispered with a nod. "I wish to pray…to settle this before it draws the shadows too tight. Afterward, we will go back. You will come with me? Pray for her repose?"

"And for strength to face what awaits us?" Wortham asked as he nodded in agreement.

"Yes," Kavan sighed. "Especially for that."

❧*❦

It could not be true. From everything he had heard over the last six months, from every morsel of gossip and news the palace staff, the Lachlans themselves, and most of Rhidam shared, that man should never have returned to Enesfel. He should be dead or at least should have learned the lesson that he was not wanted here. The Elyri bard had been gone long enough that the hawkish man had begun to believe it himself. But something, according to the furtive messenger who brought the news from Levonne, was bringing the bard back. If not stopped, he would resume his position as one of the influential forces behind the Lachlan monarchy.

There was no solid proof that the bard was coming here, only the messenger's word from a source he trusted, but that source, young and eager to please, might have misunderstood the situation. Perhaps by 'home', the messenger meant the bard was returning to Alberni. Or Bhryell. To his knowledge, the Elyri had not yet set foot in Rhidam but was due to do so soon. After putting so much effort into steering Enesfel to where it was, Kavan Cliáth could not be allowed to return.

That one man could destroy everything he was striving for. He would not allow that to happen. The Elyri bard had to be eliminated.

Madalyn was alone to see them off. Tayte had not been seen since Kavan's arrival and his absence, and the tale of hatred the duchess had told, weighed heavily on the bard as the horses were loaded with their trunks, some additional clothing that she supplied for Zelenka, and enough food and water to get them comfortably to Rhidam. Kavan attempted to argue that perhaps he should stay, that he might be able to break through to Tayte if given the opportunity, but Madalyn assured him that would not likely be the case.

And as Wortham reminded him, there was much to do in Rhidam. They could not delay their return forever.

Despite Kavan's efforts, since the troubling vision seen on Káliel had not returned, he was unable to convince Urian to remain in Levonne, though he desperately tried to do so. As Urian pointed out, the imagery of him lying on the ground in a pool of blood did not necessarily indicate it was his blood. It could belong to anyone. Death might have been present in the vision, but Kavan could not be certain that it was not someone else's death he sensed. Because the bard could not definitively give proof, the dedhá insisted he must make the journey to Rhidam, that Rhidam was where he needed to be.

Maybe, Kavan mused, if he remained in Levonne, he could not only save Tayte from himself, but Urian as well.

Or perhaps he should attempt to use the Gates.

But it was knowing what waited in Rhidam that was his primary reason for hesitancy. A few days' travel on horseback would bring him face to face with everything, everyone, he had left behind and thought never to see again. Face to face with Ártur. Face to face with Princess Diona. The dread of what lay ahead was why he resisted attempting the Gates again. He dreaded each of those moments of confrontation, and though the building anxiety during each mile of the ride would be torture, it was better, he argued, then dropping himself into the middle of the castle to be bombarded by it. He hoped that, during the course of the next three days, he would think of some way to make those moments bearable. Or that he would at least be able to come to terms with the inevitable.

No amount of avoiding the future by remaining in Levonne was going to change anything. He had to go back. It was time.

❧*❧

It felt odd for Ártur to be in Bhryell beneath the afternoon sun when it was normally dark, or nearly so, when he came home each day. It felt odder still to be going to the second home of Syl's parents, where she and his children had been staying since her return to live in Bhryell. He had not been to this spacious house of wood and brick in a long time, and though he had wanted to come sooner, his wife insisted he stay away. Reluctantly, he had followed her wishes, hoping that in doing so he would change her mind about his intentions. Today, however, seeking her out was not his choice. He was going at the command of the King of Enesfel.

Waiting for someone to respond to his knock, he ran his hand nervously through his hair. He did not expect Syl to come to Rhidam, even for a few hours, and he had expressed that belief to King Hagan, yet the young king insisted Syl be invited to his celebration. Even if she chose to reject the invitation in favor of Elyriá's security, Hagan believed not asking his surrogate mother to celebrate with him would be a rude failing. For Hagan's peace of mind, he demanded that the summons be made at once, rather than waiting for evening when Ártur would have gone to Bhryell anyhow.

And so Ártur was here.

"Ár…"

He had not expected her to open the door, though who else would have had not crossed his mind. Once she saw him, he expected her to slam it without speaking, so he barred it with one hand, taking a moment to catch his breath as he realized again how beautiful she was.

"I apologize for being here…but King Hagan demanded it…said it could not wait. May I…may I come in?"

Syl inhaled, narrowed her eyes as if expecting a trap, and replied, "Chethá is napping. If this is going to involve an argument…"

"I do not anticipate an argument; I didn't come here for that."

Satisfied, she let him inside and closed the door, but he came no further than the entranceway. He felt uncustomarily unwelcome. "The King's birth celebration is in nine days; he is planning his own event and he wants you there."

She immediately shook her head. "I cannot leave Chethá."

Ártur sighed. "I told him you would not come, that your fear for your safety is too great…rightly so…and that there are the children to consider. He wants to increase security and take every precaution so that you can attend, is willing to give you anything you demand if you will agree to be there. He asked me to remind you that you are the woman who raised him, the closest thing to a mother he has had…that you are the most important person he could invite." He felt awkward saying all of those things, certain that Syl would feel it to be emotional manipulation, but as it was Hagan's wish, he said the words he had been asked to say. "He also wants you to meet his bride-to-be."

"Bride to…" To Syl, Hagan, though king now, was still a little boy. The thought of him married, with a family of his own, seemed strange. "This banquet is to occur in the evening?" Of course it would, those were the normal hours for such celebrations, stretching into the night after a day of work and duty.

Ártur swallowed the hundreds of things he wanted to say and did his best to maintain a neutral expression as he replied, "Yes."

"And you will be there?"

He felt trapped. He swallowed and shrugged. "The King expects me, at least briefly. I may stay only long enough to convey my wishes and hear Bhyrhán's first song…that is if it the King will allow me to leave…or if you come…"

Chin tilted haughtily, Syl huffed, "You would break your promise for the…?"

"I would return after the first song…or when you wish to come back…I have no intention of staying overnight…he expects me to…"

The baby's cry upstairs interrupted him and Syl, annoyed with her turbulent feelings, started up the stairs. "Your precious Lachlans mean…"

She slid on the fifth step and fell to the bottom. Ártur rushed to catch her but she hit the floor before he could.

"Don't touch me!" She tried to rise but sank back to the floor, her grimace revealing her pain.

Ártur lifted her easily despite her pummeling fists striking his chest, neck, shoulders, and face. Holding her to him for the first time in weeks reminded him of everything they risked losing if they could not find a compromise. Impulsively he stroked her hair and murmured her name soothingly, until she grew still against his shoulder and wept. He carried her upstairs to her room, placed her reluctantly on the bed, and gathered the crying child from her crib, placing her in her mother's arms, marveling at how much she seemed to grow and change each time he saw her. Llucás he saw every night. Chethá, still nursing, was unable to leave her mother for more than a few hours and Syl did not trust Ártur with her for that long.

"Your ankle is sprained. There is little I can do except make you rest, but I can take away some of the pain…"

"I have children to care for," she began to protest.

"I can do that."

"You have a duty to…"

"It can wait." That he chose to stay, to tend her and look after the children, clearly surprised her and that pleased him. He felt her shiver as he touched her ankle and hid his smile. Moments later, her pain was relieved and she pulled her leg away. "There. I have done what I can. If you stay off it for the rest of today and tonight, you may be able to bear weight tomorrow without too much discomfort."

"And if I can't?" she asked, her tone of challenge clear.

He touched her face, smiling at her suspiciousness and her obvious internal struggle to either lean into the touch or pull away from it. "Then I will stay until you can. I told the King it might take time to be allowed to see you, and even longer to persuade you to attend, even for an hour. If necessary, I will ask Bhen to take a message to the King when he brings Llucás this evening."

Syl tried to maintain her cool resolve but had to ask, "You would do this for me?"

It hurt that she doubted him after their years together, but he understood why. "I love you. I have never stopped. You are safer in Bhryell with the children than in Rhidam…and my duty keeps me there. It forces us to be apart more than I like, but I love none of you less. You are strong…and that does not excuse my shortcomings…but I pray that someday you will understand and forgive me."

The sternness around her eyes softened. That was a start, at least, although she was not verbally going to commit to anything. "While I feed Chethá, would you be kind enough to prepare the meal you distracted me from?"

They both knew Ártur was no cook, but the request was less about his ability then it was about his willingness. He kissed, her, unable to resist, and chuckled, "I will do anything you wish while I am here."

Though she frowned, the expression did not look as disapproving as she intended. "I will hold you to that," she grumbled without looking at him.

"I hope so."

❧Chapter 24❧

Princess Diona stormed into the morning room, startling the King enough that he spilled the drink in his hand down the front of his velvet and linen tunic. "How in k'Ádhá's name could you have allowed such a thing to happen?" she cried, stopping short of telling her brother that she thought he was an idiot.

"What?" stammered the King. "What are you talking about?" Though he asked, he already knew what she meant. He too had just received the disturbing news.

"You bring some poor fellow here who claims to have the names of those responsible for k'gdhededhá Jermyn's death, you throw him in prison, you let the accused know, and then you let him go without protection? Without investigating his claims? Without learning what he knew or trying to learn the truth of any of it?" Exasperated and angry, she found it difficult to keep her voice low.

And though he was the king, Hagan, already regretting his choices and feeling defensive about them, was still cowed by his older sister. "He accused dedhá Claide…" he began to stammer.

"If any one of us in your court said the same, would you have imprisoned us too without investigation?"

"He's dedhá; what do you have against him? What would he possibly be guilty of?"

It took every ounce of willpower for Diona not to blurt out the details of evidence she and Caol were compiling. "That's not the point! You will never know if he is or isn't…if anyone is or isn't, if you don't investigate claims while the witnesses are alive! And you take a man fearful for his life, who claims to be a witness…you tell others what accusations he's making, and then you let him go without granting his request for sanctuary? What sort of king are you?"

That brought Hagan to his feet, inflamed the inadequacies and insecurities he already felt. Red-faced, he snapped, "The rightful king! I do not believe his death had a connection to what his accusations…"

Diona was not afraid. As the older sibling, she had never been afraid of her brother and it did not occur to her, in her anger, that his rank might give him power over her. "But you don't know it…you just think it! They say his death looked to be at the hands of brigands, but Enesfel is too full of brigands these days for any death to be ignored! He was too far away from Rhidam…"

"How do you know?" he snarled, eyes narrowed as he took a step forward. His sister, he believed, had too many details she should not.

"I overheard the sentries discussing it."

Suspicion relieved, as that was entirely possible, the King decided he needed to have a word with his staff and the palace guards about gossiping on the job. He grunted, "It was a mistake…"

"Enesfel can't afford such mistakes. This one cost us information and may have cost a man his life…"

"Us? You are out of line…"

"Enesfel…and you, little brother, are a fool."

She stormed from the room, not waiting to be dismissed or castigated for her ill-spoken words. When her sources told her the witness was found covered with leaves in a stretch of forest far outside Rhidam, badly decomposed as if he had been there for several days, she had gone to investigate. Bhyrhán had identified the corpse, and then the news had been sent to the King as it should already have been. From everything she had learned from Caol, brigands did not hide their kills beneath leaves and debris. Brigands on the road rarely took pains to hide their deeds, only to hide themselves.

She fumed about the discovery, their misfortune, with Asta and they rode back to Rhidam and then she had marched straight in to confront Hagan. In her opinion, he was a fool, one their father would have been ashamed of. She was likely one as well, for pointing this out to Hagan, and her father would have told her that too. As a princess, heir by default because there were no other immediate male heirs, she was subservient to her brother and there was little she could do to affect his choices except try to provide advice that he no longer seemed inclined to seek. She felt compelled to point out his errors in the hopes that it would never happen again, but she, frustrated with herself, knew she could have done so in a more appropriate way.

Not watching where she was going as she growled and muttered her annoyance to the ancient keep walls, she collided with Prince Espen as they both rounded a corner. Without taking time to realize who she had charged into, noticing it was a man only by the boots he wore, she muttered, "Pardon, my lord," as she tried to push past.

The prince caught her arms, her distress alerting him to trouble and bringing out the protectiveness he felt for her. They might not have spoken to each other in many days, but his feelings had not changed. "What is it, Diona? What has happened?" He pulled her into the library where they could speak privately, relieved that she did not protest or resist.

Grateful to see him and embarrassed by her words and behavior when they ran into each other, she found him easy to talk to without censoring her thoughts the way she should have done with Hagan. Their stalemate was, for the moment, set aside and the possibility of being overheard did not cross her mind. "The man who came here…who accused Claide…who Hagan…" She paused, growled, and shook her head. "He's been murdered, dumped on the road outside of Rhidam…and Hagan has the gall to think there's nothing he could do, that it means nothing…he does not see that he should have gotten names, found out what the man knew…"

Espen sighed, thinking about how often he and his brother, the King of Hatu, disagreed over matters of state. Fortunately, his brother had an advantage of age, experience, and innate wisdom. "He is king. You can advise him of errors, perceived faults, but you cannot make decisions for him. If he does not seek advice, you should not give even that. He is the one who must live with what he has done, with the doubt about the validity of his choices. He is the one history will hold responsible for the good and bad in Enesfel when his legacy is left…"

"That is all men care about," she exclaimed with frustration. "What others will think about you…how you'll be remembered." She did not intend to attack Espen, but in her anger, she lumped all men together. "He does not live in a void; none of us do. What he does affects everyone…not just his legacy. If he doesn't learn that soon, there won't be a legacy, an Enesfel, to remember him."

Keeping his voice calm, Espen said, "He does not have the wisdom of your years…"

She did not feel wise. She had not felt wise in a very long time. "He doesn't need wisdom…he needs common sense," she grunted. "I don't have to stay here and tolerate his folly. If there is nothing I can do except make the situation worse because he will not hear me, I will go to Levonne, visit Lady Cáner, and leave him to his mistakes…"

"There is one thing you can do…"

It was the first time they had been alone in the same room in many weeks. In her furious state, some part of Espen knew his timing was not the best, but he could not allow the opportunity to pass without reaching out one more time. When he kissed her, a gesture unexpected in the heat of her anger, it was met with equal ardor despite the irrational fear that simultaneously erupted in the back of her throat.

Eventually, compelled by a need to catch his breath, he broke the kiss, pressed his nose and forehead to hers, and breathlessly whispered, "We're not getting any younger…"

He realized immediately the mistake he had made in speaking when she made a half-hearted attempt to retreat from him and murmured, "I cannot think on this now…"

Holding her fast, his embrace tender, her body compliant in his arms, he stubbornly pressed, "When then? Fifteen years, Diona…you were a child then…my mistake…but you are a child no longer…I want an answer…"

"I have had one since Hagan's ball, but you left and I was unable to…"

The door opened, interrupting what might have been either a fruitful conversation or else another round of argument and blame. Asta poked her head around the door, her expression grave, mortified, and apologetic all at once. "I'm sorry…I apologize for…but General Agis is demanding to see you, Prince Espen. Some difficulty among your men…"

"I will be there at once," Espen growled in annoyance at the inopportune disruption. If his men did not have a damn good reason for whatever problem had arisen, he was going to have them mucking stalls as punishment for a week at least.

He looked into Diona's eyes. She did not seem angry, she did not seem determined to avoid the topic of discussion, only disappointed yet again that he was being pulled away. "This is not over."

"I am going to Levonne as soon as I pack." She wanted this conversation with Espen, but her need to escape the frustration of her brother had not evaporated in that kiss. It would take her time to be ready to travel. Perhaps he would find her before she left.

"How long will you be gone?" He intended to see her before she departed, but there was no guarantee the timing would work.

"Eight or nine days…no more…barring unforeseen events." Given the recent violence and trouble throughout Enesfel, they both knew any number of delays could detain her.

"Then I will expect to resume this when you return…if not before."

He stalked past Asta, intending harsh words with his men, and the young woman apologetically said to her cousin, "I will see that a horse and attendants are ready for you."

Sometimes, Diona mused with a frustrated, heavy heart, Asta behaved more like a servant than a princess.

❧*❦

"Let go of me!" the boy screamed as he kicked and bit and twisted away from the bony hand that had unexpectedly grabbed him. Venturing into the sanctuary in the daylight hours had been a mistake; he knew that before he had done it. He had hoped to find somewhere nearer the choir loft where he could hide to watch the choir rehearse, and had mistakenly hoped he would be as safe here as the Elyri dedhá seemed to be. Never truly safe, of course, but safe enough.

He longed to sing with those children but he did not dare. Watching through cracks between rafter beams had been as close as he had been able to come, but he had come down in hopes of stowing himself in the narrow cupboard where the robes were kept. It was when the older balding dedhá found him, the one he had overheard giving orders to someone else to find a man and kill him before he reached Rhidam. The boy did not know who the dedhá wanted to kill or why, what sort of offense someone could make that would warrant that request from a man of Faith, but he knew the man could not have thought himself overheard.

The boy had been too careful for that.

Thus when he was found, and the dedhá tried to grab him, he knew he was not being caught for eavesdropping. Perhaps it was because he was dirty, or looked like a thief, and as such was not welcome in the naós during these empty hours.

From his memories of sermons long past, however, he believed the naós welcomed everyone in need. As long as he had been alone, need was something he had in abundance.

What he knew in that touch, however, confirmed what he had believed for a long time, since first laying eyes on the beak-nosed Teren dedhá. The man hated Elyri. The youngster knew it, felt it in every fiber of himself. He broke free and ran into the city streets, away from the shouts of "filthy vagabond" that echoed after him. He had expected the Gathering Hall to be a haven, expected the Faithful to be his friends. He did not know if he would be able to return to his sleeping place, whether someone else would find him there or if he had been exposed by the other. But at least he felt confident that the dedhá who had tried to catch him did not suspect him to be Elyri. He was grateful for that.

❧*❧

Syl was a model patient, making no unnecessary demands on him, taking up no more of his time and attention then she had to, which made Ártur unexpectedly sad. He wanted the chance to do more, to prove himself, but he had been unable to do more than bring her meals, tidy the house, and take care of the children, tasks he did gladly without being asked. He was aware she was monitoring his actions, dissecting everything he did in a quest for hidden motives or a reason to doubt him. But he also knew she was finding no flaw in anything he did. He stayed with her the previous day as promised, and remained overnight to see the children tucked into sleep and the house readied for the night. They had not shared a bed, but sleeping under the same roof, in the chair near the hearth where he kept the fire burning as she slept, had given him the best night's sleep he had gotten in weeks.

When Bhríd came to see to his sister's welfare, having spoken to Bhen who had reported the Healer's dilemma to the King, Syl had encouraged Ártur to return to Enesfel with her brother. The request had been doubled-edged, and Ártur saw it at once. She wanted him to stop fussing over her, but she was also testing to see if he would hasten back at the first opportunity and prove that his first priority was the Lachlans. After speaking with Bhríd, Ártur decided to stay one more day as well, when he would be certain that Syl's ankle would support her and that there was no undue limitation of her movement.

He knew she would be fine. She was already hobbling around her room, from bed to chair to cradle, trying to show she did not need him to stay, doing her best to tempt him into leaving earlier than promised.

Ártur was determined to prove himself, to prove her wrong.

He was also staying for the children. He had missed too much of Chethá's first months and found pride in Llucás' growing interest in the family legacy of harp making. The two were growing fast, changing so much, and he did not want to miss any more than necessary. After his brush with death, his children's smallest accomplishments gave him a welcome sense of satisfaction.

Perhaps his persistence would pay off. The first step was to convince Syl to come to the King's celebration, however briefly, to extend her wishes in person. That was more for Hagan's sake, and Syl's, then for Ártur's, but he hoped the King's efforts to increase palace security would prove that Ártur was safe…and his actions and words in Bhryell would prove that he loved her, that he preferred coming to Bhryell each night to share time with his family over sleeping alone in an empty bed in Rhidam.

Asking her to return was too much, and he admitted he did not want her and the children there unless they were safe. But he was growing comfortable with this new arrangement, had grown comfortable with seeing his family again. He would like it more if Syl would forgive him.

He crumpled the letter in one hand and tossed it into his cooking stove, watching the edges curl and darken as they came in contact with the smoldering embers of his dwindling fire. There had been no need for Asta to send him word of this latest casualty. He had known the man had been hunted and killed, although, until Asta's letter, he had not known the reason for the order. He had been unaware that the man had accused Claide of conspiracy against the late k'gdhededhá, had suspected the man complicit in Jermyn's death. The dead tanner had known the names of other conspirators as well, it was said, and had given none of them to the King because Hagan had not asked. He had instead been accused of madness and threatened with confinement in St. Bhílycá's if he spoke of the matter to anyone else, and the Corylliens had felt the need to kill him.

Or they had been asked to do so by someone else.

Where that order had come from, he did not know. He just knew it had been given.

To Caol, this indicated the Corylliens guilt both in this fellow's execution and in the death of Jermyn Tythilius. It also quite damningly implicated Claide. Caol knew that proving this one crime, the torture and murder of his superior, would be enough to destroy Claide's career, likely to end his life, and bringing Claide to justice might even be enough to hobble the Corylliens activities. It was up to Caol, he believed, to make both things happen, and he intended to enjoy the outcome, when he succeeded, to an almost perverse degree. Perhaps the tanner's widow had answers. Perhaps his friends. Getting to them as Alty would be tricky, but somehow, Caol had to try.

➮*➯

The six men in unmarked, piecemeal armor, with their large hunting dogs, burst from the forest on the eastern side of the road, catching Kavan and others off guard. Hampered by the almost audible hum of the relics stowed behind him that seemed to grow louder and more persistent to the bard's ears the nearer they drew to Rhidam, and the multiple distracting thoughts that vied for his attention with annoying persistence, not even Kavan's highly tuned senses registered the hidden enemy until it was too late to avoid them. The packhorse reared, spilling the goods it carried across the road, and bolted into the trees with four of the dogs snapping at its hooves, egged on by a single word command and gesture by one of the men controlling them. Zelenka screamed. Five other dogs brought down Urian's horse while four of the men singled out and surrounded the seemingly strongest opponent. Wortham. The captain felled two without dismounting, but at Zelenka's cry, he turned his horse in time to see Kavan fall from his mount, an arrow lodged low in his back. The bowman was stalking nearer, had dropped the bow in favor of a long-bladed knife, as the last of the six men yanked Zelenka off of her horse.

Wortham was torn. Who was he supposed to protect? Kavan? Zelenka? Kavan was down, but conscious, and the captain knew the bard to be capable of defending himself, either with a weapon or with the Elyri power he wielded so well. Decision made in that split second, he turned towards Zelenka, but Urian made the choice for him as he swung his pack of whittling supplies and struck Zelenka's attacker across the back of the head. The man spun off balance and fell onto his own blade. Judging them both to be safe, judging Kavan to be the target, Wortham shook off the two men trying to apprehend him, gave an angry bellow, and lunged at the encroaching archer.

On the ground, clutching the small of his back, Kavan shuddered in pain and convulsed once, an unexpected movement that caused Wortham to trip over him. But his sword found its destination and ran the archer through, causing him to fall to one side.

Rolling to his back, the captain barely avoided the dagger's strike. Yet it was not him they wanted. By the way this second man attempted to engage and draw him away from the downed Elyri, Wortham was further convinced that the bard was their objective. Maybe they knew who he was; the White Bard was known to many. Maybe they gauged, from his hairstyle and the lines of his face, that he was Elyri. Maybe they were opportunistic thieves whom fortune favored with an Elyri target, who looked to be carrying the party's wealth.

But Wortham would never allow anyone to kill Kavan without killing him first; he hooked one leg around the combatant nearest him and brought the fellow crashing hard to the ground, winding him with the impact. The other took the opening of Wortham's distraction and lunged at the bard with a large, serrated hunting knife.

Rolling, Wortham came up to rush the man, his head down, catching him in the stomach, knocking the air out of him as well. He was able to prevent further injury to Kavan, though this time as the last, when the Elyri moved, intending to roll clear of the fight, Wortham tripped over him to land on top of the attacker. The captain wrestled with him, half-watching the man he had knocked to the ground in case he intended to rejoin the fight.

He could not continue to fight this way, against younger, spryer, outnumbering opponents. He needed his sword back in his hand.

To his surprise, as he yanked away from his wrestling adversary, the man lurched sideways and fell unmoving to the ground. Rather than take the time to see why, Wortham turned on the last of their attackers who had struggled to his feet, his knife still in hand. The man's eyes darted between Wortham and Kavan.

Wortham was unarmed. He might not be able to kill this man, but when the fellow lunged at the Elyri on the ground, hoping to sidestep the captain, Wortham dove between them. The blade ripped into his bicep as he caught the wrist of the man's weapon hand in his other big fist. Both crashed to the ground, the majority of their weight landing again on Kavan, until Wortham rolled and pulled the enemy with him.

The Elyri curled into a ball, moaning.

With a hand around the assailant's throat, Wortham knocked the knife free, and without considering the consequences beyond protecting Kavan, strangled the fellow, shaking him until his neck snapped. The corpse was tossed aside and Wortham squatted back on his knees, surveying their surroundings quickly, judging the group's condition and any damage they had received.

Of the five horses, two remained alive and still with them. The majority of their belongings, save for the reliquary, the red harp, and Urian's whittling tools, had been stowed on one horse. The dedhá's horse lay in the road, bleeding from multiple bites along its throat and belly, its nostrils flared in distress and pain as it fought for breath. The two horses that lived, Kavan's and Zelenka's, lingered at the side of the road, nickering skittishly but not running. The other two had been chased into the forest and Wortham could not spare the time or effort to find them. What if those dogs returned, he wondered? Would they return? Could he defend them against so many fierce beasts?

Zelenka looked dazed, blood on her hands, her face, her dress, near the man she had killed to save Wortham's life. Some of the blood was hers; her shoulder was bleeding where her bodice had been cut and there were scratches and bruises on her face, her neck, her arms. But she was on her feet and the wounds appeared to be minor.

She was alive.

The blind man was not beside his horse, nor was he near the man he had accidentally killed. There was blood on the ground, shredded strips of brown fabric caught on bushes at the side of the road. Something had been dragged into the brush, or had crawled there, but Wortham had neither seen the man go down nor heard him cry out.

"Stay with him. Clean his wounds but do not remove the arrow," he ordered, pointing at Kavan as he retrieved his sword from where it had fallen. Without checking, he was confident Kavan was alive and in no immediate danger of dying, even if he was in pain. He hoped Zelenka understood and obeyed his instruction. Leaving that arrow embedded where it was might be all that was keeping the bard from bleeding out, bleeding to death.

Wortham expected her to refuse, to cling to him, to try to follow him or demand he stay with her for protection, but she exhibited unusual stoicism in her shocked state as she scavenged their scattered belongings in search of water, a discarded blade in her hand.

Branches had been broken in the underbrush and blood stained the leaves, but there was no sign of the dedhá in the dense growth. It was too thick for Wortham to enter easily, and from what he could see, the trail of something dragging stopped where he stood. But there was nothing there, as if the man had vaporized as a mist.

Thinking that the blind man might have turned around and stumbled away in a dazed panic, Wortham reluctantly called, "dedhá?" If there were more rogues nearby, he had given away their location with that call, but the skirmish had likely already exposed them and Wortham believed it appropriate that he find Urian rather than let the blind man fend for himself.

"Urian?"

"Gone," called Zelenka in Trade. "Crawled." She pointed into the brush where Wortham was standing.

"There's nothing…that's not possible…"

Kavan's groan of pain interrupted and Wortham returned his attention to the bard, not liking that sound and afraid that he had misjudged the Elyri's condition without checking on him first. He was breathing, but unconscious, and when Wortham removed his bloody tunic to examine the wound he saw the multitude of darkening contusions where the captain had kicked or fallen on the already injured man. In the chaos, the arrow's wooden shaft had broken, leaving the head buried in the bard's lower back. It was, as far as Wortham could see, the most serious of his injuries and should not be life-threatening if the arrow was not allowed to penetrate any deeper.

The captain was no physician or healer, but as shallow as the arrow's entry was, he believed he could remove it. He did not want to take chances with Kavan's life, however. Rhidam was half a day away, more if they had to travel on foot with a wounded man. If the bard regained consciousness, there was even a chance he could walk with that injury, but it seemed wisest to Wortham to wait where they were for some passerby's assistance, for someone who could be sent on to Rhidam to summon the healer without risking movement causing Kavan further internal damage.

Wortham motioned Zelenka closer. "Clean this…like this…but be careful. I will collect our things…find the dedhá if I can." He could not go far, but he could watch for signs of the blind man as he picked up everything the packhorse had scattered. It was going to be a daunting task to retrieve everything and repack it, since the first trunk had been smashed, leaving only the one they had received from the ghost ship to hold as much as he could cram into it. As he worked, he constantly scanned around them for some trace of the blind man, paused occasionally to watch Zelenka who had, after tending to Kavan, used some of their water supply to wash her hands and face. She now wandered up and down the roadside apparently gathering kindling and bits of wood, as well as the discarded weapons, all of which she lay in tidy piles at Kavan's side.

The bard's manuscripts were intact, as was the reliquary and, Wortham assumed, its content. The containers of Diwi and Orec, the redwood harp, the figures Urian had recently given to Kavan, were likewise undamaged. Urian's whittling pack was missing, and the remainder of their food lay scattered in the dust, no longer fit for eating. While most of their extra clothing and their bedding was dirty now, strewn about and possibly torn, it appeared functional.

Depositing everything with Zelenka as he found it so that he could then try to rearrange the trunk's contents for the best fit of their remaining supplies, Wortham squatted and wiped his face with his forearm as he looked at the weary woman who had remained remarkably calm in the aftermath of the attack. "This road is frequently traveled. Someone will find us, help us. When he wakes up, perhaps we can travel, but there is much to carry and it will not be easy. We might have reached Rhidam by sunset…now the best we can hope for is midnight. We've lost the food…"

She nodded, understanding that they would not be eating soon. Having gone hungry many times in her life, it was not the worst fate she could suffer tonight. She continued to gather burnable material and lit a fire while Wortham brushed the hair from Kavan's face, checked his pulse, his temperature, his condition. The Elyri's skin had grown cool and moist and he was beginning to shiver despite the relatively mild temperature of the day. Wortham hastily wrapped a blanket around his friend, swearing at himself silently.

If Kavan was going into shock, perhaps the internal damage was worse than it seemed. He had seen what happened when a man's intestines leaked their contents into the body cavity. It was never a good thing. Or maybe the Elyri had lost more blood than it seemed, though there was little on the ground and his shirt, while bloody, did not suggest massive blood loss. Nor did the bruising of his white skin hint at any excessive pooling of blood from internal injuries. Wortham tried to get Kavan to drink but the water trickled out of the side of the bard's mouth. The fire, while not needed for heat or cooking tonight, combined with the warmth of the blanket, might help combat the shock and someone might see its distant glow and be inclined to assist them, despite the fact that the injured man was Elyri.

Thinking it prudent, Wortham pulled all of the dead men to the side of the road where the dogs had disappeared into the forest. and brought the remaining horses to be tethered near where they were camped. It was mid-afternoon now, and with little else they could do but wait, he squatted by the fire or paced the area, still hoping for some trace of the vanished blind man.

But the sun sank lower into the trees to the west, casting shadowy fingers across the road as it disappeared for the night. No one came. Not a wagon, not a single rider, not anyone on foot. So much for the road being well-traveled, he thought bitterly. Where were the merchants who frequented this road, conducting trade between Rhidam and Levonne's port? Was the violence in Enesfel bad enough that trade had dwindled so, or ceased entirely? Kavan did not wake and his body temperature swung between fever and chills, with only an occasional short-lived period of normal temperature in between. Refusing to show his fear, Wortham too gathered additional kindling and branches for their fire, anything to feel like he was helping when there was very little he could do.

At the fireside, adding more wood to the blaze, he heard noises from the forest's edge and looked to see several of the hunting dogs, bloodless but dirty, emerge from the treeline. Motioning for Zelenka to keep still, Wortham readied his sword in case the dogs attacked. The animals were wary, confused, and one of them came forward to nose the corpse nearest to it. One by one it sniffed at the other bodies as well, including the dead horse, and the other dogs followed suit, until they all collected at the roadside, staring at the two people who still lived as if waiting for something. A threat, a command, some indicator that the people could be trusted. They did not appear threatening now, but somewhere there were the dogs who had taken down Urian's horse and might have taken Urian as well. Wortham would not take any chances. He had the bandit's bow, and what arrows he had found, and even when the dogs lay down with their heads on their paws to watch, the captain refused to let down his guard.

The light in the west was rapidly fading as the sun sank behind the trees. Too late for travelers now. They were going to have to wait for daybreak. There was no one but Wortham to keep watch, no one but Wortham to treat Kavan's injuries and see to his health. But no one, man or beast, was going to kill them this close to home. Wortham would die a hundred times before he would let that happen.

❧*❧

"I am not afraid of the dark, Lord Zarkosta." Diona sniffed and drew back her shoulders as if the gesture would lend credence to her claim. The wool cloak she had been forced to wear when the general deemed the night chill worthy of precaution, itched at the back of her neck, and her thighs ached from the unaccustomed extended length of riding. She refused to complain, however, and as the desire to get as far away from her brother tonight as she could was the driving force behind this journey, she was determined to push on, to ignore discomfort, to be the lady of strength she wanted others to see.

The general barely avoided rolling his eyes; only her royal status kept him from doing so. He had heard such noble bravado before, from men of much higher, and lower, rank. "Your Grace, I was not implying that you are. Given the troubles in Enesfel, however, I do not think it prudent to continue traveling in the dark."

Tossing her head, hearing his point but not yet believing they were at risk, she did not look at him as she said, "It is not yet dusk; there is light in the sky. I would think you would want to travel as far as possible to avoid spending two nights in the open."

"You are a Lachlan; we are not at war. You should not have to sleep outdoors. We could have taken shelter at the last…"

"And inconvenience those people for my comfort? I think not." Her father would have done such a thing, seeing it as his right. She imagined Hagan would as well, as the powerful men she knew were more inclined to exert their authority and influence to remind their subjects who they were. The princess felt no such compulsion, no need to force others to acknowledge her rank so long as they were respectful, polite, and kind.

"If we travel until dark, how will the men see to provide a fire, set camp, prepare dinner for you?"

She could see his points, the more he made them, and she pursed her lips in annoyance. "Just a little further," she eventually conceded. She had made this trip before, usually with Bhríd or her brother, and they normally stopped at one of the homes along the way to seek lodging. They were nearly always graciously received. But as the only royal member of this party tonight, and the one whose wishes mattered, she wanted to sleep under the stars. Her brother's ill-conceived actions continued to irritate her and she did not particularly care about the difficulties her desires placed on those sent to protect her and see her safely to Levonne. Bringing so many men seemed ridiculous, but Bhríd had insisted…as had Espen.

He might be irritated, but he was still concerned for her welfare.

"The next suitable clearing," she agreed with a sigh. "Build the fires first; there will be light enough to see."

Though annoyed, he was satisfied that she was willing to compromise and see reason, and so he grunted, "Yes, Your Grace. I pray we find a suitable place before it grows much darker." Otherwise, he wagered they were in for a long night made all the longer by her uncomfortable grumbling.

He abruptly drew his horse up short, stopping the riders behind him with a raised hand after catching the reins of the princess' horse to stop her as well. There was a spot of light on the road ahead of them, a fire he was sure, but it was too far ahead to be certain if it was a stationary fire or a collection of moving torches. "Your Grace…move back. Denyan?" The soldier he summoned pulled closer, nudging his horse between the general's and the princess' so that she had no choice but to draw back several feet. "Take five with you, see what's there. If they're people, make them step aside; if they need assistance, find out what sort and report back."

"Yes, sir," the soldier replied as he pointed to five other men in the group and road with them into the fading daylight to discover what blocked their path.

The princess' interest in what was happening kept her from retreating very far. "What is it, Lord General?" she asked, excited and worried at the same time.

"We will know soon enough. But," he took his eyes off his scouts and the point of fire to look at the woman sternly. "I recommend you withdraw into the ranks for protection, My Lady. If they are brigands of any sort, we cannot protect you if you do otherwise. We can guard you better if you are…"

"Lord General…"

"No arguments. In matters such as this, the wishes of the King outrank your curiosity. Move back…or we go back."

His soldiers shifted as one until they surrounded her on every side, swallowing up any protests she wanted to make by the press of their horses' bodies that crowded so tight together that she could not consider moving regardless of her wish to do so.

Horses. Several of them. From their sudden cessation of movement, Wortham knew they had seen his fire. Such a large group, however, made him uneasy. Friends? Foes? Sword in hand, he took position in the center of the road several feet away from Kavan and

Zelenka as a handful of riders split from the group and continued forward. Their organization suggested a military unit or at least men with military training, but there seemed no need for soldiers on this stretch of road, unless it was Chamberlain Cáner traveling to Levonne.

He prayed it was so.

The dogs still at the side of the road pricked up their ears in interest and sat up expectantly.

The riders were wary, not knowing if the three individuals they could see were alone or were a prelude to a hidden ambush. "Do you need assistance, sir?" one of them called.

"Denyan?" Wortham took a few excited steps towards that familiar voice, barely able to believe his luck, knowing he would recognize his countryman's voice anywhere. But it had been several months since they had seen one another, it was possible that his hopeful ears deceived him.

The lead rider slid from his horse and rushed forward, his armor clanking as he approached and clasped Wortham's outstretched hand in sincere greeting. "Bless you, Captain; what are you doing here? Can we help you?" There were other questions he could have asked, but with a motionless figure on the road and a woman on her knees nearby, offering aid was more important than asking questions.

Before Wortham replied, Denyan waved to one of those with him and said, "Tell the General it's Captain Delamo. They may approach."

Troops then. Lachlan troops. "Battle or patrol?" Wortham inquired. Bhríd would not have brought either general with him to Levonne, so their presence here was something different.

"Nothing as grand as that," Denyan chuckled. "We are escorting the…" He stopped, however, when he identified the wrapped body on the ground. The white of his face and hair made him unmistakable, but it was difficult to tell in the twilight if the bard was alive or dead. "What has happened?"

"I will explain as we travel, if the general can spare an escort. I must get my lord to Rhidam, to Healer MacLyr, as quickly as possible…unless he is with you."

"He is not." Kneeling, Denyan felt for the bard's pulse, verifying for himself that the man was alive, rising to his feet only as General Zarkosta's horse thundered up to join them.

The rest of the unit was not far behind.

"This is an unexpected surprise, Captain."

"Aye, and a blessing for us, General. We have seen no one on the road since we were ambushed and are in sore need of another horse or two, and an escort to Rhidam if you can spare a few men."

The general was given no opportunity to reply, however, before a smaller horse, taking advantage of the loosening of her too-tight escort, was able to push to the front of the group. "What is the problem, Lord General? Are we…?"

Diona's voice cracked when her gaze met the Káliel Captain's. Her breath was sucked out of her lungs and she could not inhale to replace it. In dumbfounded shock, she looked over the woman behind Wortham, her clothes dusty and bloody, her skin the same warm brown as Espen's, and finally down to the bundled form lying at the woman's feet. The silver of his hair in the shimmer of the firelight gave his identity away and her heart felt as if it was ripped from her chest and followed her stolen breath.

"Kavan!" The word was a squeaky hiss. She struggled to get off of her horse without falling, intending to run to his side, but Wortham stepped between her and the Elyri with a growl, his hand tightening around the hilt of his sword so that his knuckles turned white.

"Do not." His tone was low and threatening, and several soldiers reached for their weapons, intending to protect the princess if necessary. Wortham was undaunted, ignored their actions, only glowered at the woman who had caused so much pain. Diona, realizing that this was neither the place nor time for words of confrontation, decided to follow Wortham's wishes.

"How bad?"

Because she stopped, because she respected the boundaries Wortham set, he was willing to answer her inquiry, albeit in a terse, cool voice. "An arrow in his back. The men who attacked us…" he gestured to the bodies on the other side of the road, "and their dogs." They killed one of our horses, chased another two away…and the blind dedhá who was traveling with us has gone missing." Maybe there had been other men he had not killed who had taken Urian, but he had not noticed them and Zelenka had not said so either. "We were attacked shortly after the noon hour, were waiting for aid or for him to awaken…but his condition has not changed and I feared to move him without assistance."

Diona nodded. She wanted to touch Kavan, see his hands, hear his voice even if it was to chastise and berate her for her foolish cruelty, but until he awoke, Wortham was not going to permit her any closer.

Though perturbed and disappointed, she was also grateful for the captain's loyalty. Without Wortham Delamo, Kavan might not be alive. Without Wortham, Kavan might not have come home.

"Were you…?"

"On our way to Rhidam," Wortham reluctantly admitted.

"Lord General," Diona said as she climbed back onto her horse. Her plans had changed, the desire to go to Levonne erased by the more pressing needs of the man she had grievously wronged. "I am canceling my visit to Levonne. Some men should stay, search for the dedhá and the horses, tend to the dead and the dogs, while the rest accompany Lord Cliáth's party to Rhidam." That she intended to be part of that escort went unsaid. The general growled softly at having his authority undermined, but since the princess was giving the same directions he would have given, he instead pointed to those he wanted to stay, those he wanted to conduct a search, and those he wanted to join him in the return to Rhidam.

"Captain, does your companion need other attire?" By not stopping, they might miss the evening meal, but a few minutes could be spared if the dirty woman in the torn, bloody dress wanted something more suitable to wear.

Wortham did not want to accept anything from the princess except a hasty escort to Rhidam, but Zelenka would be more comfortable, he knew, in something better to wear. He asked her first, purposely using her language so that Diona would not understand and felt smugly satisfied when the princess frowned at him.

Instead of answering Wortham, however, Zelenka looked at the princess, curtsied in the manner Wortham and Urian had taught her to do, and bowed her head. "Yes," she murmured. "Clothes. Please; when we stop." She seemed to recognize the nobility in the other woman, as she had in Clianthe and Gabrielle, but despite her desire for something clean to wear, she neither wanted to be watched, wanted to go into the dark forest to change, nor allow the injured member of her group to suffer longer than he needed to.

Diona, seeing this, offered her hand to the woman and Zelenka accepted the invitation to ride on the horse behind her. Denyan and two others secured the remaining trunk and the haphazard bundles Wortham had made on one of the two empty horses, and then, after Wortham was settled on Kavan's horse, they lifted the bard into the captain's arms. The general gave parting orders to the men he was leaving behind and then turned the rest back towards Rhidam.

This was not the way Kavan had expected to make his return, but perhaps, Wortham thought, it was the best way. Unconscious, he could avoid unwanted questions until he awoke and recovered, at which time he could avoid whomever he wished. The Elyri's skin had grown cool and damp again, and his hair was matted to his skull. Wortham paid no attention to anything else around them, relying on General Zarkosta and Enesfel's soldiers to protect them. He only had eyes for Kavan.

"Not much longer, my lord, and you will be in your own bed. I will not leave your side." He ignored the princess' glance back at them, not caring what she thought. To Wortham, she had no right to ask, demand, or promise anything. Not anymore.

❧*❧

It had been a dim-witted, ill-advised idea to deface the Eagle's Nest Inn, and Caol had tried to talk them out of it. The establishment was too close to the castle for vandals to avoid detection by the palace guard, and there was too much foot traffic to guarantee an adequate window of activity. Even in the middle of the night, there were sentries on patrol, guards on the walls, in the tower, and at the gate. He had tried to persuade Layton to select a different target, had suggested several candidates further away from the keep that would send the same message to the King and mean less risk to the vandals. Layton and others had scoffed that risk was part of what they did, and rather than allow Caol to beg out of the event, Layton insisted that he go too. Not as a participant, however. Since he was so worried about being caught, he was serving as a lookout to warn the others when guard activity put them at risk of being discovered.

When the soldiers, attracted by the furtive shadows flitting about the Inn's exterior, decided to investigate, as Caol had warned they would, he gave the agreed-upon warning whistle and the shadows, surprised by the accuracy of Alty's warning, scattered before much damage could be done. Caol did not loiter to see what became of them or what they tried to do in the few moments of destruction they could undertake before they were spotted. He ducked into the alley nearest his lookout point and slid into a concealed opening, a hideout known to no one outside of the Association, to wait out the foot chase of vandals through Rhidam's streets. There were others in the dingy room, men, women, and children in various stages of undress, playing cards, drinking, chatting up matters that concerned only those individuals involved. They each looked at the new arrival before turning back to whatever they were involved in. Used to disruptions, trusting that only other members would know this place existed, the intruder had to be one of theirs, even if they did not recognize him. They watched him cautiously as he listened for the sounds of running feet or anything that might indicate he had been pursued, but the alley remained silent.

Since the stranger did not bring trouble into the room, the others left him alone.

Good. He was safe. And the people behind him showed no desire to expel him into the night. He would wait a little longer, maybe enjoy a drink before he emerged from this hole, and then scurry off to the Corylliens pre-arranged rendezvous place. He did not know, however, if there would be anyone there to meet him.

❧*❦

The náós bells tolled the second hour of the new day when voices passed Gaelán's door in the corridor, but the young healer was already awake. He was not sure what had roused him, but he heard the palace gates open, the drawbridge lower, heard the sounds of people and horses coming into the courtyard. Not able to see anything from his window, he was content to lounge in bed, hoping to be summoned or else hoping to fall asleep again, until the voices and footsteps came outside of his room. He recognized Princess Diona's voice, but was sure she had left earlier for a trip to Levonne. If she had returned unexpected, perhaps someone had been injured. Expecting to be summoned, he got up and dressed quickly, listening to those outer noises for clues about what had happened.

When the collection of voices entered the room next to Gaelán's however, Kavan's room, the boy bolted from his chamber, only half-dressed, to charge into the neighboring room with breathless amazement and anticipation. He saw no one but Kavan, who lay face down on the bed, the fevered skin of his back exposed so that the dark, swollen puncture of the arrow's entry was plainly visible, marring his paleness. As if in response to the young man's presence, Kavan twitched, his head turning on the pillow in Gaelán's direction, but his eyes never opened.

The others in the room looked to see who had come in.

"Good." Sounding relieved, Wortham motioned Gaelán closer. The young man had healed Kavan extensively once before; the captain trusted he could do it again since he had already been told that Ártur was not here. "Will you tend him?"

The captain stepped aside to allow Gaelán close enough to examine the wound. The healer touched his fingertips to the surrounding discolored tissues, examining the damage with senses other than his eyes. "I can heal him," he nodded, "but I do not know how to remove an arrow…"

He could, he knew. He was simply too afraid to do something wrong and risk harming Kavan more.

"I am here." Rouvyn Talis, whom Wortham had not seen in many years, pushed to the bedside, having been directed to the room by palace staff after the princess' summons. "Master Cáner and I will see to him if the rest of you will please leave us to…"

Wortham growled. "I will not leave him. I swore I would not." He trusted this Teren doctor's medical skill and knowledge, though he did not know how he came to be here, but he trusted no one enough to leave the bard while the princess was near.

"Allow us to tend to his injuries, Lord Delamo." Rouvyn touched the man's hand to soothe him, smiling reassuringly. "By the time you have changed your clothes and seen your companion to a room, we should be finished. I do not think it irrational for you to stay with him after that. I wager he would prefer it."

Not even Diona would argue that assertion and the others, a few soldiers, General Zarkosta, Denyan, the page Peter who met them in the corridor and followed in case anything was needed, began to file from the room, shuffling feet reporting their reluctance to leave. Wortham waited until the princess went out before squeezing Kavan's hand, putting one arm protectively around Zelenka's shoulders, and escorted her from the room, ignoring Diona's efforts to stop him. He had resigned his position in the Lachlan guard to follow Kavan, and while he knew she was royalty and should thus be obeyed, he did not feel he owed allegiance to the woman who had wronged his friend and set into motion a chain of events no one could have foreseen. Until Kavan could express his wishes, Wortham chose to hold his own counsel and decide for himself.

Behind Kavan's closed door, Gaelán watched Rouvyn carefully probe the injury for the arrowhead, knowing the process hurt no matter how careful the physician was. Kavan did little more than twitch and groan in his sleep. Using the young healer's skill to pinch off the surrounding nerves, deadening the pain and controlling the blood flow, Rouvyn made two small incisions that would allow the arrow to be removed with minimal internal damage. Gaelán waited as Rouvyn worked, noting that the bard's hands no longer showed evidence of the trauma he had borne when he left Levonne. As soon as the arrow was free, Gaelán's focus changed to healing the wounded tissue, internally and externally, while Rouvyn applied a cleaning solution and salve intended to prevent infection and lower the Elyri's unstable body temperature. When he could do so, Gaelán used his talents towards the same end, speeding up the remedies so that Kavan might heal sooner while there Teren physician cleaned the exterior of the wound.

Looking at the blood on his hands, Kavan's blood, again, Gaelán listened to Rouvyn's relieved sigh. "We make a good team, Master Cáner. Thank you." The Teren wiped his hands on a damp cloth he had used for washing Kavan's back and handed it to Gaelán for the younger man to do the same.

"He will live." Though it was a statement, Rouvyn heard the question in Gaelán's tremulous voice.

"Of course." He smiled and tousled Gaelán's red hair. "There is nothing now to prevent it. He was not poisoned, there are no signs of that, and you have healed everything else. Nothing else was in the wound. Lord MacLyr will check him when he arrives in the morning, will want to be certain nothing was missed, but I assure you he will find nothing."

Twirling Kavan's matted hair with his fingers, wanting to wash it but thinking that would be inappropriate, Gaelán asked, "Would it be a wise precaution to instruct others that he is to have no visitors until he wakes…besides us healers…and of course Captain Delamo? You know…to limit exposure to infection."

"There is no need…" But Rouvyn too knew Kavan to be a private person who frequently sought his privacy. The Lachlans and many others were going to start forming a line outside of his door to see the bard, be with him, speak with him, especially when word spread through the castle that not only was the bard home, his hands had been restored.

"For me?" Gaelán begged. "I know it is what he would want."

Rubbing his shoulder as he gave the request brief consideration, Rouvyn nodded. "I see no harm in doing so." From what he understood of Kavan, limiting his exposure to the influence of others might even help speed his recovery. The possibility that too much stimulation by the demands of others would drive Kavan deeper into himself was a very real one. "No visitors until he permits them. Captain Delamo will enforce this?"

"Of course he will." Gaelán assumed Wortham would have put the condition into place without the physician's say so. "I can stay with him now…until the captain comes back."

The Teren doctor patted him on the back affectionately and stepped into the corridor to speak with those gathered there. All but the soldiers who had escorted them inside, carrying the group's belongings, remained. They had gone with Wortham; the captain had not yet returned. Rouvyn suspected he was going to have to stand in front of this door until Wortham came back. Otherwise, the princess, at least, was going to circumvent his instructions and go inside.

Alone with his uncle, Gaelán climbed into the bed beside him, not caring if it was a childish gesture or not. Nestling his head against Kavan's shoulder, as the man continued to sleep on his stomach, the young man whispered, "Welcome home, k'aendhá. I will take care of you. I promise."

He was asleep with his arm across Kavan's back by the time Wortham came in. The captain smiled and took comfort in the bedside chair. He did not have the heart or desire to ask Gaelán to leave. He had seen in the young man's eyes that he was one of the few to welcome Kavan back without reservation or demands upon him. He would not deny Gaelán his welcome.

Part 2

❧Chapter 25❧

It was too early to seek an audience with the King, but Espen was irritable and tired of waiting. He felt tired of a lot of things, resulting in an impulsive decision that consumed his every thought from the moment it jumped into his head, into the back of his throat, into the pit of his sour-feeling stomach. The sun was creeping over the horizon at an hour when many in the royal house were still abed, but it was hour enough to act.

Oh yes, the woman he loved would have her answer for him when she returned from Levonne. Knowing that, when he had heard her voice passing his room not long before, a too-early hour when she should have been miles away from Rhidam, Espen's heart began to thunder with trepidation and excitement. Such a hasty return might mean there had been trouble, but it also might mean that her answer to the long-lingering proposal might be forthcoming. Either way, he needed to see her, to learn the truth.

He dressed quickly in his finest attire and went in search of her, not knowing where he might find her at such an unholy hour, but willing to make the rounds of everywhere she seemed likely to be. The first person he found, however, was Doctor Talis who was instructing a pair of guards that no one except himself, Gaelán, or Healer MacLyr was to enter the door where they stood watch without permission from Captain Delamo.

Captain Delamo? In Rhidam? Then the sentries outside that specific room meant one thing. The Elyri bard had returned.

Duke Cliáth was home.

Espen neither hated Elyri nor feared them. And he knew the bard well enough after years of visiting the Lachlan court that he knew the man had no interest in Diona. Knowing it, however, did not keep him from feeling angry. That the Elyri's return coincided with Diona's abrupt reversal of plans meant one thing to Espen. His answer indeed.

"I am sorry to keep you waiting," Hagan muttered with a yawn behind his hand as he shuffled into the morning room. He looked disheveled and weary as if he had not slept well in days or had been up most of the night. "There has been much commotion this morning and it is barely dawn. You wanted to see me?"

There was a number of things Espen considered saying, some of which would not be appropriate for one of his station to say to the King who allowed him to stay in his home. Instead, he held his breath, released it slowly to calm himself, and asked, "Is…has Lord Cliáth returned to Rhidam? Is it true he is here?"

A hint of a smile graced the Boy-King's face, a different sort of smile than the King had expressed in months, a smile that dispelled some of the fatigue from his features. It was a smile Espen expected to see on many faces today, as the news of the Duke's return spread through the castle and beyond.

"That is the good news. Diona and her escort found him, Captain Delamo, and a traveling companion attacked on the road to Levonne. Thanks to the captain's prowess, they escaped with only minor injuries. Lord Cliáth's are the worst, nothing life-threatening according to Physician Talis, but he will be kept under supervision until he awakens to be sure. The best news is that his hands are healed, or at least Gaelán says they are. I have not seen him and they're not letting anyone in to disturb his rest. Lord MacLyr has not yet arrived to confirm his condition and I cannot spare anyone to fetch him since Lord Cáner has been out all night investigating vandalism at the Eagle's Nest. Is that what you needed to speak with me about?" It was news Espen could have gotten from anyone else and the young King felt perturbed that perhaps Hatu's prince had requested an audience for gossip when Hagan had not even eaten breakfast yet.

Sighing, Espen shook his head. "No…I have come to inform you I shall be departing Enesfel in two or three days…"

"Dep…two days? Why? For how long? Where are you going?"

Espen had known the news would be a shock, but he was determined not to let the King's reaction sway him. "Home…to Hatu. I do not know for how long. I have been away too long. I agreed to be here, to help, but there has been little I can…"

"Your men have been invaluable…"

"My men, yes. But not me. And many of those men have families they have not seen in weeks or more. I will select others, send more to rotate those in your service, but for myself…it is time to return to my brother to learn the state of things in Hatu, do my duty by my brother.”

Rising, the King poured a glass of water to have something to do with his hands. Having a foreign ally present in Rhidam had been a tremendous boost to his confidence and morale and he was reluctant to let him leave, but he had no hold over Espen and the man’s reasons were sound. “I understand…you are free to do as you must. I appreciate Hatu’s support and hope I will continue to have it. I would be indebted to you, however, if you would reconsider, and if you must go, if you would consider a favor before you do so.”

Since the King rarely asked for anything from him, Espen bowed slightly and said, “Of course.” Hagan could ask, but Espen could not guarantee it was a favor he could grant.

“Will you remain in Rhidam until Lord Cliáth’s health is resolved? The rumor of his return is likely already spreading through Rhidam…servants and soldiers talking as they do. If for any reason he does not awaken…if he dies…there will likely be a riot the likes of which we have not seen. I’ve sent word this morning to the lords closest to Rhidam, to have men ready in case I must call on them to keep the peace, but having you and your men here will be crucial. When he wakes, as Gaelán assures me he will, you are free to go. A day or two…what would that matter? And of course, I hope you will remain to celebrate my birthing day…won’t you?”

Espen pondered the King’s words, the implications and the logic of the request, and then bowed more formally. “If the injury is minor as you say, then his condition should resolve itself quickly.” Perhaps even within the next few hours. It would take that long for Espen to make all of the necessary travel preparations. “As for your…” he supposed that attending would be the diplomatically proper thing to do, since he was already here. If he left Enesfel before that, it might appear, both to Hagan and to Espen’s brother, as a slight from Hatu to Enesfel. Espen would never hear the end of that from either of them. “I will attend as you wish, of course, and in the meantime will determine which of my men I can leave when I am gone and which will travel with me.”

“Wonderful.” The King looked relieved and delighted. When servants entered with breakfast, Hagan made a sweeping gesture over the trays. “Will you join me? I have not had the opportunity to eat yet.”

“I have already done so. May I be excused to survey my men?”

“By all means. Do what you must.”

The King did not mind eating alone, nor did he mind that Prince Espen left the door open on his way out. It allowed the King to see who was passing. He liked to watch people. He saw the novice Edward pass with Gaelán and wondered what the novice might want with the apprentice Healer. Or maybe they were friends. Hagan did not know. He no longer begrudged Gaelán the ability to heal; Gaelán might be a healer, but Hagan was a king. And though Asta had not changed her affections for him with his crowning, even that no longer troubled Hagan. Sigrid had agreed to marry him. His celebration was days away. With Kavan home now, Hagan felt he would no longer need to rely on his sister's advice and perhaps his other advisors too would stop turning to her.

If, with Kavan's help, Hagan could find a way to bring an end to the troubles in Enesfel, all would be right with the world.

Except that he missed his father.

"Diona?" he called, stopping his sister as she strode by the door. Not sure she heard him, as it took several moments for her to respond, he was relieved when she came into the room. "Sit, please." She did not speak and he knew she was still angry, but she did sit as he asked. "Would you care for a drink? Something to eat?"

"I have things to do," she said coolly.

Hagan, determined to get past her bitterness, not liking to have his sister angry with him, continued in an amicable fashion. "How is Lord Cliáth?" It was a topic he believed she would be willing to talk about and the one he most wanted to hear good news about.

The question did foster a change on her face, but it was a change from bitterness to sadness to confusion, and Hagan was sorry for having brought the matter up. "No change yet...at least that is what Physician Talis says. He will not allow me into..."

"What good would it do to see him if he's asleep? After what you...what he...he should be allowed to recover and welcome visitors as he feels able, not have us waking him to appease ourselves."

It was the first wise words Diona believed she had ever heard from him, but they did not satisfy her and she scowled deeper. "I should be allowed to apologize."

"You can't do that when he's sleeping. Leave him be. He'll wake up soon enough. Has Captain Delamo said anything?"

She shook her head. "He refuses to discuss where they were, what they've done, what happened, until Kavan allows it. I commend his loyalty; I know what it means to Kavan, but he has oaths to..."

"He resigned his position when Father was alive. He might be our subject, but he's no longer in our employ…"

At the mention of their father, Diona stared out the window and pretended to shield her eyes from the early morning sun when it was tears she was shielding against. Hagan missed the man, but he had not been as close to their father as Diona had been.

It was partially in their father's memory, for family solidarity with the only close family he had left, that he murmured, "I apologize for yesterday. You are right…and I was shortsighted. Whether or not I believed the man's story, I should have investigated it before speaking to suspects, before letting him go out into harm's way. I should have heard him out and protected him. I don't believe his accusations were true, nor do I believe his death, as untimely as it was, has anything to do with his coming to me or with his claims. I should not have been angry with your efforts to point out my error. You did your duty as my advisor, my sister, a Lachlan. I should have listened."

"If you say so, my lord," she sighed. He had always had a habit of apologizing for everything, whether his fault or not, whether he meant it or not, because he did not want her, or their father, to be angry with him. He knew how to put on a demeanor of contrition, but only a change in his actions would verify if he meant it or not.

Finished with his meal, he stretched and got up. "I have to speak with Lord Bhíncári and find out what Lords Cáner and Agis have learned about last night's events…see if General Zarkosta has any news yet about Lord Cliáth's attackers. I do wish Lord Dugan would hurry back. This would be much simpler if he was here. Have you heard from him?"

She shook her head without looking at him, wondering why, if he believed things ran more smoothly when the inquisitor was here, he refused to permit the man to do his job. "No. Surely he and Wilred will be here for your celebration."

"He had better be. If not, I will be forced to summon him back. Too much is happening here. I need him. Without his expertise…"

"Expertise you do not utilize to its potential," she muttered.

Ignoring her interruption, he continued, "…and with Prince Espen returning to Hatu, I am short…

"What? When?"

The announcement made her straighten in the chair with an expression of alarm. He had said he was going to wait for her return. Yes, she had returned…that same day…but since she had not seen him since her departure and subsequent arrival, she did not know if he even knew she was home. Maybe he did. Maybe he was expecting her to come to him late last evening…or first thing this morning…or else he had been planning this retreat even while telling her he would wait.

"Not until after the celebration, thankfully. Not until Lord Cliáth's health is improved…or he dies…"

"He's not going to die!"

Hagan patted her hand. "Of course not. Prince Espen is merely waiting as a precaution in case his condition or return results in rioting. Once the celebration is over, he intends to go home to…"

"He cannot leave!" Not without speaking to her first. Whether he intended a short visit home or to go and never return, Diona could not allow him to leave without speaking to him. She rose so abruptly that the wooden legs of her chair screeched across the paneled wood floor.

"If you wish to catch him, I suggest you do so soon…"

She did not hear him as she hurried off in search of Espen.

≈*≈

The news of Kavan's return was, to Asta, as it was to many others in Rhidam's keep, the best news heard in months. She could not wait to share it with her father. While not as close to Kavan as some, the bard had assisted in saving Caol's son, Asta's brother, and had kept the inquisitor's secrets until he had been prepared to reveal them to King Arlan himself. The two had spent time traveling and working together and Asta knew her father would want to know the Elyri was home. He would also want to know because once the word spread, it would have a considerable impact on the population…though whether that impact would be good or bad she could not guess.

At the first opportunity she could find, which was easy enough with her father gone and only her tutor to hide from, Asta snuck out of the castle and ran to the street corner where she frequently met Marta. Today, however, the girl was nowhere to be found. Asta ticked off the list of places where Marta might be, checking each one, but the girl was still missing. A one-armed fellow she finally made contact with, someone she had seen her father talk to before, agreed to tell Marta that Asta wanted to see her, to make sure Marta went to the castle as soon as possible. There was no guarantee the message would be given, but she had to trust that it would be. She could stay outside no longer without being missed.

What she did verify during that outing was that, thus far, it seemed no one was aware that the White Bard had returned to Enesfel. His late-night arrival in the midst of a Lachlan military unit had kept him hidden and the soldiers, it seemed, had not yet gossiped. For the time being, things would remain as calm as they could be. That one most influential Elyri could not inadvertently cause chaos for the King.

It was unfortunate that such a peaceful man could be the centerpiece of trouble, but it was exactly what his return could be. And she knew that Kavan undoubtedly knew that too.

It was difficult to leave Kavan's side, but Zelenka needed his attention, or at least deserved his time, and Wortham knew it was unfair to leave her confined to her room in a house full of unfamiliar people and customs. When Gaelán suggested bringing gdhededhá Tusánt to see Kavan, to bless him and pray over him in the hopes that it would speed his recovery, the captain agreed and waited for the dedhá's arrival. He refused to allow other visitors until Kavan could invite them in, but the Elyri gdhededhá seemed an acceptable exception to that decision. A man of Faith who could intercede in prayer might be just what Kavan needed. Wortham stayed with him until Tusánt and a novice named Edward arrived and then he half-heartedly joined Zelenka for breakfast.

Having spent many years in this palace, he could find his way anywhere, and after a morning meal unlike any Zelenka had ever experienced, he decided to start her familiarization of the keep in the back gardens. Of all of the places in Rhidam, he believed she would be happiest there, with an abundance of flowering foliage similar to the Káliel garden she had been so taken with. The sun was warm, the day pleasant, the sky clear, and they had nowhere else to be. She could enjoy the pleasantries here without feeling rushed. For now, their travels were over. It was time she started to feel at home somewhere.

In the hot, arid, largely barren lands where Zelenka had grown up, green flowering plants rarely sprouted and lasted for only a few weeks a year except on the banks of occasional mountain-fed tributaries. Irrigation meant those in the southern lands could produce crops, enough to manage a meager existence, and there was water enough far below the surface that, as long as a person or group was prepared to dig for it and establish a well, communities could flourish. For

Zelenka, the Káliel garden, the Levonne vineyards, and the forested stretch on the road to Rhidam, had been places of awe and wonder. This perfectly manicured garden of fruit trees, groomed hedges and flowering plants kept her spellbound with a delight Wortham was happy to see. Each new blossom had to be touched, smelled, and compared to the last. She wanted to try each new fruit but he explained that it was forbidden without the King's permission. She instead turned her attention to asking questions about their flavors, their textures, the flowers, and the plants themselves.

Wortham was at a loss to answer her. Weapons he knew. Combat he knew. If she had asked about ships and life at sea, he could have fumbled his way through answers. Plants, however, gardening and agriculture, he knew little about. She was frustrated with his inability to answer, and he began to believe she thought he was intentionally withholding information in an effort to rush through the garden tour.

He was spared a potential confrontation between his willingness versus his ability when a matronly woman he recognized as one of the groundskeepers, a woman who had tended the Lachlan gardens most of her life, overheard them speaking and stepped in with the offered information. Wortham graciously accepted the woman's aid, and was grateful that, as with other women they had met on their journey, Zelenka showed only an initial shyness before eagerly beginning to open up. As soon as Zelenka realized that the woman could answer her questions, as well as ones she had not yet thought of, and was not bothered by the awkwardness of their language barrier, Zelenka latched onto her as if she was her new best friend.

Given that Wortham had witnessed little social interaction between Zelenka and anyone in her village beside her mother, perhaps this was her first friend.

It quickly became apparent that the captain's company was not required, and when he excused himself, he was surprised and pleased that Zelenka responded with a smile and wave rather than with uneasy clinginess. It was for the best. Because they would be staying in this place for the foreseeable future, Zelenka would have the chance to meet others, make friends, develop personal interests she had been unable to do while caring for her ailing mother or during the long journey north. For however long Kavan chose to stay in Rhidam, Zelenka needed things to do that would not require Wortham constantly at her side.

After the past several months of her companionship, however, the change in routine was going to be awkward for them both.

With her happily occupied, Wortham gratefully returned to where he felt he belonged. He wanted to be there when Kavan woke up, as he had promised he would be. He wanted the bard to know that he had stayed by his side from the beginning of their journey to the end.

If Tusánt had not heard the tales and believed them to be true due to the credibility and honesty of the tellers, he would not have placed such high significance on the sight he now beheld. Kavan had survived his brutal beating, and wherever his journey had taken him, he had returned home. His will, his mind, his body were strong, tenacious, and he would never be easily defeated, even by those who wished him dead, so Tusánt was not surprised by the bard's perseverance.

But he was surprised that those deformities associated with his attack had been erased from his body. His hands were as whole as they had ever been, and Tusánt was amazed. He had prayed for that very thing, yes, as had others, but had any of them expected, or believed, it was possible? There was no other word for it except miracle, and when those others, who knew the rumors of Kavan's disfigurement, learned of his healing, they would proclaim the miracle too.

Seeing the bard, seeing this healing with his own eyes, were the last things he expected when he was summoned to the castle under a veil of privacy and secrecy. The news of the bard's return, particularly while he was incapable of self-defense, would be troublesome. Some would rejoice at his homecoming, for the miracle that had made him whole. Others would greet the news with gnashing teeth and angry curses, while others would shrug and care not at all. If Rhidam was lucky, the dedhá mused as he sprinkled blessed water over Kavan's sleeping form, the first and last groups would far outweigh the second. Kavan deserved a homecoming of quiet calm. Tusánt doubted very much he would get it.

Bhríd stepped back and inspected the work the men had done in cleaning the vandalized wall of the Eagle's Nest Inn. Fortunately, because of the establishment's proximity to the keep, the palace sentries had intervened before much damage was done. What was left, however, the anti-Elyri slander and anti-Faith symbols rarely seen in the centuries since the Faith's rise to prominence, were drawn in both blood and excrement. Some had washed off easily, the rest would have to be covered with fresh plaster and whitewash or else remain visible, a reminder for the entire city, until the weather eroded it away.

There was no way of knowing if the blood was Teren, Elyri, or animal. An Elyri's attempt to read blood alone was rarely successful, as they instead read impressions left on the surface where the blood was spilled or splashed. Bhríd believed, however, that the volume of blood needed for something like this necessitated either one large donor…such as a cow or horse, or several smaller ones…people or smaller animals. With no recently reported murders or disappearances, he judged the blood to have come from animal sources, and thus he had already sent the justice off to question the local butchers, hoping there had been some unreported theft or a large recent purchase that they could track down to locate those guilty of this offense. It was a long shot, but so far there were no other leads to pursue.

Despite the proximity to the castle and the early detection of the crime in progress, none of the perpetrators had been apprehended in the subsequent chase. Anyone living near the castle or who spent enough time observing it could have determined the schedules of the duty guards and had thus chosen an adequate time to act and be gone without being caught. None of the vandals' faces had been seen, there were few witnesses except for the soldiers who had discovered them in the act, raised the alarm, and given pursuit, so finding them would be nearly impossible. The best man for that job was several day's ride northwest of Rhidam. By the time of his return, any trail would have grown cold.

Or so most of King Hagan's court thought. Few would have guessed, or believed, that Caol Dugan had been part of the night's mischief. After escaping the pursuing guards and spending a considerable amount of time in hiding, he found his way to the rendezvous point, arriving, as he expected, ahead of Layton or any of the others. Or at least there was no one in the gutted, charred remains they had chosen as a meeting place when he dashed inside. Fuming, fretting over events he had warned about, he paced in the darkness, wanting to pummel Layton, or someone, for taking such a foolish risk with their lives to prove some sort of point to the Crown.

When Layton finally appeared, along with two others who had been the primary organizers of the effort, the normally cocky stooped man was visibly shaken and it gave the inquisitor just enough of a pause to prevent him from knocking the man to the ground.

It did not keep him from snapping, "Where have you been?"

"Ducking patrols," muttered one of the others between gasps for breath. Layton was holding his side; the other was trying not to cough.

The admission caused Caol to quickly check every escape route in the building, wanting to be sure they had not been followed. "Idiots…you haven't led them here, have you?"

Layton snorted defensively though he sounded like he too was concerned about the possibility. "Don't assume the worst, Alty; we took precautions Haven't seen them in hours." The quick darting of his eyes towards their entrance point, when noises outside filtered into the building, belied his reassurance that they had lost their tail.

The second man, no longer fighting a cough, flopped down on the dirty floor and wheezed, "We kept running to be certain."

"Think we've been up and down every alley at least twice."

"Better pray that's true," Caol grunted.

Groaning as he leaned against a burnt wall, his action cautious in case the beam shifted, Layton reluctantly said, "Maybe should have listened to you, but at least we got the point across."

It was more of an apology than Caol expected, but he was not prepared to let the matter drop. "Did we? A few hastily scribbled words of hate on an inn are not going to bring about social change. They will have most of it washed off already…and we'll be lucky if no one saw our faces…"

"So what do you suggest?" From Layton's tone, it was as much an honest plea as it was a challenge for the newcomer Alty to prove he could do a better job of planning. Little did they know that at one time he had single-handedly arranged to keep the castle under siege long enough to temporarily kidnap the woman he would one day marry as a stalling tactic to keep then King Owain from engaging Prince Arlan's army too soon.

He had no immediate plan in mind, however. He had not expected to need one. "I don't know…but there has to be something…"

"Not too public," whined one of the others. "Anonymity is the whole point…"

"That was hardly anonymous," Caol snorted.

"Don't you think we would have more success if we strike closer to home, take someone close to the Crown," the man on the floor challenged the first. "If the ignorant could put a face to…"

Gauging by the eye-rolling of the other, and Layton's ignoring them, Caol guessed it was a common argument between the two. Not in the mood for debate and knowing this was not the best place for it, Caol snapped, "No." As much as he knew that having a face to represent a cause could be a good and productive thing, if the cause was right and just, he also knew that their cause was nothing of that sort. Most of the group's activities to date had been malicious or illegal or both, and the cause they were striving for happened to conflict with the position of the Crown. Any faces to connect with the activities of the cells going by the name of Coryllien were doomed to arrest, torture, and execution.

It was the end Caol wanted for all of them, but as Alty, he had to think smart to remain on the inside.

"Too risky. We will not succeed unless we turn the hearts and minds of the Lachlans against the Elyri. Killing the ones they employ will only strengthen their anger and position against us, will push them to protect them. We have to find other ways."

Layton leaned forward. "How do we do that?"

"I don't know." There were obvious answers, of course, but he happened to like the Elyri he knew and he was not about to suggest ways of killing any of them…or anyone else. Someone had already tried to lure Ártur from under the Lachlan protection. Thank k'Ádhá they had failed, largely due to the intervention of a power no Teren could have foreseen. If it had not been Layton and his group who had dreamed up that plot, however, who had it been? Was there a second cell in Rhidam he had not yet encountered. Or someone else?

Plotting and participating in terror and property destruction was one thing. Getting someone maimed or killed was another, especially if that someone might be a friend or family member.

"Well…" Layton rubbed his jaw. "It's something to think about and bring up next time. We should seek better shelter…get some rest."

Go back to their normal lives. Those were words Caol heard though they were never said.

The two others staggered out of the dilapidated building, each through a different opening and each in different directions. Before he followed them, Layton offered his hand to Caol with a sagging smile.

"Good work, Alty. You did right by us…even if they don't see it yet. Counts for a lot."

Caol accepted the handshake and nodded his gratitude. He was pleased to be gaining Layton's trust and hoped it would bring him closer to the core of the Corylliens, to that fellow named Heward. There were drawbacks, however, as he knew he might eventually have to kill to prove his loyalty. But he could not think about that risk now; he would have to deal with the possibility when it came.

Having Ártur home full time was what Syl had longed for since the day she left Rhidam to raise her children in the safety of her homeland. He was attentive, waiting on her though she no longer required it, he tended to duties around her parents' home that did not need doing, and he spent a great deal of time with the children, the way he had done, as much as duty allowed, when they lived together as a family in the castle. But he was not a man for domestic life and it did not take her long to see the restlessness creeping into his eyes. Having spent much of his life in the company of nobility, waited on and provided with a never-ending stream of people demanding attention and care, the reversal of roles did not suit him. He did not complain, but she knew.

As much as they loved one another, a fact of which she had little doubt in spite of her recent fits of anger and accusation, they were both used to the flurry of dozens of others filling their daily lives. And while Syl was mostly content with the company of her children, her parents, her family, and those friends and neighbors she had known since childhood, Ártur's life had removed him from all of those things and replaced it with the role of court healer. She did not think he would ever be able to put that behind him.

It had taken a full day of resuming her life, leaving Ártur for little to do, for Syl to realize she loved him too much to keep him caged. He spent the calm hours of his day on the porch watching people pass, or pacing as he waited for Llucás to return for the night, playing with Chethá when Syl was busy, and to Syl, he looked miserable. He was, despite her accusations, a man willing to fight for his family and be there when they needed him. A family that included his cousin. A good man trying to do right by everyone while also trying to stay true to himself. Those were things she had fallen in love with and she knew it was wrong to penalize him for it, even with the most justifiable of fears.

Their evening meal was cleaned away and the children settled into bed before she found him behind the house, staring into the darkness in the direction of Rhidam. When she stopped behind him and wrapped her arms around him for the first time in weeks, he gave a guilty start and quickly refocused his gaze on something closer.

"You seem anxious," she murmured, her cheek pressed between his shoulders.

Wanting to avoid the fight he believed was coming over a perceived preoccupation with Rhidam, but not wanting to lie, and admittedly confused by her gesture of affection, Ártur shook his head and stammered, "It is nothing…a feeling I have that something has happened…and as I do not have the Sight, I am likely imagining it."

"You long to be there."

There was no accusation her tone this time, but still he denied it. "I told you…"

She chuckled softly and turned him in her arms to face her. "My ankle is healed. You know that. Llucás is with your family during the day and I can manage Chethá on my own. It is too late today, of course, but I can care for our family during the hours when you are not here. I will worry about you constantly…fear for you…but I can bear it if I know you are coming back to me."

Wide-eyed, Ártur stared, wondering if he dared hope she meant what she said. When he did not speak, she pulled his head down and kissed his mouth.

"That does not mean that everything is right," she murmured. "As long as your life is in peril, I will be unhappy, but at least I understand. And I know you mean well by your family. All of your family." She tugged on his hands affectionately. "Stay with me…tonight…and in the morning we resume our previous arrangement. I will expect to have you back with me tomorrow night, and every night possible thereafter. And tell Hagan…I will consider his invitation."

"Of course!" he agreed eagerly. In an ideal world, there would be peace in Enesfel and he and his family would be safe together in Rhidam, the way they had been before. But as long as Syl accepted his duty, accepted him, as long as there was hope for their marriage, the world was as right as it could be and Ártur was happy.

❧ * ❧

After that hostile brush with the Teren dedhá, the boy had taken to following him around Rhidam, recording his movements on a stolen scroll, whenever the choir's rehearsal schedule or performance did not conflict with the man's movements. The boy loved the music too much to miss those rehearsals, but he was curious too, about Claide and about the person the dedhá wanted dead. In spite of his efforts, however, he had yet to find clues about who that person might be.

He knew from the spying he had done that there was little love between Claide and the Elyri dedhá with whom he served. The two men avoided each other as much as their duties to the Faith allowed. It was for gdhededhá Tusánt that the boy continued his spying, believing fervently that Tusánt was the man Claide wanted dead.

Besides, it gave him something useful to do in the too many long hours he spent alone each day.

This day, judging by the man's formal attire, Claide was going somewhere important and the boy scurrying behind him in the shadows could not wait to find out where.

When Caol first heard the rumors he was skeptical. It was well known by the Corylliens, and everyone else, that the White Bard was likely the Lachlans' closest advisor, and most beloved, which made him, of all of the Elyri in Rhidam, potentially the most dangerous, and perhaps also the most feared. Rumors, positive and negative, factual and fanciful, had surrounded Kavan all of his life, particularly after he came to Enesfel in support of Prince Arlan's bid to be king. A rumor declaring his return to Rhidam was not necessarily anything more than that. Caol had been unable to make contact with Asta to verify it, but when his early morning foray today led him to cross paths with dedhá Claide, he followed him towards the castle and stopped in the shadows upon overhearing a conversation between the dedhá and the gate guards that proved the rumor to be true.

If Wortham Delamo was in Rhidam it was likely Kavan was as well. Regardless of his state of health, the bard was in Rhidam, and alive, and Caol wondered, as he watched the dedhá enter the courtyard, why that news had brought Claide to the castle.

What Caol was certain of was that it was news Claide was not happy to hear.

❧*❧

It was the nearest the boy had been to the castle since his last attempt to make contact with the Elyri chamberlain. His failed efforts and the attitudes of the guard had led him to give the gates a wide berth out of fear of imprisonment and he had no idea the chamberlain was looking for him. Curious about his suspect's business, the boy watched the Teren dedhá disappear through the gates and decided to remain in hiding until his return rather than try to follow him inside.

The castle was teeming with Elyri. The boy did not know how many, but it was his impression that there were so many there that it made Elyri-hating Claide's visit a ridiculous thing. His decision to remain to watch, however, was sidetracked when he noticed someone else there to watch as well, someone whose stance and behavior made the boy nervous. Deciding he could not afford trouble, he opted for retreat to a distant block where Claide would have to pass on his way back to the náós…if that was where the man went upon his completion of business here.

❧*❧

It did not matter to Diona that it had been barely over a day since Kavan's return. His extended sleep concerned her, despite Rouvyn's assurance that such a period of recovery, for Kavan, was normal. The princess was certain he was awake and avoiding her, or certain there was something wrong that she was not being told about, and she voiced her worries to anyone who would listen in the hopes that someone might be able to do something to help, particularly if that something would get her into his room. She was prepared to resort to the use of royal prerogative, to force her way in uninvited, but entering the bard's room uninvited had started this nightmare, and she had learned a hard lesson from that. Never again would she invade Kavan's privacy without a solid, imperative reason.

Longing to see him was hardly imperative.

As the sun rose on the start of Kavan's second day in Rhidam, the princess was, however, preparing to use her prerogative for something else. Healer MacLyr should be here. He would be able to fix whatever was wrong, cause Kavan to wake, set everything right. She knew he was caring for his injured wife, and she did not begrudge him his time with his family after the attack that had nearly killed him. But she did not think he knew of Kavan's return, as he should, thus she planned to send Bhríd to Bhryell for him as soon as the man awoke, whether her brother approved or not. With Bhyrhán having traveled to St. Kóráhm's so that he could see the place before the King's celebration, it left only the chamberlain, and if he did not appear soon, she would wake him herself.

The sound of footsteps caused her to turn from her pacing in the corridor and when she locked eyes with the healer she had just been thinking about, she rushed to him, threw her arms around his neck and exclaimed, "Praise be you are back!"

Having noted her pacing as he stepped out of the chapel, Ártur wondered if she had been waiting for him. Her tone, her actions, filled him with dread. She had been closest to Gaelán's room when he had first seen her, thus his initial fears were for the young man he had left in his stead. "What has happened to Gaelán?"

"Not Gaelán, it is…"

"Good morning, My Lady…Healer MacLyr." gdhededhá Claide acknowledged the Elyri only because the princess was there and would expect such courtesy from him. He did not look at the Healer as he spoke, but continued, "I came as soon as I heard the news. I knew you would want someone to offer Lord Cliáth the Last Rites…"

"Last Rites?" both Diona and Ártur exclaimed at once, one in panic and disbelief before he threw open the door to his cousin's room and the other in shock and fury as she glared at the insolent clergyman.

"He is not dying! Who told you that?"

Claide, realizing too late his error, did his best to salvage the situation without making matters worse. "People talk, My Lady. You know how news changes when it spreads…"

She understood gossip, and though those that knew about Kavan's return had been sworn to silence, she knew that servants, in particular, liked to talk as they worked. It was possible the dedhá had overheard idle discussion that suggested the newly returned bard was close to death, speculation about a closed door and no one being allowed inside. It was also possible that the gleam of joy she believed she had seen in Claide's eyes and heard in his voice was her imagination because she expected that reaction from a man who hated Elyri…and Kavan most of all.

"Aye…as do you," she hissed. "It would be wise of you to learn the truth before assuming the worst…"

Her condescending, bitter tone and use of the word man in reference to the Elyri set Claide's nerves on edge but he forced a polite bow, partially to hide his annoyance, and said, "Of course, My Lady. May I see him? Having a man of Faith pray over him might…"

Diona shook her head. "No one is allowed to enter without permission from the healers…not even me."

While he knew she was angry, that she would not likely have permitted him into the room, he could also tell that her words were true. She was not keeping him out simply for spite. Perhaps the bard carried some contagion and the healers wanted to keep it from spreading. If that was true, the dedhá was not about to take such a risk with his life. When he spoke again, however, it was without another bow. "Very well. Please let them know I was here, that the offer stands. I will come at once if I'm summoned."

"I will tell them." Unable to believe he would drop whatever he was doing to rush to Kavan's bedside if summoned, she chose not to tell him that Tusánt had already been here. Any desire Claide had to see Kavan was not out of benevolence, was not meant to pray over him for healing. Any prayers the man would likely offer would be for death. And he might even try to kill the bard himself. Both possibilities seemed reason enough to keep Claide away as long as possible. Rouvyn's order made it easier to do so in a diplomatic fashion.

Inside the room, with Wortham keeping silent watch from the bedside chair, Ártur pulled his cousin into his arms and held him to his chest, weeping with joy and relief to see Kavan alive and home. Though he had prayed for this day, he had carried deep fear that it would never come. Seeing him, smelling the familiar scent of incense that always seemed to cling to Kavan, touching his skin and hair, they were all proof that he was home and to Ártur, the reality of his misplaced fear was what mattered.

He opened his eyes to look at the sun-browned and haggard captain. The man was leaner, worn and weary, but his face showed no worry for Kavan's condition. Like much else when it came to Kavan, Wortham had great faith he would be well, even when others did not.

"When did you…?"

Wortham bent forward, elbows on his knees. "Two night's past."

"No one sent for me?" Ártur was both hurt and angry.

"Lord Cáner has been engaged with pressing duties…and I'm told there was another Elyri here who is away to St. Kóráhm's. By the time the chamberlain was free last night, I was told you could not come."

He did not know why dedhá Tusánt had not been sent. Perhaps he was occupied with duty as well. There were questions in the captain's voice but he would not push for answers. He was too respectful for that. "For Kavan, I would have," the healer snorted in frustration, perturbed that his living arrangement had kept him away when Kavan needed him, and would pull him away again at day's end. He gently settled his cousin back into the pillows.

"I am sure you would have been…and I would have…" The captain's failed, fumbling words were aborted by the healer's gasp as he adjusted the sheet around Kavan and noticed the bard's hands.

Clutching them tightly, not thinking he might awaken Kavan in doing so, not certain what he was seeing was real, he poured healing energy into them to test their condition, to be assured that this was no illusion or trick. "How…?" he began. "When…?"

Wortham shook his head. "You will need to discuss that with him when he awakens." Despite whatever right Ártur had to know, Wortham knew Kavan would not be comfortable with anyone discussing his healing behind his back, not even his best friend and dearest cousin. Besides, Wortham did not know how it had been done. Only Kavan had the answers.

Knowing Kavan's concern for privacy and dislike of gossip and the proclamation of miracles, Ártur understood the captain's reluctance, but it did not satisfy the healer's curiosity. "They are fully restored. No residual fracturing…no tearing of tissue…no bruising, no scarring…this cannot be…"

"And yet it is," Wortham assured him. "You see it for yourself." Watching as the healer's hands traced over Kavan's bare arms and torso, the captain held his breath as long as he dared before asking, "He is well? Master Cáner and Healer Talis say he is…" But Ártur was more experienced, more skilled, and knew Kavan better than anyone. Wortham would feel much more secure in Ártur's diagnosis.

"I find no damage or defect," Ártur muttered, attention divided. "Only residual bruising. They have done well. What happened? Why is he…?" He had not been back long enough to hear the news but there must have been some injury, some traumatic event, for Kavan to shut down the way he had. The healer had seen this in his cousin before.

Thinking perhaps it was what awaited Kavan with others, particularly the princess, that Kavan was avoiding, Wortham chose his reply carefully. "We were attacked on the road from Levonne. He took an arrow in his back during the ambush, suffered a fall and bruising during the scuffle. I dared not remove it myself…but shock set in before I could get him adequate aid."

"Brigands?" It was possible someone had recognized Kavan and attacked him for being the White Bard, or for being Elyri, but with the general pervasive lawlessness plaguing Enesfel, the attack might have been a crime of opportunity.

"I do not know. The majority were killed for their effort. If there were others, they fled. There was no one to question."

"Good." His Healer's Oaths would permit him to harm no man, but when it came to Kavan's welfare, that oath did not prevent him from wishing harm on those who dared to hurt his cousin. "He is asleep. Once his internal equilibrium is restored, he will awaken."

"And I will be here when he does." At least, that was Wortham's intention, and he wanted to assure Ártur that even if the healer could not be here when Kavan awoke, the bard would not be alone. Day or night, Wortham wanted to be the first face Kavan saw upon waking.

Knowing he would be gone during the nights, despite his wishes to the contrary, Ártur knew there was a chance he would not be here when Kavan opened his eyes. He was jealous of anyone who could be. He considered asking Syl to grant him this one brief alteration to their agreement, to stay until Kavan awoke, but after just regaining his wife's favor, he did not dare take the risk.

If he could not be here, then it was best if the captain was. Whatever hell Kavan had endured during his months away, Wortham had remained at his side. It would not do to begrudge such loyalty this privilege.

"Stay with him, Wortham…and if he needs anything, swear to me you will let me know. I do not care how…swear to me."

Wortham nodded gravely. "If he needs you, you will know." Even if Wortham had to search all of Rhidam for another Elyri to take him to Bhryell, to the healer, himself.

❧Chapter 26 ❧

It was dark when he opened his eyes. Night. Early or late, he wondered, flexing his fingers to be certain his waking was no dream. A quick assessment of the surface beneath his hand and the canopy above that he could see without turning his head revealed that he was in a bed. His bed. Rhidam. An involuntary shudder ran through him born of anxiety and awkward discomfort. There was no recollection of how he had gotten here, forcing his thoughts backward in search of his last memories. Wortham, and others, tripping over him…more than once. The arrow in his back. The ambush.

Filled with a sudden panic for the welfare of his companions, he bolted upright and was rewarded with the sight of Wortham slouched in a nearby chair, his head hanging back, snoring steadily, unresponsive to Kavan's abrupt movement. While seeing the captain did not tell Kavan what had happened to Zelenka and Urian, for the moment he was satisfied that his best friend was safe. It allowed Kavan to relax into his pillow with a relieved sigh.

There was no pain, a realization that told him he had been under the care of a healer, Ártur or Gaelán, possibly both. That meant they, at least, knew he was here, and most likely everyone else in the Lachlan keep did too. It would have been impossible to keep a secret of that magnitude from the King or his sister. The fleeting thought of Diona pulled a groan from him and he closed his eyes with the determination of banishing those dark memories. He missed the bright little girl she had been, inquisitive and insistent, demanding to know the truth, fair-minded, honest and loyal. The child had been buried beneath the onslaught of womanhood and her determined quest to make him the object of her affections. Perhaps, as Muir indicated, she had learned her lesson, but even if they found a way past the mistakes she had made and the pain she had caused, he did not believe their relationship would ever be the same.

Nor should it be. Just as his relationship with her father had changed when Arlan had gone from lonesome boy to King of Enesfel, Diona was no longer a child to be treated as such. And Kavan was no longer the man he had been. He could forgive her, perhaps, but he would never be able to forget.

Too weary to dwell on such matters, his body eager to take advantage of the relatively safe haven the castle offered, in order to recover from months of grueling travel, Kavan gave in to the luxury of sleep. He had no wish to flee, and the only reason to rise meant facing the world and the people he had left behind. He was not prepared for that. The inevitable confrontations would come soon enough. There was no need to seek them out.

❧*❧

The last thing Saul expected to find when he stepped outside that morning was mounds of upturned earth dotting the burial grounds to the right of the heavy double doors. He frowned, looked behind him through the door he held open, and wondered whom he should tell first. It might be nothing more than the harmless prank of mischief makers, it might have been a set of hasty burials during the night, but given the political climate, and the rumors heard from nearby villages, nothing had a bad habit of turning out to be something. Most often something ugly and unfortunate.

At the front of the Gathering Hall, Edward was preparing the candles for the morning Gathering. Edward was one of the few people Saul knew he could trust, as he learned his way around Rhidam and met new faces daily. He whistled and waved for the other novice to join him. Edward lay down the flint and firestone on the closest bench and came to the summons without asking questions. Nor did he ask questions when he saw what Saul was pointing at. They shared a quick glance and in unison cautiously chose to take a closer look at the disturbed section of the náós grounds.

During the reign of King Innis, it had become necessary to create additional burial grounds, one to the northeast of Rhidam's center, one to the south. Few were interred in the náós grounds any longer; when they were, they were either wealthy patrons, people of import, or else individuals appointed to be buried there at the discretion of either the Crown or the k'gdhededhá. Frequently those burials were foreigners without kin in Enesfel, and as such, as a result of the recent anti-Elyri violence, a relatively high number of those buried here were Elyri.

With that knowledge in mind, it was a surprise for the novices to discover that each of the disturbed graves had, judging by the names on the headstones, not been Elyri. They counted six mounds of upturned earth, six holes filled with some foul-smelling, dark sticky substance which Saul guessed was a mixture of waste and blood. It was a message, but he was more concerned with what had been done with the missing remains than with what the message might be.

"We must show the dedhá," murmured Edward in a sickly tone.

"And the Justice," Saul agreed, equally revolted. "He'll want to investigate."

But to what end? There seemed to be nothing worth investigating that might offer clues, nothing worth knowing other than the obvious. But neither novice was trained for criminal investigation and both knew they might be overlooking something important. It was decided that Edward would fetch Tusánt and Justice Corbin while Saul kept watch in the desecrated graveyard. It was not a duty Saul relished, but they could allow no one to fill in the holes or disturb them until the authorities saw them. And if need be, he would keep people away; the smell alone would be enough to both attract and repel the curious. They had to do their best to stave off panic and quash rumors before they began. Rhidam did not need more reasons to be afraid.

The second time Kavan awoke it was to realize he was alone in a slightly brighter room. He sat with a lazy stretch, testing muscles as his glance at the window confirmed that the hour was just past dawn. Noises within the water closet told him he was not alone and he assumed, without testing the aura, that it would be Wortham with him still. Two harps rested on his dresser, the red kestrel that had once belonged to Eridel and the other, more familiar black kestrel he had missed so dearly. As neither instrument was in a case, Kavan guessed someone had set them to be in his line of sight, and again the odds lay with Wortham. It was the sort of thoughtful gesture the captain would make. Seeing them had the desired effect, making him smile wistfully and filling him with the long-buried need to play.

He had no desire to move yet beyond sitting, and did not want to wait for Wortham to come back into the room to bring his harp to him.

But he wanted the feel of his instrument in his hands, the perfect excuse to practice a skill he rarely used, one he had never tried in the company of anyone other than Tíbhyan. It had always seemed a lazy thing, and so Kavan rarely even tried. Today, with his heart filled to bursting with long-unused power, it was easy to extend one hand, wrap the black wooden frame in ropes of energy, and pull it towards him without the physical need of touch. It was the same way skill, the same power, he had used to collapse Pháne's cave into itself, only less destructive.

Two doors opened and two men, Wortham from the water closet and Ártur from the corridor, stared at the harp hovering in the air between them. The healer was more surprised by the unusual display of ability than Wortham, but Kavan only glanced back and forth between them, saying nothing until the harp was safely in his lap.

"It is a relief to see you awake, my lord," Wortham said, his tone more formal than he would have used if they had been alone. He maintained his dignity and allowed Kavan to keep his, though his smile and the brightness of his eyes conveyed more emotion than his words or actions. Ártur, however, did not hesitate to rush to embrace his cousin the way he had the day before, although this time expecting an embrace in return. It had been too long and the healer needed to express his relief and affection regardless of Kavan's comfort.

"You have no idea how…"

Accepting the embrace out of the same relief and affection and joy, awkwardly returning it with closed eyes, Kavan murmured, "I do, Ártur…and it is good to see you well."

The healer choked on his sudden discomfort as he drew back from the hug far enough to sink onto the edge of the bed. "I would not be…if not for you and Gaelán…"

Not wishing to discuss his contribution to saving Ártur's life, still chagrined at having taken other lives to do so though he did not regret it, Kavan leaned against the headboard and mound of pillows piled there. "It appears we both owe him our lives." He pushed his hair out of his face. "Do you know who…?"

"There was little to identify…they were all dead…but it is fair to guess that the Coryllien extremists were responsible."

That name made Kavan shiver. "How active are they?"

"Too active. Not a week goes by without something happening they claim responsibility for. Vandalism, fires, beatings, murders. In all of my years in Enesfel, I have never seen it so bad for our people. Even k'dedhá Jermyn was…"

"I know." Kavan sighed and rubbed his eyes. The memories he had been shown of that man's torturous death haunted him still when he dared to think about it. It made him feel sick and guilty that he had reacted so abysmally to his own attack when Jermyn's, and even Ártur's, had been so much worse. "I fear it will continue to worsen, but I am hopeful that matters will be set right soon."

Sensing that Kavan meant something specific, that his cousin had Seen something or had a plan, Ártur scowled. "I don't see how it can be, unless all Elyri leave Enesfel…or die."

His hopes for reassurance, answers, or a hint of what Kavan knew remained unfulfilled. Kavan only stifled a yawn before asking, "Was he given a proper burial?"

"Jermyn? Yes; at St. Kóráhm's. We thought it would be…"

"Fitting." As Alberni was the man's birthplace, and he had served in the order of St. Kóráhm until his appointment in Rhidam, there was no better place for the man to rest. His body could have been taken to Clarys, for burial amongst others of the Order, but Kavan knew he belonged there no longer. Enesfel was his home. In St. Kóráhm's plot, the man's body was safe from further defilement, defilement that would surely have raised an uproar if those in Clarys had seen it.

"Owain? Hagan?"

"Owain should be here for the King's day, or sooner if he learns you're here. Hagan…" The healer's smile faded. "He is not Arlan."

"He is young, inexperienced, and faced with a terror he is ill-equipped to fight." Even Arlan would have found combatting this evil to be a difficult thing.

"I know. I hope that is all it is. I pray every day he has a chance to learn from this…that he has a hand in restoring Enesfel's peace. It will be a shame if his name in the history annals is forever linked with the destructiveness of the Corylliens."

Feeling a cold prickle run up his back and neck and settle into a throbbing pain behind his eyes, Kavan muttered, "I hope so too." He had doubts about Hagan's future, but he would do his best to prevent any negative outcome for the young King. With the ever-present prophecy in the back of his mind, a prophecy that harkened back to the day of Diona's birth, Hagan's fate was a persistent worry. There was no way to predict what lay ahead for Arlan's youngest child; Kavan could but strive for a favorable result.

The healer took the lull in the uncomfortable subject as an opportunity to ask, "And you? How are you, sínréc?"

Though he knew what Ártur meant, that the healer was not referring to Kavan's physical well-being, he chose to reply with, "You have examined me, I'm sure. You know I am well."

"Physically, yes." The corners of his mouth twisted. "I have no doubts about how healthy you are…but you know what I mean."

Though Wortham's posture became suddenly more protective and defensive, Kavan stayed him from action or speech with a flash of his green eyes. After too many months of worry, he knew his cousin's questions would not be put off, and Kavan believed he owed it to Ártur, and a few others, to give what answers he could. "I am…better than I was, better in many ways than I have ever been. In other ways," he sighed, "I am still far from where I should be." It was a necessarily cryptic answer, but Kavan had no desire to detail his tormented journey for the healing of his hands and soul. He was home, with a mission ahead, and what he desired now was to put the past to rest.

Ártur scowled, not liking the reply because he knew he would not receive a better one. As he had once told Arlan, Kavan would divulge what he wished to reveal and no more. To the eye, Kavan appeared no different, but the healer believed it was too early to tell. The true measure of the bard's state of mind would come from watching his interactions with others. "If it is peace you need to settle your mind, you shall have it for as long as you require it. Thanks to Wortham, Gaelán, and Rouvyn's orders to keep others away until…"

"Rouvyn Talis?"

Kavan's surprise proved what Ártur already knew, that the Teren physician had known Kavan before. "He has come on as a court healer for the hours I am unable to be here, and to help in Gaelán's training."

His efforts to rush over private details failed. "Unable to be here?"

Hoping to make as much light of his situation to deter his cousin's concerns, Ártur smiled and said, "No fretting. After the attack, it was decided I should spend my nights in Bhryell with Syl and the children and be in Rhidam during the day…unless I'm needed here for an emergency of course. Gaelán's not ready for the title of healer, and I would not have my family remain here in Rhidam with things the way they are. I need to spend time with them too."

Kavan knew his cousin well enough to realize there were details he was leaving out, but he would learn the truth somehow even if Ártur would not tell him. Perhaps he should not push for particulars when he was not willing to share specifics about his own journey, but after saving his cousin's life, Kavan felt he should know the truth. Knowing would also allow him to better gauge Rhidam's climate. "It is important you remain safe; I worried I had not done enough."

"You saved my life; that is enough for me."

Lowering his gaze at the emotion in Ártur's voice, Kavan murmured, "And Bhríd? Gaelán?" To his knowledge, there were no other Elyri in the keep and Bhríd's frequent travels between Rhidam and Levonne put him at risk. "Madalyn told me about the boys…" He did not mention that he had spoken to Tayte already.

Ártur raked his hand through his short hair. "How one can be so Elyri and the other so Teren, I do not know. Bhríd is doing well, though obviously concerned about his family. Gaelán…he has been greatly affected by your attack, your absence." He chose not to bring up the strange transference of power that happened between Kavan and Gaelán, in case Wortham was not aware of the experience Kavan had that caused it. "His studies are progressing, considering his late start as a healer; he has a lot of catching up to do, but he will get there."

"I want to talk to him."

"Whenever you wish. I imagine he'll come eventually, to see how you are; he does so several times a day. You are well enough to be about your business…whatever that is…I see no need to further monitor your visitors unless you wish it."

The question in his final words was noted, but Kavan shook his head. "No…avoidance would be unproductive." There were things he had to do and hiding from the world would delay the inevitable. "I appreciate your concern for my sanity, but before anyone is allowed in, I should like to eat, bathe, dress." Not having eaten in nearly a week, his body was in desperate need of nourishment and he knew he would feel better if he bathed.

The healer's face paled and Wortham grunted and looked at his feet. Both had overlooked Kavan's immediate needs in their relief at having him awake. "I will bring breakfast and see to your bath," the captain promised with a bow.

"And I will let the King know you are awake. He might already…" If the servants knew, word would spread quickly. "He'll want confirmation. I will give you time to bathe and eat, however."

Kavan nodded, knowing that others beside Hagan would be told the news. Soon there would be a line of visitors, a plethora of questions, a flurry of greetings, embraces, kisses, and warm words.

And there would be apologies. At the moment, however, as the two men left him alone to embrace his harp and bask in the silence of solitude, he was determined to enjoy the peace for as long as it lasted.

❧*❦

With King Hagan's birthday mere days away, Prince Espen had prepared a list of men who would remain in Rhidam to serve Enesfel and a list of those who would return to Hatu and be exchanged for fresh troops. Those traveling south would either be going with him when he departed, or if he stayed, they would go alone, taking a letter to his brother that he had written explaining the need for replacement troops and his desire to establish a rotation of soldiers. The letter would only be sent if he could not discuss the matter with his brother in person, but at the moment he had every desire to deliver it himself.

Despite the efforts he knew Diona had made the day before to speak with him, he avoided her with the excuse that he was too busy, that she could wait as he had done. The news had spread quickly this morning that Lord Cliáth was awake, recovered from the injuries sustained during his travels, and thus Diona had no more excuses. He had not seen her yet this morning, in spite of her efforts the previous day, and though logically he knew she might not be awake yet, in his frustration he argued that her not coming was all of the answer he needed. Realistically, she may not have even spoken to the bard yet, but what did that matter when he believed he already knew her answer?

His efforts to evade pain and humiliation were thwarted, however, as he strode across the Great Hall intending to provide his captain with the final list of men who would be traveling. He reached the gilded double doors, pulled them open, and found the princess on the other side, her arm extended as if she had intended to open the door as well.

"My lord…" Her words were a breathless gasp, a pleasant sound to Espen's ears that sent shivers down his spine. After several days of being apart, he could tell she was pleased to see him. She, on the other hand, quickly assessed his unhappy expression and lowered her gaze, bowed her head, and extended him a rare formal curtsey. His unhappy expression, she believed, was because of her, despite her efforts the previous day to rectify the situation.

The gestures of contrition lessened his upset, but his frustration continued to roll beneath the surface and behind his eyes. He bid her rise with his fingers on her arm and allowed his touch to linger a little longer than he should have. "I hear there is good news? Lord Cliáth has recovered?" He was not convinced it was good news for him, but he did not wish for an innocent man to suffer more than he already had in order that Espen could marry the woman he adored.

Knowing the question bore multiple meanings, Diona nodded, keeping her face neutral as she replied, "So I have been told. I am on my way to speak with him shortly, if he will allow it." Her voice faltered and her gaze dropped. It was likely the bard would not want to speak with her ever again, but she needed to try. For her own peace of mind, she needed to attempt to set things right between them.

"So that you might ask his hand?" he muttered bitterly without intending to voice that thought out loud. Eyes wide, he snapped his mouth shut.

Diona sighed. He had every right to be bitter and angry and to suspect her motives, but for once he was wrong. Hoping to appease him, she inched closer and reached for his hand. The prince sidestepped away, avoiding her touch.

"No," she replied earnestly. "I want to see with my eyes that he is well…and beg for forgiveness for my offenses. I cannot properly look to my future when I carry such blackness on my soul." Espen grunted but she continued, "Where might I find you after, my lord? I…"

"I am going to speak to my captain. After that…"

"Will you dine with me at noon? In the garden?"

The hopeful, expectant note in her voice sparked within him the first ray of hope he had felt in too long, but he immediately tried to snuff it out. Regardless of the outcome of her conversation with the bard, Espen expected the same answer, and expected that the offer of a shared meal was meant only to soften the blow. As much as he feared hearing it, however, it was time for the charade between them to end. He nodded once. "Aye, mid-day. I will expect your answer."

"Aye, my lord," she promised, a nervous smile on her lips as she curtsied again. "You shall have it."

By the time Ártur located the King, Hagan was engrossed in welcoming his bride-to-be back to Rhidam for his upcoming feast. It seemed mere days ago that the last gala had ended, but the healer expected that, with the stress the kingdom was under, Hagan was not the only one seeking a diversion from unrest. Besides, once everyone knew that Kavan had returned, that he was awake and well, healed of his injuries, this revelry would become as much a homecoming for him as it would be a birth day celebration for the King. Whether it was admitted or acknowledged, those who loved Kavan would be thinking it and feeling it regardless of any wishes the King might have.

Hagan welcomed the healer's news, in spite of the interruptions it presented, and he promised to visit Kavan and extend his welcome as soon as he could. Judging by the way he then strode arm and arm out of the library with the young woman chosen to be queen, Ártur did not expect that visit to be soon. He then encountered Bhríd in the corridor greeting his wife and eldest son, who looked as if he would rather be elsewhere, and gave them the news as well. Madalyn looked stricken to hear it, as if the attack that had led to injury and perhaps a death had somehow been her fault. Even Tayte, however, assured her that she was not accountable, that sending any more men or resources would have left her vulnerable in Levonne…and who would have expected anyone to brazenly attack the White Bard and Wortham Delamo?

To Ártur, the young man's expression seemed unnervingly blasé.

Instead of choosing to go to Kavan, Bhríd opted to allow his kinsman to come to him. Knowing there would be a steady procession of visitors vying for the bard's time, the chamberlain saw no need to further inconvenience him. They would see each other soon enough.

Now, one of those visitors stood at Kavan's door, trying to still her racing heart and trembling hands. Everything that had happened to Kavan, the months he had been away, had been precipitated by her mistakes and she was afraid that he would rightly blame her as much as she blamed herself. She could avoid what waited beyond that door, pretend she had done nothing wrong, that nothing had happened, that these past several months had not existed, but she needed to go to Espen with a clear conscience and head. He deserved that and so much more for the years she had forced him to wait for her. And Kavan, for everything he had done for her and for her family, and for everything he had suffered as a result of her callous disregard, deserved an apology at the very least. She respected him too much to turn back.

Finally gathering up her courage, she sucked in a breath and lifted her hand to knock for entrance, but before her knuckles touched wood, the familiar voice on the other side said quietly, "You may enter."

She had not considered until that moment, as she swallowed the last of her fear and opened the door to see him for the first time in months, that he might already know she was there. Nor had she fully realized how much she had missed him. He stood at the window, his back to her, dressed not in the robe she was used to seeing but black breeches and a white tunic cinched at the waist…much like the clothes she had asked him to wear on the last evening they had seen one another, clothing he had at that time rejected. His hands gripped the sill and she could see the tension in his arms and in the set of his shoulders, but words failed her as she looked at him.

What could she possibly say that he would want to hear?

Kavan closed his eyes and held his breath. Of everything he had anticipated and dreaded facing during his first days back in Rhidam, this was going to be the most difficult. Anything else would be preferable to facing her. In the silence, he waited for footsteps, for her to rush him and throw her arms around him, but for many minutes, neither of them did anything. When she finally forced her feet to action, he could feel her slow approach and braced, battling the terror and turmoil that surged through him. Her words could not hurt him the way they had before; he was determined not to allow that ever again. That determination eventually enabled him to face her before she reached him, to open to her emotional state and look her in the eye.

He realized she was scared too. That knowledge made this moment unexpectedly easier.

The vision of him, as her gaze traveled down the lines of his new attire and then back to his face, combined with her fear, continued to leave her speechless. Ever since she had been a child, she had believed him to be the most beautiful person alive, a belief reinforced again as he stood with his hands behind his back, the waves of silver-white hair brushing his shoulders, the set of his mouth handsome in its tension. But she also realized that, in spite of his beauty and the special place he held in her heart, he was second to the love she felt for Espen, and that confirmation made her smile.

The smile was short-lived, however, when she met his gaze. His eyes had seemed wise and strong to her for all of the years she had known him. Now they seemed hardened, haunted, fearful, and beneath their substantial strength, she saw for the first time a layer of vulnerability unrecognized before. Had it been there all along, she wondered, or had she put it there?

"It is good to see you, my lord," she managed to whisper, her voice coming in a forced squeak that made the sound higher. To her ears, she sounded like a little girl. She felt like the little girl who was afraid to disappoint her tutor and was waiting for punishment. From him.

He bowed because he believed it was expected, though he felt little bond to her nobility anymore. "Thank you. There were times when I…but I am here to attend to duties too long neglected."

"My lord, you are beholden to us no longer…as you were to our father." He had sworn no oaths of fealty to the new king, had never sworn any to her. Any duties he felt he had were ones he chose. She had no right to expect him to stay in Rhidam and was letting him know as simply as she could that she would respect his choices for however long he elected to remain in Rhidam. "But perhaps you will be better able to influence my brother's choices and actions while you are here…for Enesfel's sake if nothing else."

"Perhaps." He did not yet have enough detail about the state of Enesfel to know what sort of advice Hagan might profit from, but based on his memories of the boy, he knew Hagan might well benefit from the trust and guidance and support of someone he valued during these crucial early days of his reign. Whether Hagan would accept and welcome such guidance, however, remained to be seen.

"Tomorrow, if you are free and feeling strong enough, I would like to bring you up to date on events in Enesfel and Rhidam. There are many things you should know, if you choose to stay."

"As you wish." With Diona's sharp and curious mind and dominant personality, he suspected she knew everything of importance there was to know in the kingdom, possibly more than the King did himself. Kavan would speak to others as well, the chamberlain, chancellor, and inquisitor in particular to formulate a well-rounded vision of the social and political climate. He would be better equipped to confront it if he knew what he faced. He did not intend to be idle as he awaited the day to purify the chapel. There had to be things he could do in the interim.

He wanted to ask how she was, whether she had married, but he could not. A glance at her wringing hands revealed no ring, which seemed to answer his second question, and she appeared well enough to give him a reasonable guess to the first. The awkward silence between them begged to be filled but he did not know what to say.

Looking at her feet, Diona broke the silence. "Your hands?"

He nodded to the uncompleted question and hesitantly brought his hands from behind his back. "It was…difficult to accomplish…but I praise k'Ádhá He saw fit to restore them."

"As do I." Warily she took a step closer. Without thinking about what he was doing or why, Kavan stepped away from her. She swallowed but did not pursue. "I am sorry for what I did…Kavan…for the things I said…for the anguish and suffering I caused. I was selfish, cruel, and what I did was unforgivable. I have yet to pardon myself for it. I know you may never pardon me either, but I pray someday you will find it in your heart to absolve me of my foolishness."

Kavan exhaled slowly, letting out a breath he had not realized he was holding and with it some of the tension in his muscles. His hands curled into fists to stop their shaking. There was no need to ask if she understood why she had been wrong, or to press for proof that she meant what she said; every sense in Kavan's body told him she was sincere and that she had indeed learned from her mistakes as Muir had said. That knowledge did not entirely relieve his anxieties, however.

"My Lady…" He considered calling her by name as she had done with him, but the word stuck in his throat. "My forgiveness you have; it was a necessary part of my healing. But forgetting…" That would be a much more difficult, much longer, process. "However," he sighed, "I have been brought back to Rhidam for a purpose, with a mission to fulfill, thus it is necessary for us to learn to live beside one another. I have no desire for there to be a rift between us…it would be unproductive and painful…for us and for others…and I have had too much of pain."

The light slowly returned to Diona's eyes as his words sank in. "Aye, my lord, I understand. It is my wish as well…and I humbly thank you." Though she outranked him in every way, she curtseyed out of honor, respect, humility, and love, and bowed her head. "Might I ask one more thing…before we put this behind us?"

Kavan's heart leaped into his throat and his chest constricted around his lungs as question after question she might ask raced through his mind. He managed to nod his head, but since she could not see the gesture with her head bowed, he swallowed and replied, "You may ask." It did not mean, however, that he would grant her request or answer her question.

"I am prepared to…do you still believe that…?" Words failed her and she sighed. Forcing an air of nobility in place of the frightened girl she felt to be, she squared her shoulders, lifted her head, and asked, "You once said Prince Espen and I were ideally matched. Do you still hold that to be true?"

It was not the question he anticipated and he stared at her. "Assuming he has not changed much in the past six months, yes."

Her face lit with a relieved smile. "Good…because I believe it as well. I am on my way to accept his proposal, if he has not changed his mind, but I needed to clear the air with you before doing so. My childishness has caused both of you grief and I intend to rectify that."

More tension bled away. Accepting Espen's marriage proposal would mean she would no longer pursue Kavan, removing the primary source of discord between them. It would aid in their ability, he hoped, to work together. "My Lady…"

She waved a dismissive hand. "I have witnessed much while you have been gone, have had too many long days and nights to reflect on life, duty, responsibility, and the nature of love. As you tried many times to teach me, I understand now that a union between myself and any Elyri…you in particular…would be devastating to the stability of Enesfel. As dear as you are to me…I love him. I cannot bear the thought of never seeing him, of losing him through my folly the way I nearly lost you. I will not allow further foolishness to destroy my friendships, my happiness, Enesfel's future, you, or Espen."

At last Kavan took a single step forward though he did not touch her. He could see her father in her face, hear Arlan in her words. Arlan too had been stubborn, rash, and prone to unrealistic notions. Arlan too had pushed Kavan away with impractical demands and expectations. And both had, in time, learned wisdom the hard way. He knew the princess had many years of learning ahead, but for Enesfel's sake, the wisdom gained during the past half-year almost made the price of his suffering worth it…although he wondered again why it was his place to suffer in order that an entire kingdom might benefit.

Overcoming the last flame of fear, he clasped her shoulders as he had often done to Arlan and murmured, "Enesfel needs such wisdom. I am grateful you have gained it."

Treasuring the gesture because he made it, because it meant that, despite having a long way to go to regain his trust, he did not hate her for her mistakes, she murmured, "My regrets are that it has been gained at the expense of Espen's patience and your esteem…and that Father is not here to see it."

He squeezed her shoulders again before dropping his hands. "Arlan knows, My Lady. Believe me, he knows."

With Kavan's words in mind and a lighter heart then she had felt in too many months, the princess searched for her prince. As he had indicated, he had met with his troops to inform them of who would be staying in Rhidam and who would be returning to Hatu. That was where she found him, but rather than interrupt as she could have done, she followed both the Hatu sensibility that women did not intrude on the business of men as well as a general level of politeness by allowing him to finish. He had waited fourteen years, waited too long; a few more minutes would harm nothing. He had waited for her; she could wait a handful of minutes for him.

After noticing several of his men glancing into the distance behind him while he talked, Espen peered over his shoulder to see Diona lingering in the courtyard, keeping her distance but obviously waiting for him. She was smiling, glowing to his eyes, for the first time he could recall. Knowing she had intended to speak with the bard and that they were not yet scheduled to meet, Espen could not imagine that smile and glow meaning anything fortuitous for him. Doing his best to hide his nervous disquiet, he completed his briefing but did not move as the men scattered, nor give further acknowledgment of her presence until the last of Hatu's soldiers were no longer in his sight.

In turn, she likewise waited, and when they were alone in the courtyard, as alone as this public place could allow, she came near enough to ask, "Walk with me, my lord?" in an eager, hopeful tone.

He stiffened as she reached for his hand, not because he did not long for her touch but because he feared the worst from her lips. "I prefer we cut to the heart of the matter, Diona." With the anxiety of anticipation knotting his stomach, he did not think he could eat a single bite until she gave her reply.

The request suited Diona. After fourteen years of coyness, indecisiveness, and courtship, there was no need for further delays.

"As you…"

As if to stave off what he believed was inevitable, Espen abruptly asked, "How is Lord Cliáth?"

She blinked, hesitated, but replied, "His body is healed but the remainder will take time." She did not know how much Espen knew of the reasons for Kavan's extended absence and she did not want to admit those failures to him now. "It appears he is willing to give me the chance to make amends and prove…"

Hearing that as confirmation of his fears, the prince did not try to hide his darkening expression as he snarled, "Then I am happy for you, My Lady," before turning to stalk away.

"Espen!" She hurried after him, confused by his behavior. She caught his arm, not caring if it was improper, and said, "I thought you desired my answer…or have you…?"

Her hand on his arm did not break his stride and she struggled to keep up with him. "You gave it. I do not need to hear the details of your plans to marry Lord Cliáth…"

"Marry…? I did not say…Espen…it is you I choose to marry…"

"I do not have to continue to…" His steps faltered. He stopped. He turned to stare in disbelief. He could not have heard her correctly.

She took the opportunity of his stunned silence to hastily continue. "I have known for some time what I truly want…but every time I tried to say it, something has gotten in the way…duty or otherwise…but no more. I say it now, Espen, I will marry you if you will have me."

His response was to pull her into a tight embrace and spin her around. He might have kissed her if not for the various people about the courtyard that prompted an adherence to an upbringing of stricter mannerisms then Enesfel followed. With no intermingling of the sexes in any personal fashion in public in Hatu, Espen was uncomfortable pushing the boundaries still, and after what had happened the last time they had kissed, he did not want to risk public embarrassment. But he was overjoyed, it was obvious in the way he held her and pressed his face to the side of her head.

"I do want it, Diona. Now and always. I have never stopped wanting it. Come…we should announce this to your brother at once and make plans…"

"No joint ceremonies," she said earnestly with a chuckle. "I will not share the attention with Hagan…and I am certain he does not want to share it with me."

"Yes," Espen agreed. Elated by her acceptance, he would have agreed to anything.

"As for plans…perhaps we can begin to discuss them over that garden meal you promised me?"

This time he agreed with a nod, kissing her ear before looping his arm around her waist to walk together towards the castle door. He had come close to giving up hope that this day would ever come. Now he could not believe it had.

❧*❧

It was several hours after the princess' visit, long after dark, before Kavan forced himself out of his room. Most of those hours were spent conversing with those who called on him. Rouvyn, Gaelán, and the newly returned Bhyrhán, whom he was surprised to see in Rhidam and was even more surprised to learn had been taken on as Court Bard during Kavan's absence. General Agis and Justice Corbin, Wortham and Zelenka, who informed him that Urian was missing though there had been no evidence at the scene of the attack to suggest his death. Asta, who entrusted him with the details of her father's activities and plan because she trusted Kavan as she did few others, and then the King with his news of an impending wedding. Ártur came again repeatedly and once more before his reluctant return to Bhryell for the night, and lastly Prince Espen, who came with a sheepish expression to welcome him home and to apologize if he had ever thought ill of the bard or given the Elyri cause to dislike or distrust him. He thanked Kavan for encouraging Diona to act, for what he had done to set her free of her infatuation and encouraging her to follow her heart. While Kavan did not believe he had that sort of influence over Diona's decisions, he understood why the prince might feel that way and accepted the words of gratitude graciously.

Now he was free, with time on his hands for reflection that he chose not to spend in the oratory as he often did, but rather somewhere he knew he had to go if he was to put the past to rest. Harp in hand, he made his way to the back garden, strolled through the moonlit paths until he stopped in front of the marker that bore Arlan's name.

Despite having been with his friend at the moment of his passing, it was difficult to accept that Arlan would not return, that the day-old infant he had greeted, the prince he had mentored and helped become king, was no longer with him. That he could not walk down a castle corridor and hear his voice. For as long as he remained in Rhidam, it would be in a castle without Arlan. Kavan understood now how Ártur felt the night Donal Lachlan died, the way he must feel having lived through the lives and deaths of so many Lachlans.

His thoughts roamed the trail of memory, of days and events shared with Arlan, some unpleasant, most not, knowing that no man lived a life devoid of grief and regret. All anyone could do was make the most of what they were given, cherish the highlights, lead a decent life and do good for others. Arlan had done each of those things to become one of the best-loved rulers in Enesfel's history.

Kavan doubted that historians would recall that Enesfel's Coryllien troubles had begun during the twilight of Arlan's reign. These dark days, he thought grimly, would forever be linked to the young King who was ill-equipped to solve the problems facing him. From the details Kavan had gleaned from those he talked to that day, particularly Agis, Justice Corbin, and Asta, he had a clearer picture of what had happened in Enesfel during his absence. He regretted he had not returned sooner to assist Hagan, but there was little else he could do beyond the path that lay before him. If Kóráhm, Orynn, and others were right, cleansing the chapel, and the time had spent obtaining the ingredients necessary to do so, would be more helpful to Enesfel and Hagan, than any words of advice Kavan might be able to provide.

Before sleeping this night, he intended to remove both the relics, the Diwi, and the Orec, to a secure location, storing them in St. Kóráhm's where he had hidden the other portion of the staff and the remaining Coryllien daggers. Only one other man, Khwílen Kesábhá, knew of that hidden vault, or had access to it, and soon there would be a handful of others, but none save Kavan would know what the vault contained. There would be books and other relics secured there, items of historical and religious relevance that few others would know about, but no one would ever have access to the daggers or the relics Kóráhm had led him to. There was no safer place for such things, beyond the reach of Teren and Elyri alike, and when the time came to use them, Kavan would return to the abbey for them.

What would happen afterward, he could not guess.

For the moment, he had music to prepare, a backlog of songs written during his travels that needed fine-tuning if he was to have something befitting the King's celebration. Wiping the dust and leaves from the marble that bore Arlan's name, he traced the letters one last time and murmured, "I am here, Arlan. For however long I can be. I will do my best to help him, protect him…to set Enesfel right. I owe you that much."

Then, harp in hand, he settled before the crypt and played tunes to the moon and the late king's memory on an instrument he had thought never to play again.

It was a bittersweet joy to hear those notes one more time.

❧Chapter 27 ❧

Heads turned as the royal entourage adorned in the amber and burgundy of the Lachlan House, black eagles emblazoned across each banner and shield, the great crest recognizable to all in Enesfel and beyond, entered the náós two by two. The attention was to be expected; while the remaining Lachlans were full supporters of the Faith, they did not frequent the náós their father had helped to rebuild, especially in recent days with the high risk of violence. That this was the nearest Gathering to the King's day of birth had increased the likelihood of their attendance, as it had become customary, since King Arlan's ascension, for the royal family to receive the blessings of the faith on such days to ensure good relations between the two most influential establishments in the Sovereignty.

What kept heads turned, however, what sent murmurs through the Faithful this day, was the attendance of the White Bard of whom so many rumors had circulated over the past half-year. Kavan could feel it, the surge of excitement and joy peppered with darker, less friendly sentiments. Rather than shut out those thoughts and emotions as he normally would, he tried to pinpoint the sources, to find those faces bound to each threatening thought and memorize them. Elyri hatred in itself was not a crime and he did not want the tide of persecution to swing the other way, for Teren to persecute Teren for their fears. But if he could connect even one face to those Asta had shown him, if even one murderer could be taken off of Rhidam's streets, Kavan believed it was his duty to help find them. There was little time for such perusal, however, as the procession made its way to the seats in the box at the front of the congregation. Royalty attending a Gathering was often less about Faith than it was about making a political statement or show of solidarity. Kavan hated it, most often did not attend with the family in this fashion, but today, his first Gathering since his return to Rhidam, he felt it necessary to be here. If nothing else, his attendance would draw out the negativity.

Painting a target on himself Wortham called it, and Kavan agreed. Believing he was capable of self-protection as long as he remained on guard, who better to expose anti-Elyri elements than the Elyri closest to the Lachlan throne, the one most easily recognized? Who he was, in addition to what he was, made him ideal bait, and though he was afraid, death itself did not trouble him. It was the potential of pain, of what came before…and what might or might not come after.

As was often the case when the King attended a Gathering, the senior gdhededhá presided and today was no exception. There was no true senior no, however, as Tusánt and Claide had come to serve at the same time, with a mere matter of days separating them. Claide was senior in age, and in tenure only by those days of arrival since both had been ceremoniously sworn to service in Rhidam on the same day. As glances were exchanged between Tusánt and the novices flanking him, Kavan guessed that the Elyri had been displaced for this service in favor of Claide and Tusánt was less than pleased by that demotion. His countryman's displeasure set Kavan on edge and made him more attentive. If something was to happen, he did not intend to miss it.

Nor had he missed the collection of freshly disrupted graves in front of the náós that Justice Corbin had reported yesterday. No one yet knew what had become of the bodies in those empty graves, but the investigation was underway, and from the few fleeting touches of the minds of those Teren dedhá seated around Tusánt, there was some suspicion that Claide had been aware of that desecration before the discovery had been made.

For the majority of the service, nothing seemed unusual. Kavan was more enthralled than ever with the children's choir and he spent much of his time studying each one, picking each voice from amongst them, matching them with the pieces he had composed during his travel. Time after time his perusal was interrupted by the proximity of a presence overhead and a faint voice that accompanied it, and he was left musing over what threat level that presence presented.

Beyond that, however, the Gathering was like any other. He attributed the lack of spiritual energies to his being focused on details other than prayer and devotion. When Claide took the platform to speak the lesson, however, it grew alarmingly certain that the lack was caused by something else. This man, who Kavan had not seen since before his departure from Enesfel, brought with him a suffocating pall of hatred that his words, which on first blush sounded uplifting and pious, spread like a tightly woven iron net over the unsuspecting

Faithful. The bard could feel the agitation of his kin, in Asta, and most especially in Princess Diona and Prince Espen beside her, agitation that blossomed into barely contained outrage when seemingly in passing the gdhededhá asserted that the holy father of their Faith in Clarys had no concern for its members outside of Elyriá beyond the donations the Teren sees brought into the coffers of the Faith.

They were words that to many rang true. If k'gdhededhá Dórímyr could not deign to oversee the appointment of new leadership in Enesfel, as he should, how could he and those around him be perceived otherwise? The response of the common folk, ever concerned about what little income they had and how it was spent, did not alarm Kavan. Powerful oratory could easily sway the masses back to reason and temperance. It was King Hagan's thoughtful expression that caused Kavan concern. He had hoped he had taught Hagan to be more discerning and critical, hoped that Diona's perceptions of her brother's naiveté were exaggerated.

Hagan had been, in many ways, a follower as he grew up, led and advised by his sister, the Cáner boys, the other children around him, and by his tutors in the absence of his father's active guidance. Arlan's death, Kavan's absence, the splintering of close relationships with Gaelán and Tayte, each had taken away many of Hagan's leadership and advisory models, at least those not of his father's court and generation. And what young man, especially a young king seeking his own voice, wanted to be directed by a woman, even if that woman was his sister, the one he had trusted most explicitly in the past? Wanting to prove his mettle, to prove himself worthy of the Lachlan name and the throne, but still uncertain and young at heart, it was not surprising that Hagan had sought counsel from someone who did not treat him as a child, someone he believed he could trust.

A man like Claide, a powerful figurehead in the Faith and capable of appearing as a father-figure, would seem a natural choice…and a man like Claide who undoubtedly, from what Kavan was learning, had a hidden political agenda, would be quick to see that need in the King and rush to fill and manipulate it.

Perhaps, thought Kavan with regret, it was not too late to turn that tide. He was home, ready for the struggle he faced ahead, and he had hopes that Hagan would trust him as his father had done, would be willing to heed his advice while there was still a chance to correct Enesfel's errant path. If the fate of the kingdom came down to a battle between Kavan and Claide for the King's allegiance, it was a battle Kavan was determined to win.

But not today. Today there would be last-minute planning for the King's festival and he would want no talk of affairs of state or Faith unless there was an emergency at hand. And before they had that talk, Kavan intended to have a face to face meeting with k'gdhededhá Dórímyr which might, he feared, be more challenging than their last confrontation had been.

Then Kavan had been a boy, easily dismissed as innocent and ignorant. This time, Dórímyr would not have that luxury. He would be faced with a powerful intellect and a man he could not bully or intimidate into submission. Without coercion and fear on his side either, Kavan was aware their clash would likely end in a stalemate.

Yet it had to be done.

❧*❦

"I told you I would have…"

Prince Muir laughed as he hugged his mentor and friend in the open courtyard not caring who witnessed his exuberant welcome. It had only been a few weeks and yet there never seemed to be enough time spent with the bard. He studied Kavan's face, smiling as he did so, pleased with what he saw…and what he did not see. "I know, but Clianthe wanted to travel by sea, and after the worry I have forced on her of late, obliging her was the least I could do. Besides," he smiled wider and stepped back to look the Elyri over more fully once again, "it guaranteed us time together we might not have enjoyed otherwise."

Kavan had to concede to that. With as much time as Muir was spending away from his new bride during their first year of marriage, they would either be forced to grow apart or else would remain as newlyweds for some time longer. He could not fault either of them for wanting a precious bit of privacy.

"Walk with me…tell me how things are." With his wife occupied by Diona, Zelenka, and Lady Sigrid, this would be the best opportunity for them to speak. Despite the bard's seemingly good health and even spirits, Muir still worried about his state of mind. He had heard, upon his arrival at the castle, about the attack on Kavan's party on the road between Levonne and Rhidam, had heard Kavan had been injured. Between that, the societal upheaval in Enesfel, and matters with his sister, Muir did not think things could be easy for Kavan.

"You need not worry I am safe, healed, and I am…well enough."

It did not surprise Muir that the bard knew his thoughts. It was a peculiarity Muir had grown used to as a child. "And Diona?"

Kavan shrugged as they walked the sunlit path where the stone columns left shadows like ladder rungs across the promenade. "Awkward…but not as bad as I feared. We have spoken on the matter and settled it…I believe…and she seems to have grown and learned from the experience as I have…as you said she had. I am hopeful those troubles are behind us." It would be a long time, however, before he felt at ease in her presence, and he was aware the prince could read that uncertainty in his face.

"That is progress at least," Muir murmured, scanning each person they passed for a possible threat even though, within the keep's wall, Kavan should be the safest he could be almost anywhere in Enesfel. Muir was not concerned for his own safety as much as he was for the man who had, for many years, shouldered the role of protector. It was odd to feel that their positions had reversed, to feel that the home he had grown up in, the world around them, might not be safe for Kavan and that he should be the one to defend him if the need arose.

"I heard about the attack…"

"I am well, Muir. I promise you. But it may be a long time before the same can be said about Enesfel." Welcoming the shift away from personal topics, Kavan gladly discussed what he knew of current affairs, save for the details of Caol's business that he had promised Asta he would reveal to no one. Diona too would welcome Muir's clearheaded insightfulness, so long as Muir did not share details with Hagan. If Hagan was more like his half-brother, Kavan mused, things in Enesfel might be much different.

As the dinner hour drew near, they circled around towards the castle's main doors, knowing there would be people waiting for them in the dining hall. "You believe there is something you can do, something that will change things?" Muir asked before reaching the door. Kavan had not said so in the midst of their dialogue, but Kavan's words on Pháne had stuck with him and Muir was certain the Elyri had a plan. He believed Kavan was capable of great feats, having witnessed some of them himself, but how could one man, one Elyri, eradicate so much hatred and fear?

"It may not be an abrupt change…and even I do not understand how it will help…nor am I convinced that change will come at my hands alone. But I am assured that what I must do is necessary for the change to begin."

"What is it?" Muir waited for a few heartbeats for a reply, and when Kavan did not, he pressed. "What must you do? It does not involve you dying…does it?"

The bard scowled. He had wondered that as well but he had no answers. He opened the door for the prince and allowed the younger man to enter first. "I do not know. I will be instructed when the time arises, until then, I am as ignorant as you. I am not afraid of dying…"

"Perhaps not, but I am afraid of you dying…and I know I am not the only one to feel thus."

Such devotion was touching, but Kavan deflected it uneasily with, "All must die…"

"Praise be not before I laid eyes on you again!"

Kavan heard the approaching footsteps but it was not until he heard the much-missed voice that he turned to greet the man joining them. The bard's smile was wider than Muir had previously seen, and it was the first time he had witnessed Kavan being the one to initiate an embrace. Though jealous, Muir could not begrudge his father that welcome, especially as he watched unshed tears break free at the corners of Owain's blue-grey eyes.

"My apologies, my lord, for not bidding you…" Kavan began.

"Nonsense," mumbled the blonde man in a voice thick with emotion. He clung to the bard, clapping him on the back to keep his hands from grasping too tightly, until he finally pulled back, almost pushing Kavan away, to resist weeping like a child with unrestrained joy. "Perfectly understandable…but praise k'Ádhá you are home."

"You have recently arrived?"

"For the King's celebration, aye. I heard rumors from the servants, from Gaelán when I came in, but I was afraid to believe it until I saw you myself. And…your hands…" He caught them both in his, brought them up where he could see them, and then squeezed them after doing so. He did not speak of a miracle, of blessings or praise, but kissed them repeatedly until he could recover his composure.

Kavan smiled back at him, grateful for the words Owain did not say. "I am glad you have come. Join us for the meal?" As much as a private discourse with Owain was desired, the public nature of the meal meant fewer awkward questions until both men had the opportunity to settle their racing hearts.

Not trusting his voice, Owain nodded, slung his arm around Muir's shoulders, and followed Kavan into the dining hall. There were others already there, various lords and ladies, dignitaries and guests arriving for the upcoming celebration or who had not left after the last one, and each turned to stare at the White Bard who had yet to dine in a public setting since his return. Murmurs flew from one to the other as the King rose to greet the three men.

"Brother…Lord Lachlan…Lord Cliáth…thank you for joining us. Welcome. Please. Sit." He indicated a collection of empty seats to his left a good distance from the royal family, although Muir moved away to join his wife much nearer to the King's chair of honor. At one time Kavan had been given the chair nearest the king, in the place where Bhyrhán sat now, but that had been during the reign of a different king, and none had known whether Kavan would join the household for this meal or not. He took no offense at being displaced, as that distant placing provided a better opportunity to watch the others in the room. Sigrid was on the King's left, in the place always reserved for the queen, and to Hagan's right, his sister fidgeted with the neckline of her gown, casting glances at Espen beside her who was clearly struggling not to say whatever was on his mind. Kavan gave them no more than a passing glimpse, uncomfortable as he was with her still, but with Owain and Wortham beside him, he was at no loss for reassuring companionship or conversation. If those in the room were expecting music from him, it would not be tonight.

He felt no enmity in the room towards any of the Elyri present, which gave him hope. While the views of those in power did not necessarily influence the masses, it seemed likely their good examples could help right the course of the kingdom, once the underlying rot and unrest were cleansed away. Knowing that the Lachlan Guard and palace staff were carefully screened to weed out potential threats, Kavan found no menace there either. He was able to relax and eat a proper repast, the likes of which he had not enjoyed in some time.

Only Ártur was missing. The healer should have been there too. Maybe Kavan needed to go to Bhryell, talk to Syl, change her mind about the restrictions on her husband's movements.

Or perhaps it was best if Kavan did not interfere.

The meal was eventually cleared away but the wine and ale still flowed when Espen finally rose to face Hagan with a formal bow. "Your Imminence…as you know, it is my duty to return to Hatu for a period, to secure new forces and confer with my brother on matters here and at home. There is one additional matter I desire to bring before him and you, if I may have permission to speak."

Hagan, distracted from his conversation with Sigrid, peered over the rim of his wine glass before setting it down to say, "What do you desire, Prince Espen?" He could imagine no matter between the Hatu prince and Hatu king that might need Hagan's permission or attention, particularly at a public occasion such as this, unless it involved a pressing need for troops of which he was unaware. Briefly, he imagined that Hatu was considering pulling all of their forces out of Rhidam, a prospect which made him anxious. That nervousness echoed in his voice.

"I will broach the subject of further cooperative agreements between Enesfel and Hatu, between Lachlans and Harcourts, more men, whatever aid my brother can spare, if Your Majesty will permit me the honor of your sister's hand."

Hagan blinked, staring at his sister with undisguised disbelief and, Kavan thought, a touch of resentment that quickly disappeared. "Diona?" Hagan asked. "Is this your wish?" There were many at the table, other than the King, who believed the princess would never accept the long-rumored union, and others who wondered if this public asking was a ploy by the Hatu prince to force the woman to answer.

The merry smile on his sister's face, however, revealed the truth. "Aye, my lord...if it pleases you." She hated adding the last few words, as she in no way wanted, or intended, to bow to her brother's wishes if, as king, he chose not to sanction the marriage.

But there was only one reason Hagan could think of not to allow it, and that reason reverberated in his words when he offered his hand to Prince Espen and said, "You have my blessings. It has been a long time coming, a happy match for our Sovereignties. Perhaps we should celebrate our unions together?"

When the prince took the offered hand and bowed again, he answered, "Your Majesty, I must decline that offer. There is no way we shall be ready by the date of your upcoming union, not with preparations to be made and my impending journey home."

"Yes, brother, forgive us...but you and Lady Niall shall have to wed without us," agreed Diona, relieved that Espen found a diplomatic way to decline an offer she knew Hagan was loath to make.

"Without..." Hagan's face paled. "You will be here, won't you?"

"Of course," she chuckled, embracing him and kissing his cheek.

"And I will endeavor to be as well, travel and my brother permitting," promised Espen.

Clearing his throat as he picked up his glass, hoping his relief sounded less desperate then he felt it to be, the King said, "Good; I am pleased to hear it." He was thankful he had misunderstood his sister's intentions, as the thought of following through with a wedding he did not feel entirely ready for terrified him despite his resolve. He wanted his older sister beside him to push him to action should his steps falter. He was also glad that she would not be sharing that day with him as a participant because he had no doubts that her marriage would somehow overshadow his no matter his efforts to avoid that. He and Sigrid would have their day of glory and honor and then he would be content to give Diona hers.

Across the vast room, Kavan closed his eyes as Espen resumed his seat at Diona's side. He had not needed the Sight to tell him Diona and Espen's intention, and despite the sigh that escaped, he felt no regret or remorse that the princess had at last committed her decision. This was as it should be. He felt no desire for her and Enesfel needed the union that the royal houses of Lachlan and Harcourt could offer.

If he had any regrets, it was that Orynn was not here to share such a life with him. No, there would be no such future for him, but at least he had learned he was capable of love, and being loved in return. Now there was no time for such things. This was the time for saving Enesfel from itself and righting the future for Elyri and Teren alike.

What started as a normal dinner turned into an engagement celebration and though Kavan refused to play, with Bhyrhán available there was no shortage of music for the dancing and drinking that followed and lasted far into the night. Kavan did not stay long, but few were concerned with his early departure. He typically left revelries early, and after what everyone imagined he had been through…the inaccurate and outlandish gossip and rumors which circled the room from the moment he had entered it, his need to retreat, to rest and recuperate, was expected.

And for some, it was enough just to have him home.

Or else, he mused, they had grown so accustomed to his absence they did not even notice he was gone.

Wortham and Owain began to follow him when he pushed away from the table, but Kavan bid them stay, assuring them with a touch that there was no cause to worry. While not weary, such a crowd as this, such merrymaking, was more than Kavan felt strong enough to shoulder for an extended time. This night brought with it memories of Arlan, of Orynn, of Myreth, and such bittersweet recollections were best endured alone. Better yet, he decided, they were best purged as he could not let such burdens distract him.

For the first time in too long, he gave in to the temptation of directionless flight.

He did not go to the lake as he normally might have, but limited his circles to Rhidam, the white raven form weaving in and out of the city streets, around the borders, along the river's edge, studying every detail, seeking clues, any hints of where the festering thorn of hatred had lodged to spread its infection through the lifeblood of Enesfel's Crown Seat. From the air, however, the city looked peaceful, at rest…untainted and sleeping, showing no hint of what poisoned her. He might gain a better view from the ground, but in his normal form that would be dangerous and it was too late tonight to consider a search in any other guise. A daytime search would raise concerns for his safety from others, but it might be necessary. He was not going to learn anything by hiding inside the castle walls.

With the first rays of dawn clawing over the eastern horizon, Kavan turned towards the castle. If he wanted to avoid his cousin's questions, he needed to be there before the healer returned. The final flight path took him over the náos where the sight of a small figure scurrying nervously towards the main door drew him out of his flight. He sensed no danger or threat in the figure, only fear of the long-standing sort, the constant need for survival rather than an immediate terror of being pursued. Kavan did not have a clear line of sight to the individual, could not gain many details, but the one thing he did believe, that he did know, was that the person was Elyri.

He took his natural shape in the secluded shadows at the side of the náos where no one would see him, and rounded the corner, intending to enter, to search for the fugitive and offer whatever aid he could. He was prevented from doing so, however, by the arrival of four Teren horsemen, each wearing the familiar ecclesiastical robes of the holy center of Faith in Clarys. These were, despite being Teren, representatives of k'gdhededhá Dórímyr, a realization that made Kavan feel sick. He recognized two of the four from his numerous past visits to the High Mother's palace and they recognized him. It was difficult not to.

"Harper Cliáth," one of the four said with a bowed head as he slid from his horse, removed his gloves, and offered his hand. "I did not expect to find you here. We were told you had been gravely injured…" The balding man looked down at the hand that clasped his and cocked his head. "Clearly one cannot believe every rumor…"

It surprised Kavan that news of his attack and disfigurement had reached Clarys. Uncomfortable admitting the truth but trusting his instinct in favor of lies and falsehoods, Kavan bowed. "gdhededhá Ensgil. There is no folly in believing the truth. I do not know what you have heard…but what you say is true. My injuries were severe…but now I am whole." As much as he did not want word of his healing to spread, he could not allow these men to return to Dórímyr and proclaim it all to be lies. Having been told that gdhededhá Kesábhá was in Elyriá trying to bring reconciliation between the Teren Faithful and the Elyri seat of leadership, allowing such lies to spread would, Kavan suspected, do more harm than good.

"What brings you to Rhidam?"

The question lifted Ensgil's gaze from the bard's hands and he released the one he held. If those rumors about Kavan's injuries were true, and if the man had been healed of them, how many other tales about him were likewise true?

"We have come to deliver this," he drew a scroll from the leather bag at his side, "to dedhá Tusánt and Claide from k'dedhá Dórímyr." Noting the bard's barely masked grimace, he scowled and asked, "Is there a problem, my lord?"

As many problems existed in Enesfel, Kavan could not provide a brief answer to that question. Though he had not read the contents of the scroll, he could guess at the words it carried, words that could be one of the biggest problems Enesfel faced. But without reading it or making an attempt to learn the thoughts burned into the page by the writer's hand, and without knowing how much of the current state of affairs Ensgil knew about, or whether the man knew what he carried, Kavan did not want to speak out of turn. "I am on my way in now; I can deliver it for you, if you wish…or I can announce you?"

Ensgil gave the offer no thought before handing the scroll to the bard whose reputation he trusted. "We have traveled safely thus far, but in truth, I would prefer to return to Elyriá before our luck runs out. We have beheld many atrocities on our journey…" He shuddered, not caring to think about the burned buildings, the mutilated bodies in ditches, the corpses and body parts hanging from trees and signposts.

Teren in Elyriá had either gone there to escape violence and better themselves, be it professionally or personally, or else had been raised there and were unexposed to the sort of horrors Enesfel suffered. Without knowing what these men had seen, Kavan understood the desire to retreat while they could. They did not even offer to wait for a reply to their message or to take refreshment and rest in the safety of the náós.

"Then k'Ádhá be with you, gdhededhá. Please, when you speak to Kyne Mórne next, convey my greetings." Kavan did not know the woman well, but she had been kind and generous to him, supportive of his career, and she was kin, no matter how distantly related.

"I shall," Ensgil promised as he put his gloves on and swung back up onto his horse. "She will be pleased to know you are well."

Kavan did not move as the four rode away, heading north at a quick clip to be free of the stirring city. More people in the streets meant a higher risk. They were wise to be clear of it. He fingered the seal on the leather tube, debating whether he should read the contents before taking it to Claide and Tusánt. But there was little need to do so. He cracked the external seal and pulled the rolled parchment out enough to read the impressions through his fingertips. As expected, the scroll itself was also sealed, but that touch told him all he needed to know.

The highest-ranking k'gdhededhá in the entirety of the Faith had opted to allow Enesfel to elect its patriarch. Under any other circumstances, Kavan might have lauded the decision to allow the Teren the freedom of this choice. But he knew that Dórímyr did not allow any of the Elyri regions to select their leaders; this, in the bard's opinion, appeared to be the slight he knew it was…and these were far from normal circumstances.

It was not that Dórímyr did not understand the dire situation in Enesfel. Kavan did not need to read the scroll to know that. Having butted heads with the Elyri patriarch before, Kavan knew it was apathy, tainted with a smudge of fear, that kept Dórímyr from doing what was right for the safety and security of Elyri and Teren alike. Unable to think of any tenant of Faith that would account for this refusal, chalking it up to a political and personal choice, Kavan slid the scroll back into the tube and stuffed it into his tunic. He could not, would not, keep it out of Tusánt and Claide's hands indefinitely, as tempting as it was to hide Dórímyr's apathy. Keeping this news from Claide for too long might prompt him to act without authorization.

When he chose to act, few, if any, would try to stop him. The outcome, an election, was going to happen with or without the k'gdhededhá's permission, but if Kavan could delay it until after the King's celebration, it would give Hagan one less worry.

And perhaps Kavan could confront Dórímyr first.

Tracking down the fleeting Elyri fugitive was momentarily set aside as he started towards the keep, pondering the implications of Dórímyr's choices, as well as his own, while keeping his senses tuned to those emerging from homes and shops. They were staring, many murmuring, and with each cluster of structures he passed, Kavan was aware of being followed. Not with maliciousness, but rather with curiosity and that awkward reverence he had uncomfortably borne before. To his surprise, he did not feel the same level of discomfort with their attention this morning, though he could not decide why. Had he changed so much during his months away? Had he finally grown into the role k'Ádhá had given him to live?

He wanted to believe it was true. It would be a hard-won victory.

The gaggle of followers stopped as he crossed the lowered drawbridge into the castle's outer courtyard. They knew they could not follow him there, and if he was not going to grace them with a song, a story, a miracle, they had to let him continue on the business that had taken in from the castle to the náós. Royal business, most likely, as everyone knew, or presumed to know, his proximity to the Lachlan King.

It was that knowledge and the fear that sometimes came with it that brought an unexpected barrage of debris hurtling across the drawbridge. Having been unaware of any hostility in the crowd, Kavan turned swiftly, hoping to catch sight of the instigator as a cry of "Go home, Elyri!" rang out.

But perhaps it was not directed at him, since Bhyrhán was now beside him, the one struck by the majority of the thrown objects. Someone in the crowd threw a punch, someone else shoved, and soon the cluster of people gave birth to a fight. Lachlan guards swarmed through the open gate, jostling past the two bards, blocking the gateway to keep any of the brawlers from spilling into the courtyard. They were content, it seemed, to let Kavan's supporters put down the anti-Elyri members of the crowd. Little by little, however, the throng grew, and spurred by the heat of the moment and the call to arms of those against the Elyri in the land, those who were disgruntled, afraid, and bitter began to outnumber the cluster of Kavan's devotees who were unfortunate enough to be unable to escape.

Though fighting each other still, some of the agitated crowd turned its attention to the soldiers at the gate, shouting taunts, hurling stones, rotten food, anything they could pick up. There were voices demanding that the King expel all Elyri from Enesfel, that he turn over those in the keep to the crowd for 'justice'. By the time Generals Agis and Zarkosta arrived, it was obvious to the witnesses that this uncontrolled rabble was not going to be dispelled by words or patience. Having Prince Espen's blessing, the Hatu soldiers were permitted their taste of action; the soldiers barring the gates parted to allow the armed men through, with the prince and the generals leading them. Rather than cause an immediate cessation of hostilities, some targeted their anger and fear at the soldiers and a full-scale riot erupted in front of the castle's moat.

"You're not going to send them anywhere," Diona barked as she and her brother watched the jumble of swinging fists and weapons tangle and untangle as the soldiers worked to subdue the troublemakers.

"They would be…"

"We need healers! You can't make exceptions for one or two and not the others. And Bhríd and Kavan are nobles. Landed, titled…and Bhríd has a family! We have no right to…"

Red-faced, Hagan looked away from the window at his sister. "I have every right! I am the king!

The roar drained the color from her face. "You wouldn't dare! What would Father…?"

"Father's not here!"

Hagan understood what his sister was saying, that she was forcing him to think like a king, as their father might have if he had been here, not as the impulsive emotional young man he was. King Arlan would not have considered sending the Elyri, his friends, away. He would have done everything in his power to protect them for as long as they chose to stay in Enesfel.

But Hagan was not his father; the Elyri were less friends then they were elders who had raised and guided him, and in truth, he had no idea how he could protect them short of locking them inside the castle or sending them away. Imprisoning them he could not do, and while he did not like the thought of banishing them from Enesfel, for the reasons his sister had given and because he liked, trusted, and relied on them, he was beginning to feel that there was no other choice but to ask them to leave.

And how, he wondered as he strained to see into the ever-growing throng, could he be angry with Diona when he understood her worry for the safety of those in the keep and the man she had finally agreed to marry who was in that crowd trying to restore order?

"I'm not saying I'm going to do it," he muttered weakly, thankful Sigrid was not here to witness this argument, or the defeat he felt to Diona's words. "I'm suggesting they would be safer somewhere else. Ask any of them; they will tell you the same thing."

"I'm going down to talk to Lord Cliáth…find out what started this," she growled as she stalked out of the room. She too knew her brother was right. Being more like their father, however, she was not prepared to concede to the wishes of the violent. There had to be some way, something they had not yet tried, to keep the Elyri safe and appease the fears of Enesfel's people. Diona might not have the answers either, but if anyone did, she believed it was Kavan. He had already hinted that he had a plan. She prayed this had not been part of it. Perhaps she could persuade him to act now, before the situation grew worse.

At least she could find out what had led to this melee. He had to have an answer for that.

❧Chapter 28❦

The unanticipated riot raged into the night, causing the King to despair that his celebration would need to be postponed. With many guests still to arrive and unable to pass the fighting, and the possibility of screaming, cursing, and weapons clashing interrupting those already inside, it would mean a meager, uneasy banquet if his generals were unable to crush the chaos. Thankfully, the inclusion of Owain and an additional three dozen soldiers, and an increase in the number of townsfolk who were tired of the violence and wanted it to end, meant that, over the course of the night hours, the Crown gradually gained the upper hand. Several arrests were made, people sentenced to short prison terms, stiff monetary fines, or both for their parts in the disturbance. Among those, three were identified from the variety of drawings Ártur had made for Caol over the past few weeks, men guilty of crimes against Teren, Elyri and the Crown in equal parts, men sentenced to a swift execution to be carried out after the King's celebration. Spending the morning hours of his day passing sentence on the guilty was a dark enough stain on his mood. Hagan refused to allow executions to mar it further.

After the fighting ended, and silence settled over Rhidam, the welcoming of delayed guests was left in the hands of his chancellor and chamberlain as the King caught up on a night's missed sleep. Having Kavan's assurance that there had been no plan to the violence of the previous day, that it had not been an attack on the royal family but a crime of opportunity against one or both of the Elyri the combatants had seen, the monarch's mind was put at ease.

It had been a bubbling up of underlying tension, believed Kavan, something Diona could not directly contribute to dedhá Claide since the bard assured her that Claide had not been in that crowd. Claide did not have the courage to engage in a show of violence. Words were his weapon of choice, words he could twist and hide behind, and if he had done anything to contribute to the riot it had come in the guise of many Faith lessons meant to inflame the discontent.

By the time the King's guests congregated in the Great Hall to long tables of feasting dishes, treats and delicacies, and the best ales and wine, the riot was relegated to the realm of gossip shared amongst clusters of guests as they ate and drank to Bhyrhán's brightly engaging music. Ártur was there because Syl had agreed to attend long enough to bestow her love and respect on the young man she had mothered from the moment of his birth. With seven Elyri in attendance, including the two Cáner boys, the King had taken great pains to make certain everything, the food, the drink the room, was secure and safe for them. Whether these precautions were successful or merely zealous, by the time Kavan entered the Hall, harp beneath his arm, everyone was confident of their safety this night.

Eyes followed as he crossed to where his usual bench had been placed, reserved for him as Bhyrhán and the other musicians attending the celebration refused to disrespect the White Bard, and Wortham had taken position at one end of it as if to secure Kavan's rightful place if anyone tried to take it. Twice the captain left that post, when he successfully convinced Zelenka to dance, and he made certain that Owain and Muir were there in his place when he was not. It seemed unnecessary to Kavan, but every one of the guests acknowledged their protectiveness and Kavan appreciated his friends' loyalty.

Syl, seeing Kavan for the first time since his departure seven months before, studied him as he perched on the bench with the black harp balanced on his knees. It was the first time seeing him without his customary robe, and knowing from her husband how damaged Kavan's hands had been, it was the first time seeing them healed as well. He would not look at her, as if embarrassed, ashamed, or apologetic, but it was Syl who bowed her head and lowered her gaze as the brass strings gave their first sweet notes to the thirsting ears of the Lachlan House.

How could she have blamed him for so many things so obviously beyond his control?

With no preamble, no introduction to the song, the first musical offering that night was a tribute to the late king Kavan had dearly loved and at that moment it was Syl who felt sad and ashamed. How much anguish had the man endured during those months away, how much had he given up, how much had he done, was he still doing, for those within these walls and without? Ártur said Kavan had a plan, but no one knew what that plan entailed, or how much personal risk it might involve. Knowing Kavan as she did, the risk was likely sizable; if he was willing to make it for all of them, how could she penalize her husband for mistakes borne out of love?

Kavan had no cause to apologize. If anything, she mused as she dried her eyes with the back of one hand while Ártur squeezed the other, she was the one who owed an apology.

The emotions in the room washed over Kavan but he looked at no one, preferring to keep his feelings behind closed lids, expressed through the notes that poured from long silent fingers. Last night, as the King sentenced the guilty and the guards cleared the streets, Kavan had spent hours composing, blocking out the sounds of battle, the thoughts of Dórímyr and Claide, and the storm that swirled around Rhidam's heart. He had feared his talent had withered during the months of disuse and had needed to prove it had not.

Now he felt relief.

For the next hour, those in the Great Hall shared his heart in the only way he could allow. The loss of Arlan. The loss of Orynn. The melancholy of missing Myreth. The fear of the present and the days ahead enmeshed with the anguish of months away from friends and family. But there was also joy in those songs, the joy of living, of a young king coming of age to rule the land, of family safe and present, the joy of healing and redemption, of learning to love and finding peace. He brought each guest on his journey through distant lands over a road of self-discovery, and in the end, brought them home to the relative calm of the castle where the brass strings then fell silent.

He rose from the bench to face the King, daring to look at no one else, and bowed, "Blessings to you, My Liege. May your days be fruitful and merry, and your reign prosperous and long." He almost choked on the final words but managed to speak them without a hint that he had misgivings about the validity of what he said.

The young man stared at the bard who had tutored him, who had, he knew given him the best chance to be a good and decent monarch. He should, perhaps, feel embarrassed by the tears on his face, but he knew others were equally moved by what they heard. He would be surprised if anyone present was not similarly affected. Having admired the bard's music in the past, he had never appreciated it the way he did now, and he realized there was no way he could realistically consider banning Kavan, or any other Elyri, if they did not want to leave. Not after everything Kavan had done to make it back to Rhidam.

"Thank you, Lord Cliáth," he whispered. It felt as if he should be the one bowing, but he could only incline his head in a gesture that gave the bard consent to retire. After that much bearing of one's soul, any man would desire solitude. Hagan knew Kavan was no exception.

What Kavan's body wanted was sleep, but his restless spirit refused to allow his mind to find solace in slumber. He knew it without trying. Grateful no one followed from the Hall, that Tusánt, Owain, and Muir had merely clasped his hands in passing and Wortham followed only as far as the doorway to keep others at bay, Kavan took his harp to his room and stood at the open window, staring across the cloudy sky. The smell of spring rain filled the air but it had not yet fallen. The possibility of rain could not deter him tonight, however. There were things he needed to do, duties he believed he alone could undertake, and though he dreaded them, they would not be put off.

The oratory Gate took Kavan to one of the many he knew existed in Elyriá's sovereign city of Clarys. He had not taken time to map the Gates scattered across his homeland as he had those he found in Enesfel, but this one he knew, one he had discovered during his many visits as a younger man called to perform for the Kyne, her family, and entourage. It would take him as close to the great Gathering Hall as he dared to get at this hour, although he did briefly consider Gating into k'gdhededhá Dórímyr's chambers. The hour would guarantee him a private meeting, but he suspected he would have frightened or angered the elderly patriarch and making a negative impression would backfire. Instead, he chose to allow the man to accept his visit unpressured. If that failed, there were other ways to get to him.

He had not brought his harp to offer music in exchange for a room, only coins in the pocket of his vest, but his face and reputation were well known in Clarys and thanks to his distant kinship to the Kyne, he knew he could gain a room in the inn nearest the náós. But knowing he could not sleep, knowing he was as close as he could get tonight he opted instead for the perpetually open náós when the tolling of the huge brass bells in the tower called to him. He knelt before the sole statue and glass painted representations of St. Kóráhm that remained in Clarys to pray.

At one time Clarys had been the center of the Heretic-Saint's cult, but as decades of conflict over his position in the annals of the Faith persisted, bits and pieces of Kavan's patron had been gradually stripped away. In a way it was as it should be; Kavan's journey had taught him that Clarys was not Kóráhm's birthplace as believed, that as revered and beloved as the man was to some, Kóráhm had been just a man, the same as Kavan. The knowledge did not dampen Kavan's adoration, but it had taught him to view Kóráhm, and the other saints, in a more realistic way.

Kóráhm's presence did not come in this place, nor did the spirits or záryph offer consolation and solace in prayer. As much as he had hoped they would soothe his agitation, something in this ancient place forbid their approach. Once, a long time ago, the first time Kavan had come to this place, there had been negativity here, a malevolent presence that had followed him briefly upon entry but evaporated when the boy turned to confront it. Now that dark energy was stronger, no longer a fleeting presence but a tightening shroud that gathered over the holy place.

It was a darkness Kavan recognized. He had felt it in the tunnels beneath Rhidam's castle, had been followed by it on the road through foreign lands, had faced it in the recently destroyed cave on Pháne. It chilled him to know that Coryllien's influence had spread so far as to reach the heart of Elyriá. Was this the root of Dórímyr's neglect and indifference, or had his apathy opened the door for this darkness to enter? What would become of the stability of the Sovereignties if Kavan failed to stop this malignancy from spreading?

As hints of dawn began to brighten the náós, dispelling the gloom as light claimed a new day and a smattering of Faithful began to enter to celebrate the early morning Gathering, Kavan, no longer able to focus on prayer or endure the power bombarding him, became aware of his surroundings again. He decided to take advantage of a Gathering in which he did not need to act the part of Lachlan courtier, ignoring as he did so the stares and murmurs of those who recognized him, either by face or by the color of his skin and hair. Even the serving gdhededhá, men and women he was not acquainted with, recognized him, and he had no doubt that by the time the service was over, Dórímyr would already know he was here.

He doubted the man would think him here for an audience, however. The two had not spoken face to face, beyond an occasional stilted greeting in Kyne Mórne's home, except that single time when Kavan was a boy.

He wondered what the ancient man would think of him now.

The service complete, with the whispers at his core strengthening his resolve, he took courage and followed an instinctual path into the core of Clarys' Faith.

There were others scattered around the waiting room outside of Dórímyr's meeting chambers when Kavan arrived, men mostly, huddled into groups speaking softly as they compared details about matters they had come to present to the patriarch, sitting alone in quiet meditation, or making slow, solitary circles of the room, admiring the artwork adorning the walls, the ceiling, the floor and decorated pedestals throughout the antechamber. The art had been collected over centuries, some dating back to the construction of the Clarys náós and the collection of living quarters, meeting rooms, libraries, alcoves, and secret chambers. Some pieces were said to be older still, bits of history that had come to Elyriá at its founding but where they had been created, by whom, how they had come to be here, were stories lost to time. The great fire that once ravaged Clarys had destroyed volumes of recorded ancient history and the stories had slipped into myth or disappeared. What he would not give, Kavan thought as he passed through the entrance arch, to learn some of that history.

To one side of the room, a younger man, barely more than a boy if Kavan guessed correctly, sat on a marble bench on a raised platform plucking a quiet hymn on an oak wood Cliáthan, a harp Kavan judged to be one of his uncle's early designs. The hush that settled as Kavan entered made the boy look up, and when he met Kavan's gaze with a shocked expression, his fingers froze on the strings. Kavan nodded in acknowledgment but motioned for the music to continue. He was neither here to play nor intrude.

The stares followed him across the chamber as he strode with obvious purpose and more visible confidence than he felt towards the door they all waited to open. No one questioned his right to be here, to go ahead of them without waiting. If the White Bard of Bhryell was in Clarys, he was either here for an appointment or else sent by the Kyne on some important state business. Or, given his association with Enesfel's royalty, he could be here on behalf of the Lachlans, a possibility that made many pairs of eyes study him more closely as he passed beneath the opposite arch that led to the patriarch's chamber.

Hwensen looked up from his desk at the end of the corridor, the desk positioned outside of Dórímyr's door, and stood with abrupt surprise. "Lord Cliáth," he exclaimed, trying to keep the pile of documents and scrolls before him from scattering as he rose.

Kavan's steps faltered. In Enesfel he was a lord, the title of Duke having been bestowed by both Prince Muir and King Arlan many years ago. In Elyriá he held no title, no rank or position that should afford him a moniker of power and respect. Perhaps the aide merely used the title given him by a king, but hearing it was unexpected.

"I have come to speak with k'gdhededhá Dórímyr," he said as evenly as he could, praying he sounded more confident than he felt. "It is an urgent matter on behalf of King Hagan of Enesfel."

"Yes, my lord, of course…let me announce you." Whatever Hwensen thought of his being here, he did not hesitate to retreat into the patriarch's chamber. The immediacy of his action disclosed that the k'gdhededhá was alone and Kavan glanced back down the hall to where the number of those awaiting audience was gradually increasing. He suspected most of those people would be kept waiting the entire day for naught. His belief in that likelihood doubled when the ashen-haired aide returned with a pensive frown on his face.

"I am sorry. k'gdhededhá is busy," he said, eyes downcast, parroting words Kavan knew he had repeated too many times before. "If you would please wait in the antechamber…"

"He will put off the meeting until I give up and return to Enesfel unseen. Is he always thus with foreign emissaries?" Such treatment was rude, impolite, and to some, might even appear hostile. "Perhaps I should take my matter to Kyne Mórne. Tell him I shall return after speaking with her."

The High Mother was the one individual in the Sovereignties who had any degree of control over the head of the Faith. As long as the Kyne's rulings and requests were not contradictory to the tenets of Faith, were not inflammatory or flagrantly immoral, even the k'gdhededhá had to abide by them. And in matters of a political nature, such as the relations with foreign nobility, the Kyne's word was the final authority. Kavan was not above using rank to gain an audience, using his relationship to the High Mother and his connection to King Hagan, to gain this audience. It might not gain him anything else, but the chance to speak would be enough.

Though Hwensen's face drained of color, his lips twisted into a small smile. "Perhaps you should. I will inform him at once."

Kavan had no intentions of going before the High Mother, however, as he bowed his head. The Matriarch had other matters to tend to, and involving her in this was not what Kavan wanted. As much as this was political, it was deeply intertwined with the religious and he believed it should be resolved by the gdhededhásur and the Faithful they served. He turned and started away, his steps slow and measured as Hwensen went back into the office. It was moments later, eight more steps taken, when the door opened and the aide called, "Lord Cliáth, k'gdhededhá will see you now," without closing the door behind him.

Kavan stopped and did not turn until his smile had faded into a once more neutral expression. The aide, however, did not hide his smile, apparently pleased and proud of the manipulation the bard had used to out-maneuver the patriarch, and when Kavan passed into the spacious office, with its host of wide windows overlooking the rear courtyard where gdhededhá roamed to and fro going about their daily routine, the aide bowed gratefully. If he had an inkling of Kavan's purpose, then it appeared he was an ally, an allegiance that Kavan could use to his benefit.

"Cliáth." The k'gdhededhá muttered the word without looking up from the manuscript he was perusing.

"k'gdhededhá," Kavan said with a formal bow. The patriarch looked older than Kavan remembered, drawn around the face and shoulders and heavier around the middle as if great age or responsibility was causing his body's mass to sag and pool around his waist. He waited for the man to speak, years of service to King Arlan enabling him to stand quiet, deep in thought with a shred of attention focused outward in order that, when he was needed, he would be able to snap abruptly to it. Whether the document Dórímyr was reading was of urgent importance or whether he was testing Kavan to see what he would do, or rudely ignoring him, the bard refused to be baited.

Grudgingly, the older man finally set the scroll aside and looked up into his guest's face.

He had not seen Kavan in years, and yet in spite of the much different attire he wore, the bard looked little different than he remembered. Only older. Having heard the rumors, both from gdhededhá Kesábhá and other, less formal sources, about the disfiguring attack on the White Bard, his pale green eyes eased slowly down to the man's hands hanging relaxed at his sides. There was no visible hint of deformity. His eyes narrowed. Had the tales been exaggeration, rumors, and lies, or had something happened to restore the use and condition of the bard's hands? Familiar with years of stories from Bhryell and as far away as the depths of Enesfel, of a man rumored to perform miracles from boyhood, the possibility that there had been some miracle was not easily dismissed. It made Dórímyr uncomfortable. Cynical.

It was much easier to believe the stories of mutilation to be false. The little boy with the heretical-bordering words could not possibly have grown into the originator of miracles. k'Ádhá would never use a heretic that way.

"What do you want?"

There was no politeness, no prelude of small talk or greeting inquiries of health or comfort. Kavan had made note of the man's assessment in that perusal of his hands and thus expected nothing less. He was here because Dórímyr preferred to keep the Kyne out of Faith business, nothing more, and likely already suspected the nature of this visit and did not want the High Mother made aware of the precarious situation poised to break in Enesfel.

But Kavan would not meet that abruptness in kind. "Your Grace, I have come to formally request, on behalf of King Hagan of Enesfel and the Faithful outside of Elyriá, that you come to Rhidam and appoint a new k'gdhededhá…"

"I will not."

Undaunted by being cut off, not surprised at the refusal, Kavan continued. "If it is your safety you fear for, I will personally guarantee it if you come at once. gdhededhá Claide is not above manipulating a vote in his favor, and if he is elected, there will be bloodshed in Enesfel the likes of…"

"What happens in Enesfel is not my concern."

"It should be. What happens within the whole of the Faith is the duty of position you were elevated into, the oaths requiring to keep the needs of all Faithful…"

"In Elyriá."

"Everywhere. I know the oaths, Your Grace. I have studied the texts. Dhágdhuán did not come for Elyri alone, but for all people…"

The patriarch scowled, resenting being called out on details and oaths that not many people knew or remembered. "That is not…"

"You know the precepts as well as I, the tenets. You know all are welcome…"

Rising with unexpected ease, his face darkening with burgeoning defiance, the older man snarled, "Do not preach to me about precepts, Cliáth. You are not gdhededhá, you are not…"

"All may read and know the holy texts; there are no hidden corners in the oaths of servitude gdhededhá take." Kavan's behavior remained calm but he knew he was dangerously close to treading the paths Kóráhm had once written and walked, words that had always been part of the Faith's teaching until they fell out of favor to the egos of men, becoming heretical as those with power strove to keep it. "Such things are not the sole privilege of the gdhededhá. By not intervening in this election, you condemn both Teren and Elyri to death…"

"Elyri should not be there."

There was silence in the chamber, both men staring at each other, aware that outside of the room Hwensen could hear every word of their exchange. Never had a k'gdhededhá spoken those words before, even if they believed them, never had Dórímyr publically voiced the opinion that Elyri should not travel beyond Elyriá's borders. Something in Kavan's calmness, or perhaps something else about him, had pulled the outburst from the older man and caused him to lose his temper and self-restraint. Attempting to be calmer, he continued in a low, strained hiss, "Going beyond the mountains invites heresy…"

"Heresy?" Kavan asked, aware of the man's agitation without understanding it.

"The Faith originates with us…"

"The Faith originated out there, in the world," Kavan retorted, pointing to the windows and the view they presented. "It came from the world, for the world, that we may know peace among all men and women. Dhágdhuán was not born here, in these walls…in Elyriá…might not have been Elyri…"

Kavan's mouth snapped shut in response to his own words, a thought voiced that he had never read anywhere, that no one had told him, that he had not even considered before. At that moment, however, he whole-heartedly believed them to be true.

"He was…"

"There is no proof," Kavan interrupted, despite the little voice in his head that suggested he should not start down the path he was about to take. "He was born long ago, in lands across the sea, lands we do not know, have not seen…" The same lands, he briefly wondered, where Kóráhm's father had gone? But what did that make him? What did that make any of them? "We know so little…"

"We know enough."

Kavan stubbornly shook his head, wondering as he spoke why he was debating history with a man so stuck in his beliefs that he would condemn Teren to suffering for the sake of being right. "He might have been Teren…or something Other…how can we know that truth when we believe the fallacy of Kóráhm being born in Clarys…”

“Of course he was…”

“I have seen his birthplace with my own eyes.”

Dórímyr had slowly worked his way around the desk until he faced Kavan closely enough that the bard could feel every emotion boiling within him, every conflicting flash of anxiety, distrust, hatred, and fear that led to the one word Kavan would not have been so shocked to hear if he had been consciously thinking about the words he used to convince the patriarch to change his mind.

“Heresy!”

Kavan looked down at the finger shoved at the center of his chest, feeling the sudden ball of power form beneath his ribs, beneath that fingertip, the ball of power that could kill if he unleashed it, a ball of power created by the fear of that one word. The one word that could ban him from the Faith and leave him even more of an outcast among his people than he already believed he was. He swallowed hard, clamping down with every discipline he had, to harness that deadly force and allowed silence to fall between them.

Eye to eye, the k’gdhededhá lowered his hand and took a step back. There was fear on his face, but fear of what? Fear of Kavan’s certainty in the words he spoke? Had he felt that power poised to kill? Or had he seen, or felt, something else…in Kavan, behind him, around him? It was that fear, Kavan believed, that erased the charge of heresy without the word being spoken again. It was that fear, Kavan thought gratefully, that might have spared him.

But it was also that fear which sealed Enesfel’s fate.

“If you will not come to Enesfel, Your Grace,” Kavan began again, more quietly, cowed by his regret for words ill-spoken, “then allow me to bring the aspirants here.” Such a suggestion was a long shot. Even if the majority of candidates held no anti-Elyri fears, that did not mean they would agree to travel to Clarys. Unless Kavan brought them by Gate, a dangerous prospect in ways that did not bear thinking about, the trip would take weeks by horse or on foot, and Kavan could not see most wanting to make a risky journey through the currently wild climate of Enesfel or over the treacherous roads that crossed the Llaethlágárá. Claide would refuse the notion outright or he would speak against it in such a way as to discourage the others from making the trip as well.

And why should they, when the Elyri patriarch was unwilling to do likewise?

"No." Dórímyr returned to his chair and reached for the nearest scroll as if to resume his work, the subject closed. To Kavan, the man's tone suggested that he found the thought of so many Teren under his roof to be repulsive. "Everything will be well. You will see."

Kavan waited a few moments to see if the man would say anything more. When he did not, the bard asked, "You desire Enesfel to elect its own k'gdhededhá?"

Dórímyr's response was a distracted grunt.

Kavan waited again and then swallowed the bitter sigh that formed in the back of his throat. "Then you condemn many people to death."

There was no reply to that, other than a flare of hostility that Kavan did not take the time to decipher or address. At the door, hand on the iron latch, he paused, his head hanging with the weight of something he only marginally understood. "May k'Ádhá forgive you," he whispered. For once, Kavan was not sure forgiveness was something he would be able to give.

Hours of flight and Gate-hopping filled the remainder of Kavan's day, taking him to the cusp of twilight and bringing him to the outskirts of Bhryell in spite of his having no intentions of going there. The patriarch's final words, his stubborn clinging to a belief that ecclesiastical elections in Enesfel would not spell disaster, left Kavan with a sense of foreboding and sickness that he did not think even time would heal. Such a belief was folly to him, unjustifiable, and yet short of forcing contact with the patriarch's mind, forcing him to see, to hear, to know what Kavan knew, he could not compel the man to change his mind. Perhaps he should have done it, but he did not think it to be his place.

Not after the tangent their argument had taken.

Hwensen, indicating he had overheard the conversation without actually admitting he had, asked Kavan if he would present the dilemma to Kyne Mórne to request her intervention. Grimly, Kavan said no. He knew the High Mother well enough to know she was unlikely to interfere in matters of Faith. While Dórímyr's choices would undoubtedly cause political turmoil in Enesfel, it was not the Kyne's place to meddle in a foreign kingdom's policies. Elyriá, like the island nation of Káliel, rarely involved itself politically with anyone else. So long as the Lachlan monarchy was not endangered and did not request aide, so long as there was no outright threat to Elyriá, the High Mother would remain neutral and allow history to take its course in the events of the shorter-lived, more volatile Teren. Kavan saw no reason to try to change her mind, not after so badly failing to change Dórímyr's.

What was left for him to do was to work against the destruction of the Faith from inside the Teren establishment and prepare for the worst, should it inevitably come to pass.

Now that he was in Bhryell, staring at the small stone and wood home before him, he knew why he had come. This was not the first time a heavy heart had brought him to the bhydáni's doorstep and he prayed, as he did every time he came here, that it would not be his last.

Someday he knew it would be.

"Kavan!"

The stooped sage's exclamation was muffled by the sudden embrace. Knowing his protégé to be reserved and restrained and reluctant when it came to physical displays of emotion, the gesture caught the old man off guard in a pleasant but slightly alarming way.

As quickly as the embrace came, it was gone, and Kavan's more familiar awkward expression followed. Tíbhyan patted his arm and said, "Come…please…sit with me." He welcomed Kavan to pass and then closed the door behind him. "You just missed your nephew…"

"Bhen was here?" He had two nephews of age to have been here alone, but Bhen was the only one he could foresee coming to the sage's home. The knowledge explained the familiar scent and lingering presence in the air.

Producing a cup of spiced tea, Tíbhyan served it without spilling and then gingerly settled across from Kavan at the table where the bard had once spent many hours each day studying. His movements spoke of growing frailty but he clung to life and showed no indication that he was ready to give it up.

"He often brings Llucás; he tends my garden and provides firewood while I train the boy."

"Another student, eh?" Kavan remarked quietly as his hands wrapped around the cup of warm liquid. The flight in the evening air had been chilling and the fire and the warmth of the tea felt good.

"Not formally. He attends lessons with the other children in the morning and trains in the shop with your kin in the afternoon. He comes here when he can. He does not require more education than that, but his father encourages learning and it is good for me to have something to do…the company of it…in exchange for what Bhen gives. I do not object."

"It is good then…for you and for him." It saddened Kavan sometimes that the sage had accepted no further private pupils when Kavan had outgrown his knowledge, as if the bhydáni might feel overshadowed by his last student. Tíbhyan swore that was not the case, that he had merely had enough private teaching in his long, productive life and that he felt he had given Kavan everything he had to give. Yet sometimes, Kavan still worried about his happiness.

"I'm glad you're here…I was…things happened that…I feared I would never see you again. I am sorry I did not come sooner."

"Nonsense," the old man chuckled. "From what I have been told, you could not come sooner…and you are here now. You did not forget me and that makes me happy."

"I could not forget you, Tíbhyan; you made me the man I am…"

"You made you the man you are; I merely educated you about what you could be…a man," he corrected with a smile, "who has found his hands."

"I…yes…" Kavan had not considered that the sage might have been shown that damage, but it did not surprise him that Ártur would share such devastating news with the bhydáni. "And myself."

"You were lost?"

The tone of the sage's question made Kavan feel warm and soothed him unexpectedly. If anyone understood that Kavan had felt lost for much of his life, in one way or another, it was the man who sat with him now. And yet the sage had never pressured him to be anything other than what he was, had accepted who and what Kavan could be, guided his student to find his own path. That supportiveness continued to be dearly appreciated.

"Not lost perhaps, but not comfortable in my skin. Maybe I still am not, but I think, at last, I am learning to be."

"Then you were blessed for such an opportunity."

Kavan nodded but said nothing else as he sipped the beverage in his cup. It was a new experience for him, something he knew from the aroma was served in some areas of Hatu and it surprised him to find it in the bhydáni's home.

"There were times," the ancient man continued, "when I felt…power. Strange events of such magnitude that I knew they stemmed from you…and I worried. It pleases me you are well."

Knowing the sage was probing for details, but not knowing what events he might have felt, Kavan sank against the back of the chair and talked. He spoke of the customs, the cultures, the exotic things he had seen, the places he had been that he knew would be of interest to his teacher. He spoke of the fragments of history he had gleaned, of Bhóité, Kóráhm and Coryllien and the ships across the sea. Of k'elyryhánag and the roots of history that stretched into those forgotten southern territories and his concerns that the troubled times facing the lands stemmed from history too long buried. He spoke of Myreth and the congregation in which the man lived and his fears of what lay ahead. He spoke of his foolish words to Dórímyr that might have condemned them all and of healing, of that terrifying experience that had resulted in the most astonishing miracle he had ever lived through.

So many things he felt he could not tell his cousin and most of his closest friends, for they would be sorely amazed, intimidated, awed and afraid in ways that Kavan was uncomfortable facing. Wortham had been there; Wortham knew, had seen, had accepted everything without question. But not many others would have been as tolerant, as understanding, as steadfast. If Tíbhyan had been with him, Kavan believed he would have accepted it all with the same excited curiosity he now listened with, would not have been afraid or intimidated by anything seen or heard. At least no more so than Kavan had been.

It was why Kavan needed to talk to him. Someone had to share those months with him, someone had to know, and when the sage recommended recording the details for posterity, Kavan was content to know he was already doing that very thing. Someday, someone might need to know of those great and wondrous events, and who else but Kavan could commit them to the page?

Eventually, as the night waned and the new day waxed, Kavan realized he might have overstayed his welcome, although the sage expressed no annoyance nor weariness during the passing hours. Leaving during daylight hours meant he risked running into family, most of whom he would rather avoid, but if he was weary, then surely the older man was as well. He really should go.

"My apologies for keeping you, bhydáni…"

"Never apologize to me, Kavan. It has been a long time since we have shared and talked; this has been most stimulating, amazing, educational. You seemed in dire need of unburdening…and I was in dire need of enjoying your company. I hope you found an old man's company of help."

"There are few who understand me as you do, few who care to try. I cannot say when I will be able to return…"

"Aye, you have a stony road before you. I do not envy your destiny. When you reach its end…if you can…come to me…or at least send word of your success." Kavan had to succeed. Tíbhyan knew that, for Kavan, failure was never an acceptable option.

"I will if I can…though if k'gdhededhá has his way, I may not be welcome in Bhryell for quite some time."

The prelate might have been too frightened to further press heresy before, but Kavan suspected that, in time, the man would turn his fear against Kavan and bar him from the Faith. Or he would try. While that would not mean he was banned from Elyriá, from Bhryell, the possible condemnation that could come with the stigma of excommunication would make him even more unwelcome in the place he called home.

"Bah. Old Marble can say what he will, but anyone who knows you knows you are no heretic." The words were meant as reassurance, but even Tíbhyan knew that, when it came to public opinion about the White Bard, views were complicated and unpredictable.

Thinking over what he had said to the prelate, words he himself might have once condemned as heresy, Kavan shook his head. "If they knew my heart…they would have no choice but to agree with him."

He may have shared those words, those beliefs, with Tíbhyan, but until he thought them through, Kavan did not want to share them with anyone other than Kóráhm. If anyone could make sense of them, it might be the Heretic-Saint.

❧Chapter 29❧

When morning came and went twice without word or sighting of Kavan, palpable panic again flew through the halls of the keep. A search was mounted for the bard, for any trace of him but there was none. The last time he had been seen was when he left the Great Hall during the King's celebration, and the fear was that, despite their precautions, some great evil had befallen the bard or that someone had said or done something that prompted him to flee again. But despite Diona's persistent questioning of the palace staff, of every soldier and guest and family member, there was no hint that any crime had been committed or that Kavan had cause to depart as he had the last time. Wortham took offense at having his loyalty to Kavan doubted after the months he had spent at the bard's side. Eventually, after leaving the princess' company in a pique of anger, he stormed out of the castle and into the city streets, intending to drink away his frustration and find the bard on his own.

Drink was plentiful today, as the yearly carnival marking the Feast of Saint Mátán was underway when he charged through the gates. The crowd was thinner than in years past, as many did not feel safe enough to journey to Rhidam, and many of those living in the city worried that merrymaking in a crowd would be an invitation for the Corylliens to strike. The King, wanting his subjects to feel safe and to continue the celebration of his sixteenth birthday into its third day, sent as many soldiers as he could reasonably spare into the streets to monitor the crowds and deter violence. While it had done that thus far, the action also dampened the celebratory spirit as people feared being mistaken for troublemakers too, should they eat or drink too much.

Remembering his last St. Mátán festival when he was nearly the King's age, Muir escorted his wife, father, and Ártur through the delights of the streets, accompanied by a gaggle of guards the King made sure they took with them. He passed the scowling captain and knew what the man was thinking without Wortham saying it.

Somewhere, his sister, the woman Zelenka, and Prince Espen would likewise be trying to enjoy the day with a similar escort, despite her continuing efforts to find Kavan. And the Cáners, minus Tayte who refused to go out in the company of his brother, were also trying to take refuge from worries in the holy festival. Soon the tournament would be underway, though this year, due to the risk to his family, Bhríd was not participating. With Caol away visiting his son and grandchild, there were no royal entries in the archery contest either.

What there was this year, which differentiated the festival from years past, was a proliferation of righteous men and women of Faith. Nearly every street corner had one, sometimes more. Some proclaimed the evils of magic…and thus Elyri…some preached love and acceptance of all people…others called for penance before k'Ádhá so that the land might be cleansed of blight and restored to more prosperous times. When an intersection held more than one of these voices, they would loudly proclaim their messages, trying to shout over one another until soldiers shooed them away. It was spiritual chaos in the streets and Muir wondered how anyone could endure it. How could there be so many differing opinions of what was right and what was wrong? Were not right and wrong obvious things?

What he also recalled of that long ago festival was that Kavan had missed the majority of that day as well. Then, as now, the prince had not known the reason for the bard's absence, but this year he knew Kavan shouldered a heavier burden than ever. Kavan was planning something dangerous, if Muir's instincts were correct, and that frightened him. If it frightened him, it must surely terrify Kavan too. Kavan had been through enough. Why must he endure more to save a kingdom, a people, who were not his? Why had k'Ádhá chosen him as a sacrifice for peace? Muir would gladly accept the responsibility himself if it would spare Kavan whatever destiny was to come.

Melting in and out of the shadows, Caol tailed his quarry, uneasily hoping to get the jump on him to learn who his intended target was. His Association contacts had alerted him to a rumored assassination, gave him the name of the expected assassin in the hopes Caol would take care of it. Assassin's worked on the fringes of the Association, necessary evils who could slip from revered to outcasts with the slitting of the wrong throat. This particular fellow must have gotten on the Association's bad side to be outed by them, and after Caol's last talk with Layton, he feared that one of the Elyri was the target. Unfortunately, they were separated into groups he could not easily monitor. Bhríd and his son in one group and Ártur in another. When he saw Asta at Gaelán's side, with little Marta tagging along at a distance, out of sight as if keeping her own watch, Caol felt better about turning his attention to the safety of the healer.

His instinct, however, told him, after more than an hour of tailing the well-protected healer, that Ártur would not be twice the target. Any expert killer would know that Ártur would be under close supervision after the last attempt on his life, making such a target a difficult one to reach. Unless Ártur had been singled out, an assassin asked to kill any one of the Lachlan Elyri would seek a more accessible mark.

Bhríd or Gaelán? Both were a threat in different ways. Bhríd because he was duke of one of the wealthiest holds in Enesfel, married to a Teren duchess, and was strong and experienced enough to be a threat to anyone who crossed him. He was the Lachlan's Champion many times over. Striking him would make the King vulnerable, and would send a message that even the strongest Elyri was not safe. Gaelán, on the other hand, though a boy, was of mixed blood, a healer, which gave birth to the fear that mixing races could eliminate all things Teren, turn the entire world Elyri. Either would be an acceptable target if a point was to be made to the King, and so Caol left the healer with the intention of finding the Cáners and his daughter.

Retracing his steps to where he had last seen those he sought, he spotted the man behind the name he had been given. While the name was only vaguely familiar to him, part of a family with a history of producing some of the best-known assassins in Cordash, it was not until Caol spotted the familiar round, childish features of the freckle-faced blonde man that Caol knew for certain who he was dealing with. Disguised in beggar's rags and a thin, dirty cloak, Caol was able to follow his target without notice as the man wove in and out of the crowd. Caol trusted that his own skills were adequate to get him near enough to prevent any intended assassination. If he was lucky, he could get word to Asta so that she would be on the lookout too. Not only did he have to avoid detection by the Lachlan guards and the killer, he had to avoid the Corylliens as well. Appreciating a challenge, he had not often had as inquisitor, he swore to himself that no one in the royal house would die this day.

❧*❧

Visiting Claide was not something Kavan looked forward too, particularly with the message he held clutched in his hand, but he knew there was no other reasonable recourse. He could withhold the news he carried, pretend that the prelate's missive had never arrived, but that would be no different than lying, and in the end, Claide would make the same decision to proceed with the elections. Though his chance of affecting the outcome was slim, at least, if Kavan met the gdhededhá, he could attempt to convince the man to be reasonable.

He intended to do a better job of that than he had with Dórímyr.

Grateful that Tusánt's novices were waiting in the thóres with him, Kavan resisted pacing but refused to sit. He did not believe Claide would harm him, particularly with others around, thought the man too much of a coward to take such an action, but the presences of those young men assured him that the gdhededhá's words and actions would be recorded by witnesses, should he somehow incriminate himself. Kavan's head turned when the tall, angular Teren entered what had once been k'gdhededhá Jermyn's chambers but he kept his expression schooled and neutral so that Claide suspected nothing.

In spite of the distaste Kavan felt swirling beneath the man's outwardly calm composure, his words came out as banally as possible. "It is good to see you up, Lord Cliáth." Kavan thought he heard a small choking sound around the word lord as if it had momentarily lodged in Claide's throat. "After such a long absence, many feared you dead."

"I am not," the bard said affably. "I am grateful for the prayers of friends, family, and supporters that saw me safely back to Rhidam."

"Indeed…it is good to have those blessings." He did not clarify if he meant prayers or friends, family, and supporters. "I was told you bring a message from k'gdhededhá Dórímyr?"

Kavan nodded. "I do. I had business in Clarys and took the opportunity to seek audience with him while I was there regarding the necessity of appointing a new k'gdhededhá in Enesfel."

Claide tensed and bristled, reactions he attempted to hide by straightening the desk's clutter. He said nothing, though Kavan waited for a question, a comment, something that would tell him what Claide was thinking without reading his thoughts. When no words were forthcoming, Kavan offered the scroll. "I was asked to deliver this."

Claide took it without looking, and though Kavan left his senses open in case there was accidental contact, Claide was too cautious to allow that. The scroll was tossed onto the desk, unread, and behind Kavan, the two novices looked at one another, perplexed.

"Is there anything else?" muttered Claide.

Because he had spoken to the prelate, there was no reason for Claide to think Kavan might have seen the scroll's contents, or read the imprints left on it. "On behalf of Enesfel…for the sake of peace, I beseech you give the k'gdhededhá time. He is fearful of the violence here but can be persuaded to come and fulfill his clerical duties if…"

Claide's bald head lifted, and for a moment he met Kavan's gaze. "Do you believe he will come?"

Kavan knew the answer was no. Dórímyr was as set in his position as Claide. Aloud, however, he replied, "I do not rule it out. Give him the chance, communicate reassurances of safety…and he may come."

The Teren grunted and lowered his gaze, but not before Kavan detected a perverse hint of desire that the prelate would come, as if he could somehow use that in his favor too. Coming or not, either event could be worked to the advantage of a man trying to manipulate the future of Enesfel. To Kavan, the die was cast no matter what path Dórímyr took. There would be an election. The question was when, and how many lives would be lost to make it come to pass. If Claide noticed the tension in the novices, it did not show.

"Elections will be held. I guarantee it."

The words made Kavan shiver with distrust as he gave the expected half-bow and backed out of the room. Edward and Saul followed, giving the bard distance while remaining close enough, and alert enough, to protect him if necessary. None spoke until they reached the náós, where Kavan paused and glanced at the empty altar.

"Tell the others…especially Tusánt…to be watchful." Explaining his fears was unnecessary. The two young men were living through Rhidam's darkest hours, serving at her heart; they were already aware of the future the prelate condemned them to.

They began to depart, but when Kavan knelt at the altar to pray they hesitated long enough for the bard to wave them away. He felt safe enough here, in spite of the various attempts made on Tusánt's life within these sacred walls. Putting the Faith's future in Enesfel into the hands of k'Ádhá, Kóráhm, and the other saints was a necessity until the princess' efforts to root out the evil thorn succeeded, or Kavan's own destiny came to fruition.

He could not say if either would happen before the election.

Outside at the far edge of town, a trumpet blared, announcing the mid-afternoon start of the jousting tournament, bringing the clatter and rumble of the festival suddenly pressing in on Kavan's awareness. He had been too focused on his mission at arrival to recall the feast day, and now that he was aware of it, its significance and the dangers this year's event held for the members of the royal house crashed around him. He should be out there, mingling, senses alert, seeking danger before it found those he loved.

Nearby movement drew him from his prayers, small, quick, near-silent, and when he lifted his head to seek the source, he caught a quick glimpse of the figure darting towards the door. A boy, perhaps ten years old, Elyri, with dark hair that spoke of phae blood in his lineage.

"Wait!" Kavan called, springing to his feet, certain this was the boy he had seen entering the day Dórímyr's message arrived. But the child, whom Kavan believed had been watching him unnoticed, did not heed his call and disappeared into the danger of Rhidam's festival filled streets. Prayers set aside, determined to find the child, he grasped onto the tail of his anxious aura to use as a beacon to lead him.

They wove through the crowd, through alleys and side streets, in between vendors and performers, Kavan doing his best not to frighten the boy. Surely the youngster must realize Kavan was Elyri as well and meant no harm. He must recognize Kavan. Nearly everyone did.

But the boy was young, possibly from some region of Elyriá where Kavan had never traveled; it was possible he might know no more about the white Bard than a name or his descriptive moniker. He might have come to Rhidam while Kavan was away, might never have seen him or heard him perform. The thought of a pure mind untainted against him by rumor and myth, combined with concern for the boy's safety, made Kavan keener to find him.

His search brought him up short when he reached the temporary wooden platform erected outside the palace gates, built on the city side of the drawbridge and meant for minstrels, mummers, actors, or other performers to use during the festival. The boy slid under it beyond the reach of seeking hands and too far beneath, Kavan guessed, for any staff or polearm to reach if some soldier poked around to flush him out. As the back of the platform was butted against the bank of the moat, it left three ways out, unless the child wanted to swim.

There were ways to draw him out, ways to manipulate the child's will, but the bard was loath to do such things. Besides, there was no need. Sooner or later the boy would come out on his own, hungry, tired and cold. Kavan would wait for him until he did.

But facing the stage, surrounded by a crowd who recognized him, whose hearts soared with expectation at his unannounced arrival, Kavan found the urge to perform to be a strong distraction from his chase. He had no harp, but he could sing. The last time he had publically sung in Rhidam had been when Farrell had been king. Conditions were different now. Now he had confidence in his unusual vocal instrument and he had something else.

Mounting the steps, taking place in the center of the stage, Kavan had conviction. His ancestral blood made righting ancient wrongs in Rhidam, in Enesfel, his accepted destiny, and if the gifts he was blessed with enabled him to reach even a handful of hearts, sway them away from hatred, it was a sufficient place to start. His music had been key in restoring the Lachlan throne to its rightful king and music could be, would be, the key again.

Eyes closed, his head lifted to the sky, he began to sing.

The platform did not muffle the voice above. Never in his short life had the boy heard a voice of such beauty and clarity. Little by little, he crabbed sideways, entranced by the sound, listening with teary eyes, until he was no longer protected by the stage, until he was crouched anxiously on the steps on the left of the platform, watching the white-skinned man draw beautiful notes from somewhere deeper than his throat, somewhere hidden and untouchable. When the singer looked at him at the close of his first song, a small prickle of fear told the boy to run and not look back. The rest, however, heart and instinct, demanded he stay, and when that silver-clear soprano began an Elyri lullaby that the boy knew by heart, he inched a little closer and began to sing too, heedless of the audience. This was what he wanted. The chance to sing like the children in the choir.

There were moments when Caol thought he lost his prey, when the suspect slipped out of view in the fluctuating mass of festival attendees. Frantically he would search the faces, dismissing each one that did not match what he had memorized. Gradually he realized they were drawing nearer to the keep, which made sense in a twisted way. A political assassination would have more impact the nearer it occurred to the castle. Caol still did not know who the target was, as it seemed the fellow was not following any particular person. Caol knew there was another staying in Rhidam, a bard, a relative of the High Mother, a target who made a gradual approach of the castle make sense. Such a target would not only send a message to the King, it would send it to Elyriá as well.

But the risk of raising Elyri ire, of causing the High Mother to act against Enesfel was a stupid one. Caol, like so many others, believed that the Elyri had the numbers, and the ability, to wipe out all of the Teren Sovereignties if they chose. It was no wonder the Association wanted this fellow stopped.

Singing filled his ears as he approached the drawbridge, boys he imagined, or else women, judging by the timbre of their voices. His prey's path veered right, towards the voices and away from the bridge. The crowd clustered around the platform would serve as an ideal place for an assassin to blend in, to hide as he waited, a place where he would not draw attention. Caol crept closer, intent on his target, ignoring the voices from the stage. Knife in his hand, he was prepared to kill the fellow without asking questions, before he was even guilty of the crime he had been commissioned to commit. There were undoubtedly other crimes for which the fellow was equally guilty and unpunished. That was good enough for Caol.

One more scan through the crowd revealed no one from the royal court nearby, none of the guards, none of the Elyri.

Except Kavan.

Unable to recall hearing the bard sing, Caol gawked, speechless, at the man he had not seen in over six months. Not dressed in the white robe he had worn nearly his entire life, Kavan looked much the same as any other man, or rather any other Elyri, save for the unusual coloration of his hair and skin. But it was the stunning notes passing from his throat that enthralled Caol, as it did the rest of the audience, leaving him breathless at the unexpected beauty.

Distracting him from the duty of his target.

This was the voice he had heard during the Gathering, the sweet distant voice in the náós rafters flawlessly mimicking the choir when they sang for the King. This was the child the Sight had shown him, the boy in the loft, the youth he had connected to without having met him. Kavan smiled at the boy affectionately, offering his hand as well as the encouragement he often wished he had received as a child. Hesitantly, the smaller hand reached back.

Caol's eyes widened with a start as Kavan's gaze met his over the unfamiliar boy's head. Even disguised, the bard recognized him, and while that should not have surprised him, it was startling. The child too, at the moment his finger's touched the bard's, turned his head to look in Caol's direction. But it was movement directly in front of the inquisitor that snapped Caol into focus. The assassin's hand came up and let his small throwing knife fly, aimed directly at the most dangerous Elyri in Enesfel. At the moment of release, Caol lurched, his long-bladed stiletto finding its mark between the killer's ribs, puncturing his lung, causing him to spit and gurgle blood.

As if having seen the attempt coming, the boy leaped at the bard with enough force to knock Kavan off his feet, allowing the instrument of assassination to fly harmlessly over them and land with a splash in the dark waters of the moat.

Kavan did not know what was happening. One moment he was trying to make contact with the boy, the next Caol was there. A prickle of danger shot up his spine, a warning, and then he was on his back on the platform, the brief connection with the inquisitor lost. Few had seen the knife, but some had. Some screamed in panic, scattering and fleeing in every direction. Some were gaping at the suddenly bleeding man falling to his knees in the middle of the crowd. A few rushed the platform to pull the boy away as if he was a threat on the White Bard's life. The child screamed and Kavan grabbed for him, drawing him into his arms and clutching him protectively against his chest.

By the time he looked through the thinning crowd to where the palace guard had begun to accumulate around the dead man, Caol Dugan could no longer be seen.

"Lord Cliáth." General Agis leaped onto the platform without using the steps and offered the bard his hand. "Are you injured?"

"No." But his voice was quietly strained as he realized that this had been an attempt, plotted or opportunistic, on his life. "Someone threw…" He pointed with one hand towards the moat, following the knife's trajectory, but he had not heard the splash. There had been too much happening for him to hear it.

The Cíbhóló general directed some of his men to the search of the moat and summoned others to the stage. "Did you see anything? What happened to him? Where the killer went?"

Understanding from Asta that, as far as anyone else in Rhidam knew, Caol was in Durham visiting his first grandchild, Kavan shook his head. "No." There was no lie. He did not see who had knifed his attacker, only guessed it had been Caol. And he had not seen where the inquisitor had gone. He could give that answer with a clear conscience while wishing for the opportunity to talk to Caol himself. He needed to know what the inquisitor knew. It would undoubtedly help his efforts against the violent scourge plaguing Enesfel.

Agis knew Kavan to be a truthful man. In the chaos, it had been unlikely the bard had seen anything. There was little reason he should have, but Agis needed to ask. "Well then, into the castle with you, my lord. If there was one attempt, there could be more, and it will be easier to secure the area and search it if I know you are safe."

Though he knew it was the wisest course, Kavan wanted to know the identity of his assailant, wanted to touch him, read him, know who had sent him and why. But he had a child in his arms that needed protection and there were already guards carrying the suspect across the drawbridge. For all Kavan knew, the fellow might still be alive.

Carrying the boy, glad the general did not question him about the youngster whose arms clung around his neck, he let Agis escort him as far as the drawbridge. The curious, and those who had heard the White Bard singing, were assembling again now that the chaos had subsided, but there was nothing to see except the imposing general and the guards who were combing the area for clues.

Not sure where he should take the boy, Kavan got as far as the library, where he set the youngster in a chair and knelt before him to be at eye level. "I owe you my life," he murmured, brushing the child's unruly hair from his forehead, "and I do not even know your name."

"Sóbhán," the boy said shakily, fidgeting beneath the scrutiny and uneasy about being inside the walls of a castle. The adrenalin of his adventure had yet to bleed away, and he gripped the arms of the chair until his knuckles turned white.

"Gift." Kavan smiled warmly. Someone loved this boy dearly to bestow such a name. His smile faltered as darker thoughts replaced his first ones. "Where is your family, Sóbhán? Where are you from? You have been hiding in the náos a long time; how have you survived?"

The boy brushed his own hair back again as his eyes perused the bard's face. The man's voice and presence were soothing, serene, and gentle; there was nothing about him that spoke of danger. The dark-skinned man had called him Lord…Lord Cliáth, and if he, as Elyri, had free run of the castle then he must be someone to be trusted. Someone had tried to kill this bard, as they tried to kill all Elyri, and that made him an ally. Sóbhán had been unable to make contact with the chamberlain, the one Elyri he had known by name, but this man had reached out to him. Perhaps he had finally found sanctuary.

"There is no one." Tears pooled in his violet-blue eyes but did not fall. "I came with my uncle from Káská…he was a sculptor, hoping to offer his services to the King for a time. He was killed the week we arrived. When they came for him…big men with masks…he told me to seek out Lord Cáner…but I could not." His shoulders shrugged and then sagged but he did not elaborate. "I ran and hid…but I could not get in. Now there is no one…in Káská…no one here."

"How long ago was that? Do you know?"

He shook his head. "It was snowing; I don't know when that was."

Snow in Rhidam likely meant his arrival had occurred at the turn of the year, at least three months ago, possibly longer. It was hard enough for an adult Elyri to survive in Rhidam now, harder, perhaps, Kavan mused, as most adults would be ill-equipped for, and uncomfortable with, a life of survival thievery. Sóbhán's innocence provided him with a purer instinct to survive, and he had been lucky enough to stay out of harm's way by finding sanctuary in the náós rather than risk trusting anyone. It was a marvel he still lived.

"When did you last eat? Bathe?" His clothes looked new enough, regal even, but his lanky frame looked ill-fed and unkempt.

"A novice brings food…he doesn't see me but brings something when he can. Clothes too." The question of a bath was unanswered.

"Come." Kavan stood, intending to thank whichever of the novices had shown such kindness. "We shall get you a bath…a meal…then a bed for tonight." What came next, Kavan could not say.

"Truly?"

"Truly." Kavan nodded and smiled again as the boy threw his arms around his waist. With no royal children to tutor and guide, this sort of innocent affection had been sorely missed. He did not know what he could offer beyond the basics, but if he had his way, if Sóbhán's story about being alone in the world was true, the boy was not going anywhere. Children needed a home, a family…and in that embrace, Kavan decided he needed this child too.

❧Chapter 30❧

"**W**here have you been?"

Both Kavan and Sóbhán looked up as the door burst open and the agitated healer stormed through it, Kavan from the writing desk and Sóbhán from the washbasin where he enjoyed his first hot bath in months. The boy was the first thing the healer saw and he stopped, his prepared tirade ripped away by the unexpected sight.

"Ártur, this is Sóbhán. Sóbhán, this is my cousin, Healer MacLyr."

"A real healer?" The boy shifted onto his knees and rested his elbows on the edge of the wooden tub.

Ártur nodded mutely. How was he to berate his cousin and learn the truth about the reported attack with a child in the room? An unfamiliar child who was not, to the healer's knowledge, kin. He knew Kavan would not speak in front of this boy.

Kavan set down his stylus, sensing that he should put his cousin's mind at ease before something unfortunate was said. "Sóbhán, finish bathing. The meal will be served soon and you should be finished by then. I shall be right outside the door."

"Yes, lásánai," the boy said with a bowed head, using a word that made both older men blink. It was not a word often used in Elyriá anymore, and Kavan was surprised the boy knew it.

Shaken, he followed Ártur into the corridor and closed the door behind him. He did not want to keep secrets, but until he knew the boy better, until he had a plan, he did not want to expose him to matters that were better left to the adults to sort out.

"What is that about?" the healer snapped, pointing at the closed door as if to the child behind it. It was not the root of his upset, but it was a place to start.

"He has been living alone in the náós rafters. I met him today…when he saved my life."

"Then it is true!" Frustrated, the healer barely resisted grasping Kavan by the shoulders and shaking him. "What in the name of…?"

"Ártur." The clipped, commanding tone silenced the older man and both stared at one another for several moments, Kavan's expression daring his cousin to continue. When it seemed Ártur was calm enough to listen, or at least willing to, Kavan continued in a gentler voice. "k'gdhededhá Dórímyr has refused to come to Rhidam, refused to appoint Jermyn's successor, has given his blessing for Claide to proceed with elections."

The healer's mouth opened and closed twice as he tried to form words. That was no excuse for Kavan's absence, but it was, he knew, more important than his fear for Kavan's safety. "How do you know?"

"I met his courier and I spoke with Dórímyr myself," he sighed.

So that was the explanation for Kavan's absence…and not one he had expected. For his cousin to have risked, and gained, an audience with the prelate meant he was more concerned about the outcome of Faith policy, the future of the Faith in Enesfel, then Ártur realized. Generally ill at ease in political matters, Ártur tried to stay out of them. He focused on the health and welfare of those in the keep. He should have guessed, however, that Kavan would not remain outside of such events if he believed he could influence them.

Kavan was not the sort of man to stand on the fringes and watch.

"You went to Clarys." He scrubbed his hand through his reddish hair. "You should have told someone."

Kavan shrugged. "It was an impulsive decision; I did not think I would be gone longer than overnight. But…things were said between us. I flew; I visited bhydáni Tíbhyan and lost track of the hours. It needed to be done. I had to try to change his mind…postpone or prevent the election."

Slumping against the closed door, he gave a defeated sound, something between a groan and a sigh. "I failed. Claide has likely sent the summons to the sees already…or he will have done so before the end of tomorrow. This election will happen unless we find some other way to delay or prevent it…and when it does, Claide will be chosen." There were few other contenders for the position as far as Kavan knew, and he could not think of anyone who might pose a serious threat to Claide and his plans.

"By the saints…" Ártur collapsed against the wall as well. "Is that why…I heard talk…someone tried to kill you?"

"I don't know." He did not believe the attempt had any connection with his visit to Claide not long before; the timing was too close. "A crime of opportunity, perhaps…since I was singing at the…"

"Singing…out there? I missed it?" The night of the King's celebration had been the first time in years that Kavan had sung before an audience of more than a handful of friends, at least the first time Ártur was aware of, and never, to the healer's knowledge, had Kavan sung in such a public way. His regret at having missed it nearly outweighed his upset over the attack.

"It seemed fitting. I was following Sóbhán, came to the stage…and singing felt like the thing to do."

There was no point in asking Kavan to explain that impetuous choice. His cousin was ruled by a set of mystical and intuitive guides that often made no sense to Ártur. With the influence of St. Kóráhm and other powers directing him, Ártur believed even Kavan did not always understand his actions. Asking why would frustrate them both.

"What are you going to do with him?"

"He will stay with me."

"Kavan…though he calls you…"

"It isn't that." Yes, he secretly admitted, being called master and lord pleased some secret corner inside, but he could not allow that title to continue to be used. He would find some other name for the boy to use for as long as he remained in Kavan's care. "He came to Rhidam from Káská with his uncle, who was killed here. He claims to have no living kin. I will learn the truth, seek out family he may not know of…but for now, he has no one else…nowhere else…and I will not send him back to the náós rafters. Besides…I need him."

Ártur faced Kavan, one shoulder propped against the wall, and studied his face as he had not done in a long time. Kavan had served as tutor for the royal children for years. Llucás and Asta had been his last students, and with Asta now in the care of lady tutors and Llucás living in Bhryell where he was educated in the manner of most Elyri children, the healer understood why Kavan might feel a significant loss of purpose. Particularly now that Arlan was gone. How many times had Ártur been denied the chance to serve as healer, and how lost had he felt during those periods? Kavan was a bard first, it was true, but Ártur had watched his love for tutoring the children grow with each additional student. In Elyriá, he would be bhydáni now. Ártur suspected that, though Kavan never said it, the unconditional, non-prejudicial love of children gave Kavan a sense of grounding he did not often feel amidst wary, opinionated adults.

"Do you want me to examine him? Be sure he is healthy? If he has lived alone for as long as you suggest…?"

It was a detail Kavan had not considered so he nodded eagerly. "Yes, please." Relieved that Ártur was not trying to talk him out of the responsibility for Sóbhán's care, Kavan intended to see that the boy received the best of everything. He would have no children of his own. For however long he stayed, if he agreed to stay, Sóbhán would be the closest, Kavan imagined, he would ever have to a son.

By the time the evening meal was served in the Dining Hall, the palace staff was aware of the young Elyri boy sheltered beneath the White Bard's wing, just as they were aware of the attempt made on Kavan's life. For unknown reasons, the assassin's body had already been disposed of, the matter quickly put to rest as if to keep the incident out of the public's eye, leaving Kavan no way to identify either the attacker or who might have sent him. Frustrated, Kavan said little to anyone during the meal, except to introduce Sóbhán and to report to a select few that within days, a few weeks at the most, Rhidam would become the seat of an ecclesiastical battle that might forever change the course of Faith history. That knowledge, and learning that he had come by it directly from k'gdhededhá Dórímyr, was enough to excuse his absence of the previous few days.

Wortham, feeling guilty for his failure to protect Kavan from potential harm, stayed close to the bard throughout the evening, though he said little, covering his shame for his failure with a lack of words as well as respecting Kavan's wish to avoid conversation. When the meal was complete, it was Wortham and Gaelán who escorted Sóbhán upstairs where, it was decided, he would share a room with Gaelán until another could be arranged. Gaelán had no intention of letting the boy sleep alone anywhere on his first night here. No longer the youngest in the keep, no longer the only Elyri youngster, he was eager to share everything with the younger orphaned boy. He was just as excited to discover that this was where his donated clothes had gone.

Sóbhán's presence meant that there were three people who no longer felt alone. Bringing him into the castle, Kavan decided, was the best thing he could have done that day.

The number of guests in the palace had not yet thinned after the feast, although Syl had departed before the party had ended and Prince Espen had already made plans to leave with a portion of his troops at dawn the morning after the festival. They would accompany Bhríd, Madalyn, and Tayte to Levonne and take a ship from there, a faster means of travel that would afford Espen a hastier return. Muir and Clianthe would travel with them, the entire retinue providing safety in numbers that would likely prevent them from meeting trouble. It was that need for safety that kept the King from complaining about the mass exodus of friends and supporters from the castle. But with Sigrid remaining for a few more days, and Kavan home, Hagan felt more confident about the direction his life was taking, and Sigrid soothed his annoyance at being left.

Even the news that Claide was already arranging the election failed to dampen the young King's spirits. On the surface, why should it, Kavan mused, as he left Sóbhán in the company of Gaelán, Asta, and Rouvyn. Hagan, like most others, believed Rhidam's Faithful had been too long without leadership and were unaware of Claide's darker side. Whether one counted or discounted Jermyn as an adequate leader, the popular consensus was that it was time for Enesfel to take the step for themselves that k'dedhá Dórímyr would not take for them.

Remembering his time with Myreth, how that small cluster of people conducted their lives of Faith without the need of such a leader, Kavan did not share that sense of need. Qol might have been afforded the respect of leader due to his extreme age and personal charisma, but from what Kavan had witnessed, his role was limited to the influence he held over Myreth and a handful of others. Except for the persecution and anti-Elyri violence rampant in Enesfel, he thought that the Faith as an entity was running smoothly without the need to elect a man who would, he believed, tear the Faithful and Enesfel apart.

Thankfully alone, without Ártur, Wortham, or Owain to question his intentions, Kavan decided to do something he had been putting off, something he dreaded doing almost as much as he had dreaded that first talk with Diona. Thus far he had received no sign, no clue as to how he was meant to purify the defiled temple below Rhidam's keep, or when the time would arrive to do so. Not knowing made him anxious, and after the attempt on his life, he was concerned that he was running out of time. His imagination about what lay in store was pushing for free rein. He hoped that going to that room, touching the despoiled altar contained by those ancient walls, would tell him what he needed to do, give him the guidance he lacked.

To his dismay, however, his attempts to Gate into the chapel proved impossible. Lingering within the k'dhín bhólibh in the upper oratory, a room considered by many to be as much Kavan's as his bedchamber was, he closed his eyes, sought out the speck of light he knew to be the destination he sought. But the point was shrouded, dim as if behind a veil, and when he reached for it, he was met with the shock of a solid wall of power blocking his efforts as if something was protecting the path, wanting to keep him away, and nothing Kavan did could punch through that separating force. Normally, such an obstacle would have caused consternation, as if the failure was somehow his. This time, however, he knew that was not true. The failure was due to that power he had released from a mummified corpse buried beneath the island of Pháne, the thing that hunted him on the road to Enesfel, the thing he had dared to believe had been destroyed or trapped when he pulled that place in upon itself. It would continue to work against him until the end, he believed, and rather than leaving him dismayed, rather than prompting him to give up, it made him angry.

Angry enough to propel him into action.

Not to be kept from where he needed to be, what he wanted to do, Kavan stormed out of the oratory, his long steps and set features telling those he strode past that he was intent on some purpose and they separated from his path as if washed aside by the waves of his annoyance. Down to the dungeon where he caused each guard and prisoner present to drop to the floor in a deep slumber without either touching them or pausing in his steps. His determination fueled the effectiveness of his gifts in a way he had not anticipated.

In the dark passage behind the secret panel, strewn with the rubble of cracked stone walls, Kavan pressed towards his destination without the use of a handlight. Having been to that room before, he knew the signature of its energy, and the signature of the evil radiating from there. Though the presence tried repeatedly to lure him down side paths, he did not waver, until it eventually took up its protective stance behind the door the bard intended to breach.

It was not locked, had no locks on it of any sort, but it took more force than it should to push it open, as if someone was on the other side pushing back. There was no need, however, to resort to psychic force to succeed, since he did not want to show the thing anymore of his abilities then he already had. He would not give it a chance to use his strengths and weaknesses against him. Straining, he braced and pushed, using natural Elyri physical strength instead of mental prowess, until he felt the blockage begin to give way. Finally, it buckled, allowing the groaning hinges to snap and the heavy wooden door to swing open with an unexpected pop. Kavan nearly lost his footing but regained his balance and, with shoulders drawn back, crossed the room to the altar, unable to see anything in the blackness but easily able to picture the details from the images of memories past.

What his mind's eye showed him, however, did not coincide with his memories. His body turned slowly in the dark, following the ethereal images drawn from the power of this place, trying to make sense of what it showed him. The images of creation, of Dhágdhuán's birth and death, and the end of time were vivid without the use of his eyes, but they were alive in a horrific way they had not been before. The animals, the foliage, the people, withered, wilted, gray and dying, twisted and deformed behind a shroud of foul smoke that reminded Kavan of burning flesh. The carved stone effigies of Gíldás, Edhriá, and Llyr wept blood from their eyes and a multitude of tiny fissures that marred their white surfaces. The fourth stone figure, the unknown saint, towered over Kavan with arms raised, not in the posture it had been standing in since carved and installed here centuries ago. Blood coursed down its arms from punctures in its wrists. Blood pooled at its feet, as if pouring from wounds beneath stone robes in a fashion Kavan recognized.

The rósádhá.

The shock of it and the force of fear that welled up in him forced him to take a hasty step back. He bumped into the altar at the center of the room. There was a screech, as much within his head as it was in the room around him, and his eyes popped open with the sensation of fetid breath moving over his face. He half expected to see something hovering above him, something with black skin and decaying fangs dripping offal. Instead, all he saw in the darkness were the faint apparitions positioned in the corners of the room. The closest wore a recognizable face, and seeing it made Kavan gasp and try to retreat again to escape what he saw. His foot caught on a chunk of stone on the floor, and when he tried to steady himself, his other foot lost tractions on the gravelly dust. This time he fell, and with a sharp crack of his skull against the earthen floor, Kavan succumbed to darkness.

Loitering in the courtyard with Gaelán and Sóbhán as Rouvyn and Ártur tended to a cluster of soldiers who had fought amongst themselves, Asta was surprised to see Marta at the castle gate. She had not seen the girl in over a week, not even during the festival although she had watched for her, as she had watched for her father the entire day. It was hard to be brave when she missed him more with each passing hour. She understood duty, the importance of what he was doing, and she believed he was skilled enough to succeed at a mission that few others probably could. But with the setting of the sun each day, she was reminded that she was barely more than a girl, without immediate family except for the King and his sister. Hagan and Gaelán were nearest to her in age, and with the King occupied by the duties of his station and Gaelán training as a healer most hours of the day, it frequently left Asta alone when she did not want to be.

Seeing Marta was a welcome distraction.

Leaving the boys to talk about Elyri skills and history, of which she knew little, Asta skipped to where the freckle-faced girl waited, aware that several sets of eyes watched her from around the courtyard. They were not suspicious, as Marta had been here often enough to be familiar, but they were cautious, and to Asta's sensibilities, overly protective. "Where have you been?" she asked quietly when she was near enough to hug the other in a friendly manner, keeping up the pretense of a close friendship.

"Busy." Marta did not say more, and in this public place, Asta did not press for details.

"Do you want to meet someone?"

"I can't stay…but I was asked to see that you got this." She pressed the doll she carried into Asta's hands with a smile as though she was bestowing some special gift. The doll was lovely and expensive, with strawberry hair similar to Asta's and a blue lace gown that reflected the blue of her painted eyes. It was the sort of doll Diona avidly collected, but this had not come from Diona…or for her. With those little details, and others, the tiny cameo necklace much like the one Gaelán had given her, the painted Lachlan signet on her hand like the one every member of the Lachlan house wore, the familiar silver combs in her hair that looked much like the ones Asta's mother had favored, Asta knew there was but one person who could have sent this, only one it could have been sent for. She also guessed it was a cover, a message in itself, for her father, more than anyone, would know Asta had little interest in dolls. What message this gift held would have to wait until she was somewhere private to retrieve it but she was excited to have received word directly from her father when he was weighing so heavily on her thoughts.

"Tell him thank you," she murmured.

Marta nodded, still smiling though her expression had turned wistful and melancholy. "I'll try."

"What? What is it?" There was something Marta was not telling her. Asta could tell, could feel it, but the other girl shook her head.

"I've got to go."

Before Asta could stop her, Marta was skipping away and Asta, feeling more alone than before, hugged the doll to her chest. Behind her, she heard Rouvyn call her name, and then Gaelán as well, and she dutifully returned to them. Once inside the castle, however, there would be no duty to bind her to their wishes, no need for their protection. Let the boys entertain themselves. She had to know what her father was trying to tell her.

❧*❧

The merciless pounding at the back of his head eventually brought Kavan to consciousness to discover he lay in the unlit silence of the ruined, underground chapel. Gone where the ghostly images, the distorted visions, and the sensation of that presence he knew he would soon confront. The latter surprised him most, as he would have expected it to take advantage of his vulnerable state. A quick self-examination revealed nothing amiss, however. Perhaps he had frightened it off, or it had grown bored and gone elsewhere to torment and manipulate someone else. Evil still lingered, heavier now, but the presence itself was gone.

Fingering his skull for the wetness he expected to find, Kavan considered what he had seen, what it meant. The distortions and bleeding saints might have been no more than their mourning for Enesfel, or might have been a darker premonition. There was no clear suggestion that either was true. But he was certain they were bad omens. The bleeding unknown saint, whom he once believed was Kóráhm, seemed now more likely to represent himself, a thought that made him sick with fear and doubt. The hair, the robes…even the rósádhá he had repeatedly endured over the last several months. He had thought the experience to be one of purification, preparing him to be worthy of using the holy items in his care, but what if the experience was something more, connected to whatever would be done to erase the stain from this room, from Enesfel?

He could endure it if he must; he had before. What he did not want to endure, what he had not previously considered or anticipated, was that the ritual he would undertake would not be done alone.

He did not want to include anyone else. He did not want those he loved to be at risk nor have them witness what could possibly be an agonizing, grisly display of sacrifice. Why could he not right the world in solitude without anyone ever needing to know? Why must there be witnesses to what he suspected would be his final moments of life?

Some of what those visions had left him with was not a surprise. Wortham had been with him for so long, at his side, it was fitting that the soldier would follow Kavan to whatever end he met. More than anyone he knew, Kavan would need the captain's strength to endure what lay ahead. But the other faces that solidified out of the mists in his mind troubled him, made him reconsider his path.

There had to be some other way. What he had Seen had to be wrong. Perhaps the visions had come from his nemesis, an attempt to lure his loved ones to death…or he had been shown their inclusion in the hopes of deterring him from following through with the purification ritual. Any entity touching his thoughts knew he desired to protect his loved ones. Discouraging action was what it wanted.

Troubled and bemused, Kavan got up, careful not to hit his head or stumble again, and cautiously found his way to the hidden compartment where he knew the Gate to be. With no resistance to the power this time, he made the connection with the upper oratory and in moments breathed easier of cleaner, lighter air, studying the blood on his fingers with a scowl.

If his enemy thought to deter him from proceeding, it would be disappointed. But if Kavan could find another way to achieve the same end without involving anyone other than Wortham, he would do it. No one else was going to be hurt. No one else was going to watch him die.

He cocked his head, listening to the unexpected sound of sniffling and sobbing from the outer chamber near the altar. The pitch sounded young, Gaelán, Sóbhán or Asta, or else one of those spirits that sometimes visited him when he prayed. A weeping spirit might be chastising him for intending to manipulate the impending ritual to suit his wishes. Feeling guilty, hoping that was not the source of the sound, he pushed the chamber curtain aside.

It was Asta on the top step in front of the altar, a collection of dismantled doll parts scattered on the stone around her. There were other items, a stiletto, a bracelet, a curling scrap of paper, and a linen bit of doll's clothing on which was a hand-drawn map. The girl dried her face as he approached, bowing her head to hide the remaining traces of tears though she made no effort to hide what lay on the stone. If the items were secret, or contained secrets, she clearly felt no need to hide them from Kavan.

"What is it, Asta?" Not one to ignore grieving, though he did not know if he could help her, the Elyri joined her on the step, looking from her face to the doll parts and then back, waiting for her to speak or in some other way indicate a need for his help.

"He's not coming back," she whispered, pressing the scroll into the bard's hand. Having grown up with Kavan, trusting him and knowing he could do things, know things, that no one else could, she did not know what she was hoping for by telling him this. Perhaps, she thought with another sniffle, she wanted to know she was wrong, wanted him to somehow change things.

Kavan unrolled the scroll and read the familiar script, his expression sad. He could not fault Caol's decision. The undercover role he had undertaken was difficult enough without constantly running the risk of being recognized by palace staff and residents. And he could not feign a visit to his son indefinitely, unless he resigned his post as inquisitor. The King might have bound his hands, but he would not easily let his uncle resign. Wilred was instructed to report, if asked, that his father had departed Durham in whatever timeframe seemed fitting when the questions of Caol's whereabouts arose. A search would be mounted, leaving his position unfulfilled for a while longer. It would not allow Asta to reach full proficiency in her chosen profession, and it was doubtful King Hagan would accept her in the position of Inquisitor even if she could prove her proficiency, but Caol's most trusted Association contacts were already instructed to rely on his daughter as if she and he were one.

His choices pushed her into the world of adult responsibility, and though many would frown at it, these desperate times required unexpected action. It was duty Asta wanted, responsibility and adventure, and with the Association's support, Kavan knew she would do well. She had trained for this, and though she lacked practical experience both Caol and Kavan believed her to be capable.

But she was still young and losing her father this way would not be easy. With her mother's death and her brother so far away, her father was the person she was closest too. Now he was leaving her under Princess Diona's guardianship.

Kavan closed his eyes and felt what the words on the paper could not tell him. Caol's emotions, his state of mind, his intentions. There were, as the bard's hand passed from one doll part to the next, flashes of imagery that could be used to identify where Caol was when he prepared this intricate message for his daughter. With luck, Kavan could find that place but it would likely be safer for Caol if he did not.

"He is safe," he murmured, "and loves you dearly. And…" He paused as the shiver of Sight ran through him, less of an image coming forth than a degree of certainty he rarely experienced, "You will see each other again soon."

He did not need to see Asta's face light up to feel the surge of hope. "We will?"

"I don't know when…or where…or how…but yes. You will." When he opened his eyes, he returned the letter to her and she carefully rolled it and returned it to the hollow of one doll leg. The other, which Kavan suspected had held the stiletto, remained empty as she began to reassemble the doll.

"Thank you." If anyone else had told her that, she would have thought them to be humoring her, trying to make her feel better about her uncertain future. Hearing it from Kavan, however, was reassuring. He would not say it if he did not know, or deeply believe, it to be true.

When the doll's head and limbs were reattached to its torso, and the necklace it had worn secured around Asta's wrist, she gave the pale blue linen underdress to Kavan. "I think this is for you…you should have it."

Eyebrow arched, he took it and studied the map drawn on the underside of the fabric garment. It depicted a coastline, mountains and rivers and cities that he did not recognize. There were no words on it, no names or details, no indication which direction was north. The area depicted could have been anywhere in the Sovereignties…except that it did not match any region of which Kavan knew.

"I don't know where it is either, or why he sent it," Asta continued, "but if it's important, if anyone can figure out what it means, it'll be you. Besides," she grinned sheepishly, "You've got the best hiding places. It probably isn't something anyone else should have."

He nodded, accepting the truth with an affectionate smile. Her father, over the years, had enlisted the aid of others in the royal house to unknowingly train his daughter, including asking them to hide objects for her to find. For reasons she was unclear of, she had only twice been able to find objects Kavan had hidden for her. She believed she knew every inch of the keep well, even corners of the royal chambers Arlan had once called his, but clearly, unless he was hiding items off of the castle grounds, she did not. If the map was a piece of the Coryllien puzzle, Kavan would be the best person to preserve and protect it.

"Find out what it means, Lord Cliáth…and stop this. All of it…if you can. Bring my father home."

Resting his hand tenderly on her head, he recalled those fleeting thoughts of manipulating events to suit him instead of as Dhágdhuán and Kóráhm and k'Ádhá commanded. Asta was a reminder of duty and responsibility. He had to do what he must, for her and for everyone like her throughout the Sovereignties who were suffering.

"I will do everything in my power, Asta."

Everything including putting those he cherished in a position to watch him die.

The possibility of watching their deaths, however, was far more terrifying.

❧Chapter 31❧

B hríd knew something was wrong as soon as he reached the iron gates that protected the path leading to the Dubuais-Cáner estate. It was not merely the absence of sentries at the gate who should have been keeping watch; it was something else, something in the air he could feel sliding against his skin like oil on water, something that burned the back of his nose and left a taste of copper and sulfur and burnt wood in his mouth. But it was not something he could hear. In fact, as he brought his family to a halt, there were no familiar sounds to be heard across the whole estate save for the rolling surf in the distance.

Even the birds and insects were still.

"Stay here," he instructed his wife and son as he drew his sword and began to inch forward, motioning three of the King's soldiers to follow while the rest closed protectively around his family.

"Bhríd?"

The chamberlain shook his head, bidding Madalyn be quiet with a wave of his hand. He expected an ambush or something similar; it would not be safe for his family until he knew what he faced.

They had made the ride from Rhidam to Levonne in good time and had seen Muir, Clianthe, and Prince Espen and his men to the port where they would find ships to take them to their mutual destinations. He wished, as he reached the open front door of the Dubuais family house, the house that had become his home as well, that he had accepted Espen's offer to accompany them to the estate. He would have found the extra men reassuring.

Especially when he eased the door open further with the tip of his sword to discover what was inside.

Pottery, china, artwork, smashed and torn throughout the house. Perhaps some items of value had been taken, but it was impossible to tell with the amount of destruction he found. More appalling, however, was the discovery of body after body, run through, hacked limb from limb, lying in dry pools of blood in many rooms of the house. Every servant, every vineyard worker, every guard who had tried to protect the innocent and had fallen where they stood. Men, women, and their children, none of whom had committed crimes save for the misfortune of being here when the butchery occurred.

All were dead.

With each new discovery, Bhríd ran room to room, gasps turning to moans, moans turning to cries, and finally, turning into a continual roar of fury, dismay, and outrage. He did not need to touch the dead to know that this slaughter was a message, nor did he need to touch them to know what that message was. These peoples only crime had been serving the Elyri Duke. He had no doubts that if Madalyn and Tayte had been here, they would have been counted amongst the dead.

It was the heartbreaking bellow that brought Madalyn running, heedless of her husband's instructions to stay where she was safe or her son's efforts to hold her back. The sight on entering the hall was enough to make her turn and vomit in horror while Tayte stared at the dead with a numb, blank expression and glazed eyes, a look that was broken when his father charged down the staircase to the summons of two soldiers sent to investigate the grounds. Between them, they dragged, limply like a rotting corpse, a man in dirty, bloody leather armor. They were about to drop him where they stood, but Bhríd shouted, "Not in my home!" He reached them as they retreated into the courtyard, and with a kick he knocked the groaning, barely living figure from their grasp onto the dusty stones.

"Who's responsible for this?"

Even if the man wanted to answer, he was weak and disoriented from blood loss and Bhríd had no patience to allow him to catch his breath, swallow, or form words. With his black hair loosed from the tie that normally held it neatly at the back of his neck, his pupils dilated enough that the blue of his eyes was barely visible, his body tense and trembling, the usually stoic King's Champion loomed over his captive, caught the man's bedraggled face between his hands, and yanked him up to stare into his eyes. "Who?"

Madalyn followed as far as the wide steps that led up to her door, but she stopped now because she dared not get any closer to her husband's wrath. She had seen him annoyed and frustrated before, but she had never seen him this angry, and she impulsively wrapped one arm around her son's shoulders. Tayte stared, as wide-eyed as his father and mother, and did not react to her protectiveness.

Some of those faces inside he had known all of his life.

The man at Bhríd's mercy began to twitch. Though he was not known for a willingness to read people, and rarely read items for the Lachlans except when no other Elyri was available to do so, he gave no consideration to the matter now as he thrust tendrils of power into his captive's head. The fellow yelped in surprise rather than physical discomfort, but as Bhríd found what he sought and began to bark names to those nearby, the injured man began to fight back. He struggled to be free, but he did not have the strength to break Bhríd's grasp. Internally, in a fight no one could see, he was trying to hide names, faces, details of their deeds from the Duke who was mercilessly seeking them.

Bhríd knew some of the names, some prominent, some not, men from Levonne and the surrounding vineyards. Some men he liked and trusted, others he had met in passing, some he had never met or seen before. Such hatred and hostility that could have led them to butcher every one of the Dubuais-Cáner staff had, until today, been beyond Bhríd's comprehension. Now, however, he understood, for the hatred he felt for these murderers was blind and all-consuming and beyond his control. He did not care that the man he held was flopping like a fish on the deck of a boat in his efforts to stop the theft of his thoughts. Bhríd wanted every guilty man found and brought to him, and if he did not find a name, he memorized physical details in order that those few could be located as well.

No one was going to get away with this crime.

"Bhríd…" Madalyn's voice was a small, scared squawk as the soldiers around them were sent into the outreaches of Levonne to bring back the guilty. He did not respond other than to throw her a look that demanded she not interfere. Normally he was content to allow her the administration of her lands and the city of Levonne. Today, however, he was taking control and interference would invite his wrath. She knew he had the right to act, for she doubted she would have the stomach to do what had to be done. This was no small offense; this was a crime against her, against their family, and Bhríd, as head of that family, had every right to seek justice.

Neither she nor Tayte moved as Bhríd dropped the convulsing man and began to pace, looking like a caged animal as he snarled, hissed, and tried to keep a leash on his fragile temper. It took nearly an hour for all but three of the twelve men identified to be dragged into the courtyard, led by Sheriff Everard who was as grim-faced as Madalyn had ever seen him.

Each captive's expression changed from neutral or outraged to one of fear when they saw the man jerking on the ground, the pile of dead bodies the guards were gathering into one place in the courtyard, and Bhríd's wrathful state. They might hate him for being Elyri, but they also feared him, both for his race and for the strength and reputation he had as a warrior. They had either believed their comrade dead or escaped with the rest of them and it was clear they had not expected to be caught.

When it seemed no more would be forthcoming today, that a longer search would be necessary to arrest the last three, Bhríd again drew his sword. He asked no questions, made no accusations. He already knew as much as he needed to. He stopped at each man long enough to press his hand against their face, their head, their neck, any accessible flesh, and force their thoughts open. Each time he did this, a man would scream with the force of it and when the Duke had his confirmation, his sword struck home, leaving decapitated bodies spurting blood across the courtyard stones. None were shown mercy. He felt none. He found perverse satisfaction in the feel of his blade biting through flesh, of bones and cartilage crunching and fracturing beneath the force of his arm. He hated warfare, hated killing, but not enough to keep him from that duty when the need arose.

And this was, in his eyes, as much of a war as he had experienced on any battlefield. This was war against him, against his family, against all Elyri, and his patience with such violence directed against innocent people was at an end.

With each man forced to kneel in a line before his father, Tayte's face grew more ashen. He struggled not to fidget, not to flee, as the awareness came that he may have misjudged his father. He thought he knew this man, but he realized now that he knew less than he could have imagined. When one of the prisoners tried to scramble to his feet, not wanting to endure the fate of those men before him, he cried, "Tayte!" as the soldier holding him shoved him back to his knees.

That was the only moment that Bhríd turned from his grisly task to stare long and hard at his trembling eldest son. Neither said a word but took measure of one another before Bhríd resumed his executions and Tayte, shaken to the core, hurried away, leaving his perplexed mother to watch the executions alone.

The last man's death was accompanied with a roar, a sound as much of defeated anguish as it was righteous indignation and fury. Bhríd's sword, his hand and arm, his chest and face, were splattered and smeared with blood but he neither noticed nor cared.

"Display them at the gates until dawn," he barked, a touch of weariness beginning to creep into his raw voice. "Make proclamation that any man or woman who dares remove them…or dares such an act of defiance again…will similarly meet death. It will not be tolerated, not here, not in Rhidam, not anywhere in Enesfel."

Sheriff Everard hurried away to carry out the duty required of him. The sentence had not been overly harsh nor unwarranted, given the nature of the crime, and the sheriff had no qualms obeying. He only hesitated long enough to see if the Duchess, whom he had served far longer, would add any orders or contradictions to her husband's decree. But the sickly pale woman wringing her hands had nothing to say, not even when her husband faced her and closed the distance between them.

"Where is Tayte?" He trusted Everard to do as he was told. Any man who defied him after what they had witnessed would be a fool.

Madalyn heard the threat, the command, in Bhríd's voice and locked her knees to remain standing. "I…"

"Where is he?"

"He is not part of this!" she cried, the need to protect her son restoring her voice. "He was with us! You cannot believe…"

Snarling, he leaned closer, his face inches from hers, but he did not touch her. "I don't want to believe it, but I will have answers."

As he pushed around her, she grabbed his bloody arm and held it fast. "You will not hurt him! You will not read him! He is your son!"

A tense hush fell over those still in the courtyard as husband and wife stared at one another, one in anger, one in fear. "They might have known one another," she continued, "but that does not mean he knew about this…or had a hand in it. They raised him! They nurtured him! They loved him! Do not read him, Bhríd. Let me talk to him!"

What she said was true. Knowing someone did not implicate a person of the other's crimes. If that were true, then Bhríd would have been as guilty as some of those men he had executed, men he had known and liked. Yet, though he had not touched Tayte or read him, he had seen something in his son as they stared at each other, had seen traces in the young man's eyes that left Bhríd little doubt that Tayte knew more about what had happened in their home than he should.

Perhaps Madalyn believed she had nothing to fear, believed Tayte to be innocent. Maybe he was. Perhaps she did not take, or want to take, his previous threats against his father and brother seriously. Bhríd did not want to take them seriously either. But he had to. Lives were at stake. His. Gaelán's. Perhaps Madalyn's. And certainly others in Levonne and throughout Enesfel if what he feared was true.

Anti-Elyri violence perpetrated against Elyri was bad enough. Anti-Elyri violence that allowed the slaughter of Teren for their association with Elyri was too much.

But the love in Madalyn's eyes, as well as the honest fear that, in his current frame of upset, Bhríd might lose control and kill his son without thinking, bled some of the need for action away. "Talk to him. Now." He did not want to appear weak as he stormed off to see to the disposal of the dead, but he could give his wife this small concession. He doubted such a talk would prove beneficial or insightful, and he feared what lay in store if his suspicions were correct. What he did know was that he was not going to be able to look at his eldest son the same again.

∾*∾

Despite Claide's announcement that elections would be held as soon as feasibly possible, or perhaps, Diona theorized, because of it, the atmosphere in Rhidam immediately following the King's Day celebration and the attempt on Kavan's life was considerably calmer than it had been. This worried her as much as any continuation of violence would have, for it suggested that something was seething and simmering beneath the surface that was going to erupt in an especially ugly manner, either as a protest against the election or in support of it…in some way that Claide could use to his advantage. Her brother scoffed at her worry, chided her for fears that were undoubtedly rooted in Prince Espen's absence, caused by serene days when she had nothing but her overactive imagination to occupy her time.

She knew it was not true; there was plenty to do. There was a gown to select, an entire wardrobe, plus she spent many hours assisting Sigrid in doing the same. And despite the lack of violence, she and Asta continued to amass every scrap of information they could about the Corylliens, researching the group's history, seeking anything that might lead to arrests and put an end to their schemes and dedhá Claide's. They found little, a name here, an empty location there, a person who knew a person who had seen another person that seemed suspicious. It was enough to lead to the arrest of two for conspiracy against the Crown but none for the perpetrators of previous violence and death. It was frustrating and frightening, particularly when Kavan insisted on behaving as if the attack on him was insignificant.

He took the threat seriously, however, despite his words. He would travel nowhere in Rhidam beyond the castle grounds, not even Hes á Redh, without Wortham, Denyan, and Avner accompanying him. The only place he dared go was the náós, traveling there with Sóbhán to retrieve the few belongings the boy had in the rafters and to make arrangements for him to join the children's choir. The boy had a good ear for tunes, and a good voice considering his lack of training or practice, and Kavan wanted to encourage that pursuit as much as Sóbhán wish to.

Sóbhán, he learned, possessed a slight trace of healing skill, able to mend cuts and scrapes and small burns but little more, and he had some of his uncle's gift for sculpture, as he was skilled with his hands, able to turn bits of wood he found along the roadside or in the courtyard into beads or blocks adorned with flowers, vines, animals and geometric patterns. He had spent hours his first night in the castle studying the carvings Urian had made, and then studying the lines of the two kestrel harps, before picking up a knife he obtained from Asta the following day and carving a variety of simple shapes and forms into a block of firewood. One of those carvings had been a miniature harp about three inches high, and in that one tiny object Kavan recognized the potential of a harp maker. He wondered, as he met with Gaelán and Sóbhán in the oratory, if Bhen would accept another apprentice…and if it was something Sóbhán might want. The boy was finding his footing, making friends and rebuilding his life after the loss of his family and months alone. Would he want to be pushed off into the care of more strangers? Did Kavan want to let him go?

"You want to teach us something?" Gaelán asked when he and Sóbhán bounced into the oratory, the two looking like conspiratorial cats. Though younger, Sóbhán was near enough in height to appear to be the same age as Gaelán, and thus far, the two seemed to get along well. Kavan motioned them to the steps at the front of the room where he sat before the altar, his harp silent in his hands.

"I want to try…but I cannot say you will be able to learn it quickly. Many Elyri do not learn it until they are older…and many never learn it at all…but with the way things are here, I believe it is an important thing for you to know. But I want a promise from you both first."

Gaelán nodded earnestly. It excited and flattered him that Kavan called him Elyri, equal in blood if not in skill and power. He felt no regret that he would not have Kavan's gifts. Kavan was unlike anyone else, different, special. It was enough for Gaelán to heal, a gift he knew the bard did not possess. Kavan had never offered to teach him anything before, and as much as he loved and respected his kinsman, Gaelán would promise him anything if it meant the chance to learn from the most powerful Elyri alive.

The dark-haired boy, having no such experience with Kavan, knew only what Gaelán and Asta told him. He did not understand that this was a rare opportunity, but as he had received very little training with the power, he was eager for it and so he too agreed to the unspoken promise with a nod.

Kavan took them into the Purification chamber and Gaelán, knowing what was there from Ártur's comings and goings, grinned. "You are going to show us how to use the Gates?"

Kneeling to keep them all at similar levels, the bard nodded. "Safety for us is a precarious thing. There may come a time when escape is necessary…when I, or Ártur, or Bhyrhán…or your father, Gaelán, are not here to take you to safety. I hope you can both learn this so that you can get to Bhryell on your own if necessary. But first, you must promise that, if I teach you, you will not use it for frivolous travels…to avoid your studies…to go anywhere else alone out of curiosity…and that you will tell no one this Gate is here."

"But everyone knows that Ártur…"

"I'm sure most do not think about his means of travel," Kavan assured Gaelán. To his knowledge, the King and his sister knew about the Gates, and most likely Asta did too, even before the day Kavan materialized in it…the day she had gotten her last message from her father. He suspected Rouvyn might know as well, and Wortham of course. But the staff, the guards, and others serving the King in the royal court did not know and must, he believed, never know. "It is too dangerous for the knowledge to spread. Teren cannot use them, but if they learn the locations, they could lay traps…kill us instantly…and I do not want that burden on my conscience."

"Nor I," Sóbhán whispered. He had not traveled by Gate, did not even know what the Gates were, but he was prepared to learn…and do anything he could to keep people from dying.

Hands out before him, Kavan instructed, "Take my hands." He considered having them take one another's hands as well, but decided against it. Until they were more experienced, he thought it best to limit their exposure to outside sources while they learned. Tíbhyan had explained when he was younger and learning the ways of power that having contact with more than one mind at a time could be confusing and overwhelming for most novices. Kavan had never been one of those, however.

"Close your eyes and look inside as if you are daydreaming…or focusing on power…"

Gaelán, having more experience with that sort of internal focus, and having traveled with Ártur through the Gate before, was the first to find the pattern of lights within his mind. Through the link Kavan's touch provided, with a little coaxing and direction from the bard, Sóbhán eventually saw them too. He was surprised by the field of stars against an internal dark sky.

"Where…? What are they?"

"Each is a destination…a Gate. Some are elsewhere in Enesfel; some are in Elyriá…or elsewhere in the Sovereignties. And some," Kavan sighed with a wistful surge of melancholy, touching the one that would take him to Myreth, "are further away still."

"Even…Neth?"

Wondering why Gaelán would ask such a question, what interest he might have in Neth, Kavan nodded, though it was a gesture unseen. "Even Neth. Elyri once lived there as well, and in Hatu, Cordash, the islands. I know of one in Neth…so there are undoubtedly more. Can you feel the power beneath our feet? Around us?"

He kept his words and explanation unspoken, words within their heads, in order that no one entering the oratory would hear them.

It was a lot to expect from the boys, he knew, expecting untrained, untested children to accomplish so much so soon, but necessity made him press on with his lesson. None could be expected to master the Gates on a first try as Kavan had. Kavan was the exception to Power, not the rule of it. He would give them the help they needed, however, because he wanted both of his young protégés to be safe should he be unavailable to provide safety for them.

Today he focused on helping them find that energy, find those contacts themselves, recognize the one that was Bhryell. Gaelán wanted more but Kavan chose not to go any further. He was about to leave them alone there, practicing that small skill, helping each other to encourage a bond between them, when a powerful psychic jolt rocked through him, throwing him off his knees against the wall of the chamber, breaking the contact with the boys in the process.

Fearing it was something they had done, Gaelán, in particular, fearing that his insistence on pushing the bard for more had somehow harmed Kavan, they knelt on either side of him, clasping his arms, his shoulders, shaking him gently.

"tydhá!" Gaelán felt it too, a bolt of something ripping through his head, leaving a throbbing in its place that was nearly as bad as what he had felt during Kavan's absence. He also felt anger and sadness on top of his fear, without knowing why he should feel anything except concern for Kavan's glassy-eyed, slack-jawed expression.

"lásánai?" Sóbhán might not know much about Power, but he did understand that this was not normal. His fear, similar to Gaelán's was that it had been some failure of his that had caused this.

Kavan blinked through the stunning pain, clawing back to a focused state though the boys' voices sounded far away. "I am…it is…something has happened."

"The Sight?"

The other boy's eyes widened at Gaelán's suggestion. The Sight was a myth. No one had that ability except for Saints and…someone else. Someone he had heard the adults talk about after their return from a trip to Clarys. A harper they wished still played for St. Kóráhm's Feast. A harper rumored to be unlike any other. A harper called…

He dropped back onto his bottom and stared. At the time, those late-night tales and sharing of rumors about a white harper had meant nothing. Even after meeting Kavan, they had not. He had not connected the two things. While he did not believe the wild tales his parents, his uncle, and their friends had bandied about, of miracles and strange abilities, he could no longer deny the man existed…and if Gaelán's claim was true, then perhaps there had been more to those mythical tales than the adults around Sóbhán had believed.

Kavan shook his head slowly, the effort making him dizzy. "No…not…but…" He had not seen anything; this was no omen of what was to come. This was happening now, a backlash of intense emotion he could almost taste as it prickled along his skin and sank into his pores. "This is…something has happened…to your father."

"My fath…"

Kavan grasped Gaelán's wrists to steady him, to keep him from bolting as he read the young man's desperate need to flee to the stables, steal a horse, and ride to Levonne alone. "He is unharmed, but something has made him…angry…and afraid…"

It was the fear that concerned Kavan. He had never known Bhríd to be afraid.

"I must go to him."

"You must stay here." Still seated on the floor, Kavan drew the boys closer, an arm around each of them, the one around Gaelán slightly tighter to restrain his impulsive nature. "It is dangerous there."

"He might need a healer! Mother might be hurt! Or Tayte!"

Kavan swallowed. That could be true. While he did not believe, from what he experienced in that intense moment, that any of his kin were hurt, he had no proof. Gaelán would not be satisfied with a guess. He would want to know, want word from his father, and he would not happily wait for days for news to reach Rhidam.

"If you will wait right here…both of you…I will go to him, find out what has happened. If a healer is needed, I will come for you. Will that suffice, Gaelán?"

It was not what Gaelán wanted, but he knew it was the best he would get. If Kavan believed there was danger where his father was, it was likely true, and for Gaelán to step into it might put his father, his family, in more peril. The reckless child in him demanded action; the maturing part understood duty, and caution bid him wait.

Before getting to his feet, Kavan kissed each boy on the side of the head, an impulsive sharing of affection he did not normally give. But the concern over what he might face in Levonne, where he believed Bhríd to be, birthed a need to express feelings he usually hid. "I will return as soon as I can."

Still stunned by the revelations he had been given, the younger boy nodded and clutched Gaelán's hand. Regardless of his push towards maturity, Gaelán did not protest. They watched Kavan's posture relax, his eyes closed, and after a silent moment of energy across their skin and a slight drop in temperature…as if a fog had entered the room…his image blurred, faded, and he was gone.

"Where…?" Sóbhán let go of Gaelán's hand and scooted to where Kavan had been.

"To my father." Gaelán drew his knees to his chin and wrapped his arms around them.

"And he wants to teach us that?" If he had not seen the man vanish in front of him, he would not have believed it possible.

"You'll learn it. We both will." And when he did, promise or no promise, when his father needed him, he would go.

Not knowing what to expect, Kavan opted for the Gate in the city's naós rather than the one in the Dubuais-Cáner home. Despite his kinsman's reassurance that he was always welcome there, Kavan was not willing to enter the house in that fashion. With Tayte's animosity towards Elyri, Kavan felt it more important not to take the liberty of appearing there uninvited. But stepping out of the Purification Chamber into the central Gathering area, in a place that brought back memories he would rather forget, bombarded Kavan with the charge of negativity. Levonne was awash with it and it took little effort to follow the darkest thread to his cousin's home. The gates were open, as the uniformed Lachlan soldiers passed back and forth dragging bodies onto low wagons. He could see movement beyond, but it was the heads, and the headless corpses, hanging on poles and ropes along the outer wall that demanded the attention of those who passed.

What, Kavan wondered with a sick feeling, had happened here?

Fearing that Bhríd or someone in his family would be one of them, concerned that his certainty for his cousin's welfare was wrong and that he himself was in mortal danger just by being here, Kavan studied each face he could see. But these were not Elyri, were instead Teren, and though the deaths continued to dismay and appall him, he was relieved that none of Bhríd's family was there. The gathered townsfolk allowed him to pass without acknowledgment, and the working soldiers did no more than look at him as they let him through the gates.

Faces in the wagons, more dead, piled high, men and women he had seen during his visits to this house. Servants, groundskeepers, cooks, stable hands, vineyard workers. All butchered and dead for several days, compared to the recent kills of those decapitated men at the wall. Kavan stopped to stare. He was trying to make sense of what his senses refused to process, oblivious to the men loading bodies for burial, when Bhríd emerged from the house. He was not immaculately dressed, as usual, was stained with blood from head to toe, and his blue eyes were black with fury and grief when Kavan met his gaze.

"I should have known you would come." It did not surprise him to see the bard there, but he had not been anticipating it.

"What has…?" Words failed Kavan as he looked left and right at the wagons flanking him.

The chamberlain's expression darkened. "Those you passed…out there…they did this." The emotion in his voice told Kavan that those displayed beyond the gate had died at Bhríd's hands and no one else's.

"All of them? All of your…?"

"Even the children." Bhríd choked before clearing his throat.

"Madalyn? Tayte?"

"Madalyn has retired…though I do not think she sleeps." How could she after what she had seen? He paused, considering how to answer the inquiry about his oldest son, and when he could not think of anything to say that would be kind or warm, he asked, "Gaelán?"

Noting the omission, Kavan replied, "He wanted to come in case a healer is needed…he felt the…backlash of power, through me. I urged him to wait until I spoke with you, learned what has happened."

"He cannot be here. It is not safe for him. I will have his things sent to Rhidam. All of them. He will not set foot in this house again."

Wanting to ease the boiling rage, Kavan laid his hand on Bhríd's bloody arm and gently, without pulling or pushing, coaxed him to walk apart from the milieu where they could speak without being overheard. "This is his home."

"Not anymore." The words were spat with finality. "Madalyn will not leave here…but I cannot stay. For Gaelán to come will mean his death. I am certain of that."

"Have there been threats?"

Bhríd snorted. "Only from his brother…who knew at least one of the perpetrators of this…" he looked at the wagons piled high with bodies, "outrage."

"You do not think he…?"

But Kavan knew that was exactly what Bhríd thought, or at least feared, and if Kavan was honest, it would not surprise him either.

"I pray not…but he has fled…and Madalyn demands I do not read him. He did not participate, as he was in Rhidam with us, but did he plan it? Did he encourage it? Did he know?" Bhríd rubbed his temples then raked his loose dark hair, damp and sticky with blood, away from his flushed face. "I do not want to believe it…but I am denied proof…and justice cannot be served until…"

Serving justice against one's own kin, particularly a child, was a fate Kavan wished on no man. Having known Tayte from birth, he did not want to believe the young man capable of such evils, even if he did hate his brother. Daring to hope for the best, wanting to give Bhríd peace and reassurance, Kavan murmured, "Give him time. Perhaps he fled from this horror…and from seeing your fury…rather than out of guilt or fear of punishment." Through the skin to skin contact of his hand on Bhríd's arm, he could see the executions his cousin had carried out, could sense Madalyn and Tayte watching in horror. Tayte was legally an adult but that did not mean he was prepared to see such bloodshed perpetrated by his father.

The chamberlain sighed. "I pray you are right, Kavan. Tell Gaelán I will return to Rhidam within the next few days…and tell him there is no need for him to come here, that it is not safe. I will explain this to him when I return."

"I shall." The news, when it reached Rhidam, would not come from Kavan. It would probably spread with the return of the Lachlan soldiers, if not through merchant gossip beforehand. Bhríd wanted the time and opportunity to deal with this matter on his own, not Crown interference. He served the King, yes, but he did not want the meddling that could come because of a well-meaning boy's effort to help. When, if, the last three men were arrested, the matter would be a closed book in Bhríd's eyes, the final notes in this chapter of his life. What would become of his marriage, his family, he could not guess. What he knew was that one thread would be left, either to tie off or cut loose, and until he saw his eldest son again, there would be no chance of finding peace of mind. He doubted he would find it even then.

<h1 style="text-align:center">❧Chapter 32❧</h1>

Word of what had happened in Levonne reached the King's ears the day Bhríd rode through the castle gates with everything Gaelán owned, and the majority of his own belongings, piled high in the wagon he had secured for this journey. The chamberlain would not speak of those events except to say that most of the perpetrators had been punished. He explained his choice of returning to Rhidam as one of necessity: Gaelán needed his protection. His wife, being non-Elyri, would be safer without him there. He had to believe that to be true or else go mad with worry. As long as he appeared to be out of her life, and his show of leaving Levonne with all he owned certainly suggested a split between them, he believed it would keep her safe. It had to. And Tayte, regardless of his shortcomings, adored his mother. Bhríd chose to believe the young man would protect her where he had failed to do so.

He might not be able to protect her in any other way, but he was trying, as he was trying to protect his youngest son whom, he felt, had been pushed aside by Madalyn in favor of Tayte and her familial lands. He could not fault her duty to the name of Dubuais; that duty had been the basis for their marriage. But it hurt that she could abandon her other son, hurt to learn that his race had proven to be a sticking point between them after all, when she had sworn it never could be.

Only Kavan, Gaelán, and Ártur knew the full story, and through Ártur, Syl as well. The grim nature of what her brother had endured was enough to bring Syl to Rhidam for a day, a day she spent sequestered with him, and later her husband, Kavan, Gaelán, and Sóbhán. They talked until the sun began to set, when she and Ártur returned to Bhryell, debating the benefits and pitfalls of remaining in Enesfel versus returning to the safety of Elyriá. None decided to retreat, duty tied the three adults to Rhidam, duty to the Crown, to each other. The boys, given the choice, opted to remain in Rhidam out of their own senses of duty, love, and respect. But Kavan felt in most of those present a wavering in their resolve to remain with the Lachlans.

Perhaps that was as it should be. He, however, had no choice but to stay. Until the sacrifice was made, whatever that sacrifice proved to be, he had to remain in Rhidam and fight for order. Destiny had, through an accident or design of lineage, made it Kavan's duty.

While the Elyri advisors debated their fate, the King found himself embroiled in his own quandary. For the first time, he openly admitted that Caol's contacts, his methods, might be the best way to find the remaining men responsible for the attack on Levonne's duke and duchess. For this instance alone, he was prepared to concede to Caol's expertise, but there had yet been no word from the inquisitor and his absence made Hagan angry. He sent a scathing, accusatory message to Durham, demanding Caol's immediate return to Rhidam.

Asta, the only one other than Kavan and Diona to know the truth, casually suggested in passing that she knew some of her father's contacts and that she could, if the King allowed, get messages to them that might result in the arrests the King sought. It would make her feel better if there was something she could do on Gaelán's behalf. She intended to reach out to those contacts whether Hagan approved or not, but this time she was pleased not to have to go behind his back to get something done. The King, not asking what sort of connection Asta had with Caol's Association contacts, assumed she would send a message to them and that would be that. He offered a bounty for any who could bring the three, alive, before the Crown, and expected that to be the end of it until the arrests were made.

The timing of the news from Levonne made Owain skittish about his own future. He should be in Fiara, tending his holdings, protecting them, but he no longer felt safe enough to attempt the journey by land across Enesfel. It was that uneasy fear that brought him to Kavan as the bard waited alone at the dayroom window, watching the resourceful young woman sneak out of the palace against everyone's better judgment. Asta was no fool, but still Kavan worried for her. Her part in the grand scheme of Enesfel's history was not yet played out and he wanted her safe.

Stopping at Kavan's side, Owain stared out the window as well, but there was nothing of interest to see by then and he could not tell what Kavan was looking at. "You will stay in Rhidam?" He did not know what the Elyri had discussed, but it was a logical topic of debate.

He recognized the pensive set of Kavan's mouth and knew something was weighing heavily on the bard's shoulders.

"I will. I must. There is too much left undone."

"You must be the one to do it?" Kavan's lack of response was answer enough. Owain scowled. "What do any of you owe any of us?"

"This is not about owing…and I cannot speak for the others. For me…this is about what is right…about the future and how to protect it. There comes a moment when we each face a choice about how to serve history…and this is mine." He looked at Owain, pushing away the ever-growing realization of how age was dogging his friend. They were barely a year apart, and yet Kavan knew he looked young enough to be the man's son. He knew Owain understood what he meant, having faced a similar difficult choice on behalf of Enesfel before. "You want to return home?"

The prince nodded. He had not spoken his wishes, but often, with Kavan, there was no need. "Duty demands I tend what is mine…but I also feel I am needed here…"

"You are…or…you will be. When the time is right…" He stopped and looked back out the window. "You should be in Fiara. I do not know when that day will come, but I will come for you then, if I may."

"Actually…I was thinking…" Leaning his elbows on the sill, he ordered his thoughts before continuing. "I don't know what it is…but I believe I must be here when the elections come. Diona sent couriers to Espen, alerting him to the immediate need for military support, and I agree with her. The need is there. When the election happens, the King may need every strong sword arm at his disposal. As I understand it, it will be another week or more before the gdhededhá convene…and then there will be a period of debate and nominations. Two or three weeks ought to give me time to set my affairs in order for a potentially longer absence. But I do not think it wise to travel across Enesfel alone, or with those few men I came with. I am hoping you might see fit to take me there."

The request brought a faint smile to Kavan's face. There was a peculiar sense of peace to be found in Owain's Fiara home, in spite of the lingering ghost of Guthrie McHador. It was the same peace Kavan found in his estate in Alberni, or in the walls of his house in Bhryell, a feeling of being home that Rhidam failed to offer. He often wondered why those places gave him that sense of belonging.

"I can take you whenever you wish. You have but to ask."

Owain smiled too, pleased to have given his friend a moment of happiness, however brief. "Then I am asking now." Others might have believed that smile an indication that Kavan felt happy to be rid of him, but Owain knew that was not so. It was being trusted enough to be asked, a legitimate excuse to use Power, and that made the prince happy too. "I have to ready my bag; I can be in the oratory in thirty minutes, if that will be acceptable."

"Thirty minutes," Kavan agreed. He did not need to ask a second time if Owain was willing to aid him in the sacrifice when the time came. The prince, like Wortham, would do anything Kavan asked of him. He might protest when the nature of his role was learned, but he would be there.

Kavan had seen it.

Rather than return to Rhidam straightaway, trusting the boys were safe in Rouvyn's care as long as they obeyed him, Kavan accepted the invitation to dine with Owain in Fiara, taking the opportunity to be free of Rhidam's oppressive air and the chance to enjoy the man's friendship. There was the prince's meager staff on hand, two kitchen cooks, four housekeepers, one stable hand and blacksmith, and another four groundskeepers, which meant the house was absent the bustle associated with the Lachlan keep. There were, he knew, some six dozen soldiers about the grounds, a necessity carried over from the days when Fiara had been part of Neth, as well as a necessity created by the cloak of violence Enesfel wore. The northernmost reaches of Enesfel knew relative peace, and the de Cormick King had not had the strength, since his defeat, to take up arms against Enesfel and the cities which had once been his. That did not mean, however, that the threat was not there. Owain could afford his small army and Kavan, as they dined in comfortable stillness, appreciated that protection more than he could express.

"My lord." One of the house staff, the man who managed the estate when Owain was away and often oversaw the day to day business even when Owain was home, came into the dining room and bowed as Owain and Kavan were finishing their meal. A loud knocking had reverberated through the halls a few minutes before, but as Owain knew no one was expecting him to be here, he assumed the visitor was someone he would not want to see and had thus ignored it, leaving the visitor to his warden to tend to. Even if there was some tragedy in Fiara, no one would come seeking a man they believed to be a way, although they might come seeking his warden.

Owain left the man to deal with it himself.

"Lord Madron has arrived, asking for an audience…"

Owain straightened and swallowed hard past the tightening in his throat and chest, locking eyes briefly with the bard. Not expecting this particular visitor, wondering how Kavan would feel about it, he motioned for the bard to follow. "Show him into the sitting room, please," he said to the warden as he started in that direction.

Kavan knew the names of each lord in Enesfel; he had made it his duty to be aware of them and, as a duke, to foster good relationships with as many as he could. Madron was a name he did not know, but it was clear that Owain did. A Nethite noble from the north, perhaps, which would explain Owain's anxiety.

"My apologies for this; I was not expecting him. I hope you do not object." He opened the sitting-room door and ushered Kavan in.

"Why should I object to guests in your home?"

Owain released the door after stepping into the room and crossed to the liquor cabinet anticipating the need for a strong drink. When it opened again, the warden ushered in a man hidden beneath a thick fur cloak, too heavy for the warmth of the year. Kavan knew it was a man from the breadth of his shoulders, the heaviness of his footsteps, and the width of his gloved hands before introductions, were made.

"Well, cousin…you do have a knack for entertaining the most interesting guests."

Cousin? There was no threat in the stranger, only amusement and eager curiosity. Cousin meant the stranger was a de Cormick, a surprise that intrigued Kavan enough to propel him forward as the stranger lowered his hood.

"Prince Kjell de Cormick…Duke Kavan Cliáth…"

"The White Bard." The blonde prince offered his hand, a gesture of trust not many Nethites would make towards an Elyri. "I did not think you would…"

"Believe me, this was not planned." Owain watched with an anxious flutter in his stomach as Kavan clasped the offered hand. He had no reason to be nervous, and yet he was. What if Kavan discovered something through that touch that he did not like? What if Kjell reacted in a hostile manner? "We arrived this evening and Lord Cliáth remained only to dine with me. I did not know you were coming."

Kjell looked at the hand he held as if expecting to feel something unusual in that handshake, something that would suggest at once that the famed bard was Elyri. He knew what he expected to see and was amazed he did not. Instead, it felt no different than any other handshake between men and he could not decide if that disappointed or pleased him. "Nor did I. I have been hunting…the best way to escape Merkar's tedious, manic, delusional moods."

"And you happened to be in the area?" Owain asked with a smirk, glad his warden was gone now. He trusted his staff, but in this delicate situation, the fewer eyes and ears involved, the better he would feel. He poured a glass of brandy and offered it to his cousin, who in turn attempted to redirect it to the bard. When Kavan shook his head no, Kjell shrugged and accepted the glass.

"Perhaps," Kjell laughed, his reply noncommittal. "If we are to work together, it is best we keep communication open, is it not? I should have sent word, but this was truly an impulsive choice."

Owain glanced at Kavan. He did not know how much, if anything, the bard knew about Diona's interest in forging a working relationship with the Nethite prince. Kjell was taking a risk mentioning that arrangement in front of the bard; Owain knew Kavan to be trustworthy, but there was no way Kjell could know that too…unless something had happened during that brief handshake.

Nothing had happened, as far as Kjell was concerned, but he was willing to take the risk on Kavan's reputation alone, willing to accept the trust Owain had in the bard. Yes, he was Elyri, a race most Nethites were taught to loathe and fear from birth. But Kavan had also served as advisor to at least one Lachlan king, and he had befriended Owain after the man was deposed. The Elyri obviously knew how to keep secrets and keep his own counsel when it came to his choice of allies. Kjell, not one for foolhardy risks, believed this one worth taking.

Kavan did not sit as the other men did, but instead bowed to them both. Though he felt shifting loyalties within Kjell in that handshake, shadows born of necessary secrecy in order to survive a life of perpetual uncertainty within Neth's ruling house, he felt something else that suggested that Prince Kjell was trustworthy. It also hinted that binding him to the Lachlan House would have both positive and negative ramifications for the futures of the Sovereignties, and since Kavan could not tell if the positives outweighed the negatives, he was prepared to give the handsome young man a chance to prove himself.

"Pardon, my lords, but I cannot stay. I have been away too long; the boys will be expecting me."

"You have children, Lord Cliáth?"

The bard shook his head, ignoring the melancholy stab in his breast. "My cousin and my ward." He was seeking an arrangement to assume legal guardianship of Sóbhán if the boy's family could not be located, but he had no desire to replace the family his ward was old enough to remember. Kavan was not his father, but he was satisfied being mentor, teacher, and friend.

Kjell nodded. So it was true the bard had not married. At least, Kjell thought, he was not the only single man here. "It is too late to travel tonight, surely…" he continued, eager to convince the bard to stay, to have further chance to talk to him, and to learn what miracle had erased the disfigurement of which Owain had told him.

As tempting as the idea was, however, Kavan felt he should not intrude on this particular conversation, felt he needed to return to Rhidam. "Do not fear for my safety. I will be well. Owain…I shall see you in a few weeks…or sooner if events require your return."

"Indeed." Owain too regretted Kavan's departure, had anticipated the man remaining to share his company far into the night, but he was eager to learn what had brought Kjell to Fiara. "I will expect you when you return. Please, keep me informed…and be careful."

"I will." Owain's worry was understandable and Kavan would not belittle him for it. "Prince Kjell, I look forward to seeing you again. I hope we will have opportunity to know one another better."

"I look forward to it." The way the bard spoke those words, as if their meeting was predestined, made Kjell all the more eager for that day to come. If, as Owain had once told him, the bard had the gift of prophecy, Kjell was interested in knowing any tidbits that might pertain to his future. This unexpected meeting was a promising start towards greater things. Greater things were what Kjell wanted.

❧*❦

The lull in the kingdom-wide storm of violence ended when a string of reports reached the Lachlans of trouble erupting in the southern reaches of Enesfel. Duke Gabersdon took leave of Rhidam to tend to criminals captured in Nelori and other southern cities. While he had left his estate for much the same reasons as Bhríd, he was not prepared to forsake his beloved city to lawlessness and had no wife or family to tend it for him. The reports had not been specific, but he hoped that some of those caught would be the ones who had abducted Dhybhé from beneath his roof. If they were, the justice he doled out would be as swift and complete as Bhríd's had been.

To Diona it seemed there could not be many more incidents left for Enesfel to endure. Many Elyri had been slaughtered, many Teren as well, and surely, she argued with her patient serving women as she sorted through another collection of gowns in search of the perfect one for her wedding, those Elyri not yet killed were wise enough to flee. How many more, save those in Rhidam and those she knew to be in St. Kóráhm's in Alberni, could remain? If few remained, and the majority of Enesfel's Teren population knew the risks in housing or aiding Elyri, who else was there left for the Corylliens to butcher?

Only those Teren known to sympathize with Elyri, whether in word, deed, or philosophy; she supposed the Corylliens would target them next. If such clashes continued, it would result in a civil war more devastating than her father had waged to return the throne to a true Lachlan's hands. Whatever her brother's strengths, waging war against Enesfel's own people, to protect the portion of the populace who deserved it, would leave a stain upon Hagan's legacy and possibly the name of Lachlan itself.

Behind her, admiring the gowns with wonder, Zelenka was quiet, listening to the princess bemoan the state of affairs in Enesfel without interrupting. Her grasp of Trade had grown stronger, allowing her to converse with these new people, but politics was beyond her experience and thus not easily comprehended. She understood there were dangers around them, understood that many were working hard to end those dangers and restore security, but within the sheltered castle walls, a city within itself to her, those dangers seemed far away, except for the attack on Kavan which she had not witnessed and which thus seemed unreal. There were other more interesting matters to think about, and one of those involved the elaborate, ornate dresses of unfamiliar richness, unfamiliar cloths and textures. She wanted one, thought Wortham would approve if she wore one, but she did not know how to obtain it.

"That is a lovely one."

Zelenka lifted her eyes, realizing the princess was speaking to her, and then curtsied as her hand dropped from the velvet she stroked.

"It is," she agreed. She had fallen into the role of handmaid to the princess, although she knew little about the customs and even less about how to find anything the woman desired or needed inside the castle or out. But as a companion, someone to talk to, she fit well enough, and teaching her the ways of Enesfel helped keep Diona's mind off of darker matters.

"You should have it."

Zelenka shook her head "I cannot…I have no need for…"

"Nonsense," Diona laughed. "One day you will need a gown for your own wedding, and before that you will have at least two to attend that will require your best gowns."

"I shall not marry."

Diona, thinking the woman sounded immeasurably sad, put her arm around Zelenka's shoulders. "Why ever not? You are still…"

"I have no kin to arrange it, and I am beyond marrying age."

"Nonsense. You can't be older than I am…and customs here are different. You do not need someone else to arrange marriage or to speak on your behalf." It was often done in Enesfel to this day, she knew, but it was not a requirement for marital union. "Besides, Captain Delamo adores you. Why wouldn't he marry you?"

The lighter-haired woman blushed but she said nothing. She adored him too, but marriage? Before meeting him, she had been resigned to a life without a husband or children, as her existence had revolved entirely around caring for her ailing mother. Her mother was gone now, Zelenka's decisions and life were hers to do with as she chose, but she could not request marriage, particularly from a man who had taken her from her home when she had nowhere else to go and had given her so much when he could have abandoned her. If not for Wortham and Kavan, her future would have been bleak, living in a city she did not know by means she could barely imagine. Because of those two men, she was here, in a foreign place, building an impossible life.

Again Diona smiled as she began to plot. "Tell me about marriage customs in your village. Is there a celebration? Feasting? Do the dedhá direct the rite? Are there vows and prayers? What is it like?"

She perched on the edge of the bed, shooing the other attendants from the room but bidding them to leave the dresses with a wave of her hand. Since none of the dresses had caught Diona's eye, a decision would be made later. Perhaps she would see more tomorrow, or gift some of these to Zelenka. She now wanted to talk weddings with the one woman, other than Asta and Belda, with whom she could freely speak. Though Sigrid too was marrying, she had already departed

Enesfel and the princes felt no bond yet with the woman who would be her brother's queen.

"It is not as elaborate as that. Normally an arrangement is made between the husband's family and the oldest male in the bride's family. Payment is arranged…livestock or seeds…crops or farming rights or a home if the match will be particularly beneficial to everyone. The bride is secluded for a week, covered, seen by none except the women in her family, and on the chosen day her husband comes to her, oversees the marking, and then a feast is held for the families, or sometimes the entire village if the husband wishes to curry special favor and can afford…

"Marking?" Diona, though intrigued by the variances in customs, thought that such a marriage sounded more like a business transaction than a personal union. While marriages were frequently still arranged in Enesfel, and often a significant exchange was sent to the bride's family by the groom's as a way of strengthening familial ties, it still struck her as peculiar and she was thankful her father had not felt it necessary to force marriage on her. It would have been his right, as father and king, and she sometimes wished he had taken the choice out of her hands. She would have married Espen long ago if he had.

"With ink…here…" Zelenka pointed to a spot on the back of her hand, on the fleshy place between her thumb and forefinger, "and on the back between the shoulders. A family mark…to show belonging."

In other words, Diona thought with barely suppressed disgust, ownership. "Is he marked too?"

Not identifying the princess' distaste as anything more than unfamiliarity, Zelenka said, "Yes, on his hand too. It proves joining."

"At least that is something." A skin mark shared was better than branding a woman as one did cattle or horses. "Then what happens?"

"We eat until there is nothing left. It is a sign of honor if the feast lasts an entire night or longer. The longer it lasts, the more fruitful the match. The bride, still covered, faces away from the fire as they eat, so that none can see her, and when the meal is done, her female relatives take her to the groom's home, where they stay until the union is joined; then they depart no longer caregivers but only kin."

Shivering at how final that sounded, the separation of a woman while they dined, then from her family, Diona whispered, "And if there are no female kin?"

"Sometimes female friends join her…or more rarely a male family member. It has happened that there is no one…but it is a bad thing for the joining to be unwitnessed."

Again, Diona shuddered. "Have you ever…?"

Zelenka shook her head. "No."

The princess decided that the other woman knew as little about the marriage night as she did. What Diona did know was that the night tended to result in a child within the year; she had seen it happen with several women at court who had married. The mechanics of it, she understood, but the act itself, or the desire for it, she could not claim to understand, in spite of once trying to force such a union onto Kavan.

"Me either," she admitted with a sigh. She stood, feeling the sudden urge to compose a letter to Espen, to ask him about Hatu's customs, in case he was expecting something equally submissive. "I must write a letter. Please, enjoy the garden, the sun…and we will talk more about dresses later." She smiled to reinforce that she was not angry, only wanted time alone for a task that no one else could help her with. By the time they met again, Diona planned to have had a long talk with a few of the men in her life, including doing what she could to secure Zelenka's future if the other woman would not.

Prince Espen found it a relief to be in Natrona after so many months away, but when he lay down to sleep that first night, after a long evening of eating and drinking with his brother the king and innumerable royal advisors, it took an hour of tossing in the thinly padded bed to realize that, while he had been born here, had grown up within these walls, missed his brother and childhood friends, Natrona was no longer his home. Those troops who had traveled with him were grateful to be on familiar, arid soil, but home for Espen was now wherever Diona was.

Eager to go back, though he had just arrived, he gave his brother a detailed, but not too detailed, report of the state of affairs in Enesfel. The kingdoms were allies, but he knew there were things that should be kept from his brother, or at least things that should not be heard from Espen's lips. He could report on Hagan's troubles as monarch without impugning him, he could point suspicious fingers at dedhá Claide and the religious establishment without making accusations, and he could speak of the hope that things would soon be resolved without revealing how slim that hope felt on most days. More honestly, he could relay the return of the White Bard, could announce him free of the disfigurement he had been subjected too. And at the end of his report, he was able to give his brother the news he had waited years to give. Princess Diona would be his wife, binding Harcourt and Lachlan bloodlines as well as their respective kingdoms, in a way that all hoped would strengthen the ties between them. It had been many generations since two kingdoms had allied through blood, and to the Harcourts, this was no small achievement.

Thinking to spend a significant amount of time with his future bride in the estate he had given her, Espen made arrangements for the grounds to be readied, for the castle to be scoured and decorated in a fashion he believed Diona would approve of, while his brother selected replacement soldiers to travel to Rhidam when Espen returned. Men were selected to avoid further need for significant troop movements back and forth, and as a wedding gift to his brother, the regiment was placed under Espen's full, singular command and control. Some would remain to provide guards for this secondary estate, while others would be riding north with Espen.

He knew the day of return would be soon. Given the impending elections in Rhidam, he knew he and his contingent were needed there. Even without the lure of his bride-to-be, the prince had invested too much time and personal energy and resources into Enesfel's success to leave the future to chance. Hagan was Enesfel's king, but Espen would not idly watch the kingdom disintegrate and leave Diona's future in peril.

❧*❦

Instinct and some inner sense led Wortham to a far corner of the castle ground, behind the stables and gardens, a place where few would think to find Kavan. It was not the garden, the library, the oratory or his private chambers, places the bard normally spent his time. With two boys to guide and teach, Elyri boys who required training of a sort different than what had been given to the Lachlan children, Kavan's haunts were increasing. It made Wortham glad that the Elyri had the boys in his life. Music and knowledge were Kavan's loves, and sharing both made the bard happy. The captain wanted, more than anything, for Kavan to be happy.

Which made him worry about the topic he needed to discuss.

A brief exchange over breakfast had informed Wortham that Kavan desired to teach the boys the rudiments of shape-changing. It would not be an easy thing to teach, or for them to learn, a more difficult thing than even the use of the Gates, but it was, in Kavan's view, an important skill for the boys to have. Given Enesfel's troubles, they deserved every possible means of escape should they need it, and he intended to give them those means, even if he could give them nothing else. Knowing Rhidam was not safe enough to permit a countryside ride in order to share that skill the way he had done with Muir years ago, Wortham guessed that a distant corner of the garden, or the remotest corner of the castle complex would afford Kavan the most privacy for these particular lessons. It was that belief that brought Wortham around a corner to find the boys laughing merrily as they roughhoused with a small white hound. The dog was the first of the three to sense him there; he stopped playing and looked at the bulky captain with a wagging tail as the curly-haired man bowed.

"My lord…a word if I may."

It was the troubled tone, more than the request itself, that caused Kavan to shift back into his normal form. Wortham was not a man easily troubled unless it was about Kavan's welfare; whatever bothered him was worth the Elyri's attention.

To the boys, whose hair he ruffled with a hand on each head, Kavan said, "Into the keep, both of you. Do not dally. Physician Talis is expecting you." Sóbhán would not be a healer or physician, but the knowledge about life, the physical body, the uses of plants and properties of food would help him gain a better grasp of Power and as Ártur and Rouvyn were both masterful readers, storytellers, and in Ártur's case painter, they were able to spend hours each day on those skills as well. It afforded Kavan hours to himself for music and personal business.

"But tydhá…"

"Another day, Gaelán. You both have studies, skills to practice, and I expect you to do it. Tidy yourselves and I will see you at dinner."

Glad that Sóbhán had yet to complain or whine when given instruction, despite having as many personal reasons to act out as Gaelán had, Kavan kept his eyes trained on the boys as they headed towards the castle until they disappeared from his view. He could still hear them, however, and continued to listen to be sure they went inside as instructed. He suspected Sóbhán's good behavior arose from the desire to be assured of his place in Kavan's life and the Lachlan household. An orphan as well, Kavan knew what it was like to worry about fitting in, belonging, about being part of a family that was not his. He hoped he would be able to give the child more security then he had ever felt.

Once alone, he gestured for Wortham to lead the way as they did not need to loiter in this isolated place to talk. "What is it?" he asked warmly, hoping to soothe his friend's agitation.

"I have come from an audience with the princess…"

Kavan scowled. The princess would be Diona, as Wortham did not often refer to Asta by her title. Knowing the first of the gdhededhá had arrived in Rhidam that morning, he presumed the news would concern Claide.

Shaking his head as if reading the bard's thoughts, the captain continued, "Less of an audience actually…then it was her hinting at matters of propriety and decorum. In truth, it is something I have considered in passing before…but I have been reluctant to pursue it or make a decision for fear how you will feel."

"How I will feel…?" Perplexed Kavan stopped walking to stare at his friend. "Whatever it is, you know I cannot hate or reject you for…"

"No?" Wortham stopped too, but he was unable to look the bard in the eyes. "I remember what it was like when we met her, how you reacted to the attention I gave…"

Zelenka. Kavan bowed his head to hide his shame. He recalled the jealousy he had exhibited, how he had feared Wortham would abandon their friendship in favor of the woman he had just met. But after so much time together on the road, Kavan had learned that it would take more than a woman to come between them. Zelenka could not destroy their friendship unless Kavan allowed her to do so.

What he had also learned during those weeks had been that, in his way, Wortham loved her. It did not appear, from what the bard could see from the outside, the same sort of adoration that King Arlan and Queen Brenna had shared. But it was more love than some who were forced to wed ever felt for one another.

"You wish to marry her." There was no need to ask. It made sense, and though he choked on the statement, the jealousy he did feel was not overwhelming or all-consuming.

"She is alone here…and I brought her…" Wortham started hastily, as if his decision needed explanation and support beyond affection.

It was not merely Zelenka's needs, however, that brought this forward; Kavan knew without Wortham admitting it. The captain had shown no inclination towards marriage in the years Kavan had known him. Undoubtedly the talk of marriage in the castle of late, both from the King and his sister, had given the captain cause to consider his future, as had having children in the castle again. Kavan did not begrudge him the wish for stability, for family, for love, but he continued to wrestle with the specter of abandonment issues he doubted he would ever shed.

"Have you spoken to her? Gauged her opinion?" He realized he was holding his breath as he asked, the struggle to breathe pushing the spoken notes higher in a way that Wortham recognized as anxiety.

Wortham clasped Kavan's hands, facing him as he replied, "I have not…for I needed to speak to you first. I wish to do nothing to cause you pain, Kavan…you know this…and I won't if you…"

"Wortham." The clutched hands were raised and he kissed them both. "You are not responsible for my happiness."

"Not even if I wish to be?"

Kavan felt the flush spread across his skin and he closed his eyes to hide the surging depths of love he felt for this man. He could feel the captain's breath on their clasped hands as Wortham leaned forward and he knew their faces were inches apart. He shivered.

"Happiness must be found within," he eventually managed to whisper, his voice rough and tremulous. "As long as you are here for me…as long as you are true in your devotion, I am happy. If marrying her will make your life complete…"

Completeness came in many forms, and as much as he selfishly longed to be the center of Wortham's universe, be everything to him, he knew that was not possible. No one person could fulfill every need of another. There were things he was unable to give Wortham, and vice versa. If Zelenka could give him those things, then it was good and right that the captain took the happiness she provided and allowed it to increase.

"I am here for you, my…Kavan." There was hesitation then, and Kavan caught an unexpected gasp, but then the feel of breath on his skin receded, the crunch of leaves indicated a step taken back, and Wortham released his hands. "I will make her understand that wherever you go, we shall go…that you will be part of our lives every day I draw breath. If she can accept that…and will accept my humble proposal…then yes, I believe marrying her is the right thing to do.

"Then you shall." Kavan was certain of it. In fact, as he released the breath he had been holding and opened his eyes, he realized he had known this outcome all along.

Head full of scattered, conflicting, chaotic emotions, memories of Orynn and Myreth rising to the surface as his feelings for them tangled with those he felt for Wortham, Kavan wandered through the gardens for over an hour before finding his way into the keep and to his room without paying much attention to his surroundings. It was as if his eyes were closed and he walked in his sleep, as he saw little and did not even realize he had left his chamber door open as he began to strip out of his dusty clothing intending to bathe before dinner. He wanted happiness for others, but when, he wondered, would he find his own.

"Such inattention is not like you, sínréc." On the contrary, Ártur could think of other times when his cousin behaved erratically, impulsively, unexpectedly, but those times were rare enough that his claim was still largely true.

Glancing over his shoulder, seeing that the door was open for his cousin was visible in the corridor, not inside the room, Kavan shrugged sheepishly. "I was distracted."

"Obviously. Want to talk about it?" Since Kavan's return to Rhidam, Ártur had been aware that there were many things his cousin was not sharing, secrets that both irritated and hurt the healer. But he knew he could not force Kavan to talk.

"Wortham." He left the reply at that, grateful that Ártur had entered and closed the door as he shed his black trousers and tossed them onto a chair.

Receiving no further clarification and doubting he would get any, Ártur nodded. "I see. I'm on my way to Bhryell. Is there anything you need before I go?"

"No." Nothing his cousin could give him at least. "There may be news by morning…I look forward to sharing it with you."

"What sort of news?" Again, Kavan refused to clarify and the healer grunted in frustration, his annoyance enough to allow him to voice what had brought him in search of Kavan to begin with. "Do you think it's wise to teach the boys about Gates, about shapeshifting, especially Gaelán, without consulting his parents?"

The water in the dresser basin was cool, and after dipping the cloth beside it into the basin, Kavan rubbed it over his arm as he shrugged. "Bhríd will not object."

"You think not? Gaelán's already in enough danger for being a healer without…"

"That is precisely why I am teaching them. If there comes a time when you, or I, or Bhríd, or even Bhyrhán or Tusánt, are not here to protect them…Gaelán can use a sword, but as a healer, he should not…and even if he does…he is not proficient enough to survive an attack."

"Attack?" The color drained from the healer's face. "What have you seen?" His tone was critical and bitter. If there was some impending danger, he wanted to know about it long before it occurred.

Irritated that his cousin would think he would hide such imperative details, Kavan muttered, "I have seen nothing, am merely taking precautions. I do not want them trapped if none of us are here to aid them."

He also intended to show the King and Diona the hidden exit beneath the castle, the one Owain had intended to use the night he had been deposed. They would not be able to use the Gates, but they would have a chance of surviving if they had an exit at hand. Kavan did not think he could save everyone, but the Elyri in Rhidam would be safe and the Lachlan bloodline would be protected if someone ever attacked the palace.

Ártur raked his hand through his hair, feeling a little calmer and chastised as well. "You will tell Bhríd?" Kavan's motives might be pure and wise, but the boy's father should still have some say in his training for as long as Gaelán was considered legally a child. As long as Kavan included Bhríd in the process, Ártur would not challenge his cousin's efforts to teach the boys the uses of Elyri power.

Both were old enough to train. In Elyriá, training would have begun years ago. Nothing, and everything, about this was unusual.

"I will," Kavan promised.

But not tonight. Stretched emotionally taut by Wortham's declaration of intent, Kavan wanted flight. He would beg pardon for missing dinner, for missing the boys' bedtime, and he would fly. It was the best outlet he knew of for the troubles that plagued his heart.

❧Chapter 33❦

By the time Kavan returned to the keep, most of the residents were asleep, but he could tell by the atmosphere that Wortham had favorable news before he found his friend in the upper oratory. It took no effort to guess that the captain assumed he had fled the castle to avoid the public announcement of marriage, and though it was accurate, it was not because Kavan was not happy for his friend. Rather he found it better, easier, to come to terms with the shift in their relationship in a way that would spare Wortham the most discomfort and awkwardness.

No words were spoken when Kavan entered; he placed his hand briefly on Wortham's shoulder then joined him on the step with his harp. Sometimes as he played, he could feel the captain's eyes on him, but mostly Wortham stared at the carved figure of Dhágdhuán or closed his eyes as he absorbed the instrument's singing voice and tried to decipher the message in the music. Kavan too remained focused on the pyre figure, but his concentration, when it was not distracted by Wortham's shifting emotions, was on the warm presences that filled the room. Kóráhm was not here this night, at least Kavan did not recognize his aura, but there were others, soothing, calming, bringing the last vestiges of peace he had not found in flight. The captain felt them too, and after a long evening of music, reflection and reveling in each other's company, he groggily staggered to his feet, intending to sleep. Kavan stopped playing and looked at him, the presences draining away until the two were alone.

"Have you chosen a date?" Kavan dared ask.

"I will follow her custom…" Not knowing what Kavan might know of that, he sheepishly continued, "We will legally wed one week from today, barring unforeseen interruptions."

So soon, the bard mused. Not that it mattered, as he knew when Wortham put his mind to something, it would come to pass.

Tomorrow, a month from now, or in a year, it would make no difference. It would happen. They would be married.

Wortham shrugged as if in response to an unvoiced question. "She does not desire our formal ceremony, not a Faith wedding. Rather, she wants something nearer to her own custom, as much as we can arrange here. Which is fortunate, for dedhá Claide immediately voiced regret that he would be too busy to officiate or attend." The captain grinned. "I wager, from his voice, that the thought of marrying a foreigner, a heathen, of sullying his hands with it, made him uncomfortable."

"I can imagine it would. He was here?"

"He dined with us…or with the King at least, as the two huddled at the head of the table together much of the evening." He leaned against the nearest bench with his arms crossed over his chest. "No one knows what they were discussing, but I admit seeing it made me uncomfortable. It was like…watching the execution of an innocent man and being unable to prevent it." Wortham knew Kavan would understand that feeling. "It is unfortunate that k'dedhá Dórímyr will not come to make this right."

"It is up to us to make it so…but it will not be easy." Even if their effort failed to change the outcome, Kavan felt obliged to try.

"Two of them have arrived. Should we talk to them?"

Laying his harp across his lap, Kavan considered the question. Tusánt and the novices would make polite inquiries in an effort to determine the leanings of the eighteen representatives from around Enesfel. Most likely the other gdhededhá in Hes á Redh would do so as well for their own edification. As Kavan understood the process, assuming that Claide followed established Faith protocols, the first step would be determining the nominees for the position, and then, after a period of debate and discussion, a vote would be taken. If there was a majority vote in the favor of one candidate, that man would be appointed the leader of the Faithful in Enesfel. If there was no majority vote, or a draw vote, further discussions would be held. Kavan was not thus far aware of any other potential candidates and was expecting this to be a short-lived election. Perhaps another would be nominated for the sake of appearances, but unless the other had comparable charisma and drive and influence, a second candidate would be a formality only.

Kavan intended to speak with each arriving gdhededhá and use his skills of persuasion and probing to gain further knowledge of what to expect of each. He drew the line, however, at flagrantly manipulating the vote. He could, he believed, force each man to vote against Claide, but then he would be guilty of the very sort of influence the Teren feared. He would not go that far, as tempting as doing so was, and he had already advised the Princess not to interfere directly as well. She could show interest in the outcome, she could show a preference between nominees if they were made publically known before the vote, but the monarchy could not involve itself in the election process.

He had not considered, however, that Wortham and others could share their views with the twenty gathering gdhededhá. Those from the outermost cities would have a strong understanding of what the Faithful in their congregations desired in a leader, and unless the men were corrupt themselves, they would vote according to their parish's wishes. Rhidam's population, however, seemed to have a biased voice, influenced by the Coryllien fear, and Claide would, of course, vote for his private agenda no matter what the will of the people was. If enough of them during the interview phase presented their voices in unison, Kavan hoped Rhidam's true voice would be heard.

"You are free to speak to whomever you wish, to make your preference known, but be careful that you do not make accusations that cannot be proven, and that you do not implicate the Princess or the King when you speak. We must be cautious or we will undo everything we hope to accomplish."

"You know I will be cautious, my lord." He began to turn, paused, and asked, "Will you see that Owain is invited to the marriage? I should like to have him here, if he will come. And Lady Gabrielle…she should know, even if she cannot attend."

"For you, yes. I will." He had intended to do so before being asked. "Goodnight, Wortham. You will be busy for the next several days…you will need your rest."

The big man chuckled. "Aye, I will. Goodnight, my lord."

It was too late for visiting after Wortham and he parted, but Kavan was able to leave a handwritten invitation for Owain where the prince would be sure to find it the following morning. He intended to go to Káliel at daybreak, but Ártur's return interrupted Kavan's departure and when the healer was given the news of Wortham's engagement he spent longer than Kavan appreciated trying to decipher how his cousin was coping with the news. Then had come an announcement, via Asta, of the arrival of four more gdhededhá, upon whom Kavan felt compelled to call before Claide exerted undue influence. As expected, some were stand-offish to the Elyri's questions and efforts at conversation, some were cagey about who they favored or supported, but even that information was useful, as the bard was able to provide it to Tusánt, the novices, and each of his allies in the keep, preparing them for who best to approach and sway.

Afterward, he spent his scheduled hours with the boys, instructing them in both Elyri skills and more mundane knowledge of history, literature, and philosophy. He had barely finished the day's lessons when Wortham found him, this time with Zelenka at his side, with the request that Kavan be the one to officiate their marriage. He wanted to decline, feeling unworthy and unqualified of such a task, but a small voice within prompted him to reconsider. If Claide would not sanction the union, as Kavan believed someone of Faith should, then someone else would have to. That small voice, mimicking Myreth's perfectly, reminded him that, in the eyes of k'Ádhá, all were equal, all were gdhededhá, thus all Faithful were authorized to carry out the tenets and commandments of the Faith. If Kavan was thus qualified, if Zelenka and Wortham felt he was the appropriate choice to tie the bonds between them, then there was no reason for him not to.

Except fear.

Once agreed, however, he spent time with them learning what her customs required. As Wortham had indicated, it was a simple thing, a few actions, a few spoken words, then it would be complete save for feasting and music. Music Kavan would gladly give, and according to Wortham, it was the best gift he could ask beyond the bard's support.

Late evening came before Kavan was free to go to Káliel. No longer did he feel the fear and trepidation he once had each time he set foot in Gabrielle's home. With her marriage to Owain and the frequency of trips back and forth to take the man to see his sons, Kavan no longer fretted over unwanted attention from the woman who had once pursued a future with him.

It was not Gabrielle in the villa study when he arrived, however, rather it was a fussing, pensive Clianthe whose pacing in front of the desk he interrupted with the opening of the closet door. She paused mid-step to stare, though she did not seem surprised to see him. Likely she had felt the energy of the Gate.

"Welcome, my lord," she curtseyed. "If you have come to see Muir, you have arrived too late. He returned to Pháne…has probably already arrived there…"

Despite the twinge of regret, he said, "It would have been good to see him, but I am here to speak to your mother."

"She has been at Council Hall much of the day; I expect her soon if you wish to wait."

"I would, yes." He could give the captain's invitation to Clianthe and be certain Gabrielle would receive it, but he would rather deliver the news in person.

"Shall we wait here or in the Hall? The dining room perhaps?" She grinned, an expression much like Gabrielle's when she had been a younger woman. The family harp was located in the dining room; the suggestion of waiting there was a not so subtle request for music. Though he had not had the chance to be alone with his harp this day, he was in no frame of mind for making song.

"I shall wait here, if that is acceptable."

"Of course. A drink perhaps?" There was regret in her voice but she did not dwell on it. Because of the Elyri in her blood and her mother's, their low alcohol tolerance meant that the carafe behind the desk was filled with something other than wine. She was already pouring two glasses before he could refuse, but the hospitality was welcome and he took the offering when she presented it. There was a jolt, a flash behind his eyes, the vision of an unfamiliar young face and other bits of imagery that passed too quickly for him to sort and he opened his mouth in a surprised O.

"What?" Though she asked the question, her tone told Kavan she already knew what he had discovered.

It explained her pensive mood, though he thought such news would please her. "You are with child."

"I know…at least, I believed I was." She quickly emptied her glass and licked her lips of the red droplets that remained.

Perhaps, he considered, it was that Muir was not here to be supportive but had instead returned to Phâne. "Muir must be…"

"He does not know. No one does."

"Not even your mother?"

"I was beginning to suspect when we were in Rhidam but did not want to speak of it until I was sure. Knowing might keep him from duty…and what he is doing is too important to have him worrying…"

"You must tell him. At once."

"At once? But…"

"He must know." Kavan could not explain why he felt this with such certainty, but he believed Muir needed this information as quickly as he could get it. It was too important to wait.

"Must know what?" Gabrielle appeared in the study doorway, smiling wearily to see this particular guest in her home. She looked expectantly between them, a wise enough woman to know she had intruded on something important.

"My lady." Kavan bowed but did not speak Clianthe's news. This was the sort of thing that should come to the mother from her daughter, and he would leave Clianthe to share it. Instead, he offered the folded parchment he carried. "I have been asked to deliver this to you."

Expecting a formal invitation from the Lachlan King or his sister to their weddings, of which Muir had already informed her and given invitation on their behalf, Gabrielle broke the seal and read it once. Then reread it. Each time, her smile grew wider.

"Wortham is to wed? The woman you traveled with? Zelenka?"

"Yes."

The awkwardness in his body language told Gabrielle more than he wanted to convey. "He deserves this. I do not know if I shall be able to attend on such short notice; recent events here are causing a stir in the Council and I am determined to solve them."

"Has there been trouble?"

Recognizing both Kavan's familiar avoidance and her daughter's relief at not being pressed for information, Gabrielle decided she would get those answers later. "Another attempted attack, successfully rebuffed without loss of life and very little damage. Then we had a quartet of traders attempting to sell an assortment of Elyri clothing and jewelry…a few days after two Elyri men, bedraggled and injured from a battle at sea, washed up on our shore with a cargo manifest of what they reported to be goods pirated from them. Their manifest and the trade wares matched…all goods stolen from their vessel before it was sunk. No others survived that attack. Such piracy is rare, and with it coinciding with events on Pháne…something must be done before their aggression turns more fully on us."

The bard's frown deepened the more she talked. It had been a matter of time before the mainland's anti-Elyri violence spread, but he had not expected the tiny island cluster to suffer because of it, beyond the efforts to breach Pháne.

"I would be willing to speak to the Lachlans, the Harcourts, the High Mother, if you wish…secure naval patrols to discourage piracy and keep the islands safe. I know the Council desires no treaties beyond trade…"

"But something must be done," Gabrielle agreed, "and we are ill-equipped to do it ourselves. There is little cause for anyone to offer us protection, but perhaps we can negotiate new trade agreements, be willing to supply a certain number of ships per month, or some other arrangement to entice them…"

"Or they might help simply because it is in the best interest of all Sovereignties to end this threat. Tell your Council, persuade them if you can, and I will do what I can to secure naval aide if they accept."

Her eyes and smile brightened for the first time since coming into the room. "Thank you. I appreciate your efforts and support whether the Council does or not. Please convey my congratulations to Wortham and tell him that, though I might not be able to attend, he is in my thoughts and I will send him something fitting. He deserves to be happy…and I am glad he is."

"As am I."

Farewells were exchanged and before he entered the closet again, he met Clianthe's gaze, bidding her to give her husband, and her mother, the news.

"Now, what is so important?" he heard Gabrielle ask as he linked to the oratory Gate. Kavan was more certain, after hearing of these recent events on Káliel, that Muir must know the truth.

By the end of the week, the day before Wortham was to wed, each of the expected gdhededhá had arrived in Rhidam. On behalf of the Lachlan Crown, though without her brother's consent, Diona provided a midday banquet and included Claide on the guest list. There was no way to tactfully exclude him, although she hoped, as the men began to arrive one by one, that the presence of the Elyri advisors would be enough to keep Claide away. Bhyrhán and Kavan sat to one side to provide gentle background music, their presence innocent enough, and because she included many of the King's advisors as guests, having Bhríd there was logical as well. By feigning a passing ailment, headaches so as not to alarm the men that they were in the presence of something contagious, it provided Diona with an excuse to have Ártur and his apprentice there as well. The majority in the room, advisors, nobles, and soldiers alike, were Teren, however, and were carefully chosen to present a picture of domestic bliss within the Lachlan House, an atmosphere where Teren and Elyri coexisted peacefully.

As it was the usual state of affairs, minus Hagan's company, Claide had no reason to believe this was the ploy the princess intended it to be. But as he entered, the last to arrive, lines of irritation etched around his frown. He looked over those present as if assessing them, but the attendance of the Elyri proved not to be enough to prompt him to leave. This was the first time the twenty gdhededhá had gathered in one room and awkward or not, Claide knew the importance of staying.

Having an innate and well-schooled grasp of political savvy, Diona did her best to keep the mood of the meal light, and though she expressed natural curiosity about the upcoming election, she kept mention of elections on the fringes of her interest and allowed her allies in the room to glean information from the ever-shifting groups they mingled and talked with. They enjoyed a buffet of treats and the music of one most had not had the pleasure of hearing in too many years. That interest in Kavan's music, in spite of any discomfort his race created, brought the guests to him in clusters of three and four. Rather than speak about important matters, he listened, with both his ears and other senses, to pick out moods, leanings, and occasional names within the thoughts of each person. He knew Ártur was squeamish about such uses of power, but he hoped the healer and Bhyrhán were doing the same. Judging by the darkness clinging to Bhríd, the chamberlain had no qualms about digging into their guests' personal lives and thoughts. He had intimately subjective reasons for wanting a peaceful, and peace-bringing, outcome to this election.

Kavan hoped he got it.

It was hours after the last of the dedhá departed, when daily duties were completed or set aside, that the princess gathered her allies, including Tusánt and his novices, into the morning room, a place she did not expect her brother to look when he returned from his survey of the military training grounds a half day's ride from Rhidam. By the time he returned, he would have heard about what she had done, but she did not know if he would be disappointed or angry.

"That was interesting," Bhríd grunted as he sank into a chair near the window.

Asta had flitted amongst the gdhededhá, cheerfully engaging each member save for Claide with flighty, girlish questions that suggested she had little working knowledge of the Faith institution. The gdhededhá had been eager to answer her, eager to educate her where they assumed she needed it, and often took pity on the inquisitor's daughter for her lack of religious education. "Boring is more like it," she groaned, stretched out on the floor before the fireplace that warmed her back. "What dull lives they lead."

"Dull if you find helping the needy or providing spiritual counsel to be boring…" chuckled Saul.

"No offense, dedhá," Asta smiled. "Such a life is not for me."

"A life of less danger than yours or mine," Gaelán reminded her.

Tusánt shook his head. "Not always," he sighed, wishing he could return to those boring days of tending the Faithful and not wallowing in political intrigue and the ever-present threat of death.

"Which returns us to business…thank you, dedhá." The grim reminder had not actually been needed, but it helped Diona to focus. "Do we know anything we did not already know?"

"I don't believe this election will be as straight forward as Claide believes," Bhríd said when no one else spoke. He knew Kavan would wait, assess what any of them said before giving his interpretation of the day's events, but Bhríd hoped someone else, anyone else, would have been the first to speak. "I think two or three support Claide already, but the rest seem divided, uncertain…confused…as to the necessity of this election and why they are here."

"The deliberations are going to be more crucial because of that," Ártur muttered, running his hand through his hair, staring at his cousin's distant expression with concern.

"Deliberations often go to the most charismatic speaker…"

Heads bobbed to Bhyrhán's assessment. "And we know what sort of speaker Claide is." That was a grim fact the princess had to accept. "But he cannot be the only one. Are there any other likely nominees? Who will stand against him? What of dedhá Karleo? He seems like an intelligent, outgoing, leader."

"One with a past," Balint had been in the gathering, having returned from his hurried trip to Nelori in response to the impending election. As a man of considerable political station, wealth and reputation, many of the attending gdhededhá had been eager to talk to him in the hopes of donations or support for their favored projects.

"But that is behind him," the princess protested. "He was cleared of those charges before he took vows."

Most of those present knew of the scandal involving the death of the man's wife and one of her brothers when Karleo was much younger. Accused of killing her by his neighbors and her brothers, Karleo of Nelori petitioned his duke for a fair hearing before the King. Duke Gabersdon, Balint's father, had been reluctant to grant the request, as the evidence the brothers presented seemed damning enough to put Karleo to death. Balint, not yet a knight, had believed in the man's innocence and beseeched his father to permit the trial: if Karleo was guilty, they would have lost nothing but a delay in his death. If he was innocent, however, they could not execute him and let those guilty of this hideous crime go free.

The accused was brought before King Arlan during the early days of his reign, and the trial was long and arduous, with many witnesses for and against failing to appear or caught lying in their testimony. In the interim, Karleo's home and business were looted and destroyed and his reputation became increasingly mired and sullied by wild, unsubstantiated rumor. In the end, it was the first trial in which Arlan called on the Elyri to read Karleo, each of the brothers, and Balint's father…and only Kavan and Bhríd were willing to do so. Afterward, what each learned was compared and Karleo was ultimately set free. Instead, two of the woman's brothers were executed for the rape and murder of their sister. Karleo's execution of the third brother in her defense was justified. That full crime, though not his, tarnished Karleo's image almost as much as the accusations had, for everywhere he journeyed afterward, people talked about the offenses against his wife and his vengeance against her killers.

Dejected and destitute, Karleo entered the Faith, took his vows, and was assigned to Durham, as far from Nelori as one could travel while remaining in Enesfel. He gained a solid following in the decades since, remained resolute in his calling, and though he was well-liked and respected, there was still a chance that he would not be able to outrun the shadow of his past to rise to the highest posting in the Faith.

"With the right support, the right backing, a little persuasion…" Asta suggested. With her father's teaching under her belt, the young woman was not above buying votes.

"No," murmured Kavan without changing expression. "That is not…if he wins, it must be on his own merits."

"But we can support him. It would be natural." With Balint being from Nelori and knowing the man, and Asta's roots in Durham, their support of Karleo would seem natural and unsuspicious.

The bard did not reply.

"Is there anyone else?" Diona prompted.

Again, Bhríd spoke. "gdhededhá Wols Hahn…of Wexel."

The name was presented tentatively, and everyone knew why. Wols had come to Enesfel from Elyriá soon after Arlan claimed the throne, at the request of the late k'gdhededhá Jermyn. They had served together in the Order of St. Kóráhm in Clarys, had known each other since boyhood, and he had been eager to accept the new post from his old friend. The man was jolly, good-natured, and much loved, but he was also of an age that any appointment he might win could be short-lived. It was no secret that many might vote for a younger candidate, although not too young, to facilitate stability in an office vacated in the cultural atmosphere of persecution.

"It is possible," Bhyrhán interjected, "that he has Elyri in his blood; there has long been speculation about him in Clarys. He could live another twenty or more years…"

Wortham grunted. "I don't think that would be something to make public…longevity might gain him support but it might also backfire."

Several reluctant sighs circled the room.

"There is one more potential nominee," Kavan said softly into the awkward void that formed behind his friend's words. It was not, he knew, a nominee likely to win, but he could pray that the man, like those already mentioned, had what it took to confront Claide and give the man a fight in the election.

"Who?" As Tusánt said the word, his eyes locked with Kavan's and he immediately felt cold and shook his head. "Me? But I am…"

"Elyri. Yet you have a substantial following in Rhidam, one much larger than you realize, and those who served with you in the Neth war are supportive too," Saul said ardently. "I see it every Gathering, every Purification Feast day, in the people I talk to in the city."

Edward nodded. "More come requesting your services, your attention, then Claide's. If the violence can be stemmed, they know you have the potential to provide the longest stability to our Faith…and though k'dedhá Dórímyr refuses to come, I believe most desire to continue our ties with the Clarys náós."

"Claide is a radical…you are not. I don't believe fanaticism is what most people wants." Diona's face brightened. "Do you think it could work, Kavan? Could Tusánt be elected?"

"But I don't want…"

Kavan knelt before the dedhá and clasped his hands, hoping to read something that would guide him as he strained to see the future. "In these days, the future is less about what we want and more about what must be done. Your path might not be an easy or safe one, but…"

"What do you mean not safe?" Tusánt stammered.

The bard continued despite the interruption. "…it must be done. Only you, your acceptance of nomination, your fight for our Faith, can prove that Enesfel is not as divided as it appears. Regardless of the outcome, however the vote falls, you can show the world that the Faith will not falter, that there is good at its heart…that the voice of the people still counts."

He raised his head, expression as tormented as that of the man to whom he spoke. He could see nothing of the man's future save for a shadowy cloud of ambiguity. He did not believe there would be easy days ahead for Tusánt, for any Elyri, but he steadfastly chose to believe that the man would live through what was to come. "Someday…what you do now…the choices you make, will matter more to Enesfel then you know."

For several minutes, those in the room held their breath. Each knew, with varying degrees of certainty from years of experience that such words from Kavan's lips were to be heeded and weighed carefully against internal arguments made for the opposite course of action. No one could wrestle with this decision except Tusánt; no one could decide his fate, his future, except for him, but even he knew there was no fighting destiny. He believed k'Ádhá spoke to him through Kavan then. Doing anything other than accepting the will of the divine was profane rebellion. But still, he struggled against personal fears in order to reach a place of submission. Whatever Kavan meant, whether Tusánt was destined for martyrdom like Jermyn or something bigger, Tusánt knew he had to accept it…or else suffer the consequences.

Head bowed, he put his hands on Kavan's head, less to bless the bard than to extract some manner of blessing from him. "If I am nominated…I will accept," he whispered roughly, "And I will fight for it as though it is my destiny." For all he knew, it was. "I will make Jermyn…k'Ádhá…all of you…proud."

"And we will be with you," Edward and Saul swore together. Their lives were about to become more dangerous, they believed, but neither saw it as an imposition. The chance to change Enesfel's path was righteous and important and both wanted to be part of it.

From the corridor beyond the closed door, the King's youthful voice bellowed, "Diona!" moments before the morning room door crashed open and the young man burst into the room, prepared with some tirade or bad news to share. He stopped short at the sight of those with her, his advisors, friends, royal staff, family, and noblemen, with

Kavan kneeling at the feet of gdhededhá Tusánt. His mouth opened, prepared to demand an explanation, but then closed again behind the breath he swallowed before barking, "Everyone…out."

With his eyes locked on Diona, it was clear the command did not apply to his sister and thus she remained seated as the others filed from the room. Asta, the last to leave, looked over her shoulder to offer the other woman support before closing the door. They had known this meeting ran the risk of upsetting the King.

When the door was closed, Hagan took another big breath and snapped, "Explain yourself!"

Diona stared at him, assessing what might be going through his mind, but as she could not tell for certain, could only guess, she asked cautiously, "What shall I explain, My Liege?"

She rarely called him by title, and normally it irked him when she did. This time, however, they both understood that he would be more peeved if she called him by name. "Why did you meet with the dedhásur behind my back?"

"Behind your back? I mentioned over a week ago that I thought we should welcome the gdhededhá to Rhidam when they arrived; you said it was a good idea…" She had not suggested how she would accomplish it, only that she wanted to do so and thought it would be the right thing to do. Hagan's agreement was as good as permission.

"I was not…"

"The last arrived while you were not here…and I impulsively invited them to dine. You know they will be sequestered soon; this was the best opportunity to…"

"To manipulate the vote!"

Diona managed a sufficiently shocked and offended expression. "Manipulate? I have done no such…"

"k'dedhá Claide told me…"

"Then dedhá," she corrected the title, refusing to give Claide the rank he aspired to until he was properly voted into that office, "misunderstood my intentions. There was no manipulation. We shared a meal, some music, and had the chance to meet one another. Introductions were made, nothing more. I did not speak of Faith politics and strove to avoid discussing the elections."

It was difficult for Hagan to interrogate his sister. She always seemed more poised than he, and he could not keep his anger at the front for long, particularly when she spoke in ways that made him doubt his perceptions. "And what of the rest? Did they?"

She shrugged. "I do not know…I did not pry to learn what others were discussing. Their discussions were between each of them. It was not my place to oversee and censor everyone. No one seemed insulted or troubled when they left. I am sorry if they were…if Claide thought I had some ulterior motive. He should have come to me to complain instead of dragging you into any disagreement he has with me."

Her pout morphed into a disarming smile and she took her brother's hand. "I am sorry you were not here to share with us. I wanted to wait, but dedhá Valgis hinted that the election process would begin almost immediately…and with you gone, I thought it important to extend Lachlan hospitality while we had the chance."

The King snorted. It was true that he had not indicated how long he would be away from the castle, and that he had failed to keep track of how many Faith representatives had collected in Rhidam, and to gauge when the elections might begin. He knew Claide was eager to proceed, and it seemed reasonable to believe that, with all of the men now in Rhidam, the gdhededhá would plan to begin the process within a day or two's time. Diona was right to offer royal hospitality. But he did not believe her motives were as pure as she presented them.

"You will not interfere, is that understood? You will not sway the deliberations, you will not give voice to any preference on behalf of the Crown, or yourself, and you will not interfere in the vote when it occurs. You and I will remain out of the process and support whoever the dedhásur deem fit to elect."

Diona clenched her jaw and her nostrils flared with the desire to voice her displeasure and defiance over her brother's passivity. Her knuckles were white as her fingers dug into the arms of her chair, but she was, without notice from Hagan, able to calm herself before saying something she would later regret. "Yes," she agreed as contritely and apologetically as she could manage. "I understand and will obey."

That did not mean, however, as Hagan grunted, "Good," and stormed back out of the room, that she would stop anyone else from seeking information or influence. She had other eyes and ears she could rely on, and other mouths to give voice to opinions she was forbidden to share. There was direction now; they would have to wait for the actual nominations before the deliberations on the Faith's future began in earnest.

❧Chapter 34 ❧

Kavan would rather have attended the first official meeting of the twenty gdhededhá in hopes of learning their religious and political leanings, but such could not be. The first meeting found the gdhededhá behind closed doors where they could put forth candidates for nomination and those with the most support would be selected for the second step of the process. While Kavan could have attended unseen, a mouse or bird in the rafters or any other small, inconspicuous creature, he chose to respect the sanctity of the process that originated centuries ago.

And though he could have used the secretive meeting as an excuse to avoid the duty before him, Kavan had made a promise, and keeping a promise to Wortham was more important than eavesdropping on a process he could not influence. Tomorrow, or as soon as the nominations were made public, the people would be allowed to speak on behalf of their favorites and given the opportunity to question their choices. If the nominations proceeded as Kavan suspected, those Teren who served the Lachlan House would give their voices as each saw fit, but the Elyri, it was decided, would remain publically silent. Enesfel was not their kingdom, and for them to show support of any one of the nominees would be, it was feared, an automatic strike against that candidate. And as none could, in good conscience, speak in favor of Claide, in case their support somehow led to his election instead of discouraging popular support, it was best to allow the Teren to decide their future for themselves.

At the mid-day hour, those closest to Wortham…his three compatriots, the King and his sister, Asta, Owain, Rouvyn, and every Elyri in the House, along with the gardening woman Betella whom Zelenka befriended soon after her arrival, gathered in the royal gardens where a bountiful meal was spread for sharing. Staying true to her custom, Zelenka had spent her week in isolation, attended by Betella who brought her meals, water for bathing, and helped her with her selected marriage gown. Once, at the start of the week, she had a brief audience with Wortham and Kavan to explain how the ceremony should commence but she had seen no one else since.

Earlier this morning, in the company of Betella, Diona, and Asta, Agis…the man Zelenka chose to represent her as a parental figure for reasons no one else understood…and Wortham, had come to bestow the mark on her hand she expected to wear throughout her life. Wortham had protested the thought of it, despoiling the woman he was marrying, but after considerable argument, he accepted that this custom was important to her, similar in meaning to an exchange of metal bands that announced her unavailability to the world. Wortham had no familial mark as her people had, but after some discussion, a small symbol in the shape of Kavan's kestrel harp was inked onto her back as she requested, and on her right hand, and on Wortham's hand as well, between the thumb and forefinger. Kavan had not known their choice until he saw the mark on Wortham's hand as he joined the circle, harp under his arm, to officiate as Zelenka requested.

Flustered, he took his place between the bride and groom, not daring to trust his voice. He had only to be here, to offer a blessing prayer on the union, and send them off to their first night together after joining their hands, an awkward responsibility but one he would fulfill with grace. He could never have expected such an honor as that mark, such a show of loyalty. It felt as if they had bound themselves to him as much as to each other.

Now Zelenka waited with her back to the others as they took seats on the cushions on the ground, forming a circle around the presented meal. She wore a gown of blazing saffron, the color of sunlight, and was covered with a veil of multicolored Káliel silk, a floral pattern expensive to produce. A gift from Diona, Kavan believed, though no one had told him so. The veil was large enough that it could later be sewn into a dress of its own or used for another purpose within the home she and Wortham would share, wherever that home would be.

On her other side, Betella gave the woman wine and food throughout the afternoon as the guests ate, drank, shared stories and songs, in a fashion different than the usual palace extravaganza. To Kavan, it seemed that, being seated on the ground, a customary request even the King agreed to, made them all equal, connected, with no obvious head, men and women gathered for enjoyment, not politics or show. Only the bride's back being to them felt out of place. Here in this garden venue, beneath the spring sky, there was no difference between Elyri and Teren, no religious battle for leadership, no need for violence or conflict.

Both Orynn and Myreth would have approved. That fleeting thought whispered across Kavan's mind as he took up his harp at the setting of the sun, and began the High Elyri prayer he had composed for this occasion. That no Teren except Zelenka could understand the words led Kavan to suspect that somewhere far back in history, their people had not been as divided as they were today. Perhaps they had been the same, as those gathered this day were the same, or at least there had been no fear between Teren and Elyri.

He wondered if he would live to see such a day return.

íth dhedhoc, íth gymae, íth hyhílag,
aiónag rásae sunít.
ít aicónys mál k'Ádhá thráaest,
hudhánaelis á kyagn elzen tesur,
lómyhás dó íthásigk elzen tesur.
mál endástás males,
gaesdág phádaes tesur dhedhoc.

The earth, the air, the water,
From which life blooms.
This union bless before k'Ádhá,
Bring them love and family,
Bring them prosperity and joy.
All holiness will be blessed
And the world be enriched with peace.

Song complete, Kavan set his harp aside and waited. There was no need to translate he had been told, and gauging by the faces around the circle, the meaning behind the words was understood in spirit if in no other way. Wortham shifted onto his knees, an action that belied his age, and smiled.

"Zelenka and I thank each of you for sharing this day with us. I, for one, did not think it would come. A year ago, if I had been told I would be married, I would not have believed it." He glanced at Kavan, knowing he would have believed anything Kavan told him, no matter how fanciful. "Please, though we take our leave, stay, enjoy what remains, and know that I am grateful to share my life with all of you."

He and Kavan got to their feet and Wortham held out his right hand to Zelenka. For the first time that day, for the first time in a week, she allowed the touch when Agis helped her to stand and placed her hand into Wortham's. Kavan clasped their joined hands between his, giving his blessing to his friend, a less formal, more heartfelt one than the prayer-song, and then he stepped away. Betella gathered the long folds of the veil and followed the couple into the castle, to the room Wortham had been given so that he no longer had to reside in the soldiers' barracks or sleep in the chair beside Kavan's bed. He had been given the room Gaelán had used, the one next to Kavan's, while Gaelán and Sóbhán took the room on the other side of the oratory, flanking the bard as closely as they could.

Zelenka had reluctantly agreed to forego the custom of having a female family member in the room on her wedding night, when it was explained that, by Enesfel custom, such a thing would have been awkward for anyone she chose, as well as for Wortham. Instead, as a compromise, Betella would remain on a stool in the corridor outside of their room until daybreak.

Kavan, however, did not intend to go to his room this night. Knowing what would transpire on the other side of the stone wall between their rooms was awkward enough. He would accept it in time, but he believed it would be easier after this first night. He watched them depart without moving, accompanied by the three former Káliel guardsmen and Betella, and then reclaimed his seat, when they were out of sight, to resume making music. It helped to keep his mind off of the fluttering in his stomach, heart, and throat.

Gradually, over the remaining hours of the evening, those around the table left as well, as staff took empty platters and plates and bowls away for cleaning. Ártur and Syl were first, as Syl, who had attended on Wortham's behalf, insisted on returning to Bhryell with her husband with the falling of night. Owain was the last to remain, the darkness not troubling him but rather giving him an excuse to remain as Kavan's protector. They might be within the royal walls, but that did not guarantee Kavan's safety.

"You wished to speak with me?" he asked after the last notes of music faded into the sounds of insects and distant night birds.

The bard's head bobbed once as he laid the harp across his lap. He was grateful for Owain's company and glad the man had agreed to attend this blessed event. Now that Wortham had retired, Owain's company helped Kavan feel less alone. "When I spoke to Gabrielle and Clianthe to invite them…there was other news. Muir does not yet know, or he did not when I left Káliel…and though he may wish to be the one to tell you, I feel it important for you to know…" It was another certainty Kavan could not explain, as he was never a man to gossip or otherwise speak out of turn. "Clianthe is with child."

Owain's expectant expression changed to one of surprise and joy. "Muir is to be a father…" He had not believed, years ago, that he would ever have children, or live long enough to have grandchildren. That he had survived to do both he could only credit to Kavan. "That is good news. Thank you for telling me." It lightened his mood as much as returning to Rhidam had done. Kavan worried about Owain being so often separated from his friends and family. The once-king spent too much of his life in relative isolation in Kavan's opinion.

He bowed his head in acknowledgment before continuing, "How are things in Fiara? Did you settle those things you needed to?"

Owain chuckled. "Despite my worry, there was little to settle, thankfully. Centuries of conditioning means most of the people are cooperative and dependable out of fear of punishment. I hope I have given them more positive reasons to do as required but…" His shoulders twitched in a shrug. "We were fortunate to have no more episodes of violence while I was away, and everything else is as expected. My staff is efficient and trustworthy, praise be."

"And Prince Kjell?"

"I admit…I was not expecting him the day you were there, but it is not easy, or possible, for him to contact me as much as he wants; we must consider Merkar at all times. He was dismayed you could not stay; he has been eager to meet you, hear you play, talk with you."

"Talk with me?" Kavan imagined a man wanting to discuss miracles, wanting to discuss Elyri power.

Owain stretched back onto his elbows and chuckled. "For a de Cormick, he is rather philosophical, with a sharper, keener mind than anyone else I've known in that place. He exhibits no outward desire for the throne, but I know it is there. It's bred into every de Cormick son and reinforced from the day of birth. But he does not want to avail himself of the methods of ascension most often employed by our family…wants to avoid the infighting and treachery that killed his father, his brothers, most of his male kin. I suspect he has the support of the military to have survived as long as he has, but I also think he is smarter than anyone realizes. He could utilize them to take the throne, but he seeks a more legitimate way, or else a more secretive one, of removing the opposition. And he wants peace…within Neth and between the Sovereignties."

"And the return of the lands Enesfel claimed, no doubt."

"I imagine so; he would not be a de Cormick, would not be royalty, if he did not want to heal those wounds his kingdom suffered and reclaim what was lost. But he is not stupid enough to go to war for it, not with a military ill-equipped and ill-staffed. Judging by his interest in you, I'd say he has in mind a cessation of centuries of Neth aggression towards Elyri as well. A Nethite king who could accomplish any of those things is one I believe Enesfel needs. Such an ally might temper the violence here as well…or so he and I hope."

"It would at least remove a sympathetic haven for those fleeing punishment. Do you expect him again soon?"

"I never expect him. He comes when he comes. Would you like me to arrange a meeting?" Kavan might be a minstrel, but he had a strong interest in affairs of state and the relationships between kingdoms, particularly during these troubled times. Or perhaps, Owain thought, it was less an interest in political affairs than it was striving for a peaceful world where he and his kin could live without fear."

"Perhaps, but not yet. I was…" He shivered at the memory of what he had Seen. "I wish to ask you to stay in Rhidam for now."

"Stay in Rhidam?" Owain's heart clenched and then soared at the thought that Kavan wanted him here.

"I do not know when, but the time will come that I must act, and I will require your assistance when that day arises. It might be tomorrow; it might not be for weeks to come." Feeling awkward for asking, he absently traced the carved wooden surface of his harp and refused to lift his gaze. "Of course, there is no need for you to stay until then…if you have duties in Fiara. One of us can come for you when the time arrives. But," he sighed and closed his eyes, realizing that part of what he was feeling was fear of that looming day, "having you at hand might save time…and I would like to have you close."

Smiling with warmth in his eyes, Owain put his hand on the bard's knee. Perhaps it was largely duty that Kavan required, but the prince had the feeling that Wortham's marriage had thrown Kavan off balance and he was looking to compensate for this new awkward situation. Yes, Owain was married too, but his wife was on Káliel. For as long as Owain could remain in Rhidam, there would be no one else to compete for his affections. "I should return home every few weeks, for a few days at a time…keep abreast of affairs…but I am otherwise free to remain for as long as you need me. You say I am to be part of your plans? May I ask what part that will be?"

"I cannot yet say as I do not know. A revelation will come, and when it does I will act."

Hearing an unfamiliar note in the Elyri's voice, Owain leaned closer. "Whatever it is…it frightens you," he murmured with concern. He did not think he had ever seen the bard afraid. Not like this. Did Kavan believe he would die? Owain could not ask the question as the fingers of that thought tightened icily around his spine. If the fear of death was what prompted Kavan to bid him stay near, Owain could not refuse. "I will be here. As much as I am able, I will be here. And if there is anything I can do, if you need anything of me, ask."

"Thank you." Kavan's head bowed again, the emotion in Owain's voice filling him with relief. The path ahead would be a stony one. Kavan wanted all of the supporters he could gather.

Though instructed not to voice her opinions throughout the elections, that did not mean Diona intended to remain home when her brother and the majority of his advisors and staff went to Hes á Redh early the following morning when the message came that the nominees were to be announced. The written votes were tallied by Rankin and Valgis and those with the highest number of votes would be presented for public examination. The tally was not to be revealed, only the names, and none were surprised to see the majority of the Lachlan staff in attendance, or to see so many noblemen and townsfolk present to bear witness to the historical event. gdhededhá Wohls, Karleo, and Claide were expected to be nominated, each having strong reputations across Enesfel as the royal advisers had indicated to the princess. It was Tusánt's nomination, however, which caught the majority, particularly Claide, off-guard. It took Claide great will-power to avoid rising in protest, from demanding a recount, or, thought Kavan without touching the dedhá's thoughts, from demanding Tusánt's immediate disqualification on the grounds that he was Elyri. Brief touches of Rankin and Valgis' thoughts, however, while refusing to take the liberty of deeper probing, surprised him.

Not only had Tusánt been nominated, he had also received the most nominating votes, with Claide trailing behind him by two. It was a possibility Kavan had not considered when he encouraged Tusánt to accept if the chance was presented to him. When Valgis questioned each candidate as to their willingness to accept nomination, Wohls judiciously declined, a wise man who knew his age would be a detriment and who preferred to leave the field open to more suitable candidates. Kavan watched the faces of the others, seeking to determine who Tusánt's supporters were. He had little luck, however, beyond guessing that Wohls was one of those voting in favor of the Elyri. Kavan was distracted from his study of the rest by both Tusánt's nervousness and Claide's cold stare that fueled it, and was pleased that Tusánt took the oath of acceptance when Rankin asked him to. The battle was on and it was up to Tusánt's backers, and the Elyri gdhededhá himself, to make enough of an impression on his equals to win the election.

The bard, however, despite believing in Tusánt, was not sure the Elyri could win. If the election came after the cleansing of the subterranean thol, an Elyri winning the highest office of Faith in a Teren kingdom might be acceptable. With the current tensions, however, with Claide seeming to wield the power of the Corylliens, an Elyri leading the Teren Faithful might be disastrous.

Or it might be precisely what Enesfel needed.

The King was called to the keep, as the assembly broke for the midday meal, by further reports of violence, this time from the southern city of Talladegah. Though he did not feel he needed his sister to deal with the matter, accepting her offer to accompany him to the castle meant he did not have to worry about her influencing the early stages of the candidates' debate. The three nominees would be questioned first by the other gdhededhá when they returned from their meal, poignant questions of Faith and morality and personal belief, questions to probe their knowledge of the teachings and tenets, that would give everyone present an opportunity to learn more about the three. What would follow would be potentially a week or more of question and answer sessions between Rhidam's public and the nominees, so that they too could learn what sort of men these were.

Such questioning also provided the other gdhededhá with a glimpse into how their fellows interacted with the public they had sworn to protect, support, and guide.

What that required, however, was honesty from the contenders. It was honesty Kavan did not believe anyone would get.

It would be a tedious process, particularly for the nominees, as they might be forced to answer the same question more than once, but it gave each a chance to contradict themselves, gave Claide a chance to make a costly verbal mistake. Kavan had already decided he would attend every day, bringing Gaelán, Sóbhán, and any other of his kin he could, making their Elyri presence known so that the real danger behind the outcome remained fresh in everyone's minds.

He had not risen from his place in the royal box at the front of the naós as others came and went. He watched, he listened, and wondered if he should have brought his harp to entertain those who, like him, remained in anticipation of the gdhededhásur's return. The excitement and consternation caused by Tusánt's nomination buzzed about the room like bees swarming in a spring field and many were excited to begin the discovery phase. While there were detractors, voices siding against him, Kavan was satisfied with the strength of support Tusánt had amongst the people of Rhidam. It gave the bard hope that Enesfel's future was not as bleak as it appeared.

Something tickled the edges of his perceptions, a sensation that made Kavan shudder, as the dedhá were brought in to take their seats across the raised stone platform behind the altar. A bench for the entrants had been pulled to one side where they could face their fellows as the questioning began, but they waited to be seated until Rankin, positioned at the podium, gave the signal to sit. Kavan perused the parishioners, the thol filled to capacity so that people were crowded around the edges and gathered in the doorways to hear. The sensation, fleeting as it was, returned, emanating from somewhere near the door, seconds before he felt the twang of a bowstring in the core of his being. Impulsively, his action out of place in the seated room, he rose and stretched out his hand, the act of a man trying to catch something as screams erupted around him. Three bolts, suggesting concurrent shots, hung midair, hovering near the dedhá who were taking their seats, aimed at the nominees. Kavan knew without gauging their trajectories, that they were targeting the man Claide would see as the biggest threat to his candidacy.

gdhededhá Tusánt.

The attendees scattered, surging towards the doors, pushing and shoving to get out of the line of fire without thinking that the assailants, whoever they were, were in that doorway, that if they were targets they were running straight into the line of fire. Their movement swept the marksmen clear of the soldiers who tried to pursue, making it unlikely the marksman would ever be found unless one of the Elyri read the three bolts. A shock of dark hair in the thrusting crowd at the back of the thol made Kavan blink, the sighting of a man he was certain was Caol, breaking his concentration. The bolts clattered to the steps at Rankin's feet and from the sidelines, Valgis scurried to retrieve them as Saul, Edward, Wortham, and Owain rushed to usher the gdhededhá out of the thol to somewhere less exposed. In the chaos, there was too high a likelihood that someone else would make an attempt on Tusánt's life and that was an unacceptable risk.

Kavan leaped over the edge of the box, intending to get to the bolts before Valgis did, but the young gdhededhá already had them and was swept along with the others to empty the room. From the side doorway, he felt eyes burning into him, a glaring harsh gaze that he knew would belong to only one man but he refused to look and brushed the shuddering itchiness away. No, he thought as Wortham and Owain came back to usher him and the other Elyri out after the gdhededhá. Surely Claide would not have been as brazen as to request an assassination in such a public place in the middle of the day…in a crowded náós full of innocent Faithful. Unless he had arranged it beforehand, or had someone prepared in case Tusánt might be chosen, it seemed unlikely Claide had been involved. Judging by the man's horrified expression when his Elyri counterpart had been nominated, he was just as shocked by it as Tusánt.

This had to be at the hands of someone else, the Corylliens most likely, but how could they have known beforehand? Could they have been lying in wait for the opportunity regardless of his nomination? Had Tusánt's guaranteed attendance been a fortuitous time for them to try? And what, Kavan groaned as he sagged against his cousin's shoulder when they stopped in the náós dining commons, had Caol to do with this? Or had it been the inquisitor he had seen? No one had seen Caol since the attempt on Kavan during the Feast of St. Mátán, and no one had heard from him except his daughter. He had suggested he would go deep underground, deep enough that he would likely not be seen until this struggle was over. If he had been here, was he interested in the outcome of the election, or something else?

"sínréc?" Ártur asked, catching Kavan and steadying him.

The bard shook his head. Others around them, the dedhá and some of the soldiers, were staring, knowing he had prevented those bolts from reaching their targets in a way no Teren could have. Most were pleased, relieved, but as none had ever seen such a feat, even the Elyri-friendly among them were dumbfounded and speechless.

"The bolts…"

"Are gone," Claide said with a sniff of disdain. Behind him, at the hearth, Valgis had just dropped them into the fire.

"Fool!" barked Owain, grabbing the badly charred items from the flames without thought of burning his skin. He screamed at the pain, dropping them, leaving them on the floor where someone had the presence of mind to douse the flames as Gaelán hurried to the prince's side to tend the burns.

"How dare you…"

"How dare you!" Wortham snarled back, stepping between the gdhededhá and the prince. "You do not destroy evidence of a crime…"

"There was no crime," Claide snorted. Many of those around them turned in shock. Realizing his error, the man drew back his shoulders and shrugged, "There was an attempt at one…but thanks to Lord Cliáth, it was prevented." It seemed to pain him to say those words, but he managed to voice what sounded like appreciation. "They are bolts, not the weapons…"

Owain snorted too. "An attempted crime is as good as an executed one. There is information to be learned from those…who forged them, who held them, who fired them. Maybe more. Now," he looked at the charred objects Asta was gingerly wrapping in her cloth kerchief, "we will be lucky if we can learn anything."

"I did not think…"

Feigned ignorance. It was all it would take to make Claide appear guiltless of that insensitive, misspoken remark. Kavan wanted to say something, but Asta was the one to cut Claide off. "We might still get something. Metal heads…metal shaft…can't be many made like this."

Her assessment and hopefulness made Wortham's lips curl into a faint triumphant sneer. "Good…at least that is something. I will take these to the keep for further study."

"In the meantime," Bhríd said, managing to keep his voice diplomatically calm, "it would be beneficial if we find a more secure location for these proceedings…"

"Elections are held in the náós," Valgis protested.

"Perhaps, but if it is not safe for us here, we should make every effort to find somewhere that is," dedhá Wohls interjected. The oldest of those present, the one with the most experience within the institutions of the Faith, and directly with the hierarchy in Clarys, his opinion would not be taken lightly.

"Unless you want to move a bunch of soldiers into the náós," offered Saul, knowing that idea would be met with even more displeasure than moving the election process somewhere else.

Edward, speaking on behalf of Tusánt, who was having difficulty breathing, asked, "Where do you suggest, Lord Chamberlain?"

"The Great Hall."

"Out of the question." Claide turned from his argument with Wortham and Owain, grateful for some topic that would distract others from his faux pas.

Balint brushed off his knees as he got up from where he was kneeling before Tusánt in an effort to calm him. "Why? It would be ideally safe and…?"

"Not easily accessible to the public," Karleo offered, rubbing his high forehead with a shaky hand. He could have been hit by one of those bolts as easily as Tusánt could have been. It was not obvious to any of them that Tusánt had been the primary, perhaps sole, target. With three bolts, any or each of the three might have been the victims.

Once those words were spoken, Claide cocked his head in thought. While conducting the election in the castle would expose the gdhededhá to constant Elyri influence, as well as to people he knew to be pro-Elyri and pro-Tusánt, it would also mean that fewer members of the public would be able to attend the questioning period. Fewer attendees meant fewer questions and thus fewer key points to influence the final vote. The questioning period would be shortened by the limited access as well. It might be to his benefit, he realized, to limit the number of pro-Elyri voices they had to contend with.

Using the Great Hall was worth consideration.

"The public can be allowed in, monitored. It is possible, if the King permits it. The Great Hall can house nearly as many as the náós, and with the Lachlan guard to secure the room, to control who comes and leaves, there will be no opportunity for a repeat of today. I will speak with the King, and if he is agreeable, we can offer rooms so that none of you will need to move back and forth between the keep and the náós, exposed to potential harm."

Tusánt rose from the bench and found his voice. "Let us discuss it, Lord Chamberlain, as you approach the King." This was not the first attempt on his life, and unlike Karleo, he was certain each of those bolts had been intended for him. He was troubled by the surprise of it, by Kavan's quick, life-saving action, by their hasty removal to this room, but he was not surprised by the attempt. It was not, however, enough to make him review his decision to accept the nomination. If anything, he felt a renewed sense of significance to doing so.

"And Lord Chamberlain and I will speak with the King," offered Balint. He could think of no reason for the King to refuse with so many lives, and such a crucial matter, at stake, but adding his voice to Bhríd's would aid in the persuasion.

Three hours later, each of the gdhededhá, their belongings, and the staff who had traveled to Rhidam with them, were housed in the first level billeting rooms of the Lachlan castle. A letter was drafted and taken to Prince Espen by Kavan, requesting both ships to Káliel and his return to Rhidam as quickly as he was able, the seriousness of the situation being explained in great detail when Kavan traveled by Gate and met with the prince and Hatu's King. Guards were posted outside of each gdhededhá's door and along the lower perimeter of the castle to lessen the possibility of anyone gaining access through doors and windows. Though that attempt appeared to have been directed at the nominees only, it did not mean that the others were not also in danger, of harm or undue influence, and King Hagan was not going to take a chance with their security.

It was too late by then to initiate the interview session as intended, thus it was decided it would begin the following afternoon. The palace staff and several men hired from Rhidam worked into the night making the required preparations for others to attend without fear. A wooden platform was erected for the gdhededhá, with benches built for them to sit, but there was not enough seating for all of those who might choose to attend, even with the workmen pressing throughout the night to build more. Many would, by necessity, remain on their feet, and despite Kavan's concern that this would compel many to stay away, the King doubted that such discomfort would deter those who were serious about attending. Word spread through Rhidam, informing the citizens of the change in plans, and by dawn, there was a crowd waiting at the outer edge of the moat for the drawbridge to be lowered. Ten days was being allotted for the public to have their voice, less if there seemed no need for the extended period. On the eleventh day, the candidates would speak for themselves and then the dedhá would sequester for the debate and vote.

Claide was hoping that ten days would not be needed.

King Hagan, though accepting of the inconvenience this placed on him and his staff, hoped it would not be needed as well. He wanted no interference in his upcoming wedding. He wanted everything to be perfect.

And though Diona would obey her brother and keep her thoughts to herself in public at least, she was determined that her voice would be heard through those in the Lachlan employ who shared her fears, her views, her beliefs. They would speak for her, when the time for questions came. She would not give Enesfel into chaos without a fight.

Nor would Kavan. But what he could do, he mused as the keep finally settled for the night, he did not know.

<h1 style="text-align:center">❧Chapter 35❦</h1>

Separation of the Teren Faithful from the Elyri establishment in Clarys was not a new idea. From the early days of the Great Persecution, the opinion that Teren should have a prelate of their own, should not be reliant on words spoken far away…by someone who would not step outside of Elyriá and often seemed less concerned about Teren parishes then they were about Elyri ones…had been a commonly reoccurring theme. Sometimes it was politically motivated, sometimes financially, sometimes racially, but most frequently it was some combination of the three and was usually resurrected by someone in power who sought to have more of it. gdhededhá, nobles, royalty, it mattered not. The question came down to power, who was perceived to have it and who wanted more.

The opinion of most common folk was one of nonchalance. Who headed the Faith mattered less than did the right and privilege of worshipping in peace and security in a place where they would not be persecuted. Their Faith was not about politics or power, but about sanctuary and comfort in life and securing a place in the life that came after. They gave little thought to the prelate at the top of the Faithful because he was not part of their daily lives.

There were times, however, when a gdhededhá, a nobleman, a prince or king, or simply someone with the gift of oration who wanted to create unrest, would strive to drive home how much better their lives could be if the Elyri establishment did not interfere. For the most part, however, the leaders in Clarys never interfered. They were just there, a lingering invisible presence. While there was no evidence that such would be true, these efforts typically coincided with periods of great troubles…pestilence, war, famine…each having a tendency to create a desire for life to be better and a need for finding somewhere to place blame for the wrongs in their lives. By default, that which was different was deemed dangerous, that which was far away, useless.

The result had historically been the oppression of Elyri and the specter of separation from Clarys rearing its head. Sometimes it lasted a period of days or weeks, but at the end of the Great Persecution, such hatred had gripped Enesfel for many years. Never since those dark days, however, had anti-Elyri sentiment resulted in the deaths of so many innocent people of both races. Not even King Bowen, for all of the death he had wrought on the land, had killed so many. And never before had it coincided with the need to replace the head of the Teren Faith establishment, or had the violence and separatist movement met with as much apathy as k'gdhededhá Dórímyr showed now.

No one was surprised when the talk of separation arose during the questioning, brought up not by the gdhededhá but rather by someone in attendance who, though offering the suggestion as his own, used rhetoric that sounded too scripted and formal to have originated in the mouth of a commoner. The odds of the man being a plant were high, but without reading him, it was impossible to know for certain and Kavan resisted trying, or allowing others to try. He had hoped the topic would fade after it was addressed, becoming buried beneath other matters as the question and answer period continued. But once each day the topic was brought up, keeping it foremost in the minds of the gdhededhá, giving the attendees cause to consider it more than ever before. Dórímyr's apathy was like a fanged worm eating its way through the soul of Enesfel.

There would be one more day of questioning before the three had their final chance to speak before the sequester. King Hagan had seen to it that the Stateroom was always prepared and the men would remain heavily guarded and escorted to and from their rooms each day to prevent contact between them and anyone who might hope to get one last argument in. Desperate to try anything, even considering visits to each of the gdhededhá in their rooms late at night while the palace staff slept, Kavan paced the oratory aisle, from door to altar and back, arguing with himself over the benefits and drawbacks of each plan his fevered brain concocted. It was obvious, from everything he heard, that Claide was the primary proponent of separation, and Kavan believed he had to uproot that idea before it took deeper hold and became a reality.

A decision finally made, a plan of action in sight, Kavan took several purposeful steps towards the Purification Chamber, confident of what he should do, but he was brought up short by a presence behind him that he had not felt since returning to Rhidam.

"Do not go to Dórímyr," the warm, familiar voice said with enough force to feel like a chain caught around Kavan's neck, pulling him back. He wanted to continue, to go where his head bid him go, but his soul and his love for the man speaking kept him from entering the alcove. After several anguished moments of silence, he took a long slow breath and turned to face the auburn-haired saint.

"If I do not…he must know what is happening…it is not too late to stop this." If he could convince Dórímyr that separation of the Faith would be detrimental to them all, Kavan might be able to convince him to come. The vote would be suspended long enough for the k'dedhá to listen, to have his say. It would show the people that the prelate cared for them, no matter what Claide claimed to the contrary.

"…or it might be construed as interference where he could not be bothered to be involved before," Kóráhm softly finished Kavan's unspoken thought as he held out his hand. The bard hesitated, fighting the urge to go to Clarys, but he could not resist the lure of that intimate gesture. Taking Kóráhm's hand was admitting the defeat of his will and desire. "There is nothing you can do, átaelás mai. As much as we both wish it…search your heart. You know it is true."

"If Claide wins, the Faith will be divided. I cannot allow that to…"

"The Faith can never be divided, not at its core. The truth will persist…"

"And be joined by those beliefs that Neth holds true. It will mean the death of every Elyri in Enesfel…in the Teren kingdoms. Doctrine that Dhágdhuán did not teach will be introduced and what is will be destroyed from the inside." Mournfully, Kavan sank onto the nearest bench and Kóráhm sat beside him.

"Do you think it will be as bad as that?"

"Do you think it will not?"

Kóráhm did not reply, other than to look away with a sigh that suggested the saint had no idea what the future held for the religious institution that had existed for centuries.

"Perhaps it is needed…to get back to what was."

Kavan stared at him then, wondering what Kóráhm meant by that, but the saint did not elaborate. Eventually, the bard groaned. "I do not know what to think, but I know what I believe. I believe if I do not cleanse the thol in time, Claide will be elected. I believe that if Claide is chosen, there will be a push towards separation. And I believe if separation comes, a shadow will fall of the sort that might remain unlifted." Again Kóráhm did not speak, and frustrated by his silence, calmed only slightly by the hand clutching his, Kavan muttered, "Why the delay? Why wait to do what must be done? When will I know, how will I know?"

"átaelás mai…I wish I could answer your questions. I sincerely do. To see what has become of the peoples, the lands, the Faith that I love…knowing I had a hand in the birth of this darkness, tears at my heart. If I knew anything that would help you, I would tell it. But I think…" His voice trailed off and for many moments there was silence between them. "I think it is my guilt that blinds me, prevents me from seeing what lies ahead for you, hides the details from me."

Feeling as well as hearing the pain and despair in Kóráhm's voice, Kavan squeezed the man's hand, using his touch to sooth the saint much the way it often soothed others. Again he took a deep breath, pushing down his own frustration. "You cannot accept the blame for what is. Your brother acted alone, turned the world on end when he could have done differently." He was not saying that Kóráhm was blameless, for he knew well the events that precipitated Coryllien's descent into darkness that had pulled the world into madness behind him. But Coryllien's choice of action had been his, and in Kavan's eyes, any blame for Enesfel's current state of affairs lay in the malevolence that had possessed him. "Perhaps you cannot help me because they do not want you to." He was not sure who 'they' were. The k'kairá perhaps, or Orynn and her people, perhaps k'Ádhá. Someone held the knowledge Kavan needed, someone controlled what he was shown and when. He was at the mercy of fate.

They all were.

"I can speak to Claide," he murmured. He may have given up on visiting Dórímyr, but there might still be a way of persuading Claide to reverse his thinking about separation. Even as he said it, however, he knew the effort would be futile, without looking to see the reluctant shake of Kóráhm's head. Kavan's interference would strengthen Claide's convictions. He could try some other guise, infiltrate the man's dreams, but that had its dangers too, not just to Claide but to himself. Kavan had done it only once before with King Donal and was reluctant to try again.

A little voice inside, however, asked if this was not the time to try, would there ever be a better one?

"Thus we wait." In the quiet of this holy place, with Kóráhm at his side, Kavan was forced to accept waiting as his only recourse. He remained on that bench, staring at the pyre figure on the wall, until the feel of the hand within his slipped away and the night turned into day. A day, Kavan suspected, that would prove a difficult burden to carry.

❧*❧

When the gdhededhá were forced to take refuge in the castle in order to be safe, King Hagan decided it was time for his inquisitor to return to Rhidam. He sent a second message via his swiftest courier, knowing it would take several days for it to reach Durham and for Caol to make it back to the castle. General Agis, with the assistance of Asta, was able to track the local maker of the crossbow bolts used against the three nominees, and together were able to narrow down the potential buyers to a dozen men from around the kingdom and beyond. The general and sheriff were doing their best to find and apprehend those buyers for questioning but the King realized, despite his dislike for his uncle's methods, that Caol did produce swift results the majority of the time. He wanted Caol home. He wanted this job done right. He wanted the men and women of Faith to be safe.

This morning, however, as he shared breakfast with his sister and cousin, a response to his summons arrived from Wilred, news the women alone expected to hear. Caol had left Durham prior to the King's celebration, intending to be there for that special event. That had been weeks ago, yet no one in Rhidam or Durham had seen or heard from him. Asta hung her head and murmured, "I will find him," before hastily leaving the room, not allowing Hagan to say a word of question or comfort. Stunned and sick with worry, he sent his sister after the girl, believing Diona had the better chance of calming her.

He, meanwhile, turned his mind to this newest problem.

How could he find a man who was capable of finding almost anything?

Puzzled about why the news seemed to upset Asta so, Diona tried to pry information out of the younger woman. She knew Caol was undercover, knew the visit to Durham was a ruse and that Caol had a plan in mind in case Hagan did recall him. Asta's reaction, however, hinted at something potentially sinister. Not knowing about the doll, Diona knew it had been a long time since the last contact between them. Too long. If the man had vanished, it did not bode well for either him or their cause. Despite being encouraged to talk, however, Asta would tell her no more than what little she knew. If Caol was gone, swallowed by the Corylliens, they would be lucky if they ever heard from him or saw him again.

The news triggered the most thorough manhunt in Enesfel since Prince Arlan's abduction decades before. Men not needed to protect the keep were sent to search every road between Rhidam and Durham. Every town, village, and home between the two cities, and every street in them, were to be scoured until the inquisitor, or some proof of his fate, was found. The King knew of no specific enemies his uncle might have, but with a man who had once been part of the Association, who had continued to utilize them as an information resource for years, and who had led investigations that had resulted in innumerable arrests and executions, such enemies undoubtedly existed.

And with the Corylliens on the prowl, there was no telling who might have gotten their hands on his inquisitor.

King Hagan tried to force Asta to give the names of Association contacts, certain she knew, from previously made claims, at least a few of the people her father had contact with. But he did not have the heart to use force beyond words on the girl he had grown up with, the girl who may have lost her father in a more horrible way than Hagan had lost his months earlier. In truth, he did not know that she knew the majority of those Caol knew, did not know how adeptly trained she was for the duties of inquisitor and the skills of the Association elite. He did not know that she had been filling some of the inquisitor's duties since her father left the keep, reporting to Diona rather than to the King. She refused to give names, refused to divulge information that might put her father at risk, wherever he was, or that might compromise her standing with the Association.

She swore only that she would get word to them and tell the King anything she learned, a concession he did not like but allowed because they were kin. It was approval in appearance, for Asta was aware of being followed when she left the castle that day. She allowed her tail to pursue her for a while, and then lost him for more than an hour before popping back up for him to follow. It thwarted the King's desire to bring in those contacts for questioning, protected the Association, and thus gained Asta a degree of respect and appreciation from the organization that she had not held before. If she was protecting them, they would, in return, protect and help her.

The efforts, however, did not bring the King any closer to finding his uncle. It was but a single day, Diona reminded him, as dusk approached and the long shadows of night seeped through the castle windows. The Rhidam Association members claimed to know nothing of his absence, according to Asta. Caol had not been in Rhidam, to their knowledge, at the time of his alleged disappearance. It was likely he had been ambushed near Durham, on the road, and it would take time for the King's men to conduct their extensive search. Hagan prayed that Wilred found some clue in Durham, that the family's long-dormant Association ties would bear fruit. In the meantime, the King was forced to appoint someone as acting inquisitor…and wait.

The man he appointed, a spry fellow with dark curly hair and a crooked nose, hailed from Hatu and came with Asta's, and then Diona's endorsement as being the best person for their needs. Like Caol, his family had been part of the Association, but he had gone into business as a farrier many years ago. The Crown was assured that while his connections to the Association were marginal, he retained enough of them to be useful and he had worked with Caol in the past.

That much was true. Since Matus Gardieu had come to Rhidam three years earlier, he had worked as a farrier while dabbling in less legitimate trades. He had been one of Caol's most reliable contacts and a man Caol occasionally shared drinks with when the stifling palace atmosphere became too much. He was, for the sake of necessity and propriety, willing to put his other enterprises on hold while he worked with the Lachlans, and most importantly he understood that the position of inquisitor belonged to Dugan's daughter, regardless of what the Crown said and what title he was given. He would gladly leave the reins of investigation in Asta's hands while assisting her as required, including wearing the face of inquisitor when the King demanded an audience or in the general public's eye.

That connection to Caol was enough for the King.

Thankful that Hagan did not question the recommendation too deeply, that the King took her word for Matus' competency and qualification, Asta and the man she respected and was willing to learn from set immediately to work, though it was not in search of her father. If Caol needed to remain hidden, Asta would respect that despite how much she missed and feared for him. Instead, the two turned their focus to finding the would-be assassins of dedhá Tusánt and feverishly hoping, as the gdhededhá prepared for seclusion to debate and vote for the man who would lead Enesfel's Faithful, that they would find enough evidence to damn the one they believed to be guilty and remove him from contention, if not from the priesthood altogether.

Kavan learned of this during the break taken between Claide's final oration and Tusánt's, which would be the last presentation of the questioning process. Having the investigation into Claide tighten and increase was good, although he suspected it came too late to be helpful. A competent and charismatic speaker, Claide eloquently addressed his audience about the need for Enesfel's Faithful to be self-sufficient, to take their future into their own hands, and not allow apathetic foreigners to continue to direct their lives, foreigners who, while sharing religious beliefs, had no more in common with the people of Enesfel than did the birds with the fish in the sea.

Why, Claide argued, should any portion of donations garnered from Enesfel be sent to Clarys when k'gdhededhá Dórímyr was unwilling to send anything to Enesfel in return except edicts, religious texts, and Elyri dedhá who were unnecessary now that Enesfel spawned enough dedhá of their own to fill the positions available?

It was a subtle dig at Tusánt, one of six Elyri dedhá in Enesfel, not including those residing in St. Kóráhm's and other Holy Houses scattered throughout the land, despite his having come to Rhidam in the days when there were few gdhededhá of any sort on Teren soil. But it was also a fact most agreed with in theory, even if they harbored no hatred towards Elyri or the Clarys church. The Faith amongst Teren had gained considerable footing in the years Arlan had been king, and Jermyn had been their head. The late k'gdhededhá strove to make the Teren Faithful self-sufficient and had, it appeared, succeeded.

That did not, to Kavan, constitute a good enough reason for the Teren Faithful to break from Clarys. Even the issue of money, in his eyes, was not an adequate reason as only a pittance was earmarked for Clarys, barely enough to make a difference either in Clarys' coffers or, if it was retained by the Enesfel náós, their own. Not that he had ever counted the money, nor seen a reckoning of how much Clarys required to balance their day to day needs, but Kavan could not imagine Enesfel's contribution to be so important.

Why not allow the Faithful outside of Elyriá to keep their resources, to tend to their own needs, and consider the matter done?

He mulled over the update about Caol that Wortham brought as he fidgeted in his seat, resisting the desire to pace. He believed he could find the inquisitor if necessary, but because he, like Asta, knew Caol did not want to be found, he chose not to offer or to try. If Asta asked him to, he would battle any obstacle to bring the man home. Not tonight, however.

"Lord Cliáth?"

Edward the novice looked anxious as he approached and Kavan immediately feared for Tusánt's life. "Yes?"

"Will you speak with dedhá Tusánt? He is…" At a loss for the right words, he shrugged. "Saul and I fear he…nothing we say offers sufficient reassurance. We think he needs…you."

Head cocked curiously, the bard followed. People often sought him out for assurance and comfort, for aid and words of wisdom to face their troubles. But no gdhededhá had ever come to him, not even Jermyn. Perhaps, he reasoned as Edward took him to the room where the three candidates had gathered to attend this one final speech, that was because Jermyn had not been Elyri…and until the end of his life, the beloved man had not faced the sort of fears Tusánt wrestled with daily because of what he was.

Ignoring Claide's icy glare that made the hair on the back of his neck stand on end as he entered, Kavan went directly to Tusánt. There was no way to speak privately here, save in soft voices still overheard, but the bard did not think words were what Tusánt needed. He clasped the man's hands, knelt before him as he had done days before, and brought the dedhá's hands to his lips.

'Do not fear,' his thoughts reached into Tusánt's unsettled mind. 'I will be with you.'

The voice in his head surprised the dedhá because he had not expected it. Many Elyri could hear the thoughts of others, particularly through physical contact; it was not a far stretch to think that sharing thoughts in communication was possible too, especially for the one man known to produce miracles. Still trembling, Tusánt tried to shake his head but decided against doing so. Claide was watching and he did not want to give the other dedhá any reason to condemn him, give him anything Claide might twist against him. He would be looking for something suspicious in that exchange as it was.

'I know not what to say. After what he…they will not hear me…'

'They will. They will here; they will listen…and they will know the truth.' Though he was convinced of the veracity of his words, Kavan could tell even without touching the other man's thoughts that Tusánt was too afraid to think clearly, too nervous to speak the way a man in his position should. Eyes closed as if in prayer in that submissive position, Kavan took a long breath. He could help, but did Tusánt want it? Did he dare try?

'Do you trust me? I can assist you…but you must relax…and be confident that you can do this. No harm will come to you, and I promise I will be with you the entire time…if you wish it.'

When he opened his eyes and looked up, it was to catch Tusánt's head bobbing yes in spite of his previous decision to remain still in front of Claide. Fortunately, Kavan stood swiftly enough that his body blocked Tusánt from Claide's view and the Teren did not see that gesture or the expression of gratitude on Tusánt's face.

"It is time," Rankin announced as he opened the door. Claide passed Kavan and Tusánt without looking at them, but there were disdain and a look of victory in the tilt of his head and set of his shoulders that made Kavan angry. Unaccustomed to that feeling, he released Tusánt's hands and murmured, "Wait for me to sit. Watch for me. You can do this, gdhededhá. I have faith in you, as did Jermyn."

Looking at his empty hands, feeling a calm flutter drift around his shoulders and settle into his throat, Tusánt murmured, "I shall."

gdhededhá Karleo had gone out as well, and he, Claide, Rankin and the soldiers who guarded them waited in the corridor for Tusánt to join them. Kavan followed as far as the door, and when Rankin escorted the candidates to the entrance nearest their seats, Saul and Edward followed Kavan to his place in the gallery. It was not a front-row spot, as Kavan had refused to draw attention to himself that way, but he was within visual distance of Tusánt with few around him to notice anything unusual should it occur.

Not, Kavan decided, that it would.

On the platform, Tusánt was the only one of the three nominees not to rely on written notes behind the ornate wooden podium, to not appear confident and convinced of his own success. His gaze swept the crowd, seeking the faces he knew. Palace staff, friends, the Faithful he served, some of them having known him from birth through the births of their children. The King, who looked bored with the long speeches, the King who was, though legally a man, barely more than a boy who had power and obligation and duty thrust onto his shoulders too soon, who wanted to still be a boy, who found politics and speeches to be tedious. Tusánt could not blame him for feeling as he did, for he too would rather have been anywhere else but in this place.

There were the princesses, allies of a sort he had not anticipated needing, and the small gathering of palace Elyri, healers who caused harm to no one, a bard who had come to Rhidam to meet Kavan and had stayed for reasons Tusánt did not know, and the chamberlain whose eyes spoke of world-weariness and the burden of hatred tearing his family apart. There were nineteen of his peers seated across from him, one of whom could not be trusted, the others he had yet to learn their mettle fully. In the audience too were his novice wardens whom he was sure he would be dead without, and others who had served Hes á Redh for years. And finally, Wortham and Owain, seated beside the bard whose eyes bid him speak, bid him address the room as a man of Faith, as a man who dared to face election for the safety and security of every person in Enesfel despite the possibility of harm to himself.

Tusánt was not doing this for glory. He was doing this for them.

But the words would not come. He opened his mouth, but instead of taking in a breath that should have given him courage, it felt as if he had swallowed a mouthful of stabbing fire. His hands balled at his sides and his eyes, wide with panic, began to tear. He did not need to see Claide to know the man was growing impatient, and he did not need to look at the others to know they were questioning his fortitude, his conviction, his ability to lead if he was unable to speak to them now, to take this final step before the vote.

He shivered. His gaze, which had strayed from Kavan to a blank space at the back of the room over the heads of the people, snapped back to the green eyes that never wavered. A tingle shot up his spine, warm and reassuring, something that reminded him of how it felt to sit beside his father as a little boy, holding the larger man's hand when he was afraid of the lightning at night. There was no darkness here, no lightning. But that calm erased the jumbled thoughts and scattered focus; he heard his voice speaking with a confidence he had forgotten he had, and words he believed in but failed to string together came out in a coherent rallying cry.

"A wise man once told me that, in the end, when we stand before k'Ádhá, we are the same. Man, woman, child, Teren, Elyri, we will be judged not for those things but according to the lives we live, the people we touch and make whole, the beauty we witness and share, the healing and concord we make real in the time we are given. Our faces, our gender, our wealth, our race…none of that matters. It is not enough, he said, to think purely, to follow mandates written by mortal hands. The spirit of holiness, the spirit of the law, is far more important than the law itself. If we cannot live in Dhágdhuán's footsteps in this life, how can we expect to follow him into the next?"

The words resonated in his ears as his gaze stayed long enough on various faces to give each person the notion he was speaking to them.

"That man you knew. That man you trusted…loved…followed until the day he was brutally taken from us by hate. That man was the sort of gdhededhá each of us here should aspire to be…the sort of man whose shoes will be impossible to fill. And yet, as is the way of things…someone must. Someone must take up the burden that fell from his shoulders when his life was stolen. Someone must be willing to face the threat that took him from us. Someone, one of us here, must be strong enough in spirit to confront the hatred that claimed that holy man and bring an end to the crushing animosity that plagues our land and makes prisoners of us all."

Gradually his hands uncurled. He did not look at Kavan but knew the words were coming from the bard who had been strangely silent on his wishes throughout the entire process. Though Kavan felt compelled to speak, he understood, as did Tusánt, that his was the one voice that must not be heard at this time. The voice believed by some to have too much influence over the Lachlans must not be thought to have influenced the elections and the outcome of Faith in the Teren kingdoms. And yet, through Tusánt, he found his voice, and Tusánt, believing Kavan's voice was the one that needed to be heard despite the arguments against him, was honored to give him that voice, and grateful for the assistance in finding his.

"I am not a perfect man. None of us are. None of us can be." His gaze lingered on Claide a second or two longer than it lingered anywhere else as Kavan, through Tusánt's eyes, tried to drive his point home. "I do not have every answer. There is no easy solution to undo everything that has been done. Darkness strives to overtake us and we must strive against it. We have already seen, through k'gdhededhá's death, through the slaughter of families, friends, neighbors, that hatred and murder is not the answer. It has brought only agony, discord, and fear. Driving out some has made life no better for the rest; it has only made us more afraid. k'gdhededhá Dórímyr is not our enemy. He has not come to oversee these proceedings, to appoint k'gdhededhá Jermyn's successor…but by your own admissions…" again his gaze lingered on Claide, "isn't that what we as a kingdom, as a people, want? The right to determine our future? Yet like a petulant child, some dare to demand more, when instead we should seek to work together, to strengthen our Faith, to follow k'Ádhá's commands, Dhágdhuán's example, strive for peace and oneness…to be a people worthy of the eternity we are promised. Wealth, political favoritism, hatred, and bigotry…these are not the ways of Faith. These are not what the Faithful are. We are more, called to more, and should live to prove it to k'Ádhá, to ourselves, and to one another."

He swallowed, feeling the tendril of Kavan's warmth retreat, realizing he was left to speak alone. The other candidates had spoken long and movingly about their credentials, but Tusánt felt no need for that. He believed his qualifications spoke for themselves. His need was to look beyond his own interests towards what was best for Enesfel and the Faith, Teren and Elyri alike. Bolstered by the words Kavan had offered through him, the words he spoke next were his own.

"Never in the history of the Sovereignties has Enesfel been at the crossroads we now face. I cannot give you an immediate solution to our troubles. No man can. I cannot offer you guarantees, for we have each seen…through k'gdhededhá Jermyn's death…that there are no guarantees except that, in the end, we shall all meet eternity. What I can give you is Faith, the belief in right and wrong, life and goodness, harmony and steadfastness. We, the Faithful, together, can bring light back into Enesfel's darkness, and I promise to lead holding the same light of Faith, conviction, and strength that k'gdhededhá Jermyn died believing in. Those things were enough for him. They are enough for me, by the grace of k'Ádhá, and I pray, when you consider the future, that those things are enough for each of you as well."

As he stepped from the podium to join his fellow candidates, Kavan's eyes closed, his body tens from exertion and the effort to act unnoticed by any in the room. Any, that was, except Wortham, who sat beside him and unconsciously slid closer on the bench as Tusánt spoke. He saw the tension in Kavan, felt the prickle of energy like ants back and forth over his skin that told him the bard was doing something. Perhaps he gave Tusánt confidence. Perhaps he was making the audience more receptive to Tusánt's words. Perhaps he was striving to bend Claide towards a more peaceful path. Or perhaps, Wortham decided as he listened to the words that sounded more like Kavan's to him than they did Tusánt's, Kavan was doing something more. Wortham did not care. He was there to support his friend and protect him if necessary.

Rankin came to the podium, his hands clasped before him. His face bore an unrealized smile and he could tell, without the bobbing heads of agreement or the short burst of audience applause, that Tusánt's words had had a powerful effect, particularly on the other gdhededhá who stood up as he joined them. Claide was not scowling, but, Rankin believed, that was because the man was in too public a position to do so. Instead, he wore a more neutral, thoughtful, suitable expression, one more likely to win the acceptance of his peers.

"Sequester will be met. Those before us have a sacred duty to search heart and soul, to choose wisely, not the one who will grant you the most favor but who is best suited to this calling of Faith put before them. Deliberation will last until the majority vote is cast, then we will return here. We pray for a swift agreement, but more importantly, we pray for your wisdom. k'Ádhá be with you, gdhededhá."

One by one, the twenty men filed out of the Great Hall, and when they were gone, the audience began to depart as well. The hour was late, and none expected deliberation until morning. None expected a swift resolution to the difficult choice they had to make. Anyone who did expect it to be swift, thought Kavan with a shudder as he allowed the ripples of thought in the room to sweep over him, were expecting a decisive vote in Claide's favor. Unfortunately, the shifting crowd was too thick as they shuffled to the exit, for Kavan to see the faces behind those expectations. Perhaps if he had, he would have found more of the Corylliens. Though there had been no violence in Enesfel during these past many days, Kavan, like everyone else, knew it was the calm before another storm.

❧Chapter 36❧

Eight days of seclusion proved that the vote was not as pre-determined as some had hoped it would be, and the tensions in Rhidam as the waiting crawled by at an excruciating pace continued to mount as those in the keep saw the twenty men escorted from their sleeping chambers to the Stateroom each morning and then back late every evening. Meals were brought to the twenty in the Stateroom, served by Saul, Edward, and a handful of other holy from Hes á Redh, while Valgis was left in charge of the daily services. Rankin, the higher ranking of the two, was charged with officiating debates, tallying votes when they were taken at the end of each day, and thus he too was kept secluded in order that no one outside of the Stateroom had an inkling of the direction the gdhededhá were leaning.

What they did know from the waiting that there was no easy victory. The longer the decision took to make, the more obvious it was that there was some matter of contention that prevented easy agreement. Some hoped it meant Claide might be defeated and some worried for that same outcome. Most did not care so long as the decision came soon. The merits of each man's position, the strengths of their speeches, and the credentials they brought to the office were topics of discussion and debate on every street corner in Rhidam, in every nook within the palace, around fires and tables and late-night candles. Few could focus on anything else.

It was an excitement of a sort most wished was behind them.

Five days into the waiting brought a welcome diversion in the form of a list of names and tiny sketches into Asta's hands, delivered by Marta but, Asta believed, having come from her father. Five of the eight matched drawings Ártur had previously done, pleasing both Diona and the King as it meant more Corylliens being brought to justice. The other three, however, were for Bhríd alone. How her father knew about the events in Levonne, Asta could but guess.

Bhríd demanded to participate in those arrests and though some had doubts about the wisdom of such a request, the King permitted his participation. The result for the last three responsible for the slaughter of the Levonne duchy's staff was a bloodbath when the three were found in the company of nearly a dozen others, surrounded by a horde of Elyri goods and crafts and evidence of captives having been held and murdered in the dilapidated stables in which they were found. Some of those stolen goods had come from the chamberlain's Levonne home. Before Agis could stop him, not that he tried, Bhríd had, in a methodical rage, beheaded and dismembered every one of them, leaving none to interrogate. The general believed the chamberlain deserved his due for what had been done to his family; he would have done the same thing in Bhríd's position.

Bhríd did such a thorough job that there was little left to read and neither Ártur, Bhyrhán nor Kavan had the stomach to sort through the parts to try. It did not matter. The recovered loot was proof enough for Hagan. Although he swore to others, when asked, that the deaths had been sanctioned by the Crown, his choice to temporarily suspend Bhríd from his duties as chamberlain, sending him to Elyriá to regain some degree of priority, led some to question the King's claim. The conflicting message of perceived punishment for a sanctioned execution left some to believe that it had not been sanctioned after all and that the Elyri chamberlain had lost his reason, turning into a cold-blooded killer. This frightened some, angered others, and fueled talk amongst anti-Elyri factions that Elyri should not be trusted in advisory positions to the Crown.

What if one of them turned on the King that way?

That the act of rage had nothing to do with Bhríd being Elyri and everything to do with the revenge of a Duke wronged was conveniently not considered.

The other men were arrested on the sixth day of the seclusion and tried on the morning of the seventh. Presented with a host of crimes that had come to Asta with the of names, as well as a smattering of witnesses willing to testify, there proved no need for the Elyri to read them. Crimes ranging from vandalism and theft to kidnapping and murder were presented, each guilty of all manner of offenses and thus impossible, in the King's opinion, to tell apart. The trial resulted in eight other names coming to light, eight other arrests being made, and though the King would not consider conducting an execution as they awaited more holy matters, he did condemn each of the thirteen to death. It was the biggest arrest in Rhidam since the Corylliens had sprung up, the strongest blow to the organization thus far, a much-needed success for King Hagan that Kavan was thankful for. The man called Anri Heward had yet to be found and none of those currently held in the castle dungeon were familiar with the name. If Caol had yet to come home, it seemed reasonable to Asta that there would be more. The King was not alone in regretting that none of those arrested knew anything about the missing inquisitor.

Late on the eighth day, as Kavan oversaw an art lesson his cousin was giving the boys and Asta in the fading light of the dayroom, Wortham brought the summons to the Great Hall they had waited anxiously to receive and a call was made to the people of the city. Though he had hoped for some clue, some premonition about the outcome, none had come, and when the Elyri in the room turned to look at him for answers or reassurance, Kavan had none to give. The Sight had shown him nothing and Kóráhm and the záryph had been unusually distant and silent. Every morning, every evening, Kavan had prayed for a sign, had prayed to conduct the ritual he had been led to believe would end the tumult, but nothing had come. Now the time of decision was here, and Kavan's words through Tusánt's mouth would be the only means he had been given of affecting the future of the Faith in Enesfel. Had it, he wondered, been enough?

The Great Hall was already filling to capacity by the time Kavan entered, but he was content to remain at the rear of the room, unwilling to be surrounded by the overflow of emotion, positive or negative, that would erupt as the announcement was made. Gaelán pushed through to his father's side, dragging Sóbhán with him, and Ártur found his way in through another door, separated from his cousin by the influx of people arriving from outside the castle. Wortham remained with Kavan, directly behind him, one hand curled near the sword he continued to carry despite no longer being a member of the Lachlan guard. Especially in these troubled days, with Kavan to protect, he would go nowhere without it.

Eyes closed, Kavan listened with both his ears and other senses, his attention divided between Rankin, at the center of the platform waiting to speak, and Karleo, Tusánt and Claide who were led into the Hall where their peers waited. The bard already knew, from the order of their thoughts without seeing them, knew without seeing the evidence of holy vestments draped over the man's shoulders and worn upon his bald head, that Claide had the position he had coveted enough to kill for. Dizziness and nausea crashed over him, intermixed with a feeling Kavan had not experienced since leaving the lands south of Hatu. The distressing warm wetness began to spread down his wrists, between his clenched palms and interlaced fingers to drip onto the stone floor. Knees buckling as his sight blurred, he was grateful Wortham caught him and noticed the bleeding before anyone else at the back of the crowd could do so. Kavan did not hear Rankin's words, did not hear the crowd's reaction or Claide's statement as the captain carried him out of the hall into the library, the closest room he could reach without worrying that someone else would see them. He dared to lock the doors after placing Kavan on the window seat and then yanked his tunic off over his head to wrap it around the bard's hands.

"My lord," Wortham did not know what to say, what to ask, or what he should do. Having witnessed this before, he recognized the rósádhá but he did not know what it meant, how or if it was connected to the path Enesfel was destined to spiral down. He did know that if anyone in the Great Hall had seen the blood they would have thought Kavan injured and a riot would have ensued. And if anyone noted the locations of the bloodletting, there would be a miracle claimed that Claide would somehow twist to be a sign of blessing on his ordination. Wortham believed that was the furthest thing from the truth, but if it was a sign, what was it a sign of?

Kavan could not reply to the unspoken query. He smelled smoke, death, and fear, tasted its bitter pungency, his senses telling him he was burning, though logically he knew he was not. What he saw, however, was not a pyre, was not his death, but a skyline ablaze. What he heard were the cries of the frightened, the dying, and the saviors struggling to their aid. He heard, smelled, tasted the crackle of burning leather and parchment and saw the pyre fall. He felt tremors beneath his feet as faceless white marble statues swayed and cracked, saw a wood-framed window of glass fly open, pushed by a familiar hand, and from somewhere far away he heard the unmistakable scream of a woman suffering. A woman he knew to be...

"Orynn."

He doubled forward, wrapped hands clenched against his stomach as he tried to breathe. k'Ádhá...what did this mean? Was there a fire in the abbey? Was Myreth in danger? Where was Orynn? Why was her cry so real, so distinct...so close to his heart and ears? There was a link, he believed, each snippet of Sight being somehow connected to the ascension of Claide to k'gdhededhá of Enesfel, but the thread that bound them was invisible, impossible to find. Confused and scared, he whispered, "Kóráhm…" as a rattling shook the library door.

"Lord Cliáth? Captain Delamo?"

It was Sóbhán's small, fearful voice on the other side, a sound which made Kavan nod slightly as consent for Wortham to open it. He did not want to scare the boy with the blood on his hands, but a child's fears needed to be addressed, and banishing him from the room would only alarm him further. Forcing a normal posture revealed the blood staining the side of his shirt as well as that on the cloth around his hands, but it could not be helped. The flow had not stopped, judging by the continuing spread of it into the fabric of Wortham's shirt, thus Kavan remained seated where he was as Wortham allowed the boy into the room. Behind Sóbhán, the healer carried Gaelán's limp body.

His own bleeding forgotten, Kavan lurched to his feet, fear for Gaelán outweighing thoughts of himself. "What is this…?" he began.

"I must ask you the same…" Ártur's gaze fell immediately on Kavan's bloodied shirt front and then to the blood-soaked cloth around his hands. "Kavan!" he cried, shoving Gaelán into Wortham's arms. He already knew there was nothing he could do for Gaelán, that he could only make the boy comfortable and allow him to come out of this state on his own. But his cousin was injured, bleeding profusely, and that was something he could tend. "Let me…"

"No." Kavan tried to back away but Ártur already had hold of his wrists and was pulling the cloth away, fearing he would see mutilation akin to what Kavan had suffered before. What he was not expecting was matching punctures on each wrist, wounds precise in their jagged diameters as if someone had driven large spikes through tender flesh and tendons. What those marks were, what they meant, was far from his thoughts as he set his focus to healing, but no matter how much energy he poured into Kavan's body, the wounds would not close, the bleeding would not stop, and the healer began to panic.

"Ártur." Kavan's plea again went unheard. Beside them, Sóbhán stared wide-eyed and pale but he did not flee. The bard thought he should say something, but his throat felt filled with dry flax and the sound that came out behind his cousin's name was a groan as weakness overtook him.

Wortham, who had placed Gaelán on the settee near the window where Kavan had previously been seated, gently grasped the healer's hands and pried them from Kavan's wrists. "There is nothing you can do until it is done. Let him be."

"But he will…"

"Kavan will be well. Let him be." Partially between the two men now, Wortham cradled the bard and helped him onto the nearest bench. "We will need water…towels…fresh clothes."

Sóbhán was the one to act, sprinting out the door as if to escape the horror of so much blood. Not sure they would see him any time soon, not sure he believed what Wortham had said, Ártur went in search of a bowl of water and the requested towels. It took him time to find what he needed and return, having to dodge palace staff and those continuing to loiter around Claide in the Great Hall offering congratulations or asking questions or seeking blessing from the newly ordained k'gdhededhá. Though he wondered, as he struggled to return to Kavan without spilling the requested water, where Tusánt had gone, where the King and the princesses were, what would happen next, he could spare no time to find out. His cousin needed him.

And if he found any of the others, or they found him, he could certainly not bring them into the library.

Or maybe Kavan did not need him, he thought bitterly, as he pushed the library door open with his elbow and entered to find Kavan staring at his wrists numbly. Though his hands and arms were bloody still, the punctures were closing, the seepage gradually ceasing. What could a man as blessed as this ever need with someone like him?

Ártur immediately chastised himself for daring to think that way again. Whatever this was, for whatever reason Kavan had to endure this obviously agonizing event, he was but a man, still cousin, still sínréc. Those facts did not change with the shedding of blood.

He knelt with Wortham at Kavan's feet and each of them reached for the man's hands. They stared at one another for several seconds and then Wortham nodded, giving in to the healer's need to help. As the blood was washed away, Wortham tugged off the bard's boots, revealing an accumulation of blood there as well, as if Kavan had been standing in a pool of it. Ártur realized with a start that he had been.

"I thought I…when this happened to Gaelán before…when I saw the marks…felt…I could not believe what I imagined…"

"No imagination," Wortham whispered, eyeing Kavan whose head lolled weakly to one side. He knew the bard could hear them, and though he worried about saying too much, there was no use in denying what the healer already knew. "It has happened before…to different degrees…but he will recover soon." He followed Kavan's nearly vacant stare towards Gaelán and, as if reading the Elyri's thought, asked, "This has happened to Master Cáner before? He has felt this?"

"I don't know. I believe so. Sometimes at least. He complained of headaches, absorbing too much power…accompanied by the feeling that Kavan was near. It has been known to leave him unconscious, and once there were marks on his wrists…bruises. I saw them, felt Kavan with him, in his head, but I do not understand how…why…" Recognizing the building of tension in Kavan's body as his muscles clenched, Ártur gently squeezed his cousin's hand. "It is not your fault. You are not harming him, nothing with any lasting effects. It may actually have strengthened his power…and he likes feeling close to you. I don't believe this is…intentional. An after-effect, a link, after the healing he gave you perhaps…or because his mind is less trained and unguarded and thus open to you."

In a way, he thought with a sigh, that mine seemingly is not. If he was honest, in the years when his mind had been most open to Kavan's, Ártur had spent too much time and effort trying to shut out contact, to keep his cousin from knowing the state of affairs around him, knowing what his life was like in Rhidam. Perhaps if he had not tried to keep Kavan out in those early years, he would have been the one to experience this peculiar bond. Or he had not experienced it because he no longer possessed the innocent openness of a child.

The door creaked open. It was Sóbhán, coming in with a pair of trousers and two shirts, one for Kavan and one for Wortham. He was still wide-eyed, but the pallor had passed. The clothing was placed on a chair, away from the bloody mess the men were trying to clean up, and wiggled his way in between Kavan and Gaelán. He took Gaelán's hand, and since he could not reach Kavan's, he put his hand on the bard's bare shoulder. Gaelán twitched and moaned softly. Kavan blinked and lifted his head to look into the boy's eyes with an unexpected start. It was a rare gift among Elyri, to be a conduit, able to naturally pass power from one to another, able to link thoughts and perhaps more. Kavan could do such things, and some healers learned to do so, but it was not a common gift or learned skill.

"That was…you had…" The boy's blue eyes traveled down Kavan's arm to his one clean hand. Kavan brought it up to stroke the child's dark hair.

"rósádhá…yes," he whispered, the admission an anguished one. "Do not be…"

"I'm not afraid. That would be being afraid of Dhágdhuán…it would be silly." He twisted Kavan's wrist around to examine both sides, to see that the evidence was gone. "Did it hurt?"

"Yes." He would not quantify the pain to spare the boy, but nor would he make it worse than it was. It hurt, yes. That was all anyone needed to know.

"But it is gone now…and you are well?"

"Just weak," Kavan said with a bob of his head. Weak, and afraid. Very afraid. Afraid enough that he wanted to get away from Rhidam. Afraid enough that he did not want to see anyone else today. On the verge of breaking into hundreds of brittle pieces that needed tending at once. "Ártur…" He locked eyes with his cousin, and the healer, disliking Kavan's tone, opened his mouth, but the bard continued, "Alberni. Now." It was where he needed to be. There was no logical reason as to why. Something there was calling him, or else his fears were pushing him to somewhere he would feel safe and isolated.

"I will go with you." Wortham set his towels aside. Kavan's feet were clean but not yet dry as he helped Kavan to stand, but the bard shook his head.

"No…you cannot…you are needed here." The man had a wife to consider, who would not understand if her new husband left her alone to be at Kavan's side somewhere else. And what Kavan needed was to be alone, or at least away from people he would not need to reassure or cater too, who might feel inclined to coddle him.

Ártur scowled. "If this is because of this," he gestured at the bloody towels, "no one else needs to know. We would not…"

"It isn't this…it is…" Shaking his head again, he was grateful that Sóbhán came to his other side to help steady him. "A few days…no more. I need to be there."

Though disappointed to have his company rejected, Wortham understood that there were times when the bard craved solitude and needed things that even Wortham could not give. And Kavan had yet to visit his estate, or St. Kóráhm's since his return to Enesfel, had not yet been to Jermyn's graveside. Given what had just occurred, who now occupied the post Jermyn had previously held, Wortham suspected Kavan wanted a dialogue with the man's spirit at his grave. Flight to Alberni was not a flight from duty, not an unrealistic request.

It was better than his disappearing for days without telling them where he intended to go.

"You should not…you are weak…"

"I will be fine." Despite his words, and Sóbhán and Wortham's support, he wobbled a little on his first step.

"We need you here…"

The healer immediately hung his head as the ill-thought words fell from his mouth. He did not see the withering look his cousin shot at him, but he did not need to see it to feel it, to know it was there. How many times, he scolded himself, would he, like so many others, put their needs ahead of Kavan's? How much more would his cousin have to give before Ártur felt it was enough…or too much?

"You will come back?" Sóbhán asked, glancing at Gaelán as he helped Kavan hobble towards the door. Wortham let them go.

Though he wondered briefly if he should take Sóbhán with him, Kavan felt strongly that this time he could not. His brooding would not be good for the boy, and though Kavan worried about his safety, he was confident that Wortham and the others in the castle would protect the boy. "I will; I promise. Someday you will come with me to Alberni. For now…listen to Captain Delamo…do as he tells you. Help Ártur clean here, and stay with Gaelán. Tell him this is not his fault and I will see him soon."

At the mention of Gaelán's name, the young man at the window seat groaned as if beginning to awaken. Sóbhán chose to let Wortham take his place, letting the captain support Kavan's weight as he went to Gaelán's side.

As weak as Kavan was, he knew he could manipulate the Gate, but he would not be able to get there on his own. "And tell Owain…"

He fell silent as Wortham swept him up, both men still shirtless, the clothes Sóbhán had brought tucked beneath his arm. Others eyed them as Wortham carried him up the stairs and the captain realized that soon he would have the princess, and possibly the King, inquiring about Kavan's welfare. Diona, in particular, would not be pleased that Kavan was leaving, but at least this time no one would question his right to tend to his own lands.

At least, Wortham mused, there was no visible blood to raise questions. What there was had soaked into the bard's dark trousers, and though it rubbed off onto Wortham's skin as he carried him, it would not be enough to cause questions he could not answer.

Maybe he would simply ignore them when asked.

Wortham stopped outside of the Purification Chamber and helped Kavan to stand. As silent as the man had been, he had believed him asleep until the oratory door was pushed open. "Orders, my lord?"

Kavan shook his head. "You do not need, orders. I ask that you watch over the boys…send for me at once if I'm needed…and tell Owain to wait for me. His presence is needed; he knows this…but I do not want him to think I am abandoning him."

"I will tell him" There was no need for jealousy. Owain was dear to Kavan, and Wortham knew, as he held the curtain for Elyri to enter the chamber, that the bard would be forever loyal to them both. Just as they were to him.

❧*❧

Sunrise gave birth to a too-elaborate ceremony meant to pass the mantle of Faith officially to Claide before the congregation of Rhidam. Princess Diona attended, along with her brother and many of the palace staff, because the King expected it. Hagan, she knew from the smile on his face, was happy for the man he seemed to view as a surrogate father, despite the fact that she and others had tried to convince him that Claide's appointment could mean the ruin of Enesfel and his future as king. Hagan, however, without the details she withheld from him, could see no connection between the Faith election and the monarchy, and as he did not share Diona's suspicions, did not see the election as anything more than Faith politics. He had no opinion on the issue of separation from the Elyri establishment, claimed that the decisions of the gdhededhá would be for the betterment of all, and would have no bearing on anything important to the ruling of the kingdom.

And though he disagreed with Claide on the issue of Elyri in Enesfel, he did not believe the new k'gdhededhá would dare to undermine the royal decrees that made all Elyri welcome. The election may have been uninteresting for the king, but the pageantry of Claide's appointment was opulent and satisfying. Afterward, it would be time to turn his attention to his upcoming wedding, and the Faith ceremony provided him with multiple ideas he hoped to incorporate. Hagan had chosen to wait until after the election in order that the new k'gdhededhá, whoever that happened to be, could officiate his marriage, and now, with the appointment made, there was last-minute planning to do in order for him to give the kingdom a queen and, if things proceeded as expected, an heir to the throne.

The pageantry, however, sickened the princess, as the candles, the brass fanfare, the flowers, and choir suggested to her that Claide saw himself as a king of sorts, a ruler worthy of a monarch's coronation. She wondered if the man had his eyes on Enesfel's throne, but when she voiced that concern to her brother, he laughed and teased her about worrying too much. To appease her, however, when he realized how serious her fears were…and because he wanted his wedding to go smoothly, he agreed to accept additional personal guards and tighten security around the castle. She might be imagining things, her fears might be unjustified, but Diona would rather be proven wrong with her brother safe than be proven right with harm befalling him.

The other man eagerly accepting increased personal security was gdhededhá Tusánt. Claide's appointment meant that Tusánt ascended to the highest-ranking gdhededhá in Rhidam. He had already been fulfilling many duties of that office since Jermyn's death, but now the shift was official. It occurred to him on waking each morning that Claide would likely stomach an Elyri in that position only as long as he was forced to. Soon, he would either reassign Tusánt to another parish, if he could, without raising the ire of the Faithful who supported the Elyri, or else he would have Tusánt killed, just as Tusánt and others believe he had ordered done to Jermyn.

As leading gdhededhá, and an Elyri, no one could deny him the right to hire attendants and bring in more novices if he chose. The four selected as guards were again at Princess Diona's recommendation and were screened by her, by the chamberlain, and lastly by Tusánt himself to be certain they were no threat to any Elyri and were not sympathetic to Claide. Edward and Saul, the moment Tusánt had become a nominee, began recruiting novices from amongst their friends and acquaintances, and after an equally thorough vetting process, four more novices with strong arms and military training were initiated into the Faith. This was to be a war unlike any other, not an obligation to take lightly in a time and atmosphere when any Elyri was a target. But it was, in Edward and Saul's eyes, the highest call to duty any could aspire to, and they used that selling point to draw in the support they needed.

With two novices sharing his room, and two guards at his door when he slept, Tusánt was as safe as he could be. But he wished, as the eighteen gdhededhá and their attendants began to trickle out of Rhidam to return to their sees, that Kavan was here to reassure him that what he had done had been worth the risk.

During the days in the afterglow of Claide's election, Kavan wished there were assurances he could give to anyone about what awaited them. He poured his heart into those words uttered through Tusánt, believed in them as he had believed Tusánt's acceptance of the nomination had been the right and necessary thing, and yet all of his efforts had failed. He wondered often as he tended to the business of his estate, if there was anything else he could have done, anything he should have done.

Yet with no guidance from the forces that so often directed his life, he had been hesitant to attempt the purification of the thol and the actions he had considered had been forbidden by Kóráhm. But there must have been something, and his failure to act, to succeed, had allowed the governance of the Faithful to fall into what he believed to be enemy hands.

Rumors persisted even in Alberni that the Teren Faith, or at least those in Enesfel, would break from the leadership in Clarys, an act that would put St. Kóráhm's in a perilous position. Their commitment was to the Faith that sanctioned their calling, and to the man who was their patron. Technically, Kavan owned the land on which the thol was built, and as a subject of Enesfel by his allegiance to the Lachlans, he was subject to the land. No one was required to belong to the Faith, and none were required to donate to it. But donating was standard practice, as those serving had to pay for their needs and the upkeep of their shelter in some fashion. Most náós did not have a wealthy patron seeing to their upkeep as Kavan did St. Kóráhm's. Most did not want those secular ties. If Teren split from Elyri, Rhidam's Faith would become the new seat of holy power in the Teren Sovereignties. Rather than send a portion of their donations to Clarys, they would be required to send them to Claide in Rhidam.

No one in St. Kóráhm's wanted to do that. Few in the Alberni congregation did either. But neither did they want to be forced to close their doors when they had only just opened.

The debate between the abbey's leaders and Kavan was long and difficult, but in the end, they decided they would follow whatever path Lord Cliáth deemed necessary when the time came. There would be no favoritism of one over the other, no siding with Clarys over Rhidam, Dórímyr over Claide, Teren over Elyri. Their best hope to support unification was to support both sides as much as they could. It might mean tightening their belts, sending equal portions of their small revenue to Clarys and Rhidam, and might mean relying even more on their benefactor's generosity, but it was what Kavan wanted, and for those inside St. Kóráhm's walls, what they wanted as well.

Jermyn's grave was no longer unmarked. Positioned in the center of the burial plot, his grave was marked with a stone spire nearly six feet tall with the man's name, his office and calling, and the year of his martyrdom extolled on the pale, green-grey stone. Because no one else had been buried here thus far, it was not difficult for Kavan to locate the site when he left the gdhededhá to their discussions about the financial details of running the abbey. It was dark by then, which he appreciated, for it meant that no one would be able to see his weeping from the windows of the bedrooms, scriptorium, or corridors that overlooked the plot.

He had not come to weep, in truth wept rarely enough that he sometimes wondered if he was flawed in some way because he found expressions of grief so difficult. Any emotion was difficult for him to express, however, unless there was a harp in his hands, and that reminder reassured him.

"I should have been here for you," he murmured to the stone, his hand on it as he tried to conjure some memory of the man that did not involve the gruesome images of his last moments alive. He wiped his eyes with his other hand, his drying tears on his skin cool in the evening air. "I should have prevented this. I should be able to…"

"You are not omnipotent, átaelás mai." The hand on his shoulder announced the man beside him. Kavan jumped, having been unaware of his presence prior to that touch. For a moment he expected it to be Jermyn, but the endearment told him otherwise.

"He may not cross over to you," the saint murmured, heart aching to see Kavan's grief. "But I assure you he is in a warm, happy, safe place. He sees you…and wants you to know that none of this is your doing, your fault."

"It should be. I should have been able to…"

"Do you remember what you told me? That each of us makes our own choices? The decisions of others do not fall on your shoulders simply because you wish to claim them. You did what you could, from where you were. You have done what you are meant to do. The rest is in the hands of others."

Kavan frowned. "I thought I was to open the door to healing…"

"You have…and you will…in time. Tusánt too, with your prompting, has taken the steps he must towards that end. The rest will come when they come."

"But he did not…"

Kóráhm smiled, bent over him, and kissed the top of his head. "He is where he needs to be. There is little else I can tell you except this…the election tipped in Claide's favor by a single vote…and the vote for separation the same. Think on that…on what that means. Even the darkest moments have their purpose in the flow of history." He chuckled at Kavan's unspoken thoughts, "Yes, even those I inadvertently caused in my own life."

Those were not easy words for Kavan to cling to as the saint's physical presence faded, leaving the warm glow of hands on his shoulders and the kiss on his head. So focused had he been on Claide's victory that he had not imagined how slim that vote might have been to put him there. A single vote was a lot when it came to the effect it could have on history, but that single vote also represented a narrower gap between the leaders then imagined. And the single vote, whoever it had been, had waivered enough that they could be swayed the other way. Whether by politics, money, fear of reprisal, it could be reversed. Tusánt had his backers and perhaps, Kavan decided as he continued to lean against the pillar of Jermyn's grave, Tusánt's being where he was would be enough to affect that change. Perhaps he, like Kavan, would have a hand in Enesfel's healing. Kavan prayed that doing so would not come at too high a price.

The lake was placid with a faint mist glittering inches above the water. Occasionally the vapor parted for the passing of a moth, an evening bird coming to roost, a fish reaching for the insects that darted and danced across the still, glassy surface. From the position of the sun, he knew it to be evening, but memory told him it should have been well past the hour of total darkness. Perplexed, he stepped across the stony path of the creek that fed the lake and crept forward until he reached the brambles that shielded the water from easy viewing. It also shielded him from the sight of whoever was there, for he knew he was not alone. He could feel the strong presence of power ahead, but heard nothing save for the chirp and whir of crickets, frogs, and night bugs. Imagining that this was how Prince Arlan had once found him, Kavan tried to see, to push the brambles aside quietly for a better view, but they would not part easily and all he could see was the surface of the lake and a hand dangling in the water.

He scowled. The position of that wrist suggested someone asleep and the shape of it, the size of the immersed hand, suggested a woman. As he had never known anyone else to come here in the years he spent visiting, except for Prince Arlan…and the rumors of phae k'kairá, and because the lake was far from the nearest villages and towns, Kavan could not imagine anyone else being here. Arlan was gone. No one else should have come. This was his lake, he thought with an irrational grunt of annoyance. That annoyance, that sense of propriety for this secret wild corner of the world, brought him around the brambles to stare down at the woman, expecting to rouse her, drive her away.

He stopped short and stared.

A seemingly lost, frightfully injured woman. Badly bruised, bloody as though beaten, wearing a torn blue gown of flimsy fabric, she lay crumpled there as if she had been thrown, or fallen, from a wagon or horse. A quick glance around revealed no tracks, no footprints, no way she could have gotten there unless, he glanced into the trees and the clouds above them, she had fallen from the sky. That thought made his scowl deepen.

"Orynn?"

In profile, she looked a little like the woman he had known for a few short months, but as he gingerly rolled her onto her back, he was relieved to see it was not. This woman's face was narrower, her torn lips fuller, and her hair, what he could see that was not caked with mud and drying blood, was the riches red he had ever seen. Not Orynn, but similar enough in small ways that they could have been siblings or cousins. It should have been impossible to assess beauty in the condition she was in, but to Kavan, she seemed flawless. It should have been impossible to know anything about her, as he chose not to test her thoughts, but as he took her hands in his long enough to learn where she had come from, a surge of blinding power punched through him with enough force to make him scream.

Scream and wake up in a sweat, his head lying on Jermyn's grave, his eyes blinking up at the moonless night sky. He jumped to his feet, the impulse to fly, to reach the lake, the strongest he had felt in weeks, but he pushed the feelings down and struggled to gain control of his impulses. It was not dusk, it was not mid-summer…and from the way the images, the sensations of hands in his, of power pulsing through his body, continued to linger at the edges of his perception, he could only conclude one thing.

It had been the Sight.

But what exactly had he Seen? Who was she and why had he been shown a stranger injured and alone in his perfect place? He wanted to believe that the importance he felt to her presence was connected to Kóráhm's past, Enesfel's future, but he was denied that potentially comforting thought by the realization that what he felt in touching her had been the most astonishing completeness of power he could imagine. Not Elyri, not in full at least, but not Teren either. Something other…an other that caused him to grasp at the crystal and half-moon crest he wore as though both talismans could offer protection. Could she have been…?

Shivering uncontrollably, he started for his estate. Someday his questions would be answered, unless the Sight proved faulty. Someday he would find her and she would tell him everything. For some baffling reason, he felt afraid of what those answers would be, the complications they would bring. He did not need any more complications.

❧Chapter 37❧

"Espen!" Diona's welcome was an exclamation of delight and relief when she entered the library at her servant's summons. Caring little about propriety or whether she looked like a demure or proper lady, she rushed to him and hugged him hard. After the tension during the days before the election which had not entirely dissipated these three weeks later, having the prince back in Rhidam was something she had been longing for every minute of the day. So, apparently, had the prince; he did not stiffen as a man from Hatu might over a dramatic public display from a woman, but rather he returned her embrace with equal emotion. She realized, when he drew back, that there was no public to be concerned about. Her ladies had been in the room when she entered, but they discreetly departed during the embrace and now she and Espen were alone.

"When I heard of Claide's election, I feared for you…we rode as hard as we could. What has happened? How are you?

"Nothing has happened…and that concerns me."

She settled on the window seat, leaving room for Espen to join her and offered her hand. "Nothing?" he murmured as he accepted her invitation.

"It has been quiet…too quiet…almost as if the violence carried out was merely a ploy to maneuver him into office. We have had no reports from anywhere in Enesfel, no vandalism, no theft, no bodies. Hagan believes it is because of the men he arrested and executed…"

"Executed?"

Her head bobbed. "It seems to have changed him…the break in the case…the arrests. He even attended the executions." Diona hoped, for Hagan's sake, that the change was not connected to Claide's election. "He does not know where the arrest tips came from, believes the new fellow acting as inquisitor until Uncle's return was the instrumental hand…"

She had told Espen of Caol's ruse because she needed to. She wanted as few secrets between them as possible. "Hagan is still intent on finding him…but I fear my uncle may not have a position when he returns." She paused, movement outside the window distracting her, Espen's men in the courtyard being accommodated by Enesfel's staff. "The executions may have sent a message to others, driving them into hiding, or the core group of Corylliens has now been stopped…"

"Or your guess is correct…and Claide's quest for power has been behind it all."

"It stopped so abruptly with his election…even with those arrests. It must look as suspicious to others as it does to me." Outside Rhidam, and even to the common folk in the street, most people likely did not look beyond the exterior, and those who noticed the abrupt calm likely attributed it to the execution of the men calling themselves Coryllien. Or they attributed it to Claide's election in a positive way…or to the near invisibility of Elyri in Rhidam. "But it's not…"

Her hands tightened around Espen's to keep him from pulling away, expecting he would misinterpret her next words. "The day the vote was cast, Kavan left Rhidam…"

"Again?" the prince snorted.

Frowning, Diona continued, "He went to Alberni…"

"That is his right and duty; he has not been there since his first flight, correct?"

"I don't believe so…but something is wrong. He has yet to return, he left the boy Sóbhán rather than take him with him. He left both harps." She did not know that Ártur had taken one of them to his cousin two days after the election, but it would not have mattered. Kavan had left without them and had not returned for them. "Uncle Owain is here, says Kavan bid him wait. He will return, I'm sure of it. But I worry that his absence bodes ill for Rhidam."

Though Espen did not share that perception of the bard's absence, he nodded. To his knowledge, Kavan no longer had an official court position; his employment had ended the night King Arlan died and there had been no appointments, no oath-taking, since then unless it had happened while Espen was in Hatu. If that had been true, he believed Diona would have told him. Despite her agreement to marry him, Espen knew she was still deeply attached to the man who had tutored her. "It is a mark of a leader to worry for your people…"

She chuckled and kissed his cheek. "I am no leader, Espen. That is my brother's burden, not mine." It was a burden she would happily share, that she believed she could carry, if Hagan asked, but there were many days of late when she was grateful she did not have to. "At least you made it back in time for his wedding. In two weeks we shall have a queen." And that would, most likely, mean the end of any dreams Diona had of one day sitting on the throne. "I am glad you are here."

"As am I." He kissed her knuckles. He was thankful Enesfel was at peace, thankful he had not come too late, but mostly he was thankful to be in her company. "I believe we have plans of our own to complete…unless you have changed your mind?"

"Never." She smiled and kissed him again, this time on the mouth. "That will never happen."

❧*❦

The upstairs oratory was quiet when he arrived, the way Kavan hoped it would be. After three weeks of the mundane tasks of overseeing the running of both his estate and St. Kóráhm's, after being assured that Alberni was in no immediate danger of succumbing to either religious troubles or anti-Elyri violence, he chose to return to Rhidam. His sheriff, a handsome bronze-skinned man named Reland who had once been a dock worker in Levonne but had returned to his home city after the death of his wife and son in childbirth, was continuing to run the city evenhandedly. Having spent his early years traveling to and from Elyriá with his merchant father before marrying and settling in Levonne, Reland held no biases between races, was proficient in multiple languages, was hardworking, educated, and well-liked. Kavan trusted him and thus far Reland had not disappointed. The Alberni estate was in the care of Martin Dary and his family, and St. Kóráhm's was in good hands, despite gdhededhá Kesábhá still traveling in Elyriá. With many competent people at his disposal, Kavan felt no need to remain in Alberni.

The city and estate could run indefinitely without him.

Nor was the emotional need present any longer. Ártur had come to him twice a week with news from Rhidam and, on the surface at least, it appeared there was peace. Though Kavan did not believe that peace would last, the immediate descent into madness he had feared upon Claide's election had not come to pass. He failed to formulate any plan for addressing those anticipated days of pandemonium, for now, a plan did not appear necessary.

What he did do, besides oversee the estate, the abbey, and fret, was face the same glimpse into the future, finding the stranger beside the lake, a woman who was becoming less a stranger in the three times the Sight 'found' her, but it frightened him nonetheless. His hope was that returning to Rhidam would end that vision so, after a late afternoon meeting with Reland, he spent one evening more in prayer at Jermyn's grave and then return to Rhidam.

If nothing else, his kin would be happy for his return, the boys and Wortham too. And being here would allow him to gauge the true state of Rhidam, the degree of calm. He could witness Claide in action and assess him better. He knew about the executions, about Hagan's decree forbidding violence of any sort against Elyri, demanding fair treatment of all people and promising swift and harsh punishment to any who disobeyed his law. Kavan heard the proclamation word for word through his cousin's mind during one of Ártur's visits.

It gave the bard hope for Hagan's successful rule, for if Hagan could find his political footing, it would be much easier to control the kingdom if, or when, that proclamation was defied.

Kavan had few doubts it would be. Claide might have achieved ecclesiastical power, but he would not be content until all Elyri were out of Enesfel. And Kavan doubted the Corylliens were finished with their reign of terror. If they were, Caol would have come home.

His plan to go to Hes á Redh upon his return, however, was cut short when he stepped from the Purification Chamber to find Gaelán and Sóbhán entering the oratory. "See?" Gaelán said, grinning widely, "I told you he was back."

Attributing Gaelán's sensitivity to the inadvertent sharing of power Kavan occasionally projected into the young man, the bard smiled, honestly glad to see them in good health and spirits. Sóbhán, relieved to learn that he had not been abandoned, ran the length of the room and threw his arms around Kavan in a clinging embrace.

"Some said you were not coming back…" he murmured.

"I told you I would. As long as I am able, I will keep my promises. Never fear for that. Were you waiting for me?

"Yes," Gaelán said, at the same time as Sóbhán shook his head and replied "No." Gaelán giggled, a more boyish sound than should have come from a young man striving hard to be an adult. "We were practicing, waiting to show you what we've learned."

"Oh?" Intrigued, Kavan looked back and forth between them "What do you have to show me?"

The younger tugged at Kavan's hand. "We have to go outside."

"It will be better there," Gaelán agreed.

Curious about what the boys intended to show him that required going outside, Kavan followed the pull of their hands. There were few about in the castle at this hour, or outside, guards and servants mostly, preparing the keep for another day. None paid the bard and boys any attention, used to seeing Kavan awake at unusually early hours and knowing the boys were safe in his company. He watched for trouble, however, and for an indication of what they planned, but even when they finally stopped in the vacant space before the Lachlan mausoleum, there was no hint of what they wanted to show him.

"Promise you'll not scold us," Gaelán said. "aendhá thinks we shouldn't try so hard, that it isn't right, but I told him we had consent."

"Consent for what?" Kavan did not recall giving them permission for anything, and because he was not Gaelán's father, permission should have come from Bhríd, not Kavan. He had no desire to scold them unless they were doing something dangerous, but implicating Kavan in possible misbehavior could not be allowed. Thankfully, Gaelán normally had more sense.

Instead of replying, the boys faced each other, holding hands with their eyes closed for nearly a minute during which time Kavan could feel the buildup of energy around them. There were not many disciplines that required joint effort, and those few there were tended to be risky skills that the bhydáni rarely taught. It was possible, however, to amplify another's power, or to guide a less experienced person in the usage of their power, and with Sóbhán being a conduit, it was not immediately clear what the boys intended to accomplish.

When Kavan felt the prickle run across his skin, however, and noted the slight shimmer in the air, he squatted to pay closer attention. A more experienced user, Gaelán seemed to be guiding Sóbhán. The younger boy was the first to change, his body giving way to the delicate shape of a dark gray dove. Moments later, his focus no longer on helping Sóbhán, Gaelán changed too, his dove form lighter with a hint of red at the tips of his feathers. Both birds fluttered on the ground as if dancing, pleased with the smile on the bard's face, and Kavan could tell they hoped he would join them.

He doubted either could maintain the shapeshift long enough for the sort of flights he normally enjoyed, but even a circle over the castle would be good experience, and, for Kavan, a delight to share with someone. He understood why Ártur discouraged them, as the healer had no fondness for shapechanging and, despite their previous talk, still had misgivings about Kavan teaching that skill.

"Once around the keep," he agreed.

He chose the same dove form, his being white as usual. They waited for him to take to the air before following, both slightly wobbly like baby birds taking to wing for the first time. But it was still flying, and that, to Kavan, was ideal. If they could learn to change without his guidance, if they could learn to do it alone without relying on each other to make it happen, it would be an invaluable means of escape to safety one day, just as Kavan intended it to be.

They reached the southern side of the keep before Kavan spotted, in the distance, a wagon bumping along the road from Levonne. It was no cause for concern, as the road was a frequent trade route for goods traveling from Hatu, Káliel, or other cities throughout southern Enesfel. Wagons, rather than pack animals, often meant the movement of a significant amount of goods, and thus he guessed this was a merchant vehicle on its way into Rhidam to trade or sell wares.

It was the half dozen men erupting from the field of tall wheat to charge the wagon that caused alarm. He could not form words, but he could communicate, and so, looking over his shoulder, his thoughts cried, "Go back; tell General Agis, Wortham, Ártur."

There was shouting below, screams and the clash of combat and Gaelán and Sóbhán had already seen the attack. "I can help!" protested Gaelán. Fighting meant injuries, and if the wounded had to wait until Ártur or Rouvyn could reach them, it might be too late.

Kavan could not refute that argument. "Sóbhán…can you…?"

"I will bring them." He sounded frightened and Kavan knew that fear could mean failure of the shapechange in a novice, but he had to trust that the small gray dove speeding back to the heart of the castle would make it. Thankfully, Sóbhán did not have far to go.

Mid-air, Kavan forced a change, morphing from the dove into his more familiar kestrel, no easy feat but one he had practiced before. For several seconds between, when the second form was not fully realized, he plummeted towards the ground, scaring Gaelán, but Kavan quickly righted his flight path and sped towards the besieged wagon. There was no time for awe or amazement; it took all of Gaelán's effort to keep up with the speed of the much larger bird. At the wagon, two masculine figures had been dragged from the seat, beaten and left for dead in the road. A few of the attackers, dressed in peasants' rags, swarmed into the wagon, bringing out what they could carry, while another hoisted the third struggling figure over his shoulder. From the screams, Kavan could tell it was a woman.

"Leave it!" the fellow shouted at those looting the wagon.

"But there's bhelts…!"

"Don't need them; got something better."

bhelts. Elyri. The knowledge filled Kavan with rage; he folded his wings, prepared to dive at the fellow carrying the woman, to force him to drop her. But when one of those jumping out of the wagon bed, shoving bhelts into his pocket grunted, "Heward better appreciate this," Kavan pulled up short.

Anri Heward? Were these men Corylliens?

He had no reason to doubt it. The name could not have been uttered for his benefit, to throw him off track or prevent his strike since these men did not know he was here. As much as Kavan feared for the woman's safety, it did not appear they intended to kill or rape her, at least not yet. If they intended to take her to Heward, Kavan could follow, find their hideout, perhaps confront Heward and end this. The man's death or arrest would be a much-needed rallying boost for King Hagan and might, Kavan hoped, help put an end to the violence.

Gaelán heard the name too, knew its significance through Asta, and shouted, "Go," into Kavan's thoughts as he dropped from the sky next to the injured men, taking his own form as he did so. The brigands ran through the field after their leader and paid no heed to a small bird morphing into a young man behind them. Briefly, the white kestrel circle back, reluctant to leave Gaelán alone. A healer was vulnerable in the open, unprotected and alone if others were to come. "The General will be here soon. Go after them!"

From his lofty vantage point, Kavan could see no one on the Levonne road as far as his eyesight stretched. No dark masses in the fields to suggest further attackers, nor any farmers. It would take anyone from the castle approximately twenty minutes to reach Gaelán and with no one else traveling who would reach him first, he would be safe enough. The men appeared in immediate need of a healer and Gaelán was the only one there.

"Go!" Gaelán shouted again, a man's voice now rather than the thoughts of a bird.

"Be careful…call if you need me…"

Picking up a sword that someone had dropped, Gaelán balanced it in his hand, looking at it grimly before kneeling beside the bloodier of the two men. "I'll be fine." The words were as much for his own reassurance as for Kavan's. Once he began healing, he would be at his most vulnerable, but it was a risk worth taking, the duty of a healer, and though he had taken no oaths, Gaelán took his calling seriously.

Near the stables inside the keep's walls, Sóbhán dropped out of the sky, landing in a rolling heap at Owain's feet as the boy's strength gave out. Breathless, afraid for his friend and mentor, he pointed at first in the direction from which he had come. Owain squawked in surprise, not expecting a boy to fall from the sky, and rushed to the child's side. The sound of his cry brought Wortham and the horses he had been saddling out of the stable. "What is it?" Owain asked, pulling the boy up by his shoulders and brushing off his dusty clothes.

"lás…Kavan…" he stammered, still pointing as he struggled to catch his breath and not collapse from the unaccustomed exertion.

Swallowing the panic, Wortham was on his horse, reaching to pull Sóbhán up with him, but Owain yanked the boy out of his grasp. "He's not going anywhere." More accustomed to childrearing, he recognized exhaustion and fear when he saw it, and if there was danger out there to face, taking the child with them would be foolish. "Where is he?" he asked the boy, grabbing the reins of his horse and moving the animal between them and Wortham. "What happened?"

"A wagon…attacked on the road to Levonne…he sent me to bring General Agis and Healer MacLyr…"

"Then bring them," Wortham barked at Owain, already digging his heels into the horse's flanks so that the beast jumped into motion. Owain could have taken offense at the command, but there was no time for something so unnecessary. No offense was meant; Wortham's only thought was Kavan.

Within minutes, Owain, Agis, Bhríd, Balint, and Ártur, plus a dozen mounted soldiers, thundered out of the keep at the fastest gallop they could manage. Wortham was far ahead of them, already circling the wagon when they caught up with him and found Gaelán, sword at his side, elbow deep in blood. "Gaelán!" shouted Bhríd, not having expected to find his son here, especially not alone. But he bit his tongue and turned his attention to the wagon instead as Ártur knelt beside Gaelán.

A healer needed focus. There would be time to reprove him later.

"Where is Kavan?" Wortham stomped through the fields on either side of the road, seeking a clue to the bard's location or fate. Other than the condition of the two merchants, Elyri father and son he wagered, and the rifling through of the wagon bed's contents, there was no other sign of a struggle, and no easily seen trace of where the attackers might have gone. They had not passed them on the road, and Wortham was near the point of concluding they had fled towards Levonne.

Weary from the unfamiliar flying and the initial life-saving healing he managed to provide before his power was drained, Gaelán rocked back on his heels and groaned, "There was a woman…they took her…to Anri Heward. He followed…" He pointed into the field.

The name Heward made many of those around him stare into the distance with increased interest. Even Bhríd, still prepared to scold his not yet adult son for this foolish risk, swallowed some of his ire and fear. The rescue of an Elyri woman, and the possibility of locating Anri Heward, and thus being that much closer to the end of the Corylliens, were necessary things. As had been the healing of two innocent men left behind. Logically, the two made the best choice they could at the moment, the more capable bard following the abductors, the healer staying with those who needed him. Knowing Kavan as he did, the choice to leave Gaelán unprotected had not been an easy one. And knowing his son, it had been a choice Gaelán would have mulishly insisted on.

"Where…?"

"I only know they went east…after that, I did not see…"

"Then we go after him."

Agis snorted. "You're no tracker, Captain. You could not even find the broken stalks." His hand brushed over the bent and torn plants that marked the men's passage into the field. "Once across the field, where would you go? How would you find them?"

"I will find them," Wortham growled stubbornly, though he knew the general had a point. But he would not wait for Kavan's return, for Kavan to be hurt or killed without his being there to help him. He knew the bard could defend himself, but it did not lessen the need to be there.

The general knew no command would prevent Wortham from trying to follow the bard, and because the former Káliel Captain was no longer part of the Lachlan Guard, Agis had no authority over him. Nor did he have any control over Prince Owain and he was not surprised when the blonde man turned his horse into place beside Wortham's and said, "I shall go with you."

"Wait." Ártur, on his knees, wiped his bloody hands on his trousers. Gaelán had taken care of the most immediately threatening damage, leaving Ártur to tend to the smaller details and the multitude of visible injuries. Years of experience allowed him to tend them quickly so that the pair, though still unconscious, would live injury-free. They could be taken to Rhidam and given shelter until their female companion was found.

Ártur rubbed the back of his hand across his brow and looked up at the morning sky. It was early. He could help locate his cousin and still return to Bhryell by nightfall, and if anyone protested, he had the excuse that they might need a healer when they found the abducted woman. He closed his eyes and sought the brilliant silver thread that was Kavan within his heart, touched it, and followed its convoluted path as far as he could from where he knelt.

"I can follow him…I can track him," he murmured, using the wooden step of the wagon to pull himself up.

"You will not be safe." As it was, there were too many Elyri in his care, and Agis did not think that Owain and Wortham alone would be enough to keep the healer safe. If he sent Ártur anywhere, or allowed him to go without protection, the Lachlans would surely strip him of rank, title, and everything he had earned over the years.

"Chamberlain? Lord Gabersdon?"

"Aye," the duke nodded at Wortham. "I will join you."

But Bhríd shook his head. "Someone has to see the wagon safely to Rhidam…while others search here…and I will not leave my son."

"I can go with you," Gaelán offered.

"Absolutely not." Seeing the young man's defiant frustration, Bhríd softened his tone and helped his son to his feet with an offered hand. "They may need your skills before reaching the keep…"

"And," Owain added, "Sóbhán is there…he will want to know what is happening. And the King will want a report."

Gaelán knew they were excuses, but they were also duty. After receiving Ártur's care, it was unlikely the two merchants would need further healing. And Sóbhán…well, he would need reassurance, but that did not necessarily have to come from Gaelán. In the end, however, he relented to his father's wishes because he knew that, other than finding out firsthand how Kavan was and perhaps witnessing Heward's end, he would be of little use to the party. He did not know how to track and could not fight as effectively as the others. They would feel compelled to protect him rather than do their jobs, and that would be counterproductive.

"Avner…Waljan…go with them." Agis knew Wortham would have fewer complaints about bringing his countrymen on the search and he knew those two men would take commands from the captain, even though he was no longer officially one of them. "We will see these men and their wares to Rhidam…and if you find Heward, bring him back alive."

The temptation would be to kill the man responsible for so much death, but such a man, in Agis' opinion, should answer for his crimes before the King. It was his duty to remind them. Whether they chose to obey that reminder was out of his hands.

As soon as Ártur, after last-minute instructions to Gaelán, was seated behind Wortham on the man's large, dappled horse, they started east across the field, leaving Agis and Bhríd to see to the merchants and their wagon. If another attack came before they reached the castle, the Lachlan soldiers could ward it off.

What this situation told them was that, despite there being so few details, the violence in Enesfel was not behind them. Claide's election had not been the cure to the Sovereignty's woes, had not been the end of the Corylliens.

They hoped the arrest of Anri Heward would be.

❧Chapter 38

Kavan expected a considerably shorter distance to travel when he began to follow the brigands through the fields to the southeast of Rhidam. If Rhidam was the hub of Coryllien activity, he thought they would be nearer to their destination. But after three hours of traipsing through crops and fallow land, then marshes, and then the swampy forest where it was difficult for Kavan to follow in kestrel form, it seemed the group was no closer to an end point. Kavan knew they were being followed, that somewhere far behind, Ártur lead Wortham, Owain, and others to find him and, they hoped, the lair of the Corylliens. But the swampy ground would slow the horses, possibly more than it slowed the men on foot. It would take several hours for them to catch up to Kavan and the offenders, and Kavan prayed that, by then, the woman would still be safe.

At first, he thought her to be the woman he had been Seeing recently, but the red crowning her head was merely a scarf and the gown she wore was typical of many Elyri women of her station. She stopped struggling after the men bound and gagged her, and Kavan suspected she feared no one would hear her scream in the wilderness. She likely possessed little training that might gain her freedom, and though he touched her thoughts to assure her that help would come, his reassurance did little. It had given her a fleeting sense of hope, but the longer they traveled away from the road, away from anyone she knew, the more that hope dwindled.

No one would think to look for her here. With the two men most likely dead, no one was likely to realize she was gone.

The men finally emerged from the copse of trees into another lightly marshy area, lands Kavan knew to lay less than two days' travel from Alberni. This marsh gave way quickly to more fields, fields that fed his people, fields that in turn bled into the forests at the foot of the Llaethlágárá Mountains. Some twenty yards from the tree line, a haphazard structure was erected, one that Kavan guessed was used for drying peat. There were other voices within, a quiet jumble of drunken men who sounded as if they were bored from too much leisure and waiting. The men he followed kicked open the door and pushed inside, eliciting shouts and the clatter of blades being drawn by startled men. The woman gave a squawk as she was deposited in the center of the room; the sight of her brought lusty chortles, catcalls, and squabbling as men jockeyed for the right to touch her, rape her, kill her.

"No one's killing or raping anyone, you cretins."

Caol's voice. Though Kavan could not see him from his perch on the eves of the structure, a structure with a single window and single door, he recognized the voice of a man long absent from Rhidam. He understood why these men had come here. If Caol wanted to remain out of sight of anyone in the keep, to be ingratiated with these people in order to get to Heward, he needed to prove himself to them. Taking them into hiding in a place far from the King's searching forces would be an efficient way to prove loyalty. He had to know the King was scouring the land for his missing inquisitor, and with the recent arrests and executions, a change in hideouts, until the heat died, was the logical choice. From the sounds of his ire, the group who had attacked the merchant wagon had acted against some standing order.

"You shouldn't have brought her here…"

"No one put you in charge. Layton said Heward wants a prize…"

"You think that means a woman? An Elyri woman?"

"But she's beautiful!"

"And Elyri!"

"Then he can kill her. What do you care? She was there for the taking and we took her…"

"Killed her men too…"

Exasperated, Caol snarled, "We're not supposed to be killing! We're supposed to lie low, keep quiet…"

"No one saw us…"

"And we weren't followed. No one knows anything…"

"Except the dead men are Elyri," snorted Caol.

"And good riddance, I say," said the one who had been carrying the woman with a cocky smirk.

"You think they'd learn to stop coming…"

"Elyri are fools."

"Crafty, sneaky fools…"

"You an Elyri-lover, Alty? Is that why you…?"

Rather than point out the paradoxes and refuting every argument those in the room were making, Caol chose instead to address the intended insult. From the sounds below, the ripping of fabric, the dragging of boots on the earthen floor, the crack of a fist into bone, the crash of wood and the loud gush of breath, Kavan imagined Caol had yanked the speaker to his feet and punched him in the face before shoving him over a table or chair, reasserting himself in the pecking order of the group of about thirty men. "What I am is a man who follows orders. You heard Layton! Heward wants us to stay put, keep our heads down…stay out of trouble and clear of the soldiers…"

"We did stay clear…" someone started again.

"Attacking travelers is not keeping your heads down or staying out of trouble…definitely not staying put…"

"We're providing food." One of the men who had pilfered the wagon dumped a burlap sack of vegetables and dried fruits and meats on the table. "It was either raid the wagon or poach the King's wildlife. Robbing Elyri traders is the lesser of two crimes, wouldn't you say?"

Caol frowned. The man had a point, at least within the philosophy of the Corylliens, but if the choice had been his, he would have taken the poaching. The Crown was less likely to notice a missing deer, a local farmer less likely to find a missing cow or pig or sheep as surprising as another Elyri attack would be. Such an attack would get them notice. A good and bad thing. Especially if any Elyri was there to read the situation. "Next time no hostages…and no killing…unless Layton and Heward say so. Understood?"

"Sure."

Oh, his words were understood, but Caol doubted they would be obeyed. For the most part, the men around him respected his strengths, but not all of them trusted him, either because he had not been around as long or because he had jumped into the position of Layton's second man in such a short period of time. A few resented him for that, but Caol did not care, as long as they did what they were told. With both Layton and his first-hand man Barris elsewhere today, Caol had been left in charge, and he knew he was being tested.

His attention turned to the frightened woman huddled on the floor, her dirty, wide-eyed face peering at him over the gag, her dress torn and stained, her skin mottled with bruises and dried blood in places that spoke of a beating to force submission and compliance. His heart ached for her, but he could not show it, not when there was a chance the men would use it against him, against her. He circled her slowly, seeming to decide her fate, when what he was trying to do was figure out how to keep her alive.

"Can we have her?" someone asked.

Caol shook his head no as he squatted in front of her, that decision made quickly as she squeaked and tried to crab away. Her legs tangled in her dress and she fell sideways. "No." There would be no raping while he was around. No killing either if he could help it. "You brought her for Heward…so we wait for Layton and Barris and let them take her."

Or Layton would contradict Caol's decision and let the men have her. Caol suspected it would be the latter, for he knew, as Layton must, that Heward, whoever he was, would have no use for an Elyri woman, no matter how lovely she might be. No Elyri woman but the high Mother would have been interesting to him.

More roughly than necessary, keeping up his callous front for the men, Caol pulled the woman up and dragged her to a corner of the room where he could protect her from those disinclined to do as they were told. "No one touches her."

A few men snickered as he perched on a mound of dried peat and began picking at his nails with his dagger. Let them believe he wanted her. It did not matter. The woman would be safe as long as he could protect her, the excuse of leaving her fate to Layton being a sound one even if some believed he had other motives.

On the roof, Kavan followed the movement of Caol's aura until he was perched above him, with the wooden rafters and shingles separating them. Having seen Kavan' shapechange before, there was a chance Caol would recognize him if he was seen, and the bard thought it best not to risk that, best for both of them. Determined to get a message to him, however, not wanting to blow the cover Caol had worked so hard to build, either by himself or by the arrival of those following Kavan from Rhidam, Kavan wiggled a tendril of thought into Caol's mind where he planted the niggling suspicion that he needed to leave this place, that they were all in danger if they stayed here. He was not in danger from the men around him, but rather something external that he could not put his finger on.

For a long time, Caol scowled and wrestled with what, to him, felt like a sliver of festering doubt. The men said they were not followed, but none of them were seasoned woodsman or farmworkers. Most knew little about stealth or covering their tracks in any setting. Most were also not professional criminals. For the most part, they were disenfranchised men, youngest sons who would inherit little, men who had lost fortunes or families and felt there was nothing else to lose, low-ranking former soldiers bored with no enemy to fight who wanted adventure, lazy and bored men who felt the world owed them their existence, men filled with undirected hatred and rage who wanted to fight or cause trouble. Blaming the Elyri, retaliating against them was a good excuse for mayhem, even if they had no actual experience or opinion on Elyri. Their lack of experience, attention, and focus could have easily led to their being followed back to this hideout.

It was a chance Caol did not believe they could afford to take. "Think we should go," he eventually said, swinging down from the peat to the floor.

Several people looked at him as his statement interrupted their games, their drinking, their napping. "Go where?"

"I know a place…Layton told me…"

"Traveling in the daylight is dangerous," someone reminded him.

"We're safe here," said someone else.

"Are we? You were out in the day…attacked a wagon in the day…came back here in the day. Who's to say you weren't followed?"

"That and you couldn't hide from your blind mama in the dark," another scoffed, ribbing the leader of the kidnap party with his elbow.

"Alty's right, we should clear out for a day or two until we're sure no one…"

"I'm already sure," the abduction leader growled. "I'm not going anywhere." He had spent hours walking to the road and back, spent hours waiting in ambush, and now only wanted sleep and the promise of the warm meal that was bubbling over the fire pit.

"Suit yourself." It had been nearly an hour since their return and no one had burst through the door yet, but the suspicion in his gut would not dissipate and Caol was done taking the chance of loitering. With a single exit available, if they were found here, his cover was blown. Or he was dead. The woman was yanked to her feet.

"Where you taking her?" her abductor protested, on his feet as well, his nap twice interrupted.

"Not leaving her here. If you were followed, she'll be your death sentence. She'll come on a little jaunt and be back with the rest of us in time to meet up with Layton. No harm done. Don't want our present ruined or taken back, do we?"

For a few moments, the charged air suggested there would be a fight. Kavan listened, holding his breath. He had not expected Caol to take the woman with him, nor to advocate everyone else leaving this place, and he worried about what he would do when Caol, the woman, and fourteen of the men emerged warily into the sun. The inquisitor paused to test the air, seeking some trace of danger, and though some sixth sense made him look up at the roof, he either did not notice or did not recognized the white kestrel perched near one corner.

Satisfied they would not be followed, at least not right away, Caol gave instruction to some of the men and they separated into two groups, intending to make a circle towards the secondary hideout and meet there by sundown. The larger group began hiking southeast, while Caol, his five men, and the Elyri woman in their custody trekked northeast. Kavan judged by the directions given that their destination was going to bring them somewhere nearer the mountains.

Trusting Caol to keep the woman safe, trusting that at least the inquisitor had gotten out of harm's way, Kavan remained at the peat shed, intending to lead the following search party here through the path his cousin followed. There were enough men within that, whether killed or arrested, their capture would prove another sizable loss to Heward's resources, just as the death of the previous thirteen had been. If there were men at the secondary location where Caol was going, Kavan had no idea how many, or how many might still be in Rhidam or how many Heward had surrounding him. Each cluster eradicated, however, meant the increasing nearness of kingdom-wide stability. He waited, watched, and only when his bird of prey eyes caught the appearance of approaching horsemen on the horizon did he consider leaving.

Those approaching were some of the best soldiers in Enesfel, men who would be able to subdue those here easily. But with his cousin among them, as well as his best friends, Kavan found he could not yet leave as intended, not without knowing they were safe. He watched from behind the peaked roof until the riders stopped a safe distance away, quietly dismounted, and then all but Ártur crept towards the door. The healer studied the shed, seeking what he could feel but not see, the source of power that was Kavan's thoughts he had followed for the last several hours. The bard had stopped here, was here now, as far as the healer could tell, but he could not see him and found that frustrating. Perhaps he was shielding his thoughts, denying contact, or perhaps he was a captive within and was unable to respond.

The only certainty Ártur had was that Kavan was alive.

Believing themselves to be safe, the seventeen men inside had set no one to guard the entrance, either inside or out, and thus when Bhríd broke in the door with a single heavy-footed kick, they had little time to scatter in search of weapons. The chamberlain dropped as he kicked, enabling Wortham and Balint to spring over him, swords slicing the air. It did not occur to them that the men they found inside might be innocent. Kavan had led them here. Besides, the collection of Elyri coins that scattered across the floor from the wobbly wooden table as men struggled to protect themselves or fight back, was damning proof enough of their guilt.

Where else could they have gotten bhelts in this forsaken stretch of marshland? Kavan could not see the coins, could not see the skirmish, but he could hear it clearly enough to imagine what was happening, and when he was confident his friends had the upper hand, he left in search of Caol and the Elyri woman he was taking away from here. Kavan had to get that woman free. He believed that was what Caol wanted as well.

The flutter of wings on the roof, combined with a burst of Elyri power that no one but Ártur could feel, brought those within the building and the healer still on horseback, to attention. Inside, several of the seventeen men lay dead, several were knocked unconscious, and a few were moaning and writhing in a disjointed, disoriented fashion. The building was searched but there was no sign of any woman here. None of their captives would speak, feeling convinced that the King's men would not stoop to torture, that they would live to make it to Rhidam where they had a chance of leniency if they proclaimed innocence. But when Ártur appeared in the open doorway, intending to tell his companions that Kavan was moving, traveling northeast, that these men were guilty according to his cousin but there were more to be had, one of the captives balked and began to babble about how they had not meant to kill anyone, how they intended to rob the wagon for food and coin but nothing more. Owain guessed the fellow would have said anything to avoid possible Elyri interrogation, and though he was not sure he believed what was said, he did trust that the grizzled fellow believed the words he spoke.

Weapons were rounded up and anything of value or use against them was confiscated. They briefly discussed sending the captives back to Rhidam with Avner and Waljan, but it was concluded that so many prisoners would require more guards on the journey. There were not enough men in their party to do so if some were to follow Kavan.

It was eventually decided that Balint, Avner, and Waljan would stay at the shed as guards until Wortham, Owain, and Ártur returned with Kavan and the woman they hoped to save.

And with luck, Heward as well.

Across the fields, against the darkening sky, Kavan flew with the sun at his back, seeking the inquisitor in the gradually morphing terrain. The forest he encountered was thin enough in this region to make spotting movement easier, but the eyes of the falcon were not well-suited for twilight and darkness…at least not for a search as intensive as the one undertaken tonight. He gained enough altitude so that, when he forced another mid-air shift, this time from kestrel to owl, he did not risk crashing into the ground as his changing wings restructured and strengthened for continued flight. He was grateful he had learned to make such shifts, to go from one animal to another without returning to his own form, as it saved time when time could not be wasted. His body had barely come out of the crossshift, his eyes adjusting to the new form, when he spotted Caol, the Elyri woman, and the five men with them creeping through the underbrush.

He could feel Caol's frustration. The woman was slowing them down. He was too small a man to carry her for any significant distance and he did not trust any of the others to do so without being crass. They could have already reached the cabin he was seeking, he believed, if they had been able to proceed at a run instead of stumbling along, her dress tearing on branches, her ill-suited slippers causing her to trip or yelp in pain as sharp sticks and stones poked her feet. What he wanted to do was find some way to lose her, some way to allow her to escape without losing face, but unless they were attacked by either bandits or beasts, Caol could think of no way to make that happen. He was haunted by the sensation of being followed, of knowing someone was there, but he could not see them, and that kept him moving, on edge, one hand on his sword, the other on the woman.

He did not ask her name. It was better he did not know and thus resisted personal intimacy. She was someone he was stuck with, someone he needed to help to freedom, or else hand over to Layton to meet whatever fate the other man decided to bestow. If it came down to that, Caol would rather not know the name of an innocent he had led to her death.

From above, Kavan listened to the inquisitor's inner monologue. He could provide the attack Caol was considering, but he hoped he would at least catch a glimpse of the one called Layton first. Accessing

Layton's thoughts would provide his best clues to finding Heward, Kavan believed, and finding him was the key needed to undermine the Corylliens and Claide. But sooner or later, Ártur and the others would catch up, long before Layton did if he was supposed to meet them at the peat shed in a few days' time. Allowing the poor woman to suffer that long was unnecessary.

The healer's presence grew stronger as the men on horseback closed the distance. Kavan could allow them to catch up, put Caol at risk of exposure, but avoiding that was as important as freeing the captive. He circled the men, got far enough ahead to land amidst the trees and make another shift, and before Caol and the Corylliens took another ten steps, the fabled White Hart burst through their midst.

Startled, men stumbled in every direction, Caol's grip on the woman dropping as the heart passed near enough to almost rake his chest with sharp silver antlers. Silver hooves caught one man in the head when the animal reared onto its back legs and crashed down with a snort, and when he spun sideways under the impact, he knocked another man off his feet causing him to land face down in the leaves, his head smashing against a rock. With its head down, the stag used its antlers to herd the woman away from the men as though urging her to run back the way they had come. The familiar stretching sound of a bowstring being drawn, an arrow knocked, turned Kavan's head towards the sound. There was no way he could avoid that arrow in this guise; if it was fired it would catch him squarely in the side, possibly a fatal shot. His thought's screamed at the woman to run, for if he was injured, he would no longer be able to provide her cover or protection.

His body twisted mid-step, hoping to avoid the shot, and he did the first thing he could think of to save himself. With all four feet off the ground, the hart changed, trading antlers and hooves for downy feathers of white. The arrow narrowly missed him, grazing the tips of his tail feathers.

"No!" screamed Caol at that same moment, his dagger let fly when he realized what, and who, had followed them. The dagger dug deep into the archer's shoulder, making him drop the bow with a cry, as the arrow that had missed the hart caught another man cleanly in the throat, a hit that made him topple over with gurgling bubbles of blood. Dumbfounded, Caol and the fellow with the dagger in his shoulder stared in disbelief as the last member of their party began to run after the escaping woman.

There was no chance to warn him. The fellow with the knife wound could not find words, and Caol had no desire to interfere. Kavan was the last person he expected to find him here. The warning he had received earlier, the urging to leave the peat shed, made sense now. In Kavan's wake had probably come soldiers, and by getting the inquisitor free, Kavan had, Caol believed, saved his life. Or at least he had protected Cao's cover. If the Elyri had chosen to act after however long he had been following, there was a reason for it, even if that reason was simply to save another Elyri from impending death.

With no warning, the fleeing man screamed as talons raked across both shoulders. He frantically flapped his arms, trying to bat the large white bird away as it clawed at his face, his eyes, the hands that tried to grab or hit. The woman kept running as Kavan had instructed.

"Let's get out of here!" Caol finally shouted, finding his voice as he tugged on the arm of the man he had injured. He did not know if the two with head injuries were alive, but the one struck by the arrow was certainly dead or would be soon. If Kavan wanted to kill the man he was currently tormenting, Caol was satisfied to allow it. He had not liked the fellow anyhow.

The wounded man yanked the dagger out of his shoulder and followed Caol, not looking back to wonder about the others' fates. Having seen the legendary hart, which had not been reported seen in years, change before his eyes into a bird of prey that promptly attacked them, he was not willing to face whatever came next. Believing as many did that the Hart was a manifestation of the phae k'kairá, none but a fool would dare to cross those mythical beings.

Better the man believed that, Kavan thought, finally disengaging from the fight and lifting into the treetops, then instill more fear of Elyri in an already skittish population.

Men shouting in the distance caused Wortham to push his horse to a gallop, a dangers thing in the thick of the forest, but he reined the animal in abruptly when a woman, her hands bound before her, burst out of the forest, crying and panting and looking back over her shoulder in terror. Owain was the first off his horse, and when he caught her, she screamed and struggled to be free.

"Let me go!"

Ártur slid down too and warily approached her, hands extended. "Do not fear; we will not harm you." He spoke in Elyri, hoping his race would instill a small bit of calm and trust. They were a long way from the nearest Gate and it was well past dark. If he was lucky, Bhríd had gone to his sister and begged Ártur's case. But he had a duty to Kavan, and to this woman, who deserved to be as safe and secure as he did. She continued to struggle, his voice, his words, having no effect until he laid one hand gently against the side of her face. The contact with another Elyri stilled her and she stared at him, dazed, blinking as if his words were finally sinking in.

"Stay here," instructed Wortham, inching his horse forward into the darkness. If something ahead had frightened her, even if only her abductors, it was better that he found it before it found them. Going alone was his only option; someone had to stay with Ártur and the woman. He trusted Owain to protect them.

"Be careful," Owain murmured. But Wortham was always careful. Any danger ahead of them was about to meet its match.

Hoping he would find Kavan, Wortham listened to every night sound, watched the movement of the branches, wishing he had his friend's ability to sense danger, to sense others around him, without seeing it. It was hard to know if they had traveled a straight line, and impossible to know where the panic-stricken woman had come from. With no audible or visual clues, Wortham had doubts, as he pushed deeper into the trees and lost sight of those behind him, about his ability to return quickly to them if they needed him.

There. He stopped his horse and stared ahead, to a place slightly right of his current trajectory. Light, faint and fluttering, a pale silver-blue glow bobbing back and forth, brightening as though it swung towards him and then fading as if retreating. A beckoning light was worth closer study, no matter what was on the other end of it. Whatever it was, Wortham was not afraid. Respectful, ready to act in self-defense, and slightly wary of a glow he did not understand, but not afraid.

Half-expecting a trap, the captain followed the light until he found the fist-sized orb hovering some ten feet in the air, high enough to illuminate the scene before Wortham's horse accidentally stepped on the groaning man on the ground. Gazing about him in surprise, he counted three bodies, dead or alive he could not easily tell, but no indication of what had happened to them. He dismounted and began examining the man at his feet. Deep puncture wounds and gouges were torn at the fellow's shoulders, his head and face, and in the dim bluish light, Wortham was certain the man had lost one eye, or at least the use of it as what had been the socket was an oozing, frightening mess.

An upward glance revealed nothing that could have done this, except for the ball of light and the treetops that swayed in the wind. It had been an airborne creature, an eagle or owl he wagered, though he had never heard of a bird attacking a person unless its nest was threatened.

He examined the other men too, once he decided the first would live. The one with the arrow through his throat was dead and Wortham yanked the bolt free, intending to keep it so one of the Elyri could read it. He crossed warily to the last two, aware that he could have spies around him, men waiting in ambush, even though he heard and felt nothing here except for the unnatural light source that guided his steps.

He passed broken branches on the other side of the clearing, blood, and the bow that had dropped where none of these men had fallen. Both lived, although he wagered they would have headaches when, if, they awoke. The signs suggested that others had been here, either attackers or part of the same group, who fled or took chase when the attack came. But who, or what, had done the attacking?

Wortham wondered if he should make chase too, but decided not to. He had three living prisoners, and Owain, Ártur, and the Elyri woman waiting for him. Continuing alone into the unknown was not practical. Getting these men healed enough to question, learning what they knew, were more productive priorities. He looked again at the glow above, pulsing and shimmering as though alive, and smiled. He did not need to chase the others. Kavan would do it for him.

The thought was followed by the glow flickering into a small pinpoint of intense blue that shot into the sky and out of sight. Embarrassed and slightly ashamed that he had not recognized the Elyri's handiwork sooner, Wortham hauled the first injured man to his horse. Perhaps he had been in the presence of the miraculous, the marvelous, long enough that he had not questioned the light's composition more deeply. If he had, he might have realized what it was and never doubted his security.

"Be careful, my lord," he murmured.

If Kavan was following those who had fled here, if he was confident of Wortham's safety, then the captain was confident too. Duty bid him go back, though his heart bid him to follow the bard. This time he chose duty over his heart. Kavan would be alright.

Night passed and dawn arrived before the men from Rhidam, along with the group of captives and the rescued woman paraded wearily over the drawbridge into the courtyard. There had been no sleep when Wortham and his companions reached the peat shed. Wary of being so far from Rhidam, outnumbered by their prisoners though the men were unarmed, and in the company of a lady they had no means to make comfortable, it was decided they should return to the keep rather than risk a period of rest. Four hours turned into five as they picked their way through the marsh, but Balint's resourcefulness provided torches of burning peat, smoky but still a light source, that kept them out of the worst of the bog and guided them back through the wheat fields. The torches did not last until they reached the road, but they no longer required light by then. Instead, they used the stars to guide them along a path many were familiar with after years in royal service. Noticeable gray crept into the sky as they reached the city's outskirts, and by the time they wove through the empty streets, the gray was joined by traces of rose, orange, and lavender. Dawn.

Even if Bhríd had gone to Bhryell, Ártur knew his wife was going to kill him.

"What in the name of…?" shouted Agis, not caring that most of the palace was still asleep when he stepped out of his barrack room into the courtyard as Captain Delamo passed through the gates. His tirade ended abruptly with the sight of the limp but living woman on the back of Healer MacLyr's horse and then the long string of men bound with ropes, reins, twine, belts…anything the Lachlan men had been able to find to keep the captives from escaping or sinking into the swamp as they crossed.

Balint, bringing up the rear as Bhríd gathered the prisoners into a huddled mass in the courtyard, said, "Sixteen Corylliens…for your disposal, Lord General. There were more…but they had a disagreement with our swords."

"And their own," Owain chuckled darkly.

"And an owl or eagle," added Wortham with a weary laugh.

"We left the dead. Some may have escaped into the forest or the mountains, but we brought back the ones we could."

It would be the best news King Hagan had heard in days, weeks perhaps, that another large group of Corylliens was brought to justice. The King and his sister had been frantic when so many of their staff had disappeared the morning before. Agis and a few of those staff members returned with Gaelán and two worse-for-wear Elyri merchants, and the news that the others were conducting a rescue, that a woman's life was at stake, kept the King from losing his temper. Of course, when night came with no further word from those they cared for, the tension escalated again and Agis was certain that none of the Lachlans, or Prince Espen, had slept as they waited for news. He wondered if he should be the one to tell them, although as he looked at the exhausted men, it seemed they each had a story to tell. It would be appropriate for them to be the ones to tell it.

"Bring them into the Hall; we will tell the King you are home."

None asked for leave to sleep, to bathe before seeing the King, to wait until a more appropriate time to present themselves and their captives. This rescue, these arrests, were too important to the well-being of Enesfel to be set aside even briefly, and they would rather do their duty and be rewarded by sleep afterward. Ártur begged for the woman to be taken to her kin, be given food, a bath, rest and further medical care if she desired it. There was little need for her to attend this audience with the King, and as she was barely able to remain on her feet from fatigue, the healer wanted her to rest. Agis agreed, and when stable hands and soldiers came from several directions to take the weary horses, two men escorted the woman to the room where her husband and father-in-law were. With the help of the general and his men, the sixteen captives were ushered into the Great Hall.

It was the first and only time any of them were likely to see the seat of ruling power they had been bucking.

"Captain! Uncle! Lord Healer!" Diona rushed into the Hall, the first to arrive, and Espen followed close behind. She noticed who was missing and the moment of joy turned into one of concern. "Where is Lord Cliáth?"

"Pursuing those who escaped…hoping to find Heward at the end," Wortham replied, his words clipped as he expected anger or accusations from the woman he had once served.

Hoping to bypass the captain's defensiveness, Ártur added, "None of us actually saw him…only the boys…"

The King entered the room then, with Bhríd at his heals, along with the two boys the healer had just mentioned who also looked disappointed at Kavan's absence. They were also, like the King, awestruck at the number of bound men gathered in the Hall. Who could have known that their efforts to show the bard what they had learned on that particular day could have led to the arrest of so many?

The King approached the throne but did not sit; before he could speak, the main door of the Hall flew open and k'gdhededhá Claide stalked into the room with a loud, "I beg leniency, My Liege."

Everyone in the room stared at the unexpected interruption, causing the newly elected Teren prelate to stop. The perplexed King, head cocked to the side, did not have to see his sister's expression to feel, and agree with for once, everything she and the others were thinking and feeling. "Charges have not been heard or made, k'dedhá," he said in a much cooler voice than any in the room had heard him use. "We have not even heard their crimes yet."

Though she kept her face blank, inside Diona crowed with victory. Most gathered knew that some of these men had been involved in the attack on the merchant wagon, the theft of their goods, the beating of two men, the abduction of the woman. That news had reached Rhidam the day before with the return of the General and Chamberlain. It was possible Claide had heard rumors of that and believed those prisoners gathered here were being charged with the same crime. But his plea was still suspect; even asking for leniency for such an attack, when the King had proclaimed crimes against Elyri punishable by incarceration or death, made him appear to be a supporter of the violence the King had outlawed.

And to those who had been told that these men bore the moniker of Corylliens, if Claide was aware of that and still asked for mercy, then he had stained his reputation irrevocably.

"What I mean," the k'dedhá continued in his most apologetic tone, bowing before the King, "is that these men…no men…should be punished before a trial is held and their statements taken…"

"We have statements," Owain grunted as King Hagan narrowed his eyes and said, "What do you think we were about to do, k'dedhá? It is my right to punish whom I choose…how I choose." He was used to being questioned and second-guessed by his sister, but not by the prelate who had been a fatherly figure prior to the election but was less so now, and Claide never verbally second-guessed him in front of so many others. "Have you ever known me not to judge a man fairly?"

To his knowledge, the poor man whose accusations against Claide he had not taken seriously was the only case that came to mind and Hagan wholeheartedly regretted the mistake of not hearing the poor fellow out. Until today, however, he had not believed Claide capable of anything that man had accused him of. Hagan still did not believe Claide had any part in Jermyn's death, but for the first time, he had caught a glimpse of something his sister hinted at long ago…that Claide was possibly as anti-Elyri as the Corylliens. Hagan had supported this man, had been eager for his election to the office of k'gdhededhá, and the possibility that he had been wrong jabbed him with a prickle of fear.

"No, Your Majesty. My apologies. That is not what I meant…"

"Would you care to tell me what you did mean?"

Claide did not shake his head, did not reply verbally, but instead took a few steps back and stopped beside the dirty, fatigued men who brought these people to be tried and judged. Annoyed that the prelate refused to answer a direct question but no longer wanting to argue, the King looked to Owain instead. "Uncle, you said there are statements?"

Owain stepped forward and bowed. He had once ruled from that throne, had once been king, and yet there was no hesitancy or regret in his bow to his nephew. "General Agis spoke of statements already taken from the men left beaten at the wagon…" he began.

Some of the captives, those who lived who had been involved in that raid, looked at one another with differing degrees of worry and anger. They had believed those two to be dead.

"As for…I swear before the throne, before the witness of these men who were present with me, that this man," Owain pointed to the one who had spoken freely in the peat shed, "indicated that the raid on the wagon was intended to steal food and coins…"

"To fund their activities?" asked the King.

"He did not say. But theft, against an Elyri or a Teren merchant, is still a punishable crime."

"Indeed," agreed the King. "As is beating two men to death…"

"They did not die," one captive cried. "We did not kill them!"

"You left them for dead," the chamberlain said evenly. "They did not die because they had fortune enough to be found by a healer."

"Something you would not have expected or counted on, I'm sure." The King paced a few steps to his left and then came back to stand before the throne. "And there is the matter of abduction…"

Someone else protested, "We do not have her!"

Balint snarled and resisted the urge to tip his sword beneath the man's chin. "You do not have her because you sent her to your leader for disposal. The intent was to abuse and kill her if your leader did not. I have the lady's word…"

"She's no lady! She's Elyri!"

"Lord Cliáth will validate her claim when he returns. Or if you prefer not to wait, ask any of the Elyri to…" Balint continued.

"They are hardly unbiased," snapped Claide, cutting the Duke off.

Again the King side-eyed him suspiciously. "Unbiased, no…no more so than you, perhaps…but they are honest. I trust them. As the others were there at the time of the statements, I request assessment by an uninformed party to read each of you." Hagan snapped his finger at the nearest page and said, "Bring Lord Bhíncári to me."

Anyone who knew anything about Elyri knew the name Bhíncári, just as they knew the name Lachlan, de Cormick, Valdis, or Harcourt. What they did not know about the High Mother, however, was where the line existed between fact and myth, and it meant that someone with that family name was perceived as a powerful sorcerer. That thought struck fear into several of the captives and the mass of men drew together for protection. None chose to speak, to condemn themselves or one another any more than they had, and Claide wisely refrained from saying anything as the musician was brought into the Hall.

"My Liege?" The tense atmosphere, the group of bound men, the King's posture, each told Bhyrhán why he had been summoned. He swallowed but bowed and waited for the request. He was not a citizen of Enesfel, had no formal obligation to this king, but he was employed here and had to weigh his choices, obedience or refusal, carefully.

"I will send each of these to you, alone, in the Stateroom. I request that you read each of them to learn what they are hiding."

"Without knowing what they are charged with, aye?" Such trials were pointless in Elyriá, as readings like this were expected and thus no one was prone to lie. Teren, however, rarely expected an Elyri at their trial. Physical torture was seldom used in Enesfel to extract information; when an Elyri was present, most anticipated torture worse than any physical pain and many spoke their crimes to avoid it.

"Correct. You," Hagan pointed to the page who had brought Bhyrhán and to two other pages as well, "will take notes on everything said and done…and you two," he gestured to two of his guards, "will remain there for his safety. I want to know everything. Everyone they know, everything they have done, everything they intended to do."

For Claide, such a command was going too far, even for a king. The men gathered were not on trial for every act, thought, word or intent in their lives, but for their part in the attack on the merchants. Yet the possibility of garnering details about the Corylliens, to seek and find a thread or connection that would put an end to the violence was something everyone in the Lachlan keep wanted, and thus no one verbally objected to this inquest. If the King wanted this done, it would be done; it was the only reason Claide swallowed back his protest.

Such a protest would not reflect well on him.

The process dragged on until after the noon hour, as some of the men fought against interrogation and others, choosing to avoid it, made their statements directly to the King. Those few were spared the necessity of confessing past wrongs, only admitting to their part in the merchant attack or the vandalism of the Eagle's Nest Inn, or any other relatively petty crime against the Crown or against the Elyri they could use. The King had long before settled on the throne and had benches brought so that his staff and family did not need to remain on their feet the entire morning as they waited. He knew they were weary, and more than once he considered dismissing them, but he felt he might need them here, and he believed they would each choose to stay to hear his proclamation once the evidence was gathered.

Eventually, Bhyrhán emerged from the Stateroom to present testimony, his expression grim as he recounted the details he had learned. Names and faces of other Coryllien members were provided. Allegations were made against themselves and each other and many not present, concerning past crimes throughout Enesfel, murder, torture, vandalism, theft and more. Unsolved crimes that now had the guilty attached to them. By the end, Bhyrhán could barely speak through his disgust, and the King, partially regretting what he had put the man through, released him.

Listening, watching, knowing what sort of torment such forced readings could be, Ártur would not be surprised if Bhyrhán chose to return to Elyriá and never set foot in Enesfel again.

Bhyrhán could have refused, but like the other Elyri in Rhidam, he felt he had an obligation to all Elyri living or traveling beyond Elyriá's borders. They deserved to be safe. What Bhyrhán had consented to do had been less for King Hagan then for every Elyri killed and everyone who might someday come to Enesfel. And he had done it, Ártur was sure, on behalf of the one Elyri who had been brutally tortured and was not here to speak on his own behalf.

With the evidence spoken, words that even Claide could not refute or ask leniency for without appearing more suspect then he already did, King Hagan stood up. He too looked pale, but he also appeared resolved, and, Diona thought, more mature then he had seemed to be weeks before. If the previous arrests and executions had bolstered Hagan's belief in himself, this one, she presumed, would convince him he was no longer a child but a man. A King. Someone to be obeyed.

For his sake, she hoped that was the case.

None of the men implicated Claide, none of their crimes, at least to their knowledge, could be linked to the k'dedhá, but to Diona, that meant that either the man was working separately from the Corylliens or that any link between them was further up the chain of command. She was not prepared to allow the man innocence, but his graying face appeared more anxious with the passing of time and spoken confession, and his hands began an absent, edgy fidgeting in his lap.

"I will think on this overnight," the King said. His words were followed by a long enough hesitation that he could almost hear the unspoken voices taunting him with perceived weakness. "Tonight, each of you will be detained in the dungeon, held without food, water or amenities. Because know this…" His chin lifted and he stared from one face to another until he met the gazes of all sixteen men. "My decree stands. Crimes against Elyri, as well as against Teren, will receive equal punishment…and crimes such as those confessed today demand nothing less than death. All that remains is to consider the most fitting way for each of you to die."

Small sounds of surprise rippled through the room.

"As for those you have revealed to us…each will be hunted, found, and they too shall join you. None shall be spared for the horrors you wreaked upon Enesfel. I reclaim our land for the people, for the good it once was. Such crimes will not go unpunished."

Near a side door, the King met Asta's gaze, the girl having been there the entire time, never missing a detail. He thought, as he spoke, that she looked frightened, but since he knew no reason why she should be, he decided he had misinterpreted what he saw.

"Lord General, take them below. The rest of you…rise and take your rest, please. What you have done this day for Enesfel will not be forgotten. Healer MacLyr?"

As the others began to shuffle in various directions, Ártur bowed and waited for the King to speak. "Lord Cáner has spoken to Lady Syl…but I shall write a letter to her as well and tell her what you have done on Enesfel's behalf. I will verify that you did not remain out of spite and that her sacrifice and yours will benefit Teren and Elyri alike. When it is done, go home for a few days, if you wish."

"I would appreciate that, My Liege." He knew how desperately he was going to need that letter when he faced Syl, no matter what Bhríd might have said on his behalf.

❧*❦

The one-room cabin in the foothills of the Llaethlágárá was the property of a patron of obvious wealth, but Kavan knew of no one residing this close to the borders of his Alberni territories who fit the description. It belonged to no one in Alberni, of that he felt certain. As he watched Caol and his wounded companion disappear into it, joining men already there, he promised he would find out who owned this parcel as soon as he could and discover how, if, they were connected to the Corylliens. He could hear the men talking inside, relaying the wild tale of the White Hart that had killed some of them, how it had morphed into a great owl to kill another, and then flew away to protect the woman who escaped during the unexpected chaos. Two wounded men sharing the same story, who had witnessed the same thing, and the fact that many in Enesfel were superstitious when it came to the White Hart or the k'kairá, meant that Caol and his partner were easily believed. They regretted the loss of their compatriots, and the loss of Heward's intended prize, but the thing that mattered most was that they were alive and that, after lying low in a place more comfortable than the peat shed for a few days, they could return there, rejoin anyone still there, and regroup with Layton. No one except Caol suspected that what they would find when they returned to the peat shed might be different than what they expected.

So many forced shape changes in the midst of such an extended pursuit, with no opportunity to resume his normal shape or recover energy, meant that Kavan was near the point of physical and mental breakdown. He could not afford collapse, however, could not afford sleep if he wanted to remain hidden yet tuned to what was happening and being said inside. What he could afford, what he allowed, was a change into his normal form perched high in a pine above the cabin where he could monitor everything without being noticed. It would, he hoped, give his body rest, and as long as he was not required to move and exert any power during the next few days of waiting, by the time the group decided to go back to the peat shed, he would have gathered enough energy to fly.

The weather was warm as the heat of summer swept across the land, but it did little to give Kavan comfort. It was difficult to be comfortably perched on a tree branch, and when a summer rain began to fall throughout the night, it did not help. He remained there as long as he could but came down with great effort to the change of form. The men inside slept by then, enabling him to take water from the well and a wild apple from the untended trees at the side of the building. It also allowed him the opportunity to investigate the perimeter for clues as to the cabin's owner, but he found nothing. He considered touching the door, reading it, for that might provide him an image of the owner's face, but movement inside, someone coming to the door, sent him in a panic as far as the sanctuary of the rooftop. He did not have the energy to hold a change any longer than that, and he prayed, heart thundering, as he lay flat and listened to the sounds of the night, that no one would think to look towards the roof. He did not believe he could defend himself if found and captured now.

The sound that spooked him came from one of the men coming out to empty his bladder, a man who came no further than the threshold, urinated in a shrub there, and after several minutes of staring into the darkness, shuffled back inside and closed the door. Kavan breathed with relief and rolled onto his back. The branches of the pine he had previously sought shelter in swayed and shivered beneath the assault of the steadily falling rain. Even if by some chance he was able to shift long enough to return there, he did not believe he would be able to maintain his balance well enough to gain any restful benefits of hiding there. The pitch of the roof sloped towards the back of the cabin, away from the door, and there was no rear entrance. If he eased further back, he might be safe enough where he was until daybreak. That ought to permit him enough energy to force a change.

Wishing for a cloak or some other shelter against the rain, Kavan closed his eyes and gave in to sleep, expecting it to be brief, trusting that Kóráhm and k'Ádhá would see to his welfare.

The executions proceeded as King Hagan promised, though because he did not want to meet blood with blood, he chose to hang the lot of them, together, along the front wall of the keep where they would be seen by everyone for as long as they would be displayed. He made a point of ordering them to stay for a full day and night, guarded so that no other Corylliens or sympathizers could take them down and no angry citizens could further desecrate the dead. All of Rhidam was made aware of their crimes by the quartet of town criers who spread the sentence to every corner of the city. The King was not the only one who hoped these additional arrests and executions would turn the tide, or be the end, of the violence and persecution.

There was concern for Kavan when the bard did not return as expected. Many feared harm had befallen him, but Ártur reassured them that he would know if that was true. The steady source of power in the thread within him suggested no stress, no injury, no fear or pain or cause for concern. His cousin was hunting and was wise enough to stay out of harm's way. Appeasing his wife was enough for Ártur to worry about, but thankfully there were no reports from Rhidam or elsewhere about violence in the aftermath of the latest executions.

Perhaps, once Kavan found Anri Heward, there would be peace in the Sovereignties. Perhaps that is what Kavan had meant about something he needed to do to end this.

On the rooftop of the hunter's cabin, it was mid-day when Kavan awoke with a start. His body hurt but it was not the ache of exertion he expected to feel. Rather it was a tight rawness of skin beneath the exposure to rain and sun. Tentative fingers touched his face, expecting to find blisters or worse, but instead, he found stretched, sunken skin in need of hydration and cooling ointment. Once he had pondered whether he could burn beneath the sun; this might be the answer to his question, but the real question was how long had he slept?

He listened. He could hear the whispers of nature, wind in the pines, birds warbling, animals moving within the shelter of the forest. There was no trace of the rain he remembered, as the rooftop was dry, his clothes were dry, and there were no clouds to be seen. It disturbed him more, however, that he heard nothing from the room beneath him. No speaking, no snoring, no movement or sounds of breath. Senses strained to their limits, he realized he was alone, that the men he had intended to set guard over and follow from this place were gone.

How long had he slept?

Unable to blame anyone for his failing, the extended exertion having caused him to slip into a place where the sounds of the world could not reach him, allowing him to rest undisturbed, Kavan dropped from the roof, braced himself for a possible but unlikely confrontation, pushed the door open with the tips of his fingers, and slid inside, cautious in case this was a trap.

But no one could have hidden from his senses today, the same senses that told him, before his eyes adjusted to the dimness of the room, that the men who remained here were dead. All of them, throats cut where they lay, asleep in dried pools of blood. Kavan scrambled to count them, to find Caol, but there was no sign of the inquisitor nor the man who had escaped the forest with him, and the bard counted a single other man missing from amongst the dead.

Having not heard them leave, seeing no sign of a struggle or fight, and desperate to know what had happened, to know what had become of Caol, the bard touched each dead man in turn. With their eyes closed, having died in their sleep, there were no death images to view and they had, apparently been dead at least four days, making any thoughts they might have had inaccessible to Kavan. No crimes endured, no glimpses of Heward or other guilty parties, no trace of what plans the future might hold for whatever Corylliens remained. What Kavan did glean, however, was the identity of their killer, and what he saw shocked him.

Caol Dugan had assassinated them all.

Why, Kavan wondered after reading the last man and collapsing onto a tall stool to relieve his shaky legs. What had been the purpose, how had he accomplished this without raising suspicions with the other two, and why had he allowed those two to live? Or had he? Had they discovered his actions and dragged him off to meet his fate at Layton or Heward's hands? Were they on their way to the peat shed? Would they already have arrived to find the rest of their company slaughtered or arrested?

He had to find Caol. Senses reaching around him in search of a trail to follow, a clue to guide him, Kavan noticed a glint of steel against the wall, a knife blade reflecting the morning sun which stretched its fingers through the open doorway. Not expecting it to be of use but hopeful still, Kavan retrieved it, eagerly absorbing the images left on it as he picked it up. Caol's knife, as he had hoped…an item left as a message for the man the inquisitor expected would find it. Swallowing past the tightness in his chest, Kavan closed his fist around the pommel.

Though there was no hint as to why Caol had done as he had, there was a single warning, something Kavan had not considered but which made sense now that it was pointed out. Suspecting that the bard would follow, would seek Layton out, the inquisitor begged Kavan not to come for him. With a large portion of the Coryllien organization dead now, Layton was Caol's best link to Heward. Yes, Kavan might expedite the process by reading Layton, but Caol expected that, by climbing through the ranks, he would be able to weed out any others remaining, any other high ranking contacts, perhaps all the way to Claide himself. Once he knew what there was to know, they could cut the cancer out of Enesfel's heart, cut off the head of the Coryllien snake. Caol had to do this his way if he was ever to return to his daughter.

Thinking it to be more a matter of ego than necessity, Kavan found a strip of cloth which he used to wrap around the blade, tucked it into the back of his trousers, and got as far as the door before a hand on his shoulder stayed him. He spun, startled that he had somehow not been alone after all and was about to be killed for that mistake. But there was no one there, just the sensation that someone had touched him, a sensation that, when his pounding heart slowed, he recognized.

He sucked in a deep breath and hung his head in surrender. Not Caol's ego on the line, he relented, but his own. He was so set on redeeming the kingdom, setting her free, being her savior, thinking he would do every man's task if he could. But Kavan's place was in Rhidam at the King's side. He was needed there, and his duty, his part in ending the cycle of persecution, was much different than Caol's. He had to let the inquisitor follow his path. Kavan needed to return to the castle to follow his.

Why then, he wondered as he covered the place on his shoulder where the ghostly hand had touched him, did it feel like he was about to step into the heart of a storm instead of making anything better?

❧Chapter 39❦

The money exchanged hands without either individual saying a word. Both knew what had to be done, what was being asked, expected, and what was being paid for with a significant sum of coin. The hand without a glove withdrew and was wiped on the dark cloak the individual wore, as if the slightest touch of another was contaminating. The other merely pocketed the soft leather pouch in the folds of rich brown cloth before its owner slid into the late-night shadows. This was but a down payment. Once the job was complete there would be more…as long as they both lived to see this through.

"Welcome home, Lord Cliáth."

Kavan had not expected the King to be the first person he saw upon his late-night return to Rhidam, but the young man was pacing the Great Hall when Kavan entered the castle through the main doors. His bedchamber windows were closed, something he did not normally do this time of year, and while he could have sought a Gate to use for entrance, he had enjoyed the opportunity of flight and felt that landing in the courtyard was the easiest way to enter while extending his flight as long as possible. He intentionally waited until this late hour in the hopes of avoiding others until morning, but the troubled young King innocently foiled his plans.

"My Liege," he said with a bow, pausing in the doorway rather than continuing past in case Hagan said more. "Did the others…?"

"Make it back? Yes. They brought several prisoners; they have already been tried and executed."

"Executed?" If that word had come from Arlan, or even the King's sister, Kavan would have found it less surprising. Hearing the Boy-King speak it so matter-of-factly was unexpected.

For a moment the young man's gaze and voice faltered. "What else could I do?" he asked in a tone that sought assurance and advice from the one man who spent more time rearing and teaching him than his father had. "Releasing them would invite continued attacks, be an invitation for others to do the same without concern for punishment."

"My Liege," Kavan murmured apologetically. "I was not questioning your decision. As much as I despise killing, there were few other choices to be made. I was…I am surprised at the haste with which justice was carried out, that is all."

"Lord Bhíncári assisted in the interrogation, between his statement and the others…and some confessions…there was no need to delay sentencing. I did not want it to interfere with the wedding. Swift action seemed wisest."

The bard smiled at Hagan's hesitant use of the last word. It was difficult, he knew, for the boy to feel wise in the middle of elders with much more experience. "It was indeed." It was good to see him beginning to fill out the role left to him too soon.

"Did you find others? Captain Delamo said you sought Heward?"

"Infighting lessened the numbers dramatically…I found many dead at the end of my search, but Heward was not among them. I cannot say how many more might exist, but I saw more than ten in the place they were hiding, meaning that no more than three escaped to my knowledge. I was unable to follow them any further."

"Well, that's some good news at least." He did not, as Kavan feared, berate or belittle him for failing to hunt down the remaining three. "Life has been quiet of late…almost normal, so maybe we have dealt with the majority of Corylliens."

"Perhaps, but do not give in to complacency too quickly…"

The King shook his head. "Oh, I know. I'm not. There is still much to do…men we need to arrest if we wish to end this…but it appears I may have a peaceful wedding at least." He smiled, warmth and embarrassment spreading across his weary face. "When it is daylight, when you have rested and eaten, you will ride with me?" Thinking Kavan about to protest he hurriedly added, "Not alone, of course. We will take soldiers and attendants. There are matters I want to discuss with you…the way my father used to…and I think it will be easier away from the interruptions here. Besides, I miss riding in the warm weather, and with life calm now, and my wedding in the offing, this might be the best chance I have for some time." The mask of rule slipped and he stared at Kavan with the pleading eyes of a little boy. "Please, Lord Cliáth…like we use to?"

Bowing his head and then bowing from the waist, Kavan sighed. Hagan's reasons were sound, and there was little need for him to remain a prisoner in his home. It would do the people good to see that their king was not afraid to be among them, even in the company of an Elyri, and the morale boost it would offer them and Hagan would be invaluable. "It has been a long while since I have ridden as well. Send for me when you wish to depart and I shall join you."

"Thank you."

The King did not dismiss him but rather bounced out of the Hall, his earlier burdened eased by the upcoming ride with his mentor and the bard's approval of his recent actions. Kavan too retired to his room, eager to avoid running into anyone else. He wanted a proper sleep in a bed, not on a rooftop, and he wanted to bathe. Bathing, however, would have to wait until morning unless he wanted to wake the staff, and since he hated waking them for personal needs when he felt like staff himself, he refused to infringe on them that way. The titles of lord and duke had not changed who he was inside, a bard in the service of the Lachlan House.

Morning and bath time was preceded by a night of restless dreams and vague, shifting images that remained largely out of the grasp of perception. That Orynn was there, her face and presence fading in and out of events Kavan could not recall was his only certainty. She seemed weary and sad, but as he could not reach out to her, could not speak to her or hear her if she was speaking, he could not ease her burden. That and the notion that what he could not recall or see was of grave import, left Kavan with a dull, heavy, unsettled feeling when he got out of bed. He chose not to use it as an excuse to forego riding, however. The King needed him, wanted his advice, his knowledge, his support, and Kavan would gladly give it if it meant steering Hagan away from k'gdhededhá Claide's tainted influence.

He had barely finished breakfast when the summons came, early enough that his cousin had not yet returned. The boys had come in briefly, with embraces and smiles, but hurried off at Bhyrhán's summons to the lessons of music and language that he offered. Despite relishing a return to tutoring, it was good, Kavan believed, for them to have a wider range of influence. Whatever lay ahead for him, he did not want to be the sole mentor the young men could turn to or rely on.

It was best they were prepared for the day when Kavan would not be there. He was convinced that day would come…and soon.

In the courtyard, the King waited with eight men at arms and two servants, none of whom were Wortham or the other men from Káliel. Their absence made Kavan scowl, but he was far enough away that Hagan could not see the expression. Deciding that the discomfort was an effect of the night's misplaced dreams, the Elyri reached the horse being held for him and swung up as Hagan grinned in greeting.

"Apologies for the delay." He could have placed the blame on Gaelán and Sóbhán, but saw no reason for it. If Hagan wanted an explanation for his tardiness, he would ask for one.

"You're here; that is what matters. It cannot be a long ride, I'm afraid. My sister asked for audience and I received word that Sigrid, Dayly and their father will be arriving later. I must welcome them."

The young woman arriving unexpectedly returned the scowl to Kavan's face, but he hid it as his horse skittishly sidestepped away from the nearest soldier. Dayly was Hagan's best friend and was often at court, so their arrival should not be a surprise. The Nialls had been a fixture of the Lachlan court throughout Arlan's reign. Today, for the first time, the unanticipated nature of the visit, which sounded as surprising to Hagan as it was to Kavan, suggested to the bard that Duke Niall was vying for deeper political favor. There was a great advantage to be found in having both children in the King's sphere of influence.

Like many others, Duke Niall was a politician, a man who regularly sought power form the monarchy, but this was the first time Kavan felt uncomfortable with the man doing so. The children could not be faulted, as it was their place to obey their father's wishes, and the bard knew he could not warn Hagan away from either his best friend or his intended bride. He could, however, advise caution when dealing with their father, and he intended to do so as their ride got underway. The soldiers with them would be watchful for danger, allowing Kavan and the King an opportunity to speak freely.

The cobbled streets were beginning to come alive as the King's entourage passed through the gates. Merchant shops were opening, tradesmen and craftsmen were lifting their shutters and awnings and setting out samples of wares to tempt passersby and residents already in search of their daily needs, a visit to the náós for spiritual feeding, or to call upon friends, relatives, or business associates. Word spread quickly that the King was among them and a crowd began to gather as the city dwellers sought access to their monarch.

Words of thanks and praise greeted the young King and people squeezed between Kavan's horse and Hagan's as they attempted to touch the King in their gratitude. The mass executions of Corylliens and the calm enjoyed since then were slowly working in Hagan's favor. It was the first time in Kavan's recollection that the majority of those in the crowd sought not to touch him for blessing but were focused on someone else. It was vaguely unsettling, but it was also, he believed, as it should be. The less of a focus Kavan was for these people, the less likely he would be seen as a threat to Enesfel. It was time to put that notion to rest.

There were some, of course, who took the opportunity to make contact with the White Bard, men and women who hoped for miracles, men and women adoring the Bhryell Saint with gratitude for some past favor, or simply those who were curious. Little by little, Kavan's horse was pushed further away from the King's as the crowd thickened and a prickle up his spine that settled at the base of his skull suggested that this situation was wrong. Giving people access to their King, allowing Hagan to boost his support with the masses he governed had its benefits, but there was danger to such a situation as well. There was certainly danger to Kavan, who was separated from both the King and his guards and thus was a target for any who sought the expulsion and destruction of Elyri in Enesfel.

An exchange of glances among the guards suggested that they were realizing the same thing, at least in regards to the safety of the King, and they began to shoo the crowd back, with words, with firm but gentle gestures, and with some degree of force when needed. Little by little, Kavan edged his horse closer to Hagan, eager to be back in the circle of the soldiers' protection.

The prickle at the back of his skull flared, making him wince. With the movement of his head, he noticed someone between them, someone in a dark, wide-brimmed hat that hid their features from view. The person, the menace, was facing Kavan, a death threat the bard was certain, but as the figure reached him, the jostling of the crowd as the soldiers pushed and pulled people away from the King made the individual turn sideways and lose his hat as Kavan was almost pushed off his horse. By the time the Elyri steadied himself in his seat, the figure was gone, the hat trampled beneath the horses' hooves as the guards urged the animals forward and away from the disappointed throng.

The threat had passed. Kavan was spared.

His pounding heart slowly settled as they left the thickest of the crowded streets and neared the bridge over the river that would take them beyond the city limits. That threat had been close, and none of those with him had noticed. It was right that they should protect the King at any cost, but not having Wortham with him, his own protection, made Kavan reconsider the wisdom of this ride. Being targeted was no surprise, but how close the would-be killer had gotten did. He would have to reconsider his actions the next time he chose to go among the people who had once loved him.

The realization made him sad.

Senses turned inward, his thoughts swarming around what had nearly happened, he did not notice the King's horse drawing nearer to his until they bumped together, and the King, startled by the unexpected contact, swayed in his saddle and nearly toppled into Kavan's lap. "Easy, My Liege," Kavan murmured, steadying him with both hands. The touch on Hagan's shoulder brought vertigo over the bard and he realized how pale and discolored the young man was.

"I'm fine, Lord Cliáth…a little dizzy but…I think we should…"

Hagan did not finish. His blue-gray eyes rolled back in his head and he slumped into Kavan's arms and off of his still walking horse. Catching him, Kavan twisted to dismount and saw a trail of red spreading down the monarch's beige leggings and onto the side of his gray horse. There was too much of it, spreading from a point where a small silver-edged orange jewel was embedded into his thigh. With one hand behind the King's head, Kavan pulled the coin-sized item free, revealing the slender pronged teeth that had held it in place. Removing it, however, allowed the blood to flow more freely, and touching it told Kavan something which made his soul cold.

"What have you done?" The guards closest, seeing the King fall, yanked Kavan away from Hagan, causing the young man to land with a thud in the dust of the road. There was blood on Kavan's hand, on his trousers where the King had bumped into him moments before, and in his hand, the weapon of attack.

One of the guards snatched it from Kavan's hand as the Elyri warned, "Don't…" but it was too late. The tines bit into the other man's palm, drawing blood before he shoved it into his breast pocket.

"You are under arrest."

"The King has been poisoned!" Kavan began to protest. "I did not…let me try to save him!" He did not know if he could. He had failed to save Prince Bertram many years ago when the boy was poisoned, but there had been considerably more toxin present then and Bertram had been a child. There was a chance, he believed, to keep the poison from doing its worst, until they returned to the castle for a healer, but he had to act immediately.

"You have done enough!" The soldier with the jewel in his pocket swung and connected his fist solidly with Kavan's jaw. Kavan would have fallen if he had not been held fast by one of the others.

"You are killing him!"

"You," the fist struck again, this time just below Kavan's ribs, "are the one killing him…and you will answer for it if he dies."

Gasping and gulping for air, reeling from the unexpected turn of events, Kavan had few choices but to allow them to drag him back to the castle past some of the men and women they had passed earlier who were now clucking and pointing wagging tongues and fingers in their direction. He could have resorted to some dramatic display of power, but he was too stunned, mentally reeling from what was transpiring, and he could not concentrate on anything except the knowledge of what seemed likely to happen. Fortunately, the worst of the blood was kept from their sight and the guards, heedful of scandal and rioting, managed to make it appear as if nothing more was wrong than the King being ill or perhaps falling from his horse. Kavan's eyes and senses sought the guilty in those they passed, hoping to find Caol among the crowd as he was confident the inquisitor could help him, but he could not focus and there seemed no allies to be found. This was worse than any death threat he had endured.

Chaos was avoided in the streets, but it erupted within the walls of the keep as the great gates were ordered closed and most of the men hastily took the pale, bloody King into the castle in search of the healers' aid. The man who had taken the jewel collapsed outside the castle walls his hand bleeding excessively the way the King's wound continued to bleed. He was taken to the healers as well. Other soldiers, no faces Kavan recognized, dragged him without a word into a dungeon cell and dumped him there, the six keeping watch outside of his prison in case he tried to escape.

But escape was an illogical option and one he did not consider. Innocent of any crime, he would not compound the trouble he faced by running, even if he felt he should be at Hagan's side, with the boy as long as possible. Instead, he retreated to the corner, away from the infliction of pain, and stared at the blood on his skin as he prayed for Hagan's life…and for strength. There was a familiar aroma on his hands, a touch of it that told Kavan his effort, and the healers' was in vain. But still, he prayed. A miracle might yet save the Boy-King.

Every bit of training, every skill and medicine he had at his disposal, was put into Ártur's efforts to divert the poison from the King's vital organs while Rouvyn and Gaelán did the same for the soldier brought in with him. This was an unfamiliar poison, the after-effects of it only seen on Gabrielle Dilyn's mother and Prince Bertram. There had been little blood when he had seen Lady Dilyn's corpse, as the body had already been prepped for burial. It had been much the same for Prince Bertram, although he knew from Muir and Wortham's reports afterward that the prince had bled heavily before succumbing to the poison's taint. Given the location of his injuries, however, such blood loss for Prince Bertram had been expected. But neither of these men in room now had suffered wounds that should result in such heavy blood loss and only the poison accounted for the difficulty in breathing both experienced.

In the corridor outside, Diona remained apart, hands clenching until her knuckles were white, accepting Espen's presence behind her, his calming hands on her arms, because she could not move away. When she learned that her brother and Kavan were going riding that morning, she tried to talk Hagan out of it. Yes, the kingdom was calmer. But the threat was still there, especially the threat to Kavan from the Corylliens who might be reduced in number but were not yet eradicated. As long as k'dedhá Claide was in charge of the Faith, the princess was convinced there could be no stability in Enesfel. It frightened her now that her brother had come under attack, that his life was at the mercy of forces beyond her control, forces she did not believe would listen to her if she prayed…but she prayed nonetheless. She had not yet thought to ask where Kavan was, or how he was, if he was a victim too. Her brother's life was all she could think about even with Wortham pacing the hall back and forth in front of her.

When the door finally opened, it was Rouvyn's grim face she saw first. She opened her mouth to ask questions, but behind the Teren doctor, she could see Ártur slumped over Hagan, his forehead on the man's chest, Hagan's hand clenched in his. She could not see Gaelán, but she could hear him crying.

"Hagan?" she whispered, the color draining from her face.

"Is gone, Your Majesty," Rouvyn choked. "The soldier as well. It was…a potent poison."

"Poison…how…?" The title had not yet registered and she was too stunned for tears. Her little brother could not be gone. She could not be the last of the Lachlan bloodline.

"Lord Cliáth…" started one of the soldiers who had brought the King home. In the room, Ártur lifted his head, his expression shaken with disbelief.

She spun to glower at the man who dared to address her and utter the bard's name in such an accusatory tone. "What of Lord Cliáth?" she barked, realizing then that the bard was not here. "Where is he?"

"In the dungeon…"

"With the murderer, I hope!"

"He is the…"

Wortham had the man pinned against the stone wall with a single hand around his throat before further words were uttered. "Mind the accusations. Lord Cliáth would never…"

Struggling for air, the soldier tried not to fight the captain's greater bulk and strength. "He had the murder weapon in his hand! He was the only one near enough to…"

"Where is this murder weapon?" Diona demanded.

The soldier pointed to the room. "He took it from Lord…" his voice faltered. "Lord Cliáth warned him to be careful…knew it was poisoned…"

"Any idiot would have guessed that," Rouvyn muttered, "by looking at the King's symptoms!" The soldier had nothing to say to that. They had seen what they had seen and acted accordingly and Diona, as angry as she was that they dared to implicate and incarcerate Kavan, knew they had done what seemed sensible at the time.

"Find it and bring it to the Stateroom…and for k'Ádhá's sake be careful! I want every man who was there present as well. Captain, you are to come with me."

Not inclined to obey the Princess' orders after the way she had hurt Kavan, Wortham grunted, "My Lady?" and then realized she was not simply 'my lady' any longer. She was Enesfel's queen and he would be forced to obey her for as long as he remained in Enesfel.

Already striding down the corridor, she replied over her shoulder, "We are going to talk to K…Lord Cliáth."

He nodded, though she could not see it, and followed swiftly, expecting her to rectify this injustice and release Kavan immediately. She quickly assumed the leadership role, despite ignoring, being unaware of, or at least avoiding the reason for that shift who lay on what had once been her father's bed. Espen, also too stunned to consider the ramifications of what had happened yet, assembled the witnessing soldiers and brought both the healers and the murder weapon, such a tiny, innocent-looking thing, to the Stateroom where she had commanded them to wait. This matter needed to be dealt with promptly and quietly before the public got wind of it. He imagined rumors were flying already; bad news always did. This had to be delicately managed or else Rhidam's previous chaos would be nothing compared to the storm to come.

Kavan did not look up when the dungeon door opened and closed. Head on his knees, he had given into weeping. Though not in the room where Hagan lay, he felt the shift within, the sudden heaviness of the half-moon pendant around his neck the moment Hagan's soul departed his body. The pendant had quickly been removed and was clutched in his hand. He had to break the binding, but did he, he mused forlornly, want to reestablish it with Diona?

He had known since the girl's birth that Diona was destined to rule Enesfel, a destiny that meant the deaths of her brothers while she was still capable of ruling. The Site had warned him of Bertram's death, though not in a way that he was able to prevent it, but this time, unless his night's unsettling vaporous dreams had been a warning, there had been no way of knowing what this day would bring. If he had known, if he had suspected, he would have refused to take that early morning ride. The boy, barely of legal age to rule alone, was gone.

Kavan knew it without anyone telling him.

"Kavan?"

He lifted his face, meeting Wortham's eyes instead of Diona's because it was easier. She had every right to blame him. He might not have killed Hagan, but he had certainly failed to protect him. "He is…"

"Yes," the captain murmured, his heart breaking as he squatted and reached through the bars for Kavan's hand. Kavan accepted the gesture, appreciating the offer of emotional strength.

"What happened?"

Kavan shook his head. As much as he wanted to talk, this was not the time or place. Diona would hear him, and likely, if he knew her at all, release him at once. But at the dawn of her rule, the too-soon release of a potential assassin would stain her. For Enesfel's sake, for hers, this had to be done correctly, no matter the cost to him.

"Not like this, My…Queen." He intentionally said the last word apart as he looked at her, hoping to remind her of the duty she now shouldered. "Try me as you would any other…"

"My lord," Wortham began to protest, aware of the hazards for an Elyri in such a trial.

"Wortham, it is necessary. Find your witnesses…for and against; try me as you would any other…not as the White Bard, not as Elyri, but as a man accused of high treason. Hear the evidence, weigh it publically and wisely. Enesfel depends on you doing this the way it should be done. It is necessary…if you want to keep the peace."

Diona stared at him for several long moments before nodding once and leaving them there. Always wise, she found no fault in his advice despite her heart's insistence on doing otherwise. It was best she limited her contact with him too. Accusations had been made and she would follow them through as she would with anyone else. There was nothing that suggested Kavan was a killer, nothing that hinted he would murder her brother, a child he had raised from birth. His grief was real, his determination to accept a trial that could end badly, his willingness to endure the indignities of an accused man, already told her what she needed to know.

It did not tell her how, did not tell her what had happened or why, but it did tell her that Kavan was not her brother's assassin. That man or woman was still on the street somewhere and while the rest of the city focused on Kavan's trial, Diona would make certain the truly guilty party was found. No matter the cost. Her brother deserved that from her…and from the kingdom he had barely had the chance to rule.

❧Chapter 40❦

K'gdhededhá Claide paced before the Stateroom door, thankful that none except for guards were present to witness it. Everything had gone wrong; this was not the way things were supposed to be, a new queen in power, a queen who had little tolerance for him and his views. But there was nothing to be done about it; he had to face her and do what needed to be done, which first meant making sure that the most dangerous Elyri in Enesfel received the penalty he deserved for what had been done. After that, Claide would fix his attention on the more reasonable-seeming Prince Espen whom he hoped would have more influence on the new Queen's choices then Claide and the Faith ever had. The shift of power could not have come at a worse time.

When the door opened and he was escorted in, it took effort not to say the first words that came to mind, make the sort of emotional plea and retort that once had an effect on the late king. He knew enough about Diona Lachlan to know he needed to be more diplomatic and cunning if he was to negotiate or influence her. He waited until she looked at him with a cool, distant expression and forced a bow.

"Your Majesty." He wondered if she could hear the way the words stuck in his throat. "It is true? King Hagan has been…murdered?"

With the news less than a day old, Diona had yet to accept those words, though on the surface she appeared calm. "What might I do for you, k'dedhá?" She knew he had not come to ask for affirmation of that news. He would have learned it from Tusánt already.

"Your Majesty, I come to demand…"

"Demand?" She cocked her head at his choice of words.

Claide stiffened and bowed his head in outward contrition. "Pardon…but this tragic news has affected my reason, as it has everyone's. Surely you understand that I, like so many others, feel that the King's assassin must be brought to justice."

"And they shall be; you need have no fear of that."

"I was told it is…that Duke Cliáth…" Accusing the Elyri duke was walking on a thin sheet of ice over a fiery pit. Accusing any noble was tricky, but accusing the White Bard, the most trusted advisor of the Lachlan House, was dangerous, especially with the new queen.

"The accused will be justly tried…"

"Excuse my ignorance," he dared to interrupt, "but it is customary to have the accused read by an Elyri." That was audibly distasteful to him. "If he is…most of those in the keep are related to the accused, Your Majesty. They can hardly be impartial."

The Queen frowned, cutting his protest short with a wave of her hand. The man had a point. There was Bhyrhán, however, the man was a bard too, a known friend, and, though most did not know it, distantly related to Kavan as well. If the bard was to be read, even for appearance's sake, it would have to be by an Elyri not employed by the Crown. The Corylliens had successfully driven all other Elyri out of Rhidam as far as she knew. She felt there was no actual need to read him; eyewitness testimony and Kavan's own words should be enough to clear him. But having someone there to read him for the record would be judicious.

"You think I do not have a contingency for that?" she asked with a bitter smile. "That I would risk his guilt or virtue on a technicality?"

Claide shook his head. "I do not, but I have had Faithful express doubts about a fair, unbiased trial, and I sought to hear it from you so that I may reassure them."

Having few doubts that many had expressed such misgivings, though believing they were more for the bard's safety than for accusations of guilt, the Queen nodded once. "Assure them, k'dedhá. I am seeking every witness and detail of import and should a trial be necessary, it will be conducted according to the law."

The man shifted his weight from one foot to the other, cleared his throat as if to speak, but bowed instead. This woman was smart and would not be easily manipulated or rattled. The game had grown more challenging, but it was a game Claide still felt confident he could win. "That is good to hear, Your Majesty. Thank you."

The Queen again waved her hand, this time dismissively, eager for the k'dedhá to be gone. With Bhríd already in Levonne to bring his family to Rhidam for the impending burial, an awkward thing she was sorry he had to face, and Bhyrhán sent to Káliel with Owain to deliver the news and seek support for Kavan from that quarter, it left Ártur to present this matter to, and she would have to do it before he returned to Elyriá for the night. She did not want to wait until morning, did not want Kavan imprisoned any longer than necessary, and if the healer knew anyone who might brave the dangers of Enesfel on Kavan's behalf, what better time to seek them out then when he was in Bhryell for the night?

Two days to bury her brother, then she would try a man she dearly loved for that brother's murder. Only then would she accept the crown. She insisted that Kavan be tried first. She wanted him at her coronation instead of weighing down on her conscience. And if, by some horrible injustice, Kavan was found guilty, she did not want to be Queen.

❧*❧

Being away from Kavan's side was a crushing thing, to know that the most innocent man Wortham knew was held in a squalid cell like any other criminal. He tried to bring him food, bedding, his harp, but Kavan accepted none of it, allowed no preferential treatment. Wortham understood his reasons, understood why he refused to speak of the events that had landed him where he was, but the captain did not like it, not when there was more he believed the bard was meant to do with his life. When he had duties to perform on Kavan's behalf, duties Kavan trusted to no one else, Owain had come to remain in the dungeon with him, not to manipulate Kavan into speaking but in the fervent desire for the Elyri not to be alone.

It had taken hours for Wortham to be allowed at King Hagan's side. There had been a multitude of examinations by Ártur, Rouvyn, Gaelán, and two of Rhidam's finest physicians to confirm that the cause of death had indeed been poison. Others had gone to him too, once the body was preserved, advisors, friends, his bride to be and her father and brother, and many others except for the new Queen who was too busy to risk exploring her grief. When Ártur finally allowed Wortham into the room, the captain was there only long enough to look at the young man's somber, peaceful face and touch the half-crescent Kavan had given him to the half that Hagan wore…and remove it from the late King's neck. Wortham did not know what the gesture meant, what it accomplished, but he did as Kavan asked. This was the first of those Lachlans Kavan had known that he was unable to escort across the void of death, and Wortham knew how difficult that was for him. By clutching Hagan's hand, memorizing his serene

❧633❧

face, Wortham hoped that, when he saw Kavan next, he would be able to relay comfort through that imagery.

That duty done, he next found Asta and Matus to study the unusual murder weapon for himself. Making sure to touch it as little as possible, in case an Elyri did read the item during the investigation and trial, and to avoid accidentally poisoning themselves, Asta put her crude drawing skills to work, sketching the item on multiple pieces of paper to allow others to try to determine its origins. Matus, the most well-traveled of the three, could not identify it and that worried her. Not of the Five Sovereignties then, but possibly somewhere in the lands south of Hatu. Wortham recalled seeing nothing similar during the months he and Kavan were in that region, but they had not traveled everywhere, and they had not been seeking anything like this. Wortham wished he had paid more attention to all of the cultural details of those lands now.

Not even Zelenka recognized it, however.

Distressed by her cousin's death and wanting to stay close in case Diona needed her, Asta did not leave the keep with her sketches but left the search of Rhidam to Matus. It was also on Matus to get a message to her father. Hagan's death was news of too high import to wait. Wortham went with Matus for a time, but he had been on another mission, one not given to him by Asta or even Kavan. There was little chance that the man he sought was in Rhidam, not when his business took him across the Sovereignties and beyond. But Rouvyn still knew people in that world, people who could put Wortham in contact with the best bounty hunter in the lands. If anyone could find King Hagan's killer and set Kavan free, Wortham chose to believe that Wace Elotti was that man.

❧*❧

Heavy-hearted, Ártur hunched before Tíbhyan's fire, awaiting his nephew Bhen and gdhededhá Bhílári, the other two men he needed to see. When he stumbled blindly through the front door of Syl's home, he wanted nothing more than to weep on her shoulder. Hagan's unexpected death and Kavan's arrest stunned him more than the attack he had endured. Hagan, little more than a boy, should not have died, not the way he had, and Ártur could not believe, no matter who might level the charges against his cousin, that Kavan was capable of such an act. Kavan could kill, had killed, the healer knew, but he loved the

Lachlans too dearly to do such a thing without reason. And if there had been a reason, Ártur refused to believe it unless that reason fell from Kavan's lips. With Kavan declining to speak about what happened, the most information anyone had were the claims of the escorting soldiers, none of which were particularly clear. The only consistency in their stories was Kavan holding the King with the tiny murder weapon in his hand.

If Kavan had wanted to kill anyone, he could have done it without the use of poison or a bloodletting instrument. If Kavan chose to kill, there would be no trace afterward and no blood on his hands.

Bhen had been there when Ártur arrived, and the healer knew at once what he needed to do. The children were left with his parents, with the promise that he would explain later, while Bhen went to the náós to fetch Bhílári. The choice of voices to speak on Kavan's behalf seemed obvious, but Ártur had no confidence that either man would accept the burden. As he, Syl, and Tíbhyan looked at the opening door, the healer's heart stopped in his throat.

Syl put warm drinks in the hands of the newcomers and waited for them to sit. Despite being summer, it was a chilly night and she knew her husband's nerves needed to be soothed. The odds were, if this was as important as his mood hinted, they would all need soothing.

"ílMairós." The sage broke the fragile silence. From those gathered in the room, he guessed the news was about Kavan and, afraid of what he would hear, the ancient man wanted to wait no longer. He had felt no great loss of Power, something he expected he would feel if Kavan died, but one did not need to die to be in distress.

"King…Hagan…has been assassinated."

Two of the others did not know Enesfel's king, but Bhen had met him and Syl, present at the boy's birth, had nurtured and raised him in place of the mother he lost when but a few days old. She gasped and wept and Bhen pulled her nearer with one arm. dedhá Bhílári genuflected and bowed his head, leaving the bhydáni to ask, "How?"

"That is under enquiry. He was riding with retainers and soldiers on hand, well-protected…but somehow he was poisoned. I tried…but I could not save him. Rhidam is in an uproar and the royal house…"

His hand tugged through his short hair and he groaned. There was no easy way to say what needed to be said next. "They do not yet know…they are accusing…" He swallowed and met the ancient man's gaze. "Kavan is being held on suspicion of murder."

"Kavan?" Bhen drew up straight. "That is absurd!"

"I know…we all know…but he will not speak of what happened, will not contradict the guards' stories, insists on a trial. The Queen has acquiesced to his demand." It felt strange to use the term queen instead of king. "Everyone is furiously seeking evidence, for and against him…including k'gdhededhá Claide…"

Bhílári frowned. "So there has been an election…"

"Claide is the prelate in Enesfel." The healer shifted to look at the others. "The Lachlans have long been proponents of enlisting Elyri in such trials…to read objects, witnesses, the accused…"

"I will do it." Bhen was not adept at reading, rarely used that ability, but for his beloved cousin, he would do, and risk, anything.

Ártur shook his head. "All of us in Rhidam are kin. Even Bhyrhán. They do not know that, but he is Bhíncári and that makes people nervous. You are kin as well. gdhededhá Tusánt will not be allowed to participate as Claide will not permit a leader of the Faith to be involved in such a way…though I suspect he will be involved somehow. The Queen seeks an Elyri who is not our kin…and as you know, with the state of things…there are no Elyri in Rhidam to choose from. If there are any still there…"

"It would be unwise of them to come forward, to make their presence known," agreed Tíbhyan. "You seek volunteers."

"I know it is a lot to ask, but I cannot hesitate in doing so. Kavan needs this. Coming to Rhidam is risky; I cannot pretend otherwise, but he needs the support of people he can trust, and I immediately thought of the two of you. I could ask others…but I doubt anyone else cares enough about his future to take the risk. I have considered asking Kyne Mórne, as I suspect she would be willing, but the risk to her life would be too great." If there were no other options, Ártur was still prepared to ask her, but he hoped he did not have to. "I can think of none better than the two of you, men of good position and standing who are not related. gdhededhá, he may not respect that you are Elyri, but you are older and have more seniority…and most people will respect that even if he does not. And no one, bhydáni, is likely to challenge your experience and wisdom."

There was no easily read expression on Tíbhyan's face as he considered the proposal. He did not fear for his life, had lived longer than many other Elyri already. For his most cherished student, such a sacrifice would be gladly given. But it had been many decades since he had traveled further than the náós from his door; the same age that gave him wisdom and removed his fear made travel difficult for his week legs. But this time…this time would be different.

"If young MacLyr will accompany an old man, lend me his strong back, legs, and shoulders…"

"Of course I will," Bhen agreed hastily, eager to help. He would go to Rhidam for Kavan regardless, but going at the request of the bhydáni was an additional excuse. Assistant and protector; Bhen accepted both responsibilities gladly.

gdhededhá Bhílári was slower to accept. "I will…need to consider this…" It was not a lack of desire to offer his aid to the man who performed miracles that deterred him, but rather that fear for his life the healer mentioned. Like the majority of his race, he had never been outside of Elyriá, and like many others, he rarely left the borders of town, save for occasional journeys to Clarys or to one of the villages within a day's travel of Bhryell.

"When will the hearing be held?" he asked pensively. He was embarrassed that the bhydáni could easily accept this challenge while he, a much younger man, found it difficult to do the same.

The healer shrugged. "I do not know. They will bury Hagan first. Day after tomorrow I am told. The Queen refuses to conduct her coronation until the matter with Kavan is resolved, so everyone is hastening to gather as much evidence as possible as quickly as they can. So far, as far as I know, no one has yet to be selected to examine the witnesses…to hear the case…"

That would be a difficult job for any man. No one would want to be remembered in the history books as the man who accused or condemned the White Bard, and if Kavan went free and the tide turned against the Lachlans for it, no man would want to be remembered as the one who allowed a possible killer to go free.

"I imagine it will be one of the guards…or perhaps the Queen will do it…" It was often customary in Enesfel for the monarch to pose questions to witnesses and suspects in high profile cases. Hagan's trial and subsequent sentencing and execution of the Corylliens had been no exception. But sometimes it was deemed necessary for the ruler to distance themselves from a case for personal reasons, and as close as Kavan was to the Lachlans, as deeply as some feared he influenced them, this might be such a time. Often the chamberlain or chancellor would be asked to fulfill such a duty, but with the chamberlain being kin to the accused, it left only the chancellor, and Ártur did not know if Flannery McGranis was up to the task.

"Give me a day or two to think about it…while you learn the date. I will," Bhílári squirmed, "have to set affairs in order if I go…"

"Thank you." To Ártur, that sounded enough like an acceptance to believe it was one. If it was not, Tíbhyan's appearance before the Crown would have to be enough.

"Have you told aendhá and aene yet?"

Ártur shook his head. "I have not had the chance and I do think any good will come of…"

"They must know," Syl sighed and lifted her tear-stained face. "I will come to Rhidam…for you, for Diona, for Hagan, for Kavan, but I will not bring the children. If they are to remain with your parents, they need to know why."

Scowling the healer scrubbed his face before sighing. He had not expected his wife to risk Rhidam for Hagan's funeral, but sometimes his wife's strength still surprised him. "You are right." They would already question Syl when she went for the children, and the news about Kavan, she felt, should come from Ártur and not from his wife. "In the morning; I will tell them before I return to Rhidam."

"And I will ready myself," Tíbhyan said. "When it is time, I will come with you."

Bhílári did not speak but nodded as if in agreement. Despite his doubts and indecision, each passing minute, each word spoken, inched him closer to taking the challenge. Ever since dedhá Kesábhá's visit, he had wondered about his place in history and what he was meant to do to help avert darkness. Aiding the miracle worker, the innocent boy he had watched grow into an equally innocent, and blessed, man, could well be his path, but it was a path he was afraid to walk.

❧*❧

Throughout the following day, the castle gradually filled with nobles and dignitaries from the lands nearest Rhidam, men and women who should have been arriving for the King's wedding and now, days before that would have transpired, found themselves attending a funeral instead. At the front of the naós, in the box where the Lachlans normally sat, a teary, devastated Sigrid sat with them, her hopes for a wedding and family and perhaps the prestige of being a Lachlan dashed in an instant. Seated with her were her brother, the new Queen, and as many of the royal advisors as Diona was able to gather, as well as the Cáners and Prime Magistrate Dilyn of Káliel, who clutched her husband's hand and listened to the recently chosen k'gdhededhá give a glowing eulogy about the great accomplishments of the late king.

Diona barely kept her expression neutral as the nasally man spoke. As much as she loved her brother, she would never have painted him as the saintly man Claide described. Some of what he said was exaggeration, or a twisting of facts, or outright fabrication of events and words she knew…or thought she knew…had never been uttered. Most of those in attendance, of course, would not know the difference, would never know the struggling Boy-King the way his sister and the royal advisors and staff had known him. She did not understand what political move the k'dedhá was trying to make by lauding her brother, but she was determined to find out…as soon as Kavan was free.

He should be here, should be present when the young man was interred in the back garden with his forbearers, but it could not be. She had thought to allow it, but while it might have been acceptable to her potential detractors if he was there under heavy guard, Diona could not subject Kavan to that public humiliation and scrutiny. There would also be, she knew, those who would view the attendance of the king's accused killer as an insult, and that was another consideration she had to make. Perhaps later that evening, when the castle was quiet and the staff asleep, she would have Kavan escorted to Hagan's burial place to pay his respects. Wouldn't that be the polite and proper thing to do for the man who had helped raise them?

Those expected to return to the castle to entomb the body, which Ártur had preserved to prevent decay, were the first to leave the náós. Many hands reached for the Queen, touched her, offered words of support and cheer. She had never given anyone cause to think ill of her, except Claide, but nor did they have any idea what sort of monarch she might be. It had been many generations since Enesfel had been ruled by a queen…a queen due to marry the Prince of Hatu…and they were equally excited and concerned. The murder of royalty was not to be taken lightly and what she did next would define her reign.

At the doorway, positioned to greet and bless the Faithful as they departed, Claide bowed to the Queen but did not offer his hand or offer her blessing. The failure was noted by many around them, and murmurs rippled through the multitude. Before he could rectify his mistake, she had moved beyond his reach and across the procession, his eyes locked on someone, or something, which kept him from pursuing her. It was a look of distraction that Owain noticed, an expression combining fury and perhaps guilt, but the prince saw nothing in the crowd that might warrant that reaction from Claide. It was enough to make Owain suspicious, especially since Claide was, for those few moments, too distracted to shake hands with or bless anyone who passed, and when he did absently resume doing so, the first hand he grasped was Gaelán's. The boy stumbled to a stop and stared, and Claide stared back with a fleeting look of disgust and the quick wiping of his hand on his robes. Then Gaelán was swept along by the rest of his family and Owain, having noticed the exchange, put one arm around Gaelán and the other around Sóbhán.

Though he was expected to attend the King's interment, Claide did not arrive, leaving Tusánt to oversee the rite as Diona preferred. There were no military plaudits to offer, no lengthy glowing speeches or remembrances to be given. Hagan had been too young, and had not been king long enough, to have garnered those things. Save for the arrest and execution of a significant number of Corylliens, the young man had barely lived. Stories told were more personal in nature and some, by those who had known King Arlan best, were comparisons between Hagan and his father. Each person present chose to believe that Hagan could have been a great king like Arlan and Innis before him, and though Diona wanted to believe it, her thoughts were colored with doubt. No one could live up to her father's legacy…not even her…and Hagan had been, in her opinion, too weak-willed to have made a great king. A good king, perhaps, but not a great one.

Not even she would live up to greatness.

When the echo of the stone marker being dropped into place faded into the early evening air and those nobles in attendance had left for their homes or had retreated inside for the meal they would savor at the Crown's expense, Diona dared to speak of other matters.

"Tomorrow, mid-morning, the trial will commence."

"So soon?" choked Ártur.

"We're not ready," Wortham growled.

"Does Kavan know?" was Gabrielle's question.

Diona shook her head. "He does not; he refuses visitors beyond Captain Delamo and Uncle…" Her decision had been made that morning, but the day's burial events had taken all of their time. She had told no one her choice, and thus no one had been able to relay the news to Kavan. "Lord MacLyr assures me he will have someone here as a reader…" she met his gaze to be certain that had not changed and when he nodded, continued, "and Lord McGranis has accepted the duty of examination. We cannot delay this inevitably…or avoid it."

Heads grimly bobbed as the collection of friends and staff accepted those assessments as valid. Lord McGranis, as Ártur had rationalized, was the most logical choice for this distasteful duty and, many hoped that his relative inexperience in such matters would work in the bard's favor and not against him.

Not satisfied, the Prime Magistrate wrung her hands. "But who will speak for him if he will not speak for himself?"

"Perhaps he will…when the time comes," murmured Wortham, though he feared Kavan was setting himself up for execution as a martyr on behalf of all Elyri, that this was somehow the purification ritual he was destined for. If it was, the items he had gathered in the Southern lands would hardly play a role, however, so Wortham clung to hope. While his death might appease some, giving them a high-profile target for their aggression, it would do little for the safety of Elyri in Enesfel. "And if he does not, I will."

He had not been with Kavan that day, but he had stories to tell that would speak on Kavan's behalf, attest to the sort of man he was, better than anyone else could.

"Flannery cannot adequately present his case without speaking with him," the chamberlain muttered.

Ártur groaned. "I'm sure he knows that." He was trying to trust his cousin's instincts, his wisdom, but it was difficult to do when Kavan's life was at stake and he appeared unwilling to defend himself.

The sound of heavy boots on dry stone intruded on their gathering and made heads turn. A young dark-haired soldier with olive skin and black eyes stopped a respectable distance away and bowed.

"Yes?" Diona asked, not knowing the soldier by name though she was beginning to recognize his face.

"Your Majesty. There is a gentleman at the gate seeking audience with Captain Delamo and Prince Owain."

The two men looked at one another, one with curiosity and the other with expectant excitement. "Might we?" Wortham asked of the Queen, finding the asking of permission to be awkward and uncomfortable.

"Of course." Though she had no reason to think the summons was of import to the trial, she hoped the captain's interest meant it was so.

"Bring him to the Stateroom," Wortham instructed the messenger, "and Lady Asta…if you would join us please?"

"Me?" Asta glanced around the group, realizing she no longer had any reason to fear who in the keep knew she acted on her father's authorization as inquisitor. Hagan's death, as horrifying and disheartening as it was, freed her to do her father's work and might, she realized with a flutter in her stomach, allow her father to come home. "Aye…yes…"

Gaelán watched her depart, heavy-hearted at the death, at Kavan's arrest, and burdened by a secret he did not know how to share or who to share it with.

Asta did not know the dark-skinned man in nomadic dress escorted into the Stateroom where she, Owain, and Wortham waited, but the two men clearly did as they greeted him with welcoming hands. Owain was surprised to see him, but because Wortham was not, Asta assumed the nomad was here at the captain's invitation.

"Thank Ethenae you received my message. I did not think you would, or that you would come in time," Wortham said, clutching the man's large hand between his.

"Hearing from you was unexpected. Prince Lachlan, it is a pleasure to see you as well." He offered his other hand to Owain but looked at the young woman, the child he believed, in the room with them. "My lady?" He could tell she was nobility by her manner of dress, but he did not recognize her.

"Asta Dugan," she said with a polite but uncomfortable curtsey. Ladies curtseyed, after all, but she hated doing it.

"Ah," the mountain of a man smiled. "Dugan's child. I should have guessed." He bowed his head politely and added, "Wace Elotti."

The bounty hunter looked older than she had pictured him, his face etched with the lines of age and his black hair peppered with curly white strands, but he still looked much the way her father and Muir had described him from the time when he had aided in the rescue of her brother and Prince Bertram from kidnappers. He knew a lot of things about a lot of people. She wondered if he knew where her father was, or if he could find him.

"An honor." He did not ask why she was here. Perhaps, she mused, he already knew.

Elotti took the drink Wortham offered and the seat Owain gestured to. It was not the sort of reception he expected for what was, undoubtedly, a business request, but he was not going to turn down either offering. "The king is dead?"

It was a relief to get to the point. "If you have heard about it," Wortham replied, dropping into a chair opposite the Cíbhóló, "then you have heard…"

"That Lord Cliáth is the accused." He sipped the expensive wine he had been given and nodded his head approvingly, despite the scowl on his face. "But surely there is no truth to that rumor."

"None of us believe it to be true…but he will not speak of the events of that day, leaving us to puzzle out what happened on our own. The soldiers who were witnesses have been placed in seclusion and been forbidden to speak to anyone save Chancellor McGranis until the trial…which the Queen has scheduled to begin tomorrow."

"Too soon," the bounty hunter huffed. From Wortham and Owain's expressions, he knew they agreed. The girl's face was, like her father's, deceptively blank. It would be impossible to track down a killer in a single night based on the lack of details he had been given thus far. "Without clues, without more information…"

Asta got up and, from the small box on the table she had been asked to bring to this meeting, she presented the nearly one-inch diameter orange jewel. "Be careful," she warned as she slid the box and its contents across the table to him. "This was laced with poison."

"And jabbed into the King's leg," Owain added. "Our healers could not determine the type or nature of the substance…"

"And no one has yet been able to identify this…beyond it being a jewelry ornament of some sort. I thought it might come from south of Hatu…" explained Wortham.

Elotti picked up the jewel gingerly and turned it to study the tines. He frowned and put it back in the box. "It is a kwolott…a ceremonial jewel worn by new brides amongst the tribes."

"Worn how?" asked Asta. The obvious answer, to her, did not seem to be a good one.

"There are usually many…as many or as large as the family can afford. This is one of the largest I have seen." He closed the box and pushed it back to Asta. "They are tapped into the skin, usually on the breasts, but sometimes on the face, neck or ears…twisted so that the barbs catch, then heated with a small bit of metal so that the skin scabs and scars around it, keeping the kwolott in place except under extreme circumstances. It marks a woman as married, for no child would wear it. They are a sign of prestige, adulthood, marriage."

"This is Cíbhóló in origin?" Wortham did not want to believe it. He had seen Cíbhóló men, but he had never seen a Cíbhóló woman in

Rhidam. Of those he knew, only Ártur had been into the desert, but the healer had never mentioned women wearing such jewels. Perhaps, once affixed to the body, the healer had never questioned how they got there and had never seen one before it was worn.

"This is no weapon of murder…"

"Perhaps not normally," Owain grunted. "Perhaps it is not intended to be…but someone used it that way against the King."

Asta leaned her elbows on the table and propped her chin on her hands. She had not shown the item to Agis, though she had shown it to many well-traveled members of the Lachlan staff and some of her contacts in Rhidam. It appears she should have. Time had been unnecessarily wasted. "As a Cíbhóló custom, these would not be typically sold or traded to outsiders?" Staring at the box she continued, "How difficult will it be to trace who might have sold such a thing?"

Impossible, she thought, but the question had to be asked.

"If it was sold," Elotti replied. "It could have been bartered, stolen, or lost and someone who did not know its origin and purpose found it. It could have been in Enesfel for years…or days."

Recalling the number of nomads in Rhidam when Arlan wrestled the throne from Owain, the men knew that jewel could have been dropped by any one of those men and found by anyone.

"Are there no other clues? No Elyri has read this?"

Wortham shook his head. "The Queen will allow no one to touch it, or even clean it, until the trial. The fear of being poisoned…if I'm not eager to touch it, I do not expect any of them to be." How Kavan had not been poisoned by it when he removed it from Hagan's thigh, Wortham did not know.

"From what I know…" Asta, as acting inquisitor, had access to what little information the chancellor could provide, as long as she shared it with no one who might taint the trial. That did not include, in her opinion, the bounty hunter who might be able to find the truth before the rest of them could. "The soldiers saw nothing suspicious at the time, and if Kavan…" If Kavan had seen anything, no one knew.

"Would he see me?"

Wortham and Owain looked at one another. "I do not know," the captain admitted. "I will ask…but I suspect he will not. He is stubbornly refusing to cooperate."

"Perhaps he knows the killer?"

It was a possibility none wanted to admit. Knowing the killer but not revealing them was as damning as having done the deed himself.

"I know…"

Heads turned towards the open door where Gaelán stood, face pale, body visibly trembling. None knew how long he had been there, or how much he had overheard, but Asta guessed it had not been long. She or Elotti would have known if he had been there all along.

"What do you know, Gaelán?" Asta asked, scooting over on her seat so that he could join her. Though there were empty chairs, including the one at her side, he took the offered positioned, her proximity seeming to give him some sense of relief.

"I know who killed him." He shrank beneath the gazes and clenched his hands under the table. "Well…not exactly…but sort of."

"Who?" Wortham asked.

"How do you know?" followed Elotti.

"How long have you…?" asked Asta beneath the other questions.

"After the service…when k'dedhá took my hand."

Uncomfortable with the hint of knowledge he shouldered, knowing it might put him in danger if he spoke, Gaelán cleared his throat as Owain exclaimed, "Claide did this?"

"It was a glimpse…a shadow of thought that came across…that Hagan's death was an accident…that he is angry about it because the target was aendhá Kavan."

Faces lost color for a host of reasons. It was the first factual hint, such as it was, of the k'dedhá's involvement in anything, and it was sobering that Kavan had been the target…and that somehow the attempt had gone so wrong as to result in the death of King Hagan.

"Well I am not sure Kavan was the target," Owain snorted stubbornly because he did not want to believe it. "After the executions of Corylliens…the way the King had begun to stand up to him…"

Asta nodded, though she did not think Gaelán was lying. "True. Perhaps he feared losing his influence."

"All the more reason to target Kavan," Wortham reminded them. "It's his influence many fear the most."

Gaelán hung his head. "From what I sensed…read…I don't believe Hagan was the target."

"Even if he feared losing influence on the King," Asta said thoughtfully, thinking out loud. "He had to know he would have less influence with the Queen. Targeting Hagan put her in the last place the k'dedhá would want her to be."

The men had to concede that point. Diona would never be manipulated the way Hagan had sometimes been. Claide would have preferred keeping the King in his pocket…particularly if he could remove Kavan's influence.

Having listened to the arguments with his arms folded over his chest, Elotti finally spoke. "With a weapon such as this…the wielder would have to be close. It could not have been fired with accuracy. It must have been hand-held, used by someone close enough to touch your King."

"One of the soldiers then. Or…"

"Lord Cliáth." They always came back to Kavan, whatever circle the arguments took, and Wortham was growing disheartened. "I know those men…and I know Kavan. I cannot believe any are guilty. But someone was…someone k'dedhá Claide knows…and in a sea of citizens in Rhidam…in Enesfel…you did not get a glimpse of the killer, my lord?" he asked Gaelán desperately.

The young healer shook his head. "His thoughts were too scattered, too vague…and I was not trying to read him. It just happened. If I could touch him again, probe his thoughts longer…"

"No." Asta shook her head. "You're not getting close enough to him for that, not if he might already suspect you know something."

"I don't think he does. I don't know how he could." But the quaver in his voice suggested otherwise, suggested his fear that Claide might well suspect him.

Wortham clasped Gaelán's shoulder. "We will not take unnecessary chances. We will find another way."

"No need for you to risk anything," Elotti agreed. "I have somewhere to start. Knowing the proximity of the assassin to the king…knowing this connection to the k'dedhá, knowing what I know…I will see where the evidence takes me. If I find the guilty I will bring him straight to you."

"Your fee?"

The dark man shook his head.

"None required. I owe Lord Cliáth a debt; I will see he is made free of these charges." Owain and Wortham looked at each other, unaware of any debt but willing to accept the man's word and his services. "If the assassin is Cíbhóló however…I demand his head."

"Fair enough," Wortham agreed hastily. The Queen might not appreciate the bounty hunter seeking revenge, but the captain had experience with both the hunter and the general. If this was a matter of Cíbhóló pride, it seemed a fair price to pay. "We should at least meet him…see him…speak to him…"

"Or her," Elotti reminded with a glance at the box. A woman's jewel could have been used by a woman just as easily, without any assassin's skill.

"Or her," agreed Owain. "The Queen will want proof of their identity…and their guilt."

"You shall have it." Elotti reached across the table to seal the deal with first Wortham, then Owain, then Asta, and lastly Gaelán. "I will let you know by morning what I learn, if anything, and will keep you updated regularly. Expect my messengers at the gate."

"We will."

There was little time. They had to use the hours available to them. Asta and Gaelán excused themselves, the young woman determined to find Marta and explain her position to Gaelán at last, now that part of her secret was revealed. He was a healer and she was the inquisitor…as much as their ages would allow them to be. The responsibilities that came with those titles meant that adulthood was upon them, but it could not be avoided. Gaelán would be introduced to Marta, and between the three of them, they too would seek details of k'dedhá Claide's involvement with whoever had been commissioned to kill King Hagan.

❧Chapter 41❦

"**I** don't care if he's dying!" the Queen exclaimed at Saul who tried not to shrink from what he considered to be a well-excused tirade. Espen, hearing her exasperated cries from the other end of the corridor, came into the room hoping to discover what was wrong and perhaps put her at ease. Her face was red as she glowered at the unfortunate novice sent to the Queen at the k'dedhá's request.

"Tell him he has two days! No more! The trial will begin the day after tomorrow, with or without him. It will wait no longer!"

"I will relay your message, Your Majesty," Saul said with a bow before backing from the room, leaving Espen with the angry Queen. The prince waited until they were alone, save for the collection of attendants and pages now required by her station to be with the woman nearly every waking moment, before choosing to speak.

"Claide?" He could think of no one else who would cause such fury.

"Is ill…allegedly. Too ill to attend the trial, and he demands we await his recovery, when he was the one pushing for swift resolution."

"Convenient." And suspicious.

"He cannot manipulate me as he did Hagan. I will not allow it. He is due to leave for Wexel, Jardin, and Nelori in less than a week and…"

"His attendance is not needed for trial, is it?" Espen was sure it would be in the bard's best interest if the k'dedhá did not attend.

"Needed, no…but he demands to be…and for something of this magnitude, the Faith should be included. If what I am told is true, I want him there to see him squirm. I will not leave Kavan under arrest indefinitely while Claide drags out delays to suit himself. He does not rule Enesfel."

"You want him here?" Espen sat in the nearby chair, watching her.

"For the trial, no. I prefer him not to be. But I don't trust him out of Rhidam, even if Sir Gabersdon is traveling with him. I would rather he be where we can watch him. As important as this trial is, I have hopes he will somehow tip his hand and implicate himself."

"Politics then."

"Of course politics. Personal feelings aside, it is the only weapon I wield…and I'll use it the best I can for the greater good…which includes removing influences such as Claide."

"You know there will be less agitation of emotions…and might protect the duke…if Claide isn't here?" Diona frowned and Espen continued, "And there are a few benefits to this delay." If she was seeking political advantages over Claide, he could think of none better.

"Which benefits?"

His calm words and demeanor soothed her, and now that she was near enough in her frustrated pacing, he caught her hand and held it.

"For Lord Cliáth's sake, the investigation is allowed to continue. This rush to justice, as important as closure is to Enesfel and your coronation, is hardly fair to him. A single day is barely enough to take statements, let alone gather evidence. Giving Captain Delamo and Prince Owain more time will benefit the duke's case."

Diona bit her lip and nodded reluctantly. As convinced as she was of Kavan's innocence, she had not thought his defense needed time to prepare. A delay had seemed moot to her. If there was evidence found to support his innocence, however, innocence beyond the bard's unsullied reputation, that would be a good thing in the end.

Espen continued. "There are many nobles still in Rhidam, those who came for the wedding, for the trial, who await your coronation. Perhaps we should take advantage of their presence and Claide's absence to do both at once…the same day perhaps…if that suits you."

"Do both?" For a moment she was confused, but slowly her expression changed, prompted by the way he squeezed her hand and the sparkle in his eyes. With Hagan's death, her own future had been the last thing she was thinking about. Preparations were being made for the coronation which would happen as soon as the trial was complete, regardless of the outcome. Enesfel needed leadership; it was her duty to provide it and she knew many expected it, including Kavan and her father. It would be expected by many for the highest-ranking leader of the Faith in Enesfel to be present at her crowning, but, to her knowledge, k'dedhá Claide had not adjusted his schedule to accommodate her, a clear indication of his lack of support and his insolence. Not having him there delighted her.

Claide's departure had been scheduled for the day after Hagan's wedding. Arrangements were already in place for a wedding and a feast, neither called off as of yet and neither originally intended for her. Many of the guests had already arrived. A few days' delay would not create significant problems for anyone, would not incur undue expense, and it would mean that none of her brother's purchases and preparations needed to go to waste. While she had not anticipated her own wedding for several more weeks, combining it with her coronation would create an event Enesfel would remember for decades. And doing it while Claide was out of Rhidam meant the man could not detract from either event. She could begin her reign as though the man was not part of her life.

"That would be…" She smiled. "I would like that. Both," she admitted. After the years she had made Espen wait, shifting their marriage date forward by a few weeks was fair. "Will you see to the arrangements?"

They were hardly his to plan, and he knew most of the details were in place. But he also knew she had inherited a substantial burden with her brother's unforeseen death, and he was eager to help where he could, even if it meant finalizing their wedding arrangements alone.

"Anything. You know I am here to aid you however I can." He had nearly given up hope of marrying her, and now that she was Enesfel's Queen, it was a rise in status that his brother would likely wish to take advantage of. Espen intended to make the most of the change to the benefit of both kingdoms, but mainly to benefit her. The road ahead was not going to be an easy one r, particularly when it began with the trial of her beloved tutor and advisor.

☙*❧

Ártur waited at his mother's table, empty ceramic cup clenched in his hands, as his parents fought over the child they had fostered when fire and plague had claimed the boy's parents too soon. Ártur did not know whether the decision for Kavan to live with them had come by default, because Kavan had already been living in their home at the time of his mother's death, if Tám had made the choice to raise his brother's peculiar child, or whether Dhaná had pressured her husband into doing what was right. Because she rarely contradicted him or argued with him when it came to Kavan, Ártur often believed she had been the force behind the reluctantly accepted adoption and that she felt obliged to let Tám have his way afterward.

This time, however, the woman was not backing down to her husband's demands, even when Tám repeated, "You will not go to Rhidam! You are needed here."

"I am going. You cannot stop me." Sámel's wife could manage the family during Dháná's absence, and much of what needed doing, Tám could handle on his own. He could feed himself, as there was enough food prepared and stocked, the clothing had been washed and hung to dry, and their home was already clean. She knew little about the man Kavan had come to be, but she could not fathom the boy she had raised becoming the murderer of kings. That was going too far. She might have failed him by relenting to her husband's demands, but she refused to fail him again. Not this time.

Red-faced, glaring at his youngest son as if to imply that this was somehow Ártur's fault, Tám snarled, "It is too dangerous."

"She will be with me," Bhen said, his tall frame poised to step between his grandparents should the disagreement escalate beyond loud voices and angry words.

"And we will be well-guarded," added Syl. Her words, however, were ignored beyond a sharp glance that suggested that, if she felt Rhidam was so safe, she should be there with her husband rather than living in Bhryell with their children. Why should she be willing to put Dháná's life at risk if she was not secure enough to risk hers?

Except this time, given what was at stake, she was.

Syl caught that glance as she tucked her hair beneath the shawl wrapped around her shoulders and covering her head as a shield against the outdoor wind. Tilting her chin in defiance, Dháná said, "This is not her decision, Tám. Nor is it Ártur's. We have turned our backs on your brother's son too often. I will not do it this time."

Tears welled in Ártur's eyes as his mother tugged him to his feet. "Come, Ártur, take me to him." She was afraid, he could feel it in her touch. Afraid of the Gate, afraid of Rhidam, afraid for Kavan, but she was not allowing fear to hinder her. Her mind was made up. When Tám reached for her, intending to pull her back, several cool, sharp gazes flashed at him, including his wife's. It was enough, for the first time in Ártur's recollection, for Tám to take a step back, snort, and then storm out of the room with defeated, angry strides.

Bhen left them long enough to bring Tíbhyan, and soon they were gathered with gdhededhá Bhílári in front of the Purification Chamber.

The dedhá had given no verbal agreement about going to Rhidam, had avoided discussing the matter, but he was waiting there with his pack for the others to arrive, dressed in his most expensive clerical robes that he hoped would be enough to impress Claide. He too was determined but frightened. The healer nodded but no one spoke until Bhen joined them many minutes later with the bhydáni on his arm.

"I can take two at a time and Syl can take one," Ártur started."

"We will go first." Tíbhyan had no fear of the Gate, though it had been a long time since he had used one, and Bhen had used it with Ártur before. If it would instill confidence in the others, the sage was eager to do it, particularly if it brought him closer to Kavan. Dháná clung to Syl's arm as the three men crowded into the small space and within moments were gone. Shortly thereafter, her son returned alone. She had known this was how her son moved so efficiently between Bhryell and Rhidam, but she had never experienced it.

"Shall we?" Syl urged the other woman tenderly. It made sense for her to leave the anxious dedhá to her husband, as long as she could convince Dháná to be at ease.

The woman nodded and followed on shaky legs, clutching tight to Syl's hands. She took a deep breath, started to nod to indicate she was ready…and then they were gone.

"It is that easy?" the dedhá murmured.

"It is if you're accustomed to doing it."

"You've certainly been doing it long enough." Ártur MacLyr had been healer to the Lachlan house for the better part of sixty years and had traveled back and forth this way between kingdoms the entire time. If he could not be trusted to take someone safely through, then no one could be. "My years in this chamber…on either side…and it never occurred to me to use this."

"There was no need I suppose…but I promise, no matter what happens in Rhidam, Kavan will appreciate you being there. Relax. Pray or meditate if it helps clear your mind. Close your eyes if you wish, and trust me."

Bhílári did not understand what happened next. Within the span of six breaths, Ártur was tugging his arm and leading him into a small, unfamiliar chapel where the others waited, joined by Bhríd, Gaelán, Wortham, and Zelenka. Shakily, Bhílári tottered as far as the altar and then paused to lean against it, his heart racing.

"Welcome to Rhidam, gdhededhá," the chamberlain said with an outstretched hand. He had not expected, when Ártur told him he had found two men to read for the Queen, that he might mean these two men. But who better than the men Kavan respected the most, two men he had grown up with. Dháná's visit, however, was even more unexpected. "There are rooms prepared, a suite where you may be together under guard. Captain Delamo has personally selected those who will see to your comfort and security and I swear to you, if you need anything, it will be provided. No one is aware of your arrival tonight; you may rest without fear. When it is time tomorrow, you will be escorted to the Hall for the hearing."

"Thank you, Lord Cáner," the sage said with a shaky half bow. If not for Bhen's aid, his old legs would have given out already."

"It is our honor, bhydáni. Come…let me take your things."

The guests were escorted down quiet corridors, down a steep curving flight of stairs, to a billeting suite on the second floor that was often used for dignitaries and visiting noble families. If any of the Lachlans numerous guests who had come expecting a wedding had been roomed here, they had been relocated in expectation of these unique visitors. Bedding had been prepared in one-half of the suite for the three men, and Syl chose to stay with Dháná and Zelenka in the other half to help the older woman feel at ease. The windows were secured and there were two guards outside of each door, Wortham's three friends and the dark-haired soldier he had met the night of Elotti's arrival. Young Mikel was eager to please Wortham and that, in the captain's reckoning, made him the ideal man to train and work with, to trust with something as important as Kavan's life.

Come morning, it was a bustle in the courtyard that woke the visitors from restless sleep in unfamiliar beds. Benches were brought from the guardhouse, the stables, from anywhere they could be found, some of them remaining from the ecclesiastical election. It filled the Great Hall with seating once again, and more were being cobbled together to one side of the courtyard. At the portcullis, townsfolk were pressed against the grating, eager to witness the trial of the White Bard of Bhryell. It would be a spectacle unseen in Rhidam, and Wortham hoped with a grunt of annoyance as he too watched the growing crowd and abundance of activity, it would be a spectacle never repeated. Whatever Kavan hoped to gain from this, or give to Enesfel, the captain hoped for success though not at the cost of the bard's life.

The Hall filled quickly once the gates opened. Seats were saved at the front for guests the Queen had been advised would be there, one of whom was the biggest Cíbhóló she had ever seen. Curious, as she sat on the throne with Espen seated beside her, she looked for the general in the crowd. When she found him, his expression revealed that he did not know who the stranger was either, but he was determined to find out. Since the stranger stayed near Owain, however, Diona judged he was meant to be there, likely on Kavan's behalf. She hoped that was true, for the bard's sake. She hoped the stranger had something significant to add to these proceedings.

Many of the others in the front row were also unrecognized faces, although she judged one to be kin to Healer MacLyr, as the woman's resemblance to him was striking. One was gdhededhá, a man Claide stared at openly, making little effort to hide his contempt. It was the last man Diona could not take her eyes from, even when Chancellor McGranis rose to order the room. She knew Elyri lived long lives. Ártur was, she knew, eighty-one years old though he looked little older than thirty. As gnarled and stooped as the wrinkled stranger was, who leaned on Bhen MacLyr for support, he had to be ancient. How old did an Elyri have to be to acquire such a frail appearance? The thought made her uncomfortably afraid. Thankfully, the sound of the side door opening, the thud of boots, clank of armor, and jangle of binding chains dragged her attention away from the old man to the one this travesty of justice was centered around.

Their gazes tore through him. Kavan could feel it, though, with his own stare fixed blankly beyond them, his head high to appear unashamed and unafraid, he did not see the size of the crowd. The Hall was full; he could smell it in the scents of anxiety, excitement, perspiration, and perfume. He could hear it in the rumbled whispers and fleeting thoughts that bombarded his guarded mind. He could taste it in the stale, pregnant, hot air when he opened his mouth slightly to breathe without smelling. And he could feel it against his skin like a million tiny needle pricks that irritated but did no lasting damage.

When his eyes did finally make contact with another living soul, it was with a man he had never expected to see in this place. Seated between Ártur and Bhen, bhydáni Tíbhyan watched him with a deceptively neutral expression that Kavan knew from experience masked scrutiny and concern. The shock of seeing him made Kavan scan the remainder of the front row. gdhededhá Bhílári. aene Dháná, another face he could not imagine being here. Wace Elotti, an unexpected attendee but one he was less surprised to see, given the man's profession. The others, friends and family, were familiar, and while their support was welcome, even expected, he wished they were not here to see or hear any of this. Thank k'Ádhá Muir was not present. This experience would be difficult enough as it was, particularly with Wortham and Ártur fretting over his possible fate, without having to endure Muir's emotions as well.

The one face he longed most to see, however, was not currently present. Hoping the man was merely detained, that he had not been prevented from attending or had chosen not to support his best friend in his hour of need, Kavan chose not to dwell on it or the cracking of his heart as he was brought to Chancellor McGranis in front of the throne, upon which the new Queen waited, the woman Kavan was not prepared to face.

"Duke Cliáth, you know the charges. For those present," the chancellor looked across the gathering, wishing he did not have to go through the formality of saying it, and continued, "the charges are the murder of King Hagan Lachlan, rightful ruler of Enesfel."

The bard nodded his head once but did not speak. A second voice spared him the need to try. "Lord Cliáth?" He faced the woman on the throne. Regardless of the outcome, he believed he was doing the right thing by insisting on this trial. He was no better than any other man, had never wanted to be treated differently. This was, he hoped, his opportunity to prove he was no different. In doing so, he hoped to lay another layer of peace over Enesfel's wounds.

"Your Majesty," he murmured with a bow.

Satisfied that he gave her that much when she had expected him to remain stubbornly silent until the end, Diona asked, "You do understand…don't you?"

"I do." Perhaps she thought to give him a way out if he claimed to not understand why he was accused of this crime. Perhaps she thought a show of incompetence might free him. But he would not lie; he understood the charges, understood what could happen as a result. That, he presumed, was the real question behind Diona's words.

Eye to eye, she tried to grasp his choices, and eye to eye he tried to make her understand, but without words there was nothing either could gain by delaying the trial. She sighed and waved her hand. "Continue, Lord Chancellor," she said, swallowing weary concern and replacing it on her face with an unfelt calm.

The chancellor, nervous in the unusual role of examiner, bid Kavan sit and called the first of the soldiers there on the day of Hagan's death to be presented to the Queen.

"Tell us what you witnessed the day of the King's death."

The man swallowed and began in a shaky voice. "The King and Duke Cliáth were to ride that day. We accompanied them through the city towards West Bridge. As we crossed, the Duke bumped his horse against the King's. The King slumped to the side and fell off."

"Fell off? To the ground?"

"No, Lord Cliáth caught him."

Nodding, the chancellor beckoned. "What happened next?"

The soldier explained in broken sentences how, when they reached the King, the murder weapon had been in the bard's hand, the hand covered with royal blood. Each of the soldiers present that day repeated much the same story, though some had not seen the horses bump together, while one said it was the King's horse that had bumped the duke's, and others had not seen the murder weapon in Kavan's hand. Each retelling of corroborating details sent ripples of whispered emotion through the room and a more satisfied smirk to k'gdhededhá Claide's face. Many in the audience expected Kavan to refute the claims, to deny what they said, to defend himself, but the Elyri said nothing throughout their testimonies.

Even when the chancellor turned to him and asked, "Do you refute these claims?" all Kavan could say was, "I do not." He could have clarified, recounted his own version of the details, things the soldiers had not seen, did not know, but on the surface, at least, their recounting of events was accurate.

In the front row, expressions were horrified and Elotti crossed his arms with a grunt.

Even the Queen was dumbfounded.

Others were brought forward in support of the soldiers' claims, though most had little to add to substantiate the tales. Accusations were made of cruelty to the downtrodden, abusive treatment of animals, slanderous words spoken against the Lachlans and against the Faith, as well as a lack of attendance to Gatherings and a lack of adherence to the Faith. After the third witness attempted to use 'he is Elyri' as proof that he was the King's killer, the queen rose in disgust and brought silence to the room. It was nearing noon, she was hungry and irritable and not interested in the games these witnesses had been pressed into playing.

She was willing to wager they had been coerced by the hands of Claide and the Corylliens.

"Being Elyri is no crime," she reminded the room coolly, "and I will hear no further allegations based on race. Nor will I hear speculative witness about his position in the Faith or the possibility of miracles." She glanced sympathetically at the bard who stared at his hands in his lap and did not react. If some were trying to paint him with the brush of heresy, then she was certain there would be those who would bring up miracle after miracle. It would embarrass Kavan and muddy the already murky trial waters. "Nor will I hear slander against his character unless it directly pertains to the events the day King Hagan died. We are here to address a murder, nothing more."

"Humbly, Your Majesty," Claide said, daring to speak, "But such accusations, if true, would serve as proof of the character of a killer..."

Diona's eyes flashed with anger at the man who dared to interrupt her, who dared attempt to contradict her decree with his own arguments. "The Duke's character is not on trial," she hissed, barely refraining from speaking the other thoughts that stampeded through her head. "His actions, his guilt or innocence of the death of my brother are in question. Nothing more. But...if you insist on pursuing such claims..." She motioned to one of the guards posted around the platform's perimeter. "Bring each man and woman who has testified to me and we shall have each of them read..."

Kavan's head came up while Claide quickly, with practiced composure painted over his surprise at having his bluff called, said, "No...that will not be necessary." The bard could feel the fingers of panic clawing at those who had spoken against him. There was no proof of any of their claims, no words of slander he had ever uttered, no cruelty or indiscretions of which he could be accused except one...and the woman he had wronged was dead. He had feared that someone from that tavern, that night long past, might be called as a witness against him, though none but Wortham knew of that failing.

"It will cause unnecessary delay," the k'dedhá continued, offering a logical excuse for avoiding what he likely knew would be an embarrassing lack of proof on behalf of those witnesses. As it was, he knew the soldiers would be read, but since the Elyri had agreed with their perceptions, there was no reason to think they were lying.

"It would indeed," the Queen muttered. "We will return in two hours and hear further witnesses." And, she prayed, prove that her faith in Kavan had never been misplaced.

Few in the crowd left the Hall, not wanting to lose their hard-won spots for the remainder of the hearing. Some had brought food with them in anticipation of this being an all-day affair. Palace servants passed loaves of bread and cups of water through the crowd so that none would faint from the physical weakness of hunger and thirst. Kavan was removed from the room, both to protect him and to prevent him from speaking to anyone, for his sake as well as theirs. Diona and Espen retreated to the Stateroom for privacy to discuss what they had heard thus far, but none of the royal advisors joined them. Syl was summoned, but whether for medical purposes or something else was not revealed even when she returned to her husband's side. Ártur, sick of heart, paced the length of the platform, ignoring Claide when he reached the side where the man was seated, half expecting to be stabbed in the back when he walked away from him.

His efforts to touch Kavan's mind failed; the bard successfully blocked his attempts to help or reassure him. It was as if Kavan wanted to be condemned and Ártur could not bear it.

"Sit, ílMairós," Tíbhyan said, catching the healer's hand and tugging him into his chair. "You are not helping your cousin with this frantic pacing about."

"I'm not helping at all, bhydáni…that is the problem. He does not appear to want our help."

"Perhaps not. Perhaps he does not need it."

"Does not…" The healer's face burned red. "He will be executed if they declare him guilty of…"

"Ártur," hissed Owain. "Lower your voice."

Ártur glanced about, aware now of people watching him, people who had heard his outburst, people who looked as devastated by the possibility of Kavan's execution as Ártur was. Annoyed at himself, he grunted, "Where is Wortham? And Asta?" It was an ill omen for the captain to be absent at such a time, unless Kavan had sent him off to do something. The princess might be ill, but Ártur had not been told of it, and with the other court physicians in the Hall, it seemed unlikely she would have been left unattended.

"She said she had something to do," Gaelán muttered bitterly. He knew now what she spent her days doing. She could not share details with him 'for his own protection', which meant he still worried too much, more than before, about her welfare, but at least he knew the truth. "I'm hoping she's doing something to help."

Owain and Elotti glanced at one another, hoping so too; they said nothing and that made the healer frown. Hoping to calm her husband, Syl held his hand and said, "Whatever happens, we will not let him face it alone."

"Whatever happens," growled Sóbhán with determination, "we will not let him die." Kavan had saved his life, given him a chance to be someone. The young Elyri, with his developing skills, would do anything it took to keep Kavan alive.

Tíbhyan patted the boy's hand. "He will not die."

"But…" began Ártur.

"ílMairós…do you believe these people will let that happen?"

Again Ártur looked around him, across the room full of those who had come to witness this trial. Save for the handful who had testified against Kavan and a smattering of others who might have, if given the chance, the majority of the faces wore varying degrees of concern and fear and adoration. Whatever Claide's sermonizing intended to accomplish in Rhidam and beyond, regardless of any anti-Elyri sentiment there might be, there was a deep, abiding love for the White Bard that wove through myth and legend to the seeds planted long ago, the seeds of hope for a better life than what King Bowen had foisted on the land, and that Owain, in his naïve inexperience, had been unable to reverse. People loved Kavan for the miracles he was said to perform, they loved him for kindness and gentleness that was never withheld, and they loved him for the music he brought back into Enesfel. Elyri or not, Kavan was adored. His death would be the death of dreams, and few in Enesfel were prepared for that.

Many would sooner accept the death of a king over the death of the Bhryell Saint. Many would riot and fan the flames of civil war if the bard faced execution.

Ártur wondered if Kavan knew that.

The Stateroom door opened to allow the Queen and Prince Espen to return. This time, the crowd did not need to be silenced. They took their seats, anxiously murmuring until the moment Kavan was brought back into the Hall. When he came, meekly accepting the chains he wore, not fighting captivity, seeming to accept his fate or else entrusting the outcome to a higher power, even the murmuring ceased. What remained of the day would either condemn or save him.

❧Chapter 42❦

He had not eaten when his guards took him back to his dungeon cell. His knotted stomach would not permit it. His head ached from his cousin's constant pounding against his defenses in an attempt to communicate, attempts Kavan was not willing to allow. Determined to succeed or fail on his personal merits as a man, to show the citizens of Enesfel that Elyri were not monsters, were not above the law, as some proclaimed, Kavan had spent his morning listening with every sense he had to the words spoken against him, the thoughts of those who uttered them, and to the reactions of the audience gathered to hear it. If they supported him as it seemed, why could they not rally together to support other Elyri as well?

Why was it just him?

When it came to his fate, however, he did not think popular support would be enough to save him. Not having spoken of the events of that day to anyone, no one had yet questioned what had happened in that crowd before they reached the bridge, before the King had fallen. None of the guards had spoken of it, if they had even noticed, the suspicious stranger in the wide hat, because he had only been suspicious to Kavan. None seemed to have thought the adoring crowd worth mentioning, and because Kavan had not spoken of it either, no one would think to question what might have happened there.

If Kavan did not speak, his fate was sealed. If he did mention it, what then? Would he seem like a man seeking excuses, trying to save his life when he should accept whatever came?

"átaelás mai…"

His head whipped up at the voice as Chancellor McGranis took his place on the platform again. It was a familiar voice, yet one no one else heard, a voice that drew Kavan's focus to the back of the room where a gray-cloaked figure lingered beneath the archway, shaking his head. Or it seemed he shook his head; Kavan was not sure. There was too much distance between them. What he knew, however, what he recognized in that chastising tone that still echoed in his head, was that he was failing, falling into that familiar trap of self-blame and the willingness to accept unnecessary suffering merely to feel worthy of love and to take pride in his ability to suffer.

Tears pricked his eyes and when he hung his head to hide them, he knew Kóráhm was gone. The Heretic-Saint had made his point. It was not Kavan's place to withhold the truth to influence the outcome. It was his duty to tell it and leave the rest in k'Ádhá's hands.

"Are there other witnesses to approach regarding the events on the day of…"

Wace Elotti was on his feet before the chancellor finished his request. "I will," he grunted.

The chancellor shifted awkwardly, glanced at the Queen who nodded, and then beckoned the big man forward. There was no reason not to hear the intimidating man's testimony, whatever it was.

"State your name and occupation for the record." It was a requirement requested of every witness save the guards, because everyone knew what those men did and their names had all been recorded prior to the hearing.

"Wace Elotti," the dark man said with a twist of his lips. "I think you all know what I do."

His words, his tone, had the desired effect. The infamous bounty hunter was known throughout the Sovereignties by people on both sides of the law. His name seeped into the dark crevices of myth where Kavan's light did not penetrate. His was a name to be feared, respected, avoided, and yet he was presented to the Queen as a proud but humble man with few knowing on whose behalf he had come.

Not even Kavan, when he lifted his teary eyes to look at the hunter he had met long ago, knew why the great bulky man was here. He, like others in the room, held his breath and waited.

"Yes." The chancellor coughed. "Well…you are a witness to…?"

"I am summoned for my expertise in many areas…to examine the murder weapon with the intent of finding the killer and where he…"

"He is there!" someone shouted, pointing at the bard from the midst of the crowd.

"Silence!" barked General Agis, his position in the Lachlan House affording him the right and duty to keep order. No other voice raised to join the lone cry of dissension and the general turned his attention back to the other Cíbhóló, whose identity he now knew, to hear what he would say. He had not been shown the murder weapon, no one had thought to ask him about it, and he wanted the truth too.

Elotti smirked. "I don't believe he is. This…" He opened the small box entrusted to him that morning and showed it first to the chancellor and then to the Queen and Prince Espen, "is not meant to be a weapon. This is a kwolott…a Cíbhóló wedding jewel worn by our women from the day of their marriage onward. It is never intended to kill, to poison. That would be dishonorable. Only someone familiar with its purpose, familiar with the way it is attached to the body, would likely choose to use it the way this has been used. I have yet to meet anyone in Enesfel, save those familiar with the desert, who know that."

"General Agis? Is this true? Is Mr. Elotti's description of the jewel and its use accurate?"

The general approached the platform to look into the box for the first time. As the jewel now lay on its side, the tines plainly visible, what it was, was obvious to him. "Aye, chancellor. It is a kwolott…the biggest I have seen from a family of great wealth I wager."

"Thank you." Flannery looked back at Wace and cleared his throat. "Why do you believe the Duke did not use this?"

"He has never been to the desert. He does not know the way of my people," Elotti replied. "If he could not identify it, he would not know its purpose. The only men I have known with kwolotts outside of my homeland have used them for decoration on saddles and leather bags. I have never known any non-Cíbhóló to be willing to press them into flesh. It is not a…pleasant…experience."

Titters and grimaces circled the room.

"Is there anything else?"

"I have seen the duke's clothing from that day…and the King's…I have seen his saddle. The degree of blood loss was too high for the brief time frame these gentlemen," he glanced at the soldiers clustered together on one side of the platform, "describe. Such blood loss from such tiny punctures in a man's thigh would have been impossible unless he had been bleeding for several minutes…even if a substance, a poison, was used to discourage clotting of the blood."

He closed the box, tempted to hand it to Kavan, but instead handed it to Owain. "Such an item could not have been shot at a distance; there would be no way to control it, to make certain it embedded in a target. Someone had to apply it by hand, someone near enough to…"

"The soldiers have all testified that Duke Cliáth was the one…"

"At the moment the King succumbed to the poison, yes…it may be true that the duke was at his side. Men riding side by side. But it took time to lose so much blood, time for the poison to travel his system. Someone needed to be near enough before that moment to wield the kwolott, to make this happen."

The guards looked at one another with concern. If the bounty hunter spoke true, then perhaps they had been negligent and none of them wanted to admit that possibility. A nearly toothless fellow seated several rows behind Prince Owain staggered to his feet and said, "We all touched him," in a grief-stricken voice.

"Touched who? Who is we?" asked Flannery.

"The King…all of us…as they passed in the street…in front of Cobbler Planitry's. We wanted to thank him…such a good boy he was…ridding Rhidam of those damned Corylliens. He shook our hands as we thanked him."

The chancellor's lips pursed in annoyance. "Is this true? Were people allowed to touch the King?" When none spoke, still exchanging glances silently with one another, Flannery turned to Kavan. "My Lord, is this true?"

No one had asked Kavan for his testimony, beyond asking whether the soldiers' recollections were accurate. No one had asked if there was more to that day than those few moments when the King fell bleeding from his horse. Elotti was the one to raise the possibility, to give Kavan a chance to speak, for which the bard was grateful. He had not planned to defend himself, but, chastised by Kóráhm, he knew he had to speak if there was any chance to clear his name.

"It is true that people gathered to greet the King," he replied meekly, head still bowed. "They crowded around his horse to touch him, shake his hand, thank him…they pushed between us…until the guards forced them back to allow us to continue on our way."

"How long did this go on?" Flannery queried.

"Five minutes…perhaps ten…no more."

"How long after that did it take to reach the bridge, the place where King Hagan fell?"

It was not a great distance, but with the horses at a walk, the King in no hurry to return to the keep, it had taken longer than it might have otherwise. "Fifteen minutes perhaps, maybe less."

Bleeding, dying, all that time, and Kavan, preoccupied with what he perceived to be an attempt on his life, had failed to notice. His head hung again, this time in shame. He might not have killed the young man, but he had failed to save his life.

"Then this weapon could have been utilized by anyone in the crowd…and could have been there nearly thirty minutes before he fell and you caught him?"

"No one would dare!" exclaimed one of Kavan's accusers, although even he knew that someone, either Kavan or someone else, had dared, making the outburst meaningless. A stern look from the chancellor silenced him and he waited with embarrassed squirming beneath the on-looking eyes of the audience.

"You may sit, Mr. Elotti. Unless there is more you wish to say?"

Smiling, satisfied that he had done what he could to prompt Kavan to speak in his own defense, and that the questions he raised threw doubt on the accusations and evidence against the bard, Elotti nodded to the Queen and returned to his seat next to Owain.

The chancellor cleared his throat again and refocused on Kavan. "My lord…a few more questions before we hear further testimony. Have you ever been in the desert, among the nomads there?"

"I have not."

"Have you ever had dealings with any Cíbhóló, beyond General Agis and Mr. Elotti."

"I met a few who had come to fight with Prince Arlan before he became…" He chose not to finish in deference to Owain. "I did not know them, only met them in passing."

"Were there women among them? Any who wore this kwolott?"

"There were no women with them."

"Did you, or did you not, know what the item was when you removed it from the King's person?"

"I did not." There was other information he could volunteer, but he decided against doing so. Explaining that he knew it had been the source of the poison, that he believed he knew what poison had been used, would open the door to a discussion of Elyri abilities that did not belong in this hearing.

"When the King was greeting his subjects, did you see, hear, or detect anything unusual? Anything or anyone out of place?"

Kavan began to shake his head no but that stab of guilt returned along with the weight of familiar hands pressing on his shoulders. He sighed. "There was someone…I could not see their face, only a hat…a wide-brimmed brown felt hat. I thought he…I believe it was a man…intended me harm…but as the crowd jostled and pushed back against the guards I lost sight of whoever it was, lost sense of them. I thought I was the target, so when I could not see him, I thought the danger past. I lost track of him and did not think they might have…that they could have…that King Hagan could have been…"

There had been no reason for him to suspect that. The King had been too innocent to be an assassin's target. "I am sorry, My Queen," he murmured without making eye-contact with her.

Diona opened her mouth to speak but refrained. Anything she did, a show of sympathy or anger, could be used against her and against Kavan. Instead, she looked away, across the sea of subjects in her Hall, as if gauging their reactions and moods.

"Thank you, my lord, that will be all. Sit. Please." The chancellor too, studied the audience before asking, "Are there any present who witness the greeting of King Hagan?" He would have previously questioned the townspeople if he had been told about that crowd, but the soldiers had not mentioned it and Kavan refused to speak. It made Flannery feel like a fool but he was determined to make the best of the task he had been given.

One by one, hands were raised, peasants and merchants alike with tales of touching the King. They described how he had been dressed that day, the location, identifying details that helped prove they were present on the day of King Hagan's ill-fated ride through his city. There was a possibility that some were merely reciting details previously spoken by others, but even Claide knew he could not demand a reading of those witnesses without exposing the opposing witnesses to the same. Many spoke as well of reaching out to Kavan to touch him in the hopes of a miracle or in gratitude for the kindnesses he so often bestowed on those in need.

There was finger-pointing and name-dropping as some sought to lay blame for the monarch's death on the shoulders of some disliked rival or neighbor. The sheriff, present at the side of the room, took down each name to probe the claims but few believed those allegations to be factual. What the testimonies did suggest, however, was that enough people had been near the King that day to make an unseen, unnoticed attack too easy. It was, by appearances, negligence and the King's own stubbornness that allowed an assassin to draw close, although none of them, guards, Kavan, or the King himself, could have anticipated an assassination attempt on a man with no known enemies…

…except the Corylliens.

The chancellor bid the last witness to resume her seat. None of Kavan's family had spoken, but the Queen suspected that was because she had forbidden unnecessary statements regarding the bard's character. Diona knew his character better than most. The man who had forgiven her cruelty, who had advised her father through hardship and war was not, she believed, a man capable of killing her brother. While the revelation of a crowd around the King did not prove innocence, nor did the soldiers' stories prove guilt. What the revelation did was raise doubt, enough doubt to draw a sour expression over Claide's face, enough doubt for the Queen to proceed to the next phase of the trial. She nodded to the chancellor who bowed and called, "The evidence, please," to the palace staff at the side of the room.

Clothing, both the King's and Kavan's, was brought to a table set on the platform. The King's riding saddle was produced and Owain brought forward the box with the murder weapon. When the prince was seated and the staff had resumed their places, Flannery spoke.

"To avoid the bias of family performing the readings, two men of renown have been presented to the Queen for this purpose. gdhededhá Bhílári…bhydáni Tíbhyan, please come forward."

Bhen assisted the sage to his feet and to the platform, while Bhílári brought the old man's chair for him. Those who had not already noticed the wrinkled, stooped Elyri noticed him now; curiosity aroused, they craned their necks to see him better. On the other side of the room, Claide's expression grew darker and when Bhílári remained at the sage's side, Claide felt he had been tolerant long enough.

"The Faith is not to be involved," he said as he rose again.

"It seems to me," Bhílári said with a hint of anxiety in his voice, "That you have involved the Faith with your presence and continued interruptions…"

The bald man glowered, "I forbid…"

Perplexed expression on her face, the Queen stared at Claide as if daring him to continue as she said, "Forbid? These gentlemen are here at my summons, to resolve the matter in accordance with your request that no family member be permitted to do the readings. I require two witnesses to be read, one for and one against, to determine the validity of the accusations and rebuttals. Who better than a respected member of the Faith? The Crown recognizes his long-standing service and accepts his offer to aid in uncovering the truth. You cannot," she added wryly, "expect Master Tíbhyan to do it alone. You have no authority over either of them, k'dedhá."

Particularly, she thought bitterly, as they were debating the separation of Teren and Elyri Faithful. She did not need to mention that for Claide to understand her.

Unsurprised by his resistance, she imagined anger rolling off of Claide like steam whistling out of a heated kettle. When he presented no further argument and did not attempt to interrupt again, she turned to her guests. "Are either of you blood kin to the accused?"

"No, Your Majesty," both said in near unison.

"Do you swear to speak of everything you learn from these things, speak the truth regardless of who is harmed by the revelations?" She did not know how such matters were conducted in Elyriá if either man had ever been called upon to serve publically in this capacity, but the questions had to be asked for the record, for the sake of those present, and to appease the increasingly angry k'dedhá.

He likely would not believe anything they said unless it condemned Kavan irrevocably, but at least she would have obeyed the law and custom of Enesfel.

The sage bowed his head. "You have my oath."

"And mine," added Bhílári.

"Then proceed, Lord Chancellor. Call your witnesses."

As the items were presented one by one to Tíbhyan so that he did not need to stand at the table to read them, Bhílári faced the daunting task of reading the four individuals brought to him, two of the soldiers and two of those from the audience who claimed to have touched the King on his last day alive. The dedhá said nothing as he touched each frightened, anxious person, aware that it was his position in the faith that permitted them enough calm to allow the process to be completed.

The bhydáni, however, spoke his findings aloud as he progressed from one item to the next, describing in detail everything he could see, feel, hear, smell, and even taste, of the King's final hour alive. He spoke of how the King had been elated by the attention, how he resisted the efforts of the guards to interfere. How there had been a slap on his thigh as the crowd was forced back, how he believed that smack had come from one of the soldiers attempting to spur his horse into action. How he had bled without noticing as he gradually grew weaker, disoriented, out of breath. How he clung to the bard as he fell and asked to return to the keep because he did not feel well. Tíbhyan revealed how Kavan had caught the falling man and removed the jeweled object when it was noticed, thinking it harmless until its removal resulted in increased blood flow. He told how Kavan had been yanked away from the King, despite his insistence that he thought he might be able to save Hagan, how the King landed on the ground uncaught. How the jewel had been snatched from his hand by the soldier who had in turn been poisoned. How Kavan had been kept under guard until he was placed in the dungeon.

Tíbhyan was prepared to read the murder weapon, a dangerous task since he was aware that the tines had been coated with some manner of lethal toxin, but the door at the rear of the Hall flew open, jarring everyone's attention. Bhílári's hands fell away from the nervous soldier he had just finished reading.

Asta Dugan strode through the room, down the center aisle, her long strides reminding many of her father as she led Matus, Captain Delamo and their captive to stand before the throne.

"Your Majesty," Asta said with a grin and a bow. Behind her, Wortham likewise bowed but he did not speak. He was, instead, watching the tension in Kavan's posture, trying to determine what he had missed of the trial, to gauge whether the testimonies were working in the bard's favor or against.

No matter. He believed he had the answer in front of him.

"Please excuse our absence…our late arrival…as we present to you Arvis Bayle…the man who killed King Hagan."

"It was an accident!" The man cried in tandem with the murmurs and gasps that washed through the room. "k'dedhá Claide bid me kill Duke Cliáth and I…"

More roars of dissent but this time the prelate erupted to his feet with a shout. "Lies! I have never seen this man! I would not…"

"But you did, Your Grace…you know you…"

"k'dedhá." The Queen's voice was clipped and cold and tinted with outrage at the man interrupting the trial, Claide's impertinence yet again, and the accusations and mutterings flying around the Hall.

"I demand the truth!"

"k'dedhá…one more outburst and you shall be removed from Our Hall…by force and in chains if necessary. Sit down!"

For several moments, the prelate remained still, glaring gaze locked with the Queen's as though debating how far he could push her, how far he was willing to dare. Finally, he did as commanded, arms across his chest, face flushed, his knees bouncing up and down furiously. But he no longer looked at the Queen. He was, instead, glowering at his accuser. The fit young man with scarred hands inched away from the prelate as far as the captain's hold would allow.

"Chancellor McGranis…if you would."

As stunned as everyone else by this sudden turn of events, Flannery cleared his throat. "Mr. Bayle," he stammered, afraid he would somehow create a disaster out of this gift he had been given. "You say there was an accident…that Duke Cliáth was your intended target…not the King. If this is true, tell us how it came to be that the King is dead and Duke Cliáth is seated here, accused of your crime?"

"It is true, my lord. The crowd was too thick. I couldn't reach the duke. I was nearly to him but the guards pushed us back. My hat was knocked off; when I tried to get it, I was put off balance. I put my hand out to steady myself, realized too late what was done. I didn't know who I…I hoped I'd poisoned the horse…or hit the saddle…or anyone else…then I heard…and I knew…" His teeth were chattering, his body shuddering from head to toe with fear and remorse but with his hands bound behind his back he could not brush away the tears that dribbled down his cheeks and chin.

"How did you come in possession of such a unique weapon? Was it yours? Was it your idea?"

"I ain't that smart, sir…no, my lord, it was given to me…"

"By whom?"

"Don't know." He shuffled his feet and hastily continued. "Didn't see his face. I was going home from the Boar's Garden when this fellow grabbed me by the throat and pushed me into the alley. Thought he was going to rob me…kill me…but he asked if I was serious about wanting to be rid of the Elyri influences on the King. Of course, I said, and he gave me the jewel, the poison, told me what to do…how to do it…that Faith would give me my chance. When he left me, he dropped his hat…so I took it…thought he'd get the blame…"

Claide's face bled from bright red to dark crimson as he fought for each outraged breath. Kavan watched both, their agitation chaffing against his perceptions like a too loose shoe. He detected no falsity in either man's words, both were firm in their beliefs and convictions, but the prelate's demeanor suggested there was something that neither was admitting to.

"You say k'dedhá Claide instructed you…"

"He did! Many times."

"But the individual in the Boar's Garden alley was a stranger?"

"Aye, that is true."

"bhydáni?"

The ancient sage, still hunched on his platform chair with both Bhen and Bhílári behind him, was listening to these new details while his gnarled fingers traced the orange jewel in the box on his lap. He could read this man's imprint on it, but there were traces of something more troublesome as well, someone stronger in will than the man the chancellor was interrogating, if not also stronger in body. Something…female. Something meant for Kavan. The puzzle put a scowl on his face, and he thought his expression prompted the Queen's address. He closed the box and raised his head.

"Your majesty?"

"Will you read him. Please. The day wanes and I would like this finished before the sun sets."

"I will." He handed the box to Bhen, the brush of his fingers against the other man's telling Bhen to hold on to it, not to put it on the table with the other items. "…if someone will bring him to me."

"No Elyri will touch me," Bayle spat, struggling against Wortham's iron grip.

Weary of interruptions and being defied too many times this day, the Queen crossed the platform and yanked Wortham's sword from its scabbard. She did not know how to wield it, but when the captain forced Bayle to his knees in front of the bhydáni, she pressed the blade to the back of Bayle's neck.

His inhaled breath robbed the breath from everyone in the Hall.

"He will, or I shall execute you here, now, for my brother's death," she hissed in a voice unlike any ever heard from her. There was a similar note of fury and retribution that some had heard from her father on the night he won the throne, a resolve to right wrongs that were an offense to earth and Ethenae, to Teren and Elyri alike.

Bayle blinked, swallowed hard, and slowly nodded, accepting the wrinkled hands on his head in spite of his outrage. Undoubtedly he would be punished, but he hoped that the accidental nature of the crime would provide him leniency. Living the rest of his life in the dungeon would be preferred to a humiliating public execution.

A few moments later, the sage's hands fell away. "He speaks true. His directives from the k'gdhededhá came in the form of altar teachings…directives such as suffering practitioners of sorcery not to live…keeping the law pure…that those who lead others astray should be condemned to death lest others be brought low."

Claide relaxed enough that Kavan could feel it, though there was no visible evidence and the bard shivered. These were words he knew well from decades of Faith teachings from the Holy Texts read during the Gatherings. Taken out of context, such quotes could easily be manipulated to foster hatred and violence, just as they had been done for this poor man's hearing. Kavan could not help but feel pity for the fellow, but not so much pity as to wish the man to go free.

Sermonizing aside, men had a mind, a will of their own. It was his own choice to act upon the words he had heard.

"He had been drinking in the Boar's Garden, discussing anti-Elyri propaganda," the old man's voice rattled as he shivered and swayed on his seat. Bhen steadied him between his young hands. "Others were there. Some left before him…a hat…a…woman…"

He shook his head to be rid of the suddenly distorted image that tried to form in his mind's eye and abruptly evaporated. "It was not her…it was someone else…tall…strong…wiry. The stranger offered the weapon…the instruction…promised ecclesiastical favor in Ethenae…and the rest you know.

The Queen lowered the sword and returned it to Wortham's hand. "Did you learn anything from the weapon?"

"Nothing we have not already heard. Whoever handled it before him wore gloves, for there is no trace of the touch of this other."

The room was silent now, save for the creak of benches and chairs beneath anticipatory shifting. Diona looked around the Hall, using the stillness to settle her racing heart. She remembered being where they were, awaiting rulings from her father, her brother, quick to make judgment and not quite understanding what it meant to be on this throne as the judge of men. Not understanding how the fate of the kingdom would teeter before her, waiting for the balanced scales to tip one way or the other. The quick to judge, impetuous part of her nature already screamed at her, telling her what she should do, and though she believed that assessment to be right, she realized she must make it appear that she was giving the matter considerable thought.

Diona returned to the throne, resisting the impulse to take strength in the touch of Espen's hand. She had to appear strong on her own and make do with his comforting presence beside her. Any decree she made must be made from this throne. Not yet crowned though still legally the rightful ruler of Enesfel, she needed the act of speaking from the Lachlan throne to lend weight to what she was about to say.

Her gaze settled on the soldiers who had been with the King and Kavan on that fateful day. "Gentlemen. Your negligence in protecting the Duke and the King has resulted in an unfortunate chain of events.

Your actions were not malicious, not intentional, and knowing my brother as I did, I am sure he ordered you back to allow the people to come to him. Because of this…because you could not have foreseen what was to come, you will be spared execution or fines. However," she continued before they could enjoy any sense of relief, "you should have intervened faster when the crowd grew too large, should have sought to protect the Duke as well, and you jumped to conclusions rather than permit the Duke to make an effort to save my brother. If you had done any of those things, Hagan might still be alive. Negligence and bias and rash judgment cost us a king, and for that, you will each be suspended from duty for thirty days without pay, demoted to the lowest ranking, and receive the appropriate cut in salary. Serve well, learn from this unfortunate affair, and you may regain what rank you have lost."

Each man bowed, ill-pleased with suspension, demotion, and diminished pay, but at least their lives had been spared and they had not been dismissed from duty or banished from Enesfel. They could start again, something their late King could not do.

Her next words were spat as if bitter. "General Agis, will you and Mr. Gardieu take Mr. Bayle to the dungeon. You, sir, will be held while I decide your fate. You may not have intended to murder the King, but you did intend murder, and that cannot go unpunished, particularly since your target was nobility…and because my brother died as a result of your choices. Your future will be decided within twenty-four hours and seen to swiftly, no matter what course it takes."

Bayle's face paled when he realized he might yet face death, but the Queen's gaze did not linger. Instead, it lighted on Claide. There were many decrees she desired to make against him, but his position in the faith and the relationship of the Faith to the Crown made such decrees tricky. As yet she had no solid proof to level against him, to accuse him of high treason as she desired, and was forced to ignore her instincts in favor of diplomacy and patience.

Finally, she looked at Kavan, whose long-suffering expression of exhaustion and sorrow cut into her enough to bring the grief she had not yet faced bubbling to the surface. Confining him to the dungeon had not been the worst punishment she had given…for a crime he had not committed. The worst she had done had been denying him the right to grieve with the rest of his family. On top of her other offenses against him, she wondered if the bard would ever forgive her or love her again as he had when she was a child.

"Lord Chancellor, release Duke Cliáth." There was no wild cheering, but friends, family, and supporters clasped one another's hands, smiled, or sighed and murmured praise in relief. The Queen did not offer an apology here in the public eye, believing that would be inappropriate in this instance, but most in the Hall were satisfied with her decision. The guilty had confessed. There was no need to hold Kavan. "My lord, the Crown is satisfied with your innocence. Go in peace; this matter is hereby resolved."

She wanted to remain, to speak to him, to those who had come on Kavan's behalf, but duty commanded her to be the first to exit the Hall. With the prisoner no longer in his control, Wortham gestured to Ártur and the others to follow him, though he remained long enough to watch the chancellor unbind the bard's wrist. He spoke low into Asta's ear and it was the inquisitor-princess who approached Kavan, took his hand, and drew him out of the impending crush of the crowd the Lachlan guards were herding towards the doors.

It would be too like Kavan to fly, to seek solitude now that he was cleared of charges and freed, but Wortham believed that this time what the bard needed most was to be loved by those who had come to support him.

With the Queen out of the room, there came shouts in the thinning crowd, words of blessings and congratulations and offerings of prayer for his continued well-being. There were no spoken slurs, no threats, though Kavan could feel those negative emotions too. For the moment, he kept his feelings inside, unexplored and unacknowledged. Had he expected, even hoped, to be found guilty, he wondered, as he entered the library where friends and family waited. Had he believed it would help, or he admitted with a sense of shame, had he felt he deserved punishment for not having prevented Hagan's death, not having warned him, for not being able to save him?

"Praise k'Ádhá you are free and that's over!" Not surprisingly, Ártur was the one to speak first and throw his arms around his cousin. "We knew you were innocent!"

"But we admit your refusal to speak frightened us." Owain saw no reason not to be honest about his fear and no reason not to speak on behalf of the others who had felt the same way.

"I..." Kavan tried to extract himself from his cousin's embrace.

"...could have been executed!" the healer finished.

Tíbhyan shook his head, using a hand hooked around Kavan's arm to pull him away from Ártur. "The Queen needed this," the sage said.

"A public trial?" asked Bhílári.

"The opportunity to show no bias," Kavan replied, thankful that the bhydáni understood. "To show Enesfel where her convictions lie, to do right by Hagan in bringing his killer to justice." He looked at Wortham. "How did you find…?"

"It was all Princess Asta, my lord," Wortham said with a grin. "I no more than aided in the capture."

Though Asta was beaming, waiting with the bounty hunter who seemed to be part of the group even as he remained apart from it, she looked at the much larger man and said, "The three of us, and Matus, together…"

The door opened as she spoke; the Queen and Espen entered. "Together?" Diona asked.

"A man full of drunken remorse and bitter failure leaves a trail," Asta explained. "Mr. Elotti found it, Matus and I followed it, and the captain executed the arrest."

"I still think k'dedhá is guilty," muttered Gaelán as he and Sóbhán replaced the healer by hugging Kavan from each side.

Diona, unaware of what Gaelán knew, asked, "What do you mean?"

Intuitively, sensing Diona's frustration and upset, Kavan's body turned as if to shield his nephew from her though he knew she would not strike him.

"He gave no orders," Bhílári began.

Bhyrhán grunted, "With such lessons from the lectern, he did not need to."

Gaelán shook his head, his brow knit in annoyance. "I don't know if he did or did not…but he knew. He knew about the attempt on k'aendhá…he knew that it failed and was angry about it…angry that Hagan had been…" He choked on the final unspoken words and Sóbhán rubbed his arm with one hand to comfort him.

"You should have said…"

"No." The chamberlain did not care if he was interrupting or contradicting. "He told Asta…that is enough. I would not have my son made a target for making public accusation against the k'dedhá."

Madalyn, clutching his hand, her other arm around her too-quiet eldest son's shoulders, agreed. She could see that Gaelán refused to look at his brother, and she worried about Tayte's too cool stare. "It would be too easy to claim he learned of the plan, the attempt, the failure during Purification. There would be no proof."

"Proof or no," snorted Tayte, pulling out of his mother's protective embrace as though embarrassed, "I would have spoken. Cowardice will allow…"

"Tayte." His father's stern tone made Tayte bite his tongue and the two stared at one another, the older man trying to deduce if Tayte actually believed that such a risk would have helped against Claide or if his words were intended as an inflammatory accusation against his brother. There was nothing in Tayte's expression to suggest either prospect and that blankness concerned Bhríd as much as the truth would have.

Diona swallowed a breath, held it, then exhaled slowly. "You are right, Lord Chamberlain. I do not wish threats to come upon Gaelán any more than on the rest of you. It is enough…too much that…"

Again Kavan bowed his head, this time to avoid the woman's gaze. "Such threats are a product of who I am…what I…"

"No," protested Ártur.

"…do," Kavan continued. "And yes, Ártur…what I am. Accept it. You, Bhríd, Gaelán…those of us who serve the Lachlans do so at great risk. It is a risk we have chosen to accept, but we cannot foolishly deny the risk exists. My position is well-known, as I am -known. As long as I remain…we remain…the threats will continue against us."

"You are not leaving." The thought of ruling Enesfel without Kavan, without the advice and guidance the bard had given her father, her brothers, her friends, but more importantly without his support, spoken or not, was unfathomable.

"My Queen." Kavan released the boys in order to face her. "That day may come…but it is not this one. There are duties I am sworn to perform. If my efforts prove successful, there may be no need for any of us to consider withdrawing from Enesfel. If they are not…we will confront that possibility when the day arrives. For now, be assured that I will remain in your service, should you wish it."

"And I," Bhríd said emphatically.

"And I," added Ártur; and though he suspected his wife was less than pleased about his decision, he knew it did not surprise her.

"And me," Gaelán exclaimed, having no desire to be left out. From the side of the room, Asta smiled.

Diona looked at each one, lingered briefly on Bhyrhán who grinned with a shrug and said only, "I have not grown bored of Rhidam yet," before returning to Kavan.

"Your loyalty and devotion are appreciated…though I can hardly claim to deserve it." Lachlan or not, queen or not, she had made too many serious mistakes to believe she deserved loyalty from any of them. "Mr. Elotti." Looking at him meant she could, she hoped, avoid the emotions surging within that she had not yet faced. "Whatever Prince Owain and Captain Delamo offered for your services, I shall double it for what you have done for the Crown and for Lord Cliáth."

The big Cíbhóló shook his head. "I didn't do it for a fee, Your Majesty. What I have done was for Lord Cliáth, nothing more." Kavan nodded gratefully and Elotti smiled. While they had not known each other well, had barely spoken in fact, there had been a peculiar instant bond between them. He had known they would meet again, and now they had met a second time. Neither man believed in coincidence. "Protect him…rule long and well…and I'll consider the debt cleared."

"That is an agreement I shall endeavor to uphold as long as the throne is mine," she promised. As Enesfel's first female ruler in centuries, as the second Lachlan woman to reign from Enesfel's throne, and following on the heels of her father's success and her brother's short-lived, tumultuous reign, Diona understood that she had a difficult future ahead, particularly with the weight of Elyri persecution on her shoulders. But she was a fighter, stubborn like her father, and she had every intention of being the queen Enesfel needed.

She crossed the room, leaving Espen near the door, and offered her hand to Tíbhyan and then Bhílári. "Gentlemen…I cannot thank you enough for the risk you took in coming. Ártur told me little about you, but the duke must be dear to both of you for you to have come. Please know you are welcome here for as long as you wish to stay."

Tíbhyan smiled, but his warm expression was directed at the man behind her. "I have known him most of his life, and if there is one thing I know, it is that he would not have done the acts he was accused of. I have every faith in him; his freedom is reward enough."

"My only regret is that we could not do more." Bhílári had secretly hoped, when coming to Rhidam, to find the shreds of proof in Claide that would lend credence to gdhededhá Khwílen's accusations. He felt darkness in Claide's stare, in his voice and words, but beyond the apprentice healer's accusations, there was no actual proof that could lead to the new prelate's downfall…or that might connect him to something Dórímyr could use against him. Such proof was not going to fall into his lap, however. It would only be found through the hard work and risk that men like Khwílen and Kavan were taking. Bhílári had come for the trial, but he was too much of a coward to do more.

"You aided in procuring my freedom," Kavan murmured. "I could not ask for more..." He looked at Bhen, then Syl, then his aunt, still surprised to see her here, and added, "...from any of you."

Intimidated by those in the room, royalty, nobility, men in armor, men with swords, Dháná bobbed her head. These were people her son had known all of their lives, a queen he had helped to birth and raise, a place he had lived for as long as he had been a healer. She had known it, but she had not imagined what his life here could be like. She was beginning to understand. What she was also beginning to understand, based on the reactions of the crowd gathered for Kavan's trial, based on the expressions and devotions of the people in this room, was how controversial...how adored and loved yet also feared and hated...her nephew was. In this place, in this world, the peculiar boy she had raised had grown to be larger than life, and more influential, it appeared, then she or her husband could ever have realized. How she wished Tám had come to see this. Wished he could have seen that Kavan had become something more important than an embarrassment to the name of Cliáth. It would have done both Kavan and Tám significant good to have the air cleared between them.

"We are honored to have helped you, my lord," Wortham reminded him, his gruff, gravelly voice quavering.

Owain reached across the space between them and brushed his fingers over Kavan's hand. "You have done too much for each of us not to desire to return the favor." There were too few occasions when Kavan needed, or would accept, help and support from those who loved him. Most often it was him supporting or helping them. They needed to return some small measure of the love he gave. Arlan would have said and done the same had he been here.

"Muir will regret being unable to be part of today...but there was no time," Gabrielle said, worry in her voice still despite the danger being past. "Word was sent, of course, but he will have just received it, or be on his way home."

Kavan suspected as much. In truth, he was surprised that so many had come together so quickly and was deeply touched by their efforts. "Tell him..." Kavan shook his head, changing his mind. "I will send a letter home with you for him, if you will deliver it, my lady." There was something he felt he needed to say to the Lachlan prince that he could not deliver via the mouths of others. His message would raise questions for which he did not yet have answers.

Angry voices clashed in the courtyard, a short-lived spat of anti-Elyri protest against Kavan's stalwart supporters. The palace guards broke up the confrontation, but not before Bhílári's face lost color. "I must get back," he muttered. Hearing about the persecution, about the slurs and attacks in Enesfel, was much different than hearing those things himself. He had no desire to remain long enough to experience anything more deadly than words overheard through an open window.

"You need not fear, dedhá," the Queen assured him.

"No, he is right," Kavan sighed. "I want no more blood on my hands."

"My brother's blood is not…"

"I did not cause it…but I could not prevent it either. I could not save him. That is blame enough. You are all safe here, but there is always a chance…"

"Please…Kavan. Before we leave you…a song or two?" Gabrielle felt no shame in asking. It was rare that she had the chance to hear him play, and there were those in the room she suspected who had not heard him in far longer. After coming close to losing him, a celebration song seemed the perfect form of communion.

And she suspected that after his days in confinement, after the turmoil of the trial, Kavan needed that outlet too.

Those around him, save for Dháná and, to a degree Bhílári, were the core support that Kavan relied on. But even those two had served their time and duty as his protectors when he was a child. Muir, Clianthe, and Caol were missing, along with those who had gone before them, but that could not be helped. If these people desired the gift of a song, after attending to show their backing, it was a debt Kavan would somberly repay.

"Sóbhán."

"Yes." The boy raced from the room without instruction needed.

Soon the instrument was in his hands and he gave his supporters songs of gratitude for their friendship, their strength, their love. Though he refrained for playing for Hagan, the way he wanted to do, the songs flowed for over an hour, past the dinner chime, to the cusp of nightfall as the last of the summer sun set behind the western edges of the country. The need of some to depart, the need to retreat from Rhidam faded into the sharing of a late evening meal as the Queen would not hear of sending guests away hungry and no one felt the compulsion to break up the fellowship too soon.

Dháná and Syl were the first to leave, the older woman not once speaking to her nephew but rather settling for a touch on his hand to convey words she could not form. Kavan had left her care at fourteen; in her eyes, he was still the boy she had raised that she was never able to care for as she thought she should have. Today she realized he was that child no longer. This was a man, a powerful, beautiful man who inspired devotion in commoners and royalty alike, whose music spoke of altruism in a way she had never been aware of. This was a man who, no matter what her husband believed, was no embarrassment to the ancient name he bore. This was a man they should be proud of. She returned to Bhryell hoping to convince Tám to give their nephew a respectful chance to be someone of worth. Tám was a difficult man to sway, his mind set against Kavan almost from the day of his birth, but perhaps she finally had what was needed to change his mind.

Ártur took Gabrielle back to Káliel with Kavan's handwritten messages for Muir and Clianthe. The Prime Magistrate felt no jealousy for that; she knew her daughter's pregnancy with Muir's child made her important to Kavan, and any discussion about that child, or about the support the two could not be here to offer, was best left between them and Kavan. Afterward, with Tíbhyan seeking private words with the bard, the healer returned with Bhílári to Bhryell and left Bhen in Wortham's company to wait for the sage. One by one the others left the library, Wortham most reluctantly.

The sage, to Kavan, looked as weary and frail as the bard felt. But he knew the man to be one of the strongest in spirit he knew. It was what had allowed him to be in Rhidam today.

"Thank you, bhydáni."

"Tíbhyan," the older Elyri reminded him with a smile.

"Tíbhyan." It was often difficult for Kavan to remember to call his mentor by name. "I did not think you would…that Ártur would ask…"

He squeezed Kavan's hand between his. "You needed me. It was good for this old soul to be needed. It doesn't happen often anymore, and it has been a long time since you needed me. When your cousin came, I could not refuse."

"You could have…but I am grateful you did not. Seeing you…all of you…the support from…"

"Perhaps it has made you realize you are not as much a monster as you sometimes think." Tíbhyan was teasing, but Kavan also knew the words were true. Being Elyri, yet different even from them, it was difficult to remember that he was not as alone as he often felt.

"Yes." Agreeing was logical, even if awkward. "You wanted to speak to me?"

"I do." From the pocket of his tunic, Tíbhyan produced the small box he had read earlier, which Bhen had slipped back into his care as the Great Hall cleared. Seeing that the sage still had it made Kavan's brow furrow.

"Read this."

Kavan took the box and opened it. "I have already held it," he reminded Tíbhyan. "I saw nothing…"

"Your focus was on a dying king, in saving a life. You did not look…but I believe you must."

Wondering if there was something Tíbhyan had withheld from the Queen and the court, something that could have condemned him, Kavan pressed one fingertip to the orange stone and opened his senses to see what his mentor had seen. It was not his eyes that saw, however, not even an image in his mind's eye. There, in the darkness of an object devoid of the usually expected flood of contact images, was a presence. A rancid, clawing, familiar presence contained within the aura of a spiteful, vengeful woman. He did not know her, had never seen her…felt her…but through her, the malicious spirit that had followed Kavan through his voyage back to Rhidam could be felt. Her darkness made him physically ill and he dropped the box and its contents as he doubled forward, clutching his stomach.

"You know her?"

Kavan shook his head. "I do not." And yet, the loathing she felt seemed too personal to come from a stranger, too personal to be the product of anti-Elyri hatred. Perhaps she was the woman he had Seen in his visions of the lake, though he had felt no such hatred in those glimpses of Sight. Perhaps she served as host to that spirit, the spirit of Coryllien, a spirit that hated him, wanted him dead. "And yet…there is familiarity."

"Watch for her, Kavan. Do not let her too close. Do not allow her to…win." Tíbhyan scowled as he said those words, wondering what had prompted him to say them. He did not have the Sight, and yet he knew there would be danger for Kavan ahead. Kavan was strong, but was he strong enough for her?

Was there anything else Tíbhyan could offer his favorite student that would make him stronger?

"Yes." He needed to be more vigilant. Kavan could feel the time of action drawing nigh and he could not allow her, or anyone else, to divert him from the healing path. She had tried, both through attempted assassination and through his pride, to remove him from play, had caused him to attempt to assume blame for Hagan's death in order to hinder his success.

Kavan made a promise to himself as he carefully closed the box. She would not come this close again.

❧Chapter 43❦

"Good evening, dedhá."

The man to whom he spoke inclined his head without lowering the hood but the soldier thought nothing of it. A late summer's rain had fallen since early evening, a welcome rain that relieved some of the stifling heat, and at this dark hour, no one could be too careful in shielding themselves for a trek across the city. It had been decreed that morning that the King's assassin would be beheaded in two days, to put his death, and the late King's murder, to rest before the Queen was crowned and wed. With k'gdhededhá Claide said to be far from Rhidam on official Faith business, seeing to the soul of the condemned had fallen to Tusánt or Rankin to carry out. The soldier at the dungeon door was not surprised to see familiar clerical robes, even if he was surprised at the late hour of the man's arrival. But a dedhá's work knew no set hours, regulated as it was by the needs of the faithful, and thus the lateness of this visit was not questioned. The soldier allowed him to pass saying, "Shouldn't be hard to find him. No one else is here."

Again with a silent nod, the dedhá strode past into the dimly lit, musty stench of the dungeon. It did not matter if the area was empty. The dying decay of previous prisoners seeped from the ancient stone to permeate the entire area.

Bayle looked up at the sound of approaching steps, a sound not accompanied by the usual clatter and creak of armor or weaponry. "dedhá," he said with relief. He was not in a cell but had instead been shackled in a dusty corner scattered with dry straw and a chamber pot. He got up from where he had crouched in the corner to kneel before his visitor. "dedhá, I repent truly for what I have done. I meant no harm to the King. You must believe me. Surely k'Ádhá understands that I was trying to do his will…"

"Ssh," the dedhá said, finger to Bayle's lips. His other hand rested on Bayle's head to bless him, calm him, but he said nothing more.

Bayle bowed his head. He did not need words, but rather blessing and forgiveness and, perhaps, someone to intercede on his behalf with the Queen. "Please beg her for mercy," he pleaded, trembling beneath that touch, finding comfort in the sound of long, rustling robes.

They were his final words. His hands grasped at his neck in reaction to the stinging slice that split his throat from ear to ear. He looked up with surprise, eyes wide, to peer inside the hood, and then he fell, twitching and convulsing, to one side, his body giving up its blood to the stone on which he lay.

The knife was wiped across his ragged trousers. Making sure they were alone, that they had not been overheard, the visitor lifted the hem of his robes to avoid dragging it through the blood, and with his other hand in his pocket, he left the dungeon with another nod at the attending soldier at the door who had heard and seen nothing.

ϟ*ϟ

With Kavan's trial behind them and Hagan Lachlan put to rest, the palace staff and residents turned attention to more positive matters: the coronation of Queen Diona and preparation for a simultaneous wedding. Little involved in the planning, wanting to maintain a low profile in the eyes of Rhidam's citizens, Kavan spent his time with Gaelán and Sóbhán in Bhryell with Tíbhyan, seeking the security of childhood and any form of training the sage could conjure to confront the woman they had both sensed, whenever that day came. Or he spent hours in front of the marble plaque that bore the names of the late Lachlan monarchs. Try as he did, he was unable to apologize enough to the young man, or the young man's father, for his failure to keep Hagan safe. He had known that some event would pass that would leave Diona as queen, but it did little to lessen his grief. If Kavan had the mercy of the dead, they would not reveal it, not even through the soothing presence of Saint Kóráhm or the hovering záryph.

It was there, at the resting place of kings, that Diona found him in the pre-dawn hours of another new day. He looked at her as she approached but then looked back at the etched stone. It was easier, as he still felt awkward and uncomfortable in her company.

"I am sorry you were not here when we buried him," she said softly, acknowledging his grief by avoiding physical contact.

"It could not be helped."

"It could have been." But they both understood why it had not been permitted, and Kavan accepted that as a necessity. "He was too young; it should not have been this way."

Running trembling fingers across the young king's name, Kavan swallowed his sigh. "I think, perhaps, it was as it was meant to be."

"Meant?"

He nodded but did not look at her. "I knew on the day you and Bertram were born that you were destined to rule. I knew he would have to…while you were sound enough in mind and body to be queen. There was no glimpse, no shadow, not a whisper revealing how it would come to pass…or when…or why…but I knew it would…and feared it all of his life."

Surprised by the revelation, Diona smoothed her dress beneath her nervous hands. "Did Father know?"

"Why do you think…?"

"He never allowed himself to get close to Hagan. He pushed him away the way he did Muir, left others to…"

"No. Arlan did not know until the night he died. Hagan reminded him of your mother, of her death…and he was never able to get beyond that. I tried to help him…"

"But we Lachlans are too stubborn for our own good…or the good of those we love." She tried to laugh but the sound was flat and feeble. "I…" She brushed tears from her lashes, refusing to cry. She remembered her father doing the same after her mother's death, remembered how grief had eaten at him through his life, and though she did not want to give into grieving when there were other matters that needed attention, she knew it would have to be done in time. "Since you knew...do you know what sort of ruler I will be?"

"That, My Queen, is up to you. The Sight has never shown me."

"Even if it had, you would not tell me…allowing me to forge my own future." She gave a half-smirk. "See, I have learned some things."

"Enough to be a great queen if you allow yourself to be."

"I would settle for a good Queen. Great may be too much to ask for. But I admit…I am afraid."

"Of what?" Fear was understandable after having endured the assassination of her brother. Any wise person facing the challenges that plagued Enesfel would feel fear. But Kavan hoped that, by addressing specific fears, he could offer enough comfort and peace of mind for her to rule with a steady hand.

"Failing…not being the monarch my father was…"

"You are not your father. As beloved as he was, he was not without shortcomings. You have what it takes to succeed. Do not strive to be like him; strive to be the best you can be. Your legacy will take care of itself."

"It isn't that…it's…marrying." She shuffled awkwardly, having never admitted that fear out loud. Now that she had tucked her infatuation with the bard into a box and locked it away, she wanted to return to the days when he had been willing to talk her through her troubles. "I remember little of their marriage…but I do remember how devastated Father was when she was gone. I remember…I see the difficulties between Lord Chamberlain and Madalyn…between Lord and Lady Healer…and I do not know if I am up to that task. It seems it must be…more difficult…in some ways than ruling Enesfel."

The bard shrugged, relieved the dialogue remained in relatively neutral territory. "I know little of marriage…except to say that any lengthy relationship between people will have its difficult moments. Even between friends. You are a strong woman, independent and intelligent, and Espen is a wise, patient, steadfast man. I believe, as long as you do not abuse that patience and he continues to accept your strengths without feeling threatened by them, you will have a long, healthy marriage. If nothing else, your joint stubbornness should allow you both to conquer difficulties that would destroy others."

"Or be what destroys us." Again she smoothed the front of her dress. "I hope your belief in my worth and abilities is justified." She knew he would not lie to her, but she did not feel assured, in these early days of reigning, in the strengths he praised. His words also did little to assure her that her marriage would be a good one. "At least I shall not have to contend with k'dedhá Claide for a few weeks."

"He has departed without incident?"

"Yesterday eve I am told, though why he did not wait until morning I cannot say. With him away, we can hope for calm and a chance for Rhidam to heal."

"We can hope," Kavan agreed. His hand dropped from the marble faceplate and after several moments listening to the early morning songbirds in the trees, he said, "You know I will be here for you…as I was for your father and Hagan. You have but to ask." He had not chosen to reinitiate the binding connection afforded by the half-moon pendants he and Arlan had shared. The thought of being bound to her in that fashion after the way she had hurt him was one he could not yet face. "I was hoping, however, if it is acceptable, to travel, to Alberni for a time, see to my estates…if Your Majesty allows."

It would also allow him time away from the marriage preparations, though he did not say that. The talk, the excitement, was making him uncomfortable. Tending to his estate was a logical excuse, a necessary duty to be performed periodically though he had recently been there and knew there was little there he needed to do.

"Of course, Kavan. Alberni is likely awash with rumors about your trial and you should put them at ease. See to it, but please return in time for the coronation."

Diona understood what Kavan did not say. He did not want to be in Rhidam for the execution of Hagan's killer, the man who had intended to kill him instead. She could not blame him for that, though she looked forward to that moment, that particular death, with uncharacteristic anticipation. His execution would be the turning of a page for her, the end of one chapter and the beginning of another.

It needed to be done.

The flutter of relief in Kavan's belly was undercut by Wortham's arrival. The captain's expression was grim and troubled, easily interpreted as the herald for disquieting news.

"What is it now?" Diona snorted, perceptive enough to also determine that Wortham was not bringing her pleasant information.

"Your Majesty." Kavan could hear how much it rankled his friend to address Diona that way after everything that had happened. Wortham had believed he would interact with her more easily than Kavan. Both men were aware that it was not so. "I am sent to report that the man held, Mr. Bayle, is dead."

"Dead? How can he be dead?" she exclaimed. The man appeared healthy, and though he had been given no special treatment during his incarceration, he had not, to her knowledge, been beaten or tortured.

"His throat was cut…"

"How? That is not…no one could have gotten near him."

This time, Wortham kept his mouth shut. It did him little good to begin to speak only to be continually interrupted. The Queen waited, and when he said nothing more, she barked, "Out with it, Captain."

"Perhaps, Your Majesty," Kavan murmured behind her, "If you would allow him to speak without interruption…"

She almost said something demeaning but bit her tongue instead. Though she was Queen, it did not give her the right to be impolite. She took a single deep breath and then tried to speak more calmly. "Captain…if you would…continue."

"Someone got in…someone professional it appears, or at least familiar with a blade, as the cut was clean and straight. There was no obvious sign of a struggle. The guards on watch overnight were taken to the barracks, where General Agis is interrogating them, under Princess Asta's supervision. No one else went in except two servants, one bringing dinner and the other breakfast…at which time he was already dead…and one of the dedhá…"

"Which one?"

This time, Wortham did not appear to mind the interruption. "I do not know. The guard on duty indicated the dedhá came late to pray with the prisoner and was cloaked, face hidden from the rain. He did not think it suspicious…"

"If their face was not seen, how does he know it was a dedhá?"

"The robes, Your Majesty."

"Then it should be easy to discover which one came. Captain, Lord Cliáth, come with me." Kavan's request to travel to Alberni was temporarily shelved. If a dedhá had come alone, it ruled out Tusánt, and Claide was last seen riding out of Rhidam in Duke Gabersdon's company. There were still many others it could have been, men and women alike, novices too.

The knot in Kavan's stomach demanded loosening, so rather than protest the command, he followed. It made little sense for a leader of the faith to bloody their hands with murder and none were, to his knowledge, experienced enough in combat to have slit a man's throat without a struggle. Some of the novices the Queen had helped select to protect Tusánt might have the skill, but Kavan could think of no reason why any would choose to kill a man scheduled for execution.

With the Queen on hand to oversee the interrogation in the náós, after the three of them and a gaggle of soldiers stormed through city streets to get there, in spite of many peoples' insistence that they could do their jobs better if they did not have to worry about her safety, every dedhá serving Hes á Redh was gathered in the thol for questioning while guards searched each room, each bedding area, each trunk and closet for a knife, a missing or soiled robe, or any other bit of evidence there could be. Valgis was not present, having previously gone out to visit a selection of housebound Faithful as he had been appointed to do by Tusánt the night before. He was being sought and summoned back while the investigation proceeded without him.

"I have not had mine since the day of the trial," dedhá Rankin said defensively when a searching soldier revealed that a robe matching the guard's description was not to be found in the dedhá's room. "They have to be cleaned, and sometimes go missing. I spilled serbháló during the Gathering that morning…I thought there some delay in the cleaning or that perhaps it was ruined and another was being provided in its stead."

"Is it true?" The Queen looked at the other clergy as Asta poked through the trunks and bags the soldiers continued to bring out. She knew that Tusánt and Claide had been at the castle for the trial and Rankin had arrived later, after the morning Gathering. Rankin had come in wearing different robes than the usual dark gray ones dedhá wore for everyday Gatherings, but even that had not seemed unusual as it was not the first time she had seen one of them wearing the pale blue robes typically worn during Purification and Initiation services.

"It is," said one of the female dedhá. "I cleaned the mantle and robe myself and hung them to dry."

"Then anyone could have taken it…"

"Including dedhá Tusánt." The soldier who spoke, a scarred man with a crooked nose held up two identical robes removed from Tusánt's trunk. One was clean and freshly folded, unworn recently. The other was rumpled with traces of staining on the breast, dust along the hem, and another darker substance along the edge of one sleeve. The Elyri dedhá grew pale.

"I would never…"

"Nor is it possible for him to have committed such a crime," Saul protested. "We were here, last night, in the náós."

"In the náós? At such a late hour?"

Kavan took Tusánt's trembling hand as the Queen spoke. Tusánt, understanding the bard's intent and trusting him, clasped the offered hand and clutched it to his chest.

"In prayer," Kavan murmured, seeing it, hearing in his head the voices gathered in supplication. It had been a gathering of those united against Claide, uncomfortable with his power, his beliefs, his position, a gathering to pray for the prisoner awaiting execution, for the Queen, for peace and prosperity for the ravaged sovereignty. Prayer for an end to violence. Nothing underhanded or suspicious, save for the late hour and their underlying unity against their elected k'dedhá.

Unwilling to expose them should they be trying to keep their feelings hidden from the man with control over their futures, Kavan said, "Offering prayers for the one to be executed…and for you, My Queen…from after the evening meal until after the midnight tolling."

"The guard said the dedhá came at the tenth tolling…which means it could not have been dedhá Tusánt." Asta was relieved to hear Kavan say it. Capturing and arresting Hagan's killer was one thing. Arresting a dedhá, a man she liked, would be something else. "The question remains; how did this get into your trunk?"

"I know not, I swear," Tusánt cried as Kavan dropped his hand.

"The trunk is kept locked, but the room is often empty as duty calls," Edward said. "Our rooms are not locked. Anyone could enter."

The bard held out his hand to Asta. "Perhaps if I…"

"No." The Queen shook her head. "Not here. Bring the evidence, the trunk and the robes, to the keep. None of you," she looked across the servants of the Faith with a warm yet stern expression, "are being accused or arrested, but I want none of you to leave Rhidam, to leave this náós, until this is settled." As steadfast dedhásur who lived beneath this roof, she knew it unlikely any would leave, but it was a command she felt compelled to give. "dedhá Tusánt, when dedhá Valgis returns, keep him here and send word to me at once."

He was no more a suspect than anyone else, but he was the only one, except for Claide, who had not been questioned.

"We will," Rankin assured her as he sidestepped to support his weak-kneed friend. Most of the group, those Kavan recognized from the prayer circle the night before, remained in the náós as the soldiers continued their search under the sheriff's supervision while Asta followed the Queen, Kavan, and captain back to the castle.

They passed the chamberlain as they arrived, the man's face strained and weary, and Diona motioned for him to join them. Bhríd was not having an easy time with his wife and both sons in Rhidam. Gaelán avoided his brother as much as possible, the responsibilities of his education and training consuming most of his time. The rest of his hours were spent with either Asta or Sóbhán. It had not kept Tayte from finding him, from hurling insults often overheard by his father, who chastised him soundly, and by his mother, who gave him long-suffering, troubled, disapproving looks but publically said nothing.

Kavan felt fear in Madalyn every time he caught sight of her, but he was unable to tell what she feared, or who, and he was never alone with her to ask. Perhaps Bhríd knew. Or perhaps, Kavan thought with a sigh as they entered the Stateroom, he did not need to ask. Fear for her children was reason enough for such a look.

"Lord Chamberlain," Diona said as the flock of attending guards was dismissed and Wortham closed the door. "Read this for us; tell us who wore it last."

Kavan frowned, wondering why the Queen had commanded him not to do it when he had offered. Bhríd, not knowing what was under investigation, however, seeing the various stains upon the fabric, took it from Asta without speaking. Such requests were commonplace enough that he had no cause to be suspect. It was in his hands only a few seconds before it fell to the floor. Bhríd, shaking his head, backed out of the room with a sickly expression of horror.

"Lord Chamberlain…come back…"

"Wortham, follow him." As uneasy as Bhríd had been of late, if he had seen something distressing in that contact, Kavan did not want him to be alone to do something foolish. And though Wortham would rather remain at Kavan's side, he obeyed out of respect.

Kavan squatted to retrieve the robe from the floor. "Reading clothing can be difficult, My Queen, and frequently unreliable. They pick up impressions from others we touch or brush against throughout the day…those we embrace or carry or bump against…"

"Then I want every name you can give me," she began, though she stopped at the grimace on Kavan's face as he curled his hand into the gray fabric.

"dedhá Rankin…dedhá Valgis…dedhá Tusánt," he murmured, picking out faces he knew from the forest of those available. Rankin was an affectionate man, prone to hugging, which led to an array of suspects. "There are many parishioners faces I do not know from after the Gathering. dedhá Hazen, Idal Gottfrid, young Lord Niall. He swallowed hard, "Tayte…"

"Tayte?" That explained her chamberlain's reaction, although it did not identify the cause of his distress. Kavan's reedy tense tone, however, made her suspicious. "Who wore it last? Can you tell? Are there any you judge to be a killer?"

"I cannot read someone's heart from such contact," Kavan murmured. "Rankin first…and it has not been cleaned since; he would have done so if he had." A fastidious man, and a wise one, he would not have stuffed the robe away without cleaning the evidence, whether into his own trunk or anyone else's. "The others…I cannot tell…"

"Then each will be summoned and questioned."

"Your Majesty, there are too many. An entire congregation. It will take Ártur too long to…"

"Then he had better start…"

"My Lady," Asta cleared her throat as she took the robe from the bard. "Is it necessary? I mean…the man was to be executed anyhow. We have been spared the expense of public execution. Does it matter who did it when he was already…?"

"It matters because it could have been any one of us!" Clergy access was not restricted to the keep; they came and went with the Lachlans' blessing. Yet if one of them was a killer, or if someone else had used holy robes to gain access, then the Queen would need to change the policy of unrestricted passage in and out of the castle. She was loath to do it, but she could see no readily available alternative.

In a softer tone she said, "And it matters because the people expect to see their King's murderer punished. There is nothing to show…"

"Then we execute someone in his stead." Asta shrugged as she said it. There was no lack of criminals in the city gaol, some destined to remain until death claimed them. Some were ill, already at death's door from dysentery or the pox, thus a swift execution would be a blessing. As Bayle was to have been beheaded, and the beheaded usually wore hoods over their faces, disguising the victim's identity would be a relatively simple arrangement, at least in Asta's eyes.

"I will not execute the innocent for…"

"Not the innocent, but rather…"

Diona lifted a hand to stay Asta's words. She would hear her cousin out because she valued the girl's training, knew the advice she gave would have been much the same as if coming directly from Caol. But she did not need to discuss the matter in front of Kavan.

"Lord Cliáth, have Ártur begin sketches. Start with the dozen you deem most suspect. Lady Asta will come for them later. We must begin somewhere; this matter cannot remain idle and ignored."

Kavan bowed, though he was reluctant to waste time with Ártur this way, and retreated from the room. There was no obvious suspect except one…and Kavan was as sickened at the thought as the young man's father had been.

Tayte was not an affectionate man. Even as a child he had been aloof, unwilling to be touched by any save his mother, and he was not known to attend Gatherings regularly now that he was old enough to manage his own schedule. When he did attend, it was at Madalyn's insistence, but she rarely did so. Kavan wondered if perhaps she had been too lenient and forgiving with him, but he could not, in good faith, blame Tayte's shortcomings or failings on his parents. No, whatever his faults were, they had sprung up recently without cause or priming by his family.

Why then was his presence strong on Rankin's robe? It was as if, to Kavan, Tayte had been the last to touch it. But it was impossible to tell if he had worn it as he gained no image of anyone putting it on or removing it, and with no other evidence yet to test, there was no way to guess what might have happened. Perhaps Bhríd could get the truth out of his son, but Kavan prayed the truth did not break his kinsman.

Sketches were created until well into the evening, with breaks taken for meals or whenever Ártur's cramping hands demanded rest. As each was finished it was sent out with the inquisitor's team of soldiers in order that each could be found and questioned. Asta would have done the questioning, but most saw her as too young to be taken seriously, thus Matus did the talking, his questions prepared beforehand and the same for each person. After the interview, each story was verified by Bhyrhán, the only other Elyri in the keep.

Bhríd was not in the castle, was seeking his son. No one had seen Tayte since the last insults he had hurled at his brother. More and more it made the eldest Cáner heir look guilty of something, or else the victim of foul play…even if he was guilty of no more than knowing the truth and not sharing it.

Kavan was not the only one left nervous and unable to sleep because of it. Tayte was trailing a silent storm in his wake and whether he intended it or not, Kavan suspected it would soon erupt.

Asta was kept busy with her investigation so that, when her brother Wilred and his wife Bianca arrived for the coronation, she had no time to give him beyond a quick, delighted greeting. They were not particularly close as siblings, with Wilred being several years older than her. But they were Dugans, and as Dugans, they were fiercely loyal to one another. Centuries of tradition as part of the Association formed bonds among Dugans that could not be broken. She would make time for him as soon as her duty to the Queen was complete. They had much to catch up on.

The setting sun continued to build tension throughout the keep, and the brought the return of the bedraggled, drunken Cáner boy who staggered into the dining room, singing, swearing, barely able to stand upright. He was a spectacle that every guest in the Lachlan house was witness to. Bhríd, infuriated and embarrassed and disinclined to give in to his wife's clutching hand, lurched to his feet, stormed across the room, and grabbed his son's arms to get control of him.

"Don't touch me, Elyri!" Tayte roared as he swung a balled fist at his father's face. The impact bloodied the man's nose, gave birth to shocked murmurs around the room, and further angered his father. Several attending guards stepped forward to intervene, but a cold glare from the chamberlain stayed them. He could handle his son. Tayte might be younger, but he carried few of the traits borne in his father's blood. Bhríd had the advantage of experience in combat and a greater than normal Elyri strength, all of which allowed him to subdue Tayte without further bloodshed.

"Damn you for eternity," Tayte bellowed as Bhríd dragged him out of the dining room. Madalyn followed, as did Kavan and Asta, but no one else dared move. The Queen had a duty to maintain order and resume dinner, and this was, mainly, a private matter for the Cáners. Gaelán was wise enough to stay out of it. If he was needed, he would be summoned. And if there was anything the Queen needed to know, Asta would tell her later.

In the dayroom, far enough from the guests that he hoped their conversation would not be overheard, Bhríd hissed, "Calm yourself if you want me to release you." He was grateful that Kavan had come, for if anyone could prevent him from doing something he would later regret it would be his white-skinned cousin.

"Where have you been?" Madalyn cried at the same time. "Two days! Two days without a word! We've been worried sick…"

"You've been worried sick. Father," he spat the last word, "did not care." His body relaxed enough that Bhríd believed it safe to release him. The moment he did so, however, Tayte turned, intending to lunge for the door. Kavan blocked his way, and though Tayte had no idea whether his uncle knew how to fight, he knew Kavan could do other things, was rumored to do other things, and that knowledge prevented him from pushing past. He eyed the windows but thought better of charging through one of them.

Bhríd scowled as he watched his son seek escape and growled, "Of course I care! I have done nothing but look for you for the last…"

"For me, or for your suspect?" The question prompted Bhríd to shut his mouth. "Well? Did you look for your son or your suspect?"

There was accusation in his tone and Bhríd could not deny the truth. But if Tayte knew that Bhríd and others were seeking a suspect, then he knew what that suspect had done. It meant he had known, in order to flee, before anyone else had. That knowing put guilt on Tayte's shoulders and made Bhríd tremble with remorse.

"You are a suspect, son."

"You would not have looked for me if I wasn't."

"I would not have known you were missing. There was no reason to believe you were…"

"I was not missing. I was drinking."

Madalyn rested a hand gently on her son's arm. "We can see that, Tayte. No one is passing judgment…"

"Someone should." There was nothing inherently wrong with drinking, except when one let the drink get the better of them as Tayte had done. Likely, Bhríd thought bitterly, the alcohol was powering his son's rage, but it was not the sole reason for it. It was but fuel on an otherwise smoldering fire. "It could kill you…"

"I am NOT Elyri!"

The room was silent. Was this the first time his son had indulged in drink? Had it been a test to see how much Elyri was in his blood? Or was it something he had already determined, a vice he could indulge in to prove the birthright of his blood to the world, to prove he did not share those characteristics with his father and brother that marked them as part of a race he despised?

"Is that why you did it?" Kavan asked as casually as he could, given the knot in his throat. "Because he failed to kill me?" He was not convinced Tayte had killed anyone, but what better reason might he have to attempt it, or participate in it, then if he wanted his uncle dead? Tayte had not expressed direct hatred for Kavan, but it was well known now that he had issued threats against his brother. Wishing Kavan dead as well was not unimaginable.

"Why must everything be about you?" When Kavan did not reply but blinked and stared at him as he, and the others in the room, attempted to discern if that was an admission of guilt, Tayte growled and strode to the liquor cabinet, taking out a bottle of strong ale without bothering with a glass.

"You've had enough," scolded Bhríd.

He took several gulps before grunting, "You are not my father."

"Tayte…please…"

He looked at his mother over the tipped glass as he drank more, and for a moment it appeared that she might be reaching him as his expression softened and the bottle lowered. But the quantity of potent liquor hit bottom in his stomach and brought up a bitter snarl. "Stop defending him, Mother. You don't need him to protect the lands any longer. I can do it. The estate is safe with me."

"Is it?" Bhríd was not surprised by the words, though it appeared his wife was. She was not naïve, never had been in Bhríd's opinion; she seemed wise enough to make a bargain to protect what was hers by marrying him instead of losing the estate to someone else. "Do you think murdering a man will leave you a future to manage anything?"

"k'Ádhá's breath!" Tayte swore, the words making Kavan scowl and the violence in them making Asta inch closer to the bard, either to protect him or seeking protection herself. "I haven't killed anyone!"

"No?" Bhríd wanted to believe him, wanted to believe that his child was not capable of murder, but he grimly admitted he no longer knew this son…if he had ever known him at all. "Then what were you doing with dedhá Rankin's robe?"

"dedhá Ran…" He stammered, his expression confused. "It was not…I thought…"

Some of his anger deflated beneath bewilderment and he dropped into the nearest chair, rubbing his forehead with one shaky hand. "He told me to take it to the náós…return it to the dedhá…I didn't ask…I assumed…" He had assumed that if anyone wanted to frame a dedhá, they would frame the Elyri dedhá. He had put the robe where he thought it belonged.

Now that he was no longer yelling, Asta drew back her shoulders and perched on the footstool in front of him. They had been friends once. Surely he would trust her now. "Who? Who gave it to you?" she prompted, hoping that, by sounding less threatening than his parents, the drunken young man would confide in her. Madalyn, hoping that too, waved her husband back when it looked like Bhríd was about to intervene.

"It was his right," Tayte muttered. "It was hers too…but you can't expect a lady to do such things. It was his right to do it for her."

Kavan's face softened. He understood.

Tayte continued. "He didn't know how to…would've gotten caught or killed or…but I told him it would be easy…"

"It was your idea?" He still had not given a name, but Asta was, for the moment, letting him lead with any information he would give.

"Getting in was Idal's idea, but I said he needed a cover. Thought he was going as a soldier; he could have used his father's armor." He pouted and rubbed his head. "I told him that would be stupid."

Bhríd met Kavan's gaze across the room. A soldier's son. Idal Gottfrid? The man's connections made no sense. A son defending a girl. A sister…but Idal had none…nor a cousin or other kin that might have crossed paths with Bayle. If it was a sister wronged, her honor besmirched or…

Dayly Niall.

The men thought it simultaneously, the spark in their eyes revealing the same conclusion as Tayte continued, "But he had every right. He took everything from them…from her…her future…her life. It wasn't fair. She should have been allowed the right to avenge…"

"And because she didn't…Dayly took it."

Asta had come to the same conclusion. The Niall children had spent considerable time with the royal family and with the Cáner boys as they grew up, before Sigrid had been kept at home for more feminine studies while the boys learned fighting, hunting, and leadership skills she would never need. Asta's training had gone in an entirely different direction, but it had been a direction that continued to keep her close to the boys. As Hagan's best friend, it would be reasonable for Dayly to be devastated, angry and bitter over his friend's murder, and with Sigrid undoubtedly distraught about losing her future husband so close to their wedding day, it was also easy to imagine that Dayly felt it was his right and duty to avenge his sister's loss as well as his friend's death.

Whether the Queen agreed was another question.

"Do you know where he is? Did he return home?" The elder Niall had been seen in Rhidam, had attended Kavan's trial with his son, and most had assumed he would remain in Rhidam for the coronation and the Queen's wedding. No matter how heartbreaking the events might be, Duke Niall knew the Queen was not at fault for her brother's death, and as a career politician, he would not likely miss the opportunity to seek favor from her as he had been doing with Hagan.

Tayte shook his head and winced, the alcohol in his blood making the abrupt movement an uncomfortable one. "Think he took her home…she couldn't stay…not when everyone would have stared…"

"Thoughtful of him." Asta glanced ag Bhríd. He would see to it that Dayly was brought back to Rhidam to face the Queen. With the wedding and coronation before them, there was little time to reach him and bring him back beforehand, thus it made sense to allow the matter to rest until after Diona was officially made Queen. That, however, would be for Diona to decide. And if Idal Gottfrid had a part to play in this tale, he would need to be brought in and questioned as well.

"She deserves that much after what she lost." Tayte rose, swayed, and smiled at his mother when she came to steady him.

"Come to your room and sleep," Madalyn said gently. Asta came to his other side to help.

"Haven't slept lately…could use a good bed…"

Kavan stepped aside to allow them to pass, nodded when Asta caught his eye, and watched the women steer Tayte towards the stairs. Asta would make certain guards were posted at Tayte's door, whether Madalyn approved or not. Tayte might not have killed Bayle, but he had been an accessory, and if the Queen saw fit, she could exact the same punishment from him that she chose to mete out to Dayly. Knowing that grim truth too, Bhríd groaned and turned to the window to stare into the darkness.

"Perhaps the Queen will understand," Kavan offered when they were alone.

"And perhaps she won't. I could not blame her either way." Dayly had his rights. They were the same rights Bhríd had exercised when he had executed the men who had butchered his household, another incident where he was sure his son had been involved, however marginally. King Hagan had not sought to punish Bhríd for his actions, but he could have. The Queen was not her brother. And Tayte, it appeared to him, was setting up for a lifetime of subterfuge and violence. What his choices might mean to the future of the Dubuais-Cáner estate made Bhríd cold to think about.

Kavan crossed the room and stood beside him at the window. "I will do my best to sway her ruling. Tayte deserves…"

"What he gets." Bhríd wanted to believe there was good in his son still, but more and more he was faced with diminishing hope that it was true.

"He is your son. That is reason enough to deserve a chance."

"I do not expect favoritism. That would be detrimental to the future of Elyri…and," he groaned, "perhaps to Tayte as well…and Gaelán and Madalyn. Leave the matter to the Queen, tydhá. I will defend him as I can…" It was his duty as Tayte's father, and he felt perhaps he had failed him in some way. "…but he is no longer a child. His future is in his own hands. And hers."

❧*❦

"Asta?"

Having seen Tayte safely to his room and to bed, leaving him to his mother's care, Asta came downstairs to arrange for guards outside of Tayte's door and to locate Matus to have him investigate the details of Tayte's story. She did not doubt him; he was too drunk to have fabricated a consistent tale, one she had gotten him to repeat as she and Madalyn got his boots off his feet and his tunic over his head. Dayly's desire to avenge Hagan and Sigrid was fathomable and it did not particularly offend her that Tayte was willing to help him. Tayte was close to Dayly and Hagan, and no doubt had entertained the idea of revenge himself. What did disturb her was his admission to dumping evidence, or part of the evidence, in dedhá Tusánt's trunk. Whether he had specifically targeted the Elyri dedhá or not, he had been willing to allow a leader of the Faith to be implicated in a murder when he could as easily have destroyed the robe to keep anyone from finding it. What, she mused, did that say about Tayte? What did it say about him that she did not already know?

"Ah…Will…you're up late." She smiled at her brother and accepted his hug. He was not her father, but it felt good all the same.

"Coriana is crying nonstop…I thought it best to escape before one of us turns to violence," he quipped.

"Wilred Dugan! You should be helping, not running away!" Unlike many nobles, Wilred and Bianca had not hired much outside help to manage their home. A husband and wife who helped with the housework and maintenance, and assisted Wilred with his trade business. But they had come to Rhidam alone, meaning they had no one else to care for their child, and insisting that Bianca do it all alone did not seem fair to Asta.

"Oh, I would be helping…if Bianca would allow it. She says I make it worse…that I make her cry more." He imagined his wife was so doting on their daughter because she had lost her own mother at a very young age. While Wilred did not interfere with his wife's child-rearing as a rule, he did worry about that relationship sometimes. But an infant needed its mother and for now, he accepted that need. "Come into the chapel with me? Talk?"

The only one likely to be in the oratory at this hour would be Kavan, but the room was empty, lit by a single candle on the altar that Kavan often kept lit there. It made the room a good place for private discussion, and it was not far from his room if Bianca needed him.

"Being a father suits you then?"

"I think so. Nothing is perfect, but we are happy. And you? You seem to be well." He sat on the nearest bench and stretched out his legs. "I worry about you, about whether I should bring you to Durham or leave you here while Father is doing…whatever he is doing."

"I'm in Diona's care…not that I need it. I'm fine here…besides, I could not serve as inquisitor from Durham."

"Is that working out? You are safe? Do you need anything?"

"You worry too much, Will," she giggled. "I know what I'm doing. I'm probably safer than most in Rhidam." Every time she left the castle she had the eyes of the Association watching her back, better protection, she believed, then a host of palace guards trailing behind her. The palace guards had been unable to protect the King; she was less confident they could protect her.

That realization again darkened her expression. "I want news from Father…want him to come home…but I do not think he will…"

"Ah, Asta, of course he will…"

She shook her head. "Perhaps for Diona…but he was frustrated with Hagan tying his hands, preventing him from doing his duty. I think without Mother, he was bored…and lonely…"

"He has you. He knows you need him. He knows he has Durham."

Though resolute to do her best, to prove her worthiness to the Queen, to Enesfel, and to her father, Asta felt equally certain that success would show him she did not need him after all and give him an excuse to remain where he was, an undercover agent for the Crown. "He trusts me to do my job without him. He doesn't need to be here for that…and he knows it. You haven't heard from him, have you?"

"No," Wilred admitted, hearing what his sister was not saying. His knowledge of the Association was limited to his abduction as a child, and as those were memories he preferred not to think about, he had not been inclined to follow his father's path. He was proud of his sister's successes, proud of the ability she must have to be trusted by their father and the queen, but he worried for her being in Rhidam without him. "I last heard when his latter came instructing me in the story about his failed return from Durham. You know more than I do."

"I hear nothing directly…and not enough of what I do here. I know he was okay a few weeks ago…Lord Cliáth saw him in the wilds southeast of the city, beyond the marshes. In hiding. He could tell me no more…and Father has not sent word since."

"If anyone can survive out there doing what he does, it's Father." He pulled her close with an arm around her. "We'll see him again, Asta. I know we will."

❧Chapter 44❧

Queen Diona chose to put off the hearing and sentencing of Tayte Cáner until after her coronation, until Idal Gottfrid and Dayly Niall were located and brought to the keep. Both dukes claimed no knowledge of their sons' whereabouts, only that, as Tayte said, the younger Niall had escorted Sigrid back to the family estate. Idal Gottfrid, leading his own life, was no longer under his father's control and not even his brother Kent knew his whereabouts. Both dukes were indignant to learn that their sons might be implicated in a crime, though what that crime was had not yet been made public. High profile crimes reflected badly on their family names and, in Duke Niall's case, would damage his hopes of ingratiating himself with the Queen. Duke Gottfrid, an older, frailer man, cared little for such political games any longer. It was Duke Niall's willingness to please the Queen that led her to believe he was not lying about her son's location. She suspected he would sell his son's soul if it meant keeping royal favor for the family, which made her feel sorry for Dayly. There would have to be sentencing, but what, she wondered, would she decide to do when that moment arrived?

She was surrounded with retainers, Asta, Bianca, Zelenka, Madalyn, Gabrielle and Clianthe, the last two having recently arrived from Káliel. She wanted to see her brother, but Muir had no desire to discuss dresses and the plans she was making for the day of pageantry and ceremony. In her excitement, she allowed the women to sweep her along and left her half-brother, the closest kin she had left, to go in search of the person she knew he wanted most to see.

Muir found Kavan in the place he was most likely to be, the third-floor oratory kneeling with his harp before the altar. He did not know Kavan had spent less time in that place since his return; events had kept him too busy to allow opportunity for meditation and music. If Muir had known, he would have understood the added tension around the bard's eyes, tugging his mouth into a frown as the door opened. It was a look of annoyance that melted quickly as he saw who had entered, as Muir reached him and caught him in an embrace.

"Praise be! When I heard…I took the first ship back…but by the time of my arrival Clianthe said you were freed. You scared me to death, Kavan." He choked on his emotion and restrained the impulse to weep. "I should have returned to the outpost perhaps, but with Hagan…the wedding and the coronation…I thought it best to wait, to be here. If the men fault me for attending to my sister, so be it."

"I doubt they will," Kavan murmured into the satisfying hug. Normally he avoided such intimacy, but in moments such as this, he rejoiced in friendships that were dear to him. "They would likely be more disturbed if you chose not to. I understand why you were not here before…but I am happy to see you now."

The prince pulled back to look at him. "You were not hurt, were you? And the man who did these things…he was punished…"

"Not by Diona…but yes, he is no longer a threat and I am well. Weary, but well." He had hoped for a few days of tranquility in Alberni, but events had conspired against him. The soonest he would be able to travel there would be the day after the coronation. He would be less missed then and he felt it would be best if he was not here.

"Good. You will tell me everything, I pray, this evening after dinner? We came via the náós for Clianthe wanted a word with dedhá Tusánt…and I have yet to unpack. She is with Diona discussing weddings and children no doubt," he grinned widely, indicating that he had gotten the good news from his wife. "I should seek my father now, announce my arrival lest he think I have forgotten him."

"He will be as pleased to see you as I." Muir rose but Kavan's hand on his arm held him back. "I…I must beg something of you…"

"Anything, Lord Cliáth.

Feeling that Muir might think quite differently if he knew what lay ahead, he continued, "When the coronation is over and the wedding behind us, I ask you and Clianthe to remain in Rhidam for a time…for me."

Muir sat again, expression somber and fretful. "Why? What is wrong?" The request did not sound as if it was made simply because the Elyri wanted company. There was no mistaking the anxious tone. "Is this regarding what we discussed before? The cleansing?"

"Yes." Kavan looked at the pyre figure. "The time draws nearer when I will need to push Enesfel along its path towards healing."

Muir's eyes narrowed and he pulled Kavan around to face him. "You wouldn't tell me before; what must you do? Is it dangerous? Will you be harmed?"

"I do not…I cannot say. What I must do, and when, has not yet been revealed, but I feel it is nearer. There are some who must aid me, who are a part of what must be done…though I do not know what is required or how you will be able to assist. But I am certain you and Clianthe are part of the puzzle." All three of them, Kavan realized, for the unborn child was as important to what lay ahead as the parents. "I need you here until the day arrives, for I may not have the time, once I know what is expected, to send for you and bring you here."

Though the prince's scowl did not change, he nodded his agreement. "Aye, then we shall stay. What shall I tell Clianthe and Gabrielle, if they question me?"

"Tell them the truth. I have nothing to hide." He had not yet felt compelled to request Gabrielle's attendance and he fretted that she might feel excluded. It could not be helped. He would follow instinct, what they and Kóráhm advised or instructed, and take no unnecessary chances with Enesfel's future, or his own.

"I will. You know you have but to ask. I'll stay as long as I must."

Muir's promise made Kavan feel a little better. There were those he knew must be with him, but something deep down told him that there would be more, that his fate would be witnessed by several and he feared what they would think of him. He did not, however, fear it enough to refuse to act. At least, not yet.

The parting of the Chamber curtain, after Muir's departure, gave the next glimmer of insight and he groaned. He had little doubt about the man's willingness to be there for him, but convincing his cousin's wife of the necessity would be far more difficult.

He bowed his head. "I did not expect to see you until tomorrow."

Suspecting nothing, Syl smiled in greeting. "Nor did I. But when Ártur told me Bianca was here…well, I am sure the Queen will demand a great deal of attention tomorrow. I would be remiss not to attend her, but I would like time to see Bianca and Coriana."

Bianca had been a surrogate daughter, born and adopted before Syl conceived children of her own. Since her marriage to Wilred had taken her to Durham, Syl had seen little of her. She hoped to make some arrangement to rectify that during this visit.

"Then it is good you are here. Prince Muir and Clianthe have just arrived, Lady Dilyn as well. I suspect Bianca is with them and the Queen. You will be staying tonight?"

Syl's expression wavered but she nodded. "Perhaps. We shall see." Head cocked, she asked, "Why do you ask?" Kavan was not known to ask trivial questions. If he was asking, there was a reason.

"I…perhaps you would spare a moment for me later…if you have time." It felt ridiculous to be afraid of the petite woman who had married his cousin, but he did not want to be the cause of further friction in their marriage.

"If you have something to say, Kavan, do so. Do not hesitate for a moment we may miss later."

He nodded, relieved she felt that way but no less worried about what he wanted to ask as he got to his feet so that she did not have to look down on him. "I…you know I have spoken of something I must do, something I believe is necessary for the healing of Enesfel."

"We feared you were aiming for that by sacrificing yourself over Hagan's death," she said, low and sad. "We were relieved that was not the case. There is something else then?"

"I don't know when, or what, or how it will come to pass, but before I speak to Ártur, I want you to know I must ask for his help."

"His help?" Her eyes creased around the corners. "You mean to put him in danger?"

Kavan shook his head but it was a reassurance he did not feel certain of. "I cannot promise he won't be…but I do not believe he or anyone else will be in danger." Only himself, but he did not say so.

"You believe? That is not good enough, Kavan. He has a family…he has children…"

"I know. I would not ask if this was not imperative to the safety of Elyri in Enesfel…"

"What about his safety? Do you not care about that?"

The bard's cheeks flushed with indignation. "You know me better than that, Syl," he muttered as he looked at his hands. "Have I ever willingly, knowingly, said or done anything to put him in harm's way? Do you think I ask this lightly? Do you think I lack concern for you and the children? If it were so, I would not be speaking of this with you before even mentioning it to him."

It was Syl's turn to blush, her gaze also casting down though the rest of her frightened expression did not change. She knew her husband well; any danger he had ever been in he had brought upon himself with his MacLyr obstinacy. The fact that Kavan was asking her first was both reassuring and troubling. "When will you…?"

"Soon, but that is all I know. Kóráhm will tell me when it is time."

"Kóráhm?" The saint's involvement was not as reassuring as it should have been. "He is…?"

"Involved? I think not. He is guiding me, and when the moment comes, there may be no time to ask permission. I will ask Ártur when I must, because I must, because not to could be devastating, but I want you to know, to not be angry with him, with me, when it is time."

She bit her lip, nodded, and began to depart, intending to think about what he had said. She made it as far as the oratory door before pausing with her hand on the latch. With her head turned, not enough to see him but to the side so that he might hear her better, she said, "I will think about what you said, Kavan…but I promise you nothing."

"I do not want promises Syl. I want to do what is asked of me."

He hoped, as she closed the door behind her, that it did not include dying in front of those he loved the most.

The days in Rhidam were hot and dry as summer past its zenith and began its steady march towards autumn. Though the rains seldom fell in Enesfel's seat of power at this time of year, it was normally pleasant in its warmth, knowing few days of unbearable heat such as blanketed the land now. Such weather made the evening, night, and early morning hours the most enjoyable, and on this day, Diona lingered before the tall mirror surrounded with ebony and gold etchings and studied her reflection.

She had risen earlier than most after a night of nervous sleep. This would be an exceptional day in Enesfel's history, the crowning of a queen and her marriage at the same time. Everything had been neatly planned but still she fretted about the possibility of something going wrong. She could not afford mistakes. The future depended on her to appear perfect, flawless, and flawless she intended to be.

Beneath the sky's predawn glow, a flurry of activity was already underway in the courtyard as soldiers took position, last-minute guests from across the Sovereignties arrived, and servants tended to horses and wagons and the delivery and preparation of food. The Grand Hall would be awash in final decorating, adorned with the unfurled Lachlan banners of amber, crimson and black, candelabra tied with crimson and amber ribbon to allow more light then the torch sconces could offer, and benches were placed at the front of the room near the throne for those the Queen deemed important enough to be worthy of seating. Most would remain on their feet throughout, as was expected when anointing a monarch, and as the ceremonies were to be merged, she expected them to remain standing for both. None would consider that expectation rude. None would dare.

Today, she thought, toying with her hair, undecided on a style she had settled on only yesterday. Today she would stand in her father's place. Today she would make her father and mother, in their eternal resting place, proud. Today she would marry the man she could not fathom living without, after years of his patiently waiting for her to decide. Today Enesfel would begin a new path, without k'dedhá Claide to hinder or ruin the event. dedhá Tusánt would arrive soon to oversee the elements of the day he needed to have in place, and in another room, not far away, Espen was preparing as she was. If he had any misgivings about marrying a queen, he had not voiced them.

Indeed, when salutations arrived from his brother, the King of Hatu ribbed him gently about marrying a woman of power, a queen, something that could never happen in Hatu. Espen smiled, laughed, and told his bride-to-be that he would have it no other way. Her rise to the throne changed nothing for him. He had known her so well for so long that he could not imagine marrying a woman he was meant only to bed and breed with, a woman he could not converse with or spend time with privately or publically. Let his brother cling to the old ways. Espen was where he wanted to be, with the woman, the people, he wanted to be with. Yes, there were times when he missed home, missed his brother, but he already knew that, when away from Diona, he missed her more. He was where he should be and would gladly accept his brother's teasing for it.

Belda was directing the staff in the room behind her, women who prepared her bath, laid out the gown and accessories she would wear, while others transported her personal belongings to the chamber that would become hers and Espen's now that she was to be officially queen. Hagan's belongings had been removed, wedding gifts received had been sent to the Nialls as Diona felt wrong keeping them, his clothing given to Gaelán, Sóbhán, Tayte, some to the náós for sharing with those in need, or otherwise stored if it was deemed too expensive to give to the poor. That was a custom, a distinction, Diona hated, but one she followed for the sake of propriety.

Perhaps someday her own sons could wear it.

She shivered. Children. How could she be a mother? Did she dare, as Queen, take the risk? Did she dare, as Queen, not do so? Those were questions that deserved long, careful consideration, but not today. Today she had more important matters to fret over…like the ceremony that would begin at noon.

A knock on the door, and then Belda, who answered it promptly, returned with a young man, impeccably and richly dressed. An Elyri man whom the Queen did not know. He bowed formally before placing the small trunk he carried on the table Belda indicated.

"Welcome to Enesfel, to Rhidam," she said, grateful she was dressed to receive this intriguing visitor. Most asking to see her would be put off until some other day. But no Elyri traveled through Enesfel on a whim any longer; he had taken great risk in coming here and Diona appreciated her staff seeing him in.

If he was afraid of the risks he had taken to come, it did not show.

"Greetings, Your Majesty, from Kyne Mórne, on behalf of the Sovereignty of Elyriá."

She blinked and stared, rising out of respect for the woman he represented. "The High Mother honors me?"

She did not know if her father had received such a salutation or honor from the High Mother. She knew her grandfather had been gifted with an expensive sword by the oldest ruler in the lands, a woman he had liked and respected and who paid him the same kindnesses in return. Diona did know that no such acknowledgment had come for Hagan. Perhaps it was because she too was a woman. Perhaps it was because the Kyne, like Kavan, had felt that Hagan's time on Enesfel's throne was doomed to be short.

"Aye. She extends the hand of alliance and wishes you a long and prosperous reign. Please accept these tokens of offered friendship and know that, should you have need of her, you have but to ask."

Diona's hand lingered over the trunk, hesitantly opening it as she pondered the messenger's words. Elyriá was not offering military support. If Elyriá had a military, it was a well-kept secret, for no one in the sovereignties knew of any permanent combat unit except for those men guarding the limited mountain passes and those who personally guarded the High Mother, her residence, and those guarding the halls of the seat of Faith. They, as far as Diona knew, were more for show than for combat. Violence in Elyriá was so low it was practically unheard of.

Monetary aid, perhaps, as the violence throughout Enesfel was taking its toll on the kingdom's coffers and would, if not stemmed soon, create other problems as well. If there was some other form of assistance being offered, Diona assumed she would learn of it in time.

Within the trunk was a collection of gifts she was not expecting. A jeweled knife of the sort many noblewomen wore at their waists, a gold hinged bracelet inlaid with ruby and amber stones, a smattering of gold bhelts that alone was worth a considerable fortune, and a pale lace veil of the fashion rarely worn outside of Elyri weddings but that, with its silver beaded edges and gold-threaded finery, was too beautiful not to wear. It was not customary for a Teren woman to wear such a thing, but Diona decided she would wear it this day, wear it for the coronation and the wedding as well. She would wear each of the items in honor of the woman who gave them, in spite of how abysmally her kingdom had treated the High Mother's people. She would wear it as a show of solidarity for those persecuted throughout Enesfel, in the honor of those who had died and those who still lived.

With the expected silken belt at her waist that King Harcourt had given her, the one Hatu custom Espen had asked her to observe this day, she would present a picture of unity between many of the lands. Her gowns were Káliel silk, given by the Prime Magistrate as an accord with the islands, even if the Council was slow to open their borders to relations with the outside world. Around her left bicep, she wore the hammered bronze wedding cuff of the Cíbhóló, a less permanent, less painful symbol than the Cíbhóló kwolott. While Cordash's gift of a carriage and eight fine, sturdy horses to draw it could not be worn, it too was a symbol of friendship between their lands. The kingdom of Neth was, not surprisingly, not represented, but she did not need de Cormick support or acknowledgment so long as the other lands kept faith with her. Working together, she believed the world would again know amity.

"Please, tell the High Mother I appreciate her gifts and thank her for them. She does me great honor and I pray I may return this honor in just and fair fashion. Tell her I likewise pledge Enesfel's support to Elyriá, and that my goal is to restore Enesfel so Elyri may again travel freely. She has my word I will not rest until I see it done."

The messenger bowed. "I will relay your words." He seemed pleased with the sentiment as he backed from the room. Diona did not know if he would stay for the coronation and wedding. A gesture and quick word to Belda to see to the messenger's safety for as long as he was in Rhidam, and then she removed the items she would wear and closed the trunk. An unexpected gift on an unexpected day. She wondered what other surprised the day would hold.

❧*❧

"A queen?" King Merkar spat the words and chortled with distaste before swishing his wine around in his mouth as if to wash away the flavor of the words. "A woman is a disgrace to the throne! Enesfel will fall soon; you shall see. When it does, we will take back what is ours and grind this queen's bones into the dust of the road to victory!"

The King continued on as toast after toast was made in mocking honor of the woman due to come to power this day. It was too early, in Kjell's opinion, to be drinking so much, but as Kjell never drank to excess, a show of weakness that Merkar belittled at every opportunity, no one noticed that he did not share in the merrymaking.

Kjell's true reason for abstinence today, however, was less about keeping his head than it was about respecting the woman he had yet to meet but whom he had, through his cousin, agreed to aid in any way he could from his place within the de Cormick court. No matter what his brother believed, no matter what lies his advisors chose to feed the King, this was no weak-willed, fickle, foolish woman about to sit on Enesfel's throne. Diona Lachlan was potentially as strong, as cunning, and as deadly to Neth as her father had been. Any ill-conceived action on Merkar's part might result in the destruction of Neth, and while Kjell had no love for his brother, or the majority of the man's advisors and so-called friends, he loved his homeland. He would support the new Queen as far as he could, but not to the destruction of Neth. Neth could be a better place, but only if she were allowed to remain free.

A message would reach her late, but Kjell would send his felicitations, and some manner of gift if he could think of something. She would know he still waited, to move, to act, to change the course of history, and she would know that, whatever path she chose, he would do his utmost to support her. His cousin, he thought as he locked his bedroom door to write in solitude, would be pleased. He was the only other person of de Cormick blood who would be.

❧*❧

"You have no regrets about this?"

Kavan glanced at Ártur, thinking that an odd thing to ask as he tuned his harp. "Why should I? Diona is destined to rule. I mourn Hagan's passing…he deserved better…" His voice faded and his fingers faltered on the strings. "But I cannot mourn destiny. I am happy for her…and for Enesfel."

"You believe she will be good for Enesfel?"

"If she chooses to be." And if, he mused, he was successful on the path that lay ahead for him as well.

The healer nodded, agreeing with his cousin's words, although he was less convinced that she had the level-headedness to rule after what she had done to Kavan. She did, however, have determination and stubbornness, and if she was, as it appeared, over her infatuation with Kavan, then perhaps Enesfel would know stability again.

"You do not regret she is marrying?" He was teasing, in part, and Kavan's scowl faded when he realized it.

"I have no desire to marry her."

"I know."

Kavan was grateful Ártur did not continue with the words he suspected would have come next. It was not unusual for an Elyri his age to be unmarried, and for an Elyri amongst Teren, who had little chance to meet others of his kind, it was especially difficult. When Kavan looked at those he loved around him, most of whom, save for the children, were wed, it was painful, at times, to feel out of place. The women he had been closest to belonged to others…or to a world beyond his reach.

"Espen is good for her, and that is good for Enesfel. I do not love her that way. Their union is as it should be. I have no regrets."

Relieved, Ártur said, "Good. I believe you." Sometimes he thought his cousin deluded himself by not admitting to regrets or hurts or offenses received, but this time he believed Kavan was telling the truth. "Will you sing today?"

"I have not decided yet."

"I hope you do. I think we will all benefit from the beauty of your music. Now…I have to see to the boys. Prince Owain is serving in the procession and Syl and I are making sure Piran and Llucás are on their best behavior. Shall I see to Gaelán and Sóbhán as well?"

"They will behave…but yes, see to them if you would." Kavan would have little time for the young men. He and Bhyrhán were expected downstairs to meet the minstrels as they arrived. As that would happen at any time, he wanted to make the most of a few quiet minutes in prayer beforehand. There would be no other chance for solitude for the remainder of the day, no other chance to be alone.

❧*❧

There was no need to see into the Great Hall to know that the room was packed from one wall to the other, from the rear doors to the back of the two benches located before the empty Lachlan throne. Not entirely empty, she reminded herself. It was missing a ruler to sit on it, but it contained the royal scepter and crown, symbols of the destiny fate was about to bestow on her, and the ghosts of every Lachlan monarch to come before her. She could hear the excited murmuring of the guests, feel the anticipation in the air, and held her breath when the brass trumpets began their welcoming fanfare.

"Father," she whispered to the air. "Be with me." She wished he could be; strong, self-assured, confident Arlan Lachlan would surely have known what she was supposed to do after today. Compared to his memory, she felt tiny and insignificant.

She was surrounded by gdhededhá and soldiers and those advisors nearest to her heart. When Kavan refused to take part in the procession, a refusal Ártur had mimicked, she was at first indignant and hurt. With the door opened to reveal the sea of faces turned towards her, she understood and approved of their choice. It was right that Kavan and the healers appear to be no more than trappings to the Queen, there to serve but not, at least to the public eye, advise. One Elyri in her true inner court, her Lord High Chamberlain Bhríd Cáner, was enough, too many for some people. With the other advisory and law-keeping positions filled by Teren, it appeared to those attending that the royal house was not the teeming den of Elyri influence many believed. They knew, of course, that there were healers, and that the White Bard was an integral part of court life, but the Queen intended to give the impression that she did not need Elyri advice to rule.

She was strong enough to stand on her own.

The awaited cue sounded and she stepped through the swath that opened before her as those in the crowd moved to allow her to enter. At the front of the procession, gdhededhá Tusánt carried the pyre image, with Valgis and Rankin following behind, each carrying the other holy items required for this ceremony to be fulfilled. Then there were members of the Lachlan Guard in their brightly burnished armor and finally the young Queen with her chamberlain, chancellor, general, justice, and inquisitor-cousin at her back, along with Muir and Wilred. Matus was not in the procession, though his position as inquisitor was the official one. Diona was prepared, if anyone questioned the omission, to publically appoint Asta as her inquisitor today if necessary. As the young woman was royal kin, however, entering with the Lachlan princes, and Matus was in attendance near the front of the room, she hoped that Asta's position would be viewed only as the inclusion of kin. The matter of Court Inquisitor did not need to be settled today.

Few cared one way or the other about it. Their eyes were on the pageantry, the clothing, and the new Queen. If any did care, it would be about the lack of Elyri at her side.

On the benches to her left, as she step by step inched nearer the dais, the amber and burgundy cloak her mother had made for her father feeling hot and heavy on her shoulders, waited some of those she had been unable to have beside her. Her uncle and his son. Muir's wife and the young woman's mother, the Prime Magistrate of Káliel. Madalyn had been offered one of the two remaining seats of distinction, but as she could not choose one son over the other to sit with her, and dared not seat the two of them together in front of such a crowd, the last two prime positions were given to Kavan and Sóbhán. Wortham stood directly behind the bard, a shield from the rest of the guests, and with him sat Zelenka, the MacLyrs, Bianca Dugan, the Dubuais-Cáners, Physician Talis, and Bhyrhán. The bards were due to perform later, but for now, they held place to greet the Queen on her way up the two steps of the platform. Those who had served in the procession broke away to occupy the benches to her right, with the Lachlan guard taking places along the lower step and the three gdhededhá stopping directly in front of the throne. Valgis and Rankin flanked the young woman and Tusánt, the gdhededhá given the honor of crowning her this day by the seniority of his post, standing at her side.

The fanfare's echo ended and one by one the regalia were bestowed on the kneeling woman. There were few words to be spoken in a customary coronation, as each participant understood their role and each guest knew what the bestowal of the regalia meant. The amber ring, resized to fit her smaller finger, signified the marriage of the Queen to the kingdom, her oneness and partnership with it. The ornately beaded collar of gold, amber, garnets, and black stones, wide enough to cover her from shoulder to shoulder from chin to upper chest and back, had been worn by one other woman in Lachlan history, and though wearing it was unnecessary, Diona chose to do it in honor and remembrance of a strong woman recalled favorably in Enesfel's historical annals. The scepter signifying her right to the throne, her sovereignty, the strength and duty of the monarch to rule justly and with fair impartiality over the people entrusted to her care. The blessed water sprinkled on her shoulders that consecrated her royal responsibility before k'Ádhá and the censer of incense waved about her to cleanse her of impurities and drive away negative spirits that might threaten Enesfel's prosperity. And finally the crown, an elaborate ruby and amber encrusted circlet of intertwined gold branches that had been worn by Lachlan rulers for decades. It was too heavy, too bulky, to be worn as an everyday symbol of the monarchy, but for the coronation and other important affairs of state, wearing it was a requirement established by centuries of Lachlan tradition. At various times its passage from one monarch to another had been bestowed by a relative, the Lord High Chamberlain, and even the Lord High General, but in the years when the Faith was strong, the responsibility of crowning a new ruler fell to the leader of the Faith.

k'gdhededhá Claide had knowingly bypassed this honor and left it to the second-ranking dedhá in Rhidam. An Elyri. It was a slight, an indication of a potential rift between the Faith and the Crown, but today there appeared to be no such rift as dedhá Tusánt bestowed on Queen Diona, through the placing of the royal crown on her head, the blessings of the Faith on her right to rule. Her succession was sanctioned before k'Ádhá and an Elyri had sanctioned her rise to power. Nothing Claide could do could undo that now.

The Elyri veil she wore, its upper fringes woven into her loose, ebony hair, trailed down her back to the floor, the weight of its beaded border keeping it straight and elegant in appearance, even when the royal diadem was placed on her head. She imagined, as Tusánt's hands rested in blessing on her shoulders, that it was her father's hands she felt there, an image that brought tears to her eyes. He had never, until his dying breaths, imagined she might be where she was.

Tusánt backed away after helping her to her feet so that she could turn and face the audience without a word being uttered as she was presented to her subjects as the Queen of Enesfel. The fanfare rang again, loud enough that the sound carried through the open doors and windows of the place into the streets of Rhidam. Her city, her land, would know that she was, until the day of her death, their rightfully appointed Queen.

But there was no time for greeting, no time for cheering in the Hall as Tusánt came near again with a gesture that summoned Prince Espen to rise and join them on the platform. The Hatu prince, dressed in the Harcourt blue of his ancestors, was positioned at the far right side of the front bench during the procession and coronation, beaming with pride and adoration at the accomplishment and beauty of the woman he was to wed. Some would not see her ascension as an accomplishment, coming as it had as the result of the tragic death of her brother. But in each Teren land save Káliel, women rarely gained the power to rule from their father, even if she was the only living child the king possessed. If a woman was deemed unreliable, weak, or otherwise unfit to rule, she could be bypassed in favor of some other male of the bloodline. That Diona had the support of her advisors, her kin, her generals and the gdhededhá, was something to be proud of, and Espen was certainly proud.

dedhá Valgis presented the new Queen with the marriage bowl, a shallow ceramic dish of pale blue painted in a darker blue with flowers, beasts, birds and the sun, images of perceived prosperity. From a sewn burlap pouch he had been given before the ceremony, Espen sprinkled a pinch of ground powdery herbs into the bowl as though planting in springtime. It was a special, potent mixture, pungent to smell and full of treated oils. When he took the bowl from Diona, it was for her to light the mixture with one of the wedding candles from the nearest sconce. Treated as it was, the herbs sparked and smoked as the bowl was returned to her again, the passing of the fire of life between spouses, the joining of their life forces to be as one. They had agreed to set the smoking bowl on the throne, a symbol for them of a land ruled jointly, though both understood, as did those in the room, that the true burden of ruling Enesfel rested on the shoulders of the Queen.

Into Diona's hands was placed a small chalice, fashioned of the same clay, at the same time, as the wedding bowl, and painted with the same designs, the representation of continuity between the fire and water of life, liquid poured into the cup from a glass decanter by Espen as another giving gesture. The water, wine, and oil mixture was sweetly spiced but with a bitter aftertaste, the way moments of life often could be, and after she lifted the cup to Espen's lips so that he could drink of what he had given her, he took the cup and likewise shared it with her, making sure to leave a small dab in the cup with which to complete the ritual.

It was an ancient custom, handed down from the earliest days of Teren throughout the Sovereignties, believed to have been brought into the lands with them when they had come, although none knew the certainty of those primordial legends. The sharing of hearth fire and well water, life and resources, was a more practical matter for the people of the land, but even amongst nobility, it held the same meaning, in symbol if not in actuality. It was a custom practiced less in the houses of townsfolk and nobles once the Faith was introduced into the lands, but one that still existed in the lower rungs of society through all of the Teren kingdoms. Diona, in her desire to bind herself and her husband to the whole of Enesfel, had chosen to combine the ancient with the new, the secular with the sacred, the common with the noble, to produce a new light for the future of the Sovereignty.

It was with the hope of new light that they lifted the bowl between them, each with a hand on it, each with one hand around the cup, and then, with the silken Hatu belt draped over their wrists as they held the bowl, poured the remaining dribble of fluid from the cup into it. Many in the audience held their breath. In the lore of the bowl and the cup, if the liquid doused the flame, the marriage would be plagued with bad luck. If the mixture of water, oil, and wine fueled the flame and caused it to flare, the new couple's life would be a blessed one. The powder flame spluttered, crackled, threatened to go out, and then flared brightly with a powerful but short-lived flame that burned itself out moments after Tusánt lifted it high for everyone to see.

It was the sign they wanted, the sign of a blessed marriage and happy life, but in that short burning blue flame, Kavan felt it. A slice, a piercing in his ribs, a burn that stole breath and brought momentary darkness pooling behind his eyes. He swayed, believed he would collapse, but Wortham gripped his arms and kept him on his feet. He could not interrupt the Queen's day with fainting, even if the Sight was trying to tell him something. What it meant, however, he did not know. He was left with a cold feeling of foreboding as the Sight faded.

His strength, balance, and vision returned in time to be summoned, along with Bhyrhán, to present themselves to the Queen and her Consort who waited with raised hands draped with the silken belt that bound them until the ceremony was complete. It was customary for the officiant, either dedhá, village leader, or eldest member of the family, to bestow prayers and blessings on the new couple, but Diona insisted that Kavan be the one to do so. She could think of no one better, no one more likely to be heard by k'Ádhá, and Tusánt had eagerly agreed. Was it a miracle, she wanted, Kavan wondered as he shakily mounted the platform steps to a position between the couple and the throne, facing them, facing the audience and the world beyond the open Hall doors? Or was it, he mused as memories of Myreth and his time in that sacred place returned, merely that she, like those people, believed he had some powerful blessing to give?

Perhaps, he admitted as he put a hand on each royal head and felt the surge of energy erupt around him, he did.

He did not think they felt it, and a brief glance at the faces of the audience revealed that most did not. None but the Elyri in the room, and if he judged rightly, Wortham, noticed anything extraordinary. Nothing more happened as he lifted his heart in song, not the one he had planned but another that came to him, unbidden, from the ether around him, a sound joined by his kin's solemn piping, giving a soulful voice to an ancient High Elyri wedding prayer that he could not remember hearing or learning but knew was ancient nonetheless. New to him, he did not know how Bhyrhán knew it and could carry the tune. The warmth that gathered in his hands passed through him and into them both, and when the words faded, so too did the warmth, leaving Kavan staring at them both with a flicker of panic.

Not her too. Of anyone in Rhidam…why her?

He suppressed the emotion and took the unsteady, staggering steps back to his place in the congregation. Tusánt touched his fingers over the Queen's heart, over the Prince's heart, and then place their free hands to the others breast.

"With k'Ádhá's blessing you are joined. The two are one to serve Him, each other, and the people of Enesfel. Rejoice in peace. Prosper and bless the lands with your union."

The trumpets took up the fanfare again and this time, as the royal procession formed to escort the Queen and her Prince out of the Hall, there was cheering and applause and the throwing of petals and greenery at their feed to adorn their path into the world with life. The guests were shooed into the courtyard, where an abundance of drink awaited them, so that, with a flurry of activity, a great feast could be set for the nobles, advisors, gdhededhá, and handful of others who would be welcome back in to attend.

The people of Rhidam would drink in the courtyard for a time before being herded out. The rest would gather in the Great Hall to celebrate for as long as there was food and drink to sustain them.

"My lord?" Wortham helped the bard from the room but they went only as far as the library, where Kavan hoped he could be alone until he was needed again. He would put in his appearance at dinner as long as necessary, and then go to Alberni as he had intended to do days ago.

The Elyri shook his head. "It is nothing…"

"It is something; do not tell me otherwise. Do not take me for a blind man or fool," the captain scolded lightly. "I saw no miracle, but there was power there and you are too unsteady for it to be nothing."

"It was not that." The power he felt, he was reasonably certain, had been the sudden accumulation of záryph or k'kairá…whatever entities followed him and appeared at their whim and pleasure. They had passed on some blessing through him into Diona and Espen, but that was not what had unsettled him. "It is…that she…"

The door opened, interrupting, for which Kavan was grateful. Perhaps if he did not speak of what he knew, it would cease to be true.

"tydhá," Bhyrhán said with a bow as he entered with Gaelán and Sóbhán behind him. The dark-haired boy was staring at his guardian with awe, impressed yet again with the man's musical talent.

"My apologies for the change in program." Somehow, despite the imbalance he still felt, Kavan returned the bow. "Praise be you were able to follow without difficulty."

"If not for your voice in my head, guiding my notes, I do not believe I could have."

Kavan twitched. Voice in his head? He had done no such thing…had he? Or perhaps that was the miracle, that he had learned and taught a song without being aware of doing so.

"Did you compose that, tyne?" asked Gaelán.

"No…I…it is old…far older than bhydáni Tíbhyan I believe." How did he know that? Perhaps the knowledge came from the same source as the words, as the notes in Bhyrhán's head. Perhaps, he thought with a shiver at the brush of a familiar unseen hand across the back of his neck, none of it had come from him at all. "I believe it was Kóráhm's choice to bless this day."

Wortham's eyes grew round. "Aye, that would explain much."

"The minstrels…they are waiting," Bhyrhán continued a little nervously. He had heard the tales in Clarys, those that had filtered in from Bhryell and later Enesfel and spread throughout the lands, rumors of a man blessed with miracles and visited by saints…or at least one particular saint. He wondered if Kavan knew of the rise in reported sightings of Saint Kóráhm and others in their homeland. He wondered what Kavan would think if he knew. Bhyrhán did not know what he had experienced in that Hall, but he believed it had been something more than Elyri power, no matter how adept his kinsman was rumored to be. It did not frighten him, but it did make him curious. "We are asked to play as the room is set, or at least," he smiled, "I have been. I hoped you might accompany me." Kavan would be expected to play later, but there was no reason he could not play now if he wished to.

The chance to mingle with other musicians was a welcome one, particularly since it took him away from Wortham's questions and occupied his thoughts with something other than what awaited at a still unspecified point in his future. The vagueness surrounding what must be done and the expanding list of those who would be part of it filled Kavan with gnawing fear.

By the time the Queen and Prince returned to the Hall, faces flushed with smiles and kisses, tables had been arranged in a giant horseshoe around the room, leaving ample space in the center for guests to come and go as they chose, ample space to dance as the feasting stretched into the night. Lords and ladies were steered away from private areas with velvet ropes and innumerable formally adorned Lachlan guards, an unfortunate but necessary safeguard after the death of her brother and the still prevalent air of persecution and violence. Guests could enter the hall or mingle in the courtyard, however, and many chose the marginally cooler fresh outdoor air over the heavy air of the Hall perfumed with flowers, beeswax candles, and the sweetness of the ample meal and wine there to be shared.

Kavan avoided looking at the Queen, avoided eye contact with anyone as he struggled against the constricting knot inside. Too many stray bits of details swam in his head, none of which he could put together yet as there was no time to allow serious consideration. Some of them he was reluctant to ponder too closely, as he was afraid of what they would reveal, and so he happily gave in to the music, to the camaraderie of other musicians. A few of them, chosen by Prince Espen, hailed from the southern reaches of Hatu and Kavan asked, with little hope, if they knew, or had known, a young harper named Eridel. One did know the name, but he had not seen or heard from the man in many months. The news caused Kavan to regret asking, but he continued to hope that it had not been Eridel he had buried in that arid land so far to the south. He also inquired after Cedric O'Grady, a name which was much more familiar to the Hatu musicians. They promised to pass on Kavan's greetings and to send Cedric to Enesfel the first chance they could. A familiar face and the chance to know the fellow better provided a positive focus for Kavan throughout the evening.

Gifts were arranged in elegant mountains around the throne for the bride and groom to peruse in private later. It was not customary for them to be viewed before other guests, lest the giver feel shamed for not matching the opulence of the gifts of his peers. Diona had chosen to open gifts every year for her celebration day but this night she chose to do differently. Over the course of the evening, as the accumulation occasionally grew, servants found time to take trunks, bags, satchels, and cloth-bound items out of the Hall to some other location to prevent thievery. Kavan's gift, however, could not be bound in cloth or contained in a trunk adorned with sparkling metal shavings or floral arrangements or silk ribbons threaded with gold and silver. His gift was music, a song without words allowed to rain down over the pair and drench them with the love he felt, the joy of beginnings, the hope for the future and the family they would build together. It was no short tune, and set as it was for the brass strings of his harp alone, there was no dancing. Instead, the Queen and her guests listened and wept openly for the beauty he painted in their hearts and minds and stirred within their souls.

And when it was over, the chiming of the last notes lingering in the smoky, late-night air, Kavan bowed to the Queen he had raised, the child he had tutored, the young woman he had guided, kissed her hand in deference and respect, and took his leave. The thought of what lay ahead for her this night, an intimacy she once tried to force on him, accompanied by his already tumultuous thoughts, told him it was wisest to leave, to retreat to Alberni as she had previously given him permission to do. He would find refuge there, solace, time to be alone with his thoughts. True to his premonitions, he knew no harm would befall the couple in the near future. They were safe without him.

<h2 style="text-align:center">❧Chapter 45❧</h2>

ot yellow light was clawing its fingers through the cracks and crevices of window coverings and shutters by the time the new Queen and her husband retired to the room that once belonged to her father and the majority of Lachlan rulers before her. She was too exhausted for anything more than sleep, and Espen, drunk on the elation of having gained his prized bride and too much expensive wine, needed to be carried to the royal bedchamber. Not wanting to be disturbed, and finding the thought of sharing her parents' bed suddenly nerve-wracking, she instructed the men who carried him to place in in the bed in the secondary chamber…the bed she had been born in…and then collapsed barely out of the day's finery, on the bed that was now hers. She was aware that Kavan had departed the celebration earlier than most, but as that was not uncommon, and he had not seemed unduly distressed, she had little reason to find his departure suspect.

Except that the night had, for many reasons, brought back the memories of another night in the not so distant past when she had crept into his chambers and tried to force her way into his bed, force him to love her. How many lives had she nearly destroyed that night? How much pain had she caused?

And why, she mused, as the arms of sleep claimed her, was she afraid of sharing her bed with the man she had just married.

Wedding nights and bed-sharing and memories of past trauma were the furthest things from Kavan's mind as he awoke with the sun in the Alberni manor house and set to the duties of Lord. When his thoughts strayed to Rhidam it was to darker concerns for what lay ahead there, and what would come after. The past was over, done and behind him, and he wanted to dwell on it no more. There were duties here, journals and records and finances to study, staff to talk with, buildings and animals to inspect, a town to tend, all of which were enough to keep his mind off of whatever was transpiring in Rhidam.

Syl would have returned home, and Gabrielle too as each had their own duties and responsibilities to manage. If Muir had told Gabrielle that the bard wanted him and Clianthe to remain, the woman had said nothing of it to Kavan as he bid her farewell before taking his leave of the celebration. Clianthe's friendship with the new Queen was worth cultivating if the future between Enesfel and the islands was to change, and Gabrielle would have accepted that reason on its own. And for now, she and Owain agreed that Káliel was the safest place for Piran to be. Owain would have seen them off with the rising of the sun.

Other guests would have begun to depart, or they would the following day if the night's revelry had not kept them up too late drinking. Kavan suspected the next few days for the Queen would consist of lords and nobles jockeying for positions in her court and by the continuing search for Idal and Dayly.

Kavan did not feel his presence in Rhidam would affect the outcomes of any of those things. Besides, if he was needed or wanted, Ártur would come for him.

Come the eve of the second day of her reign, after having slept much of the first, Physician Talis closed the door to the woman's room and shook his head to Espen's unspoken question. "She is resting."

"Is it serious?"

Espen was not the only one concerned. The Queen had eaten little that day and had seemed to many to be sluggish, weary still, and obviously out of sorts and distracted. Whether anyone else believed in omens or not, Espen had seen the quick extinguishing of the flame in the wedding bowl, the bright flash and the too quick burning out, and he was concerned with its meaning. What if the portents were of her early death? What if she was too ill to rule? Who, he wondered, would reign in her stead?

But the physician smiled and bowed. "Do not fret, Your Majesty. She is of strong health and constitution. She has a mild stomach malady and general weariness but no fever or other symptoms. I have given her mint and ginger tea, to drink as much as she can, and suspect she will be well after a day or two of rest. She has endured much of late, the election of the k'dedhá, the death of her brother, Lord Cliáth's trial, the excitement of a wedding and coronation…with little chance for adequate meals, rest, or mourning. With the excitement behind her, rest should settle her nerves and her stomach and she will be back on her feet quickly."

The prince scowled but nodded. What Rouvyn said was true. Her brother's death had precipitated a rush to make the wedding happen, to try Kavan quickly yet fairly for the sake of the coronation, and he knew she had yet to grieve Hagan's untimely loss. The pressure of maintaining her composure in order to accomplish as much as she had done in such a short time would have been too much for most people. It was likely she had, indeed, grown sick with worry, guilt, grief, and stress. Those worries, many of them at least, were behind her now, and thus he hoped the overwhelming stress would be as well. If she would face her grief, he believed she would be strong enough for the task of guiding Enesfel on its proper path.

Inside, however, Espen suspected something more, some other reason for her hiding from the world and most especially from him. Perhaps she was regretting the decision to marry. Perhaps he had said or done something in his rare drunken state to offend her. Or perhaps, he thought with bitter nervousness, Lord Cliáth's early departure from the feast had upset her and made her regret her choice of husbands. He was confident that Kavan had no interest in Diona as lover or spouse, knew that she did not love him enough for that either. But did she love Espen enough to leave the bard behind and commit to marriage?

"I will see to her duties as well as I can," he promised, determined to shorten his wife's recovery time by relieving her burden.

"And I will continue to monitor her health for signs of anything more serious. But I assure you, Your Majesty, this will pass."

Thankfully, Espen found the initial days of ruling the kingdom, as Diona spent yet another day and night locked in her chamber, to be relatively uneventful. There were reports from the southernmost reaches of Enesfel of Elyri persecution and violence, a riot in the city of Wexel following dedhá Claide's arrival there, but Lord Gabersdon, with the help of his retainers, had quickly put down the uprising. The duke would continue on to Nelori, to spend a few days at his own estate before returning to Rhidam. He sent his regrets for missing the coronation and wedding, but traveling south with Claide had been a duty on behalf of the Crown, and thus his absence was understandable. He would pledge the Queen his support upon his return, and pledge his sword against the violence until the Coryllien threat was put to rest.

The report and a handful of others referring to similar small pockets of violence all, oddly enough, from the southern cities of Enesfel, gave Espen little to do, however, and Rhidam itself was calm, serene, much like the city had been when he had first come here as a young man. The change in Rhidam, the changes in the towns and villages of the south, lent credence to the Queen's theory that it was dedhá Claide who stirred the people to violence. The prince wondered, as he wrote yet another report, if the man realized how such events made him look. He wondered if Claide cared.

His first true duty came late on the third day, after more fretting and quashing rumors regarding the Queen's health, when Justice Corbin dragged both Idal Gottfried and Dayly Niall into the keep, the former stoic and quiet, the other kicking and swearing and lashing out with fists and words in his fear of punishment. With Tayte still detained in his room in the keep, under guard lest he think of fleeing as he tried twice to do, the three men were kept apart, kept from seeing each other after Espen met with Idal and Dayly alone. The prince did not question their actions or their motives but asked if each knew why they had been arrested. When he was satisfied that both were clear-headed and aware of the situation in which they found themselves, he had them detained in clean cells, as far apart from each other as the dungeon would allow, with adequate bedding and a good meal and the promise that the Queen would see to them as soon as she was able.

For Diona, unwell or not, that meeting came as soon as she heard from one of the servants about the men's capture. She tried to be angry with Espen for not telling her, but as she had denied everyone access to her except Physician Talis and her servants, there was no way Espen could have told her. It was not his fault. It was the fault of fear, fear that she was going to have to get beyond, though she did not know how. This, she knew, was not a matter that Kavan could help her with. She had to find her way through it alone…or risk losing everything.

Wan and thin, with dark shadows under her eyes and sunken cheeks that spoke of little sleep, Diona dressed and forced herself to the Great Hall, with Belda and Chancellor McGranis aiding her. Fortunately, no one other than staff saw her slow, shaky journey down the stairs and she was already seated on the throne by the time word of her arrival reached Espen and he found her there.

"Diona!" he exclaimed with relief, rushing to kneel before her, clasping her hand to his lips with a sigh. If anyone thought his display unseemly, the prince did not care. His brother certainly would have derided his behavior, but Espen had grown beyond Hatu's customary separation of the sexes. It occurred to him at that moment that what he felt during the days she had kept apart must be much the way the women in his homeland felt when denied access to their husbands. He determined then to strive harder not to judge her actions and have more patience. It would help, however, is she told him what was wrong, but he could see that she had, indeed, been unwell. Her health was the kingdom's top priority.

"Espen." The word was breathy, Diona surprised by both his joy at seeing her and her own at seeing him. Why, she wondered, caressing his dark hair with her free hand, was she being such a fool?

She was about to apologize, beg forgiveness, when the door opened and the chamberlain ushered his eldest son into the room. Tayte's initial expression of defiance faded when he saw the Queen's condition. He looked momentarily guilty as Espen rose and stepped behind and to the side of her to a supportive but subservient position.

But that expression of guilt passed too soon when the barely closed door reopened to allow Lord High Justice Corbin and three soldiers to escort Dayly Niall and Idal Gottfrid into the room. The queen watched anger, resentment, fear and guilt flash over each young man's face. Two were younger than her by enough years that she had spent many hours reading to them, telling them stories or supervising their play as they had been in the company of her brother. She knew them well, or thought she did. With the events of late, she was beginning to believe she no longer knew many of those around her. The boys she had known had changed, and not entirely for the better. Idal was a stranger, older, a face she recognized from among the nobles who attended her father's court but she knew nothing of his personage. What she did know was that he and his brother Kent were friendly with k'dedhá Claide, occupying a suspicious house that Caol had watched from the onset of the Coryllien persecution.

Asta, having bid her brother and his family a safe journey for their trip back to Durham, had been summoned as well; she came into the room with Lord Niall at her heels to received heated glares from the youngest two men. It was no secret to either of them that the girl they had grown up with, that both had shown interest in over the years, was the acting Inquisitor, if not yet Inquisitor by royal appointment. Neither felt she could be trusted any longer and betrayal sparked from them as she took her place beside the Queen.

Idal ignored her.

"Lord Niall," the Queen said to the younger Niall, striving to voice her authority as much as she could muster in her weakness. Lord Gottfrid lived too far away to attend, but word of his son's arrest had been sent. "It has come to my attention that you have taken the laws of Enesfel into your own hands by executing a prisoner of the Crown."

"It was my right to see him dead!" Dayly exclaimed bitterly, despite his father's presence. He might have been fearful of castigation, might have been afraid of his father's judgment and opinion, but he held to his convictions regarding his rights and his sister's honor. "He took my sister's husband…her life! He killed my best friend. He murdered the King!"

"Offenses he was slated to be punished for, I assure you…or do you doubt my ability to follow through on sentencing a man to death?"

"I…" Dayly's eyes still flashed with anger but then he lowered them with a deep breath. Hagan had been the squeamish one, the one prone to avoiding violence. He knew Diona was not like that. "No, Your Majesty, but…"

"But?"

Dayly spluttered, his eloquent words failing. Once he might have spoken plainly, bluntly, to the princess, despite her being a Lachlan and being older. But she was the princess no more; she was his sovereign and that made their relationship different. "It was my right," he repeated.

The Queen took a breath, staring at him, leaving a long silence not to think but to make him uncomfortable, a tactic she had often witness her father employ. When the breath was released, it took some of her anger with it. In truth, she was less angry about the execution she had been unable to carry out than she was at someone taking the law into their hands without her permission, of undermining her authority.

"You should have come to me," she said finally, voice cool and even. "If you had expressed your desire to be his executioner, the right to avenge your sister's honor, we might have come to a mutually agreeable accord." Seeing his effort to protest, she held up a hand to silence him. "Avenging your sister I can understand. Avenging Hagan, I can understand. Stealing a dedhá's robe to frame him for murder, however, is a crime of a more serious nature."

"I did not steal the robe! I was not framing…"

"Weren't you? Do you deny you wore dedhá robes to gain access to the dungeon?"

Dayly glanced at Idal and Tayte, wondering what, if anything, either man had already confessed to the Queen. Idal's entire demeanor was blank, while Tayte's face was flushed dark with indignation, but there was no way for Dayly to know if the Queen's information came from one of them or from some other source, a witness or an Elyri reading of the dead man's corpse, perhaps. Rather than accuse Tayte, however, a man he considered a friend, for his part in the planning, he squared his shoulders and said, "No…I do not deny it."

"And do you deny that you instructed Lord Cáner to return it to the dedhá's trunk?"

"I told him to return it," Dayly squeaked, blinking in surprise, "to where Idal got it…"

The Queen looked at Idal, who did not react.

"The dedhá's trunk…" countered Tayte.

There was a slight faltering in Gottfrid's façade. "I did not say the trunk. I meant to return it to the washroom where I…"

Tayte's eyes narrowed. "You did not say…"

"You didn't ask. I thought you knew…"

"How could I know where you found it? Why would I have thought of the washroom?"

"You think I could have snuck into the náós and broken into locked trunks?"

"How did you know they were locked?" interjected Asta. Dayly, meanwhile was content to be silent, letting the other two condemn themselves while taking focus off of him.

"Of course they would be locked," Idal shot back with a snort. "Who wouldn't lock their belongings?"

The look on Tayte's face suggested a different answer, and birthed a spark of fright, for he had gotten into Tusánt's room and trunk to return the robe without a second thought as to where else to return it.

The two continued to glare at each other, their quarrel revealing as much to the Queen and her advisors as it did to the two of them. Each had made assumptions of the other in their inexperience. Dayly had acted out of a sense of revenge for his sister and had used the disguise most likely to gain him unquestioned access, suggested by Idal. They had trusted the older man's advice and Dayly had trusted his friend with evidence, or at least part of the evidence, without considering that Tayte would also be implicated for helping him.

Tayte's motives were less clear, beyond the desire to help his friend. Perhaps, Diona thought, that was enough to win him leniency. The argument revealed that Tayte had known the trunk was locked, and yet he had successfully gained access to it, which suggested a skill with locks that he had no reason to have. Perhaps he had foolishly thought he was following Idal's directions by putting the robe in the dedhá's trunk, but there was a reason he chose Tusánt, a reason he had picked the lock of that particular trunk rather than find a more convenient place to dispose of evidence. And Idal, the elder of the three, the mastermind, had given the two younger men enough leeway in that idea to damn them while hoping to remain free of the charges. If Diona questioned them one at a time, Idal might have been able to talk his way out of this situation. As it was, he knew he could not.

"Lord Cáner."

Bhríd squared his shoulders, expecting to be addressed, though Diona's eyes were on his son. It made the chamberlain no less nervous, as he too had serious questions about his son's motives and actions.

"Your Majesty?" Tayte's voice quavered but he showed no other sign of apprehension.

"Why dedhá Tusánt's trunk?"

It was the one question everyone wanted to be answered, and Tayte was prepared for it. "Someone was in dedhá Rankin's room…and dedhá Valgis' room was locked."

Bhríd did not need to touch his son to know Tayte was telling the truth. He was familiar with the young man's aura, his body language. That Elyri skill had taught the Cáner boys early on that they could not easily lie to their father. It was another reason Bhríd was bitter about his wife demanding he did not read Tayte or pursue the deaths of their staff further. Despite the dedhásur's insistence that their rooms were rarely locked, which begged the question of why Valgis' room was, and some interest in who had been in Rankin's room if not Rankin himself at that hour, it seemed an all too convenient truth that covered the underlying reason for Tayte's choice.

"Why take the time to look for a trunk, open a locked one, when you could have burned the evidence?" asked Asta, who wanted to know where he had learned to open locks that way. She had promised to keep her special education secret which won her the opportunity to learn such things, and she knew Caol had taught none of those skills to Tayte. Nor had she.'

"I…." He faltered. "I did not think of that…"

"But you did think about disposal enough to pick a lock." It was not a question.

"And the blade?"

Tayte shrugged. He had never seen the weapon. Getting rid of the robe had been his only charge. Dayly glanced at Idal, who continued to stare silently straight ahead. The implication in that exchange was that Dayly had either disposed of it, with Idal's instruction, or that the blade had been given to Idal for disposal or safe-keeping. Neither was inclined, however, to answer Asta's question.

The Queen had heard enough to feel confident of their guilt, leaving her with the dilemma of how to punish them. None of the crimes necessitated death, but such crimes could not be lightly overlooked either, particularly Dayly's. Any choice she made would bring grief to the men's families, but the trio, as far as Diona was concerned, had brought punishment upon themselves.

"Dayly Niall." It was difficult to condemn her brother's friends. Her friends. But as her first challenge as Queen, it was expected. Kavan's trial had been a necessary formality as she had not doubted his innocence. And Bayle's sentencing had been a simple matter because the man was a stranger and had killed her brother, their King. No other sentence but death had been possible. Now she was faced with a more personal set of rulings which helped her understand how difficult her father's duties had been for him.

"For acting against the wishes of your Queen, for taking the right of execution of an already judged man upon yourself, for imitating a dedhá to gain unlawful access to this keep and the dungeon, you are hereby sentenced for the crime of treason against the Crown…"

"Your Majesty!" the elder Niall gasped, afraid of her next words, the sentence that usually came with a treason charge. A stern look from the woman, however, and the movement of a pair of guards to flank him if he made any physical threat against her, caused the white-haired man to remain where he was and fall silent.

She continued. "Because it was a crime of passion, a crime of honor, you shall be spared the sentence of death. However, because it was not such a passion crime that you took time to plan your entrance, your disguise, the disposal of evidence, I cannot ignore what you have done. You are hereby banished from Enesfel for no less than ten years. Should," she glanced at the elderly man behind Dayly, "the Duke become incapable of upholding his responsibilities to the Crown during those years, the estates and titles will be granted to Lady Sigrid and any family she might have. If the titles and lands are maintained by the Duke until your return, you may petition the Crown to be reinstated as the heir to the title and the privileges that come with it."

Dayly's face darkened but he nodded his acceptance. To a young man, ten years seemed but a short span, and he believed his father to be a fit and healthy man who would surely live until his son came back. And if by some fate he died before Dayly's return, he was satisfied with his sister gaining both title and lands. If Hagan had lived, if the wedding had been performed and consummated before his death, she would have had so much more. Becoming a duchess would be a small compensation. His father, he suspected, was more upset by the ruling then he was. Dayly bowed and murmured, "Yes, Your Majesty. If it pleases you, I will go to my mother's family in Cordash?"

It was where the Queen expected he would go and she bobbed her head once. "That is agreeable." It was penance, but it was not unbearable. She was grateful neither he nor his father fought her.

Idal, with no one to support him, not even his brother, took his sentence as stoically as he had most of the questioning. He, as the thief and the mastermind of the break-in, would remain incarcerated until a hefty fine was paid to both the Crown and the Faith, amounts he did not know if his father would be willing to pay. He believed, however, that his imprisonment would not be long. After the sum was paid, he too would be banished from the kingdom, but as he had no known kin in lands outside of Enesfel, his future was less certain. Perhaps he would follow Dayly. At least he was given time to consider his destination while he waited for his fine to be paid.

When Diona looked at the Cáners, however, she felt no such comfort. She could not banish Tayte to his father's people, for if his hatred for Elyri was as strong as it appeared, that would likely only deepen it. And with the potential for a sound relationship with the High Mother at stake, it would be foolish to send a potentially violent man into exile in Elyriá. Madalyn's family had lived for generations in Enesfel. There was nowhere to send him. She considered briefly imprisonment and a fine as well, but her chamberlain did not deserve to be financially penalized for the wrongs of his son, and she did not believe a short prison sentence would teach Tayte anything. With no evidence to prove that he had intentionally targeted Tusánt, the worst crimes she could punish him for were breaking into the náos and the dedhá's trunk, and acting as a knowing accomplice to murder.

That was no small thing.

"Tayte Cáner. You have served as a willing accomplice to murder, both in the planning, the disposal of evidence, and withholding knowledge of the crime from the Crown. You broke into a man's lodgings and belongings, a crime in its own right, and planted evidence to accuse an innocent man of these crimes. As those acts were all directly connected to the crime perpetrated against the Crown by Dayly Niall, you, also, are indicted on the charge of treason."

Unlike Lord Niall, Bhríd did not speak, did not protest, and he refused to hang his head. Tayte interpreted that as yet another betrayal by the man who had sired him and spat, "Execute me then! I will not be sent to Elyriá. I will not go!"

"Nor would I send you where you might endanger the lives of others," the Queen growled, color rising into her cheeks at his challenge. The fact that she called him on his anti-Elyri stance took him aback. He had made no secret of it, but he had not expected her to make a public statement of her knowledge. "I have too much respect for your father to execute you for your foolishness…this time."

But, she implied with her stare, she might not be so lenient next time, for she, like his father, felt reasonably certain there would be a next time. Tayte's fury had become a driving force in his life and as long as that held root, she would continue to see him as a potential threat to the Crown and to Enesfel.

It was that threat that tempered her next words. "You are hereby stripped of any right or chance to bear the title of Duke of Levonne, or any other estate, for the next ten years, and are barred from Rhidam for that same term. Should your parents become unable to fulfill the duties of their titles during that time, your brother will gain the rights of title and estate…"

"No!" Tayte roared. He was no healer, he had no skill he deemed marketable beyond his knowledge of the vineyards. And his father would outlive them all. To lose the right to the title he had been born to…to his father, to his blood-tainted brother…was worse than death.

The Queen ignored his outburst and continued. "…should he desire it. If he does not desire it, the estate shall revert to the Crown until such time as you are deemed fit to carry the title with respect and honor. And if," her voice dropped to a venomous tone that none in the room had heard her use before except once or twice in reference to k'dedhá Claide, "harm befalls your father or brother…if there is any reason to suspect your hand in their harm, I will not hesitate to give you the headman's ax. Do you understand?"

Bhríd blanched, his face losing color and most traces of life to the shock of the Queen's words. He had spoken little of Tayte's threats, his attitudes, to anyone outside of immediate family, although perhaps Gaelán or Princess Asta, who overheard much and whom his youngest fully trusted, had spoken with the Queen. Perhaps Madalyn had done so. Or perhaps Diona was more sensitive to these things, and smarter, then some gave her credit for. Those Kavan raised and tutored, who paid the most attention to his teachings, seemed to be that way, so perhaps she would prove worthy of her crown.

Perhaps, he mused, he should have placed Tayte and Gaelán's education in his kinsman's hands.

The sentence laid on Tayte was not a light one, and would not, he knew, be easily borne. He expected Tayte to be more difficult to live with now, at least for him and Gaelán, which guaranteed that the two of them would not return to Levonne so long as Tayte remained there. The sentence was not on Bhríd, but it was heavy to shoulder. At least he hoped the decree would provide Gaelán protection. Bhríd could protect himself. Gaelán, on the other hand, started on the healing path, would find it difficult to protect himself from his brother's wrath. If the boy was lucky, the Queen's threat would be enough to shield him.

It took effort for Tayte to resist either launching into a tirade or else pulling free of his guards to storm from the room in fury. He was smart enough to realize that doing either would gain further sanctions. He swallowed his breath and more violent impulses and began a stiff bow as Diona added, "I say this to you again. You shall not set foot within this city without a summons from the Crown. Should you desire audience, you will petition the Crown and await a response." As she saw it, anyone willing to disguise themselves to sneak into the castle once, or were willing to help another do the same, could not be trusted not to do it again. "Lord Justice. Take Mr. Gottfrid into custody. The rest of you are dismissed."

They were difficult sentences to pass, but Diona felt there was no other choice. She could see in the elder Niall's face his anger at his son and his disappointment that his son's action would likely mean he would never be fully trusted by the Crown again. His hopes for political advancement had been undercut by his heir. How troublesome then, that it seemed the chamberlain's position was secure, although it had not been the Elyri's boy who had killed anyone. But banishment for a term was better than execution. In time, Dayly would come back to him. From what he could see between the chamberlain and his son, there would be no going back for them. The final wedge had been driven into place.

❧Chapter 46❧

If Espen had not been beside her when Diona rose from the seat of her latest ruling and then collapsed in a faint, he might have thought she was trying to avoid him again. One moment she was standing, facing him, murmuring, "Thank you for being here," the next she was in his arms as limp as a sleeping child. Undoubtedly, he thought with concern as he carried her to her chambers, such a ruling against friends, against her brother's friends, had taken its toll on the physically weak woman and sapped what strength she had mustered to be here. Physician Talis stayed with her, checking her over one more time, but there was little Espen could do except fret and make certain her wishes were carried out…

…and wonder why she did not want Healer MacLyr to tend her.

There was wailing from the chamberlain's rooms, a sound that made Espen sigh. Lady Cáner was less pleased, it appeared, than her husband with the ruling against their eldest child, or at least she was more vocal with her upset than Bhríd had been. Normally soft-spoken Bhríd was heard trying to reason with her, to assure her that it was far better, this punishment, then having Tayte sent away, imprisoned, or executed. If Tayte used his time wisely to improve himself, make a name, mold his life into something the Crown accepted, there was a chance the Queen would one day overturn her ruling. That was the purpose of the ten-year marker. When Madalyn decided she would speak to the Queen and beg her to reconsider on Tayte's behalf, her husband reminded her that this was something Tayte, an adult now who had chosen his own actions, would have to face alone. If they attempted to take his punishment for him, lessen it, or otherwise coddle him, he was going to learn nothing except that he could get away with any crime he chose because his parents…at least one of them…would shield him from the consequences.

The duchess, in grief and frustration, swore that Bhríd allowed Tayte to be punished because he was not Elyri enough to deserve his father's love, that he would move every obstacle if such a ruling was made against Gaelán but again turned his back on Tayte. Stunned, knowing it was untrue, that he had never turned his back on Tayte and that had Gaelán committed, treason, he would have been expected to endure the consequences, Bhríd bit back the argumentative words that first came to mind. Broken by his wife's accusations, knowing they were a product of her pain but stinging no less because of that knowledge, he stalked stoically from his room saying that he expected Tayte to be out of the castle by the time he returned. He fully expected that, when he did, he would find Madalyn gone as well.

He had tried from the start to believe that their racial differences could never come between them, but the blade of a child's misdeeds and suffering, rooted in those very differences, was cutting them apart and there was nothing anyone, not even the youngest Cáner who waited in the corridor outside of his parents' room listening with horror to every word, could do to change it.

The brewing storm in the keep, to which the Queen was blissfully oblivious, was matched by a hot, oppressive pall over Rhidam, as if the stifling late summer air was a tightening noose around the throat of the city. Further rumors of persecuting violence made their way to Espen's ear, accompanied by a few reports of a scattering of brawls in Rhidam's taverns that spoke of heat-induced tension roiling beneath the surface. He assigned more soldiers to patrol the streets in case alcohol and the day's temperatures sparked more than brawls, but that was the most the prince could do beyond pray the day passed quickly and the night brought a drop in temperature and, if they were so blessed, rain to wash the tension away.

Diona stirred in the hottest hour of the day and tried to recall how she had gotten to her bed when the last thing she remembered was speaking to Espen after the ruling against the trio of young lords. She must have fainted, a thought which embarrassed her as she had never been prone to such weakness. But she could not recall having ever faced this much continuing adversity. If this was her body's reaction to such stress, she would never survive as queen and Enesfel was doomed. She hoped, as she drank two cups of water in succession, that the suffocating heat was to blame. Perhaps she could consult Ártur, but she already knew the truth and did not want to hear him say it.

Maybe she should request a consultation with the healer's wife. Perhaps another woman, one who had experienced what Diona faced, could belay her fears.

At least she had slept a little, something she had not done much of during recent nights, and she felt hungry for the first time in days. Emotionally, she even felt ready to face the evening ahead of her. She might be too weak to make a long evening of it, but she was determined to speak to Espen and seek a resolution to her troubles before they created an even larger issue.

Espen, however, could not be found. Chancellor McGranis reported that Espen, Owain, and Muir had ridden into the city to offer a show of royal presence, an effort to quell the day's heat-spawned unrest and prove that nobles too were forced to endure the summer's heat. Left to her own amusements, Diona ended up beneath the shade trees in the courtyard with Zelenka and Clianthe, taking advantage of the southerly breeze. With Ártur already gone for the night and not wanting to trouble the other two Elyri men with fetching Syl for her…particularly when one of the men was undoubtedly burdened with the fallout of his son's sentence…and unable to share her thoughts with Espen, she instead spoke to the pair of women about the topic most on her mind…the wedding night she had not yet had.

She had heard from Asta about the fight between her chamberlain and his wife that had precipitated the duchess leaving with her son, but though offending the woman who had been a friend of her family had not been Diona's intention, that was less troubling than the need for this particular talk. As patient as he had been over the years, as patient as he still was, she understood that no man would wait forever for his wife to come to him, and she could not risk the option of annulment. Being Espen's wife, and everything that came with that, was what she wanted. If only she was not afraid.

They ate beneath the setting sun and still Espen, Owain, and Muir did not return. They were fighting men, capable of taking care of themselves, and Diona knew they were men inclined towards hunting and adventure. It was better that her husband was out there, tending to duty, then moping about the castle over her health. Hopefully, when he came in he would be pleased to see her out of bed and be willing to sit and talk with her. Yet the tolling of the náós bell rang the eighth evening hour and then the ninth and still he had not returned. The air was still hot but the sun's light had finally left the sky. Weary still from the plaguing weakness and frustrated that her evening had not gone as planned, Diona retired to her room. At least she felt, through her talk with the other two recently married young women, that she understood her fears at last and might be able to help Espen understand them too. Together, they might be able to address them, erase them, and move forward with their marriage.

❧*❧

Rarely did he dose mid-day or in the early hours of evening, but the hot day sapped Kavan's energy during the tour of Alberni businesses and finally, in the refreshing cool of St. Kóráhm's grotto, he was able to sit and rest and shed the sticky heat. He came to the grotto every evening during his stay in Alberni, as the tranquility of the abbey soothed him. Having heard nothing from Rhidam, he presumed everything was peaceful, at ease, and that Dayly Niall and Idal Gottfrid had not yet been found. With the boys secure in Ártur, Rouvyn, and Bhyrhán's care, Kavan was not concerned with their welfare either. Being free from duty and expectation was something Kavan needed as he awaited answers about his own future.

But there were no answers forthcoming in the abbey either, not from Kóráhm, who was conspicuously absent, not from the presences that came when he meditated with his harp in prayer in this place. He felt heavy inside, and though he was certain his time was nearer, he had yet to be given an indication when it would come, what he was meant to do. The elusive truth made him anxious so that he spent longer and longer hours at the pool's edge in the monastery trying to dispel the internal discomfort his burden brought with it.

Dozing in prayer, however, was rarer still, but what startled him awake led him to believe that the period of sleep, brief though it was, had been the precursor to the Sight, to a vision of flame, soot, and screaming. Heat searing his skin, the hairs there prickling on edge, and thick smoke that he could smell still and see, now that his eyes were open, as well as taste upon his oddly dry, cracked lips. It felt as though he was in the middle of a monstrous fire, though there was nothing but the residual fog of Sight-smoke. The abbey was not ablaze. Something to come then, he presumed, or something happening now, though he had no hint of location or time. As his thoughts had been focused on what awaited him in the underground chapel, he wondered if that snippet of vision was intended to answer his plea for direction.

He clutched his harp to his chest, closed his eyes, and rocked back and forth on his knees as he resumed his prayers. *Not the pyre, Dhágdhuán,* he prayed. It was distressing enough to share the rósádhá with the cornerstone of his Faith. He did not think he could endure the same fate as the Holy Founder, which would undoubtedly raise future comparisons between the two men in the hearts and mouths of the people in every Sovereignty. He could endure the suffering, but the implications, the parallels between them, he could not. Kóráhm had suffered that same death. Kavan did not want to be a third in that particular trinity. He did not envision himself as worthy of being equated with them in the same breath.

But he wanted to know what the vision meant.

❧*❧

Out of her gown, into her nightdress, Diona was about to douse the candles for the night when the naós bells began to toll. Another hour had not passed and this was no steady march of peels to mark the hourly change. This was a frantic clamor that brought her to the window, heart hammering in trepidation. Such chaos might indicate a riot, an attack, or some other calamity.

What it announced this night was easily identified from her chamber window.

On the northern horizon, near the western edge of Rhidam at the bank of the Tegid River, a deadly orange glow was accompanied by shouts of fear and panic. It had been a long time since there had been any fire in Rhidam larger than a single structure. She could not recall one during her lifetime and her father had never mentioned one from his years as king, but it was something every urban dweller feared. Narrow streets lined with closely packed wood, brick, and clay houses, some that jutted out over the alleys and streets to block out the light of the sky, were a breeding ground for the worst fires imaginable. It was, she mused as she stared in horrified fascination, a risk most city folks lived with, and one most were careful to avoid as they knew what carelessness could cost them.

The dryness of the timbers and cracking clay in the summer heat meant the easy spreading of flames; as she watched she could see its growth. In the courtyard, soldiers and servants scrambled about, some dousing buildings with water pulled from the moat and well as fast as they could draw it, in order to protect them from catching fire should it spread to the keep, while others ran into the streets in the direction of the blaze. Rich or poor, man or woman, young or old, they either lent a hand in the effort to hold the fire at bay or else helped to get the old, infirm, or very young out of the fire's path.

Diona took enough time to draw a robe over her nightdress and shove her feet into slippers before running into the courtyard. She did not know what she could do to help; going to the fire, putting her life in danger that way was inconceivable, but she had to do something. Finally, she joined the line of water bearers at the well, where Zelenka and Clianthe already lent their strength to the efforts to protect the keep. Diona nodded at them both. She might not be able to do much in her weak condition, but she, like they, could draw and carry water.

Wortham and Bhríd found Owain in the thick of the firefighting efforts near the point of the blaze's origin, the warehouse that, to their knowledge, had not been used since k'dedhá Tythilius' body was discovered there months earlier. The dry air and drier building timbers made an ample meal for the hungry flames; they devoured the warehouse in less than thirty minutes and jumped to two of the closest buildings to begin feasting there. Espen and Muir, working side by side further along the wide-cobblestone path that traveled beside the river, issued orders to tear down a series of nearby wooden buildings with the hopes that it would slow the fire's spread so that they might gain the upper hand and contain the fire to a small section of the city. Keep its spread to the north and it would burn itself out. They hoped. Townsfolk scurried here and there, showering the flames with waters from the river, but it seemed that, for every pail poured on it, the fire roared hotter and wilder. One by one, the buildings in the northwest quadrant began to succumb, in spite of their efforts, so that by dawn, nearly the entire quarter was burning.

The glow of it, the smoke, brought farmers from the surrounding countryside, and when Ártur returned to Rhidam that morning to learn of it, it was to promptly return to Bhryell for his wife. Healers would be needed, and Bhen, on hearing the news, demanded to come as well, to lend his hands and strong back in an effort to save Enesfel's Crown seat. gdhededhá Tusánt had much the same idea; his efforts to find aid sent him to his home city of Clarys, and while he was not as successful as he hoped, he returned with two dozen young men and women to fight the fire, four gdhededhá to assist the displaced and those weary from fighting the flames, and three healers. Saul and Edward led the twenty-four volunteers to the encroaching eastern front of the firestorm, Rankin oversaw the establishment of a triage center from which the healers could work in the naós, while Valgis, despite the awkwardness he felt around so many Elyri dedhá, directed the arranging of pallets, provisions of food and drink, and gifts of clothing for those who needed it. The spacious náós had rarely been bursting with so much activity.

Ártur, however, refused to remain in the náós with the healers and physicians, despite his wife's unspoken protests. Men would be suffering burns, cuts, and other injuries out there, near the fire. As a healer who had spent his earliest years on the battlefield, Ártur was prepared to be where the action was, where he felt most needed, regardless of the risk. No one, he believed, would be interested in assaulting him today. The survival of Rhidam was more important than the life of a single Elyri, particularly when that one Elyri might save their lives before the end of the day.

"General Wyndham!"

It was not a man Agis expected to see today, and he had to wipe his sooty hand across his eyes, clearing them of smoke, to look again to be certain he had seen the former Lachlan general correctly. The ex-general dodged the falling timbers of the building Agis and others were defending and stopped when he reached the Cíbhóló's side. "Came to see the Queen…to apologize for not being here…" Another timber cracked, popped and then fell before them. Agis grabbed the older man's arm and yanked him to safety as someone thrust a bucket into the old man's hand. The ex-general threw the water on the flames, handed the bucket to one of the boys running pails back and forth between the nearest water source and the fire's front as fast as they could, and then took another. "Wasn't expecting this."

"No one was. Appreciate the help."

Ternce nodded and kept working. He might have retired from service, but he was not going to allow Rhidam to burn without doing his utmost to save it. The city continued to burn. Though exhausted, the people of Rhidam continued to fight for their homes and Ternce Wyndham was there alongside them.

The images of flame and the smell and taste of smoke refused to leave Kavan once he noted them, and by the time he finished his meal, he was anxious enough about the premonition to decide to return to Rhidam. If it was his death he was sensing, fate haunting him, it made sense to confront that destiny head-on. Harp in hand, it took the moment of emerging from the Gate into the oratory to know that something in Rhidam was wrong. He could see nothing in the windowless room, nor hear anything, but he could feel it. He could smell it. Leaving his harp on the altar, the safest place for it until he knew what was happening, he stepped into the corridor to be hit by a wall of smoke so thick he could barely breathe.

But it was not the keep that burned. The sounds of shouted commands, screams of panic and pain, were too distant. He went to his cousin's north-facing room, one that afforded a better view of the city than his east-facing room did, and from there witnessed the horror enveloping Rhidam. Smoke rose from the riverside point of origin, with small pockets of flame still sparking there, but the body of the fire had surged east and south, despite efforts to contain it to the north, through the collection of houses that constituted Rhidam's poorer north quarter. It was nearing the city's center, and if it spread much further it would reach Hes á Redh. Some of the embers the hot day carried into the sky had found nests in buildings elsewhere throughout the city, some of those buildings had been doused and the biting sparks on their wet thatched, planked, or tiled roofs extinguished before they could ignite. Other structures were not as lucky, meaning there were smatterings of flame dotting the entire city skyline. Men were spread thin in their efforts to take control, but it did not appear to Kavan that such control would be gained soon.

"k'Ádhá…Dhágdhuán…Kóráhm…" he begged as he scanned the view from one side of Rhidam to the other, wondering how far south the fire had jumped. "Please. Show mercy."

"Prayer is not going to help, Lord Cliáth." He turned from the window towards the Queen. Smudged with soot and mud, her hair disheveled, her nightdress and robe torn and soiled and hanging ripped from one shoulder, she had clearly been helping the efforts in some way which made Kavan proud.

"My Queen…"

"Don't. I don't know where you've been…or why you're arriving at this hour…but we need you out there."

She sounded terse, angry, but Kavan did not take it personally. Her mood was not directed at him but brandished in his direction because he happened to be the target in her path. He also understood that she was not saying they needed him in particular, but rather that they needed every able body to win the battle before Rhidam was destroyed. She did not know, unless Muir or Owain had told her, how he had once helped control another, much smaller fire. That had been long ago, when Prince Bertram had still been alive and Prince Hagan newly born. But as the cries in the courtyard sent servants and staff running towards the guardhouse, where the roof now began to smoke, Kavan believed he could offer much the same aid here. Perhaps it would not be enough to save the city, but it would be of more use, he imagined, then carrying buckets would be.

Diona did not wait for a reply but continued on about her business. Alone, Kavan chose flight, dodging falling ash and embers, in order to quickly reach the strongest area of the fire, the southern-most line where Espen, Muir, Owain, and Wortham had formed a united front against the flames. Further to the east, where the fire was relentlessly pushing towards the náos, Kavan spotted Agis and Ternce Wyndham, as well as the justice, the chancellor, and Wace Elotti also battling as one. The fire's proximity to the náos concerned Kavan, but it was the blaze's southern edge that was the biggest threat. If the flames reached the city center, recovering from the devastation would take far longer. The weather was hot and dry now, but the chill and damp of autumn, and then winter, would be on them soon. The fewer citizens left homeless by disaster, the better off Rhidam would be.

No one saw him land behind the front line of firefighters. No one noticed the arms outstretched as if to embrace the whole of the fire. No one noticed the surge of power that pushed out from the Elyri's core, spread east and west as far as his senses would allow, forming an impenetrable firebreak. What Wortham did notice, the first to do so, was that the storm of flame that suddenly erupted between two buildings in front of them, which should have sprayed over them and killed every man around him, blasted against some invisible wall and shot into the air over their heads. Nothing should have held those flames at bay. Nothing except…"

He looked back in relieved elation to behold the bard there, eyes closed, concentration directed against the threat and not on his best friend or those men around him. Wortham had seen this before, had watched Kavan pull fire into itself to be extinguished by the efforts of men's hands, and though he did not know if Kavan's attempt would be enough to put down a fire of this size, Wortham was not going to allow Kavan's effort to be wasted.

"Here!" he shouted. "More water here!"

If anyone other than Owain and Muir connected Kavan's arrival with the miracle that saved them, if anyone thought to question why the bard was in the middle of the fire with his eyes closed and arms open, they did not. They were too busy fighting the flames to ask.

Asta scurried through the alleys and streets with messages, meals, and water, anything she could get her hands on that might help. She was small, light, and for a woman brought up in the Lachlan keep, knew the streets of her city well. With Gaelán and Sóbhán helping in the náós, and the other women fighting to protect structures within the bailey's walls, it left Asta to help in other ways. Each trip out and back had shown her that the fire was marching ever closer to the haven of injured and displaced and this time, as she had gone to the Queen seeking permission to direct people to the castle courtyard, in the event the náós was threatened, she skirted close enough to the eastern edge of the fire to get a better idea of how far away it was and how fast the flames were moving. She determined that the possibility of the náós burning did indeed exist. Another few hours at most, and the flames, if not stopped, were going to devour the náós.

She spotted Elotti first, as the bounty hunter tried to lift a charred beam with a glowing center from the body of a man fallen beneath the collapse of a ruined structure. Some burned from the top down, others, igniting below, collapsed under the weight of their upper floors and roofs as the timbers and clay at the bottom gave way to the fire's gnawing teeth and the eroding wash of the water used to douse them. Agis, trying to get to the fallen man as well, was prevented from pushing forward as the flames sprung up in front of him. His shout, the name of General Wyndham, sounded like a distant buzz in Asta's ears over the roar of the flames. Seeing her opening, she darted forward, intending to help pull the fallen man to safety, but a hand grabbed her shoulder and shoved her back as someone else in dark, wet, clothing flew past. The stranger dragged the ex-general by both arms until he was clear of debris, out of danger of falling flames, to drop him at Asta's feet. The stranger hesitated long enough to meet the young woman's eyes, his lower face and head hidden by the wet cloth he had wrapped around him. His eyes, however, were visible…and familiar.

"Father…" Asta whispered in shock.

But just as quickly, he was gone, not risking further recognition as the bounty hunter reached the fallen man. She spluttered for words, eyes darting about to find where her father had gone while Wace lifted Ternce over his shoulder. There was no trace of him. He had vanished as quickly as he had appeared.

But he was alive…and in Rhidam.

"Come," she shouted, motioning for the bounty hunter to follow her. She knew the quickest way to reach the healers and she figured quick was what the injured man needed. Elotti did not speak of the stranger, of recognition, or even question where she was leading. She was Dugan's daughter, and strangely enough, he trusted her for it.

Asta did not care if he trusted her or not.

Her father was alive.

Darkness brought little relief from the sweltering heat of the fires dotted across the city landscape. One after another had erupted, creating more than a dozen small fires which were, compared to the main inferno in the northern parts of the city, more easily contained. For every fire put out, however, another began, and even the roof of the guardhouse within the keep, half of the servants' quarters, and the horse stable had not been spared from burning. Those battling smaller fires were left to do it alone as Kavan kept his focus on the main body of flame. Little by little, the townspeople gained control of it, but the threat continued to push towards the náós and that was where Wortham dragged Kavan to next. The bard dared not lower his guard, dared not take his attention off the fire, for he feared that if he did so, he would not have the strength to start again. It took less effort to maintain the wall around a portion of flame then it did to reestablish it each time he moved, and thus when the line of defense shifted to some other front, Wortham and Owain took Kavan to it. Each worried the man would collapse, as the lack of food and sleep, and the exhausting work continued to dog them, but they did not beg him to stop. As much as they needed him to do this, Wortham understood that Kavan needed it too if they were to save Rhidam.

The kindling trees scattered through the burial ground already glowed like torches scratching at the sky, and some of those grave markers made of wood instead of stone already burned as well, a morbidly fascinating spectacle. People worked to douse the outer náós walls to protect them from flying embers, but in some places, exposed wood on the outer façade, such as the doors and frames of the windows on the west and north sides, already smoked. Should they be consumed by the flames, the fire would gain entrance to the combustible benches, kneeling bars, fabrics and holy oils that filled the thóres.

Supplies meant for the firefighters had already been relocated to the keep, and as quickly as they were able, the injured, the dead, the dying, the exhausted were being moved as well. Some of the dedhá lingered to protect their holy home while others escorted their charges to safety. Tusánt would be the last to leave, if it came to complete evacuation, like a sea captain refusing to leave his sinking ship. With him, Gaelán, Sóbhán, Edward, and Saul struggled to get the wealth of the Faithful, the holy relics, as well as the people, to safety while pouring every drop of water they could on the smoldering frames. Tusánt saw spot after spot of fire snuff out as if blown, but the five men could not work fast enough to get ahead of the risk. Finally, three of them ran out, their arms loaded with objects of importance and wealth. The smoking front door banged closed behind them, crackled and burst into flame with a force that shot sparks into the building, showering the two men who still remained inside.

Tusánt and Gaelán.

"Gaelán!" Bhríd roared, his voice barely heard over the gnashing fire and something else.

The growl of thunder above them.

Heads lifted to the sky to be drenched with an unexpected deluge. The smoke spread so thickly over the city that no one had been aware of storm clouds or impending rain, and if there had been previous warning thunder or lightening, none had heard or seen it, deafened as they were by the continual roar of fire and the blinding brightness of dancing orange flame. Was there lightning too? No one could see, but the fear presented by lightning was a very real one amidst so many already burning locations.

"I…can go in…" Kavan rasped; the damp covering Wortham had wrapped around his mouth and nose to keep out the worst of the smoke made speaking difficult.

"You'll be killed," Espen cried, his hand grasping for the bard who was already pushing forward, having been snapped out of his daze by his cousin's cry and the fear of those inside that crowded around the edges of his concentration. Espen came up empty-handed, held back by Wortham and Owain who, begrudgingly, allowed Kavan to proceed. They had witnessed Kavan entering a burning building to save victims before. They had faith in his ability but less, the look they gave one another said, in his strength to do so for long.

"Lord Cliáth!" Sóbhán, who had made it halfway across the náos grounds with an armload of books, watched the man disappear into the fire in horror. He dropped his cargo to turn and run after him, but Muir tackled him and held him to the ground, keeping him from the fate Gaelán and Tusánt faced.

The shield used to contain the exterior fire was drawn tighter, forming a second skin around himself that would protect Kavan's clothing and body from the fire, allowing him to pass through the flaming doorway unharmed. He strained to see through the smoke that billowed in from the outside, coming through the door, a few small holes in the glass windows, and through the sporadically burned and open rafters above. Behind the smoke and flame came the rain, but Kavan did not feel it. He felt the heat, the pressure of the smoky air as he stumbled forward, straining to see his targets, hands occasionally seeking the support of the nearest bench as he forced himself forward.

Soon he found the men he sought, both of whom had retreated to the front of the náos to crouch near the altar where, thus far, the fire had not touched anything. Both stared at the pale vision as he reached them, their eyes wide with fear and wonder, but they did not move until he held out his hands and croaked, "Come to me."

They flanked him, one on his left, one on his right, and Kavan held them there, an arm around each, eyes closed as he stretched the protective shell to encompass them as well. He was weak, exhausted, the limits of his Power already pushed past the point where he expected depletion, past the point where he thought he should have collapsed. Willpower alone, and perhaps the hand of the divine, allowed him to go on, enabled him to steer the men towards where the door of the náos should be. It no longer burned, but it belched black smoke that obscured everything in their path. Kavan stumbled, but Tusánt drew him back up. Try as he did now, however, Kavan's legs refused to support him, the last of his strength straining to keep all three of them from burning to death.

Gaelán, sensing his mentor's growing weakness, opened his smaller well of power and allowed Kavan to draw on what strength he possessed after so many hours spent healing and assisting the other healers and physicians in their efforts to do the same. Tusánt did not have the skill to share his Elyri gifts that way, did not know how Kavan was protecting them from the flames, but he could gird his spirit with prayer and push forward, dragging Kavan along with physical strength he rarely used, until he found the doorless opening and, rushing to escape the building, they tumbled down the stone steps because no one could see them.

Seeing them emerge was Wortham's cue to release Espen and charge towards the trio. Others were fighting the fire around the door and Edward and Saul dragged Tusánt to his feet. Muir and Sóbhán, having scooped up the dropped books, pulled Gaelán along too, while the captain lifted the bard and carried him far enough away from the smoldering náós to be safe, the man cradled against the captain's chest. Kavan did not stir as the men regrouped and hurriedly marched to the keep. He did not hear the thunder, did not feel the rain, no longer noticed the fire. There would be no more aid from Kavan.

But his help was less important now that the sky had seen fit to bless the city with a lathing kiss of overdue rain. While Kavan lay unconscious on the pallet he was placed on, attended by the boy he had taken in and his cousin's healer wife, the fires that had spread across Rhidam one by one began to disappear. The streets ran black with soot as the downpour washed every structure, destroyed or not, clean of the fire's inky dust. The Queen saw her chamberlain carrying his eldest son past her, the young man's arm, neck, and cheek blistered, bloody and scarred, and for the moment she set aside her decree. She had forbidden Tayte to enter the castle, but under the circumstances, the barely conscious young man had nowhere to go and she was not about to cast him back into the burning city in his condition. Later, when the fires were dark and the city settled into grieving silence, when he was healed and rested, that would be soon enough to send him on his way. Tonight, no one was leaving the protective confines of the keep.

The graying sky of morning brought Rhidam the last dying gasps of the fire as the final pocket of burning structures nearest the city center were torn down by the hands of men and extinguished by the rain. Those with strength remaining, including Owain, Agis, and Espen, continued to roam the streets for several more hours, searching out burning rubble to expose to the dwindling rain while, in the courtyard of the Lachlan castle, the wounded were tended, families reunited, and little by little began to push back into the city to discover whether their homes had been spared.

Exhaustion was too heavy on most to do more, however, and many slept, passing that day and into the night in the cooling, open-aired rain. There would be weeks of cleanup and rebuilding ahead, but no one cared to think about that yet. Those here had survived, and that was a blessing not to be ruined too soon by the reality of the struggle ahead. Diona saw to it that her staff was sent to bed, save for those still combing Rhidam for fires, victims and survivors, and those keeping watch in the courtyard. Kavan was taken to his room. Then she too collapsed from exhaustion. A long, peaceful sleep, even if in bedding that smelled strongly of smoke, would do every one of them good.

Bhríd collapsed into the chair at his sleeping son's side, wishing he could shake Tayte for his impulsive mulishness but choosing, instead, to respect his unorthodox choice, no matter how much it pained him. The Eagle's Nest immediately outside the castle's outer walls had burned, the mortar between its old stones had blazed, cracked, and crumbled, causing the collapse of walls beneath its own weight. Madalyn, shaken almost to speechlessness, told her husband how she had gone back into the structure to retrieve any belongings that might still be intact. Something, a bottle of wine perhaps, or a flask of lamp oil, exploded at the touch of a single ember, throwing a wall of fire from one side of the inn to the other. Tayte, covered in a heavy blanket soaked in water, had charged inside after his mother to save her. As he caught hold of her, the sleeve of his shirt ignited and the flame raced up his arm to his shoulder, his neck, and the side of his face before he was able to bring it, and his mother, under the dubious safety of the shielding wet blanket. He had gotten her outside with only her clothing and hair singed, but at least she was alive. The burns to his sword arm proved to be more severe than he expected, and his face and neck were forever marked.

That was where Bhríd had found them, both leaning against a street lamp, moaning in agony and barely able to remain upright. Surprisingly, Tayte did not protest when his father lifted him with strength Tayte would never have, nor did he complain when he was brought within the safety of the castle walls, his mother trailing close behind, crying in fear for her son and with the shock of how close she had come to dying. When Tayte did protest, however, was when Bhríd set him down in front of one of the Elyri healers and the woman pulled back the blanket to view the damage. Tayte snatched the blanket back, the effort aggravating his pain, and spat, "No!" refusing to be touched.

Hoping his reluctance was solely due to having a stranger tend him, Bhríd found first Ártur, and then Syl, to take care of his difficult son. And still Tayte refused, demanding that only a Teren physician could attend him, that he would sooner suffer the scars and crippling effects of the injury than the touch of Elyri magic. Dismayed and disappointed, the chamberlain turned his back on Tayte and left him to his mother's pleading, hoping that she would be able to talk sense into him, convince him to accept healing. As young and stubborn as he was, Bhríd suspected Tayte had no inkling of the life he would be condemned to if his sword arm was not properly tended, the looks he would receive throughout his life. Already denied the duchy, at least for the foreseeable future until he changed his views and attitudes, Tayte would have only his hands and wits to forge a life. If he lost even partial use of an arm or hand, Bhríd hated to think what that would mean. But Tayte, like Bhríd's brother Phaedr, was as stubborn as any Cáner. He might not acknowledge his Elyri blood, but he was a Cáner down to his bones. Phaedr had refused to allow blindness to hinder him, refused to allow it to keep him off the battlefield in defense of Prince Arlan. He had lost his life because of it. Bhríd hoped that, regardless of his chosen path, Tayte's stubbornness would be similarly put to good use and would not result in a similar end.

But come dawn, Tayte and Madalyn were gone, riding back to Levonne without a goodbye, and Bhríd believed he would never see his eldest son again. As for the future with his wife, that was a matter to be worked out later, when both had opportunity to settle once more into life's routines. He had expected to outlive her, to lose her one day, but he had not expected that day would come so soon, while they were still young enough to enjoy their lives together. Regardless of their differences or difficulties, he did not want to say farewell to their marriage. He loved her still, just as he did both of his sons.

❧*❧

With Matus and Elotti's help, Asta scoured Rhidam, seeking her contacts, making sure they were well, but mostly seeking her father, who she swore she had seen that day in spite of what both Diona and Gaelán said. Perhaps she thought she had seen him because she wanted to. Perhaps it was someone who looked like him. Asta refused to believe that, though neither she, Matus, nor the bounty hunter turned up any evidence of Caol being in Rhidam during the long hours of the fire. What they did find, with Matus' help, was the fire's point of origin, the building where k'dedhá Tythilius had been tortured and killed. Nothing of the outer building remained, the stone walls had been reduced to rubble, burying the secret basement opening into that chamber of death.

Asta, in her capacity as inquisitor, thinking the fire starting in this building to have been more than a coincidence, ordered men to clear the rubble to expose the trap door and then, using a strong ox to pull on ropes fastened to the metal hatch handle, worked the surprisingly undamaged door open to investigate the room beneath. It seemed suspicious to her that someone had bothered to destroy the building now and she wanted to know what secret was hidden here. The building had been periodically monitored since its discovery; there should have been nothing there to find.

But the stench as the hatch was opened told them otherwise, and it was to her horror and sickening shock that she, Elotti, and Matus found a room full of mutilated corpses. Some had been dead for weeks, possibly months. Others were more recently deceased, and a few, judging by the bloody scratches on the underside of the hatch door and the torn, broken fingers of some of the emaciated bodies, had died clawing for escape as the fire brought the exterior of the building crashing down on their tomb. Odds were, she thought with a grimace, her stomach trying to express its revulsion against her wishes, they had been too weak to survive or escape, whether they had been locked in or not, and the fire above had drawn out the last of the air from the room, causing suffocation before the building's timbers and stone collapsed on the hatch. There was no way anyone could have survived.

Rather than remove the bodies, taking them to the castle or the naós for identification, Bhríd and Bhyrhán were brought to identify as many of the dead as possible. Most were young, barely more than children, and Teren, from the far reaches of Enesfel. Only a few were from Rhidam. Some had been dead too long to identify by sight or touch, and if they bore no distinguishing marks or jewelry or other possessions, it was impossible to determine who they were. Some had been strangled or beaten. Most had died with their throats or wrists slit…sometimes both…as if they had been executed…or sacrificed. That possibility, once Bhyrhán commented on it, chilled the investigators. If all of these people had been sacrificed in some sort of ritual, there was a single organization to blame.

The one that called itself Coryllien.

The consensus was that, without an order from the Queen, the ill-fated victims should be interred where they were. Wace was the last to leave the room, and when he did, he closed the trapped door so that, at Asta's orders, it could be sealed to remain perpetually unopened. It was the only tomb big enough to hold so many dead at once.

The list of names Bhyrhán compiled was taken to the keep where the bleary-eyed Queen tried not to slouch on the throne in the Great Hall while overseeing the duties of her staff and advisors as the task of getting Rhidam back on its feet began. Rubble needed to be moved, the reusable materials gathered and those not useable disposed of in some way. The interiors of fire-gutted buildings had to be cleared for repairs to begin, while others merely needed cleaning to be made functional. With so many collapsed and destroyed structures, it was going to take a substantial amount of time, resources and money to rebuild them.

Diona had already sent formal pleas to the Kings of Hatu and Cordash, a message to Káliel's Prime Magistrate, and one to the Elyri High Mother. Lords from across Enesfel were sent requests for aid, materials, and labor, in lieu of a portion of the tax burden each was expected to pay by year's end. General Agis sent word to his kin in the desert, hoping his messenger found them in a timely manner and that they might be willing to assist with manpower if not reconstruction goods. Owain, weary though he was as he had not yet collapsed into sleep, wrote to his own staff in Fiara with instructions for the transport and delivery of lumber to be brought to Rhidam. With that request, he sent a secret letter to Prince Kjell. Help from Neth was unlikely, but the situation in Rhidam was desperate enough to prompt the seeking of aid from every avenue available. If some portion of the city could not be repaired and rebuilt before the arrival of winter in three months' time, there would be too many homeless, too much suffering, for Rhidam to support. Diona did not want to think about what would happen to her city then.

She did not want to think about it any more than she wanted to dwell on the declaration she held in one trembling hand on her lap.

"Your Majesty," Asta said with a bow before placing the list of names into her cousin's empty hand. "These are the names of the deceased, those we could identify, found in the chamber where k'dedhá Tythilius was murd…"

"What?"

"Uncle and Prince Espen pointed us to where the fire originated. With the help of Mr. Elotti, Matus, and the justice, we determined their assessment to be accurate. Those names," Asta pointed at the list, "some have been dead for weeks, some died as recently as a few days hence, possibly before or during the fire. Lord Bhíncári and Chamberlain Cáner identified those they could…but there were at least two dozen beyond identification. As there were too many to relocate for burial…there is already dead beginning to line the streets as they're pulled from the debris…I ordered the basement room sealed so that none will enter and find them. Not the most sacred tomb…but a tomb all the same. Saul and Edward spoke prayers for their souls, giving them the best burial we could…under the circumstances."

"Children?" There were still so many people reported missing from across Enesfel, mostly children, that even this number, as large as it was, would not account for all of them. Diona wondered how many other basements in Rhidam and elsewhere were similarly filled.

"Children and young adults mostly," Bhríd answered, his voice rough with the sickness of their find. "All Teren." Those could have been his own children…except for one disturbing fact. "Beaten, strangled, most dying from a cut to their throat…"

"Like Bayle," Diona muttered.

The similarity of the deaths struck the chamberlain, and it was a short leap of disbelieving logic to wonder if Dayly was connected to the Corylliens and if, in turn, his son was too. One hand balled at his side, the other tightened around the hilt of his sword. Bhyrhán clasped his shoulder, staying his anger, and Bhríd gave a forced sigh. Who could he be angry at? He had no facts, no proof, just a sickening suspicion he prayed was the product of his overactive, overtired mind.

"Read this." Diona gave the chamberlain the other document she held, its curling parchment indicating it had arrived in a scroll tube though there was none visible. The proclamation read:

> *'We, the Corylliens, do hereby claim cause and effect*
> *of the fire meant to purge Rhidam of its sin and the*
> *taint of those who have corrupted our great kingdom.*
> *There will be no rest until each of them is gone from*
> *within the borders of Enesfel and the innocent are*
> *made free. This is our solemn vow.'*

Bhríd tried to read the impressions left on the parchment, tried to gain some imagery from it that might reveal who had written it. Whether it was his exhaustion or some other reason, all he could draw from the page was a sense of darkness that made no sense. But it did confirm what those at that basement had already guessed. Whether the fire had been accidental or intentional, it made too much sense for the Corylliens to be responsible or to claim accountability if they had not been the cause. That persistent anti-Elyri voice continued to cry out for the expulsion or death of every Elyri in Enesfel. As long as they remained, Enesfel would have no peace.

How sickened they must be, he mused, to know that so many Elyri, healers, clergy, and others, people who had never stepped foot out of Elyriá, had come to Rhidam in her hour of need to help those who required it, without thought for their own safety or a request for compensation. It made Bhríd proud to be Elyri, regardless of what his eldest son thought of him.

"If it would please Your Majesty," Elotti said with a bow, "I offer my services in eradicating these vermin." He met her gaze for many long, silent moments. He was not asking for payment, not expecting any. He was offering his assistance for reasons that were entirely private, entirely personal. The man was known to excel at his line of work, and if his involvement would help bring an end to Enesfel's nightmare, the Queen knew she would be a fool to refuse.

From the beaming look of excitement on Asta's face, she knew her cousin thought so too. "Very well. Lady Dugan will see that your needs are met. You will work with her as she deems suitable. And Lord Chamberlain?" She motioned for the parchment and he returned it to her. "As soon as Lord Cliáth is available, see to it that he reads this…and get some sleep." If anyone could learn anything from this curious proclamation, it would be the Lachlan's court bard.

❧Chapter 47❧

The worst pain he could imagine, radiating from his spine, around his abdomen, and back again, jarred Kavan out of his exhausted sleep, the burning of it creeping in progression from his ribcage to his groin leaving him breathless and sweating, an unfamiliar sensation since Elyri were not known to sweat except under extreme physical duress. Scarcely able to stand or walk, he waddled to his cousin's room where he found Syl, barely awake but still in Rhidam. It had taken this tragedy to seemingly reunite his cousin and his wife but Kavan doubted she would remain in the castle much longer. There were the children in Bhryell to consider, and it was too dangerous in Enesfel still to bring the little ones back.

Kavan described his symptoms but was unable to determine if the pain was real or a phantom product of the Sight. Syl had barely placed one hand on his stomach before looking up into his face, wide-eyed. "If you were a woman," she said, "I would say you were giving birth."

"Birth? That's absurd." But then his eyes widened too, and he ran from the room, pushing that pain aside in favor of action. "Clianthe!"

Syl followed, afraid that the Sight had shown Kavan something she would need to address. If Clianthe was experiencing labor pains so early in her pregnancy, it would not be good for either child or mother. But Clianthe and Muir were found in the morning room, sharing breakfast with Diona, and it took only a glance to see that the young woman was healthy, not suffering, and not in labor.

That realization brought Kavan up short.

If not Clianthe, who? The Sight, surely, as it had been known to cause physical symptoms of injury and pain before. He might have thought Diona, but they had not yet shared the bonding the half-moon pendants had afforded him with her father and brother and she too did not appear to be suffering. He knew of no one else who might be with child, and deduced that this suffering, a birth was to be of someone who would become important to him, or to Enesfel, in the future.

Just as the Sight had brought him to Prince Arlan long ago.

"Is everything alright?" Muir came to his feet as the bard burst into the room; Syl behind him did little good to ease the prince's mind.

"I…yes…the Sight…"

"What have you Seen?" Diona had observed the effects of the Sight on Kavan before and no longer doubted his claims.

Kavan shook his head. "It is…I'm not certain. It is too soon to say what it means…"

"Lord Cliáth."

That was a note of command that made him close his eyes. Why, he wondered, was hearing it in her voice more difficult than it had been hearing it from her father?

"Someone is giving birth," Syl replied, interpreting Kavan's distress though not understanding it. The lady healer smiled at Clianthe and added, "And clearly you are not."

"I should think not…it is too soon," Muir said with relief, although beside him his wife frowned with worry. As she was near enough to touch, Kavan put his hand on the woman's arm, knowing that, if there was anything to read, that was touch enough to do so.

What he read made his head cock curiously, the voice of a child calling to him, beseeching, from far away in the darkness. He was not sure what it meant, what he heard, but he was comforted enough to share that with her.

"Your son is well…and will be a man to be proud of."

"A son?" Clianthe's lips turned from the frown and into a smile as she looked first at her husband and then to Syl as if seeking a healer's affirmation. Syl put her hand on the woman's belly but read nothing.

"It is too soon for me to tell."

"A son," beamed Muir. If Kavan claimed it, then a son they would have. If Kavan said the boy would live to be a man, the prince needed no other reassurance.

The talk of children was enough to make Diona squirm, something Kavan noticed and was about to comment on but she, seeing his expression and not wanting to discuss that personal issue with him, took an object from the table and offered it to him.

"I received this the day the fire was out; I wanted you to see it."

He could feel the darkness in that rolled parchment without touching it, as if it were claws reaching for his skin, raking him with needle nails. He took a step back and shook his head. "I cannot…." Or rather, his unexpected fear suggested to him that he should not.

"Cannot?" She untied the leather cord that bound it and spread it on the end table at her side.

"The Corylliens claim responsibility for the fire," Muir explained, "And there were bodies in the basement where…dozens of them…"

The image of the dead, piled high in a room Kavan had never been in but had Seen once before, brought the bile to the back of his throat. Jermyn had suffered there. Jermyn had died there. "So young," he whispered before again squeezing his eyes shut. He swayed and reached a hand out for support, his knee pressing against the table next to the Queen…and against the parchment spread there. A strangled sound forced its way into the back of his throat from suddenly constricting air forced from his longs. Darkness descended over his consciousness. Unable to breathe, Kavan sank to his knees and then crumpled at Diona's feet.

"Kavan!" The formality of titles was bypassed in her panic and concern. Syl knelt beside him, loosened the button nearest his throat, and tilted his head to allow air to flow more easily. It did little to help, as he continued to gasp, his eyes rolling back in their sockets, his face mottling with the lack of oxygen and the strain of his body fighting towards consciousness and away from the darkness trying to swallow him. Images one after another, faster than eye blinks in a dust storm, faster than the beat of his heart or a lightning flash, raced through his head, too fast to see, too fast to recognize or decipher, each no more than a fleeting moment before being obscured by the next. Their rapidity produced a thundering in his skull that added to the pain, and when joined by another of those peculiar contractions, his body reacted by curling into a ball.

Syl tried to push him flat. He would be unable to breathe in that contracted position, and since he looked to be gasping for air still, keeping him breathing was her priority. Even with Diona's help, however, he would not uncurl, and Syl did not know what to do. Equally afraid for his mentor, Muir knelt with the women, and with two hands on Kavan's shoulders, attempted to hold him down as the women pulled his legs. The moment Muir touched Kavan, however, the bard's body lurched into a rigid, straight posture with enough force to send the prince sprawling backward across the room, knocking him far enough that he crashed into the wall beneath one of the windows.

"What…have…you…done?" Each word was a forced challenge as air refilled Kavan's straining lungs and his paralyzed body fought against the force that held him. A power unseen by the others attacked the prince in that touch; Kavan felt it. Muir appeared stunned but otherwise unharmed, but the Elyri could see it, the deep orange glow of power that seeped slowly into the young man's body through his mouth, his nose, his ears, and eyes. Every orifice became a gateway until the glow was gone.

Kavan sprang up, leaped across the room and grabbed Muir's shoulders, not sure what he expected to find or feel, but after what he had witnessed, he did not expect it to be good.

The prince stared at him. Kavan stared back. Muir, confused by the bard's behavior, opened his mouth to ask what was wrong, but he could not form words as his focus on Kavan's face registered one emotion after another. Anger, fear, confusion, guarded relief. Kavan expected something to be there, some energy or unnatural force nesting in Muir's core. But he sensed nothing. No matter how deep he probed, how deep he pushed power in Muir, there was nothing there that should not be. If it was, Kavan could not detect it, and that thought, more than anything else, frightened him. How could he combat something he could not detect?

It was a cold blast of realization that caused him to fall off his knees to the stone floor and clutch his pounding head between his hands. Now he was afraid for an entirely different reason, almost incapacitated by the weight of obligation staring at him through Muir's eyes. He had wanted to know when, had hoped for time to prepare for the destiny Kóráhm had placed before him, but there was none. No time to prepare except the remaining hours of this day.

The time was at hand.

Muir clutched Kavan's arm and he murmured earnestly, "I am well, Kavan. Do not fear. No harm has come to me."

But it could. There was a concern Kavan had to face, for he did not know if he could protect those whose help he required from what was to come. "My…Queen…" He struggled to his feet, body sore, the muscles of his stomach and lower back beginning to ache from the continuing contracting sensation. k'Ádhá, he begged silently before speaking, let this child, wherever it was, be born soon.

It was a male child. He knew it.

"Kavan?" Muir whispered. "What do you need?"

What do I need? The words crossed the Elyri's mind with an almost bitter, unvoiced laugh. I need this duty taken from me. Then he shook his head in silent argument and frowned. What he needed was to take up the burden fate had given and carry it obediently, see this through to the end. To resist or refuse meant the damnation of his soul, if not in k'Ádhá's eyes then at least in his own. If he failed to act, to do his part to purge Enesfel, he would not be able to live with himself.

"Tonight…an hour before midnight…meet me before the throne. And Clianthe…and you…My Queen…" Voice thick and tense, he turned his face to look at Syl, the only one he was able to look in the eye, and added, "Ártur too…"

"No…"

"He must." He clutched her hand, relaying his apprehension and distress in that touch. "Without him…I will fail…without any of you…without those…I will fail…"

"Fail what…?" Diona asked.

"It is time," said Muir, cutting off his sister's question. She seemed not to mind.

"Tonight…bring your father, my prince…nothing more. I will have…everything else that is needed."

"Kavan." He bristled at the Queen's tone. "What do you mean?"

"Wear the crown, Diona," he replied, dropping formality to speak with her as an equal, as a man who had taught her and cared for her as a child. "The collar…the ring…they should protect you."

It was rare that he called her by name any longer, and while it thrilled her to hear it, it also made her frown. "Why do I need protecting? What are you saying?"

"Do not be late…be prompt. I cannot wait…and if one of you fails…I shall fail as well." Syl's hand tightened around Kavan's conveying questions she did not voice and he added. "If Enesfel is to be purged of the darkness in its heart, set back on its proper course, failure is an option I do not have."

The healer's hand dropped and her gaze lowered. There was no dishonesty in his words, his tone, his touch. Whatever he intended to do, whatever lay ahead of him, was hidden from her during that contact, but his belief in his need for others was certain. She dared not deprive him, deprive Enesfel and Elyriá, for the deaths that could come of failure, if his words were true, would be too great a burden for her to stomach.

And Ártur would never forgive her if harm came to Kavan because he was not there beside him.

"I will tell him," she reluctantly agreed. "He will ask me why…but I will tell him."

"Just tell him I need him there." That would be enough. They both knew Ártur well enough to know that.

Having no more to say, no more that he could say as even he did not yet know the full details, Kavan staggered out of the room leaving silence behind him. He could hear them, as he leaned wearily against the wall outside the closed door, murmuring amongst themselves as to what this meant, what they were being asked to do, whether they would be safe…whether Kavan would be. He wished he had answers. They would know tonight, when he knew. He prayed that they, and he, would be strong enough to face whatever those answers were.]

Without providing details, without telling them they would be included in the night's endeavors, Kavan set Gaelán and Sóbhán to the task of getting a message to Tusánt and finding the candles Kavan was going to need. Some items the dedhá would be able to supply and others were tasked to Wortham to acquire, with no explanation given as to their intended purpose. Wortham thought nothing of the peculiar request until Kavan asked him to bring all of the items to the Great Hall at the specified hour, to come dressed in his armor, to be ready for anything. It took little imagination, and a quick assessment of the stress in Kavan's eyes, for the captain to guess that the time of cleansing was at hand. Having vowed long ago to be beside him when this time came, to do whatever Kavan needed of him, Wortham hastened to obey. He would have insisted on being there, on helping, even if Kavan forbid it. Wortham would never allow Kavan to shoulder a burden of this magnitude alone.

The remaining items necessary, those hidden for safekeeping, were retrieved and lay before him on the altar steps in the oratory, where he knelt in prayer without his harp through the midday meal and dinner hour as well. The regular contractions continued throughout the day, removing any desire to eat, which coincided well with the powerful feeling that fasting was needed this day, a purging of his body to accompany the purging of mind and spirit he sought in those hours of prayer. Ártur came, but when Kavan refused to speak or acknowledge him, he left again with a frustrated huffing sound. The boys came too, after their noon meal, their sack of candles full and added to the collection of objects on the steps. Their curiosity about the items there, particularly what was in the wooden box that radiated such power, was met with a stern glance, a look that was enough to prevent them from touching it. When Kavan instead offered his hands to them, they each took one and knelt to pray with him. They stayed until the dinner summons came and then slipped away without disturbing him and without, they thought, even being noticed.

They knelt with him long enough, however, for Kavan to be assured that both would be ready for their roles this night. He tried, in his prayers, to argue against including them, to resist their attendance, as he thought them too young to witness whatever was to come. After their departure, however, he gave in to the inevitable and accepted their presence as another necessary component of the ritual he was preparing. No one, he decided, not even him, would be prepared for what lay in store. Age did not matter. Nothing mattered except that the pieces of the puzzle be in their proper places.

"I wish I could be with you, átaelás mai."

Kavan did not need to open his eyes to know who was beside him. "I wish so as well," he whispered. "Do you know what I must…?"

Kóráhm shook his head with an unhappy frown. "I wish I could give you that, at least. You deserve better than the fate my actions, and inactions, have bequeathed you with."

At the mention of fate, Kavan opened his eyes to stare at the pyre above him. His fate, he thought, surely meant he was destined to die tonight. Wanting to relieve Kóráhm of that emotional burden, he murmured, "You are not responsible for his actions. His choices were his. He is the defiler…not you."

Though true, it did not prevent the saint from feeling that this duty should be his. "Is there anything I can give? Courage? Strength?"

"Comfort." Kavan met his gaze. "I want to know that, no matter what happens to me, the others will be safe. Can you give me that?"

Again Kóráhm shook his head. "I wish I could…but I cannot see through the veil of shadow surrounding the night ahead. If not for what I see in you, I would not even know who is to be there with you…or that the time has come. I'm pleased you do not have to endure this alone…that you will have support…since I cannot be there. I am sorry I cannot give you more."

The Elyri's head bobbed once. "So am I." He held out his hand, palm up, and asked for the one thing he could think of that he desired right then. "Wait with me, my lord…until it is time?"

Kóráhm covered Kavan's hand with his and both tightened at once. It was a touch that gave Kavan the needed strength and comfort, and the saint's words, "It would be my honor and joy," lifted his spirit. Anything else would have to be found deep within.

∻Chapter 48∽

There were others already gathered in the throne room by the time Tusánt arrived with the requested decanter of water he had spent his day ritually blessing with every manner of prayer, incantation, and ritual he knew. He doubted there had ever been water more blessed except for water blessed by Dhágdhuán himself. He had been told to be prompt, and though there were still ten minutes to wait, he was happy he was not there alone, nor the last to arrive. His robes, those worn for the holiest feast days, were clean and pressed and he had spent considerable time in additional prayer, despite not knowing what he was preparing himself for. The message received had made the matter sound urgent, had been a plea for a willingness to offer whatever the White Bard required. It sounded ominous enough to warrant preparation of a spiritual nature. Edward and Saul insisted on traveling with him for the silent trek across Rhidam's dark, deserted streets. The fire had sapped the life from the city, draining away much of the late-night activity normal around inns and taverns. Despite the deserted nature of his chosen route, however, Tusánt felt safer with the novices beside him, and when, if, he returned to the naós, he did not want to walk alone then either.

He nodded to each of the others as he nervously took his place among them. Wortham nodded too, sword clutched in his hand, his armor impeccable, his bearlike features stern and focused as though he had waited there much longer than anyone else…as if he was intending to go into battle and was only awaiting the command to go. Owain stood near him, similarly dressed with an identical sword in one hand, fidgeting with his armor with the other. Beside him, his son and the young man's wife waited silently. Muir, unarmored, adorned in the formality of one about to wed, with his arms around Clianthe who was similarly dressed, pressed his mouth against her loose hair over her ear. He appeared to speak to her in whispers as her head occasionally bobbed or shook as if in answer, but Tusánt could not hear what Muir was saying. Both were dressed in whites and creams, expensive fabrics of clothing newly tailored.

Pacing the room, circling the throne in anxious anticipation, Ártur's distorted expression belied his frustration and anxiety about not knowing what was going on. The yellow healer robes he rarely wore swished about his feet, one of the few sounds in the room, loud and ominous in the Hall's midnight silence. It seemed an odd group, but they all had one thing in common: each was much loved by the bard who bid them assemble and each loved him dearly in return.

Soon the Queen hustled into the room, her face flushed as if she had run to join them. She was relieved to find she was not late, nor was the last to arrive, as the bard had yet to join them. It had taken considerable argument with Espen to be free of him, an argument that ended badly, she feared, with his threat that, if she regretted her decision to marry him, she should tell him in order that the marriage be annulled and he be free to return to Hatu before further shame was brought on him or his family. She made the wise, but difficult, decision not to tell him that Kavan's request was her reason for again avoiding their marriage bed. She claimed lingering exhaustion, a partial truth based on the unending trauma of the fire and the duty it had thrust on her already weary shoulders. Pushing his patience was not her desire, and she aimed to have the discussion with him that she had intended the night the fire sparked, but again it would have to wait. Whatever Kavan intended to undertake this night was for the benefit of the kingdom, thus this was a matter of duty, not frivolity or fear. She hoped the night would prove worth it and that Espen would wait until the evening hours were over.

With a crackle of static in the air around them, anxious faces looked at one another in anticipation and turned when three sets of footfalls echoed through the main entrance. Kavan, Gaelán, and Sóbhán entered, arms full of a variety of items. The white robe Kavan wore was different than those he had worn in years past. It looked to be little more than a thin bed sheet cinched at his waist with a length of coarse rope, with a hole cut in it for his head. It was large enough to hang so loosely from his shoulders that it threatened to slide off as he moved. The boys in their Feast Day finery looked excited about the adventure they were included in, but Kavan showed none of their enthusiasm. His expression was mostly blank, save for the tension around his eyes and mouth and a haunted resolve in his face that each could see when he reached the group. He looked at Saul and Edward and nodded once.

"Good. It is good you have come. You will not be able to follow the entire way…but the dedhá will require your aid later."

"We thought he might," Saul said solemnly. "Whatever you ask, Lord Cliáth…know we are with you."

The bard bowed his head in acceptance and appreciation before addressing the others. "Ask your questions now, for once we are below, there must be no speaking, no interruptions. I will…you will each be given items once in position, and you will do as instructed with them, nothing more."

"What is this about?" Ártur, while afraid of the reply, was not afraid to ask the question and demand an answer. What his wife had told him had been cryptic and vague and, to Ártur, disconcerting. "Are we in danger?"

It took willpower not to roll his eyes or sigh. Someone was bound to ask those questions although he dreaded answering and instilling fear in the others.

"I…"

"Speak honestly, Kavan. You know each of us would face death for you."

"Aye." Owain agreed with Wortham, although he was less certain that most of the others in the room felt the same. He had never seen that resolve or devotion to Kavan in either Tusánt, the Queen, or Clianthe, but perhaps that was because they had yet to be tested.

Kavan bowed his head. "I do not know, Wortham…for I do not know precisely what lies ahead. But I do believe you will all be safe."

Wortham nodded with a grunt. "That is enough."

Diona, with a kingdom to lead and duty to uphold, had no desire to face death yet. She was young and the needs of her people lay stretched before her. But if, as Kavan said, this would somehow benefit the land, then it was her charge to see that through too. "You believe this will break the cycle of persecution and death? Will bring us peace?"

"It will make peace possible…though I do not expect it to be an instant remedy." He did not even know how it would bring about those changes, but he had faith that it would. "As in any birth…" Another contraction ripped through his belly and he wondered if the words he had begun to say were a result of those sensations or if the pains were a result of the statement, "there is pain…birth…and then much growth to be undertaken before maturity can be attained…and anything can happen during those stages. Consider tonight a birth…which you will attend so that the Sovereignties can emerge from darkness into a new maturity. Whatever you see tonight, regardless of what you hear or feel, I beg you hold your ground, beg you to remain strong and do not interfere. I need that of you…for I have no idea what I shall face."

"You have our word," Muir and Clianthe said in unison. A chorus of agreeing voices followed.

"Are we to come too?" Sóbhán asked as Kavan knelt, opened the wooden box, and withdrew the three staff pieces contained therein. Two of them Wortham had never seen before, but the third he recognized with a snort. He met Kavan's gaze, a look passing between them that made the captain fall silent but added to his watchfulness. He recognized the box from their travels but had never seen inside of it. Memories of events during that journey, the evil that followed them after they gained the box, made the captain more aware than any other, except Kavan, of what might await them. What the rest of them would endure would likely pale in comparison to the burden Kavan would bear. Wortham chose then, as was his way, to support his friend however the man deemed necessary.

"Yes. Both of you." Kavan side-eyed Ártur, aware the healer was about to ask if Bhríd knew what his son was about to do. The healer bit his tongue. "You will know what to do when it needs to be done."

How that could be when Kavan was not yet aware of what might be asked of any of them, he could not say, but he believed the bond formed when they knelt in earlier prayer would allow the boys to anticipate his needs and respond accordingly. The power guiding him this night was setting his path. He had to follow it, wherever it led, and trust he was not being led astray.

The boys, not yet in tune with the seriousness of their mission, grinned in excitement as Kavan assembled the lower two portions of the staff and then positioned the crown piece and twisted it into place. The moment it was done, its carved crown of gold filigree shaped like a writhing flame lit from within, a white glow that filled the dark Hall with the light of many torches. Kavan blinked, as surprised by the unexpected brightness as everyone else.

"Sóbhán, carry this. You and Gaelán stay behind me; it will light the way for the others." It worried him to put an object of such power into a child's hands, but Sóbhán's innocence seemed to shield him as he did not react in any way as he closed his hand around the staff.

Muir took the bundle the boy had carried in order that the youngest could carry the staff that towered above him by nearly two feet. No command to follow was given. As Kavan crossed to the passage behind the throne that led into the dungeon, everyone in the group joined him. Ártur realized where they were going and his frown deepened. Of those in their company, only Wortham and Ártur had been there before, and it was a place Ártur had hoped to avoid ever returning to.

"Are we…?"

A glance over the bard's shoulder silenced the healer, though he was still tempted to talk Kavan out of the insanity he had planned.

There were no guards at the dungeon door and none within when Kavan opened it to allow the others through. Diona scowled; unless this was Kavan's arrangement for there to be no guards, no witnesses, she was going to have words with Agis in the morning.

"Saul, Edward, you are to wait here for our return. Allow no one to follow us, no one to enter."

The novices looked past Kavan to Tusánt for approval. They trusted Kavan, had promised whatever he required of them, and had already been told that they could not go where the others went this night, but neither were happy about being left there and letting their charge out of their sight. The dedhá nodded, however, reassuring them enough that they took up the swords left by the door. They took position as if they were Lachlan guards, but when the dungeon door closed, removing the others from sight, they looked at each other with matching scowls. This promised to be a long night.

It took no searching this time for Kavan to find the small stone that allowed the path to open before them. The pop of a spring release was followed by the deafening echo of stone scraping over stone and each could see for themselves the start of the convoluted, debris-laden path that led into the labyrinth beneath Rhidam's keep. Diona's first thought was of palace security; such an entrance must have an exit somewhere. If it did, should she not know about it, find it, guard it against use to avoid invasion? Yet Kavan had known it was here and apparently never feared that possibility. Perhaps there was but this single way in and out. These tunnels might have served some other function in centuries past instead of invasion. She decided, as her half-brother pushed her gently through the doorway after his wife, that she would not worry about it now but concentrate on the present.

With Wortham before them, directly behind Kavan and the boys, and Owain behind them, each walked slowly to avoid tripping over broken rock and an occasional fallen timber, all within the circle of the light emitted by the staff. Kavan led at a steady even pace so that none felt any reason to fear becoming lost in the unfamiliar maze. The bard was known to keep his secrets and Ártur, despite his annoyance, was not surprised by his cousin's silence. He fretted less about becoming lost than he did Kavan's tight-lipped behavior.

None could see his face, the advantage of being the leader, for which Kavan was grateful as he turned another corner into the final stretch of corridor. He had walked with eyes closed, allowing the internal beacon of power to pull him towards his destination. The strength of it, even across the stretching distance, made him rethink this endeavor more than once, made him question his motives, tested his resolve. For the strength of what he found here at this threshold was greater than it had been a few short weeks ago, fed, he suspected, by the continual sacrifices the Corylliens made. Such sacrifices did not need to be in this place, it seemed, to fuel the malevolent spirit, which made Kavan question whether what he did tonight would be sufficient. How could it be when there were still men and women performing such deeds in the name of that man's memory?

When the door loomed before them, forcing him to open his eyes to look up at the ancient writing above, his resolved solidified as strongly as the wall of power beyond the door was solidified. In that moment of facing it head-on, Kavan lifted his chin defiantly and pushed open the door. He was not afraid of Coryllien's power. He had faced it before and he had won. However difficult this might be, he was determined to defeat it this time as well.

Shoulders squared, bracing with enough power from the humming chest in his hand to drive the force away before him, he felt whatever was in the room balk, reacting, it seemed to what was in the reliquary. Taking that as a positive thing, Kavan spoke a High Elyri prayer, words of protection that Ártur and Tusánt alone understood, Tusánt only in part. It did not matter if others knew the words he uttered. Each felt calmer, safer, upon hearing them. He opened the door the rest of the way and passed through at the moment his internal clock told him it was midnight, the turn of a new day. He was sprinkled with dust falling from the mantle as he had been every time he passed through that door. The sensation of it, like tiny wings dancing over his head and against his bare neck, robbed him of breath and he turned to watch the others enter, curious to see if anyone else felt what he had. Each person was similarly showered, each looked up to see what had fallen on them, but none appeared unsettled or disturbed by it, taking it as nothing more than falling dust. Kavan interpreted it much differently, like a baptism and blessing.

Each person stopped a few steps inside to gawk in awe at the faded ancient murals on the wall and the polished white saints keeping watch from the corners of the room. Such a place should not exist beneath the Lachlan keep, such a place of ancient ritual and holiness should not bear the stench of decay and defilement.

And yet it did.

Beginning with Diona, Kavan led each person to the place he wanted them, finding the logic of each, the words he uttered, to be reasonable and right though he had given no previous consideration to where they should stand or what he should say.

"My Queen…the north star, the rightful ruler installed in the face of catastrophe that threatens the world."

He brought her before the northern wall with its mural of the apocalypse believed to await the world's end, a dim collection of fire and chaotic death with tiny figures leaping into the air as if they could escape the flames and their fleshly shells. From the items brought with them, he placed a candle in her left hand and in the other, the small silver scales, which was oddly weighted on one side as though something of great mass was placed on it. From around his neck where he had been wearing both half-moon pendants since Hagan's death, one was removed, snagging in his hair before coming off over his head. He stared at it for several moments, fighting a different sort of reluctance, but he eventually pressed it against her chest, over her heart, where it warmed in his palm. Then it was placed with a trembling hand on the lighter side of the scale. Knowing what it would mean, should the pendants touch each other now but being unable to escape that bond to the Lachlan House, he removed his pendant as well and placed it on the scale with hers. The weights swayed but steadied, with the empty side still tipped beneath its invisible burden.

"The power is yours, now and in the days ahead. Hold steady, hold true, and balance will come."

Muir and Clianthe, hand in hand, were situated before the portrayal of Dhágdhuán's birth on a flat plain overlooking a vast churning sea on the cracking eastern wall where the sun always rose. A candle was given to each, lit as Diona's had been by the peculiar smokeless glow of the staff's flameless light. They held them in their free hands as he readjusted his robe to keep it from falling when he removed the cord at his waist to wrap it around their joined hands. "Love…and the triumph of it over the ills of the world. Rebirth," Kavan bowed his head to Clianthe, "and dedication," he bowed to Muir as well, "the completeness of unity before opposition."

Something tickled his senses, pressing around him by the opposing force that seemed intent to push between him and the prince. Kavan's eyes narrowed reflexively as he impulsively threw a shield of protection around Muir. The force retreated, but to the Elyri's senses, it seemed to laugh at his actions. Kavan resisted frowning, not wanting to trouble the prince any more than the young man was already after seeing the change on Kavan's face. The bard forced his expression to be neutral again, squeezed their hands between his, and then returned to those still awaiting direction.

"As the shields against the finality of death, the world is graced with healing and faith, that our lives not be short and our hearts not be heavy with the separation from the divine, from whence we come and to which we shall return."

The nagging questions about his Faith were pushed into the recesses of his mind as Kavan moved Ártur and Tusánt to the western wall's depiction of the martyrdom of Dhágdhuán the Intercessor on the Pyre of Sanctity. He could feel each man's anxiety, both being more nervous and fearful than anyone else in the room. Tusánt, sensing the aura of the chamber was not a holy one, despite the images around them and the presence of Saints in the shadowed corners at the edges of the light's glow, held the clay decanter of consecrated water in one shaking hand as Kavan placed a lit candle in his other.

"The Word spread to the world that all might share in the awareness of clemency and Faith. Without you, darkness would prevail; with you, there is the possibility of eternity."

Though Kavan tried to offer Ártur a soothing expression, the healer did not accept it. He was worried for the others, worried for Kavan, and uncomfortable beneath the weight of the force of power he could sense but not understand. When he had been here before, the negativity had been confined to the altar. Now it filled the room, pulsed and undulated like something liquid and alive. If he could feel it, he knew Kavan could too, for he knew how sensitive Kavan was to such things. He suspected it was that negativity that Kavan intended to face. Kavan was the most powerful ágdháni Ártur had ever heard tell of, but that did not mean he had the strength or ability to win against something as strong as what seemed to be with them.

A flask of serbháló was pressed into Ártur's left hand, a candle into his right. The flask seemed an odd thing to be given, but Ártur obediently remained silent. "You are the healing of the world, that which bathes the wounds, cleanses them, makes us whole. You are the gift given to all mankind, that which saves us from ourselves and gives us the strength to find and know peace and life."

Ártur flushed, not knowing if the words were addressed to him personally or healers as a united group. He decided it did not matter. Kavan's words made him view his life's calling in a new light. If Kavan needed a healer's strength this night, Ártur was satisfied knowing he had been chosen to stand with him when his cousin could as easily have chosen Rouvyn or someone else.

Before either of the short benches flanking the door they had entered through, a door now closed to cut them off from the outside, Wortham and Owain were placed, swords in hand, the tips of their blades touching the dusty floor between their feet. Neither held a candle, leaving the creation mural behind them dimly lit by the light of the staff. It was vital, Kavan felt, that their strengths guard the portal to this room, though he expected nothing to come through that door. What must be fought was already here. It might, however, try to escape, although no mortal man, no normal sword, was going to prevent it should Kavan fail and that happened.

It was up to Kavan to contain it, destroy it, prevent it from spreading malignancy any further into the world.

"Swords of Justice," Kavan said to both, pressing one palm to each sword, aware that the audible static pop that ignited the blades with a dim silver-blue glow was heard by everyone. Now, he thought. Now if that negativity tried to pass through this door, it would be contained by the two men defending it. "Guards against chaos, protectors against that which seeks harm to the innocent."

Owain blinked away suddenly rising tears, nervously clenching his fists around the now heavier sword. Wortham, beside him, seemed not to react to the change. Of those here, Owain was, he felt, the guiltiest of harming the innocent, for it had been at his command, his oversight, that the most innocent man he knew had suffered and been sentenced to death. Thank k'Ádhá he had failed, that Kavan had escaped his grasp and had gone on to spare his life and give him a new purpose. Being King had not been Owain's destiny. Here, at Kavan's side, intending to rid the kingdom, the world, of the evil Kavan believed resided here…that was a destiny Owain felt worth living for. And dying for, if necessary.

A hand, a touch light enough he almost did not feel it, brushed over his. He looked into the bard's eyes and, finding pardon and acceptance, straightened his shoulders and lifted his chin. He was a shield now. Those things were but shadows of his past. That man was gone. The man Kavan had enabled him to become was ready to act.

Gaelán and Sóbhán were positioned at the ends of the worn, altar, on the primary floor rather than on the raised platform. Handheld censers of holy Gathering incense mixed with a pinch each of Diwi, that Kavan and Wortham had spent months procuring, were placed at each of the four corners of the platform and lit with the one candle that remained. The room quickly began to fill with its pungent, sweet fragrance while Kavan set four more censers before each limestone saint, praying to each in the language of his ancestors.

"Gíldás…grant us strength. Mátán…grant us life. Edhriá…grant us safety." He stopped before the unmarked, unnamed saint, wondering who he was to direct his final supplication to. He settled for calling out to the one saint he felt closest to. Kóráhm might not be able to be with him now, but wherever Kóráhm was, Kavan believed he would hear. "Kóráhm…grant us success."

They were each things desperately needed tonight.

Burning incense in place, Kavan returned to the altar, opened the reliquary that waited on the floor before it, and removed from its cushioned center a large golden chalice, inlaid with bone-white circular stones, etchings of black and silver, and a stone on each cardinal side, one blood red, one royal blue, one spring grass green, and the last pale lavender tinted with flecks of deeper purple. It was no flimsy item, nor one made of some other material and overlaid with gold. The chalice was heavy, made heavier by the power emanating from it. He prayed that the Chalice of Llyr would enhance his gifts tonight not interfere with them as it had during their journey north.

If their powers conflicted here, he feared what might happen.

The Chalice of Llyr. Again the words were High Elyri, the name of the object drawing Ártur's focus. Was there a coincidence to the name, he wondered, a meaning for it? Kavan did not explain, but put the Chalice in Gaelán's empty hands after dripping wax near the center of the altar and pressing the last burning candle into it so that it remained upright on its own. Praying in earnest, elaborate words,

Kavan half-filled the Chalice with the consecrated water Tusánt had brought, and then used the majority of what remained to bless each participant in the room and finally the staff. When the water touched the glow emanating from the Staff of Drebhoti, the negative energy in the room flared with such intensity that even the Teren could feel it, like icy water splashed against their skin. When Kavan did not react to it, however, failed to show surprise or fear, the others found the strength to remain calm.

He returned the decanter to the gdhededhá.

A small silver cup, brought with the candles the boys had procured, was filled with serbháló and offered to each participant. It was rare to have the slightly fermented elixir outside of a Gathering, as it was used almost exclusively for Holy ritual purposes. But on this night, the benefit of the blessing such sweetness offered against the spiritual battle to come was a requirement. Kavan could think of no purpose more holy than what was to come, and did not believe any member of the Faith, except most likely k'dedhá Claide and k'dedhá Dórímyr, would object. What remained in the cup after each had partaken was added into the Chalice, mixed with the sanctified water.

The negative presence flashed again. The stone walls around, above, and below grumbled. Heads turned, fearful of being buried alive beneath Enesfel's castle, but Kavan ignored the tantrum tremors. The force wanted acknowledgment, wanted to frighten him into stopping, but Kavan was not going to give it the satisfaction, even when the scales in Diona's hand temporarily tipped towards the opposite balance. It was a false reading, and when Kavan ignored the sight, the presence battered him with petulant fists of power.

The remaining Diwi in the clay pot was taken around the room and with steady fingers, Kavan marked each of his friends, touching the yellow powder to their ears, their foreheads, eyelids, and chins. The last of it, as with the ingredients before, was added to the Chalice, the contents mixed again. Yellow stained fingers were swiped over his tongue, the bitterness of the herb a sharp contrast to the sweet smell it produced when burning. The smell of death in Hatu, for Diwi was frequently used in funeral services. Would Espen recognize that scent on Diona's skin, her hair and clothing, when he saw her next?

It was a stray, random thought that Kavan pushed away as quickly as it came. He had to concentrate. Focus was one of the few tools he could control tonight.

He began to swirl the cup in his hands for further mixing as he spoke, this time in Trade so that each in the room understood him. He relayed to them the tale he had recently learned, a story lost to history until this day, of Dawid Coryllien and Kóráhm di Curnydhá, half-brothers of an Elyri mother, brothers torn asunder by their love of a single woman, a woman whose death lay at the center of the history the rest of the known world had come to suffer. For in that woman's death, one man learned regret and brought his skills and knowledge to the city of Clarys, a city who would come to claim him as its own…and one man sank into the pathos of hatred and revenge which would lead to the single greatest persecution of Elyri the Five Sovereignties had ever known.

That Coryllien had carried Elyri blood was a shock for most, but not as great of a shock as it was to learn that the two men, one hated and reviled, the other loved and cherished by some, had been blood kin. That this room, this tiny ancient place of prayer and worship far older than either Kóráhm and Coryllien, had been the site of death and sacrifice in the name of madness and revenge, was cause enough to want to cleanse it. But learning that it had been those two men at the heart of what would grow into the Great Persecution, was a shock that left the night's participants cold.

Kavan did not know how one man, kin to both Saint and Defiler, could be called upon to cleanse this place.

With the Chalice in his hands, Kavan began several slow circles around the room, around the altar, cup raised as if in offering, reciting in the ancient Elyri tongue what was quickly recognized as a genealogy. Most were names that no one recognized, including Ártur, although he picked up the usage of Drebhoti as the name Kavan had used with the staff. At the moment Kóráhm's name was spoken, however, it was obvious this would be the lineage of the Saint. It was a surprise to learn that he had fathered children. Name after name, unfamiliar, unknown, dating back so many thousands of years that none alive had been there to know the men and women now put forth.

Gradually, however, Ártur began to recognized names, vaguely familiar ones heard from parents and grandparents in stories told to him as a little boy. He feared, as the familiar names were spoken, that he was the individual Kavan referred to as being the blood kin necessary to cleanse this place. Or perhaps it was Gaelán or even Sóbhán since he knew little about the boy. Names like MacLyr, Cliáth, Bhíncári. Names that at first filled the healer with horrified amazement. Not Kóráhm's genealogy, but rather the listing of his ancestors, his descendants, culminating in a pair of names, a man and woman the healer knew well.

The final name of the matriarchal line stopped then, and as Kavan reversed the direction of his circle, he began a second lineage, the patriarchal line that was often only considered in the passing of a family name in business, such as the Cliáthan harp makers. But that too, Ártur quickly deduced, was working its way toward the final revelation, how the man before him, the man he called sínréc, was the blood kin on both matriarchal and patriarchal sides of his bloodline to the saint who dearly favored him…and the scourge who had birthed the Persecution for the sake of hatred and revenge.

Kavan Cliáth.

Kavan did not utter his own name. No one in the room needed to hear it, though he knew that, by the time he was finished, Ártur knew the truth and Tusánt most certainly suspected it. To the others, it was merely a long recitation of names that served to lull them with its sing-song chant quality.

The Chalice, when returned to Gaelán, was icy cold. The young man flinched but took it as instructed though it was with a troubled look that threatened to topple into an outburst of tears. This was more than the young man had bargained for, not the sort of adventure he had anticipated, and his fear, so close to the altar, was something Kavan had to address. He lay both hands on Gaelán's head and kissed his hair tenderly, channeling love and reassurance through his touch. Gaelán, not expecting that either and having never felt such intense love, looked into his cousin's eyes with adoration that brought tears to both. He was loved. Kavan would allow nothing bad to happen to him tonight. He was safe.

The final ingredient, the stoppered vial of the tangy spiced smell of Orec, was opened and also lifted in prayer. Wortham, focused more intently on the bard because he knew what that vial contained, swallowed hard as some of it was dabbed on Kavan's fingers to be placed in tiny smudges on his forehead and over his heart where the white robe had slid low enough to expose unbroken flesh. Could it be absorbed through the skin? Wortham could not recall if it could be, but the possibility made him more fearful.

Fortunately, the contents of the vial were emptied into the Chalice, not into Kavan's throat. When it came into contact with what was already in the Chalice, the consecrated water, serbháló, and Diwi, a smoky blue-green flame erupted, startling Gaelán so that he nearly dropped it. The bard was there to steady him before that happened, his prayer faltering with the near mishap but resuming as soon as the Chalice was again steady in Gaelán's hands.

The smell of what burned and bubbled in that cold Chalice made Kavan's stomach churn as another wave of contracting muscles careened over him, more strongly than before, a signal in his mind that he was closer to the culmination of this ritual night. Thus far it felt to be no more than set up, but that was, he knew, an important component of any ritual. Despite having stepped into the ancient chapel not knowing what he was to do, he continued to follow his instincts, to trust the guiding spirits to lead him towards the desired end. He relieved Gaelán of the Chalice when his prayer was complete, the power in it burning his hands with its stinging chill, and tipped the cup to allow the contents to run across the surface of the rough marble altar, pooling mostly in the depression at the center worn with age and usage. The cup was returned to Gaelán, its iciness peeling bits of flesh from the bard's hands when he let it go.

Heart in his throat, Kavan stared at his hands, bleeding and raw, and then at the altar through the open spaces between his fingers. Following instinct was putting his life at risk, for such open wounds were a sure way of absorbing the Orec into his body. The presence with him, vacillating in strength with each action taken, laughed. Kavan could hear it, feel it, attacking the edges of his power. It was a sound that braced him instead of making him shrink from duty.

He had known since accepting this call, despite Qol's claim that he would live, that his life might be lost before the night ended. It was his burden to face, to bear, whether he wished it or not. To shrink from it meant the lasting damnation of Enesfel and, perhaps, the continued oppression of his people. Ignoring duty might even damn him, and he had no inkling what effect, if any, it might have on Kóráhm.

Facing this was the only option Kavan believed he had.

Decision made, he began to spread the spiced water and oil mixture over the top of the altar with flat hands, an action that brought a distressed squawk from the captain who had, from his position behind Kavan, been able to see the open wounds on the bard's hands. If he had suspected what Kavan was to do, he would have prevented it. Both men knew that to be true. It was too late, however, and all Wortham could do was tighten his grip around the hilt of his sword and move his lips in prayer…prayer that Kavan made it through what he needed to do, prayer that his friend would survive the deadliest poison he knew of, poison that had killed King Hagan in less than an hour and was known to be twice as lethal to Elyri.

The mixture burned, stinging as it seeped into those wounds. Kavan shared Wortham's fears, though he refused to listen to the small voice in his core that loudly proclaimed him to be a dead man. He doubled forward beneath the strength of another contraction, and his forehead cracked against the marble. Breaths caught around the room at the sound of the impact, but as Kavan instructed, none of them moved though they wanted to. Vision blurred by that startling pain, Kavan stood up straight and beckoned Wortham and Owain to join him, ignoring the trickle that crept down his forehead.

"These swords, weapons of war and peace, have never known the tempering of battle and blood. Lay them across the altar, crossing from corner to corner, resting upon one another at the center."

With the hilts on the southern corners, the natural direction for them as the men had come from the south side of the room, the swords were placed as Kavan bid, positioned so that the still flickering candle was in the northern quarter of the X. The touch of glowing, virgin steel against the anointed marble filled the room with a vibrating hum loud enough that each heard it, a buzzing that came from without and within and shook the walls and the air around them. The center point, where the swords crossed, began to glow a faint purple, a glow that increased when Kavan touched the crown of Drebhoti's staff to the place. As the staff was then taken around the room, to crown each limestone saint with its touch, the line of light followed, purple threads being drawn from the altar's center to the head of each saint. It formed arcs of light crisscrossing the room, an X in the center of a square that followed the paths the swords designated. The room continued to tremble and the power at the periphery of his senses snapped with what felt like hungry, angry jaws. The threads of light sparked and hissed like lightning. Little by little, Kavan tightened his hold around the net of power he had woven, but the poison eating through is body as it snaked towards his lungs left him doubtful that he would be able to continue long enough to complete what he had begun.

Would any of the others, he wondered, as he returned the staff to Sóbhán, be able to complete the ritual without him? Would they need to, or would his death complete it?

It was with great difficulty that he hoisted himself onto the altar, straddled over the cross point of the swords, one bare foot to the east, one to the west. No one had noticed before that moment that the bard had come into this once holy place without shoes. Facing the door, the black maw looked far away. It devoured his gradually blackening vision as he paused, hesitating, with his back to the Queen. Unable to avoid the moment in spite of his dread of it, he tore open the front of his robe, rending it from top to bottom, and let it fall, leaving him nude, exposed, vulnerable not just to the poison in his blood and the power around him, but to the eyes and judgment of those in the room. He could feel them staring, in shock, in surprise, in awe and wonder, their gazes cutting like knives against his fair skin. Their thoughts too bombarded him, but he struggled to shut them out, not wanting to know, despite some level of morbid curiosity, what they saw, what they thought, what they felt to see him like that…the man so modest, proper, afraid of what others thought of him. But it was not them he was exposing himself to. It was k'Ádhá and Dhágdhuán and Kóráhm and the vengeful spirit of Dawid Coryllien that continued to stab at him with increasing desperation.

The robe dropped into Gaelán's hands after the young man placed the Chalice in the front-most quarter of the altar X, and he spread the cloth on the floor and platform step between himself and Sóbhán like a royal carpet spread before the feet of a king. The young men knelt on it, together holding the staff, their hands alternating one above the other to keep it steady, the central pole to the tent of purple lightning crackles crisscrossing the room.

Head hung forward, hair covering his face, with his hands clasped either in prayer or as a means of hiding his maleness from the eyes of others, Kavan continued a new prayer, his rough voice becoming harder to hear over the hum that was, with each moment that dragged by, growing into a roar. Ártur could no longer understand the words Kavan spoke, was not certain they were words any longer though their cadence reminded him of speech even if the sounds of the words did not. He strained to hear them, hoping that focusing on Kavan's voice would take his attention away from the noise around them and his own fears.

Hearing no longer mattered. When it appeared that Kavan was about to slump forward off the altar in front of the boys, the roar was pierced with a sharp cry, the sound accompanying the throwing up of first one of the bard's arms above his head, then the other, stretching him erect as if hanging by his wrists into a posture familiar to every adherent of the Faith. The position might have meant less if not accompanied by the sudden eruption of blood spurting and trickling down his arms from what appeared to be fresh punctures in his wrists. Similar wounds appeared in the crowns of his feet. The red trails from his arms snaked their way to Kavan's torso, the blood flowing from his still spread feet, intermingling with the substances already christening the altar, seeping into the ancient cracks and fissures in the stone, filling the gouges left from one sacrifice after another that had left the taint of defilement in a time long past.

Gaelán screamed and squeezed his eyes shut against the sudden burst of pain in his head, his arms, and legs. He knew now, he understood, and only his grip on the staff kept him from clutching his head and curling into a ball on the floor.

The blood on the altar bubbled and smoked as if it were grease on a hot pan. The air grew thick with smoke and one by one those in the room began to cough on the choking air. Kavan's head lolled back, his eyes rolling into his skull, appearing dead or unconscious, although his mouth continued to move in prayer. Over the roar that became a shriek of fury and agony, the movements of Kavan's mouth formed not words but song, a simple monosyllabic sound of pure tone and emotion akin to the song he had formed the day he had stood in the abbey of Gorbesh, bleeding, feeling as if he was dying, as the process of blessing and healing beneath the unmatched power of k'Ádhá's will began for each resident there. This time, with the poison churning within him, Kavan had little expectation of living. He was losing more blood than he ever had before, much more, he presumed, then Hagan had judging by the weakness of his body. If the poison did not kill him, blood loss certainly would.

In unison, as his body convulsed in that suspended position wracked by another contraction, the boys lifted the staff and touched it to the lip of the Chalice where it rested on the altar at Kavan's feet. The glow within the staff's twisted, molded flames sputtered as if to go out and was masked and muted by the smoke that began to draw into it with a great sucking sound. Little by little the air grew cleaner, though the shrill shrieking was too loud to hear much else. The slight movement of Kavan's mouth told Wortham the bard was still singing.

The captain ached to go to him, gather him in his arms, hold him and still his weeping until the pain in his limp body passed. Kavan's arms flopped to his sides and his nude form dropped to his spread knees, a position that placed the struggling candle near his hairless groin and made the men in the room wince to see it. With the smoke cleared, those in the room could see more clearly the spasm of Kavan's body as muscles continued to roll and contract beneath his bloody skin. Streaks of something else, dark and scary looking, spidered up his arms, alerting Ártur for the first time that something Kavan was using was poisonous…and that poison was working its way through his body as quickly, he guessed, as the bard's blood was flowing out of him. How, he wondered as he cried, "Kavan!" and took a step forward, was the man even functioning?

Kavan shot one arm out as the other palm pressed to the uncomfortably hot marble to steady himself. Thinking the action was meant to stay and silence him, the healer stopped midstep and snapped his mouth shut, silently cursing himself for disobeying the only command Kavan had made of them tonight. Stay and be silent. But that demand was nearly impossible to obey now that he was faced with the fact that his cousin was dying.

What Kavan wanted, however, was not to silence him, but for the final piece of the ritual that must be included, while he still had strength enough to act. Wortham, the one person Kavan had entrusted this particular item to, other than a man who was not with them tonight, pulled the unmistakable Coryllien dagger from the leather pouch he carried it in and placed it carefully in Kavan's hands. His fingers brushed lightly against the bard's skin and Kavan moaned. Hand closing around the gargoyle hilt, Kavan drew in a long, struggling breath, fingertips brushing Wortham's skin in return, and only then did Wortham step back to his place with visible regret.

k'Ádhá help him, he prayed. Do not let that be our final moment.

The negativity battered against Kavan's shields harder as it sensed the danger in the object the bard held. Trapped by the blood Kavan had spilled, the ultimate sacrifice, the blood of kin, the blood of brother it had long waited to taste in revenge for she whom Kóráhm had not saved, it circled the room, taunting him, screaming in frustration and delight but also in fear, for the one thing that could spoil every dark dream of vengeance was trembling in a rapidly weakening hand. The struggle of power against power, as it sought to break free of Kavan's net of energy made the temperature in the room soar. What it thought should be an easy escape in the Elyri's weakened state proved otherwise. His body was weak, and growing more so, but his spirit, his mind, his power stayed strong and focused on the force with which Kavan battled. In a supreme effort of will, Kavan straightened, leaning back on his knees, his weight settled on his toes, and wrapped both hands around the Coryllien dagger's hilt.

His cold green gaze focused straight ahead, on the chasm that should be the door but looked to him like an endless black throat into the abyss. With a final cry, all of his physical strength pushed into the sound and the action, Kavan slammed the dagger downward, between his legs, and in his mind's eye blood splattered the floor, the ceiling, and every wall around him.

The earth shook, throwing those in the room to the floor, to the benches behind them, or against the limestone saints that creaked and swayed but miraculously remained upright. The force of it cracked the northern wall, allowing skulls to tumble out from it around the Queen's feet. She screamed, but Kavan could not tell if the vision was real or something in his head as he slouched on the altar. Metal shattered metal, metal cracked stone as the fullness of his training drew the energy in the room down through his arms into the blade between his hands. The vacuum of power snuffed out the arcs of lights from the saints to the swords, from the crown of Drebhoti's staff, and for a few moments, drew enough energy to cast each candle into darkness. Nothing could be seen except for the glow between Kavan's hands. After the span of a few panicked breaths, the tiny flames reignited one by one as the temperature in the room slowly edged towards its previous subterranean chill. The terrified shrieking grew more frantic the fainter it became.

Each person in the room expected there to be blood, expected that, in that powerful thrust of unusual Elyri strength and power, Kavan had emasculated himself. And while there was blood, still too much of it flowing from wrists and feet to fill the cracks of shattered metal and fractured marble, there no evidence of castration. The last great contraction at the moment of the dagger's impact had eased and left a feeling of relief that the birth he had overseen had been a successful one. The force that was Coryllien, that which had remained of him over the centuries, lingering in search of appeasement, in its need for vengeance against the brother who had wronged him, had found satisfaction, foolishly, perhaps, in the blood of the one man able to trap and destroy him. The shattering of earth and metal bathed in familial blood had, to Coryllien's surprise, shattered his hold on existence as well. The bonds that had held him to earth and kept him from passing to the after were severed, the splinters of power and spirit that remained dispersed into the elements of eternity where they belonged.

Coryllien was free and the sovereignties were free of him.

Kavan tried to push to his feet but there was no strength left in his failing body. What he felt was a pouring into his core of something he did not understand, a sucking of power through his pores, but it did nothing to give him the strength to rise.

No longer feeling bound to the promise to stay put, both Wortham and Owain were at his side before he fell from the altar, holding him, keeping him upright as he seemed determined to be. Words of benediction formed in Kavan's mind, made it to his lips, but there was no voice to utter them. It was Sóbhán's youthful voice that took up Kavan's song, his gift as conduit allowing sounds of a language he did not speak to be uttered with the surety of someone native to the words. Beneath those words, Kavan could hear an infant crying, perhaps two as there seemed to be an echo of a second voice behind the first. The softness of it, tiny strength in feeble lungs, made him long for a smile he could not muster. Somewhere, he thought thankfully, a brand new life, perhaps two, had come into being on the cusp of a new age for Teren and Elyri. He could think of no better legacy to leave the world than giving new life, new hope, in the wake of his death.

"Kavan."

He did not know the voice that called from behind, the voice that seemed to come from far away to the stuffiness in his head and ears. Bleeding still, though the flow had slowed as his body's supply neared depletion, Kavan turned his head to look, noting absently that no one else appeared to have heard what he had. It was a trick of the dim lighting, perhaps, that for the span of a few slowing heartbeats his face seemed to overlay on the featureless limestone figure in the northwest corner of the room. The sight shook him, for no part of his mind, body, or spirit could accept the possibility of sainthood, not even in the way Myreth had once explained that every man and woman were saints in the eyes of the divine. The thought of anyone using that title to refer to him still hurt and frightened him, no matter how much he had grown and changed during the last year.

But who was he to argue with the will of k'Ádhá? And how could he have any sway over what others made of him after his death? That would be between them and k'Ádhá, between the establishment and the Faithful. Kavan was but one man…a man who hoped he had restored the land to the path of peace and prosperity.

Too weak to cry in earnest, or to fight the tears that bled from his eyes, he hung his head and wept, giving in to what he could not fight, divine will and the frailty of his body. The last thing he knew was Wortham hoisting him into his thick, strong arms and cradling him like a child…or a lover. Everything after was darkness.

The sound of screaming filled the empty room with unbelievable agony as some part of her, a piece of her soul that had guided her since the earliest days of memory was ripped free, an abrupt sensation that tore a jagged hole in her psyche, bleeding orange and crimson and black into her vision, into her core. That which had led her, directed her, was gone, and with nothing to plug that gaping psychic wound, she lapsed into a deathlike stillness. Those who found her later found a woman breathing, eyes open, but obviously not aware of her surroundings. They tried to shut her lids, but her eyes refused to close. Nor would she wake. Afraid of what she had become, thinking her possessed of a demon, some of them fled. Others remained and some were chosen to guard her, feed her, care for her until the day she could fend for herself again.

Locked in the prison of her bleeding thoughts, clawing for escape and healing, she vowed again that the defiler, the destroyer, would pay. Pay with his life, the lives of those he loved, with his soul. She did not know how, or when, but that day would come when she was free of this prison and would see it done. It was a vow to her ancestors she had every intention of keeping, even if locked forever in the chains of her mind.

The ancient man struggled up from the floor where the shaking earth and blast of power had thrown him. He had felt death before, had felt great power, but he had never, in so many centuries of life, felt the destruction of power and the reabsorption of it. What had happened to cause such devastation…and where had that power gone?

Any guesses he could make would be just that, not based on solid evidence or proof. But the one guess he could settle on, as he checked his thin body for injury and then closed his eyes to examine himself psychically, was that he knew of a single earthly source possibly potent enough to cause such a worldwide event of power.

If that one source had not destroyed itself as well in that attempt, then Tíbhyan believed that no greater source of power existed in all the lands than the one he had once called student.

"Live, Kavan," he said aloud, words on a thread of energy cast into the night, set adrift on the fluctuating sea of power set in motion by whatever the younger Elyri had done. "Live and tell me what this means."

<h1 style="text-align:center">❧Chapter 49❧</h1>

ortham refused to leave Kavan's side, in spite of Ártur's insistence that there was nothing to be done. There was no further decline due to the poison in his blood; though his body was weak because of it and the incredible amount of blood lost, he did not, as yet, appear to be dying. Rather he appeared to be in some sort of stasis, neither improving nor getting worse, but in a deep sleep from which he would not wake. The discolored streaks beneath his skin, where the Orec raced through his veins and turned them ugly shades of purple and black remained, but the blood, all of it, had been washed away by Gaelán, Sóbhán, and Wortham while the older healer did everything he could to save his cousin's life. Those who had been in the chapel with the bard were gathered in his room, not ready to separate while Kavan's future remained uncertain, each knowing they had been through something powerful and miraculous that they would never experience again.

"You do not need to do more," Wortham said quietly to Ártur, his voice unusually calm considering the circumstances. "Kavan has been in k'Ádhá's hands this night…it is fitting we leave him there. k'Ádhá will choose his fate."

"But which fate?" Ártur muttered as Muir choked, "I wish I could be as calm as you, Captain." The prince had one arm around Clianthe, the other around Diona, and all three appeared stunned and wary. He had seen many amazing things in the years he had known Kavan, but nothing compared to the last few hours. Without Kavan to lead them from the maze, and with each one fearing their stubby candles would go out before they were free of that place, they expected to have to find their way without guidance. No one was confident of their path. The light of the staff continued to glow dimly but it would not be enough to guide them. Fortunately, Ártur remembered the Gate as the first candle spluttered out, and he took both Tusánt and Diona through at once. The Queen because there would undoubtedly be chaos caused by the shaking of the earth and Tusánt because he would have similar duties, and the men left at the dungeon door, to tend to. The dedhá could pray for Kavan as easily from the náós and there would be those there in a panic if they could not find him.

The others had come here, to Kavan's room, and the need to stay together had brought the Queen to them as dawn broke the night with promising feathers of golden light. She had excused her absence during the night and her behavior, with the fact that Kavan had been poisoned, the truth if not all of it, and Espen and others awaited news of the bard's condition, some in the corridor outside of his room though Espen went about the business of addressing the earthquake-induced problems an already fragile Rhidam faced.

Some buildings damaged in the firestorm had succumbed to the shaking and collapsed, causing more deaths, more destruction that needed clearing, more rebuilding to undertake. Though Espen was angry that Diona had not told him of the poisoning sooner, had waited until morning to share news he felt he deserved to know, he at least understood the importance of her concern. Whether he liked his wife's fondness for the bard or not, he knew the bard's importance to Rhidam, to Enesfel, stretched beyond his influence on the Lachlans. It was the sole reason Espen accepted his wife's choice to go to Kavan to check on his condition.

"We must be cautious," she said wearily, the stress of a night without sleep, her worry for Kavan, and the duties she still faced this day giving her voice a strained, grated edge. "No one outside of this room, this group, must ever know what happened last night." There was one she would tell, one from whom such secrets could not be kept if he was to rule effectively at her side, and perhaps Kavan would deem it important for others to know, but that would be up to him. How could she, or any of them, ever explain those events, what they had witnessed and experienced? How could she expect Espen or anyone else to accept the story, understand it, when she could barely understand or accept it herself? Never in her life had she witnessed such a display of Elyri power, not even a single miracle. She had seen healers work, had seen Kavan use the handlight, had seen the Sight at work in his life. Each of those gifts, however, paled in comparison to what they had seen and felt last night.

"Who would believe us?" Clianthe said through chattering teeth. They did not chatter, she did not shiver, out of cold but rather from the shock of such an awe-inspiring experience.

"Where Kavan is concerned, many…but you know what would happen." Heads bobbed in agreement with Owain's unspoken inference. The elder Lachlan prince looked older, wearier and more worn then he had early last evening, as if the night had aged him. With the use of the Gate to take them from the chapel, he understood how Arlan had come into the castle that fateful night the throne had been wrested from Owain's hands. He felt no hostility, no umbrage towards the bard who had likely been the one to bring Arlan inside. The understanding was surprisingly welcome. It had been Kavan to bring Arlan here, Kavan who saved Owain's life when he could have allowed him to die. Kavan who welcomed him back into Rhidam with an open heart. Kavan who introduced him to his son, his wife, to a world of possibilities he had not thought within his reach. Every event of import in his life had been in some way because of Kavan, perhaps even his banishment to Neth as a boy, although that likely would have happened without that foolish childhood fight. Owain saw no reason to think that what he had participated in last night would be any different. His life was likely to change again and he did not know if he should be afraid or if he should embrace and welcome the change.

"Indeed, unless we want to bombard him with the adoration of miracles, with a public push for sanctification…keeping this quiet is best."

Ártur adjusted the sheet over Kavan after inspecting his wrists, his hands, his feet one more time. There was no hint of bleeding, only the dark veins that roped up his arms and spoke of poison still inside, and the holy wounds that Ártur had not been able to seal despite every healing skill he had tried. They no longer bled, but he could not close them. He had given his cousin every purgative he had that was safe for an Elyri, but they could only purge a poison from the stomach, not the blood. He had done his best to block poison from the vital organs, but he could not do so indefinitely and in spite of his efforts, he knew a cure was out of his hands. Coryllien's poison had already permeated every cell and fiber of Kavan's body. Perhaps that was why those wounds would not heal. If it was going to kill Kavan, there was nothing Ártur could do.

Muir squeezed his wife's trembling shoulders. "We cannot stay. You need rest, love…and we are raising too many questions as it is." They could hear voices in the corridor, voices wondering, worrying, voices that needed appeasing. "Unless we want more questions…we must attend to duty as if last night did not happen."

"Espen already knows of the poison," Diona murmured.

"And likely others will too by now. But gossip will spread regardless, and if we allow the gossip to seem no more than gossip based on him being sick…"

Gaelán lifted his teary face. "And if he dies?" He had helped Ártur as best he could, but the pain of the rósádhá which Kavan had unknowingly cast onto the young man had left Gaelán ill-fit to heal or do anything more than cry. How could he call himself a man, he thought bitterly during the last several hours of the night, if he spent so much time crying?

"He won't die." Sóbhán clung to that belief as any child might, though not because he had any foolish notions about the mortality of man. He had seen his parents die, his uncle be killed. He was no stranger to the ravages of death. But his belief would not be taken from him. Kavan would live and everything would be right again.

The healer tousled the youngster's dark hair. "Of course he won't." He wanted to reassure them all, even though he had little faith in those words himself.

"k'Ádhá's will," Wortham reminded them, keeping his fears stoically hidden. "I will stay with him and come for you, Lord MacLyr, as soon as any change comes. Your wife is waiting…"

"As is yours."

"Zelenka understands."

Ártur groaned, nodded, and stepped away from the bed. Zelenka accepted the bond between Wortham and Kavan, did not fret, to Ártur's knowledge, that Kavan would somehow displace her in the captain's life. Zelenka was content with what she had of Wortham, a difference in culture or certainly in personality. Syl, on the other hand, had reason to fear that relationship. Because of it, Ártur had nearly died once. He needed to go to her, assure her that he had lived through the ordeal. He owed her that for her acceptance of his participation at Kavan's side last night. Not to respect her sacrifice, her worry, meant risking his marriage again, risking his family. He did not want that.

"Gaelán…Sóbhán…come away…"

"But aendhá…"

"Will sleep without you…and your father will be looking for you." The healer was surprised the chamberlain had not already come in search of his son. Perhaps he thought Gaelán was with Asta or was busy healing somewhere in the keep after the earthquake. Perhaps Kavan had told him that he needed Gaelán with him. But until he saw that his son was well, the man would worry, and Ártur felt his kinsman had enough to worry about.

"I'll go with you, Gaelán…and I will know…we will know…if he needs us." There was an undeniable bond between the two young men and Kavan, a bond stronger than before. If Sóbhán believed he would know of any significant changes in Kavan's condition without being here, Ártur suspected it was so.

One by one they filed from the room, with Ártur the last, leaving Wortham at Kavan's side. The captain waited until they were alone to stalk with balled fists to the window where he could watch the sun finish its emergence over the distant horizon and the Llaethlágárá Mountains he could not see. Kavan would live. He had to live. No loving deity, no benevolent power, would put a man through so much suffering, leave him lingering on the brink this long, to deprive him of life in the end. Kavan had done what was asked of him, repaid a debt that had not, in Wortham's eyes, been his to pay, and suffered for it. If that poison was to kill him, the captain believed it would have done its work already. Orec killed swiftly. Wortham knew this. And yet, hours later, Kavan still clung to the fragile tendrils of life. The power, his or k'Ádhá's or even Kóráhm's, that had kept Kavan alive this long would surely overcome death in the end.

"You are right to blame me." The voice drew Wortham from the window towards the man lingering at the foot of the bed. "I knew this would come, that the deb would be settled, but I did not imagine…"

"No, you did not," Wortham growled. The saint was the last person he expected to see, a man that rarely showed himself to anyone but Kavan. Then, his tone apologetic for addressing the saint in that fashion, he added, "I don't believe anyone could have imagined that…not even him." He knew that Kavan had no previous plan for that ritual, no idea what would need to be done to right the balance. Perhaps he had suspected, as Wortham had, the repeated incidents of the rósádhá would come into play, but could he have guessed he would be poisoned as well? Could he have guessed at the earthquake that shattered lives throughout Rhidam or the way the night would have affected those who had been asked to help him? "He did what he had to…what he knew no one else could do. He did what you could not." There was no condemnation in those words. "Should he have to die for the sins of the past as well? Hasn't he given enough?"

Kóráhm sullenly shook his head. "I do not know. I wish I did. I do not believe his story…is over…but I do not know what that means."

Wortham took that for proof that Kavan would live, though he did not know what sort of life that might be. Perhaps the bard would spend the rest of his days in the state he was currently in. That was not living, but it was, for Wortham and others, a selfishly hoped for thing, better than the bard's death and absence from their lives.

"Did it work?" he asked the man who rounded the side of the bed to touch Kavan's hand and kiss his forehead. "Did his sacrifice…was it enough?"

"I believe so. Time will reveal that for certain." Kóráhm offered Wortham his hand. "You are the best friend and companion a man could hope for. I wish there had been someone like you for me in those days." It was an accolade Wortham clung too as he clutched the saint's quite real, flesh and blood real, hand. "Stay with him, Captain. Do not leave him. He will always need you, whether he admits it or not."

"I know he does." It was one of the few certainties Wortham held true, the one he most needed. His life held little meaning without Kavan in it. He would endure anything as long as Kavan was there for him, and as long as he could be there for Kavan in return.

❮*❯

"Espen." The Queen found her husband in the morning room, a bottle of brandy on the table beside him as he watched the movement of men in the courtyard, troops coming and going as the inspection of Rhidam continued and the slow process of cleanup and rebuilding prepared to begin. He did not look at her as she entered, and from the position of his hands and arms, she guessed he was toying with his turban. He had not worn it since taking residence in Rhidam, save for their wedding day. It was as if the turban represented the life he had left behind and here, in Rhidam, it had little meaning. If he had it now it meant one thing.

"You are going home?"

The thought that he might be leaving her, might intend not to return, cut like a blade through her heart and made her cold. The prince, numerous retorts in mind as he turned to face her, found that each failed at the sight of her tear-streaked, tension-filled face and the pained, frightened tone of her voice. Sometimes, in moments like this, she reminded him of the child he had first met, a young girl with an adult mind who was out of place in the lives of the men around her. Becoming Queen had not changed who Diona was, but it had added strain to the woman who had, in his view, never entirely grown up. Perhaps, having been so sheltered by those men, she had not needed to do so.

"I am going to my brother for aid. I know we have both written to him, but I think the request may be more profitable if I present it personally and escort that which can be spared back to Rhidam. My brother will act more promptly if I am there to force his hand."

That made sense, but Diona did not believe his choice to go, and his choice of times, was created by the timing of the fire and the night's earthquake. "Will you be gone long?"

"That…" Espen studied her, trying to read her feelings in her eyes, her face, her posture, "is up to my brother and his generosity. I am sure you can control the situation without me."

"Perhaps…but I would prefer you to be here at my side."

Rather than question the truth of her statement, a truth he doubted, he bowed his head. "Then I shall endeavor to return as swiftly as I can. Is there something you require? My horse and men are waiting…"

"Yes, actually, there is something I have been meaning to say…"

"What in k'Ádhá's name has happened?"

The unanticipated interruption of k'dedhá Claide, whose return to Rhidam had not been expected for several more days, was enough for Diona to long to hit someone, preferably the arrogant looking, hawkish thin man whose clerical robes bore no hint of the effects of travel or even passage through Rhidam's still sooty streets. If she had not known from communications with Sir Gabersdon and from the reports of violence from Wexel, Nelori, and the other cities of the south, Diona would have suspected the k'dedhá had been hiding in Rhidam, even in her castle, the entire time he was reported to have been away.

"Happened?" she growled, frustrated that her attempts to speak privately with her husband were thwarted yet again, this time by a man who did not have the decency to announce his arrival properly or the politeness to knock before bursting into a closed room to speak to the Queen. "What has happened is that you have lost all manner of etiquette, k'dedhá, and I pray you find it before I take in on myself to teach you how one approaches the Queen."

The rattled man, angry at the scolding, bowed formally. "I apologize, Your Majesty," he muttered with a hint of distaste for those words. How an apology must irk him, she thought bitterly. "I just arrived; the city…Rhidam…its streets…who has done this thing?"

"Why must someone have done something? There was a fire…a fire now extinguished. Last night the land shook, but that is over as well. The fire was obvious to even you, surely…"

"Are the people being provided for? Shelter? Food? Rebuilding aid?"

Diona's eyes narrowed further. "What do you take me for?" she hissed. He had entered through a courtyard full of Rhidam's displaced. If he had been to the náós, which he might not have been, he would have seen many sheltered there as well. He would have passed Lachlan guards in the street, searching for bodies, aiding in the cleanup of debris, assessing the damage of roads and buildings and bridges over the Tegid. There was no way he could not have seen at least some of the work the Crown was undertaking.

"Messages have been sent to all lords and lands as well," Espen began diplomatically, hoping to give his wife time to calm her righteous fury, "and I am on my way to my brother to seek Hatu's aid. I believe the chamberlain is traveling to Bhryell, and Lord Bhíncári is likewise journeying to Clarys for the same.' He did not mention the Elyri assistance already being given in Rhidam. The k'dedhá would learn of that soon enough if he had not already noticed.

"Good…good…" Though Claide sounded relieved at the requests being made for aid, the seeking of it from Elyriá obviously did not please him. "The náós? Is it…?"

"Damaged, but largely intact." Diona was grateful for Espen's wisdom and discretion. He rarely interrupted her or spoke in her place when she was there to do so, but in some moments, particularly with Claide when her patience reached its end, he had proven adept at diverting her anger, speaking for her, long enough for her to regain dignity and control. If he left her, she would be hard-pressed to find anyone capable of doing likewise…or who was willing to. "I have already discussed the matter with the gdhededhásur; for now, the Faith will handle the needs of the people…food, clothing, and arranging shelter for those who do not have it…"

"It should not be…" Claide began indignantly.

"It is the Faith's duty to tend the poor and misfortunate, is it not? Royal funds are being directed into repair and restoration of homes, businesses and public structures…including the náós, if our funds allow. But neither the Crown nor the Faith can tend every need alone. We have agreed that this is the most equitable and logical arrangement, since the Faith lacks the experience to rebuild the city."

Nose in the air as if insulted, Claide huffed, "They have no authority…"

"They have every right to decide how to aid the Faithful in your absence," Diona reminded him, having made a thorough inquiry into the matter before meeting with all of the gdhededhásur to decide how best to help Rhidam's suffering. "And you must agree, the Faith cannot provide every need, repairing their homes, rebuilding their businesses, as well as offering their daily life requirements. The Crown has resources for that, and the Faith has the capacity to accept donations of food and clothing, to redistribute such things as needed. Do you have some other suggestion that we did not consider?"

The twitching at the corner of the man's mouth and eyes was the sole indicator of his rapidly whirring thoughts. As much as he wanted to undercut what had likely been Tusánt's ruling, as the Elyri was the second in leadership of Hes á Redh, there was no good way to do so. It was a fair and equitable division of resources that he could not realistically deny, but it irked him that the credit for such a compromise, for the aiding of Rhidam's suffering people, would be given to the Elyri instead of to him.

When he did not speak, the Queen continued, "Repairs are already underway on the náós; the roof is solid enough to give shelter for those who may still need it when the rain comes, and any roof repairs should be completed by then."

"In the náós?" The thin man choked and covered the response with a cough. His expression, and the idea that his interest in charitable aid to Rhidam's displaced population did not include the Faith providing for their sheltering needs…as Faith tenets demanded, made the Queen want to laugh.

"They will not all fit in the courtyard, as you must have seen upon your arrival," she replied. "After what happened to Hagan, there are risks to keeping them here for too long. Others are putting up friends, neighbors, and kin, but that still leaves many without homes as they rebuild. The Faithful appreciate the generosity."

"Well…yes…they should…"

Diona glanced at Espen who smiled and nodded with a hand on Claide's elbow to escort him from the room saying, "Come…allow me to show you the worst of the damage…what is being done…"

The Queen was grateful for being relieved of the prelate's irritating company, even though it came at the expense of her conversation with Espen. As his departure was now delayed, she hoped he would see her before he left for Hatu, and that they would be able to separate on a positive note. He might be angry and disappointed with her, but he did love her, as she loved him. If they could talk plainly, they would survive this awkward period. Espen would come home, Kavan would live, and everything would return to the way it should be.

❧*❧

Days ticked by with little indication of improvement or worsening in Kavan's condition. He did not move beyond the shallow rise and fall of his chest. To keep his body from wasting, Ártur turned him in the bed every few hours and saw to it that he was given food and water several times a day, soup and grain mash mixed with milk and honey easily swallowed without choking. The wounds on his wrists and feet were kept clean, covered with salve and bandages twice a day. The healer's care had no visible effect, but gradually Wortham noticed the fading of discolored veining in Kavan's body where the poison had left behind its trail. Little by little, the holy punctures began to close. Daily examinations convinced Ártur too that the poison that should have killed him was disappearing, either being expelled by his body or absorbed into it. They were the only signs that gave those in the castle hope. If the poison was dissipating and not killing him, if the punctures on his extremities were healing, then the odds seemed in favor of recovery. For those who had stood with him in that chapel, that day could not come soon enough.

Unable to delay the inevitable, Muir and Clianthe returned to Káliel and the resumption of their lives and duties. Only by returning home might they have some chance of swaying the Council to lend aid to the broken city of Rhidam. Though Muir longed to remain at Kavan's side until the bard opened his eyes, that night's events had taught him something worth remembering, that most often duty came first. Returning to duty was what Kavan would want him to do, and Ártur promised that, should there be any change, he would be sure to let Muir know, even if it meant flying to the prince.

Owain likewise felt compelled by the situation to journey to Fiara, to gather as many materials and able-bodied aid as he could assemble. Offering land-owners a reduction in their yearly taxation if they would journey to Rhidam, donate goods and food and time to the recovery efforts, seemed a fair thing if it meant lessening the burden on Rhidam.

The kingdom might suffer for a time over shortness of funds, but they would recover more quickly if the people Enesfel depended on were able to return to their homes and livelihoods. Bhyrhán made multiple journeys to Clarys with similar requests for aid and Bhríd, uncomfortable going to Levonne and preferring to leave Levonne's aid in his wife's hands, journeyed to Bhryell to seek assistance from the surrounding areas. With the healers and physicians, including those who had come to help from Elyriá continuing to assist with the assortment of medical issues created by smoke and fire and the injuries caused while men moved debris and bodies, it left Wortham and Sóbhán most frequently at Kavan's side. They too, however, helped in Rhidam's recovery where they could. It was a joint effort by high and lowborn alike in those initial three weeks. With all of the focus on rebuilding, there was little occasion or energy for violence.

Despite the apparent healing of his body, the longer Kavan remained unconscious, the more everyone, Wortham included, feared he would not awaken.

The day after Duke Gabersdon returned leading several wagons of carved stone blocks, followed not long after by Owain's return with a trail of lumber-laden wagons, lumber both cut and uncut, a proper state memorial was held in honor of Ternce Wyndham who had lost his life during the fire, a man who had been a boon and friend to Enesfel for many years, a man Owain Lachlan had once called comrade. His body had been taken home by his family to be buried with his kin in northern Enesfel, but the Queen, setting aside any bitterness over the man leaving royal service when Hagan needed him, insisted on marking his funeral with the pomp someone of his rank and service deserved. The memorial, held in the open area in front of the castle gates as the náós was not yet fit for such things, was also used to commemorate others who had perished in both the fire and the subsequent earthquake. The thoughtfulness the Queen gave to the people's feelings, the attention to their hardships, the help her troops, her staff, her advisors were providing, went far in keeping the disorganized populace appeased.

But she feared it would not be enough. As the ninth month of the year was ushered in, the oppressive heat broke and cooler weather began to stretch across the middle portion of the kingdom. It had yet to grow cold, but as the nighttime temperatures eased lower, fear crept in and unrest began to blossom among those who felt their homes were not being given the priority they believed they deserved. It did not help that rumors were circulating of Lord Cliáth's death. He was last seen carried out of the burning náós after saving dedhá Tusánt's life. With no official statement forthcoming from the Crown, and whispers of death by fire, smoke, or poison racing through the streets, his absence rubbed across Rhidam's open wounds like grit and sand.

The Corylliens, or at least the anti-Elyri factions in Rhidam, seemed in as much disarray as Kavan's supporters were at his absence. As news of the number of Elyri healers in Rhidam spread, and a shipment of grains, dried fruit, clothing, and workable leather arrived from Alberni in response to the word sent to Saint Kóráhm's, attempt after attempt was made against any Elyri who dared go into the streets alone…except, peculiarly gdhededhá Tusánt. The hard work the dedhá put out day and night to help the citizens, the efforts he took to treat everyone fairly, his leadership during and immediately after the fire and earthquake when Claide had been absent, won the Elyri cleric support and begrudging respect from those who might otherwise shun and threaten him. Even Claide's return to Rhidam did not dampen that support, despite the man's attempts to pull Tusánt out of the community eye by giving him less public duties to undertake.

Tusánt, however, held no illusions that he was safe. How could he be, when attacks continued on his countrymen and threatening anti-Elyri messages were left around Rhidam as constant reminders of the Corylliens' presence?

❧*❧

"That's the brilliance of it." General Glucke thumped his fist on the pine and iron table with fervor, easily taking the idea as his, though the notion had originated with Kjell when Owain's message reached him. It had taken almost a week for the news of the great fire in Rhidam to reach Merkar through official channels. It was not enough time for Kjell to covertly gather any sort of assistance for Enesfel's Queen, but it was time enough for him to formulate an idea and slip it discreetly into conversation with Glucke, knowing that, if he could convince the general, the general, in turn, was likely to convince Merkar of its merits. Kjell sat at the far end of the dining table in his normal place, as far from the King as possible, as far from the usual rabble of advisors and family that clustered around Merkar, listening to the men without appearing to. It was part of Kjell's ongoing effort to stay out of the path of Merkar's sword arm. The less intelligent, less interested in politics Kjell appeared to be, the less likely it was that Merkar would attempt to take his life. He still believed his brother had orchestrated the deaths of the rest of their brothers and their father; Kjell's cunning was all that spared him thus far.

"I could not go; they will kill me on sight," Merkar choked.

Not as dumb as he appears, Kjell thought as he absently twirled his fork through something unidentifiable on his plate. To covertly build goodwill with the Lachlans, then to use that friendship against them, was the sort of play Merkar appreciated, but Kjell had not believed for an instant that the King would consider undertaking the mission on his own. He, justifiably, believed the Lachlans would rather kill him than risk trusting him. And, Kjell thought as he side-eyed the general, he might have an inkling that the general hoped the Lachlans would do just that, for if King Merkar died, Prince Kjell would have the throne, and Glucke like many others, believed Kjell would be easily manipulated if that day came.

"Send someone else…one of the advisors…your daughter…"

The King scowled as he pondered the suggestion. He did not trust his advisors…or his daughter. Truth be told, few de Cormick's trusted anyone, especially their kin. But something in the King's eyes changed when his ponderous gaze fell on the prince across the table.

"Yes…yes…we could do that. Send Kjell."

As if he had heard his name but was unaware of the topic of discussion, Kjell lifted his head with his very best bored expression and whined, "Me? Send me where?" as if being sent away was an unwarranted, unwanted, imposition.

"I don't know if that would be wise…" began Glucke half-heartedly. Sending the prince on such a mission had its good points: he was amiable and likable, more trustworthy, Glucke believed, from an outsider's point of view, and he and the King could surely manipulate the prince into doing what they desired while in Enesfel. The plan's primary drawback, however, was that Kjell's simple-mindedness might prompt him to do or say something that would fall back on Merkar…or that he might do something to get himself killed. If Kjell was to die, there was no suitable heir to Neth's throne. King Merkar had daughters thus far, girls too young to be married off to potential kings…if any could be found worthy of Merkar's approval. Kjell's death could mean civil war that could further weaken the kingdom and an eventual defeat by either Cordash or Enesfel.

No, Glucke thought; sending Kjell was too risky.

Unless Kjell's death left the path open for his own ascension to the throne.

But it was not up to him. King Merkar's mind, now that he had been given a small shred of idea, would not be swayed. "Of course it is. Owain was fond of him…sentimental fool probably still is. And he's harmless. No one will suspect him of anything. He's the perfect envoy for this sort of thing."

"Envoy? To where?"

"To Enesfel…to Rhidam," crowed Merkar, proud of his idea.

Kjell looked suitably anxious and excited at once. "To do what?"

Merkar clucked his tongue and shook his head. "Now don't you fret your little blond head about a thing. Nothing for you to worry about. The general and I will take care of everything. All you need to do is pack some clothes and be ready to travel when I command it."

"What if I don't want to?" Kjell began, trying to sound like he was afraid of this imposition, afraid of the unfamiliar.

"Think of it as an adventure. You like adventures, don't you? You hunt for them often enough."

Years of practice kept the smile off of Kjell's face and the table's distance between them kept the man, and his general, from noting the satisfied flicker in Kjell's eyes. This was exactly what he wanted, what he had hoped for, the opportunity to help the new Queen and offer his services legitimately…with Merkar believing he was doing it for him, for Neth. For Neth, yes, but never for Merkar and the hosts of parasites who ran the kingdom and battled constantly for favor. It would take a week or more to gather supplies and materials to donate, giving Kjell time to plan. In the meantime, he would strive to make sure that the typically fickle de Cormick King did not change his mind…about sending Kjell or sending aid.

❧*❧

"You owe him! You owe us both!"

Claide eyed the much younger man with barely disguised scorn. The claim was true…to a point. Without the financial backing and the initial idea sharing of the two Gottfrid sons, his plans might have proven unfruitful. But that had been long enough ago, the newly elected k'dedhá felt, that he was no longer beholden to anyone now that events had unfolded as he had anticipated. He had consolidated enough power and influence to accomplish what he had set out to do, and no one, particularly the youngest displaced son of a barely influential duke, mattered to his plans.

"His actions were his own," the hawkish man snorted. "I applaud his ingenuity, his bravery, but I will not risk implication in his schemes."

"There is no risk! I require only the money for his fine…consider it interest due on the money we gave you. Give it to me and I will assume all of the risk. When he is released, we shall see that he…"

"There will be no fines paid." There were limited sources from which Claide could get that sort of money. His widowed benefactor had been displaced by fire damage to her home and was spending much of what she had on repairs. Taking money from the coffers of the Faith would leave a trail to him that he would be hard-pressed to explain should anyone notice the deficit. And his own personal wealth…wealth that had come in part from the contributions of men such as the Gottfrid brothers…well, that would remain untouched until the day he was forced, by age, by health, by circumstance, into retirement. He did not trust them to pay it back. He did not trust anyone enough to let them know he had such a stash.

"He will have to wait until the reconstruction of Rhidam is…"

"He will die before then!" Winter in a dank, cold dungeon might not kill Idal, but his health would undoubtedly suffer.

"k'Ádhá will…" started Claide.

Kent Gottfrid's eyes narrowed and flashed as he snarled, "If you do not free him…if he dies…so shall you."

He rose from the table in the Boar's Head Tavern and stalked away, unruffled by the piercing look the k'dedhá gave him. Claide might have private resources, a means of threatening others, but Kent had resources too. He could summon up the strength of the entire Coryllien organization if he had to. Kent was not afraid of Claide.

Bhríd put the letter on his desk, reading the impressions left on it as he absently smoothed the parchment with the flat of his palm. This was hardly the sort of news he expected and the ill-timing of it left him cold and sick when he believed he should be excited and pleased. Children were a blessing. Why should he not welcome a third?

By allowing his thoughts to stray to his sons, he found the answer to that question. He was proud of his youngest, not because he carried

Elyri gifts but because Gaelán respected life and was working diligently to build a life that helped others. His eldest son, on the other hand, had brought shame on the family name, on their title, and appeared to be as much a force for destruction as his brother was one for healing. With Tayte still at his mother's side, what chance for survival and a good life did a new child have…a child who too would carry mixed blood through no doing of its own? The possibility that Tayte might find some way to kill a new child was one Bhríd could not shake or ignore, even if his wife would refuse to believe that Tayte could do such a thing.

But Madalyn would not abandon their eldest son, as she still hoped she could find in him the generous, intelligent child he had once been. Though Tayte was forbidden to hold the duchy, there was nowhere else for him to go where he knew people and could attempt to build a new life, and Madalyn would, Bhríd knew, keep the young man close as long as she was able. He could work the vineyards; he could manage her books. He could continue to contribute to the family, to the duchy's wealth, and perhaps someday his position would change.

Bhríd could demand otherwise by right of Enesfel law, but it was not the Elyri way. A woman ran the household, and the vineyard was Madalyn's familial home. What right did he have to demand that their son leave the only home he too had ever known in order that his father could return to his wife's side and protect the unborn?

They needed to talk. Soon. But for now, she was safe. And Rhidam needed him.

❧Chapter 50❧

The room was bright with sunlight, still and peaceful despite the sounds of reconstruction that rumbled in through his open window. Midday, he judged, groaning as he tried to rise. The air was hot, though not as heavy as the stifling heat of the day he last remembered. He felt frail and exhausted and though he had no idea how much time had passed, he judged by the exaggerated thinness of his fingers, his hand, his arm when he looked at it, that it had been much longer than he had ever been unconscious before. There were no dark streaks snaking up his arms and the places on his palms where the skin had been ripped away had been healed, leaving no trace of damage.

He had survived the Orec, he mused in amazement. How could that have happened?

Had it happened?

The shiny scar tissue visible on each wrist assured him it had.

They were the only scars, those and the two on the crowns of his feet, that his body had ever borne.

Fear strangled him, filling him with a surge of survival-related instinct that enabled him to struggle to his feet, wobble in place long enough to snatch the long tunic hanging on the nearest bedpost, pull it over his head and stumble towards the door. It occurred to him that he was alone, causing him to both fear that the others had died in the event that seemed unreal to him now, and worry that they had given up on his survival. Staggering steps brought him into the empty corridor, to the door of the adjoining oratory and the Gate it contained. He had to go there. He had to see with his own eyes.

Though physically weak, he felt stronger, in mind, in spirit, and in power, than he had ever felt. That power enabled him to journey easily through the Gate to arrive, moments later, in the abandoned chapel that had haunted him since he first discovered it. With a handlight to see by, he studied the room. There were no traces of blood on the floor or walls as he remembered, but it remained on the altar, where the shattered blades still crisscrossed the marble. The blood there, pooled around the embedded Coryllien blade, was dry, a dark brown powder that flaked and peeled when he attempted to pull the dagger free. He did not expect it to come out, but his conscience would not allow him to leave the blunted instrument of death to taint a room that now felt clean and new. The hilt broke from the dagger with a snap and remained in Kavan's hand as he stared at the trapped blade that was now flush with the top of the cracked marble, leaving a tri-tipped metal shape in the stone. Perplexed and curious, he rubbed his finger over the mark before turning slowly to inspect the room.

The skulls he recalled tumbling from the fractured north wall and its apocalyptic mural, lay scattered about, delicately shaped skulls bleached with age that he had not been able to examine. There were fewer of them than he had thought, not the hundreds he expected to see, and he wondered as he knelt and studied one, whether he had imagined that number or whether it had been real and those skulls had somehow disappeared as the blood splattered around the room had done. What he did know was that the broken swords and dagger hilt on the altar proved that some, if not all, of his memories were accurate. He had been here with the others. The ritual had been completed.

But had it worked?

Beneath his fingers, the skull he touched was warm, warm as though living, which made him jerk his hand back in shock. There was another sensation there as well, one that told him these were no children's' skulls. Young, perhaps, but not children…not Teren…and far more ancient than the sacrifices in this room could have made them. He scanned the cracked mural in the glow of his handlight. Perhaps they were fissures caused by the earthquake, but the shape of them, the similar squareness and size and their spacing across the wall suggested they were man-made…chambers created, perhaps, to house the skulls of those who had built this place, people entombed within the sacred spaces carved with loving hands.

He shivered and pushed to his feet. How old were those people…and how long ago had this place been built and originally used? He got no sense of it from the skull, but the k'kairá writing over the entrance doorway suggested an age long before the Elyri had come to these lands, or at least a time concurrent with their arrival. It opened unanswerable questions, questions he believed would tell him much about his own history if he could find the answers.

Most of the items used that night had been taken away, carried out by the participants when Ártur brought them back to the rooms above their heads. It had to have been Ártur, for surely they had not found their way through the maze to the dungeon entrance. Other than the broken blades, which Kavan did not move, the Chalice still lay tipped on its side on the altar where Gaelán put it, cold to the touch and clean of traces of liquid and blood Kavan knew had filled it. On the floor before the altar, his robe was spread, stained the crimson of blood, the blood, he wondered, that it had absorbed from the rest of the room? There was no proof of that, as the fabric was dry and no red came away on his fingertips when he touched it, but that seemed the only explanation for the change in color. The idea made his body as cold as the Chalice surface had been and raised tiny pebbles across his skin. The staff, still assembled in one piece, lay on the cloth, its now dark crown pointed towards the wooden box the Chalice and crown piece had been transported in, which remained where Kavan had placed it, open, empty, and waiting, he believed, for its contents to be returned.

The Chalice vibrated with faint power as he picked it up and returned it to its velvet nest. The power he could feel was like a hum, a purr, something warm despite the metal's coolness, soothing and less likely, he believed, to interfere with his own power. That should mean, he hoped, that he would be able to take it from this room by Gate without a stumbling trip through the crumbling dark corridors he was currently physically unable to make. He wanted to get these things to his room where they should be safe until he could take them back where they belonged.

But perhaps, he mused, as he took the staff apart piece by piece, this was the safest place for them, for now. None but Elyri were able to easily come here. Sóbhán and Gaelán were not yet proficient with the Gates, and the odds against his cousin or Tusánt wanting to return here alone were high. Kavan trusted those who had been here not to speak of those events to outsiders, thus no one should be aware of the items being here. Perhaps if they remained a few more days, until Kavan was stronger, he would return them to their proper home so that no one would ever find or tamper with them.

The staff crown was nested in the box with the Chalice and the box closed and latched. The hum of power increased, a sensation he thought was like a recharging between the objects, but it was still too weak to interfere with his gifts. How long might it take them to fully recharge? How long would he have, he wondered, before the power was too strong to Gate them? That would mean another trip over land to the south, a trip Kavan had no interest in making again…but one he would undertake if necessary. Qol had demanded it.

There was a way to further protect the sacred items until he was well enough for that long trip. The chest was of a size that would fit snuggly into one of the vacated holes where the skulls had been in the wall. One was cleaned out with his hands, loose rock and debris scooped out onto the ground without consideration that the dust might once have been a person, and when it was empty, he slid the box into place. It was a tight fit, and he believed others would find removing it to be a challenge. The remaining two staff pieces were too long to fit in any of the carved niches, and Kavan did not want to leave the Coryllien's hilt here. He decided to bring them to his room. Without the crown, the staff would be useless, and the hilt, at least, he did not want to discard.

With the torn, red fabric draped over his shoulder, he leaned against the altar, his hands spread flat, and bowed his head in prayer. There was a peculiar yawning emptiness inside of him, the feeling that something had been lost that could not be regained. Unlike the first time he had touched this ancient marble, the power felt right, untainted, pure. There was no longer darkness lingering over it, save for a tiny withering spark buried far in the earth below…a spark that screamed impotently at him. Not Coryllien that. No, Coryllien's spark, his soul, had been dispersed, sent on to find what peace it could. This little flicker was a more ancient evil, one Kavan believed would trouble them no more. As long as no man set foot in this room to do evil on this portal to Ethenae, the flicker was powerless.

What Kavan had done, some of the memories vague and others pushed away because he did not want to think about them, appeared to have worked.

"Kóráhm…tell me…is it done?" If the saint would reply, he would be reassured and thankful that his life's purpose had been fulfilled.

"Thought I'd find you here." The tickle of power that indicated the use of the Gate pierced Kavan's concentration before he heard the words behind him. He had not thought his cousin would risk that Gate, but in search of Kavan, Ártur was capable of many unexpected things. The healer's tone was full of partially relieved worry as he assessed his cousin's too thin, trembling form. "You should be in bed."

Kavan sighed. "I know." That rare agreement was an expression of how weak the bard was, for he normally resisted confinement to bed. "But I had to see…to know…"

The healer nodded. "That's why I figured you would be here when you were not in your room or the oratory."

"It was real…wasn't it? All of it?"

"Sometimes I awaken and feel I am still here. Other times I am about my day and it feels as if none of it could have happened. But," he looked around as he reached Kavan's side but dared not touch the altar. He had no desire to glimpse the sort of great power residing there. Seeing it in his cousin was enough. "seeing it again…there is no doubt about what we shared here…as insane as it was."

Kavan, again overcome by that sense of loss, closed his eyes, dropped his head forward, and when he swayed on his feet, leaned against Ártur's shoulder for support, another rare admission of weakness. This far beneath the ground, the air, the stones beneath the bard's bare feet were icy, and Kavan, dressed only in that tunic, did not have the physical capability to withstand it. Nor, it seemed to Ártur, was Kavan making any attempt to regulate his body temperature. Whether he was unable, was too weak, or was otherwise focused, the healer could not tell. But it made no difference.

"Come…I'm taking you back to bed. Anything here will keep until you are rested and strong."

Kavan picked up the staff pieces and the broken dagger hilt and allowed Ártur to steer him to the Gate. He made no attempt to take them through, merely shut down his defenses so that his cousin could do the work. He relinquished the objects so that Ártur placed them next to his harp on the dresser and climbed gingerly into bed as though the movement hurt and robbed him of any remaining energy. When the healer helped him out of the tunic and adjusted the sheet and blanket over him, knowing his cousin did not sleep well unless covered, Kavan murmured, "Will you send Wortham to me…please?"

There was a jealous pang in the healer's chest but he nodded. "As soon as I find him, yes. He was to assist in clearing the debris from the Eagle's Nest. The Queen decided she wants the inn restored before the rains come."

"How are…?"

"Everyone is well. Muir and Clianthe returned to Káliel. Owain has brought supplies from Fiara and Bhyrhán has gone to Clarys to seek aid. Bhríd made a request from the Bhryell Council…but who knows how successful that will be." A few young Elyri had taken it upon themselves in the past to aid Neth's beleaguered population; Ártur's niece had been one of them and had died for her generosity. Whether any would be daring enough to transport supplies across Enesfel's troubled landscape, whether the Council would approve of them doing so, was hard to say. Ártur was reasonably sure that Bhen intended to do just that…alone if necessary. "Prince Espen is seeking aid from his brother. There has been a smattering of violence, but it seems the Coryllien's efforts are small- in scale and sporadic. At least Tusánt has found favor…though not with Claide…"

"Claide is back? How long have I…?"

"Over four weeks."

That was why he felt week in body, though it did not explain the emptiness inside. And since Ártur claimed everything was well, no one harmed or dead, the feeling made even less sense than before. He groaned and sank into his pillows.

"He came back before…the day after we…" We did not do anything, the healer reminded himself. They had been silent observers to what Kavan had done. He was still unclear of their purpose for being there, but if it had been for nothing more than moral support for Kavan, Ártur felt honored to have been trusted enough to be included. "It seems suspicious, and odd…but everything he does seems that way now. We do know he was not in Rhidam at the time of the fire, so his early return may have been coincidental."

Kavan tended not to believe in coincidence where Claide was concerned, but without contrary proof, there was nothing to be done. He was too weary to consider the implications of the man's return. Though he closed his eyes, he still heard the footsteps retreating towards the door. "Don't forget…send Wortham."

Having thought him already asleep, Ártur replied, "I won't forget." He wondered, as he left, if Kavan would stay awake until Wortham came or if he wanted the captain with him as he slept.

It was not Wortham, however, who came into the bard's room not long after Ártur left. Having heard voices as he passed, Bhríd changed out of his sooty clothes and came back to Kavan's room to find the healer gone and the bard seemingly asleep. He was pleased to know Kavan had recovered from whatever had happened to him. Not even his own son would say; if he wanted the story he would have to get it from Kavan, but he doubted the bard would share it with him.

For reasons he could not adequately explain, he felt compelled to share his news with Kavan, news he had not yet shared with Gaelán or anyone else. Not wanting to disturb the almost skeletal man in his sleep, however, he began to back from the room before hearing his name spoken in a raspy whisper.

Embarrassed at being discovered, thinking he had roused Kavan, Bhríd came to the bed, poured a cup of water, and gave it to the pale man. "My apologies…I heard speaking…I thought you to be awake."

"I was…I am," Kavan reassured him, gratefully swallowing the water. He was so thirsty.

"I heard it was…poison?" He did not know the source of exposure; he was merely grateful the bard lived.

Kavan bobbed his head and motioned for more water. "It seems I have recovered."

"Gaelán will be pleased to hear it. He has been insufferable ever since this happened and not even Sóbhán's conviction that you would live has soothed him." The refilled cup was put in Kavan's hand. The skin to skin contact at that moment made Kavan jerk as if his hand had been burned and he stared at his cousin, seeing both the man and something else at the same moment, an image, an impression, that stunned and dismayed him.

"Madalyn is with…" Perhaps this explained the peculiar heavy emptiness inside.

"…child…aye." It did not surprise him that Kavan learned the details through that touch. This unborn child was at the top of his mind most moments of the day, the child, its mother, his marriage, the two sons at odds as far apart as possible. "I learned of it three days ago…and I cannot…" He shook his head. "The timing of it could be better…there are so many dangers…"

"Go to her, Bhríd. Stay with her."

"But Tayte…" It was difficult to admit that on some level he was afraid of his son, or rather what his son had become.

"Go to her, to your home," Kavan repeated emphatically. "If you do not…you will regret it the rest of your days."

The chamberlain blinked, eyes wide as Kavan's words, their intent, sunk in. There was warning in them, warning of danger to the child, Madalyn, or perhaps to Tayte. Perhaps to all of them. A warning of things to come, either so that he could prevent it by being there, or that he could not but should be there to see them through to the conclusion Kavan Saw. Perhaps Kavan did not actually see anything but sensed it, sensed something coming, a shadow across his world.

Bhríd got to his feet, struggling not to surrender to the pain in his breast and the darkness threatening his vision. He did not need to ask for details. If there were any that Kavan thought he should know, Bhríd believed Kavan would tell him. It was the sort of man Kavan was. All of his ponderings, his wrestling with choices and the future, were decided in Kavan's command and he knew what he had to do.

"And Gaelán?" he asked. It was his only question, his one uncertainty. No matter what he did, Gaelán could not go to Levonne. He could not study healing there, and going would get him killed.

"He will be safe in Ártur and Rouvyn's care…and in mine. You know we will do our best to see that no harm comes to him."

Then it was not his youngest son at risk. That, at lease, settled Bhríd's mind a little. "I must speak with him." And then would follow a more difficult task. Words with the Queen.

➤*➥

Three of the assisting Elyri healers and Wortham were among those clearing debris from the damaged Eagle's Nest Inn. There had been few requests for healers or physicians this day, and the men, wanting to do something constructive, voted to aid those working on the Queen's project of the day. It was the safest place, other than the náós, for Elyri to work, since both locations swarmed with Lachlan soldiers and a fair number of the sheriff and justice's personal staff and Queen's advisors. The Eagles Nest had the added advantage of being within running distance of the castle gates and bridge across the moat, providing sanctuary should trouble arise. For Wortham, it kept him close to Kavan, should the bard awaken and need him…or worsen and need him too. He suspected that was the primary reason the Queen had made the inn a priority project, to give those who wanted to help but felt compelled to stay close to the bard something to do.

Most of the heavy debris had been removed, the usable stone set to one side, unbroken items that had not perished in the flames collected and place in a pile where a group of children was lending their small hands to the restoration efforts by washing the soot away in large wooden pails of water from the moat. There were women washing the walls, looking for areas that needed patching or repair, while the men carefully made their way in and out with broken beams, collapsed stone, and tools and supplies to shore up and repair as much as was required to make the building safe to work in. The efforts had steadily progressed for the last week, the building almost ready for the efforts of carpenters and stonemasons, and there had been no incidents of note, either among those laboring to restore the inn nor those passing to and from other projects throughout the city.

That string of luck, however, in a city licking its wounds and occasionally seething with those looking to lay blame for their ill fortune, was too good to last. When angry shouts and the screams of startled women and children erupted outside the gutted inn, Wortham, the healers, and other men working within poured through the doorless entry to find a dozen or more men shouting curses at the workers and the Queen for spending resources on an inn when there were citizens who were homeless and hungry.

They seemed not to care that the inn could house and feed some of those, if restored, and the owners had just as much right for assistance as anyone else.

"Ungrateful wretches!" the captain shouted as a stone sailed over his head and struck one of the healers behind him, despite his efforts to shield them from harm. That healer cried out and dropped to the ground. Women and children scattered and the soldiers in the group pushed into the gaggle of assailants to end the ruckus and make arrests.

Ártur had the bad luck of arriving at the onset of violence in his search for Wortham, and the captain, certain the appearance of the Lachlan healer meant news about Kavan, shoved past others to protect the bard's cousin.

"So many of you cursed Elyri," someone shouted. Unable to reach Ártur in time, Wortham watched in horror as the barrage of rocks from an increasingly larger crowd shifted from the majority of the workers at the inn to the Elyri among them. Men who were not soldiers but who worked side by side with the healers on this project did their best to surround them, two standing and one who had fallen, and move them back into the inn for protection. It trapped them, but it was more protection than remaining out in the open provided.

What began as a handful of individuals protesting the Crown's choice of priority projects became an assault on the outsiders, a much easier emotional target than the Queen. Balint, helping there today as well, shouldered up to Wortham and together they reached Ártur to protect him from the hailing debris. The healer was cut and bruised but not badly injured, and the two soldiers were determined to keep it that way as they muscled him towards the castle gate. They were weaponless, without armor, but their bodies were big enough, broad enough, and strong enough, that they did not fear serious injury from rocks and decaying food.

A clay pot of wine caught Wortham in the face, shattering on impact, causing the man to scream. Balint shifted to look, keeping the three moving, but Wortham was going down, a jagged shard of pottery embedded in the left side of his face, in his eye. By now the palace guards, those on duty at the gate and stationed in the bailey, had charged into the fray. Seeing their wine-drenched comrade with blood streaming down his face, several sought to get him, and the healer who could save his life and sight, to safety. With armed men involved, both those from within the castle and those from nearby streets who had heard the commotion, the assailants began to fall back, some being apprehended, others falling beneath blows or beneath the press of their fellow rioters. Men and women wanting to reclaim Rhidam from too much anti-Elyri violence joined in, attacking their fellow citizens, while others, high on the emotions left in the fire's wake, entered the fighting simply to relieve the tension that had simmered too long. With the sun setting, torches and lanterns were brought into the mix, as was the fear that another fire would ravage Rhidam.

Wortham, however, was unaware of it.

❧*❧

Wortham's arrival was not the one of quiet joy Kavan hoped for. Rather it came with cries, chaos in the corridor, shouting voices and thundering boots. Kavan did not immediately recognize any of the voices save for the captain's bellowing roar, "Kavan!" that reverberated through the stone floor and walls and burned into Kavan's center like a hot, heavy molten stone. It brought him instantly awake, immediately to sitting, and despite his weakness and nudity, the cry of obvious pain and distress brought the bard stumbling from his room in time to see those bulky men, Balint among them, wrestling the captain through the doorway of his room. Zelenka followed, her face pale and panic-stricken as her footsteps tracked through the trail of blood left behind.

Wortham's blood.

Door thrown open, Kavan pushed to the bedside where Wortham thrashed and fought to be free of the multitude of hands that held him, his only thought being to get to Kavan. There was a gash across his left eye, short but deep, and the blood that poured down his face as he tried to cover it was thick and copious, reminding Kavan of a day years ago when Wortham had come close to losing sight in that same eye.

But the memory of what came after, that followed that night, was something Kavan chose not to think about as he held the man's head between his hands to allow Ártur and Gaelán and Rouvyn to work. He could not anticipate when such a miracle would be granted and knew that the ones he prayed for most fervently were often the ones not given. That knowledge did not prevent him from sending up his most heartfelt prayers while lowering his face towards Wortham's to whisper in his ear, a quiet song to soothe him and draw his focus away from his pain and the work the healers were undertaking. At the first note, Wortham's whole body grew rigid and his good eye, which had been blinking away tears of pain and blood, closed as he concentrated on the sound.

It took little effort, despite his lingering weakness, for Kavan to focus on Wortham, the song, and also on the effort his kin were making on the captain's behalf. Through the flow of power, Kavan was aware of Ártur's wounds, but true to his calling, the healer was more interested in Wortham's far more serious injury. Kavan lent as much power as the healer needed to increase their efficiency and Gaelán, unable to get his hands near Wortham's face, was instead healing Ártur's visible wounds.

Minutes passed, their efforts pooled towards a single goal, but in the end, it was not enough. The blood ceased flowing, tearing and bruising and cutting were repaired as near to the original condition as possible, considering the injury. But healers, regardless of their skill, regardless of what Teren thought of their gifts, were not miracle workers. Wortham would live a long, healthy life, but unless that miracle came through Kavan's hands, the sight in Wortham's eye would be forever lost. Head on the pillow next to the captain's, one hand against the man's face entwined in his dark curls and the other resting on the reassuring rise and fall of Wortham's chest, Kavan wept silently, his tears soaking the pillow and Wortham's still wine-soaked hair. No one, not even Ártur or Zelenka, had the heart to separate them. With Wortham out of danger, Gaelán pulled the blanket free to cover the bard's naked shoulders and followed the others from the room.

Zelenka sank to the floor in the hallway, willing to wait there until she was needed, wiping away frightened tears but speaking to no one..

Perhaps, thought Kavan, he was too weak. Four weeks of little food or water, four weeks without music and prayer, had certainly taken its toll. He might not have come soon enough, or his well-meant prayer for his dearest friend had been met with disapproval. It had surely not fallen on the deaf ears of the divine. Perhaps there was something Kavan had failed to do in the underground chapel, or something that had been done incorrectly. Perhaps the energy, the effort, the power it had taken to achieve that cleansing had taken every bit of that within that had once allowed the awkward capacity for miracles to pass from the divine to the mortal.

What if there were no more miracles? Was that not what he wanted, to be the same as everyone rather than a tool of the divine?

The sensation of hands lightly squeezing his shoulders stilled his mind. He shivered, sighed, and sagged further into the mattress over which he hunched. It soothed him a little, calmed his spirit, but it did not take away the emptiness.

Or this blindness might be k'Ádhá's will and Kavan and Wortham would both be forced to accept that the world, and k'Ádhá, did not bend to conform to their desires. There was still time…so long as both men breathed…a chance, in k'Ádhá's time, for healing to come to pass. And if it did not, Kavan would love Wortham no less. If he could not restore his sight, he would give the man other things and, he knew, as he dropped into sleep, that he would do anything Wortham needed.

Her dungeon was full, as was the sheriff's holding facility in the heart of the city. The fighting lessened quickly with the onset of night; the freshness of fire memories made most reluctant to fight beneath the glow of torch and lamp. Arrests had been made indiscriminately, leaving the sorting out of gilt to the Queen and Inquisitor. Some rioters were set free shortly after their arrest, those deemed lesser threats, those who had, as it turned out, been brought into the chaos either in self-defense or in the defense of family or the Elyri targets now huddled in the dayroom under Bhríd's protection. Every Elyri in Rhidam, at least those who could be found, except for dedhá Tusánt, were gathered into the safety of the castle to be guarded until the chaos was under control. Enough were questioned and either released or detained for further interrogation later, to be certain that there was no overflow of capacity, and then the Queen sent everyone to bed.

Diona, however, could not sleep. The Great Hall was empty now, save for the handful of soldiers and attendants who seemed to hover about her too much these days. Gone were the times when she could flit about the castle alone or with one or two of her ladies. The crown on her head and the heavy weight of Rhidam's health on her shoulders necessitated a level of protection she was not accustomed to. They were easy enough to ignore, however, seeming little more than the shadows of the room or extra décor that would not intrude on her pacing or her thoughts unless she needed them.

The news of Kavan's waking had come not long before the riot, but Wortham's attack brought her elation to an abrupt end. One of the visiting Elyri healers had suffered a blow to the head from which he had yet to wake, in spite of Ártur's efforts to heal him. It was the nature of some head injuries, the healer explained. Sometimes the damage was of a sort that it, or the bleeding inside that accompanied it, left irreparable impressions within that head that resulted in a damaged man…or a dead one. Which fate lay ahead for the comatose healer was not yet clear.

Ártur said much the same about the captain's eyesight, a more personally painful fact for Diona as she strode here and there about the Hall. She recalled a similar injury he had sustained when she was a child, an injury that should have blinded him except for something, a miracle at Kavan's hands, that spared him. Captain Delamo was no longer in her service, had not been on the Lachlan staff since his resignation to follow Kavan on his long-ago quest, but he was still a soldier she knew she could depend on as long as an order or request did not compromise Kavan's safety or wishes. But would he continue to be a fighting man if he could not see the way he had before? Some men continued to serve as soldiers, acting as guards or training staff, but Diona could not imagine Wortham settling for something so mundane. Others gave up, retired into obscurity, or found a more permanent end to what they considered to be uselessness. She could not imagine that end for the captain either, not so long as Kavan lived.

No. As long as Kavan was in Wortham's life, the two men would find their way forward and Wortham, she believed, would not allow a handicap to stop him from serving the man he was most faithful to.

There was other news that troubled her and left her in a quandary, vacillating between anger, understanding, and perplexity over what to do with the vacancy it gave her. Like many others, Bhríd Cáner had served the Lachlan House since the ascension of her father to the throne, far longer than many people lived. If he were Teren, he would have retired or passed on already. It was unfair to expect him to serve Enesfel, a country that was not his, for the long decades or centuries of his life, and with the threat of anti-Elyri violence ever-looming around them, it was illogical to expect him, or any other Elyri, to remain where they did not feel safe.

Nor, she admitted grimly, was it fair for her to expect him to stay as his family disintegrated. His wife was with child, and his troubled eldest son deserved the effort necessary to reach him, thus Bhríd's request to resign his post to join his family was a respectable one. But what, she wondered, was she to do for a chamberlain? Who in Rhidam, other than Kavan who would never accept the position, was suitable?

At least he was leaving Gaelán in Rhidam so the young man could continue his education. Father and son had mutually agreed that Gaelán was safer here, so long as he did nothing foolish, where the Lachlan Guard could protect him. Both understood the dangers of Gaelán returning to the sparsely-manned Dubuais-Cáner house with a brother who wished him ill. Bhríd knew the dangers he faced by returning to confront his son, but Gaelán was under no such obligation and Bhríd felt better leaving his youngest son in Rhidam.

Boots on stone drew her out of her thoughts, out of her head, to the man at the other end of the Hall. She smiled to see him.

"I paced many nights in this room," Owain said. "These walls have heard more confessions and secrets, more desperate prayers, than any dedhá, and have seen many strange and wondrous things. I pray you are not adding to their burden."

"I pray not…but I fear I am. What brings you here so late, Uncle?"

"Like you, I could not sleep. I checked on Captain Delamo…saw Kavan with him…and it made me…"

He was not sure what the sight made him feel. Jealous to not be a part of that shared intimate moment? Thankful that Wortham lived? Sad that the man had suffered an injury that would undoubtedly affect his future? Grateful that his friend had the love and support of the Elyri bard? Honored that he too could claim to share Kavan's respect, support, and love? Elated that Kavan lived through the poison that should have killed him and had returned to them once more? There had been so many emotions washing through Owain and, unable to return to sleep with those things colliding inside of him, he had come here to do what years of habit had instilled in him. The exact thing the Queen was doing.

"I'm praying for him…for both of them." Though the injury had not been to Kavan's flesh, the bard would suffer as surely as Wortham, perhaps in some ways more. It was Kavan's nature to suffer for those he loved, and Diona wished she could ease his burden. Offhandedly, she voiced her other wish out loud without intending to do so. "I wish Espen was here."

"He will return soon with much-needed supplies and manpower."

"I hope so."

"Why would he not?" He was unaware of any issues between Diona and her husband, but given their stormy, extended courtship, he imagined there were problems he knew nothing about.

Regardless of his history, her uncle, by blood or not, made Diona feel safe, secure. He had been in her place once, after all. He knew the challenges she faced, knew the weights she carried. He was a steady calm man, no matter what he had been as a youth that had caused her father to take the throne from him. She was glad Owain supported her. Perhaps she could talk to him. He might provide advice she had not already heard from others…or at least he might reassure her.

"With everything that has happened…Kavan's trial, the fire, the earthquake…Kavan's…whatever that was…down there…" she stared at the floor as if she could see the chapel far below them. "And my illness…we have not…" Words failed her out of embarrassment and she looked away at one of the random soldiers attending her in this room. Perhaps they should not hear this. But it was too late now.

If not for the self-conscious pause, Owain would have had no idea what she meant. Her embarrassment, however, made it easy enough to guess. "Surely he understands those reasons. Any man would."

"If those were the only causes, perhaps, but frankly, I am afraid."

Owain nodded. "Fear is common for both parties the first time."

"It is not the first time I fear…it is…what comes after."

"After?" Owain was perplexed, but the confusion quickly faded. He had not been here to witness Diona's childhood, but he had heard many stories from Muir, and he knew that any young woman growing up in those shadows would be fearful too. "What your mother endured…it is not common." Common enough, he knew, but there were more safe births, to his knowledge, than unsafe ones, particularly with an Elyri healer in attendance. "Your mother died after childbirth, but that does not mean you shall too. You are younger. You are strong. She was a small woman…too small, perhaps, for bearing children."

He had heard of that possibility but he did not understand what such things meant. "And perhaps," he sighed morosely, "her suffering was because of me, because of what I did. I mourn the stupidity of my youth. I could not take it back…could not give her back what I took, and I pray often that I was not the cause of her troubles. I am deeply sorry for what I may have taken from you as well."

Diona squeezed his hand. He was not the only one to make foolish mistakes, not the only one to bring others pain, to cause heartache and tragedy by unthinking acts. She could not hold such a thing against him when he had spent years striving to atone for those earlier errors in impulsive judgment, not if she too wanted forgiveness for her own.

"Mother forgave you. It showed in her steadfast love and care for Muir. She did not blame you for her problems…even if my father did."

"Because she was a better person than either of us." That was a fact Owain had been certain of even as a younger man. "Tell your fears to Espen. He will understand…and if he loves you, he will help you."

"I have tried, yet something invariably interferes whenever we…"

"Do not let it. Accept no interferences. When he returns, take him aside at once and speak to him. Tell him. And tell him things will change…if you believe they will."

"Oh, they will. I watch all of you…Kavan, Ártur, Bhríd, you…you continue to do what must be done without allowing fear to hinder you. I cannot live in fear. I will not."

The mention of Bhríd sparked an idea, one she was surprised she had not considered sooner. It was the best possible solution, so long as her uncle agreed.

"What I will also do, Uncle, is ask you this once. Think about it carefully, for I do not want you to regret the decision you make. When Bhríd leaves Rhidam after my celebration day, to be with his family until the birth of his third child, I will lack a suitable chamberlain."

She saw his surprise and continued hastily, thinking he was preparing to object. "You are a Lachlan prince, a man who once ruled from this throne…whether you were born to it or not is irrelevant. It is that experience that I believe can benefit me in ways that no one else's can. You know what the obligation means; you know what it takes to rule from this throne. You know the challenges and pitfalls. I am asking, as Queen and niece…if you would be my chamberlain…to give me your advice and experience so that Enesfel can thrive."

Owain found nothing offensive or belittling in the request. Yes, he had once been Enesfel's king; despite being a prince, he was no

Lachlan by blood. He had long ago accepted the loss of the throne to Arlan. Kavan's sparing his life had given him a perspective that allowed him to grow beyond resentment into acceptance and calm not felt before. How many years had he spent coming to Rhidam as a guest, a visitor, to see his son, to see Kavan, as a pathway to visit his wife and second child? He had lent his sword, his back, his presence to any situation that required it, something that even Arlan had begrudgingly come to accept, but he had never lingered in Rhidam with a true sense of duty and purpose. Serving as chamberlain rather than as a courtesan was an unconsidered possibility.

It was a fitting choice. He knew the duties, he knew Rhidam and Enesfel. He knew the lords of the realm and the nobility of other kingdoms. He already knew, as Diona said, the challenges she faced as he had been part of her inner circle through every turn her path had made since her father's death. And he knew what she needed to be a good monarch, better than anyone in her court except, perhaps, the bard who would never take a position of power in the Lachlan court.

Arrangements could be made for the upkeep of Fiara for extended periods. Other lords did the same, notably Kavan and Bhríd and more recently Balint. He trusted his people to take care of matters in his absence and to keep his house and lands prosperous and in good repair. Being in Rhidam on a more permanent basis also meant being closer to his wife, his sons, and soon a grandchild, for there would be Elyri to take him to Káliel through the Gates as often as he wished…as long, of course, as they did not flee Enesfel. And it would keep him nearer to Kavan, something he longed for every time he was away.

Owain did not need to think about the offer. Nor did he care what others might think of a man who had once been king serving as chamberlain. He wanted to be useful, he wanted a reason to be in Rhidam. And he wanted Enesfel to have stability, something he was unable to provide when he was king. Diona's offer seemed perfect.

He bowed. "I will gladly accept, My Queen, and serve the Crown and Enesfel with all my heart, loyalty, and honor. This I swear."

She brought him to his feet with her fingers beneath his chin. "Enough formalities, Uncle," she chuckled with a relieved smile. "A simple yes will suffice."

He laughed too, nodded and accepted the embrace she gave, the same one she had shared with him as a little girl. "Yes, Diona. I will be your chamberlain."

❧Chapter 51❧

I think it for the best," Kavan said quietly, his arms wrapped around his middle as they had been often over the last several weeks, watching Wortham across the room as the man insisted on dancing despite his handicap. On the first day of waking, the man bemoaned his fate, the lack of a saving miracle. Come the second, however, there was a dynamic change in his demeanor, as if everything was a challenge to be vigorously met so that he could continue to be what he had been: Kavan's right-hand man and protector. Something had come over him, a dream, a visitation, an epiphany, which shifted his point of view more abruptly than Kavan had been able to do, and whatever had caused it was something Wortham would not speak of. Over the last month, as the efforts to restore Rhidam continued, Wortham practiced everything, from eating to sword fighting, determined to continue to be the best swordsman Kavan would ever have at his back, determined to be unhindered by his diminished eye-sight. He was thriving, his drive and focus and need to be useful to Kavan pushing him to try harder, to overcome failure, to succeed.

He was, Kavan believed, a better swordsman than he had been.

Wortham would not, however, serve the Queen in the capacity he had once served her father, something Diona accepted with regret. He had no intention of taking an oath to the Crown. It was why she knew he would leave with Kavan, now that the bard had made up his mind.

"There is too much violence in Enesfel still…too much fear and distrust. With Bhríd going to Levonne," his melancholy gaze found his kinsman in the crowd dancing with Asta because she demanded it on what would be his last night in Rhidam for the foreseeable future, "and Bhyrhán choosing to stay in Clarys, it removes most of the Elyri advisors from the Lachlan court."

"You are more than an advisor, Kavan," Diona reminded him. "You are my friend…I hope."

Kavan bowed his head, considering her words as the band of minstrels hired for the Queen's celebration began another song. Not long ago he had believed he could not get past what she had done to him, or rather what she had prompted him to do to himself. But time and wisdom had changed him, and everything in his life felt different. She was different too.

"It does not change the facts. Without me here, I believe Rhidam will find a quicker path to peace. They will not begrudge you your healers…Ártur and Gaelán will be safe."

It had not surprised Kavan or Syl that Ártur chose to continue to serve his days in the Lachlan court, spending his nights in Bhryell, in spite of Kavan choosing to leave the castle, leave Rhidam, with Sóbhán, Wortham, and Zelenka. Ártur was, first and foremost, a healer…the healer to the Lachlan House, which he had been since his first official posting to Diona's grandfather. As long as the Lachlans needed him, as long as he lived, he would likely feel compelled to serve them. Not even his wife begrudged him that any longer, as long as he returned home to her each night, although Kavan wondered if she would feel differently when she realized that her husband no longer had Kavan's presence in Rhidam to pull him there.

"And dedhá Tusánt?" Every other Elyri she knew had left Rhidam. The healers who had volunteered their assistance to the wounded of Rhidam had, after the Eagle's Nest incident, taken their fallen comrade back to Elyriá. Perhaps more would come with aid for the slowly recovering city, but none were expected to stay, not when it was clear their lives could be at risk if they did so. The Corylliens, for all of the seeming disarray, were still an active force and until their heart was excised from the land they would continue to be a thorn in the Queen's side. They would continue to stir hatred and discontent until they were eradicated. It made sense to limit the number of Elyri in the castle, removing targets and, perhaps, allowing the land to continue to heal without that one source of ongoing contention.

Tusánt would be target enough, the one Elyri left in Rhidam with significant influence, but it seemed it was influence that the majority of Rhidam either welcomed or at least tolerated. Kavan had discussed his choice with the dedhá, given him the option of serving in St. Kóráhm's until the soul of the kingdom was settled, but Tusánt would not hear of retreat. He believed, because of the popular support he now carried, that he was the balm, the salve, which would ease the way for stability and welcome for all Elyri. Kavan prayed he was right, although he knew the man would have no easy road ahead with Claide in control of the Enesfel Faithful and, if he had his way, the entire Teren Faith in four of the Five Sovereignties. That was a goal to strive against, and Kavan wished Tusánt success.

He would help if he could, but he did not see any other way to do so at this time. And Tusánt knew he had sanctuary in St. Kóráhm's should he require it.

"He will remain your ally," Kavan assured the Queen. "He and Rankin, Saul and Edward, will be your eyes, your ears, within the Faith…and I pray…" The main doors of the Great Hall opened and the k'gdhededhá strode into the room. "I pray that should any news come you believe I should know of, you will send word at once."

"You know I will."

Anything more they intended to say was interrupted by the angular-faced k'dedhá who this time remembered to bow and wait to be addressed before speaking. She was tempted to ignore him, let him stand there quietly for longer than she needed, but she would rather not endure his presence near her that long. "What is it, k'dedhá?" she asked, trying to sound more interested than she felt.

She had not expected him to put in an appearance this evening as the friction between the Lachlan Queen and the head of Enesfel's Faithful was well-known. Perhaps, she mused as she watched him straighten, he was here for some public show that might make it appear that the animosity between them was one-sided.

A variety of heads in the room turned to gawk, though most continued eating, drinking, and dancing, paying the trio no attention.

"I have just received news I thought Your Majesty should know."

"News?" The word did get her attention, for she could not imagine any news he might receive that she would not have already gotten, or that she would be interested in…except bad news.

"I have received this." He offered a rolled parchment, its seal already broken. She motioned for Kavan to take it, which he did, but not without Claide recoiling and looking as if he would rather have snatched the message away. "k'gdhededhá Dórímyr intends to be in Rhidam in three weeks."

Diona looked at Kavan, who's gaze lifted from the scroll he had begun unrolling, to look first at her and then at Claide. He was tempted to think the other man a liar, to think him mad, but even without reading the words on the scroll, he knew this was no madness, at least not on Claide's part. If anyone was mad, it was Dórímyr, for the message, written by the Elyri prelate and not his aide, was entirely serious. This was no fanciful jest nor a formality meant to appease the Teren Faithful with platitudes he had no intention of carrying out. The k'gdhededhá of Clarys had finally decided to come to Rhidam for a long-overdue visit…at the worst possible time in Rhidam's healing.

Kavan's baffled expression of consternation told the Queen what she wanted to know of Claide's honesty. The k'dedhá looked as if he would be sick at the thought of the arrival of a man who had ignored the Teren Faithful too long, but there was something else in his eyes, a glimmer of expectancy that neither Diona nor Kavan liked.

"You may expect our repair efforts to double," the Queen promised, "to have the náós more fit for his visit. I will have more men and supplies brought to you in the morning. You will keep me informed of his plans and expected arrival date as you learn them." It was an order, not a question. She wanted to know everything the Elyri k'gdhededhá intended to do, where he intended to visit, when he would arrive, to make sure the man was as safe as possible. She did not want to contemplate what would happen if the man was attacked, injured or killed within her city, her kingdom.

"Of course, Your Majesty," he said with another outwardly respectful bow after taking the scroll back from Kavan. "May I have leave to speak of this with gdhededhá Rankin and Tusánt?"

Surprised that he had not already told them, that he might have come to her first with the news, she knew he was not asking permission to speak to them. Instead, he was asking to be released from her company, permission she gladly gave with a wave. She made a point of not watching him retreat. Kavan, however, did watch him, glad to have something other than physical discomfort to focus on.

Ártur had already examined him, had found nothing wrong…and yet the discomfort lingered. An after effect of the Orec, perhaps. It seemed a realistic possibility.

"Do you think he will come?" Diona asked under her breath when Claide was out of earshot.

Kavan frowned. "He intends to, or he did when this was written. I will go to Clarys, speak to him myself, dissuade him if I can."

"And if you cannot?" She did not need to tell him that Dórímyr's presence in Rhidam as the city was fighting to recover from more than a year of devastation and unrest would result in further turmoil. Perhaps he was contemplating challenging Claide's right to his position. With Claide possessing a small degree of popular support, and Dórímyr's history of nonchalance towards the Teren náós and faithful, his arrival bore a strong likelihood of being the interference no one now wanted. Interference that had come too late.

"Then I will be here when he comes." What good it would do, Kavan could not guess. It might irritate the wounds that Dórímyr's arrival would tear open, but Kavan hoped he would be able to protect both the k'gdhededhá and Rhidam from the worst of it.

From his pocket, he removed the two half-moon pendants he had not worn since the night of the ritual. Together on that scale, the power had again fused Kavan to the Lachlan House, specifically to the Queen, but he had not yet bestowed the Lachlan portion upon her. He had been reluctant to give it to her, to initiate that bond, but the ritual had initiated it for him and he had no choice but to honor it. Keeping both halves would cause them both to suffer. In fact, he wondered as he turned to place her half in her hand, if perhaps that was the cause of his discomfort and emptiness of late.

"Wear this. As long as you do, if you need me, I will know."

Diona looked at it somberly, looked at Kavan, and then slipped it over her head. Her father had worn it. Hagan had worn it. Whatever its purpose, she would wear it too. Hand on the metal that warmed against her skin, understanding what this meant on the surface if not on the same level that Kavan understood it, she nodded and then smiled as Owain came and offered his hand for a dance. He filled the role of chamberlain so easily that Bhríd's upcoming absence might not even be noticed by many in Rhidam. Eventually, the absence of the Lachlan's Champion and the White Bard would be obvious, would be questioned, would be missed by some, but Bhríd retiring to his family estate to be with his pregnant wife would be understood and accepted as, Kavan hoped, would be Owain's place in the Queen's court. He was happy for the man, that Owain had found purpose, peace with himself that would allow him to carry on when Kavan and Wortham were not here. He did not want Owain to be alone. If he could, he would have asked the prince to come to Elyriá as well, but Owain had family, an estate, and a duty to uphold. Saying farewell, for a time at least, would be hard enough without worry for the man's future.

Kavan watched them dance, watched his cousin and his wife, watched Gaelán and Asta and Sóbhán, holding himself, unsettled and restless and peculiarly lost. Restoring the pendant to a Lachlan wearer had not rid him of those feelings. Perhaps it would take more time.

Muir was not here for his sister, but that was understandable, if slightly frustrating for the bard who felt a deep need to see him. Soon. He wondered, as the dancing continued, if that feeling of need and the feeling of loss and restlessness were connected. If so, their connection was not obvious.

The evening wound down and the hour approached when Syl and Ártur would leave and Kavan, his bags already packed in the upstairs oratory, would follow, returning to Bhryell for his first extended stay in years. The tapestry of St. Kóráhm had already been taken there the night before, given to Ártur to deliver to his home, where Bhen would hang it on Kavan's bedroom wall where it originally hung. He knew he would return here, that this was not goodbye to Rhidam or anyone in it, but he could not gauge when that return would be beyond his visit when the k'gdhededhá came to Rhidam. For however long he remained in Bhryell, he did not want to be without his few most treasured possessions.

No one asked him for a dance as they had on Diona's last celebration day and he was content with that. The Queen had learned a difficult lesson after that night exactly one year ago, and though her husband had not made it back to Rhidam in time to celebrate with her, she had no desire to pursue Kavan or anyone else. Her chamberlain-uncle and her departing chamberlain were the only men she shared dances with. The two others she might have considered would have been her absent half-brother and her other uncle, had either been here to share this night. But Muir had his own duties and no word, no sign, had been heard from Caol since Asta's fire sighting. No one, not even his son and daughter, knew if he was alive or dead. But Kavan believed he was out there, and believed he would see that man again as well. The circle had not yet come around for any of them except Kavan. He was in Rhidam, on Diona Lachlans birth day, and he was whole. Tonight he would leave Rhidam again, but for an entirely different reason. And this time, he knew he would come back.

When the moment came for his gift, a parting song that would be the last his harp and voice would be heard in Rhidam for the foreseeable future, he did not sing alone. With Sóbhán at his side, Kavan gave the Queen the only gift he had.

dhór bhi_dhór,
hwae deanár á daeár.
bhí íth chaiit phuíbh.

zálágk ást dhór.
ebh ibh llán,
ebhed,
ergothé naeth,
sayrád, zilhád, kyánád.

Circles within circles,
Lessons taught and learned.
In the rising sun
A new year dawns
We face ourselves,
Each other,
And find the strength
To live, to hope, to love.

Voices woven in unison, in harmony, intricately entangled with the tinkling chime of brass harp strings, rising and falling, pulling each listener with the sound into the heights of the soul and then gently depositing them, filled with the hope and love of which Kavan sang, into the room at Enesfel's heart. Kavan closed his eyes and waited.

The emotion he could feel from each one around him was praise enough. It was the single affirmation of talent and acceptance he needed. The affirmation of the healing that lay ahead.

❧Chapter 52❧

"Lord Cliáth…a moment before you go…there are visitors to see you…"

Wortham, Zelenka, Sóbhán, and Syl had already passed through the Gate to Bhryell and were awaiting Kavan's arrival in the náós where Kavan had spent so many hours growing up. Ártur had come back to Rhidam to share a few parting words with Bhríd who would be riding south to Levonne with the rising of the sun, and to give instructions for Gaelán for the night. Kavan too had shared words with his young kinsman, who was fretting and sulking about the possibility of never seeing Kavan or Sóbhán again. Arrangements were already made for the boys to travel between Bhryell and Rhidam with the healer on occasions to allow them to see one another and permit them to take advantage of the educational opportunities available on both sides of the Gate. That reassurance, that Kavan was not abandoning him, had been enough to send Gaelán back to his father's room so that the two could share a final evening together for what could be a long time.

Kavan turned from the altar when Chancellor McGranis spoke, surprised that anyone had come visiting Rhidam, to the castle, at such a late hour. The Queen's feast was still underway downstairs, where Kavan had spoken his farewells to her and Owain before retreating here. None had felt emotionally strong enough to follow him to the oratory, choosing instead to see this as the temporary parting it was intended to be, not the extended one it felt like. Thinking of Kavan's absence as a long term thing was more painful than any of them cared to admit. He exchanged words with Asta and with Tusánt and Rankin as well, so who, he wondered, had come to see him off?

Wace Elotti was the only person who came to mind, but he was only one visitor, not plural, and was, to Kavan's knowledge, not currently in Rhidam.

He did not recognize the middle-aged man who followed the chancellor into the oratory, nor the younger woman behind him, but from their manner of dress and the sun-browned skin of their faces and hands and the deep rich brown-black of their hair, he guessed that they had traveled to Rhidam from somewhere south of Hatu. News of Myreth, he wondered with a skipping, excited flutter of his heart. He did not recognize them from the Gorbesh abbey, but that did not mean they were not from there or from the region surrounding it. Perhaps even Zelenka's own village.

That was the hope, his belief, until he saw the bundle in the woman's arms. An infant.

His heart seized in his chest. He could not breathe.

"My lord." The man bowed shakily, weary, and perhaps afraid by the people before him, the strange land to which he had come, and the message he was sent to deliver. He spoke in stilted, heavily accented Trade, the language obviously not his primary one. "The Lady Orynn instructed us to…"

"No." Kavan shook his head as long scattered puzzle pieces collided in his heart. It took all of his strength to remain on his feet.

"She had not the strength for two…they have kept the other…to be trained in her mother's stead…but this one, we were told to bring to you."

Kavan's head continued to shake as darkness began to pool around the edges of his vision and he struggled not to faint. "She is…dead?"

"Ailing when we left her," the man replied sadly. "I know not of dead, but perhaps. They would have spared her as long as they could, but they were, she said, displeased with her choices."

Which choices, Kavan wanted to scream. He wanted to shake the old man, demand answers, but he suspected that neither of these two knew what he wanted to know. He doubted they even knew who she really was. Kavan already had the answers, or thought he did, but this…this he could never have imagined in a millennium of guesses.

"This is not…no…it cannot be…"

"Then what shall we do with him, my lord, if you will not take him?"

Him.

Kavan blinked and stared at the small wiggling bundle as the young woman edged closer. Pink skin topped with black curls, little about that to speak the truth, but for his eyes, sleepy, almond-shaped eyes like hers. But they were not hers…at least not hers alone.

The man was right. If not Kavan, who? What should they do with the child if he turned his back on the last bit of Orynn he would ever touch, ever hold, ever see? With trembling hands, he took the babe. He squirmed and began to whimper in discomfort at the change of position. Kavan rested the child against his shoulder as the young woman rejoined the man Kavan presumed was her father, though he might have been her husband or her much older brother. She must have been feeding the child during their journey, but now that responsibility was pushed onto Kavan. "You will stay? You are welcome." He would find a use for them, should they choose to stay.

But wasn't he due in Bhryell?

"We cannot. We have carried out k'ílshwythnec's command and must report that it is done."

They knew. But how much did they know? Did they know what this child was to him?

The man was already backing through the oratory door. Chancellor McGranis shrugged and followed, not about to allow strangers to roam the halls of the Lachlan keep.

The chapel was quiet, save for the soft cooing and faint sucking sound as the child found his own fingers to soothe his disquiet. Kavan did not move, was still struggling for air, and resisted looking at his cousin who had stared at the entire proceedings with a wide-eyed, perplexed expression. How, Kavan wondered, could he ever explain this when it made little sense to him? How could he tell his cousin things which, until this moment, he had tried not to think about out of embarrassment and confusion? How, he wondered, could he explain this to anyone?

"Who…?" began the healer, looking back and forth between the child in Kavan's arms and the couple who had disappeared from sight. He had heard no mention of anyone named Orynn before, but he understood the title and presumed this woman was someone Kavan had met while searching for healing. He wanted to know more, who she was, and why she would choose to entrust a child, her child, into Kavan's care. "Who…?"

"Dhóri," whispered Kavan. "My son."

The End

Character Index Book 4

Agis, General--The only Cíbhóló nomad to serve in the Enesfel military. King Hagan promotes him to Lord High General after Ternce Wyndham retires the post.

Aleski MacLyr--Ártur The oldest son of Sámel MacLyr, Ártur MacLyr's nephew and Kavan Cliáth's cousin.

Anri "Hugh" Heward--A Nethite suspected of involvement with the upsurge of anti-Elyri violence during the reigns of King Arlan, his son Hagan, and daughter Diona

Arlan Trebor Lachlan--The youngest son of King Innis of Enesfel. He was the 25th king of Enesfel, responsible for peaceful relations with Hatu, increasing Enesfel's size via the war with Neth, and opening a dialogue with the islands of Káliel.

Ártur MacLyr--Elyri healer, employed by Kings Innis, Donal, Arlan, and Hagan Lachlan. He is married to Syl Cáner and is cousin to Kavan Cliáth.

Arvis Bayle-- a man who attempts to assassinate Kavan.

Asta Deidre Dugan--The daughter of Princess Deidre Lachlan and Lord High Inquisitor Caol Dugan, she has been groomed to assume the position of High Inquisitor.

Avner--One of the five Káliel guards sent by Gabrielle Dilyn to serve Arlan in his quest for the Enesfel throne.

Balint Gabersdon, Sir--Once the youngest knight in Enesfel, he is the Duke of Nelori.

Barris--Layton's second in command.

Belda--Diona Lachlan's personal maidservant.

Bertram Earl Lachlan--The eldest son of Arlan Lachlan and twin of Diona Lachlan, he was killed at the age of nine by a Coryllien dagger in a skirmish between Caol Dugan and Halstatt Tarmajien.

Betel--Lachlan's gardener who befriends Zelenka and serves during her marriage.

Bhenádíctus, málneag--He was a Teren herbalist. Though never ordained, he wandered the known territories preaching repentance, poverty, and forgiveness. He owned nothing in his life other than his clothing and his walking stick; those in his order take vows of poverty and become wandering missionaries. He died on Káliel in the shrine he built there, though since his body was never found some people believe that k'Ádhá took him directly to heaven. He became the patron of travelers, the poor, and those in need of spiritual forgiveness and enlightenment.

Bhendhámyn MacLyr--The youngest son of Sámel MacLyr, nephew of Ártur MacLyr. He is a harp maker in the Cliáth tradition who agrees to apprentice Ártur's son Llucás.

Bhílári, gdhededhá--head clergy of Hes Índári, Bhryell, who witnessed many of Kavan's "miracles" and has known him since childhood.

Bhyrhán Bhíncári--One of many grandsons of Kyne Mórne Bhíncári, the High Mother. He has chosen the life of a minstrel and plays the shawm. He is distantly related to Kavan Cliáth, whose mother's maiden name was Bhíncári.

Bhóité--An extremely ancient Elyri, living near the Hatu city of Enda, who was the keeper of the keys that sent Kavan on his quest into the barbarian lands. Also the name of the gentleman to whom Kóráhm entrusted this information many centuries ago, though it is uncertain if these two individuals are the same or different.

Bhríd Cáner, Lord High Chamberlain--A distant cousin of the MacLyr's, employed by King Arlan Lachlan as his chancellor, he resumed the post of Chamberlain upon the death of Guthrie McHador. He is known as the best swordsman in the Five Sovereignties, and is the King's Champion.

Bianca MacLyr Dugan--An orphaned Teren, adopted by Ártur and Syl MacLyr, she is married to Wilred Dugan.

Caol Dugan, Lord High Inquisitor--Originally the son of a member of the Association, now part of the Lachlan court and family, since he married Princess Deidre Lachlan, King Arlan's sister. He has maintained the post of Lord High Inquisitor for his entire time in Rhidam.

Cedric O'Grady--The nephew of Sir Paul O'Grady, Duke of Eleva in Cordash. He is a minstrel whom Kavan meets in Yd Haszafni, Hatu.

Chethá Llyárá MacLyr--The infant daughter of Ártur and Syl MacLyr.

Claide, gdhededhá--A Teren gdhededhá in Enesfel who serves with k'gdhededhá Jermyn Tythilius

Clianthe Dilyn Lachlan--The daughter of Gabrielle Dilyn she marries Prince Muir Lachlan.

Cora--A Levonne prostitute.

Coriana Deidre Dugan--Wilred Dugan's firstborn child, granddaughter of Caol Dugan.

Darius Corbin, Lord High Justice--A soldier of the Lachlan ranks, who rose to the rank of Justice when Minos Cornell assumed the post of Chancellor after the death of Guthrie McHador.

Dawid Coryllien--A figure once thought of as mythical, whose name is connected with the death of many Elyri and many Terens during the historical period known as the Persecution. His name was given to the daggers connected with those murders. Very little is known about him in the Five Sovereignties.

Dayly Niall--The eldest son of Duke Symon Niall of Dorshur, he is a close friend and companion of Prince Hagan who spends much time at the castle.

Denyan--One of the five Káliel guards sent by Gabrielle Dilyn to serve Prince Arlan in his quest for the throne.

Dháná MacLyr--The wife of Tám MacLyr, mother of Sámel and Ártur MacLyr, Kavan Cliáth's aunt.

Dhóri –Kavan's son with Orynn.

Dhybhé--An Elyri jeweler who settled in Nelori with her brother, only to have her brother disappear and then be kidnapped herself while under Sir Balint's care.

Diona Cordelia Lachlan--The only daughter of King Arlan Lachlan; heir apparent after the death of her father makes Hagan king.

Dórímyr, k'gdhededhá--The highest religious leader in the Faith of Elyriá.

Drebhoti--A mythical/historical figure connected to the staff that Kavan needs to cleanse the thur thol below the Rhidam keep.

Ealdun Gottfrid--The eldest son of Charles Gottfrid, he is currently the acting Duke of Erleta.

Edhriá, málneag--An ancient saint

Edward Lindunn--The son of a wealthy Rhidam resident, whose mother was from Cordash. He was to serve in the Cordashian military, but instead returned to Rhidam and eagerly agreed to enter the priesthood while serving as a guard for Father Tusánt.

Eleza, gdhededhá--The gdhededhá of *Shepherd's Heart Church* in Fiara

Ensgil, gdhededhá--one of four Teren emissaries sent to Rhidam with instructions from Dórímyr for the Teren Faithful to elect their own k'gdhededhá

Eridel--A young harper whom Kavan meets while in Hatu during his quest for healing.

Espen Harcourt, Prince--The second son of King Geir of Hatu, he is the brother of King Noreis.

Flannery McGranis--The former squire of Bhríd Cáner who is elevated to the post of Chancellor upon the death of Minos Cornell.

Gabrielle Dilyn Lachlan--Prime Magistrate of Káliel, mother of Clianthe and Piran, she is the wife of Owain Lachlan.

Gaelán Ágdhrán Cáner--The youngest son of Bhríd Cáner and Madalyn Dubuais who has shown that he possesses the Elyri talent to heal despite being half-Teren.

Garrett, gdhededhá--The acting head of Saint Kóráhm's while Khwílen Kesábhá is in Elyriá attempting to gain ammunition to confront k'gdhededhá Dórímyr.

Gíldás, málneag--An ancient saint

Glucke, General--Neth's leading General, with personal aspirations towards the Neth throne.

Guthrie McHador--Once the general of Enesfel's army under Kings Innis and Donal, he reared Prince Arlan and assisted him in his bid for Enesfel's throne. He remained at court as Arlan's Chamberlain and died during the fight with Neth that resulted in Enesfel obtaining the territory surrounding south of Lake Curo.

Hagan Guthrie Brennan Lachlan--The youngest child of Arlan Lachlan, he is the 26 king of Enesfel.

Hazen--A female gdhededhá serving in Hes á Redh Náós Rhidam during the reigns of Kings Arlan and Hagan Lachlan.

Hwensen-k'gdhededhá Dórímyr's personal aide

Idal Gottfrid--The second oldest son of Charles Gottfrid of Erleta. He and his brother Kent have purchased a modest home in Rhidam, which is currently under suspicion by the inquisitor and Princess Diona.

Jermyn Tythilius, k'gdhededhá--A former brother in the Order of málneag Kóráhm in Clarys, Elyriá, he was ordained as the k'gdhededhá of Rhidam and is later murdered in the outbreak of violence.

Jilletta McPhelan--The daughter of General Liron McPhelan, she is greatly interested in Prince Hagan and the prospect of being his queen.

Johann Alty--Lord High Inquisitor Caol Dugan's assumed name when he infiltrates the Corylliens.

Karleo, gdhededhá--a formerly married man who became gdhededhá after the death of his wife at the hands of her brothers.

Kavan Kóráhm Cliáth--Last of the Cliáth's, only child of Rístyrd and Llyárá, cousin of Ártur MacLyr. He is an admired harper, possessor of the Sight, holder of great psionic capabilities. Known as the White Bard of Bhryell for his tremendous musical talent and unique physical appearance, he was employed by Arlan as his court bard until his flight from Rhidam to the lands south of Hatu. He is also the Duke of Alberni and the founder of málneag Kóráhm's Abbey.

Kent Gottfrid--The third oldest son of Charles Gottfrid of Erleta. He and his brother Idal have purchased a modest home in Rhidam which is currently under suspicion by the inquisitor and Princess Diona.

Khweltz Coryllien--The stepfather of Kóráhm, he was the father of Dawid Coryllien.

Khwílen Kesábhá, gdhededhá--Once an aide to k'gdhededhá Dórímyr, he was selected as the abbot of málneag Kóráhm's Abbey in Alberni due to his gifts of oratory, learning, and painting.

Kjell de Cormick--The youngest son of Loris of Neth, he is the brother of King Merkar de Cormick and is the current heir to the Neth throne.

Kóráhm di Curnydhá, málneag--Elyri málneag for whom Kavan was named, also known as Kóráhm the Rón by many in Elyriá because of some controversial writings he made before the time of his martyrdom. Few of his books are available and he is not commonly discussed. Originally born in the town of Ergoth, he is the half-brother of Dawid Coryllien.

Layton--A member of the Corylliens from who Johan Alty takes instruction

Lira Brocke--a young woman from the wealthiest family in Rhidam, whom King Hagan considers marrying

Llucás Phaedr MacLyr--The oldest child of Ártur and Syl MacLyr.

Llyr--A mythical/historic figure learned to be a gdhededhá and a fighter, responsible for the creation of the chalice Kavan seeks in connection to the thur thol below the Rhidam keep.

Loefel, gdhededhá--A gdhededhá from the Fiara area who died prior to Ártur MacLyr's attack.

Madalyn Dubuais Cáner, Duchess--The Duchess of Levonne, she is the only woman in Enesfel to have control of her own lands; she is married to Bhríd Cáner.

Marta--An Association member used as a contact by Caol and Asta Dugan.

Martin Dary--the master of the Alberni estate while Kavan is away.

Matus Gardieu--a farrier from Hatu, member of the Association, who serves as the 'face' of inquisitor for Diona Lachlan while Asta Dugan is underage

Merkar Rousset de Cormick--One of the sons of the late King Loris of Neth, he is currently the ruling Neth king.

Mikel--a young soldier being groomed by Captain Wortham Delamo to serve Kavan.

Mórne, High Mother (Kyne)--The matriarchal ruler of Elyriá; she is head of the Elyri High Council.

Muir Innis Lachlan--The bastard son of Owain Lachlan and Brenna Weylin Lachlan, he was raised as Arlan Lachlan's son. Upon reaching adulthood he gave his land and title as Duke of Alberni to Kavan Cliáth and moved to Fiara with his father. He is now married to Clianthe Dilyn and lives on Káliel.

Myreth--A singer of extraordinary talent he is a man of unknown mixed heritage who was raised in the cloister of Gorbesh.

Narn--The name of someone suspected of being connected to the anti-Elyri violence in Enesfel, possibly a Cíbhóló nomad.

Noreis Harcourt--The current King of Hatu, he is the elder brother of Prince Espen Harcourt.

Onea Pantel--The woman who heads the Fiara branch of the Association.

Ordelia Cornell--The oldest of seven children, five of whom are girls, of Duke Rostryn Cornell, the son of Minos Cornell of Theron.

Orynn--A member of all three known races (k'kairá, Elyri, and Teren) she was chosen by Kóráhm and her own people to make contact with Kavan and assist in his quest for healing, redemption, and the items needed to cleanse the thur thol below the Rhidam keep. She is known among the people in the barbarian territories as k'ílshwythnec, "she who sees," because of her tremendous knowledge of the past, present, and future.

Owain Ustes Lachlan--He was believed to be the 5th child of Innis, son of Ula de Cormick of Neth; he was the 24th king of Enesfel. He is actually the only child of Guthrie McHador. He relinquished the throne to Arlan Lachlan and has lived in the Neth city of Fiara since then. He assumed the title of Duke of Fiara when the area of Neth south of Lake Curo seceded and became part of Enesfel. He is the father of Muir Innis and Piran Guthrie Lachlan.

Paul O'Grady, Sir--The Duke of Eleva, Cordash

Peter--A page in Hagan Lachlan's court

Piran Guthrie Lachlan--The son of Owain Lachlan and Gabrielle Dilyn-Lachlan.

Qol--A member of the race known as the phae k'kairá who has been serving as k'gdhededhá in the cloister of Gorbesh, and acting as the keeper of the relics Kavan seeks.

Rankin, gdhededhá--A Teren gdhededhá in Hes á Redh Náós, Rhidam.

Reland, Sheriff--the sheriff of Alberni

Renfrid Valdis--The current king of Cordash.

Rouvyn Talis--A Teren physician who traveled with Kavan many years ago on his search for the kidnapped Princes Bertram and Wilred. A native of Rhidam, he returned there when his services to Kavan were no longer needed, and has lived in the area since. He has remained on speaking terms with Justice Darius Corbin and becomes the Lachlans Teren court healer after the attack on Ártur MacLyr.

Sámel MacLyr--Ártur's older brother and Kavan's cousin. He is a harp maker in the Cliáth tradition, like his father.

Sigrid Niall--The daughter of Duke Symon Niall of Dorshur and the younger sister of Dayly Niall.

Saul Peado--A Teren from Alberni who came to Rhidam to serve in the Lachlan guard but is chosen by Princess Diona to act as Father Tusánt's guard while studying as a novice for the priesthood.

Sóbhán--An orphaned Elyri boy who manages to survive the ravages in Rhidam; Kavan adopts him as his son, making him a Cliáth.

Sósáná--Kóráhm's mother.

Syl Cáner MacLyr--The wife of Ártur MacLyr, she is also a healer, and sister of Bhríd Cáner. She is the mother of Llucás and Chethá.

Symon Niall, Duke--The Duke of Dorshur

Tám MacLyr--The father of Ártur MacLyr, he is a harp maker in the Cliáth tradition, and uncle of Kavan Cliáth.

Tayte McHador Cáner--The eldest son of Bhríd Cáner and Madalyn Dubuais, he is the heir to the Levonne estate.

Ternce Wyndham, Lord High General--He served as both Owain's second general, then as first general. He was asked to keep his position by King Arlan and has served as such since Arlan's ascension, retiring from the post upon the monarch's death.

Tíbhyan --Elyri Bhydáni, who was Kavan's private tutor. He is the oldest man in Bhryell and one of the top 10 sages in Elyriá.

Tusánt, gdhededhá--The only Elyri gdhededhá serving in Rhidam.

Urian Jayr--A wandering monk of the Order of málneag Bhenádíctus who joins Kavan on his journey.

Valgis, gdhededhá--A newly ordained Teren gdhededhá from Levonne, currently serving in Hes á Redh Náós, Rhidam.

Waljan--One of the five Káliel guards sent by Gabrielle Dilyn to serve Prince Arlan in his quest for Enesfel's throne.

Wilred Douglas Dugan--The son of Caol Dugan and Deidre Lachlan, he is the acting Duke of Durham, husband of Bianca MacLyr, and father of Coriana Dugan.

Wohls Hahn, gdhededhá--a former member of the Order of St. Kóráhm who came to Enesfel to serve the Faith at the request of k'gdhededhá Jermyn.

Wortham Delamo, Captain--Captain of the five elite Káliel guards sent by Gabrielle Dilyn to serve Arlan. He is the closest of Kavan's friend and considers himself the bard's protector and servant.

Yhsábhel--A woman with whom Kóráhm was involved at the time of the Persecution who was murdered in the violence by Dawid Coryllien.

Yorick Zarkosta, General--He had joined Arlan's quest for the throne, and has risen to the rank of General in his years of service since then. He acts as the Captain of the Lachlan house guard when not in a state of war.

Zelenka--A young woman from Gorbesh with whom Wortham Delamo falls in love and who travels with them when her mother dies.

Elyri Phonetics

á--ä (as in m**o**p)

a--ă (as in c**at**)

ae--ā (as in **a**ce)

ag--ä (as in m**o**p) (HE**)

ai--ī (as in **i**ce)

au--aů (as in **ou**t)

é--ŭ (as in b**u**t)

e--ĕ (as in b**e**t

i--ē (as in b**e**)

í--ĭ (as in s**i**t)

ó--ō (as in g**o**)

o--ŏ (as in m**o**p)

u--ū (as in bl**ue**)

y--ē (as in b**e**)

yh--y (as in **y**es)

b--b

bh--v

c--k

ch--ch

d--d

dh--j

gae--gwā

gdh--zh (as in vi**s**ion)

gh--g (as in go)

gk--k̲ as in loch (HE)

h--h

hw--w (breathy, as in whale)

k'--k

k--k

l--l

Ll--l

m--m

mh--m (slightly breathy)

n--n

ne--nyä

p--p

ph--f

r--r

s--sh

t--t

th--th (as in thistle)

z--z

• C is always pronounced **K** but the letter **K** is most often used to designate this sound. **C** mainly appears at the beginning of some proper surnames and place names and occasionally in the center or at the end of a word. This is believed to be a carryover from the earliest days of the Elyri language, or to have been influenced by the Teren languages, but Elyri linguists and scholars have not yet determined its significance. However, in keeping with this unspoken, unexplained rule, no Elyri have first names, or middle names, starting with **C**.

•   The combination **gk** (pronounced as in the German ich) occurs only at the end of words, unless there is a verb suffix or plural suffix behind it, and only in those words of High Elyri origin.

•   The letter combination **ag** occurs at the end of words of High Elyri origin. If the combination appears elsewhere in a word, it will either be as a product of two words having been combined or will be the result of a suffix having been added. Though some Standard Elyri words have retained their **ag** ending, most words carried into the standard will have the **ag** combination replaced with **á** when written, though they sound alike when spoken.

•   The **H** sound only appears in High Elyri words and in some names carried over from ancient sources; Standard Elyri derivatives will normally drop the **h** from the original word but there are exceptions to the rule

•   Double **L**'s are found at the beginnings of words, single **l**'s in the body or at the end. When words do have the double **L** in a location other than the beginning, it is always the result of two words being combined into one.

•   In the High Elyri there were no naturally occurring **B, P,** or **ow** (as in cow) sounds. These did not get introduced until Elyri acquired their current religious faith. Even then, the sounds were not commonly used until the standard Trade tongue influenced everyday life. These sounds mainly appear in proper names or religious settings.

•   The combination of the letter **ne** occurs almost exclusively at the end of a word, and is always pronounced **nya**, regardless of where it occurs.

•   The **ee** sound at the beginning or end of a word is always represented with an **I**. In the center of words, it is represented by a **Y**. When the **ee** sound is represented in the center of a word by the letter **I** it is a result of two words being combined into one. In some cases, as with the name Cliáth, the original words may no longer be known. The few exceptions where Standard or High Elyri words begin with a Y for the ee sound are believed to have originated as intentional misspellings.

- There is no **S** sound in the Elyri language. **S**'s are always pronounced **sh**.

- The letter **Z** appears only in the High Elyri or in words derived from the High Elyri or originated as misspellings in one of the Teren languages and were absorbed back into Elyri in the aberrant form.

Elyri Grammar

In most Elyri words, the stress falls on the second to last. Words where the stress falls on the final syllable (or on the first syllable in words with more than two syllables) are either names, the result of an Elyri translation of a Teren word, caused by the addition of a prefix or suffix, or the result of a word being truncated, having dropped the last syllable over time.

The **k'** at the beginning of a word signifies importance or singularity. It is applied to a word that can have a common meaning and a special meaning: k'tyne would be a favorite niece or female cousin, whereas tyne is simply a niece or female cousin. In the case of the phae k'kairá, when the Terens translated the term into "the Others" it is the **k'** that indicates the O to be capitalized; not just any others but the Others.

The Elyri written language does not have additional characters for capitalization. The first letters words may carry a dot beneath them to signify that the word is a proper name, a place, or a title, but first letters of sentences are not capitalized.

Sentence breaks are characterized by either a new line of text or by a symbol that looks similar to an s. This has resulted in many mistranslations from Elyri into other languages.

Nouns

Noun forms of verbs do not have gender. When these nouns are made plural they take the plural inclusive suffix sur.

The prefix **íl** added to a verb makes it into a noun; the word then means "one who" as in "ílDaeni"-one who instructs, i.e.: teacher.

Some nouns are formed by adding the prefix **ai** to a verb; the verb dhesá means touch, aidhesá also means touch but is a noun. Not all verbs can accept the **ai** prefix.

-thé: the standard plural suffix

Nouns ending in **I** are both singular and plural and do not take the -**thé** ending

Elyri monetary denominations are both singular and plural.

There are other exceptions to the singular/plural rule, most being words carried over from the High Elyri. High Elyri contains very few words that are NOT both plural and singular. Any exceptions to the rule are noted.

Some words have gender. A word ending in **ne** is feminine and a word ending in **dhá** is masculine. Both are made plural in the same way (with the **thé** ending). Some gender-neutral words that have been altered from their original form may have either ending.

Some words in Standard, those referring to a group that includes both male and female individuals, require the **-sur** ending, creating the plural inclusive form of the word. The same ending exists in High Elyri.

Adjectives

There are few adjectives in the Elyri language. Instead of saying someone is beautiful, or wise, and Elyri would say they possess beauty or they possess wisdom.

To modify such qualities, an Elyri speaker would say:

bhykólé aelá shwyth: She possesses wisdom. Teren: She is wise.

ochbhykóle aelá shwyth: She possesses more wisdom. Teren: She is wiser.

utbhykólé aelá shwyth: She possesses the most wisdom. Teren: She is wisest.

naimbhykólé aelá shwyth: She possesses no wisdom. Teren: She is not wise; or She is a fool.

The few adjectives that do exist come through the High Elyri and are believed by most linguists to have their origins in some language other than the Elyri.

Verbs

When **ibh** modifies a verb (ie: is singing, is looking) it is attached as a suffix to the verb. In all other instances, it is a separate word (bhydáni ibh gaeth: He is bhydáni.)

When **im** modifies a verb (ie: was singing, was looking) it is attached as a suffix to the verb. In all other instances, it is a separate word (ílDaeni im gaeth: He was a teacher)

There is no "be" in the Elyri language. Whereas a Teren would say, "He will be singing" the Elyri would say "He will sing." Instead of "I will be there" it would be "I will come" or I will go"; instead of "I will be here" it would be "I will stay", "I will attend," or "I am here."

Rather than using verbs such as "strengthened" or "beautified", in Elyri they would say "given strength" or "given beauty"

Verb Tenses

(present) do, does	(past) (ár) did, have done	(present) (ibh) am, are, is doing	(past) (im) was, is, were doing	(future) (ád) will do, to do, be done
aelá	aelár	aelibh	aelim	aelád
ándás	ándásár	ándásibh	ándásim	ándásád
árá	árár	áráibh	áráim	árád
bhaeá	bhaeár	bhaeibh	bhaeim	bhaeád
bheken	bhekár	bhekibh	bhenim	bhekád
bhair	bhairár	bhairibh	bhairim	bhairád
bhólon	bhólár	bhólibh	bhólim	bhólád
chóne	chóneár	chóníbh	chónim	chónád
daeni	daenár	daenibh	daenim	daenád
dhesá	dhesár	dhesibh	dhesim	dhesád
dhys	dhysár	dhysibh	dhysim	dhysád
donai	donár	donaiibh	donim	donád
ghlaiph	ghlaiphár	ghlaiphibh	ghlaiphim	ghlaiphád
ghytae	ghytár	ghytibh	ghytim	ghytád
kelém	kelémár	kelémibh	kelémim	kelémád
mairós	mairár	mairibh	mairim	mairád
naeth	naethár	naethibh	naethim	naethád
yháth	yháthár	yháthibh	yháthim	yháthád
zene	zenár	zenibh	zenim	zenád
zólágk	zólágkár	zólágkibh	zólágkim	zólágkád

Verb/Noun Tenses

	noun form 1(íl)	**noun 2(ai)**
aelá	ílAelá (one who owns)	
ándás	ílAndás (one who honors)	aiándás
bhaeá	ílBhaeá (one who asks)	
bheken	ílBheken	
bhair	ílBhair (one who accepts)	aibhair (acceptance)
bhólon	ílBhólon (one who purifies)	
chóne	ílChóne (one who brings)	
daeni	ílDaeni (one who instructs)	
dhesá	ílDhesá (one who touches)	aidhesá
donai	ílDonai (one who endures)	aidonai
ghlaiph	ílGhlaiph (one who sleeps)	aiglaiph
ghytae	ílGhytae (one who threatens)	aighytae (threat)
kelém	ílKelém (one who passes)	
mairós	ílMairós (one who heals)	aimairós
naeth	ílNaeth (one who finds)	
zene	ílZene (one who gives)	
zólágk	ílZólágk (one who reveals)	

Verb Tenses (High Elyri)

(present)	(past)(-ár)	(future)(-es)
aelás	aelásár	aeles
bhánys	bhánár	bhánes
dytae	dytár	dytes
ghai	ghaiár	ghaies
síndóbhaene	síndóbhaenár	síndóbhaenes
zugdhu	zugdhuár	zugdhues
tyreth	tyrethár	tyrethes
pháló	phálóár	phálóes
scenyhur	scenyhár	scenhyures
elzen	elzenár	elzenes

Verb/Noun Tenses (High Elyri)

(noun 1) (bhe-)	(noun 2) (ae-)
bheaelás (one who owns)	aeaelás (possession)
bhehánys (one who makes music)	
bhedytae (one who obeys)	aedytae (obedience)
bheghai (one who does)	
bhesíndóbhaene (one who forgives)	aesíndóbhaene (forgiveness)
bhezugdhu (one who protects)	aezugdhu (protection)
bhetyreth (one who knows/scholar)	aetyreth (knowledge)
bhepháló (one who buries/gravedigger)	aepháló (grave)
bhescenyhur (one who names)	aescenyur (name)
bhelzen (one who gives)	aeelzen (gift)

Foreign Phrase Index

ELYRI WORDS

HE: High Elyri   SE: Standard Elyri
n--noun   v--verb   adj—adjective
adv--adverb   prn--pronoun   prp--preposition
pl--plural   sng--singular   psv—possessive
pl in--plural inclusive

á (ä) (prp)--HE/SE; and, also, together with, together

Ádhá (Ä-jä) (n)--HE/SE; god; k'Ádhá-supreme deity in the Elyri monotheistic religion

Adhár (ă-JÄR) (n)--HE; first Equal day, referring to the Holy Feast day on the spring equinox or any festival, party, or religious observation in honor of that day.

aene (Ā-nyä) (n) (pl: aenethé)--SE; A father's female relatives, including his mother, grandmothers, aunts, sisters, and cousins.

ágdháni (ä-ZHÄ-nē) (n) (sng and pl)--HE; the title for any Elyri trained in the use of nature's energy. Humans have no word that can be used, though they often translate it as sorcerer, wizard, or some other similar term. In common science fiction parlance, it can be translated as psionist. In sources predating the earliest known High Elyri documents, this word would be translated the same as dhesádhá.

aicónys (ī-KŌ-nēsh) (n) (sng and pl)--HE; bond, union, joining, marriage, friendship

aiónag (ī-Ō-nä) (n) (pl: aiónagthé)--HE; path, destiny, life

ást (äsht) (adj)--SE; new

bhelts (vĕltsh) (n) (sng and pl)--SE; Elyri gold currency.

bhí (vĭ) (prp)--SE; in, within, inside

bhydáni (vē-DÄN-ē) (n) (sng and pl)--HE; This is both a title and a social standing. It can be translated teacher, master, sage, or wise one, though it actually encompasses all of these meanings. The title is given to those who, through their exceptional psionic capabilities, wisdom, and intelligence, have demonstrated their worth. Psionic ability is the key to the title, though great ability without wisdom and intelligence will not gain the title. With the title comes the privilege of teaching their knowledge to the children, particularly their psionic knowledge. Each city, town, or village will have at least one bhydáni. Either the bhydáni will ask another into their ranks, or, in the event that a location has no functioning bhydáni, the inhabitants will select someone to fill the position. In extremely rare cases, someone can become bhydáni by accident; they accept mentorship of someone and others begin to ask for the privilege of learning from them as well. By becoming an unofficial teacher, the individual has become bhydáni. A little less than 2/3 of all bhydáni are female.

bhydhá (VĒ-jä) (n) (pl: bhydháthé)--SE; Father.

chaiit(chī-ĒT) (n)--SE; sun

dedhá (DĚ-jä) (n) (sng and pl)--SE; priest or monk; the term makes no distinction between the two. The shortened form came into use after the Teren came into the lands and adopted the Faith as their own.

Dhágdhuán (JÄ-zhū-än) (n)--HE/OE; the Intercessor, considered to be the founder of the Faith because his death is said to make it possible for mortals to reach the divine,

dhedhoc (JĚ-däk) (n) (pl: dhedhocthé)--HE; earth, world, land, place

dhesádhá (jěsh-Ä-jä) (adj)--HE; This word origins reach far back in the High Elyri; its original meaning was touched by the deities, but when the Elyri embraced their current belief system the word came to mean touched by k'Ádhá. It is a conjunction of two words dhesá-touched and ádhá god or deity.

dhór (jōr) (n) (sng and pl)--HE/SE; circle, cycle

ebh (ěv) (pn)--HE/SE; we, us

ebhed (ě-VĚD) (prp)--SE; other, each other, one another

elzen (ěl-ZĚN) (v)--HE; give, bring

endástás (ěn-DÄSH-täsh) (sng) (n)--HE; all, everything

ergothé (ěr-GÄ-thŭ) (n) (sng and pl)--SE; strength, fortitude

gaesdág (gwāsh-DÄ) (n) (sng and pl)--HE; peace, calm, state of stillness

gaetió (gwā-TĒ-ō) (n) (sng and pl)--HE; High Elyri boat or sailing vessel. It is known in Elyria that the term was once used for a specific type of boat but the nature of the vessel is no longer known.

gdhededhá (zhě-DĚ-jä) (n) (sng and pl)--HE/SE; priest or faith teacher or disciple; the term makes no distinction between them.

gdhededhásur (zhě-DĚ-jä-shūr) (n) (pl.in)--HE/SE; A group of faith teachers/clergy of both sexes.

ghymae (gē-MÄ) (n) (sng and pl)--HE; air, sky

hes (hěsh) (n) (sng and pl)--HE; heart

hudhánaelís (hū-jän-Ā-lĭsh) (n) (sng and pl)--HE; family

hwae (hwā) (n) (pl: hwaethé)--HE/SE; lesson, parable, teaching, story

hyhílag (hē-Hĭ-lä) (n)--HE; water

ibh (ēv) (v)--HE/SE; Is, are, am; its translation is dependent upon the rest of the sentence.

íth (ĭth) (prp)--HE/SE; the

íthásigk (ĭth-ÄSH-ēk) (n)--HE; prosperity

ithnás (ĒTH-näsh) (n) (pl: ithnásthé)--HE joy, happiness, pleasure

k'aendhá (k-ĀN-jä) (n) (pl: k'aendáthé)--SE; A favorite paternal male relatives, including father, grandfathers, uncles, brothers, and cousins.

k'dhín bhólibh (jĭn vō-LĒV) (n) (pl: dhín bhólibhthé)--SE; Purification Chamber; a place within the náós where the Faithful confess their hearts to k'Ádhá and receive forgiveness and blessings from the gdhededhá

k'elyryhánag (k ĕl-ēr-ē-ÄN-ä) (n); when Kavan first encounters the word, it has no translation as it is a word outside of any forms of the languages spoken, but it appears to be the word from which Elyri was originally derived.

k'gdhededhá (k zhĕ-DĔ-jä) (n) (sng and pl)--HE/SE; The Elyri designation for the male individual who is elected as the head of the Faith.

k'ílshwythnec (k ĭl-SHWĒTH-nyĕk) (n)--HE; She (who) sees; Prophetess. The K indicates a particular individual. Any prophetess would be ílshwythnec.

k'rylag (k RĒ-lä) (n) (pl: k'rylagthé)--HE; Once Korahm chose the word rylag for his method of travel, k'rylag was carried over into standard Elyri and came to refer strictly to the Gates, not a standard gate.

kyá (KĒ-ä) (n) (pl: kyáthé)-- SE; Beloved, dearest one

kyag (KĒ-ä) (n) (pl: kyágthé)--HE; Beloved, dearest one.

kyagn (KĒ-än) (n) HE; love, affection

Kyne (KĒ-nyä) (n) (sng and pl)--HE/SE; The High Mother, the Matriarchal ruler of Elyriá. It includes the translation "Mother ruler", "Mother protector", and "exalted mother". Since nearly all Elyri families can trace some familial link to the Bhíncári, the Kyne is both a figurative, and near-literal, mother of all Elyri. This position is both hereditary and elected, chosen from among all of the women in the Bhíncári family.

lásánai (LÄ-shän-ī) (n) (sng and pl)--HE; my master/lord or mistress/lady; one to whom an individual has chosen to be subservient. This is a strictly voluntary status which may or may not be acknowledged or honored by the one being given superior status, but it gives the title bearer no more power over the speaker than the speaker wishes to allow. Not to be confused with a title of nobility or landholders since there is no such status in Elyriá. It can be used for either women or men, though it is more commonly used for men.

Llaethlágárá (LĀTH-lä-gār-ä) (n)--HE; The mountains separating Elyriá from Neth and Enesfel.

llán (län) (v)--HE/SE; see

lómyhás (lōm-YÄSH) (n)--SE; prosperity, wealth

mál (mäl) (v)--HE/SE; bless

máles (mäl-ĚSH) (v)--HE; will be blessed, will bless

málneag (mäl-NYÄ-ä) (n) (pl: málneagthé)--HE; it can mean one who possesses a quality of blessedness, sacredness, or holiness; its most common translation into the Trade languages is saint.

naeth (nāth) (v)--SE; find

náós (nä-ŌSH) (n) (sng and pl)--HE/SE; a place of worship, temple; also occasionally used to refer to the altar.

phádaes (fā-DĀSH) (v)--HE; enrich, make better, improve

Pháne (FÄ-nyä) (n)--HE; An island in possession of Káliel. Its name is translated as tiny or small.

rásae (rä-SHĀ) (v)--HE; grow

redh (rĕj) (n) (sng and pl)--HE grace, sometimes used as forgiveness in a religious sense

rón (rōn) (n) (sng) (pl: rónthé)--SE; one whose beliefs run contrary to the teachings of the Faith; a heretic

rósádhá (rō-SHÄ-jä) (n)--HE; Literally translated as the Wounds of the God, it refers to the manifestation of the death wounds of Dhágdhuán which inflicted many saints and holy individuals. These include punctures in both wrists from where the founder was hung by his wrists, sometimes accompanied by the burn of a rope on the left wrist, punctures in both ankles where his feet were secured to the pyre post, possibly the scars of ropes on the ankles as well, and, very rarely, the marks of burning flesh on the lower body.

rylag (RĒ-lä) (n) (pl: rylagthé)--HE; gate, doorway

saeitá (shā-Ē-chä) (n)--HE: ghost or spirit

serbháló (shĕr-VÄ-lō) (n)--SE; A form of Elyri wine with almost no alcohol content, used only for the purposes of religious ceremony.

sínréc (shĭn-RŬK) (n) (sng and pl)--HE; This word has no direct translation. Blood kin with a special bond, is about the closest it can be described. Any blood kin can be sínréc, but saying "he is my cousin," is different from saying "he is my sínréc" (or "he is sínréc."). It is sometimes used for non-relatives who are extremely close.

sunít (shū-NĬT) (prp)--HE; from

tádóbhmátá (TÄ-dōv-mä-tä) (n)--SE; place of eternal anger, the place where those who are not followers of Dhágdhuán go after their death

tágdhá (TÄ-zhä) (n)--SE; brother

tesur (tĕ-SHŪR) (prp)--SE/HE; they, them, their

thol (thäl) (n)--SE; church, temple, place of worship

thóres (THŌ-rĕsh) (n) (pl: thóresĕth)--SE; the room or rooms in a náós that serves as clergy offices and residences.

thráaest (thrä-ĂSHT) (prp)--HE; before, according to, in front of

zálágk (ZÄ-läk̲) (v)--SE; begins, starts, dawns

záryph (zä-RĒF) (n) (sng and pl)--HE/SE; winged beings connected to the realm of the holy; angels

Translations

Sósáná saeitá gaetió   The ship of Sósáná's ghost

íth dhedhoc, íth gymae, íth hyhílag,   The earth, the air, the water
aiónag rásae sunít.   From which life blooms
ít aicónys mál k'Ádhá thráaest,   This union bless before k'Ádhá
hudhánaelis á kyagn elzen tesur,   Bring them love and family
lómyhás dó íthásigk elzen tesur.   Bring them prosperity and joy
mál endástás males,   All holiness will be blessed
gaesdág phádaes tesur dhedhoc.   And the world be enriched with
     peace.

dhór bhí_dhór,   Circles within circles,
hwae deanár á daeár.   Lessons taught and learned.
bhí íth chaiit phuíbh.   In the rising sun
zálágk ást dhór.   A new year dawns.
ebh ibh llán,   We face ourselves,
ebhed,   Each other,
ergothé naeth,   And find the strength,
sayrád, zilhád, kyánád.   To live, to hope, to love.

Pronunciation of Elyri Names

Ágdhrán (Ä-zhrän)
Aleski (ăl-ĔSH-kē)
Ártur (är-TŪR)
Bhendhámyn (VĔN-jä-mēn)
Bhílári (vĭ-LÄR-ē)
Bhíncári (vĭn-CÄ-rē)
Bhyrhán (vēr HÄN)
Bhóité (vō-Ē-tŭ)
Bhríd (vrĭd)
Bhryell (bhrē-ĔL)
Cáner (KÄ-nyär)
Chethá (CHĔ-thä)
Cíbhóló (kih-VOH-loh)
Clarys (klär-ĒSH)
Cyllyá (kē-LĒ-ä)
Cliáth (klē-ÄTH)
Dhábhiyhá (jä-VĒ-yä)
Dháná (JÄ-nä)
Dhóri (JŌR ē)
Dhyóti-(jē-Ō-tē)
Dórímyr (DŌR-ĭ-mēr)
Drebhoti (drĕ VÄ tē)
Elyri (ĕ-LĒR-ē)
Elyriá (ĕ-LĒR-ē-ä)
Gaelán (GWÄ-län)
Hwensen (HWĔN-shĕn)
Kátá (KÄ-tä)
Kavan (KĂ-vän) (in Elyri his
    name is spelt Kabhan)
Khwílen Kesábhá (KHWĬL-
    ĕn kĕsh-ä-vä)
Kílyn (kĭ-LĒN)
Kóráhm di Curnydhá (KŌR-
    äm DĒ kūr-NĒ-jä)
Llucás (LŪ-cäsh)
Llyr (lēr)
MacLyr (mäk-LĒR)
Mórne (MŌR-nyä)

Sámel (SHÄ-mĕl)
Sóbhán (shō-VÄN)
Syl (shēl)
Tám (täm)
Tíbhyan (TĬ-vē-ăn)
Tusánt (tū-SHÄNT)
Yhsábhel (ĒSH-ä-vĕl)

The Lineage of Kavan Cliáth

(These dates are years prior to the birth of Kavan Kóráhm Cliáth)

Maternal Line	born	spouse/name change
Ísaié di Bhíncári (f)	5678	Gaed di Cliáth
Llyrá (f)	5115	
Bhásá (f)	4552	
Rene (f)	4358	Drasi
Kmholás (m)	4280	
Srono (m)	4180	
Dá Llaoá (f)	3955	
Bhílís (f)	3538	
Sosáná (f)	3434	Dhesádhá di Curnydhá
Kóráhm (m)	3063	Yhsábhel **
Kaeará (f)****	2852	Phailó Cliáth
Dhyne (f)	2752	Asdár MacLyr
Bháóli (f)	2614	
Sonrus (m)	2373	
Raeóne (f)	2294	
Gaer (m)	1938	
Ylne (f)	1826	
Lláó (m)	1532	
Mhálus (m)	1442	
Ósári (f)	1241	
Ílyn (f)	985	Murs Bhíncári
Kmhártu (m)	908	
Ahná (f)	804	
Ándhru (m)	504	
Mháráó (f)	433	*****
Estr (f)	242	
Bháni (f)	197	
Llyárá (f)	94	Rístyrd Cliáth
Kavan (m)	0	

**Yhsábhel was an adopted child of unknown parentage; believed to
  be phae

****Kaeará's mother was unidentified

*****Mhárao' father was unidentified

Paternal Line	**born**	**spouse**
Dhedec di Curnydhá (m)	5254	di Bhíncári
Gaesrun (m)	4971	
Llubhá (m)	4844	
Aeórdhyá (m)	4373	
Churás (m)	4159	
Durdhári (m)	3877	
Cáóbhyr (m)	3679	
Tyrín (m)	3434	
Kóráhm (m)	3063	Yhsábhel **
Dhyóti (f)***	2916	Sámorá Cliáth
Phailó (m)	2647	
Bhárne (m)	2514	
Lláns (m)	2389	
Mhílbhr (m)	2120	
Thórís (m)	1750	
Cátán (m)	1621	
Kmhynyn (m)	1578	
Pháól (m)	1387	
Pherís (m)	1087	
Gaeríc (m)	836	
Dhóryn (m)	643	
Mhárd (m)	558	
Márc (m)	393	Esbhít Dhurbhín
Rístyrd (m)	193	
Kavan (m)	0	

The Five Sovereignties - City Legend

<u>Enesfel</u>
1-*Rhidam
2-Alberni
3-Bryn
4-Chantel
5-Dorshur
6-Durham
7-Erleta
8-Jardin
9-Kamin
10-Kilmacud
11-Levonne
12-Nelori
13-Seres
14-Talladegah
15-Tarsee
16-Theron
17-Wexel

<u>Cordash</u>
1-*Aralt
2-Anzet
3-Ediug
4-Eleva
5-Jassett
6-Kakkoris
7-Korr
8-Liatti
9-Lindumn
10-Matina
11-Pesek
12-Sebring
13-Trallan
14-Verbier
15-Vioe
16-Vron
17-Wynett

<u>Elyriá</u>
1-Clarys
2-Ánásair
3-Bhastyán
4-Bhórdh
5-Bhryell
6-Cármycá
7-Cylleá
8-Dhánthes
9-Ibhórys
10-Káská
11-Khwíncanon
12-Rísóri
13-Sábhóne
14-Sídhári
15-Turyn

<u>Hatu</u>
1-*Natrona
2-Avarrou
3-Cran Ufa
4-Drisoge
5-Enda
6-Fa Ruqi
7-Furr Katio
8-Kílyn
9-Palil
10-Wasilla
11-Yd Haszafn

<u>Neth</u>
1-*Glevum
2-Fiara
3-Gorea
4-Mawr
5-Nogero
6-Pravek
7-Ruidoso
8-Venago

<u>Káliel</u>
1-*Káliel
2-Jaffe
3-Mara Qin
4-Pháne
5-Shola

The Five Sovereignties

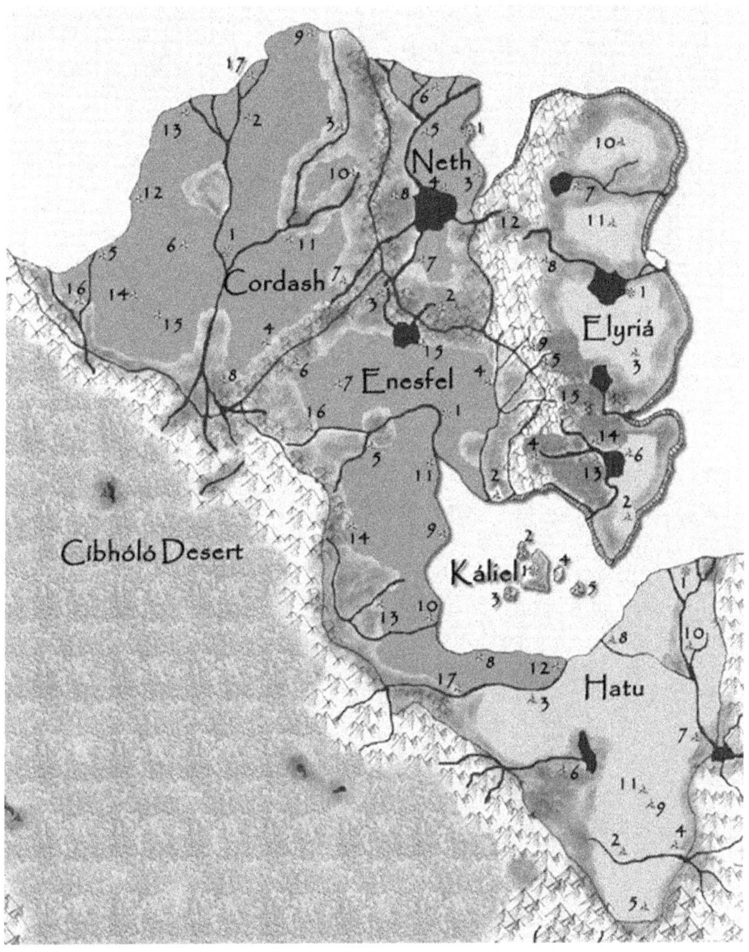

The Southern Lands - City Legend

1 - Hatu city of Enda
2 - Fikahr
3 - Ergoth
4 - Yashir
5 - Zabin
6 - Gorbesh
7 - Pa'aliaka

⊕ - Monastery of Gorbesh

Southern Lands

About the Author

Unsatisfied with 'how the story ends' as a young reader, Tamara took on the challenge of crafting endings to the tales of others to better suit her vision of the world. That desire to mold reality into how she imagined it should be, gave birth to a life-long fascination with the written word, and its capacity, particularly through realms of fantasy and science fiction, to foster an understanding of the people, events, thoughts and emotions that make us who we are.

A long-time resident of Clearlake, California, after a life that took her back and forth across the country, Tamara is owned by a pack of papillions, a pride of cats, and an eclectic arsenal of films she enjoys in her off-moments.

White Purgator

Kestrel Harper Saga Book 5

(excerpt)

It appeared to take great effort but one old hand eventually came up to Kavan's face, flexing and trembling as it drew closer, until five now bloody fingers raked down Kavan's white cheek. Running footsteps burst through the still open double doors, but Kavan ignored them. "You…" Dórímyr choked, making one final effort to reach his mind. The feeling of malevolence and defeat that Kavan felt in the k'gdhededhá's expression and body seemed stronger in that short moment of utterance, in that brief contact Kavan decided he should allow, but then the prelate's body stiffened and was lost when collapse came, his arm flopping back onto the floor, splattering blood droplets across the stone when it hit.